A Soul to Guide

Duskwalker Brides

Book Four

Opal Reyne

ISBN: 978-0-6458301-1-8

Cover art: Sam Griffin
Editor 1: The fiction and friction
Editor 2/ proofreader: Messenger's Memos

**Trigger Warning**
Major spoiler below

Please only read further if you have triggers, otherwise you will seriously spoil the book for yourself.

Firstly, I will list what triggers **AREN'T** in the book so you can stop reading in order not to spoil it: No rape, non-con, purposeful harm done to the FMC by the MMC, torture, suicide/self-harm, death or detailed grieving over death, ow/om drama, abortion, pregnancy, mental/emotional abuse, incest, or drug/alcohol abuse.

Please consider stopping here if your trigger has been detailed above as the rest are spoilers.

There are some depictions of depression and mental health. Childhood trauma. Memory of loss of death. Vivid memory of bullying and violence within a school featuring young children, with an emotional attachment to the perpetrator.
As always, my books have gore.

<u>Author's note on language</u>

I'm from AUSTRALIA.

My English is not the same as American English.
I love my American English spoken readers to bits. You're
cute, you all make me giggle, and I just wanna give you a big
'ol hug. However, there are many of you who don't seem to
realise that your English was born from British English, which
is what I use (although a bastardised version since Australians
like to take all language and strangle it until it's a ruined
carcass of slang, missing letters, and randomly added o's).

We don't seem to like the letter z.

We write colour instead of color. Recognise instead of
recognize. Travelling instead of traveling. Skilful instead of
skillfull. Mum instead of mom. Smelt is a past participle of
smell. We omit the full-stop in Mr. Name, so it's Mr Name.
Aussies cradle the word cunt like it's a sweet little puppy,
rather than an insult to be launched at your face.

Anyway, happy reading!

Pronunciation guide

People:
Merikh – Merr-ick
Raewyn – Ray-wen
Daefaren – Day-far-in
Cykran – Cy-kran
Aurea – Aur-ea
Ulair – Ul-lair
Mericato – Merry-cato
Jabez – Ja-bez
Weldir – Wel-dur
Lindiwe – Lind-di-we

Races:
Elysian – E-lee-see-an
Anzúli – An-zoo-li
Bansu – Ban-zu
Taihee – Ta-he
Nanteth – Nan-tee-th

Places:
Nyl'theria – Nyl-ther-ria
Lezekos – Lee-zee-key-os
Anzúla – An-zoo-la

Other:
Synedrus – Sa-ni-drius
Draflium – Dra-flume
Rankae – Ran-kay

To all the MonsterFuckers out there that love a good grumpy/sunshine trope,

this book is for you.

We like 'em mean, we like 'em keen, and we like confusing the fuck out of the grump. It's even better when we can flit around them like a pretty fairy, dazzling them with our charm.

I would like to give a big shoutout to the wonderful **sensitivity readers** who helped to make this book a safe place for those I am trying to positively represent. As you all know, representation is a big part of what I want to do, but I want to do so in a way that isn't harmful.

Thank you to Diamond, Erin, Geornesha, and Nicole for your contribution towards POC sensitivity.

Thank you to Anica, and Trev for your contribution towards POC and disability sensitivity.

Thank you to Joanna, Kristin, Pearl, and Vanessa for your contribution towards disability sensitivity.

I would also like to give a special thank you to Crystal for your contribution towards POC, disability, and overall sensitivity.

I appreciate all the time and effort you put into helping me with this book. You will forever have a place in my heart.

PROLOGUE

If one had eyes that could see, they would probably note the mess in this high-ceilinged, spacious laboratory. How the walls and ceiling were made of white tree branches, while obsidian glittered on the ground. They would note the gold ore that filled in the gaps between branches and helped to support the glass in the roof.

They would see that every wall in this octagonal, nearly circular room, either had a writing board or a gold-and-black marble bench against it.

They would try to figure out what ingredients the cupboards, windowsills, and benches were covered in, since there were glass beakers, tubes, and metal jars from one end of the room to the other. Some contained ground-up dust, others whole items such as plant roots, flowers, and leaves. There were a few that held liquids of different colours.

A person might even gape at the lovely round white light that looked like an exploding star hanging from the very centre of this triangular roof, and marvel at how it was powered by magic. Or stare in awe at the little red, blue, green, and silver orbs that hung from the ceiling and changed locations to mimic their current astronomical points in the sky.

Without a doubt, they would be scratching their heads at the mathematical equations written on every surface available.

For Raewyn, who could not see, she knew the state of her precious laboratory by what she could smell, by what she could feel, and by what she could hear – like the papers loosely fluttering on their clipped stacks from the wind gently pushing in.

"Cykran, could you please close the window for me?" she murmured as she frowned at the paper in her right hand, too distracted to raise her voice.

She brushed her fingers over the bumps etched into the paper to read what was there.

Cykran said nothing, but her pointed ear twitched at his light footsteps heading towards the only open window in her spacious laboratory. Despite his general quietness, Raewyn could hear where he was by his deep breaths, and lately, she'd even noticed him by the general shift of his clothing.

The window made a muted clicking noise, and the smallest smile spread over her lips.

A few had been nervous about a *Demon* working as her assistant, considering how many of his kind had slaughtered the Elvish people. Raewyn, on the other hand, couldn't think of anyone more tolerable.

Since the day she'd accidentally blinded herself with magic, people's attitudes towards her had changed. Some were wary of her hurting herself in her laboratory, while others were worried she'd hurt others by exploding this part of the council palace – it wouldn't be the first time, and that was before she lost her sight.

Of course, there were many more who knew Raewyn wouldn't stop her experiments, no matter where she was, so it was safer for her to work where she was isolated and could be monitored.

Many had come forward, wanting to be her assistant, but none were as patient as Cykran. None were as quiet, even in the way they breathed. None were as thankful as he was.

What's more, none knew how to distinguish what she truly

needed against what they thought she did.

Others would get in the way by being overly helpful, but he rarely crowded her and stuck to leaning against one of the cabinets, since there was barely any free wall space. He also only spoke when necessary – except for when he wanted to be a sarcastic little bastard, but that was part of his charm.

From the right, she tentatively felt out and picked up a vial with a distinct peppery scent, then one that was musky.

"Yellowcrest and bellsage," he commented, which caused her to put down the musky scented one and grab the container on the left instead. "Yellowcrest and ringsage."

After bringing both closer, she fingered the paper with bumps of *elbraille* on it so she could read her notes.

Letters made up of triangles and lines told her what was written, both in Elvish and mathematically, and she was thankful such writing craft was available. With just a small amount of magical ink, the elbraille would form raised patterns on the parchment.

It also allowed everyone, no matter if they were visually impaired or not, to read what was written.

The rest of her experiment she could do without Cykran's help, since she had all the tools she needed with elbraille etched into the handles to inform her of their measuring amounts. Each spoon had a swiper mechanism, so she didn't need to touch whatever it was – like spotted green and pink polleshrooms, which could be quite poisonous.

After pouring a tiny amount of yellowcrest into a glass container already filled with other ingredients, most of them liquid, Raewyn paused as she went to tip in a gram of ringsage.

This spell required the perfect amounts of every ingredient. An incorrect ratio could lead to different results: some funny, most not.

Last time, when she had been trying to uncover the spell through her equations, she'd accidentally turned her dark-brown skin a bright purple. People had, jokingly, called her hufflepumpkin for a week!

When she paused for too long, Cykran chuckled. "I wonder if you'll turn *into* a hufflepumpkin this time, rather than just colouring yourself as one."

Raewyn pouted. "That's mean, Cykran." She stepped back and gestured to the glass container. "Excuse me, assistant, but I require help."

His dark laugh was warm but hissy from his Demon fangs. "By the holy Gilded Maiden, no. You do it, councilwoman. I don't think I'm truly capable of such wonderful scientific breakthroughs; that is best left to our most valuable asset, the great Raewyn Daefaren."

Raewyn rolled her eyes at his mocking words. "Then don't tease me. Since you're in the room with me, you'll likely turn purple too."

His fangs clipping shut in concern and his clothing ruffling with movement had her laughing.

She could almost picture him with an annoyed pout and his arms folded. She remembered what he looked like, since they'd been friends long before she'd lost her sight.

She didn't know if his hair was still long and tied back into a high ponytail, but he had the same white hair and taupe-brown skin, similar to the Elysian Elves, despite being born a Demon. He was a little taller than the average Elysian height of six foot four inches, but he was just as lean, with defined muscle tone.

Since he wasn't a true Elysian Elf, Cykran lacked the magical symbols printed over their skin, which was indicative of the type of magic they best wielded. He also had red eyes, whereas theirs were predominantly a variation of brown or green. He hated his red eyes, claws, fangs, and horns, considering they made it obvious what he was.

She had never minded them.

Most Elysians didn't. As long as Demons fully obtained Elysianity and intelligence, and weren't mindless, bloodthirsty monsters, they were accepted.

Which, unfortunately, were few and far between.

Delysian was the race of Demons who had become so Elf-like, they were basically the same. It was the name given to them when they entered through the gates and were granted permission to stay within the city.

Outside the council palace, past the beachside landscape of Lezekos City – the only place Elysians could now live – was an infestation of Demons. This beautiful world, once free for all, was now owned by the Demon scourge: a never-ending wave of fangs.

Poor Cykran still battled the fact that he became this way from eating a vast amount of her kind. Many Elysians were wary of him in general, as they feared he would turn on them, but as long as he consumed some kind of meat every day, he was as harmless as a tukdeer.

Except for his sarcasm, apparently.

"I thought you cared about me, Cykran," she falsely whined.

"I am thankful for you, councilwoman, as your family is the reason we Delysians are allowed to live here, protected from the Demons." Then, his tone became snidely humorous as he said, "But no, you can turn yourself into a vegetable, and I'll make sure no one eats you."

Raewyn groaned in dismay.

The reason she was trying to make hufflepumpkin grow was so she could help feed the city. Food was free, although monitored, since they would never make someone work for the necessities of life. Anything that a person required to live, whether it be food, water, a home, or even sanitary products, was freely available to all.

Elysians only paid for nonessentials.

A small home with very little was provided for free, but if they wished for a bigger home, furniture other than a bed, table, and chairs, they had to work for it. Artwork was considered a luxury.

Most just wished to support the city in any way they could.

However, food was becoming scarcer as their numbers, thankfully, began to flourish. Over two-thirds of their people had been slaughtered when the Demons arrived, and since they were non-violent, they had no way of fighting back.

They never ate meat, so fruits, vegetables, nuts, and legumes were essential. It was odd for them to have livestock, but if the Delysians didn't have meat to eat, they couldn't remain in the city.

Besides their slowly dwindling food, they were also running out of space. Currently, thousands were working to expand the city's walls *before* overpopulation became an issue.

People had already – after learning the new practice of fighting – cleared the surrounding forests of Demons. The magical barrier protecting the city had recently been expanded, and construction of the new areas was firmly underway.

Now, she was working to make sure her people were always fed.

"Are you sure you need to take this risk, Rae?" Cykran asked, his low, firm tone filled with worry.

Despite not being able to see, she turned her face up towards him. "Yes. We have learned how to make other vegetables and fruits, but they are easy to grow. Hufflepumpkin is so high in many nutrients and is more filling. It will be better for both our peoples if we can grow it quicker, since it will help feed the Delysians as well."

With just that bit of self-encouragement, she poured in the ringsage. Finally, the last ingredient was dropped inside – a single hufflepumpkin seed.

She hovered her hands above the container and took in a deep breath, letting her magic freely flow through her body. Cold lines wound up her forearms in geometric hexagons and patterns, glowing as she used her magic.

It was the only thing she could see, as if her blindness was purely physical. She'd never been able to see tendrils of magic before her accident, and it was a comforting sight now that she lived in darkness. Hers glowed a neutral grey that lacked any elemental colouring. It was exceedingly rare, but powerful.

Once she poured enough magic into the concoction, there was resistance, as though she was pressing against a large ball. She shoved in spirit, a replenishable source that came from within, and the grey glow of her magic spun with bright green to signify the spell had shifted into more of an earthy element.

Something burst to life in the middle with a wave of pressure, and she stopped. Seconds ticked by as Raewyn waited.

"Did it work?" she asked Cykran, before patting down her arms. She would have touched it to double check, but she didn't want to be harmed by something unknown that could potentially be dangerous. "Or am I purple?"

"Nothing is happening."

"It failed," she sighed. She would have slapped the table in frustration, but her left ear twitched at footsteps approaching from the hallway. "Can I never get a moment of peace?"

"Someone is approaching? I'll get the door."

Cykran's bare feet slapped against the stone floor as he headed to the doorway. His feet squeaked as he sidestepped two of her benches overflowing with either paperwork or ingredients – all of which she knew by memory.

The room was partly made of a gigantic tree that sat close to the centre of the city; it housed many within its white, sun-bleached trunk and branches. Within the *unnatural* formation, they'd set carved marble and smelted ore, such as gold, platinum, and bronze, into its foundations.

The council palace was at the very top of the trunk, which is where she was currently – on the fringes of it.

"Sometimes it amazes me how good your hearing has become," Cykran said as he moved.

"Your other senses can sometimes get better when you lose one." But not always. "Our head of security claims he only obtained his council position because he was always a better listener, since he doesn't talk like everyone else."

Mericato had injured his throat as a child, but it was the infection that affected his speech. Now, he used sign language to communicate, more out of comfort than necessity. He was often in pain.

She was just extremely lucky her sense of smell, hearing, and touch had improved in the last few years. Before that... she'd been as clumsy as they came. She'd tripped on air one too many times.

Just as Cykran made it to the door, soft tapping resonated through the thick timber.

The clack of the locking mechanism being opened was followed by the door creaking, which brought in the rush of fresh, earthy scents from within the palace's corridors. The starfir tree pollen was cleansing and uplifting, but she always tried to keep it out of her laboratory, so as to not contaminate her experiments.

She'd only had the window open since two of the three suns had been shining on her side of the palace, making the temperature inside nearly unbearable.

"Raewyn, you are late for the meeting, and the other councilmembers grow impatient," Aurea, a general council assistant, stated. "If you don't come immediately, you know how Ulair will be."

She was likely shaking her head, since Ulair was the most annoying and temperamental of all the councilmembers.

Raewyn also had a feeling Aurea had her hands on her wide hips and was narrowing her deep-green eyes. They were delicately set in her dark, taupe-ish complexion. Aurea's hair had always been shaved on one side, with the rest swept to the right, in the years Raewyn had known her. She was short for an Elysian, probably six foot two, which had always made Raewyn's six foot seven feel even taller than usual.

They both shared the Elysian white hair, but Aurea's short hair was straight, whereas Raewyn's was long and coily, worn loose and full around her head. Still, they shared similar willowy

Elvish figures.

Elysians came in all shapes and sizes, with different features, such as noses and lips that were full, perky, or thin. Even their eyes were of differing shapes – although they were generally brown or green coloured. Their brown skin ranged from light to dark, with the same grey undertone of their Elysian heritage.

Though she hadn't looked in a mirror in over six years, she remembered most of her own features, as well as those of the people she'd encountered regularly before she lost her sight. However, as time passed, details were beginning to fade – which terrified her, as she didn't want to lose them.

"Oh yeah... I forgot about the meeting." Her forgetfulness was due to her obsessive, workaholic nature, and it was probably one of her biggest faults. "Do you mind guiding me so I'm quicker? I'm sure if I make Ulair wait much longer, he'll have a hissy fit and give himself indigestion again."

Just as she stepped forward to grab her guide cane, the sharp sound of glass shattering next to her made her gasp. Raewyn jumped back as a billow of peppery and sweet scents exploded against her senses.

A bright pink magical glow grew in size, but it had been so small before that she hadn't noticed it. It was a terrible mistake on her part, one likely caused by Aurea's interruption.

"Raewyn, watch out!" Cykran yelled as something vine-like grabbed her arm.

By the clattering glass and the mixture of smells, Raewyn suspected more vines were growing from the vial she'd tried to make a hufflepumpkin grow from. Other containers were knocked over as the vines grabbed or flicked them with their tendrils, the cacophony of sounds and smells almost overwhelming her.

Oh no! she thought, realising random ingredients were mixing with her still-activating spell. Raewyn struggled to free her arm, only to wince when the vines tightened in reaction.

Cykran's rushing steps made her stomp her foot in his

direction. A barrier, made from the root-like vines of the starfir tree, formed between them. She didn't know what was about to happen, but she wouldn't put another in harm's way for her sake.

If they took her to the medical facilities in time, she would be fine, so long as it wasn't fatal.

"Rae, let me through. Please!" Cykran's claws tore at the wooden vines as he tried to fight his way through.

From experience, she knew the barrier she'd formed would be hexagonal, so she was able to hear his voice clearly through the spaces in the vines.

"Just stay there," she begged, throwing her free hand over the vines ensnaring her in the hopes she could sever them or gather enough magic to incinerate them.

"I'll get the guards," Aurea said with a panicked shout before she ran off.

Cykran's voice was strained and distressed. "I'm supposed to protect you. I can't do that if you don't let me through."

A tornado of wind began to form, her growth spell changing into something else entirely. It was the sucking sensation in the air and the yellow magic of a seam cracking open that alerted her to what it was.

The cold dread of fear trickled down her spine.

She let go of the vine to grip the closest bench, praying to the Gilded Maiden she had the strength to hold on. Her feet lifted off the ground, and her long, billowy skirt whipped around her ankles.

It's a chaos portal. Raewyn shut her eyes tight as she held on with all her strength, despite feeling her hand slipping from the marble edge. *It's an unknown rift.*

Since it had opened, it meant the world on the other side hadn't blocked the Elysians from entering. It was an unknown place, with unknown people... and unknown dangers. What if she went to the Demons' home realm... or somewhere worse? What if she couldn't get back home?

Her pulse quickened, pounding wildly in her ears from the

fear pummelling its way through her veins.

"Cykran," she sobbed out, as she was pulled so far back she lost her grip on the bench's edge.

She scrambled to grab something else, unsure of what could tether her to Nyl'theria, their realm, when she wrapped her hand around a cold pole. Fearful tears escaped from her clenched eyes, and they were sucked away instead of falling down her face.

"Cykran." Her voice broke as she pleaded, "*Please* save me."

She suddenly wished she hadn't barred him from reaching her, but she hadn't wanted him to come to harm. This wouldn't harm them, though, only remove them from this realm.

She couldn't lower the barrier without using at least one of her hands. One was tangled in vines trying to yank her closer, as if they were alive, while the other was holding on for dear life.

"I'm coming, Rae! Just hold on."

The cracking of vines, as Cykran struggled to break through, was quiet in comparison to the ferocious roar of the portal at her feet.

With a crunch, whatever she was gripping broke under the force of the powerful vortex. Raewyn still held the metal pole when she was sucked through.

Cykran's beastly roar was the last thing she heard, her answering scream eaten up by the swallow of magic before she disappeared.

I just wanted to feed my people!

ONE

Raewyn tightened the thin hood of the cloak she wore over her head with her right hand to make sure it didn't fall back. With her left, she glided the backs of her fingers over the side of a building to guide herself through the town.

Despite the fact that it was apparently summer here, the heat was rather cool to an Elysian Elf. Nyl'theria was hotter than this even in winter, and it was likely brighter as well.

My hair isn't showing, is it?

She doubled checked again, worried that the head wrap she wore beneath the hood had untied. She wore it to hide her hair's white colouring.

The sound of chatting, in a language she was growing familiar with but had never properly spoken before, was loud as she passed person after person.

Raewyn spoke very little. Her accent was weird to them, and they'd comment on it whenever she spoke.

Her father had taught her many Earth and Elvish languages, but she hadn't spoken them since she was a teenager.

Of all the realms I could have teleported to with sentient beings, why did it have to be Earth? She sighed with discontent. *Why couldn't I have teleported near a town with Anzúli?*

Why did it have to be *this* realm? Sure, it was better than the few realms with poisonous gas for air, but every day she worried about being discovered.

The Elysians had made sure the Demons who travelled through the many permanent portals to Earth couldn't return to Nyl'theria. She dearly hoped the humans didn't know that.

She didn't know how much Earth had changed, but when her people had come here last, the humans had been rather fearful and violent towards anything different from them.

And Raewyn was *very* different.

She'd studied many human biology books before she lost her sight. She'd read humans came in varying shapes, sizes, skin tones, and ethnicities.

One thing she did know is that they didn't have the long, pointed ears she had, nor were the women generally as tall and willowy as she was. Add the fact that she had very striking white hair, and to these people, she was an oddity. She'd already been asked a flock of questions when she arrived.

After walking towards the only sound of life she could hear in the forest, the guard who had found her had barely understood her.

However, the moment he'd spoken, her heart had nearly burst with fright when she realised he was human.

She hadn't been able to explain how she found herself outside the town, nor had she been able to explain where her special gown came from – one that had malleable gold etched into the white silk. She struggled to answer *what* the golden jewellery cresting over her forehead was, but they gave her the word *diadem*. She also couldn't explain where someone like her had gotten the many bangles that rested around her ankles and wrists.

They questioned the colour of her hair, her height, her willowy physique. Her ears had been hidden underneath her curls, which was lucky since it had fallen from her original half-up, half-down tie up.

Raewyn pretended she had amnesia and had no idea why she looked the way she did, or how she came to be in the forest.

They eventually stopped questioning her.

She asked for a cloak so she could hide her identity when they let her go, which they thankfully gave her. She'd ripped the bottom of it so she could place a strip of cloth over her eyes to hide them, and, more importantly, her white eyebrows.

Other than the golden chain around her waist, a special contraception spell she hadn't been fond of parting with, no matter the reason, she no longer owned any of the jewellery she came here with.

She'd found a merchant after they released her from questioning, and she'd sold most of her jewellery so she could make transactions within the town. That was after she discovered humans were so cruel, they wouldn't feed those who were hungry.

Raewyn refused to be hungry, or to not sleep in a proper bed because they wouldn't house anyone without money. Ridiculous!

They also weren't beyond trying to rip someone off. Unfortunately for the dear, unsuspecting merchant she'd sold her jewellery to, she knew what gold, silver, and copper felt like, and that they had their own unique smell. They also had their own distinct tone when tapped against a hard surface.

She'd gotten most of what it was worth, and half of that was a very weighty bag tied to her waist. The rest was hidden underneath a glamour spell at the inn she was staying at.

The long sleeves of the itchy dress she wore helped to hide a skin-deep geometric band glowing around her left forearm – the only indication she was currently using magic. It was easy to do on an inanimate object, but to glamour a person required a much more advanced spell – which she couldn't do without a mana stone.

I can't let anyone know I can use magic. She just needed to remain hidden until she got home.

That meant she needed to leave this town and find some Anzúli. When she'd asked if there were any people who could use magic, she'd found they were referred to as Priests and Priestesses here.

There were none in this town, or in any of those close by. She wouldn't have faced the outside world to go to them, even if they *had* been nearby. Not alone, at least.

She'd been inquiring for the past Earth month about travellers leaving this town, Clawhaven. The few who were brave enough to leave refused to take a visually impaired person with them, or a woman in general.

Cowards! She wasn't going to let them tamp down her fight.

She continued every day, determined to find someone who would travel with her. Of course, she'd do the best she could with what she had. She'd grown up rather pampered, perhaps a little spoilt, but she'd learned to be resilient, no matter the battles she faced.

It didn't help she couldn't share with them that she had superhuman hearing, or a superhuman sense of smell, or that she could probably lift and throw them a few metres. These weren't normal qualities for a human, and her lean frame gave everyone the impression she was underfed – which wasn't the case.

She was just... tall, which meant all her limbs were longer, and the healthy fat she had on her was evenly spread out.

They called her lanky, and she'd wanted to smack them on the nose!

Most were nice to her, though, probably out of pity. She wasn't fond of that, since she'd rarely received pity from anyone back in Nyl'theria. She was just Raewyn, a person who couldn't see.

Her people didn't pity her, or think less of her, or anyone else who had an impairment. They just made sure they were comfortable, happy, and had all the assistance they needed without complaint. If something wasn't available, they would find a way to make it so.

Humans were different. She'd already seen they were mean, judgemental creatures, and their morals were only as strong as the laws that suppressed them.

I miss home, she thought as she tried to navigate the town and return to the markets by the paths she walked every day. They were easy to locate by the smell of freshly cooked food and chatter. *Dear Gilded Maiden, I miss my laboratory.*

She missed being buried underneath paperwork, and experiments, and being forced to listen to Cykran's sarcasm. She missed the freedom of dressing in flowy gowns that showed off a little shoulder or thigh, rather than this heavy layered winter dress.

She sighed as she raised her face to the sun washing over her, wishing this apparent summer heat was hotter. Time seemed to pass quicker here, and it was disorientating. Night came often in comparison to Nyl'theria.

From what she'd learned, Clawhaven was relatively small. Distressed, rough timber formed a barrier around the town. Housing and markets were all mixed together, most people selling their wares outside of the very places they lived.

Those who were better off lived in the middle of the town. The inn she stayed at was located towards one of the four exits, which is why it was so cheap.

When her fingertips brushed over a smooth wood carving, she crossed the street so she could turn right down a pathway. The area was narrow, but most streets, except the four main veins to each gate, weren't wide.

The path beneath her shoes became hard-pressed dirt. One more right turn, after which she could smell the scent of a particular flower, and the markets should be right ahead of her. She hoped to leave the town before they withered due to seasonal changes, since they weren't a reliable landmark.

The softest breeze pushed the wind forward from behind her, but she could still smell the *lavender* – as she had been told it was called. Someone had placed a pot of it on their windowsill.

Just as chatter became loud, Raewyn turned and ran straight into a solid wall.

"Uck!" she yelped, stumbling backwards onto her arse while supporting her hood so it didn't fall.

"Watch where you're going," a gruff voice demanded, causing her ears to twitch under her hood.

Her brows drew together. *I didn't hear him coming.*

Raewyn could always hear people approaching. Whether it be the sound of their feet hitting the ground, the subtle shift of dirt under their shoes, their very breath... Raewyn could always hear who was around.

This person had been silent.

She turned her head up with a pout, her cheeks puffing with annoyance, before waving her hand back and forth centimetres in front of her face. *Like hellooooo, can't see here.* Her eyes were literally covered with a cloth!

Raewyn waited for an apology, a gesture to help her to her feet. *Something.*

The smell of cinnamon and orange, what she'd learned were popular foods here, infiltrated her senses. Except it was different, and the combined scent made her chest warm.

He smells like draflium. Draflium was a rare, highly sought-after flower that glowed bright red at night with a purple pollen centre.

"You should be careful of your footing," he said, before the shift of material, likely a cloak, brushed over her shoulder as he stepped around her. "Walking down the narrow side streets is dangerous by yourself, even in the daytime."

Facing forward, Raewyn gaped. *How rude!*

She stomped her way to her feet with a huff, storming forward to greet the markets. She threw her hands up, exasperated by humans and their behaviour.

An Elysian would never treat another like this. Her steps were hard, in an attempt to vent her frustration. *You knock someone over, the least you could do is offer assistance. It was his fault as much as mine.*

"You should watch where *you're* going," she almost growled

to herself.

She touched the wall, making sure the brick building was familiar in case she found herself turned around by their kerfuffle.

"There has to be one person in this awful town who would be willing to travel with me."

For most of the precious night, she'd sat in the tavern of the inn. She'd inquired with two people who were leaving town soon to go to the beach to fish, hoping to bring fresh ocean life for the town to eat.

She'd received the same answer. Both declined allowing her to accompany them. She'd begged and offered to pay them, but apparently, she was too much of a liability.

The man had just flat out refused, but the woman said she didn't think she could handle the guilt if she accidentally lost Raewyn or was unable to protect her on their journey.

Now that she was deep in the markets, Raewyn's search for the day began.

It was mostly pointless; she was just an unwanted listener in people's private conversations. She'd learnt much about the people who lived here, but it was mostly irrelevant to what she needed.

With just the sound of their voices, their tones, the words they spoke, most appeared tired and weary. Although the daytime brought sun and generally brighter moods, there was a weight resting over every single person living here.

It was the Elysians' fault they were suffering. Would humans have advanced greatly in the last three hundred and forty years if her people hadn't brought the Demons upon them by accident?

It wasn't hard to feel guilty about it, despite it not being *her* fault personally. Still, she often wore her heart on her sleeve, and she, as a councilwoman, bore the weight of her people's problems and faults.

There is nothing I can do for them.

One thing that often caught her attention was the warmth-inducing scent of draflium flowers. Periodically throughout the day while she ventured around the markets, the stranger from earlier had been nearby.

She tried to ignore it as she slowly made her way behind stalls so she could stay off the busy path. She didn't want to be knocked around or get in anyone's way, and it was easier to guide herself with the walls since she didn't have her cane.

However, her ears twitched, that deep voice close. It was the storekeeper's response that truly grabbed her attention, though.

"Leaving so soon, are you?" the woman said in a lazy, uncaring voice. "You haven't been around long."

"Yes. I have overstayed my welcome," he answered plainly and with great thought, as though he was looking over what she had available.

He's leaving? Raewyn nibbled the inside of her cheek before making her way, subtly and hopefully without notice, just a bit closer.

The woman laughed and changed her tone. "I have potatoes, pumpkin, beetroot, just about anything that'll last you, at least to get you to the nearest towns. If you're looking for the best produce for your travels, there's not a shop in Clawhaven as fresh as what I have."

"I highly doubt that," he answered with a scoff. "The farmers have the best produce, and I didn't come here for food. I wanted to inquire if you had dill."

The woman let out a huff, no doubt frowning at his rude tone in the same way Raewyn was.

"I picked all my food fresh from my garden just this morning! The farmers add strange things to their produce to make it grow bigger and faster, but it doesn't have the natural vitamins our good people need."

Raewyn had heard of this kind of mass production of food. The Elysian council had considered doing this themselves, but decided a healthy belly eating slightly less was far better than a full one lacking in nutrients. It's why she'd been working so hard on magically growing hufflepumpkin.

"Do you have dill in the back or not?"

Gosh, he sounded so rough and arrogant!

"No. I don't have dill," she bit. "Go ask Peter. He's three doors down."

Within seconds, Raewyn lost his scent when he'd moved through the crowd of people without responding. She turned her head one way, then the other, unsure of which direction he'd gone.

She took a gamble, and it paid off when his scent became stronger.

"You're looking for dill?" Peter asked, his voice louder the closer she got. "I don't have much left. It's a favourite herb for most since it tastes so good."

"I don't care – whatever you have left."

"Hmm," he hummed thoughtfully. The next time he spoke, Peter's voice was coy. "It'll cost you a lot then."

The sigh the stranger let out gave Raewyn the impression he was rolling his eyes at the storekeeper's antics. "Just give me the fucking herb. I don't care how much it costs."

Peter laughed, just as her ears pressed flat against her head. Swearing was an uncommon practice for her people, and it tended to show a lack of respect. She was learning it was quite common for humans.

It made her strangely uncomfortable, like she wanted to squirm.

The front door creaked open as Peter went inside his home to collect the dill. Raewyn turned and pretended to check the bag she had strapped across her torso just in case the stranger looked around while he waited.

He's leaving town. Despite her aversion to him, since he seemed to be a grumpy pants, she desperately wanted to ask him if she could tag along.

I gather he's tall. He felt pretty big when he knocked me over, so does that mean he's strong? She lifted a hand and tapped her full, pouty lips. *Maybe if I play to his masculinity, call him a coward if he won't take me, I can manipulate him into travelling with me.*

Raewyn was willing to punch below the belt if it got her what she wanted. Once he took her to a different town, she could dust her hands of him. Hell, if he was willing to take her to a town with Anzúli, she'd pat him on the bum and tell him he did a superb job.

But how do I go about approaching him? She chewed at her bottom lip as she thought. *I can't just walk up to him and say, "Hi there! This might seem weird, but I've been stalking you and heard, because I was eavesdropping, that you're leaving! Wouldn't it just be amazing if you took me with you?"*

She scrunched up her nose. Yeah, that *wasn't* going to help her at all.

"There you go," Peter exclaimed, just as his door slammed shut. "One pouch of dill. That'll be five silvers."

"I think you should look me over once more and reconsider just how deeply you wish to con me," the stranger bit out.

"T-three silvers?" Peter said, his tone losing its confidence.

"How many guards do you think it'll take to restrain me if I bash your skull in?" This time, he laughed, but there was true mirth in his voice, like the idea of skull bashing brought him immense joy.

"Fine! One silver."

"That's better." Coins rattled as he searched his pouch. "Next time you wish to con someone, take into consideration that this much dill is barely worth four coppers."

"It's always better to negotiate." Peter laughed weakly. "Most people aren't as big and scary as you."

"Yeah, but people like me will likely strangle you for being a general annoyance."

Peter gulped, and Raewyn only knew the stranger had moved on by the subtle jingle of his coin pouch shifting as it settled and the diminishing of his smell. He was moving, and she was quick to follow him.

She lost him a few times, but she always managed to pick up his scent or voice in the crowd of pedestrians. Within minutes, she would find him somewhere else, just casually speaking with storekeepers, asking about their wares.

"I'm leaving in two days," he answered someone as he traded coin for fishing hooks, lure, and wire. "I'm stocking up now, as I wish to leave early in the morning."

"Ah yes," the man chuckled. "It's always best to leave an hour after sunup. The Demons have usually scattered by then, and it gives you a full day to vacate from the town's proximity safely."

As he often did, the stranger sighed. "Why are you explaining something to me as though I don't know? Why is it you think I wish to leave early in the day?"

"Oh, sorry," he answered nervously. "Was just making general conversation. I didn't mean to offend you."

"You didn't offend me. I just don't wish to be spoken to as though I'm an idiot."

Okay, so the stranger had a point. Nothing got Raewyn more fired up than being told something she already knew. She couldn't fault him on that.

By the end of the day, she was exhausted from following him, from hiding around corners or stalls. She tried to figure out a suitable way to approach him without having to enter the street full of people, but the opportunity never came.

Then... he was gone.

TWO

After following the stranger, Raewyn didn't take into consideration that he would lead her on a strange path. She'd gotten herself lost.

She could tell night was falling when the world got quieter, as if everyone was afraid to be out in the dark.

This market street was generally busy throughout the day. The scattered footsteps and chatter were lessening every minute, and the drop in temperature informed her the sun, *singular*, was disappearing again.

Night was coming, and Raewyn had already discovered that being out past it brought danger – and not only because of the Demons.

Raewyn had to ask for directions multiple times to find her way back to the inn. She knew her room step for step, having mapped it out, and now she knew it by pure memory. It was small and modest, but that was fine with her. She didn't need anything lavish.

Thankfully, the inn was the most well-known one nearest to the western gate and was easy to find. She was walking back along a path she wasn't particularly familiar with, but apparently, she'd find it on the right if she kept going. Once she was in its direct vicinity, she should be able to locate it by the smell of alcohol that permeated the air from the tavern taking up its bottom half.

She brushed the back of her hand over every surface to find her way, making sure she didn't carelessly bump into anything. She tripped a few times, but she was so used to that now, she was quick to right herself.

The once-clumsy Raewyn was now one of the sturdiest people on her feet, even more so when she wasn't forced to wear shoes to fit in with weird people who liked to cover them.

Okay. So, the stranger said he'd be leaving early in the morning in two days from the south gate. If she couldn't find him again, she'd just wait at the gate, packed and ready to go. She already got the impression that if she met him there empty-handed, he'd leave her behind.

She weighed the probabilities, already formulating excuses to any rejection he could give her so she could be prepared. She *would* be going with him, even if she had to wrap her hand around his ankle and drag along behind him.

No good person would leave her to wander the forest by herself if she just casually followed him out of the gate. She didn't care if he hated her the entire time.

She leaned her shoulder against the wall of the somewhat quiet street she found herself on, wishing things were easier. Then, she turned so she could place her back against it, willing for just a small shred of hope.

The town was beginning to feel like a prison. For Raewyn, who was a free spirit by nature, it was becoming unbearable.

I'm worried that the longer I stay here, the likelier it is I'll be targeted. How long would it be before Raewyn had to beat the heck out of someone to protect herself, where it would be discovered that she wasn't 'normal' to them?

Despite this, she wasn't the kind of person to weep. She was used to high stakes and high pressure; it was just the unfamiliarity getting to her.

She didn't know how much longer she had to go before she made it to the inn, but the smell of burnt food and hay wafted under her nose. She covered it when it became stronger.

Either the food here is terrible, or people just don't know how to cook.

"Well, well, well, what do we have here?" A woman softly chuckled a few feet away from her.

She paused when three, maybe four, people entered the path in front of her.

It wasn't very narrow, so if she asked politely, there was surely no issue in her passing – that's if they didn't stop her to make fun of her accent. Raewyn was constantly listening and learning, gaining experience before she started fully communicating with humans.

"Please excuse me," Raewyn greeted kindly while hugging the wall with her shoulder.

Someone stepped in front of her.

"We've been watching you. Haven't we, Jackson?" a woman said with a haughty undertone. She smelt awful, like burnt food and mouldy hay.

"You always come back to this inn around this time of day," Jackson answered with a smugness in his voice.

Her back stiffened, realising she'd been cornered on purpose. She could almost picture their rapacious expressions as they leaned against houses or fencing in plain sight, Raewyn none the wiser.

This path wasn't narrow, which gave her a lot of freedom to run. However, she would never consider doing so, since she didn't want to fall on her face or run into something.

A small breeze ruffled her cloak and dress, pushing them forward as she considered her options.

I know how to fight in hand-to-hand combat, but what if they have weapons? She'd never had to fight before without being watched by an instructor, nor had she ever wielded a weapon – or fought against one.

"Let me through," Raewyn stated firmly, before adding, "please."

She tried to step around the woman, who was obviously much shorter than her as her voice came from below, but the sound and scent of a different person blocked her way.

"How does a blind lady find herself in such nice living quarters?" a man asked, his voice deep but not comforting.

Raewyn's ears twitched nervously under her hood as she backed up a step.

"Seems a little suspicious to me," said a younger man on the other side of the pathway, as though to block that exit as well.

Raewyn noticed someone's scuffling feet as they manoeuvred behind her. She was completely blocked in.

She almost laughed. They probably thought they had her trapped and defenceless. Perhaps if she were a human woman, she might have been. Unfortunately for them, she'd trained her reflexes and, participated in hand-to-hand combat to sharpen her skills.

Before the accident, she'd never had much interest in learning to fight, and she never needed to. She'd only signed up for the courses to teach herself how to wield her senses, and she learned she had a rather good knack for fighting.

Not to boast, but she was kind of good at everything she put her heart and – more importantly – her *brain* to.

She wasn't the strongest, or the fastest, and definitely not the bravest, but against humans? A child Elysian could beat them with their eyes closed and both hands tied behind their back. She'd studied their physiological makeup – they were one of the slowest species of sentient creatures.

"I bought my stay, just like anyone else," she answered as she squared her shoulders and lifted her nose. "But I'm guessing you don't particularly care how I obtained my gold. Your questions are more to rouse fear in me like a feeble, helpless person."

The woman to her left laughed. "Listen to the way she speaks! *Liwke a veeble, welplezz purrrson.* Where the hell did the guards pick you up from? Was that supposed to be scary?"

Raewyn's left ear twitched in annoyance while both heated in embarrassment. She thought she'd spoken quite well that time, but for goodness' sake, she was trying to speak a language she'd learnt when she was young!

She also hadn't paid attention to her father. She liked mathematical equations, not off-realm languages. She never thought she'd need to learn them.

"Shut it, Lori," the guy behind her bit. "I already feel bad about robbin' her. Don't make me feel worse by pickin' on the way she speaks."

"The sun is going down, lady," one of the men from behind said as they crept closer.

"Just give us the money, and no one has to get hurt," Jackson, warned. He was the one near Lori.

"We don't actually want to hurt you," the second man from behind her sighed – the same one who'd asked Lori not to tease Raewyn about the way she spoke. He seemed kinder than the rest. "I already feel bad about this, but if I don't pay my taxes, I'll lose my market permit."

Raewyn clenched her hands tightly. "And what about me?"

"We'll leave you with enough to eat for a few days," Lori answered, followed by the distinct sound of metal sliding out of a casing. It must be some kind of dagger or knife.

"I need to pay the inn for my stay." Her nose scrunched up tightly in anger and worry. "If I don't, I'll have nowhere else to sleep."

"Someone will help you," the kinder one said. "Someone will feed you or give you a home."

"Really?" Raewyn scoffed. "Because as far as I'm aware, there are already those without homes within the town. How can you justify your own actions when the next time you see me, I may be living on the street?"

"Did you understand that, Greg?" Lori laughed. "Because I only got a few words."

Greg, the kinder one, sighed. "I don't know why you're bein' a bitch when it's obvious what she said. Open your ears, Lori."

"Oh, shove off." Lori stepped closer. "No matter what choice you make, you *will* be walking away lighter. So, choose whether it will be painful or not."

Raewyn unclenched her hands and lifted her chin. "I'll scream."

"Good for you," Jackson sneered. "No one will come save you. I imagine everyone is already watching us from their windows, and yet... where are they?"

"The guards?" Raewyn answered, her voice growing small.

"They won't care," Jackson chuckled. "Not if we pay them off."

"Oh, screw this! Just grab her!" Lori shouted, and all four rushed her.

From behind, both her elbows were grabbed.

"Get off me!" she shouted, lifting her feet and kicking them forward. The bottom of her boots made contact with someone's stomach, and they keeled forward enough that when she kicked again, she bashed them in the face.

A lot was happening. The sounds of huffs, light coin purses rattling, clothing, and feet scuffling were the only reasons she sensed where they were. Their scents banded together as one mass of violent, grabbing hands, and Raewyn let out a grunted scream.

Someone grabbed her coin pouch and tried to undo the double knotted ties. She shoved her head backwards in a diagonal motion, and the back of her skull smacked into the side of someone's face. She stomped her heel down at the same time on their foot, and both actions forced a pained yelp from them.

Their hands around her biceps loosened just enough that she was able to shove her fist forward and hit the person who had grabbed her coin pouch.

No one came to help; no one came to stop them. Despite her yells and their barked commands to each other, no one cared enough to save Raewyn.

"You're so fucking dumb, Jackson," Lori spat from the side, making it obvious she was the one Raewyn had kicked earlier. "Just cut it off!"

"Oh... yeah." The low chime of a blade being withdrawn rang in Raewyn's ears.

She had more money in her room in the inn. Raewyn knew she wouldn't be without a safe place to eat, sleep, or bathe, but this money was all she had in this world. She doubted she'd be able to get more.

"Please," she begged as she kicked and fought, her frantic squirming allowing her to grab at Jackson's hair and yank on it. "Please stop. Please just leave me alone. This isn't fair."

"Wow! She's so damn strong. It's like trying to fight off a giant flailing fish."

One arm was still being held back by someone unnamed, while Jackson fought to get her to free her death grip on his hair, whining as he did. Lori was pushing between Raewyn and Jackson, probably trying to go for her coin pouch as she wildly kicked.

"Fuck," Greg muttered under his breath, his voice a few steps away and growing quieter, as though he was retreating. "I can't do this. You guys were right; I don't have the stomach for this."

"It's a bit late to make that decision," a familiar, deep, mean voice said. The smell of draflium flowers washed over her senses, carried in by the breeze flowing behind her. A shiver ran down her spine. "I feel like this brings a new level to the saying 'rob someone blind.' I didn't think idiots meant it literally. Leave the woman alone."

"Oh, fuck off," the nameless man behind her spat before he must have turned around to look at him. "Holy shit. You are the biggest fucker I've ever seen."

"You," Jackson bit out. "What do you want? We won't share, if that's what you're after."

"I have my own money," he answered. The following sound was a thwack and then a thump, as if someone had been struck so hard, they'd hit the ground. Within seconds, the man holding her other arm was gone. "I heard a commotion; I came to investigate."

"Hey, what the hell?" Lori cried, moving away from Raewyn.

Jackson pulled away, and Raewyn let him so she could get closer to the stranger she'd been following all day.

Okay, so maybe he wasn't as bad as she originally thought.

"This isn't what was–" Jackson's voice was cut off with a choke, like his throat had been grabbed.

Lori's scream was next, followed by a groan from Jackson next to her, as though he'd been thrown at the woman. Their combined slapping thuds reverberated through the ground as they fell into what she assumed was a pile.

"I told you to leave her alone," the stranger said calmly but firmly. "Now fuck off, the lot of you."

Only two sets of footsteps echoed, one from behind and the other from in front. By the lack of burnt cooking that wafted in the air, Lori had run, while someone behind her had gotten to their feet to do so as well.

Greg's leather scent disappeared, while Jackson's and the unnamed assailant's scents remained.

Until now, Raewyn hadn't realised her heart was pumping wildly in adrenaline and fear. She also hadn't noticed tears were dampening the cloth over her eyes. Her hands were trembling, and it was only now that she was safe, and everything was okay, that she understood just how frightened she'd been.

In the moment, she'd just been so worried about fighting back, nothing else had registered. Now, all she wanted was to sink to her knees in relief.

Raewyn let out a little sniffle.

"Stop crying. They're gone." He made a thoughtful hum before he added, "At least the conscious ones are."

His warm scent of oranges and cinnamon suddenly became comforting, like the big hug she'd needed since she arrived in this stupid realm. Her tears pooled heavier rather than disappearing.

"T-thank you for saving me."

"I said stop crying, and stop being afraid." He gave a grunt before pushing her to the side – albeit gently. "You'll just bring Demons, if they aren't already heading to this town."

"I know, I'm sorry, but I just can't seem to stop."

Gosh, she wanted to stop! She hated how gross her cloth was becoming against her face.

"Well, the inn you stay at is just around the corner, so you're not far from being safe. We better leave, before the guards come around and start asking questions. Since we're the ones still standing, they'll think we were the ones at fault."

Wiping her nose as she frowned, she asked, "H-how did you know I was staying at the inn?"

"I come to this part of town often. I've seen you around."

"Oh." Her ears twitched at the shifting of dirt, as though he'd begun walking away, and Raewyn leapt forward. "Wait! Please don't leave me alone here."

She managed to grab ahold of his large wrist, both her thin, nimble hands barely wrapping around the thick limb.

He paused and turned, and Raewyn knew, just knew, he was staring down at her.

"I can take you back to the inn, if you would prefer."

"Yes, please," she answered, gripping his arm tighter. The thick, coarse clothing covering it crinkled in her palms. "I also wanted to ask you something."

"Fine. What is it?" he grumbled out as he started walking.

"I overheard you were leaving today."

With an odd sense of humour in his voice, he said, "Did you now?"

Knowing she was getting further away from those people and closer to the safety of her room, her trembling subsided. She could even smell the food and alcohol from the tavern, and the owner had been nothing but caring and protective towards his patrons.

She still held onto the stranger's arm by tightening her fingers around his shirt, refusing to let go of her saviour, but her hands eased their panicked strength.

He saved me from those people. Maybe he'll travel with me. He appeared to be far nicer than he first seemed. Why would he help a stranger when he gained nothing from it?

Her grip strengthened, and Raewyn opened her mouth to speak. *Okay, here goes...*

THREE

Standing at the south gate, Raewyn adjusted her bag straps before she fiddled with her hood, checking to make sure she had everything in place. Freshly bathed, with plenty of food and water, she was ready to leave this town.

She'd been waiting there since dawn, making sure the stranger didn't leave without her.

When she'd asked if he would be willing to take her on his travels, he'd agreed without argument. She'd released a sigh of relief, especially since he hadn't asked for compensation.

He'd only asked her two questions.

The first was if she'd menstruated recently. She lied and said she had – Elysian women's cycles were different to humans due to the time difference. If she'd said no, he wouldn't have understood she was only in the middle of her cycle and wouldn't bleed for quite some time.

She figured he worried she'd bring Demons upon them. It'd been an uncomfortable discussion to have with a complete stranger, a human male at that, but she understood the necessity of it.

Secondly, he asked if she was a fearful person, as the scent of fear she could produce during the nights in the forest could bring danger.

Although she wasn't impervious to being afraid, she

informed him that she should mostly be fine. Probably a lie, considering Raewyn had never been face-to-face with a bloodthirsty Demon before, but they'd cross that bridge if they ever came to it.

When just a fraction of warmth hit the side of her face, she knew the sun was beginning to rise and fidgeted further.

Did I bring enough food and water? He said he wouldn't be sharing his own with her unless he found food along the way. *What about my sleep blanket? Should I have bought a second?* She'd bought it recently, since she found Earth's summer just a little chilly at night.

She'd also brought cleaning products – not just for her body, but also for her second dress and socks. She had no underwear since she didn't like the ones available here.

She turned her face downward and sneered at the boots on her feet. She didn't just hate them; she *despised* them with a passion.

However, the humans had made unkind comments about her not wearing them within the streets.

Elysians didn't wear shoes, wishing to feel the soil beneath their feet, to connect with it on a spiritual level. They often wore cloth or gold over their arches for decoration.

These shoes not only disconnected her with this world, but all worlds in general.

Raewyn touched her head wrapping, feeling the bumpy texture of the two braids she had in her hair for ease of management during their travels. She expected that privacy was about to become scarce, so being able to wash her hair freely without him seeing the whiteness of it would be difficult.

"Ready?" the stranger said right next to her.

Raewyn started and let out a squeal.

She turned to him with a few huffs, trying to recover from being startled. "How long have you been standing there? I didn't hear you approaching."

"I've learnt to be quiet on my feet." Now that he was close, his scent washed over her. "They're opening the gate. Have you obtained everything you need?"

"Yes," she answered, pushing her satchel behind her so it would be more comfortable. Between her medium-sized breasts, she gripped the strap tightly. "You won't need to worry about me, I promise."

"Good, because I'll only look out for you if I must. I will protect you, though, if we encounter any Demons, Duskwalkers, or bandits."

Raewyn's pointed ears twitched under her hood. *What's a Duskwalker?* She'd never heard or read about those in any of her texts. Were they a new creature on Earth, one that arrived after the Elves left?

She didn't question him on it, knowing it was best she didn't reveal just how little knowledge she had of this world. She gave him a weak smile instead.

"This is for you." He handed her a rope with fragrant pouches attached to it. "Tie it around your waist. It's filled with herbs and spices, and it will help to hide your scent from all those who may hunt it."

"Thank you," she said as she took it and wrapped it around her centre. "That's very astute of you."

Silence bled between them, and Raewyn nervously shifted her weight back and forth between her feet. Why did she get the impression he was looking over her with an assessing gaze?

"You said you found my footsteps quiet, and a cart is too noisy for safe travelling. Will you have trouble following me on foot? I don't talk much."

"Maybe a little..." She wouldn't feign confidence when the alternative would be getting lost in a potentially Demon-filled forest.

He gave a rough huff, and material shifted as though he folded his arms across his chest. "I won't hold your hand."

Her dark complexion hid from him any redness from her flushing in chagrin, but she hoped her hands curling into fists were obvious. If her eyes weren't covered, she would have glared in his direction.

"I'm not a child. I don't need you to hold my hand or arm. If you have a rope, you can tie it to yourself, and I can hold it."

"You want to walk me like I'm a fucking dog?"

Her ears flattened at him so freely swearing at her, but she puffed her cheeks and folded her arms.

"What else do you want to do? It's either I hold it, or you hold it, and I imagine holding something the entire way will annoy you. Attaching ourselves together permanently would be foolish if we needed to be apart because of danger, or even if we went the wrong way around a tree to each other."

"Hmm... I guess that's all true."

"Exactly, so don't be so rude when you haven't come forth with any ideas."

"You're quick to use your tongue. I'm offering to take you through the forest. Shouldn't you be more cautious of the way you speak to me?"

Raewyn's right hand curled into a fist around her bag strap. "Well? Is it the rope idea, or do you have something better?"

Without answering, he dug through a bag filled with metal, like tools and coins, as well as... bells? Yes, there was definitely the chime of little bells.

Within moments, he grunted and said, "Here."

She tentatively reached her hand out and found a long piece of rope in his outreached hand. When she yanked on it, there was resistance, as though he'd already tied it around his waist.

Suddenly she was hurtled forward when he walked forward without even saying anything! Raewyn nearly tripped over her own feet in surprise, but skilfully righted herself and jogged a few steps to keep up.

The whirring of wheels and clanking of chains started up, followed by loud creaking. The gate was opening, and Raewyn took in a long, calming breath.

"You got a name?" he asked as they waited. "It would be

impolite if I just called you woman along the way."

"Raewyn, but my friends call me Rae. You?"

"Call me Merc, since I don't particularly like it when people call me big fucker like you heard the other day."

Raewyn laughed. It wasn't that she found what he said funny – she was just so nervous about leaving the safety of this town, but also excited to finally get away from it. If she found some Anzúli, they might be able to help her get home.

When the rope went from slack to taut, she stepped forward after him. He grunted when she stepped on the back of his shoe, and she blushed as she looked down.

She spent a few moments feeling the length of the rope, then held it further down with her right hand, and grasped the end with her left. She made the rope taut enough that she could feel which way he moved, but would still remain at a distance so she wouldn't accidentally step on his heel again. Yes, she was always behind him, but she didn't particularly mind that.

The less he looked at her, the less he'd pay attention to her features. It also meant she could basically walk in his exact path, and in doing so, she'd never run into anything like she might if she were next to him.

After a few minutes of walking, him in complete and utter silence while she tried everything to make sure they could walk with ease together, she lifted her head. She listened to the quietness that had fallen around her.

It's been a month since I heard true silence. Every day, every night, every minute of both, Raewyn heard people.

She smiled slightly, taking in the earthy, rich scents of fresh trees and shrubs, even the very grass. She took in the birds squawking in the distance, and the insects that made chirping songs. It was peaceful, calm, and serene.

The tall forests in Nyl'theria were the perfect place for Demons to hide and travel in the daytime, giving plenty of cover from the three suns. For hundreds of years, her people hadn't been able to travel through them. They were stuck, imprisoned by the very magical barrier that protected them.

When she smelt the sap of a tree as it grew closer, she dropped the tip of the rope and reached her hand out just to... touch it. Feel its bark. Get to know the tree on an intimate level.

Her joy grew brighter.

"Why the hell are you smiling for?" Merc asked in a curt tone. "The trees may be sparse, but Demons can still travel in the daytime."

All joy fled out of her in one quick swish. She grabbed the rope again while turning her head to the side to dismiss him.

"Thank you for allowing me to come with you," she said to take the power away from his rudeness. "You haven't told me what town you're going to, or why. Do you mind if I ask?"

"There's no reason, I'm just travelling." Then, as if he were incapable of being kind, he added, "You know... you talk strange. Where are you from?"

Raewyn swallowed the lump that formed in her throat.

"My parents aren't from here. I picked up their accent, I guess." At least *that* entire statement was completely true.

"Where did they come from then? I've been all over this country, and I've never heard anyone speak like you."

"Where are you from?" Raewyn asked, desperate to get away from the conversation.

"North of here. The guards said they found you wandering the forest by yourself. How did someone such as yourself navigate the forest without being guided as you are now?"

"I don't know," she answered. "I can't remember. I think I hurt my head and got separated from those I was travelling with."

Raewyn nibbled at her bottom lip. *He inquired about me? Why?* She wasn't comfortable knowing that. Then again... she did follow him around the market like a stalker. It would be awfully hypocritical of her to judge him.

She was a stranger to him, and he may have wanted to make sure she was safe to travel with.

"They said you were suffering from amnesia, but sometimes people begin regaining their memories over time. You remember nothing? Then how do you know your parents aren't from here?"

"I was making an educated guess," Raewyn said, gritting her molars in frustration. "I thought you said you don't talk much."

He bit out a grunt, and once more went quiet.

She didn't know why she let out a giggle she'd tried so hard to suppress. He was often mean and short with those he'd spoken to when she'd followed him in the markets, and it didn't seem like he appreciated people acting that way back to him.

Which meant she just wanted to do it more to get a rise out of him. Unbeknownst to most, Raewyn was an instigator when she wanted to be. Not a cruel one, and only to those she thought deserved it.

"What's so funny?" he asked.

She thought she'd skilfully hid her giggle. "I didn't mean to offend you."

She really hadn't, but she was glad it'd stopped his interrogation.

"It will be impossible for you to offend me, Raewyn. I've heard worse things than a little woman like you could ever possibly say to me."

Little? I'm not little! She was tall, even for an Elysian woman. She was offended, which made little sense, but she thought that might also be because he was a human. She didn't want him to think her inferior when she was certain she would be faster and stronger than him, even with her thin, tall frame.

"I told you my friends call me Rae," she offered with a smile to defuse the situation.

"I'm not your friend. By the end of this trip, you will see that."

Her bottom lip stuck forward into a forced pout. "Has anyone ever said you're grouchy?"

"I've been called many things, but I'll add that to the list."

Her smile grew at his answer. "I'll add it to the bottom where I care the least."

"You know what then, Merc?" she asked in a playful, yet nondescript tone.

"I don't particularly care to know what you'll say," he said, just as the leaves rustled.

Her smile grew so wide that it crinkled the outer creases of her eyes and revealed her even teeth. "By the end of this trip, I'm going to hear you call me Rae."

She would make him see her as his friend. Not because she needed the validation of him doing so, but because she thought it would be entertaining.

Complicated people were always the best to crack open. He would be a fun puzzle to solve, and Raewyn did love anything that was puzzling and difficult.

It was why she became a scientist to begin with.

She just hoped nothing bad happened to him by the end of this journey.

FOUR

The first night of their travels, Raewyn discovered the ground was hard, cold, and dirty. She'd hated every moment, especially since she had to *pretend* to be asleep the entire time.

Anytime she tried to sit up, he told her to lie down, and, in his words, 'go the fuck to sleep.'

Perhaps he was angry with her because she'd begged for rest, even when he'd wanted to march through the night like an unstoppable force.

He'd added that she didn't need to be worried and that he'd wake up and protect her if an enemy were to come.

She appreciated that he seemed to be saying this to soothe her, like that was the issue with her sleeplessness, but she didn't need soothing – she was just hopelessly bored.

Even if she did have the same sleeping habits as a human, she doubted she would have been able to sleep. Starting a fire would be an unwise decision, which is why she'd never asked for one, so she shivered the entire night.

It was especially windy, and the one blanket she'd brought was nowhere near enough.

Merc never offered his own, nor his cloak, or for her to lie behind him to stay warm. Then again, why would he? It was summer; she was sure this was hot for him.

Most nights were spent like this, while their days were

mostly filled with silence.

When they'd passed a freshwater lake, he offered her privacy if she desired to bathe. She wanted to, more than anything in the world. He didn't seem to be a pervert or attracted to her in general, but the white hair on her head was not the only place she had it on her body.

Even when he led her away from the lake, she had her nose turned to its fresh, inviting scent. The grass and plants surrounding it smelt livelier, and her heart soared with the idea of belly flopping into it if it meant she could also be cleansed.

At least it gave her fresh water to drink. Merc boiled it for her so it would be safe from bacteria. He'd grumbled the entire time, since she demanded he do so.

They'd also had an argument over it.

"I'll leave you here. Don't test me," he threatened when she stamped her foot and folded her arms across her chest, refusing to leave until he set up a fire and boiled the water.

"We can leave, but you can't complain when you have to carry me when I'm suffering from dehydration or because I'm sick with a fever, all because you wouldn't spend a few minutes ensuring my safety." Then she'd tapped at her lips and spouted, "What was it you promised me? You'd keep me safe? I didn't realise you were a man who broke his promises."

She'd tried, really tried, not to appear smug when he caved. Whenever she annoyed him, he threatened to leave her behind, but never stuck to his word. She had the feeling he wouldn't, so she poked and prodded him as much as she could.

Two days had passed since they left Clawhaven.

She really tried to keep her spirits high, even when she tripped over a tree root, or smacked into a branch he ducked under. But there was one thing wearing her down... these silly shoes!

Her feet weren't made to wear them, and they pinched. She had sores she wouldn't have formed had she been barefooted. She'd almost started crying when there was a rock in her shoe she couldn't get rid of until she realised it was actually inside her sock. She didn't even know how it got there.

Oh, and what about when her sock got wet somehow? It was absolutely gross.

Raewyn had never been so thankful when the third night approached, and Merc managed to find them an abandoned cottage to stay in. The door was already open, and he kindly cleared away the spiderwebs and their creators.

His footsteps were usually quiet, but not even he could hide how the porch steps creaked under his weight. So, when he came back outside while she was holding onto the broken porch railing, she heard him approach.

She also smelt him, since he was covered in soot, as though he'd cleaned a fireplace or chimney out.

"Inside is safe," he stated, while slapping his hands together as if he were dusting them. "There's evidence of a Demon nest, but it looks as though it's abandoned."

Raewyn cocked her head. "Demons will build a nest inside old houses?"

"Of course. It's perfect shade from the sun. Half the time, Demons will kill the people and take their place inside their home. It's easier for them since they don't have to go back to the Veil or the mountains to hide."

A shiver coursed down her spine, one that even shuddered her shoulders. From what she'd learned of the Veil through her texts, it was similar to the forests of Nyl'theria – just with different vegetation.

She didn't want to be anywhere near it.

"Go inside," he demanded. "I saw through one of the windows there's a well. I'll go check if the *princess* can have more water. Maybe she'll even take a bath so she doesn't stink."

Her lips parted in mortification, and honestly, just in shock that he would say something like that.

"I don't smell that bad!" she yelled when he walked down the steps. Then most of his sounds became muted when he touched dirt.

He was completely gone when the slight jingling of bells ceased around a bend.

"I don't... do I?"

She'd been rubbing the pouches tied around her waist against her body, so she didn't smell too bad. She sneaked a sniff at her armpit, and she thought she smelt just fine.

She reached her hands forward so she could guide her way to the door and then made her way inside. She touched all the walls to familiarise herself with the layout, counting her steps as she did.

There was very little furniture, as if it'd been ransacked over time. There was, however, a singular chair and a low table.

There were two rooms, one that was empty, and another that had broken bits of timber and a de-fluffed mattress. She went cold when she understood this was the 'nest' he spoke of and backed out of the room in horror.

Once she mapped out the walls of the house in its entirety, she did the dimension math in her head of how many steps each wall was from each other. She went through it all in her mind's eye, and once she had, her confidence within the space grew.

Merc came in not long after and placed a sloshing bucket on the ground with a metallic thud. He then started up the fireplace and set the water container to boil.

Since he was crouched down in front of it, she accidentally bumped his side as she crouched next to him, following the sounds and smells to know where the fireplace was. The fire crackled as it came to life, and the heat that billowed from it was utterly pleasant, as was the sweetness of the wood burning.

"Can I really have a bath?"

"No, there's no tub, but I'm sure you want to get clean. I'll leave so you can have some privacy to wipe yourself down."

She leaned closer and rudely sniffed at the air right next to him. Over the course of their time together, she'd grown fond of his scent, like that of a draflium flower, and she'd already missed it.

"You need one now as well. You smell like ash."

"I'll wash myself outside near the well. I'm not so picky about the quality of my water, so long as it's clear."

Along with his smell, she also found his voice nice – even when it was being used for rudeness or to curse. She'd never really touched him, so she had no way to gauge what he looked like. All she knew was that he was very tall, and very strong. From the times she'd accidentally bumped into him, he appeared dense, with thick, large muscles.

Were he not a human, she may have tried to get to know him on a less friendly and more intimate level. His personality, although abrasive, wasn't truly unpleasant to her. Raewyn had always been soft but resilient. She could handle anyone, and most people tended to like her because of it.

Her parents had been reclusive, preferring to throw themselves into their work, which is why they'd never applied to join the council. She, on the other hand, had been invited when most were supposed to submit forms.

Underneath Merc's callousness was actually a person who cared on a deeper level. He wouldn't have obtained the water for her, cleaned away the spiderwebs, or offered her privacy if he didn't. Sure, he let her go a little cold at night, but that was her own fault, since she'd never voiced her displeasure.

Bubbles began to pop at the top of the water heating inside the fire. Merc removed the bucket and put it on the ground, the muted thud informing her he'd placed a cloth underneath it, so he didn't burn the flooring.

"Do I really smell that bad?" she playfully asked, with her lips pursed but curling upward.

"No, but women tend to their hygiene better than men." His clothing rustled as he stood. "Eat while it cools down. I'll go outside, wash, and check the surrounding area to make sure it's safe."

When the door thudded shut, Raewyn sat down and finally

removed her bag from her torso. She dug through it, and her shoulders turned inward at how much food she had left. She'd been rationing it, but Merc said the closest town was still a few days' walk. He'd never told her how many more, oddly vague about it, but she was beginning to worry about how much she had left.

She ate the last of what was soft and likely to begin spoiling.

Once she was done, she finally removed her boots and massaged her feet through her socks. They ached terribly, and she was relieved to have freedom from her foot prisons.

The bucket was hot to the touch, but she wrapped whatever was beneath it around the handle and lifted it off the ground. From feeling the main room before, she'd determined two of the windows didn't have curtains or blinds.

However, the room that wasn't once a Demon's nest had only one window, and its curtain was fully intact.

Even if she trusted that Merc wouldn't spy on her like a face-pressing creep through the window, she didn't want him accidentally seeing her from outside.

Knowing her chance at privacy could be limited, Raewyn got to work undressing. For the first time in three days, she removed her cloak, blindfold, and head wrappings.

She opened a jar of oil, poured a few drops into her palm, and rubbed her hands together until she'd smeared it evenly. She then worked it through her two braids, taking particular care with her hair to ensure it would continue to stay protected throughout their travels.

Once done, she wiped her body down. She also scrubbed at her eyes, noticing the sensitive skin on her face was irritated with tiny bumps from the blindfold.

The oil she'd used for her hair was also good for the skin, so she smeared a small amount across her face. She also took extra care with her feet, trying to soothe her blisters and the general aches she obtained just from walking on them. Even her knees got attention due to their stiffness.

The entire time, she listened carefully to make sure Merc hadn't come back or called out to her. The floors were old and creaky, and that gave her comfort in her ability to sense him.

When she was clean from head to toe, she sat there on the ground for a long while with her knees to her chest.

I hate this, she thought as she rested her chin on her knees. *I hate having to hide. It's terrible for my skin, and it's making this journey far more unpleasant than it needs to be.*

If she could, she'd spend the night locked away in this room just to be free of her clothes and feel more like herself. But, when her ear twitched at a random noise outside, she sighed and reached for her dirty clothes.

With the last of the water, she scrubbed them clean with the bar of fabric soap she had. She left them in the water to soak as she pulled out clean clothes from her bag and dressed before wrapping her hair once more.

She threw on her cloak and a pair of socks, but she refused to put her shoes back on for now.

She opened the door, and while carrying the bucket of washed clothes, poked her head out. "Merc?"

She received no answer.

She made her way outside so she could wring her clothes of excess water and brought them back inside to dry them in front of the fire. She sat in front of it as well.

Just as she was wondering where Merc was, the chime of jingle bells moved around the house. At each corner, those chimes dwindled in number until the last one, and then there was complete silence, apart from her breathing and the low flames.

Footsteps creaked on the porch, and a gust of wind blew his fresh, clean-of-soot scent into the house.

"You've been gone a while," she stated.

As usual, Merc grunted instead of replying. The door closed, and she followed the sound of his movements, mapping where he was in the house. The fire crackled when something large was placed inside it, likely more fuel.

Then he sat down against the wall next to the fireplace. Despite the size of the house, he'd chosen to sit relatively close to her.

"Why are you wearing your cloak?" She flinched when a fingertip brushed against her cheek, as though he was pushing the hood back. "We're inside; you don't need it."

She shoved it back over her head properly.

"I just prefer to wear it," she answered, before shining a smile his way.

His back shifted against the wall as though he'd leaned to the side to view her face better.

"What are you hiding under there? I didn't expect to see you dressed from head to toe again."

"I'm not hiding anything." The lie wasn't very convincing, especially since she'd said it rather defensively.

He sighed with true annoyance, as if his patience was wearing thin.

"You're even wearing a new piece of material over your face. I'm sure it's uncomfortable to wear all that. It's summer, for pity's sake. Most people bake in the heat even while wearing very little."

"I get cold really easily," she admitted. "Even now, I find it a little chilly in here."

"I noticed you shiver a lot, but that still doesn't explain why you are dressed for winter. No one is this cold during summer."

"I-I heard you moving around the house before with bells. Why?"

Merc gave a hum. "You heard that, did you? You've got pretty good hearing."

It was why she found his constant silent footsteps so alarming all the damn time. Then again, many Elysians were quiet on their feet, and Cykran was the worst for sneaking up on her.

"What were you doing?" she pressed, knowing Merc could be evasive with his own answers just as much as she was.

"I was placing charms out to protect the house. For tonight, neither of us will be eaten by Demons, no matter how much sound, fear, or blood we make."

Raewyn's back stiffened. "You didn't bring me here to kill me, did you?"

The chuckle that came from Merc was sickeningly dark, the moment ominous. She didn't know if he was being frightful with his words on purpose to make fun of her, but she really didn't appreciate it.

"If I wanted you dead, I would have done that the first day."

Raewyn laughed, hoping to break the tension, even when her stomach suddenly twisted with uncertainty. She was glad her eyes were covered, since it hid how far her eyebrows shot up in worry.

"So, back to the main topic." Her hood was moved again. "What are you hiding under there?"

With an annoyed hiss, Raewyn shoved her hood back and turned to him. She showed him her face and head wrapping, but skilfully made sure she didn't uncover her ears.

"Nothing, see?" She shoved it back up just as quickly. "I'm just cold, so leave me alone. It's not like you've shared a thing about yourself other than your name and that you come from the north."

"I'm nothing but a traveller. I visit towns, get what I need, and then move on to the next place."

"Do you not have a home, then?"

"I do, but like I said, it's north. For someone who has lost their memory, you'd have no idea where it is, even if I told you. Do you even know where Rivenspire is?"

Raewyn grumbled, "Well... no."

"Exactly, so what's the point in sharing anything about me?"

"I don't know." She rubbed at her arm, seeking to soothe herself.

"How badly is your memory affected?"

She shrugged, trying to feign the memory loss he expected.

"I remember some things. I know my parents, my family, my home, but I can't tell you where they are. I can't even tell you where *we* are."

"Have you always been without sight?"

"No," Raewyn answered truthfully. "Why are you asking me all this?"

"I'm just curious about you, is all. It's not like I'm asking you to lift your dress, so why are you acting so skittish?"

Raewyn's cheeks heated in embarrassment. *Gosh! He's so blunt and churlish. Why does he have to say things like that?*

"I wouldn't lift my dress for you even if you begged."

"Why not? I'm a handsome fellow." She hoped he was just being playful, rather than a creep.

"I really don't feel like being interrogated, Merc."

"Interrogated? Most people would call this 'getting to know each other.' It's perfectly normal for someone to inquire about their travel partner. Don't people usually share conversation over food?"

Raewyn opened her mouth, but closed it when she had no retort. She tipped her head forward as she bit her tongue. *I guess he's not wrong. Most people would do that.*

"Your constant evasion of questions, the way you hide your face and body constantly... you have to understand, I find you rather suspicious."

She hugged her torso. She didn't want to have to hide from him, but she couldn't trust a human not to react badly to what she was. The history her people had with his wasn't kind towards the Elysians.

Sure, the Demons were worse, but humans had trapped her people in the hopes they could grant their wishes, like they were all-powerful genies. That, or they would just kill or imprison them because they were different, showing off the pointy-eared 'freaks' they had in cages to other humans.

What if Merc turned on her when they got to the next town? Raewyn didn't want to feel that kind of betrayal.

"I showed you my face," she quietly answered. "What more do you want from me?"

Merc's voice turned deep and firm as he stated, "I want to know *who* you are."

Raewyn patted the floor until she touched her clothing, finding they still weren't dry.

"I'm going to sleep, so please don't touch my clothes," she bit as she scooped up her bag. "Maybe I can sleep properly for the first time since we left Clawhaven."

Raewyn went to the wall furthest from Merc. Then she curled up into a ball, pulling her blanket over her body until she'd even covered her head. She crossed her ankles, hoping to make herself as small as possible.

Please, let this be over soon.

FIVE

Raewyn only fell asleep for an hour, maybe two, when orange and cinnamon saturated her senses. However, it was her hood being pushed back that caused her to quickly sit up and knock Merc's arm away.

"What are you doing?" she snapped, pushing herself against the wall while propping her knees protectively against her chest.

"Wake up, the sun is rising."

She pulled her hood more firmly over her head. "Why were you touching my cloak?"

"I wasn't," he argued with a huff. "I was about to tap your cheek to wake you."

The lie was obvious, and the trust she'd felt in Merc's presence over the past two days was beginning to die.

"H-how long will it be before we get to the next town?" she asked, remaining seated on the ground while he stepped away from her.

"A few days."

"You've been saying that since we left Clawhaven."

"It's a few days," he bit out. "But I travel faster alone, and your need to sleep all night is slowing me down. So, Raewyn, I'm saying a few days because I have no idea how long it's going to take us."

Her shoulders hunched in as she drew her legs tighter against her chest. For the first time in their journey together, her heart picked up its speed.

Merc sighed. "Sorry, I'm just being impatient. I want this to end as much as you do. I'm not used to being around the same person for so long. It's why I travel a lot, and usually alone."

The smile Raewyn gave was weak. "It's fine, I guess. We all have our days."

"Here," Merc said, and the thump of something landing near her feet startled her. "Let's get going."

As she was putting on her boots, she carefully listened to his movements around the house. *What does he want from me?* She was beginning to feel like he hadn't allowed her to travel with him just to be nice.

Then a thought crossed her mind. *What if he is just being nice and I'm worried for no reason?*

Merc had never hurt her, had never tried to touch her or rob her. He'd given her no reason to not trust him, other than his questioning her and wanting to see her face properly.

Raewyn rubbed at her neck self-consciously.

It is pretty suspicious of me to keep my hood on all the time. Maybe I can tuck my ears into my hair wrapping so I can lower it?

She was choosing to trust Merc, but at the same time, he was also trusting her. Her secrecy might be worrying him.

Her lips pulled to one side as her ears drooped. *If it were the other way around...*

"Hurry up. You can look conflicted on our travels."

Raewyn tried to tie up her boots faster. "I really am slowing us down, aren't I?"

Once she was fully ready for their travels, they finally started back on their journey. He led her outside, and she firmly held the rope and followed his steps.

The forest was quiet save for the odd bird chirp, but the wind was light and warmer than the previous day.

"You're right," Merc eventually sighed.

"People often say that about me," she answered in a playful tone, hoping to erase whatever misgivings they both had about each other. "You'll have to be more specific."

"I haven't really shared much about myself."

"Makes it hard to trust someone you barely know."

We're as bad as each other.

Raewyn then stayed quiet, hoping her patience in not poking him further would get him to finally reveal something.

It paid off.

"So, like I said, I come from the north. Rivenspire is far from here, but it's pretty big. I live about two days' walk from it – at least, it's a two-day walk for me. I grew up with my mother and father, who, thankfully, died of old age. I'm not quite sure where my brothers are, but I'm sure they're around, or dead – who knows these days."

"How old are they?" she asked.

"Now? One would be... thirty? The other thirty-four or something."

The smile that spread across her lips was real. "What about you, then?"

"Twenty-nine. You?"

"Ah." Raewyn almost giggled when she realised in human years, she would be nearly four hundred and ninety. "I'm thirty-two."

"Have any siblings?"

Raewyn's smile died as a cold, painful lance stabbed her heart. "I have an older half-brother, but I don't know how he is doing. I haven't seen him since I was really young."

"I haven't seen my family since I was young either. I left home after my parents died. Guess I started travelling as a way to grieve, especially since my brothers went off to do their own things. I wanted to figure out my place in the world and haven't really stopped travelling since."

Holding the guiding rope connected to him, she raised her hand nearest the end and rubbed her chin in thought. What else could she ask him?

The question that came to mind made her grin like a deviant. "Ever had a lover?"

His steps faltered and stumbled. "What the fuck?"

She grinned. "Is that a no?"

"Of course, I have."

Her expression softened. "What were they like?"

"All of them have been nice enough."

"But I'm guessing the traveller in you couldn't stay with them?"

"You can say that. I've broken a lot of hearts on my travels."

Their day continued with a general back and forth, and Raewyn spun as many truths as she could into her lies and evasions. She felt terrible lying to Merc, but the trust required between them for her to reveal what she was, where she came from, was just too much of a risk.

He, however, was being oddly chatty. She learned much about him, and every bit she did added to his personality. She found herself softening towards him, and the awkward night before was washed away.

It also aided her to forget about their journey through the forest as she listened to every word he said. Apparently, his town had been a farming place that fed the mining villages nearby, which in return gave ore to the smithing and carpentry town. The whole area worked as a unit and traded regularly with each other – and came to each other's aid when needed.

He'd apparently been one of the few brave enough to go into the forest to chop wood, and he said he still wore the lumberjack shirt to go with it – it was rather coarse against her skin whenever her hands brushed over it. She figured that was why he'd been confident outside of the protective walls of towns and villages.

When the temperature began to drop, Merc informed her they'd need to be quieter now, since night was falling. He was always alert during it.

"I've always wanted to ask," Raewyn whispered, despite his warning. "Do you carry weapons? You know... for fighting against Demons?"

"What kind of question is that?" he snapped back in a low tone. "Of course, I do. Only an idiot would walk around the forest without a weapon."

Raewyn bit her tongue. *Did he just call me an idiot?* She didn't have any weapons! *I guess he is my weapon, though. Go forth, meat shield.*

"I'm surprised we haven't come across any Demons on our travels," she said, turning her head so she could listen around them.

"You really don't know anything, do you?" Merc sighed, his gruff voice disapproving. "We're in the southlands. There's a border wall made of logs that cuts this part of the continent completely off from the rest of it. It keeps most of the Demons out, or, at least, the ones that aren't good at climbing."

"Oh... does that mean people can't get through it?"

"There are gates, just like in the towns. Now shut up."

Ignoring him, she asked, "Do people monitor the gates?"

"No. You have to open them yourself."

"That sounds like an awfully difficult–"

Merc suddenly turned around and grabbed her entire face to quieten her. Her eyes clenched under her blindfold, and she bashed on his forearm, barely able to breathe. Her mouth was covered by his large palm, and the purlicue between his thumb and forefinger partially blocked her nose.

He was right in front of her, merely inches away, and she could feel his hot breath washing over her forehead.

"Shhh," he demanded, getting even closer. "Something is coming."

Raewyn's ears pulled back, a natural twitch that made her hearing more alert. Great. Did her words conjure the very creatures she'd just been asking about?

Only when she calmed her rapidly beating pulse from

thinking Merc was trying to hurt her did she finally notice the thud of paws. Something was running towards them on all fours, and it was faster than anything she'd ever heard.

Raewyn shook her head in his palm to reject the idea of a monster coming their way, although barely, since his grip was tight.

"Stay still and keep yourself calm. Don't smell like fear."

He brought her closer to his body, and for the first time, she got a grasp of what he truly felt like.

He was much bigger than she thought he'd be. His body was dense with muscle, thick and wide with it. He had a slightly bulging gut, like he had a layer of fat under an eight pack of abdomen muscles.

As though he was trying to hide her, he wrapped a big strong arm around her waist. His cloak fell around her to shield her further.

Forcing them together pushed his hand down so it was only covering her mouth, but it also allowed her to feel the trunks he called legs.

Her eyelids fluttered at his draflium scent. Despite the danger she could clearly hear nearby, her body went warm with arousal. His body heat, mixing with the freshness of that scent, had a strange coil of desire tightening in her gut.

Raewyn tightly clenched her eyes shut. *It's a placebo. It's not real.*

The draflium flower, when glowing at night, was a powerful aphrodisiac when ingested. It did nothing when touched or smelled, but she'd played with its effects once or twice for fun.

Get your head together, Rae, she demanded. She was forced to suck in another draw of his scent, and her nipples tightened. She clenched her thighs together when liquid began to pool at her entrance. *He does smell nice, though.*

She almost wanted to drool.

"Fuck," Merc bit out. "It's too late. It's picked up your scent."

Her lazy, desirous haze was cut through when he picked her up and shoved her into the curve of a tree trunk. He let her go, and fresh, non-arousal-inducing air cleared her lungs.

"Stay there and don't even think about moving."

"Wait–"

A ferocious roar cut her off this time, and she shrunk into the tree. It was close now, not even a few metres. Beastly and frightening, it sounded massive.

A long, heavy material fell over Raewyn, causing her to flinch.

"Put that over you. It'll disorientate it while I fight it."

When she pushed the material to her face, feeling its thick, worn texture with her fingertips, she realised it was his cloak. Her chest fluttered with ease. He cared about her safety and wasn't planning to use her as a diversion to save himself.

It'd been something she was worried about.

"Will you be okay?" she asked quietly, wrapping his cloak around her.

"If something growling is coming for you, do whatever you need to protect yourself. Don't think, just do."

Her brows furrowed deeper, but as she opened her mouth to respond, those approaching steps halted. The creature had leapt. A roar shot right past her and ended right where Merc was standing.

A deep thud had her whimpering, but she covered her mouth with both hands to stay quiet. Her heart squeezed so tightly she thought the tendons holding it in place would snap.

Other than a singular yell, Merc was quiet, while his attacker was a mixture of snapping fangs, rattling bones, and growling snarls. Whatever it was, a Demon or the Duskwalker thing he'd mentioned, it sounded bigger than him.

The creature smelt odd, but it was smothered, like it was evolving into something to be pleasant. It made it sweet.

That sweetness was drowned out when coppery blood penetrated the air.

A sharp inhale of breath hissed out, and Raewyn's eyes crinkled into bows. *Merc's hurt.* She wanted to go to him, to help, but knew she would only get in the way.

"Give her to me," a distorted, rumbling voice demanded.

"Fuck," Merc spat.

Raewyn's scream was loud to her own ears when her calf was grabbed, and she was flipped to her back. As she was dragged across the ground, the action dislodged her blindfold, and she saw a bright glow of two red orbs sparking in the darkness now that it was no longer blocking her vision. She was too frightened to linger on why she saw them.

Dread crawled down her spine like a ghastly cold finger trying to tear its way to bone. She kicked her feet, hitting against a hard face, while sticks and rocks scraped her back.

The monster let out a yelp of pain, not due to her actions, and she was freed.

On her hands and knees, Raewyn trembled, her arms shaky, as she crawled back to the tree where Merc's cloak lay upon the ground. She threw it over herself and huddled into the overarching roots while adjusting her blindfold.

Raewyn was ready.

Whatever Merc was fighting, it wasn't a normal Demon. He was a human. He would be too slow, too weak, to battle something like that.

Even an Elf would lose this fight.

She was ready, gathering magic in her hands so she could protect herself when she needed to.

All he has to do is weaken it. If he weakened it, and she made sure they weren't connected in a lock of limbs, she might be able to help kill it.

She'd explain where the magic came from later. *I'll just claim I'm an Anzúli.*

Just as a booming, ear-splitting roar shook the very foundation of her core, another yelp rang out. It was cut short by the crunching snap of tiny bones; a neck had been twisted.

Eerie silence descended upon the area.

Raewyn held her breath, like that was enough to hide her presence. Someone had died, and the mixture of blood and scents made it too hard to distinguish who.

No... it wasn't actually silence.

There was the tiniest rumble, and she wasn't sure if it was a quiet growl or not. It was too difficult to hear over her own panic, her heartbeat, and the crackle of magic that radiated just below her skin, vibrating against all her bones. Only she could hear it.

She braved slowly getting to her feet. She wanted freedom to run should she need it.

Her spit clogged in her throat when grass and leaves crunched under footsteps approaching her. Who or whatever it was, it was covered in too many smells, especially tangy and weird blood, and their breaths were deep and booming.

"Stay back," she warned.

"Calm your fear. You're not helping." Merc's voice was strained, deeper than usual. "You might bring more."

Tears of relief welled in her eyes.

"Merc!" she cried as she leapt forward and wrapped her arms around the base of his head. "By the holy Gilded Maiden, I thought you were dead."

While she was clinging to him, Merc stepped back. She could feel he'd put his hands in the air as though he wanted to avoid touching her.

"Let go," he demanded, his gruff voice right next to her ear. "I don't like being touched."

Well, he better get used to it! Because, right now, she was so elated he was okay, she thought she'd never want to let go.

"Thank you," she whispered, burying her head against his neck, ignoring the texture that brushed against her forehead. She thought it might be his hair. "Thank you so much for protecting me. I don't know what I would have done without you."

Raewyn went to kiss his cheek, to physically show just how

thankful she was. Instead, she headbutted something long and hard. Like *super* hard. Her hand pressed against his face to push herself away as she nursed her stinging brow bone.

"Ow, what is–" Raewyn paused when she realised what she was holding didn't feel like flesh, but rather bone.

Her hands patted once, only to discover that it wasn't flat but felt more like a... bony snout?

That's not a human face. Actually, it wasn't even a face at all, more like the skull of an animal. Fangs parting made her realise it was real and not some strange hallucination.

With a high-pitched scream, Raewyn shoved herself away and crashed against the ground. She scooted backwards on her backside to get away from him.

"What..." Her heart was nearly in her throat as she yelled, "What are you?!"

The low, quiet laughter that echoed from him was dark, and almost *cruel*. "Now, why did you have to go and do that?"

Foreboding terror washed over her from the tip of her forehead to send a chill down her spine. Raewyn's ears flattened backwards in her choking fear.

"W-where's Merc? What did you do to him?"

The Demon, or creature... whatever it was. It must have taken his voice somehow. That was it. It *had* to be it. Demons could obtain deceitful magic by consuming those who had the affinity for it – like Elysian Elves.

"The Demon is dead, Raewyn." Her jaw fell at her name being said, her mouth dry. "You've been travelling with me all along."

One thing became frighteningly obvious when he stepped forward, and she heard the distinct scrape of claws digging into the soil. The reason she'd never been able to hear his footsteps... the reason he'd been hard to track... was because he'd never been wearing shoes.

She'd been travelling with a monster.

Raewyn stood, and with her hands cupped to her chest, she

stepped back from him.

"Don't you dare run," he warned.

Of course, Raewyn ran.

Maniacal laughter boomed from him and carried over the distance, no matter how far she managed to get. With branches and leaves cutting across her clothing and face, it had her heart racing. Her breaths stuttered, warming her lips as the air froze them.

Nothing could shake her of the fear pummelling through her.

All she could think was, *he lied to me.*

SIX

Merikh let out a humour-filled, dark chuckle as he watched Raewyn scamper away, knowing she would.

With her hands forward, she bounced herself off tree after tree, and he just laughed. No matter how far or fast she ran, he would inevitably catch up to his *prey*.

Yet his laughter was also a product of frustration because, for three fucking days, he'd been taking this woman on a silly goose chase through the damn forest!

The nearest town to Clawhaven was merely a two-day walk, and he'd been guiding this woman in circles, hoping she would just tell him what the *fuck* she was.

Because Merikh knew... he knew this woman wasn't human, and he'd known it back in Clawhaven. She'd smelled ripe with strong magic; he'd even noticed it through the snout cloth he used to dilute scents.

So, what in the hell was she?

For a week, he'd been following this woman around those scum-filled streets, wondering how to best approach her so he could get her to follow him into the forest. Being straight forward and asking seemed far too suspicious – especially when her constant, near pathetic, begging for a traveller had been rejected so many times. And she'd already revealed she was cautious of people, since she rarely interacted with anyone except when necessary.

So, he watched, and he waited, and he planned.

Being the 'knight in shining armour' was the best approach he could think of. He was an unsociable bastard at the best of times, so he needed a protective guise to mask his true nature and intentions.

Did he feel terrible that he paid those four humans to harass this woman? Not. One. Bit. Not when all her troubles would shortly end, alongside her life.

The only reason he wasn't dashing after her was because he was shoving back those wretched, demanding hands that pleaded with him to chase his fleeing prey and tear her to pieces.

He would, eventually, but Merikh wanted to know *what* he was eating first... and where he might be able to find more.

After a deep, pacifying breath, one that gave him confidence he'd suppressed the worst of his hunger for sweet, delectable meat, he picked up his cloak. He slung it across his shoulders and calmly walked after her.

Run, little bunny. Run.

Her heartbeat was deafening over the distance, a scared little flutter, and it was a pretty beat as he followed. Her scent was sweet, split into three different kinds.

One of undeniable fear, so delicious it made him salivate despite his snout cloth.

One of her scent, which had annoyingly sometimes made his seam twitch. Convallaria majalis, or lily of the valley, was the closest he could come up with to naming it. It had been wrapping around his mind like a horrible little ache for the past three days. It was just as pleasant as it was toxic.

Then, finally, her magical scent that intertwined with her lily body odour: clary sage – so earthy, so vibrant, and so rich with power.

It was that clary sage scent he was interested in the most. He not only wanted it, but needed it, if he ever wanted out of this hellhole of a realm.

A small growl tore from the back of his throat, a sound he'd been hiding as grunts.

Every day that Raewyn acted coy, tiptoeing around him to not share a shred of information about what she was, was a day he'd lost figuring his way out of this realm.

He'd been hoping to get her to lower her hood, but it was like the damn thing was stuck to her head. Any time he tried to get close to her while she was sleeping, she'd wake suddenly, and he'd pretend he was doing something else.

The urge to rip it from her had been near undeniable, but he needed her to give her information *willingly*. A confused and frightened woman would do him no good.

Seemed it was too late for that.

He'd been hoping the Demon would get her to trust him more. Instead, it meant she now knew he wasn't human.

Oh! And that damn lame, made-up story he gave her today... The one about having a human family, coming from a farming town – the whole thing had been bullshitted to get her to talk. Which, in fact, it had, but everything she'd shared was utterly useless.

His friendly, chatty approach had failed, but he'd realised it might have been the key to her finally slipping up and telling him something of value. She'd seemed rather sincere when he pretended to be choked up over his 'parents.'

He'd been hoping to play on that in the future.

Instead, now he was being forced to take a new approach.

She would talk, whether she wanted to or not, and he'd promise it would all be okay, when, in fact, it would not be. She had too much magic, something he hunted for whenever he visited human towns – with them none the wiser about the monster walking among them.

Raewyn would just be another person added to the list of faces he couldn't remember he'd eaten.

Merikh continued to follow her, his naturally red orbs brightening from hunger, when he saw her between the gaps in the trees.

His new future could be within his grasp – all he had to do was grab the potential key trying to escape.

Merikh launched forward and tackled her to the ground, being careless of both of their bodies. He wrapped his arm around her thin torso and lifted it as he knelt above her.

Her little shoves were cute, holding strength, but not enough to part them.

"Let go of me!" she screamed through gritted teeth.

"Let's see what you've been hiding," he growled as he grabbed her cloak and hair wrappings. He even had his claws curled underneath the strip of cloth covering her eyes, and he pulled all three back to finally reveal her.

Merikh's aggression swiftly deflated out of him.

Long white hair freely fell as two big braids down her back. Even her eyelashes and high arching eyebrows were white, and they were stark against her complexion.

Her skin was a smooth, dark, taupe-brown, but it had the strangest grey undertone to it, rather than pink or olive. Dark spots dotted her button nose and sharp cheekbones as freckles, with an even darker beauty mark beneath her right eye.

Both her cheeks and jaw were rounded, rather than being sharp, and they made her look sweet. Her full, pouty lips were twisted as she fought against his hold, but they were ignored.

Her eyes drew his attention.

With a near-black ring encasing a tawny brown, it was her *glowing* pupils that struck him. Rather than being black, her pupils glimmered like white starbursts that forked through her irises, and he realised she was truly sightless because of them.

Holy shit. She was the most beautiful thing he'd ever seen, and he'd seen almost everything in his long life.

It took him longer than it should have for him to notice her long, pointed ears, or the strange black symbols that followed her hairline.

For a long moment, he was stuck staring at her ridiculously

mesmerising face. He'd never seen someone so pretty.

When he did notice the combination of her hair and ears, the familiarity of them dawned on him.

"Holy shit," he rasped out. "You're a fucking Elf."

Her eyelids, tipped with long, full, white eyelashes, widened in shock. "Let go of me!"

Her sage scent intensified – after having been soft since they left Clawhaven – and the strange symbols in her hairline glowed grey. Then, they pulsated with green.

Merikh grunted when vines made of long grass, spun to be rope-like, wound around his limbs, including his throat. He was yanked back like he was nothing but a rag doll.

He was unprepared for it; he lost his grip on her and slammed against a tree. A yell ripped from him when his spine cracked as he wrapped around the somewhat thin trunk.

She turned to her hands and knees, about to spring to her feet, but Merikh roared and leapt for her. Before she could get away, he grabbed her ankle and pulled.

Raewyn let out a pained cry when she didn't fully come with him, and he looked up to see she had wound more grass vines around her forearm to keep herself away. Then she kicked him underneath the jaw, shoving his fangs together before his head went back.

The kick had been strong, far more powerful than a human, and it'd almost sent him hurling to his back. Fortunately, he remained on his knees, but she'd managed to get out of his hold.

With her scent ripe with fear, the only thing that was saving her from Merikh going into a frenzy was the special cloth resting over the nose hole of his bony bear snout. He could smell through it, but it was heavily diluted.

He was going to lose control, her squirming and struggling exciting a dark part within him he'd embraced for far too long. His hunger, his desire to increase his humanity.

The problem was... now that he knew what she was, he was no longer interested in eating her. Okay, maybe a little, and much later, but he had plans for her first. He would take her help, whether she wanted to assist him or not.

With a snarl, Merikh pounced on her again.

She heard him coming, and a shield formed above her like a basket of thick grass. Its links appeared like hexagons, and his snarl deepened as he tried to dig through it to get to her. Yet, when he ripped a link away, another quickly formed in its place. He threw grass stalks from his fists so he could dig again.

He dug and dug, going faster and faster until he was quicker than her pesky spell. Once he could get both hands gripping the hole he'd made, he tore her shield in two.

"Please," she whimpered, but he just reached down and grabbed her throat and shoulders with his large hand.

He brought her closer, his heart racing with a thrill – not just from this difficult battle, but at the potential that lay before him. He was vibrating with exhilaration.

"How did you get here?" he asked, his voice husky with excitement. "How did you get to Earth? Where's the portal?"

"Leave me alone!"

Vines tried to wrap around him again, but he heard their rustling this time and rolled to the side to dodge. He took her with him, uncaring if he hurt her in the process.

"Can we get back there?" He shook her when she didn't answer. "Is that why you were desperate to leave Clawhaven? To go back to a portal?"

Her eyes were tightly clenched shut, as were her fists. She was so afraid of him that she was visibly shaking, and tiny droplets had collected on her long eyelashes.

In a small, trembling voice she cried, "Are-are you going to kill me?"

It was a like a punch to the gut that sobered him straight.

He looked up and around at their environment. He'd been freaking her out, scaring the hell out of her, and just because he was using a scent barrier to hide himself from fear and blood scents didn't mean it was actually hidden.

I need to calm her down or she'll bring a horde of Demons upon us.

Awkwardly, as he'd never comforted another before − a predator soothing prey would be strange − he petted her head. Honestly... it was the best he could think of.

Yet he kept doing it, petting this trembling female Elf's hair, as he said, "I told you yesterday, if I wanted you dead, you'd be dead."

That did absolutely *nothing* to ease her. His claws scraping over her probably wasn't aiding him.

It was already too late.

Within moments, the foul scent of rot fluttered on the wind, as did the quick thumps of a speedy Demon making its way closer.

Merikh went to scoop her up in his arms and run with her, his precious, valuable prize, but a whoosh of wings from above made him look up. He despised winged Demons for this very reason: they were hard to track, as they could glide near silently, and their scents never reached him in time.

It swooped down the moment he turned his sight upward, and he threw himself over Raewyn to protect her.

Bat-like chirping mixed with the mangled cry it gave as it dived. "A Mavka! I'll be rewarded if I bring your skull to the Veil!"

The Demons always said that these days, although they hadn't two years ago. *You'll just be another added to the number of Demons I've slaughtered.*

The humour that tightened his chest was filled with malice. He tensed, stiffening the bases of the long, sharp quills that usually laid flat over his back, calves, and forearms. His quills lifted, creating a dense layer of deadly spikes that tore through his red flannel shirt, his black pant legs, and dark-brown cloak.

The bat-like Demon's shriek was ear-piercing as it stabbed its clawed feet on the quills.

In her fear and confusion, unable to see what was happening,

Raewyn beat at his shoulders. He doubted she was able to sense anything happening around them with his body and cloak shielding her. He'd be a barrier of sound and scent.

Her fear also may not be allowing her to register what was truly going on around her.

The upward pointing bull horns on top of his head were enough to ward the Demon away from grabbing his skull. At the moment, from above, Merikh was untouchable.

Still, if he didn't calm the woman shaking beneath him, who was even trying to crawl out from under him, more Demons would come.

He raised his forearm in preparation to impale the one coming on all fours from the side. It was yet to break through the tree line.

"Raewyn, I need you to–"

The agonised choke that came from Merikh was profound, cutting his words off, when she kicked him in the fucking seam. His entire body went rigid. His red glowing orbs turned white from the pain, and the solid ball of his orbs wavered, as though he was about to cry ethereal tears.

The Elf's lithe body was deceiving as to just how much strength she could wield. His groin radiated with agony, to the point his hidden tail coiled around his leg in aversion.

Then, just as the second Demon broke into the area and leapt for them, impaling itself with the quills on the back of his forearm, she did it again. Merikh yelped as his arm buckled and his knees tried to turn inward so he could protect his groin.

Pointless, since she was between his legs.

The Demon's scream made her jump in fright and gasp. "What was that?"

Merikh yelped again when the Demon above swooped and cut him right across the arse. He had no quills to protect him there. Usually, he had his tail free to swat with defensively.

The Demon currently stuck to his forearm thrashed, since it had impaled itself in the stomach. It made his limb heavy, and the constant, agonised screams as it desperately pushed to free itself were annoying. He yanked his arm back to dislodge it with a grunt.

With a whimper, the Demon backed up, leaving a trail of dripping purple blood. It didn't leave, but its pain and fear made it wary of coming close again – at least while he was protecting what it wanted to feed on.

"Don't you dare kick me in the cock again," Merikh growled, the white of his orbs flaring into red. "Currently, I am the only thing that stands between you and the Demons you are foolishly bringing upon us with your fear."

"Demons?" she squeaked, before she stupidly tried to poke her head out from between his arms so she could... hear them or smell them, maybe?

He tucked her back in by cupping the top of her head, just as the swooping one dived. It must have thought better of it when it realised it was going to hit his quills, and it flew upwards to assess the best way to attack.

The space between his back and calf quills was small, and if it didn't strike accurately, it'd cop a face full of quills. Hitting him there last time had been lucky, but he figured the Demon understood just how much of a risk going for it again would be.

"Control your fear. I've muted my sense of smell, but it will eventually get to me, and then the Demons will have to fight me for your corpse."

Merikh winced when her scent deepened. Fuck, he'd said the wrong thing.

"Aren't you going to eat me anyway?" She covered her face. *"Olee Giildeed Maydin!"* she gasped in another language he didn't understand. "That's why you said I'd find out you weren't my friend!"

"I'm not going to eat you!" he bellowed.

Okay, he might eat her, but right now, he needed her to just calm down! Currently, he was protecting her with his very body, but they were stuck with the Demons unless he took matters into his own claws.

"I need you to trust me." Then, he asked softly, beseechingly even, "You've been doing that for days, remember?"

She shook her head as her strange eyes crinkled with the hurt of betrayal. "You lied to me."

I could strangle her. He could snuff out the scent himself if he rendered her unconscious, saving them both from further trouble. She was obviously in a state of complete panic, and he was starting to doubt whether he could calm her at all.

But he didn't move, didn't even try.

It would solve the current issue, but it would only create problems later. He was going to need her trust, even if it was broken, because he was no longer going to let this Elf out of his grasp until he was done with her.

She was stuck with him – for now.

Merikh took in a long breath while facing the gust of wind ruffling his spikes, using its freshness to help clear his mind.

I could use her blood to make a shield.

That brought on a bunch of issues.

It would saturate the air with blood momentarily until he healed her, making her fear scent even more delectable to them *all.* He would have to hurt her, and that would make her trust him even less.

The other issue was he'd be stuck inside the shield with her, since he could only project a shield around himself.

The solution was clear, and he turned his face back down as he hovered above her.

"We can only have this conversation later if you survive this. Right now, if I move, you'll be attacked. I am all that protects you, all that is keeping you safe."

He *swore* he heard her whimper.

Great, so his protection wasn't good enough for the Elf?

"If you want to get out of this, I'll need your help."

The winged Demon finally made its decision, and it swooped down behind Merikh. With sharp toe claws, it grabbed one of his feet and started to lift off.

With a terribly irritated growl, he yanked his leg back, incidentally forcing the creature closer. When it let go because he brought it too close to his back quills, he kicked the thing in the gut, and it flew backwards into a tree.

The other Demon had taken the opening and tried to scuttle its way between his body and the ground, so he kneed it in the back. He then dragged his knee backwards and to the side so it was no longer beneath him, swiping at it with his claws so it would back up.

She squealed when it must have touched her, and she brought her legs up closer between their bodies into a ball.

It scared some sense into her. "What-what do you want me to do?"

"Create that shield around yourself again, the one made of grass."

With a trembling nod, she pressed her forehead against his chest and the sweet smell of her clary sage magic saturated the air. He realised the reason her magical scent had been so light the past few days was because it strengthened when she was using it.

She must have actively been using a spell or two in the town.
If she hadn't, he may never have noticed it to begin with.

Grass began to grow around his legs, and he shook them. Instead, it grew beneath them, as if she understood he meant for her to only shield herself and not them both.

Merikh lifted his body to give her space while keeping her protected. When her shield formed, he laid on it so he could move his arms and legs into a better position.

Once he was essentially crouching over her on his hands and feet, the winged Demon above stood no chance. Without warning, Merikh leapt into the air with one powerful kick of his thick legs.

The moment he was gone, the Demon on the ground rushed forward, as he figured it would. It was slow, and her grass shield was enough to keep it at bay.

Grabbing the flying Demon by both ankles, Merikh swung his arms as he was falling back to solid ground and slammed the Demon into the dirt. The satisfying *crack* of multiple bones had his chest swelling with humour, and it only deepened as the winged one inhaled a deep breath before it shrieked.

Still holding its ankles, he slid it against the ground before he launched it into the side of a tree. Hollow bones snapped as one of its wings bent in on itself.

Since it was down for the moment, he checked on Raewyn when he noticed the slightest scent of her blood. Her shield was bigger, and the Demon was climbing around on top of it while poking its arm through the hexagonal gaps. It was smaller than Merikh, so it was able to fit a slim limb through the shield as it swiped.

Merikh twisted his head in surprise when it let out a cry right after a bone snapped. It pulled its arm back, and he noticed its elbow was broken, as if she'd kicked it against the inside of her shield for trying to claw her.

Movement in front of him caught his attention, and he turned forward once more to find the winged Demon rousing from its temporary nap.

"I'm sorry," it wheezed as it weakly tried to crawl away, one wing scraping against the dirt, grass, and leaf matter. "I'm sorry. Keep it. I don't want it anymore."

Merikh tilted his head. *Is it begging for its life?* How pathetic, especially since he was sure plenty of humans had pleaded to live while it ate them.

It didn't grow to be this large, with pale skin growing over its features, to not have.

Its movements remained languid, like it didn't have the strength to flee any faster. Merikh stepped closer. No remorse filled him as he grabbed it by the head and snapped its neck. He finished the job by pulverising its entire skull with both hands in an explosion of brain matter – just to make sure it was truly dead.

When he approached the smaller Demon, it hissed at him like a feral creature while standing on all fours on top of Raewyn's shield. It was reaching inside with its other arm, just begging to be kicked again.

Like he'd done to the winged one, he grabbed it by the ankles and slammed it against the ground.

"You call yourself a Demon?" he bit. "You're nothing but a nuisance."

He shattered its skull by bringing his knee high to his chest and then stomping on it with every bit of force he had in his strong legs. Brain and blood splattered with a cracking plop beneath his foot. It didn't even have a chance to make a noise, but its body did flail for a second.

Merikh looked himself over – his clothing was ruined from his quills and the Demon blood that covered him.

See? he thought as he looked around at the two dead Demons. *All she had to do was help, and now I'm done.*

It'd taken, what, less than two minutes when he'd been trying to get her to calm down for around five or ten?

The scent of her fear was still present in the air. He snorted out a huff, the material covering his snout billowing away before laying over his nose hole again.

"You should control your fear before more Demons come. I can protect you all night, but that would only exhaust you."

Merikh approached her shield and stood over her, watching her through the gaps of her grass vines. He purposefully stepped on a bundle of sticks to make sure she knew he was in front of her, and her left ear twitched at the sound.

In the dark of night, her glowing starburst pupils gave off a small amount of light. They moved towards where she heard him step, and he tilted his bony head curiously. He'd figured her hearing was sensitive from their travels, so he wondered just how impeccable her other senses were.

Her lips tightened and turned inward, and the expression she wore was one of great struggle. Her thick white brows twitched as they slowly drew together.

She didn't trust him, didn't want to go with him. Then again, who would want to willingly go with him?

"It's either me or the forest, Elf," he stated firmly. "Make your decision, or I will do so for you."

Her trembling worsened. "What if I say no?"

His tone was cold and unfeeling as he said, "I think it's best if you tell yourself I'm giving you a choice."

When her jaw muscles ticked, as though she'd gritted her teeth, he knew she'd made her decision.

Her grass shield disintegrated, withering of life as it opened above her. She raised her hand up to grab the fading edge so she could get to her feet.

Merikh shot forward and grabbed her wrist, pulling her from her shield. Her gasp was cut short by her squeal as he hoisted her until her stomach lay over his shoulder and her upper body hung down his back.

Before she could say anything on the matter, he bolted. She gasped and groaned as she bounced, the wind constantly being knocked out of her from the speed at which he ran.

"Put-put..." She struggled to speak. "Put me down!"

She kicked and kneed at his chest while she punched at his back. She was extremely lucky his quills were laying slimline down his body; otherwise, she would have stabbed herself.

"The area will become a feeding ground for nearby Demons. The death of their brethren, alongside your fear and blood scent, will bring more." He held her legs down firmly to settle her bouncing so as not to pain her. "If we stay too close, we will get caught in their hunting. If we get far away enough, we'll be able to avoid another fight."

Merikh wasted no time as he sidestepped around trees, shrubs, and fallen logs, occasionally jumping over what he could. The wind whistled in his sensitive ears, as did the light thumping of his footsteps.

She was silent for a few moments, as if she'd accepted his response. Then she whispered, "Please... slow down."

With an irritated growl, refusing to slow down at all, Merikh pulled her from his shoulder and cradled her tall and lithe body in his bulky arms. She crossed her arms over her stomach with a hiss, and he looked down momentarily to notice the drying cut across her cheek.

Well... that wouldn't do. Her face was far too supreme to be marred.

He could have chosen to only heal her face, but Merikh took any and all wounds she could possibly have. He healed her, the sacrifice being he must bear them instead. His ankle felt a little tender, but at least she didn't have any major wounds.

Once more, she gasped, this time in pleasant surprise. She even touched at her unmarred cheek.

"You can wield magic as well?"

He grunted in response as he listened to their surroundings.

When he heard a flap of wings, he stopped, put her on her feet, and shoved her between his body and a tree. He made sure his cloak covered her completely as he placed his palm over her mouth and turned his head upwards to watch through the gap in the tree canopy.

The cold moonlight cast halos between the sections of leaves, streaking white beams of light throughout the shroud of darkness.

A smallish, winged Demon flew overhead, circling. When it spotted Merikh, it hissed at him and flew off in the direction of the dead Demons. It kept searching, occasionally doubling back in an attempt to find Raewyn.

He could feel her heart pounding deeply against his torso, how her lungs rushed for air, heavy and rapid. She was still giving off a delectable fear scent, but it'd at least lessened during their small run.

He slowly drew his hand away, allowing her to breathe comfortably as he waited to make sure the Demon was truly gone.

"I thought you said they don't come here because of the border," she whispered so quietly that he doubted her voice went past the barrier of his body.

"No. I said those who cannot climb cannot get through it."

The Demon perched itself nearby, scouting the area, since Raewyn's scent here was fresh. The subtle chirp of crickets went quiet, as if they, too, were wary of it.

"However, that brings more dangerous Demons to the southlands, such as those who can fly or are strong enough to climb."

When it flew off, she didn't squeal as he swiped his arms around her so he could cradle her light weight. Once more, he ran.

Merikh wouldn't allow anything else to have his prey, and anything that tried... would die. Raewyn, currently, was the luckiest creature on this very planet. She had, what he knew to be true, the fiercest and most ruthless protector – unless he turned on her.

Until he decided on what he would do with her, she was safe.

As long as she does not try to kill me... If she set off his rage, which he often freely let off its leash, she'd be dead within seconds.

When Merikh arrived at the old, empty cottage house, he set her feet on the porch. By this point, her fear had dissipated almost completely.

"Go inside and stay in there," he demanded.

"How?" she bit, throwing her hands to the sides. "I don't even know where we are."

Great. She was being feisty all of a sudden. It was cute that she thought she had any way to defend herself against him. She may have magic, she may be able to fight him off, but there had been one guarantee in Merikh's life.

He. *Always*. Won.

"You are standing on the very porch you were standing on

this morning," he informed her as he dug through one of the two satchels strapped to his waist. "I know you know your way around it, *step* for *step*."

Out the corner of his sight, he noticed her lips part as her jaw fell in disbelief.

"You..." With her hands clenched into tight fists, she stamped her boot. "You were taking me in circles!"

She must have realised it'd only taken them about twenty minutes to get here when they'd been walking all day and most of the night. He was fast, but unless he was on all fours, he wasn't *that* fast.

"Not really circles," he admitted as he pulled four charms from his bag. "More like wiggly lines. Just go inside." He waved his hand to shoo her before realising she couldn't see the action. "Before a Demon runs off with you."

He didn't catch her reaction other than her stamping her foot again. He was too busy making his way down the side of the house, putting up the charms he'd made the day before.

On each corner of the house, he placed an ornament made from dill, red berries, a small animal bone, and a jingle bell, all tied together by a white ribbon. They would create a magical barrier over the house, protecting her completely from any kind of predator.

He'd once taught someone how to make these so she could show another of his kind how to, but he reflected very little on that fact whenever he used them.

SEVEN

Once Raewyn sobered up from her trepidation and her confusion, fury settled in.

Okay, so maybe she wasn't handling navigating a new realm she couldn't even see in very well, a realm that had little to almost no defences against a horrible enemy. Then, to top it off, it had something even more monstrous in it! Something she wasn't familiar with... and had been travelling with.

Despite the fact he'd protected her, she wasn't foolish enough to believe it was from the goodness of his heart – if he even had one.

Raewyn was now at the mercy of a *something* she had no idea how to fight. What were his strengths and weaknesses? Could he die?

She didn't even know what he looked like! Even though he'd barely made a move when he'd been trapping her against the ground, just hovering above her, one of the Demons had literally screamed in agony. He hadn't even moved a muscle.

The thought of running crossed her mind, but she rolled her eyes. Where? Where could she run that she would be safe? He'd either catch her or a Demon would.

She couldn't outrun him – that had already been made obvious. She doubted she'd even be able to if she *could* see where she was going. Where did that leave her?

It's either me or the forest, he'd said, which meant he knew exactly the predicament she found herself in.

As she turned to go inside, Raewyn shuddered with repulsion before rubbing at her cheek in tiredness. Just as her left hand touched the distressed timber of the door, the smoothness of her cheek reminded her of how he'd healed her.

If he was intending to be cruel or hurt her, he wouldn't have taken care of her wound... would he? *Or am I just reaching for hope that everything will be okay?*

She slammed the door behind her and hugged her midsection, wishing she could barricade the entryway. Her stomach was tied into knots of uncertainty and worry, unsure of where she stood with her scary, unknown companion. He killed two Demons with little effort, in a matter of breaths, so just how quickly could he dispose of Raewyn?

He knew I was an Elf just from looking at me. She nibbled at the inside of her bottom lip. *What does he want from me?*

The creak of weight bearing down on the timber slats had her ears pressing backwards and lowering. Raewyn backed up even before the door opened, and his scent mixed with fresh air billowed in from outside.

She hated that she found his orange and cinnamon smell comforting.

When the door closed, the silence was so distinct it was almost deafening. All she could hear was her own startled heartbeat overtop of her breaths. Her thoughts went quiet, giving her a reprieve so she could quickly make a decision, depending on his next move.

Raewyn shivered, her expended adrenaline now leaving her colder than ever.

She flinched when he stepped forward, but other than the flooring, she heard nothing from him; not his breaths, nor the material of whatever he wore shifting.

He was frightfully quiet. A true predator.

The clacking of two different kinds of stones boomed in the

silence, but it was the sweet smell of fire that had her settling. He was lighting the fireplace. Considering he'd been able to track her and fight those Demons, she didn't think he needed the light.

Is he warming the house for me? Regardless, she refused to step closer, despite the urge to. Even when the fire was in full roar, seeming to ease the quiet and bring life to the house, she stayed put.

"Is... is Merc even your real name?" She didn't know why that was the first question that spewed from her shaking lips, but she wanted to know just how deeply he'd lied.

"No," he answered.

His response immediately made her pulse spike, and her hands shook as she wiped them on the skirt of her dress. "What about that story you told me? The one of your parents, the farm town, your brothers? Does Rivenspire even exist?"

"Absolutely, it does, but it was destroyed about fifty years ago. It's nothing but ruins now."

The saliva in her mouth thickened.

The tears that pooled in her eyes were of betrayal. She hated the hurt that cut through her, making it feel as though a lump had formed right behind her sternum. She hadn't had much trust in him to begin with, but even the smallest amount being chopped away was painful.

Raewyn hated being lied to, especially since she had nothing to gauge a person by but their words.

"Your family?" she asked with her lips quivering. "Brothers?"

"I've got many brothers, none of which I care for," he answered nonchalantly, having no idea just how much each word cut her up further. "My parents? Somewhere out in this world, and I couldn't give a fuck about them either."

The worst thing about crying when she didn't want to was having to wipe her cheek and chin because it tickled her skin. She didn't want to cry, didn't want to show any kind of weakness, and yet she was incapable of stopping her tears, no matter how much she tried.

"You lied to me," she angrily sobbed.

"I lie to everyone. Don't take it personally." Gosh, he sounded so cruel! "And you have quite the hide to spout that, when you've been prancing around under a cloak and mask to conceal that you're really an Elf."

She didn't have a violent bone in her body, but she sincerely wished to go straight up to him and punch him in the face. She was exceptionally glad she'd kicked him in the balls, or cock, or whatever! Not just once, but twice.

"What even are you?!" she yelled, her breath sputtering with anxiety. The warmth in her swelling, tear-stained face drained away when he stomped closer, his footsteps echoing with thumps. "St-stay back!"

"Or what?" He chuckled deeply. "You're going to smack me with those little hands of yours?"

She quickly knelt so her hands could touch the timber and let magic flow through her palms. Brown, glittering magic lit up, and a barrier formed between them – a really, *really* pointless one.

With what could only be a singular forearm smack, her barrier shattered. Since the component she'd used wasn't alive and tied to the soil, which made it brittle, he barrelled his way through with ease.

Raewyn fell back on her arse and hands, and she scooted backwards until her back met the wall. She curled her hands against her chest, as though she wanted to protect it.

She perceived him crouching over her by the sharpness of his scent and the warmth that radiated from him. She considered kicking him between his squatting legs but decided against it. She didn't want his retaliation.

"I'm a Duskwalker." When she shook her head, he made a thoughtful hum. "A Mavka, then?"

Raewyn shook her head again. "I've never heard of that

before. We didn't know anything other than Demons was here."

"Fine. It's better if I show you then."

Raewyn flinched when he slowly curled his *clawed* fingers around her wrists, practically swallowing them in his palms. She uselessly pulled on her arms. She fought, afraid of what he was about to do to her, squirming to get free.

Her fingertips touched bone, and Raewyn paused.

He's making me touch his face?

The texture that greeted her palms was smooth, cool, and it didn't take her long to gather the courage to explore. She needed to know what he looked like, to know what was currently towering over her like a massive ball of menace.

His bony snout wasn't particularly long, but it wasn't short either.

"A skull?" she asked, before her fingers halted at a distinct cut over the top of the snout.

"A bear skull, to be exact."

She tried to remember if she'd ever read about a creature such as him as she brushed her thumb over that cut.

"Careful with playing with any scarring on my face. It's sensitive."

She moved up and gingerly touched at the eye sockets, noticing they were... empty? There were claw marks going down the right one.

"How do you see?"

"My sight is made of two orbs that float within my eye sockets. They are predominantly red, but they will change colour depending on my mood."

Is that why I saw red sparks before? She saw nothing now, but when he'd been fighting off the first Demon and her blindfold had dislodged, she'd noticed two glowing red lights in the dark of her vision.

"How were you able to walk around Clawhaven with a face like this?" Or rather... lack thereof.

"I wear an amulet that creates a human glamour." He pushed

her hands higher so she could feel it across his brow. The metal chain links were cold against her fingertips, as was the crystal that sat in the middle and tapped against his skull when she fingered it. "It has a twin, which protects the wearer from Demons touching them."

"So that's why I thought you were human."

She'd thought it was her lack of sight, but it wouldn't have mattered at all. Everyone thought he was human. It was relieving to know she hadn't been the ultimate fool in this scenario.

When she palmed higher, she frowned at the two large protrusions she felt sticking out from his skull. If she remembered correctly, she thought Earth bears didn't have horns.

Nyl'therian cervaursa were similar bear creatures, but they had deer antlers. If any of them were still alive, of course.

She noticed his horns were somewhat wide, pointed upward and forward, with a slight curve on the top.

"Bull horns," he informed her. "I am made up of many creatures, although these are two out of three of my most distinct."

When she slid her hands back down, fear was replaced by awe. The scientist within her desired to know every part of him, to know how a creature could live without skin upon its face.

He was an anomaly, one that made her wish to discover more of him. Oh, how she would love to dissect him and find out how he ticked!

Her fingers hesitated when she touched sharp fangs. Any movement he'd given before, the slightest muscle twitch or sway from breaths, halted completely. His steadiness gave her the impression he was being still for her sake rather than out of aversion to her touch.

As she touched them further, coming to the tip of his snout, she understood he had a bite that could kill. There was no material covering his jaw, but there was a cloth tied around his upper fangs, covering his nose hole.

"It helps to minimise the scent of fear and blood."

This was why I found it so difficult to hear him breathe. His breaths were muted by the material.

"How did you come to be?" she asked in breathless wonder as she began to touch down his throat, and the softest fur she'd ever felt tickled her fingertips.

"I was born, obviously."

"By?" Just as she touched the fur around his shoulders and chest, he grabbed her hands to stop her.

"You Elves really don't have any idea what Weldir has been up to?"

Her brows drew together. "Weldir?" She scoffed. "That demi-god has no power to create creatures."

His laugh was cold and empty. "Sure, he does. Give him a mate, something he can touch by binding it to himself, and he is able to create life."

Raewyn's eyes widened as her lips parted. "But he doesn't have a physical form! He was born half-created."

"So, therefore, he has half the ability, as long as he is in his own realm," he added. "The one your kind gave him the power to control."

"Well... not us," Raewyn grumbled, retracting her hands completely to cup them to her chest. "Thank you for allowing me to touch you."

She wasn't sure if he understood the significance of what he'd done, allowing her to see in her own way, but it calmed some of her fear. She didn't like the unknown, and she'd been fretting the entire time that he was a Demon.

He could definitely be much worse, and there was still much she didn't know, but at least she could picture the face in front of her now.

A white bear skull with two scars, one across his snout and another down his right eye socket. He likely had dark brown or black bull horns. She knew he had fangs, claws, and fur, and he also said he had red orbs for eyes? She imagined they floated in his empty sockets, but she hadn't been able to feel them.

"I don't like being touched because I don't like others discovering what I am."

"Anything else I should know?" she asked nervously. "Do you have wings or a tail? Venom?"

"No wings or venom, but I do have a bull tail I keep hidden." Then, after some thought, he added, "Be careful of my back, forearms, and calves. I have echidna quills I can extend as protection, and they are exceptionally sharp. When I'm calm, they lay flat against me, but if you walk into them while I'm aggravated, you'll likely impale yourself."

Raewyn swallowed thickly. "G-good to know."

From what she knew of his body, he was taller than her by a few inches, but not that many. Since she was six foot seven, she thought he might be around six foot ten, maybe eleven? He was bulky from what she'd ran into a few times, strong, and he was chubby – he had a meaty gut that wasn't thin but like he had fat surrounding his muscles.

He was huge, then, to her as an Elysian. Her kind were often tall and lean because of their high metabolism and Elvish physique. He was tall and near three times the width of her.

She scratched at the side of her neck awkwardly. "Even with your glamour, the humans were still a little scared of you."

"The glamour does nothing to my height or frame. It only makes me appear human."

Maybe if I hadn't been wearing my blindfold when the magic was active, I might have seen the glow of the spell and realised something was wrong.

She'd worn it to protect her identity, but she held a little regret for it now. She wouldn't have followed him into the forest.

She saw nothing currently, since he'd removed her blindfold, so it must mean it was only active while humans were nearby.

Raewyn thought he'd back away from her now, but he

remained crouching over her. She was cornered.

Her right ear flattened when he pinched the pointed tip of the left one. "I knew you were hiding something under that cloak. I just didn't expect it to be your hair and ears. I, at first, thought you were seeking to find the Priests and Priestesses because you were one of them, just someone special."

"I never told you I was looking for them." Her lips pursed in realisation before she narrowed her brows in his direction. "You were following me in Clawhaven."

"Says the person who followed me through the market," he bit back. "Do you know how many times I lost you because you couldn't keep up?"

"It's not like I could see where you kept running off to!" she yelled, full of chagrin. "There were so many people that following your scent and stupid voice was really difficult."

"Why are you looking for people from the magic temples?"

Raewyn folded her arms and turned her head to the side. "No reason."

All false pleasantness faded as he gave a terrifying snarl. His hand shot forward to grip her cheeks firmly and force her head forward. His claws stabbed into her flesh, and they were the only reason she didn't fight him.

"Currently, your life is in my hands. I can either be your willing guide in this world, or I can make you my prisoner. You will give me the answers I seek. The *how* is completely up to you."

"Were..." Raewyn worried her bottom lip as her heart shrivelled in her chest. "Were you ever planning to take me to another town?"

"Sure. It just depended on what you were."

Why did she feel like that was a lie?

"So, Raewyn... Why were you looking for those people? Are they the key to helping you go back to the Elven realm? I know they're not human. Their scents are different, and I long ago realised their skin glows with magical symbols – as do their eyes

– when they are stripped of their garments."

It took her a long while to answer him, unsure if she should share the truth. He was right: her life was in his hands, and she *did* need someone to help her navigate this unknown world.

He wasn't hurting her. Although there were minor threats in his words, he hadn't truly said anything frightful... yet.

In reality, she cared very little about what he was. Delysians were Demons accepted by the Elysian. They had killed and eaten her kind, but they had transformed into a species that could be trusted.

Could he, a Duskwalker or Mavka or whatever, be trusted as well? He obviously wasn't a mindless, bloodthirsty monster. They wouldn't be having this conversation otherwise.

He knows what I am. He knows I'm not from here. She didn't have to hide from him about what she was, her needs. *He knows I'm trying to get back home.*

Raewyn let out a defeated sigh. "Yes, I'm looking for the Anzúli... urm, the Priests and Priestesses of this world?" When he let her face go, probably satisfied she was answering him, she rubbed at her arm. "The portal that brought me here was one I created by accident."

"Where is it? If you tell me about the location, I can take you back there."

Raewyn laughed, but it was so hollow and sad that it stung all the way to her soul. "It's gone. Portals like that, accidental ones, don't have a lasting power source. Once I was sucked through, I doubt it lasted more than a minute."

Her hands clenched tightly. *Had I been able to hold on just a little longer, I wouldn't have been sucked through.* She would have remained in Nyl'theria, wouldn't have suffered for a single second on Earth.

"These... Ansthulie you spoke of."

"Anzúli," she corrected, and a deep but quiet growl rumbled from him. "What? If you're going to say their name, you should say it properly!"

"These Anstthúli you spoke of," he repeated. At least his pronunciation was a little closer this time. "Can they help you make a new portal to the Elven realm?"

"Maybe?" She gave a one-handed shrug. "We don't know if they have been sending more of their kind across to this realm. If so, they may have a way to redirect their portal, or make a new one temporarily for me to cross through."

The slightest shift from him and a small *tap tap* gave her the impression he'd raised his hand and was tapping a claw on the hardness of his face in thought.

"Their magic has been growing weaker over the years," he admitted with a high pitch hum of thought.

"I have to try," she answered sadly. "Elysians, uh, my kind of Elf, are forbidden from practising portal magic." Of course, she'd studied it, but it was insanely complex. It was a speciality field, one that required a minimum of ten years' experience – which she didn't have. "I can't make a new portal myself, since I don't know how. Like I said, the one I made was an accident."

"Then they're your only possible path home?"

The shudder that racked her body was deep. "No, but the alternative is too dangerous."

"You're not wrong about that. Jabez's portal is so guarded that not even I can get to it."

Raewyn tilted her head in surprise. "You know of Jabez?"

"Of course, I fucking do," he bit with a growl. "That half-Elf is a menace, and your kind made sure he had a fun playground to mess with."

Her ears flattened again. "We are sorry for whatever he has done." The sincerity of her words rang true, and every day, her people bore the weight of the horror they had knowingly left the humans to deal with. "We were hoping to find a way to fix both our realms, but every year, we're met with failure. No matter what we try, or how much research we do, we can't–"

He interrupted her with a growl. "Save your breath. I don't care about the war between the Elves and the Demons. I don't care who is at fault, who is wrong, who is good or evil. All I care about is one thing."

"Which is?"

"You."

Her lips parted in surprise. "Me?"

"Yes," he answered, his tone just a little too perverse. "Because you're going to get me off this sad, dreadful rock they call Earth."

"You want to go to Nyl'theria?" she squeaked.

"Is that what your realm is called? I don't care if it's Nyl'theria or not, just anywhere that isn't here."

Raewyn scratched at the side of her head in annoyance, before pushing her braid over her shoulder.

She didn't know how to feel about that. Bringing him to her realm could lead to trouble. Just because she was a councilmember didn't mean she could allow whomever to enter their realm. They already had issues with monsters crawling everywhere; they were essentially imprisoned in a pretty city.

Bringing him, an unknown entity, into their already overrun home could lead to further devastation.

As a councilmember, she needed to make sacrifices to protect her people. Her needs were second to the overall.

But I don't want to be stuck here. The inner turmoil she faced twisted her gut. *And I am one of the head scientists.*

Sure, there were others who could take over her work, but they would be years – probably ten Nyl'theria years – behind her progress. There were things only she knew, differential equations only she had conjured up. Without her, the Elysians would slip backwards in their progress to fixing their world, as well as Earth.

They need me.

Was that true, or was she just coming up with excuses?

Then again, she could just pretend she was going to allow him to come to Nyl'theria, and then cast a barrier so he couldn't. She was sure the Anzúli would help ensure he didn't pass through the portal.

"So, the idea is that you'll help me get back home so long as you get to come with me?" She wished her voice didn't shake with uncertainty.

To be fair, she wasn't the greatest liar. She wore her heart on her sleeve. All her emotions, her truths and lies, were easily seen and read.

"Don't sound so concerned," he said as he slipped a claw under her chin to make sure she faced him, most likely to add power to his next words. "If your people are like the humans, I have no interest in staying there, either. You – and they – only have to fear me if you don't give me what I want. We'll all get along just fine otherwise."

Raewyn's lips tightened before she narrowed her eyes into a glare. "And what is it you want? Power? To take control of a clan of people who are already suffering?"

"Power? Why would I want something as ridiculous as that? I have no interest in ruling or governing over a bunch of Elvish people I know little about. What I want is freedom." She felt him come closer, his breaths billowing through the material covering his nose hole. "And, Raewyn, I will kill and maim anything and everything until I have it."

"You expect me to trust you after saying that?" she snapped.

"I can already see the cogs turning in that head of yours. It is a warning, that is all. It should only be frightening if you intend to betray me. Otherwise, it is empty and pointless, and you and your people have nothing to fear."

She opened her mouth to refute him, then instantly shut it. *So, we won't come to harm as long as we don't betray him?* The fact he had no interest in taking over her people, or harming them, was exceptionally relieving.

Hopefully, he wasn't lying.

"What did you mean by freedom?" she couldn't help asking.

His scent softened as he leaned back and then stood.

"Go to sleep. We will be leaving this house the moment the

sun has fully risen." He finally stepped away to give her some space, and she took a proper breath. "I will take you to some Anstthúli."

"I'll be honest with you," she said, rubbing at her eyes in emotional and physical tiredness. "I've only been pretending to sleep. Earth's planetary cycle is different to mine."

"I know, which is why I didn't rip your cloak off earlier. You're also a very light sleeper and your hearing is better than a human's. Not better than mine, but you have been awfully difficult these past few days." The fireplace crackled as if he disturbed it, likely so its flames would burn better. "Still, it's best you try. If you can travel throughout the night, then we will. Your pretending to sleep has been endangering you the entire time, as remaining in one location is just begging for the Demons to find us."

Raewyn sighed, hating that she'd been putting herself in danger.

"Fine. I'll try to sleep." He did wake her the previous night by trying to remove her hood, and she was tired after the events that unfolded this night. "What is your name, then? If it isn't Merc."

"Merikh," he grunted.

Her whole body drained of heat as her blood ran cold. *His name means death and slaughter.*

What did she just agree to?

EIGHT

Merikh kept a relatively slow pace in comparison to how he usually travelled, but it was at least faster than how he and the Elf had been travelling the past few days.

Now that he'd discovered what she was, he didn't have to take into consideration a human's capabilities. She was easily able to keep up with his pace, though he still slowed so she didn't trip too often, and her endurance was strong.

She never ran into him, and he figured she measured how close she was to him by the length of rope around his waist. It was barely taut, but the moment there was slack, she slowed along with him.

She's clever.

Despite her inability to see, with the guide rope and her essentially stepping in his exact path, she was just as capable of making a long and treacherous journey as anyone else. He liked people who took their life and everything it'd given them by the reins, whether it be good or bad.

Those who were in pain, he understood.

Merikh had lived pain, breathed it, bled it. There were times when he'd done nothing but lie in the forest in a ball with his quills extended for protection. There were nights he'd spent whimpering in agony, where he was utterly incapable of moving.

He had more reasons than anyone else living in this vile world to lie down in the dirt belly up and allow wallowing pity to crawl all over him.

But he didn't, and neither did the little Elf, which sparked a sense of pride within him.

She also seems to be resilient.

Especially when a few warm drops splattered against the coolness of his skull, and he turned to see she had raised her face to the canopy of leaves with a small smile. After last night, discovering all his lies, what he was, and that she was essentially his prisoner, the fact she'd smile at all was proof of her resilience.

With her eyes closed, she allowed the starting raindrops to cleanse her face. Her hood was up, protecting her hair from leaf debris, and she pulled it further up when she brought her face forward.

The rain was inconsistent. One moment, it drizzled, and the next, the sun baked them with enough heat to dry their clothing.

Merikh was wearing a new red flannel shirt and black breeches, the others abandoned at the house alongside his torn cloak. He didn't have to replace his clothing often, but he also didn't regularly have to fight with Demons.

He was known, and she was the only reason he'd been attacked at all. Usually, they left him be when they saw him in the wilderness. Though they'd begun attacking him in recent years due to the Demon King's orders, most were still wary of doing so.

Raewyn was wearing the same plain grey dress she'd worn the previous day, but had forced him to step out of the house so she could bathe. He'd taken that time to retrieve his charms and pull them apart.

He'd kept the bone, bells, and ribbon, while tossing the dill and red berries upon the ground, as they were already beginning to wither. He'd also filled her water sack again via the well, not requiring one himself.

He didn't eat food nor drink water, which is why he'd told her he'd never share with her. He had nothing to share, and he wouldn't weigh himself down with useless items just to play pretend.

Not when he'd been originally planning to make her his meal.

However, her presence was offering him something far more valuable than the magic she held – which was what he'd wanted all along.

After years of searching for a way, have I finally found it?

She could be the only answer to his problem, and he'd grip that lifeline by the throat if he needed to. After a hundred and eighty years of searching for it, could anyone blame him?

He looked behind him once more, curious about the woman. Her face was turned off to the side, as if she were listening to the creature he could hear digging through the bushes nearby.

His sight found her throat, the tiny pulse of her jugular.

Okay, so maybe no gripping by the throat, since it looked rather delicate, but he wasn't letting her go. Not until he got what he wanted.

His sight then found her round face, unobstructed by material, and her beauty was just as mesmerising as the first moment he'd seen it.

Her freckles were dark little spots dotting over a cute nose and high cheek bones, while the brief sun streaking across her already rich complexion gave it a glitter of bronze. Her white eyelashes reminded him of the soft, fuzzy wings of a colourless moth, and they framed those brown irises and starburst-pupil eyes with supreme contrast.

When his sight dropped to her full lips – that had a merlot colour on the inside seam – and stubborn chin, Merikh lightly growled at himself and brought his skull forward to stop looking. He was a little relieved he couldn't see her behind him, and that her other pretty features were hidden by her cloak.

Regardless of her angel-like appearance, Merikh had little

interest in her. He had no aspirations of acquiring a bride. She was a means to an end, that was all.

The humour that twisted his gut was one he was familiar with, full of dark realities. *Only a fool would think anyone would want to be eternally tied to one of us.*

He could think of a certain blue-orbed Mavka who had uselessly tried.

He lifted a branch to make way for his horns just as he thought, *I wonder when Orpheus will realise it's pointless and give up. Shouldn't be too much longer.* Orpheus' mind, from what Merikh had observed, was twisting further and further into hopelessness. *He will eventually turn out like me.*

Maybe then, Merikh would have someone who understood him.

He was just about to absentmindedly release the leafy branch, but instead held it to make sure it didn't harm the Elf behind him. Once her head was clear, he let it go, and it swiped right where her face would have been a second ago.

"Thank you," she chirped, her voice just as lovely as her face.

He grunted in response and continued making sure his path would be of even footing, for her sake.

Just as a new bout of drizzle fell, she asked, "Where do you live, if not in a human town?"

"Nowhere," he abruptly answered.

"You don't have a home?"

"Yes, I have a home." He looked around the familiar forest he'd walked many times in his long life. "I just haven't *lived* in it for nearly a hundred years."

"A hundred years?" Her voice was thoughtful, and he suspected her white brows were furrowed. "How long do you live, then?"

"Unendingly forever. From what I know, I'm at least three hundred years old, if not more. How much longer I live is solely up to the world and if it wishes to break me."

"So, you can die. How, if you can supposedly live forever?"

His tone was nonchalant as he asked, "Why do you wish to know?"

It wouldn't be the first time something wished to gain the knowledge of how to kill his kind.

"Just curious about what you are, to be honest. We Elysian Elves can live around fifteen hundred Earth years, sometimes more, sometimes less. I guess it would be like... a hundred, for a human?" She made a squeak, as though her foot had almost come out from under her because of how slippery the ground had gotten. "But we can die just as easily as a human."

Merikh did the math in his head, but he wasn't very confident about his guess. *One year equates to about fifteen of ours?* He'd confirm that later, but there was a real possibility that she may be older than him.

"Mavka, or Duskwalkers, as the humans call us, can only be destroyed by breaking our skulls. Many have tried, and many have lost their lives to my claws, so I wouldn't try doing so yourself."

Raewyn snorted an empty laugh. "Oh yeah, just kill my Earth guide. How stupid do you think I am?"

"When creatures feel cornered, they tend to do idiotic things. It has nothing to do with intelligence, and everything to do with fear."

"Okay, so if you *do* have a home, where is it?"

He tilted his head in thought. Her questions weren't unwelcome. He didn't care what she learnt, nor was her chattering annoying. Merikh was just so accustomed to silence, or others thinking he was human, that he just wasn't used to it.

It helped that he found her voice, and even her little Elvish accent, pleasant. It was almost musical, in its own way. It was so gentle and feminine he thought she could lull any creature into a calm stupor if she tried.

"My cave is situated in the southland area of the Veil's walls. Do you know of the Veil?"

When he peeked over his shoulder, he saw her head bounce

up and down as she nodded. Then, her lips parted as she gasped, right as her left leg slipped to the side on a patch of mud. She righted herself by tugging the rope.

Since he'd seen the whole scene, he could have caught her, but he also didn't want to. He shrugged.

"You seem to know much about Earth. Elves are known creatures to humans, though believed to be a myth. I'm assuming your kind came here often?"

"We studied this world before we sent the Demons here." Raewyn rubbed at her neck in what he thought might be awkwardness. "Honestly, we only chose Earth because Jabez had already created a portal here. We thought it best if we only infected one world, rather than many."

"I wouldn't be alive had your kind not."

The smile she wore was bright. Merikh softly growled at her for it and turned forward.

His statement hadn't been a thankful one, but rather, resentful. Had it not been for them sending more Demons here, Weldir's magic wouldn't have been spread so thin on Earth. He wouldn't have sought a mate to empower him.

The sun came back to warm the world and dry them, and Merikh looked through the sparse treetops to see that the light rain would eventually return. Grey clouds still circled, casting a dangerous, looming shade over them.

Another squeal came from her, and this time, she actually fell into his back. Catching herself by gripping two bundles of his long quills, she was lucky his thick shirt had protected her hands.

"Ugh! I can't do this anymore!" she blurted.

The tension of the rope faded, and he turned around to see she was no longer following him. "I can't help that the ground has become wet. I am taking us on the safest path."

"It has nothing to do with you or me!" she bit, as she bent over and unlaced her boots. "It's these stupid foot prisons! How can anyone walk in these things? You can't feel the ground, can't steady yourself through it."

Merikh looked at his own bare feet with paw-like toes. He never wore shoes, as they never fit. He cared very little if the humans raised an eyebrow that he often appeared barefooted, considering the glamour only made him appear human but didn't clothe him.

She removed both shoes and then her socks. "Since you know I'm an Elysian, there's no point in me wearing them anymore."

Just like that, she tossed them into the forest as though they were the foulest things in the world.

She stamped one foot like a demonstration. "There, much better. I shouldn't lose my footing anymore."

With a sigh and a shake of his head, Merikh chased after her boots. Once he'd collected both, he tied the laces together and slung them over one of his shoulders.

"You'll need to wear them when we're in town. You'll already appear odd with the hood over your head, and I doubt you'll be able to handle people stepping all over your toes."

He could handle the odd boot crunch, but he wondered if her feet could withstand such pain. They were dainty for her size, but large simply because she was inhumanly tall.

Then, Merikh tilted his head and got down on one knee. Yellow shifted into his sight, taking over its usual red.

He lifted her foot to inspect the arrow markings on her flesh in deep curiosity. *Why does she have these markings? They are like tattoos.* Three points in a row ran over the arch of her foot towards her toes, and, upon further inspection, he noticed more wrapped around her ankles.

Merikh drew her skirt up a little to see how far they went, noticing rings around the tops of her calves. He was about to go higher, but she smacked him in the forehead with the bottom of her fist and ripped herself away from him.

Merikh grunted. "What the fuck did you hit me for?"

"You were lifting up my dress!"

Curiosity had gotten the better of him, and he'd acted without thought. When she went to bash his skull again, he grabbed her wrist and shoved up her dress sleeve.

"I noticed the black rings on your fingers, but I didn't realise there were more. Are you covered all over in tattoos such as these?"

Her hand had similar arrow markings that circled her wrist. However, her arm was free of any markings until right below her elbow, where she had an intricate looping knot all the way around.

She ripped her arm away from his large palm, and she placed her hand over the marking around her elbow.

"Yes, I am. All Elysians are." Her tone was defensive, and her puffed cheeks and tight lips told him she hadn't liked being inspected. "They're magical symbols, and they grow over time. They aren't tattoos."

With an annoyed exhale, Merikh stood.

"You don't get to ask me a million questions and then scold me for my own."

"Sure, I can," she pouted. "My questions don't involve me undressing you."

If Merikh had eyes, he would have rolled them. Instead, he rolled his head.

"Let's move on. We're wasting time."

He turned and waited for her to grab the rope again. She remained pouted for quite some time, and he accepted the silence with ease.

She ate while they walked, never losing her pace.

"Merikh," she said, causing his quills to shudder and short fur to puff slightly as a thrill swept through him.

It was the first time she'd said his *real* name to him in her melodic and heavenly voice. His reaction was so shocking to him that his orbs turned a reddish pink in embarrassment.

When others said his name, it was brash. It sounded like what it was: an omen and warning of death. From her lips, she'd somehow twisted it to sound... inviting, rich.

"What?" he grated.

"How long will it be until we're there? Don't you dare say 'a few days' like you have been."

He considered their new pace, since she was much faster and steadier without her boots on.

"At this rate, we'll likely reach the only Anstthúli temple in the southlands within two to three days." Then, with a curt tone, he asked, "Is that a *problem* for you?"

"I'll be honest... I'm almost out of food."

"Then you should have rationed it."

"It's been five days. I have rationed it, but I only brought as much as I could carry."

Merikh raised a hand to the underside of his snout.

It won't do either of us any good if she goes hungry. He wasn't interested in needlessly torturing her for a necessity. Plus, she'd likely start whining or slowing down if she didn't have enough sustenance.

"I'll find food along the way."

NINE

Knee-deep in faintly moving pond water, Merikh had his claws tensed and ready. His long black trousers were rolled up as far as his thighs would allow, the bottoms of them wet. His shirt, however, couldn't manage the same feat, and it currently lay on the shore.

The short fur around his thick thighs was the only thing moving, and it gently swayed with the river's natural motion. He was so still that even his long, thin bull tail, curled up within his trousers, was unmoving.

In that position, poised to strike, he waited.

He'd waited so long that Raewyn eventually sighed with boredom from the riverbed. She was sitting on her arse, her arms wrapped around her bent knees.

The water here was fresh, as it hadn't been polluted by seawater running back up the river yet. This was also a good place to refill her water sack.

All these necessities were irksome to a creature who'd never needed to consider them, but he wasn't annoyed at her for having them.

"Does fishing usually take this long?"

Does fishing usually take this long? he mentally mocked, refusing to answer in case it frightened off an unsuspecting fish.

She wasn't the one getting drenched just so she could catch

someone else's dinner. No, instead *he* was doing it, and she was being highly ungrateful.

Then, she snuck her toes into the water and kicked!

"Is this water sanitary? If so, I'd love to have a bath once you're done swimming around in there."

Just as he was about to quieten her, his sight snagged on movement. It seemed her little kick had frightened a small school of fish his way.

He dived both his hands into the water, and his cage of claws struck two fish, wedging them between his palms and the muddy river bottom. The rest left bubbles behind as they scattered. He yanked both free of the water and inspected their sizeable bodies.

Now that his task was done, he headed in her direction, and the water sloshed around his legs as he approached.

"Well done." She clapped, like he'd completed an amazing feat.

"Why are you clapping?" he asked, his head tilting in confusion. "With a fishing line, I'm sure you could have done this."

"Really?" Her smile was an oddity to their conversation, and it only caused his orbs to morph to yellow in curiosity. "I've never held or seen a fish before. Can I touch it?"

He didn't really understand her excitement, but he didn't mind handing it to her. It would free up one of his hands so he could begin preparing them.

"Don't lose it," he stated, as he plonked one of the fish in her outstretched hands.

She let out a squeal when the flailing fish wobbled in her grip, but she held it tightly as she fought against its strength, her entire body shaking along with it.

"Why is it moving?!"

"Because it's still alive," he answered while tilting his head the other way, unsure of how she wouldn't have known that.

Didn't they fish in their realm? *I just thought she hadn't held a live fish.*

In his own way, he was a little excited to find out just how different this... Nyl'theria was to Earth. Was it just like–

"Gross! Put it back in the water."

Merikh practically dived for it when it looked as though she was about to toss it forward into the river. He only had enough time to catch himself with his elbow, otherwise he would have ended up in the river instead.

With a grimace, she touched the natural slime coat of the fish that covered her hands before she manoeuvred herself so she could wash them in the river.

As Merikh was righting himself, holding both flailing fish, Raewyn sat back next to the fire with her chin lifted.

"That was disgusting." Her lips pulled back in a cringe. "I can't believe you're going to eat that."

"Me?" he exclaimed as his head reared back. "I'm not eating these. I caught them for you."

She crawled around on her hands and knees to evade the smoke when it began blowing in her face. She paused once she was clear, and then sat on her knees facing him with her brows pinched in concern.

"Oh, I didn't know you were doing that for me." Then she lifted a forefinger and bashfully scratched at her cheek. "I can't eat them."

The wind changed directions and blew the smoke right back into her face. She gently coughed. She could keep moving as much as she wanted, but it no doubt would happen again.

A small, cruel chuckle would have left him, but it didn't, not when realisation sunk in.

"What the hell are you talking about?" A small growl bubbled from his throat as his orbs flared bright red. "You said you needed food, and I found you food."

Her brows and cheeks crinkled into a wince. "You should have told me sooner that you were catching the fish for me."

"Who else would I catch it for?" He couldn't believe it. He'd literally gotten himself wet and caught this for her, and she didn't want it? "You will eat this, or you'll go hungry. There is nothing else edible along the way."

"Elysians don't eat meat!"

"Well, you do today," he bit, grabbing her ankle when she started crawling away. "Whatever reservations your people have about food, in this realm, you eat what you find or you starve. There is no in between, no choice."

Just how rich were the Elvish people that they could survive without meat as an additional life force? Humans couldn't spare not to eat it. When travelling, there sometimes wasn't any alternative. They hunted because they *had* to hunt.

"Then I choose nothing when the alternative is sickness. I can survive a few days without food, but my physiological makeup is incapable of consuming meat. It brings on a sickness, a curse, if you will."

"Then why did we come here?"

With a deep snarl, Merikh threw the fish into the water, doubtful they would survive after being exposed to the air for so long. She flinched in surprise at his snarl and the splash, before her knees knocked inward self-consciously.

Merikh sat back on his haunches and palmed his skull in frustration.

I thought she would be like taking care of a human. Merikh had never taken care of a human before. He'd only ever observed and read about them so he could pass off as one without suspicion.

He was their death and destruction. If he took one in like some sort of pet, it'd be like fattening up a pig for slaughter.

This just got a lot harder than it needed to be.

"You should have told me first what food I should have been looking for, rather than making the assumption I had any idea," he growled out, just as he rose to his feet. "How the fuck am I supposed to know what you can or can't eat?"

"Well, you didn't think to ask me either." She bit at her

bottom lip before wiping her hands on her dress. "You're not going to eat them then?"

She looked wary of him. Then again, she always looked torn between being wary or warm. Her 'friendliness' was likely nothing but a façade to placate the monster she was travelling with.

Which meant he hated it when she showed him even a smidge of warmth. He'd rather she glare like everyone else who knew what he was.

"No, as that would be utterly pointless. No amount of food satisfies a Duskwalker's hunger. I am *always* hungry, always on the cusp of starvation, with no end in sight. *That* is my curse."

"Well, that sounds terrible," she muttered with a forced pout, and he bet she thought she looked cute, yet it only soured him further.

He looked at the water, sparkling gold from the bright sunlight. He had half a mind to toss her into the river.

"Tell me about it," he scoffed.

Cupping his hands in the water, he collected a large amount so he could dump it on the fire he'd made for absolutely no reason.

"It will take us an additional day to get to the temple, but there is a small farm town we stop at. I will get you food you can eat."

He was not above torturing her if she truly intended to back out on her end of the deal, but he had no interest in starving her. He didn't want to make the rest of their – hopefully – short journey unbearable.

He bet she'd whine and groan and bitch at him. That was normal... right? He was sure the humans had coined a specific word for it, *hangry* or something. Starving her would only torture himself.

"Any other requirements I should know about?"

"Nope." Then, she had the gall to bat her pretty, fluttery eyelashes at him before she dipped her big toe into the water and swirled it. "So... about that bath."

"No," he bit as he collected all the fire and fishing tools he'd prepared for her uneaten meal so he could place it all back in one of his satchels. He also donned his shirt. "For wasting my time, you can suffer."

Honestly, he was just feeling more irritable than usual, and she had truly wasted their time.

"I promise it'll only be five minutes."

Merikh folded his arms when he stood, prepped and ready to go. "Another five minutes lost."

Without a shred of warning, she bounced to her feet and placed her hands on her hips. "You know what? I don't have to ask for your permission."

When she began undoing the ties at the front of her dress, Merikh let out a deep growl.

"I said no! Dusk is beginning to colour the sky, and we have left our scents here for too long. This is how you endanger yourself."

Raewyn lifted her chin stubbornly. "I guess you're not as strong as you claim to be," she sang, just as she lowered her dress past her shoulders.

With his growl growing fiercer, Merikh turned before he could see any more of her body, surprised she was willing to strip in front of him just for a bath. Weren't most women shy about their nudity?

"You have five minutes," he snapped as he walked just past the trees and bushes. "Or I'll leave you here."

The giggle that came from her was light and airy, full of mischief. "No, you won't."

He peeked back to see she'd literally stuck her tongue out at him like he'd seen children do to each other.

Merikh disliked that the truth of her words was so obvious; he didn't have a hope of convincing her otherwise. She was more irksome than he'd originally anticipated.

I should have just eaten her...

TEN

Even after another day of travel, Raewyn kept her lips mostly shut. Merikh was still irritated, and he'd limited his responses to her as short grunts.

She wasn't interested in annoying him further.

She did feel bad he'd gone through all that trouble for her, and it probably seemed as though she was ungrateful. She wasn't. She appreciated his attempt to feed her.

Raewyn wasn't so disillusioned as to believe they were friends. In reality, she was his captive, and she was allowing it because she needed his help.

I shouldn't have assumed he'd understand I can't eat meat. She was just so used to that common fact among her people that it had skipped her mind.

There was a lot going on. She was in a strange place, with a strange... *something*, having to go on a strange journey just so she could skip to another world. There were so many variables, and she felt lost in a forest filled with sharp teeth.

Saying she was overwhelmed was an understatement.

Raewyn was also tired, physically exhausted from constantly walking, and she'd been hungry the entire time. Her stomach often quivered from emptiness, soon to start loudly gurgling. She'd been rationing her food when she realised days ago things were taking longer than she'd estimated. Since then, she'd eaten as little as she could, filling herself with water rather than food.

She wasn't at her optimal thinking capacity. Would anyone be in her position?

It didn't help that she didn't fully understand what he was. Okay, so he had a skull for a face. What else? What else was different about Merikh, other than the oddity of his exterior?

As Raewyn had done all her life, when given a subject of interest she knew little about, she poked and prodded her subject until it cracked. If she'd had paper and the magical ink that created her elbraille, she would have begun writing a thesis.

Instead, she was mentally categorising everything she learned about him and classifying it as research. She wanted to be able to catalogue what he was so she could inform her fellow councilmembers of what was happening on Earth.

She'd share the horrible state of the humans and how they were being forced to live because of their actions. She'd share that the Demons had completely overrun this world, and that Merikh's kind seemed to be more dominant than them. She needed to tell them as much as she could about Weldir and what he was doing, perhaps even speak to a prophet who had the rare ability to speak to their gods – currently, out of thousands of Elysian people, there were only three.

A prophet for each deity that remained, a horrible story for another time.

She wanted to explain everything she could about Duskwalkers, and Merikh in particular, especially since she was still so unsure of him.

His personality was churlish, and Raewyn had been constantly testing his boundaries to see if she could figure him out.

She'd been surprised by his honesty when she asked him questions about what he was and how to kill him. She expected him to keep anything pertaining to himself a secret, worried she'd try to off him the first chance she got.

It either meant he was an idiot for telling her, or he was as awesome in strength as he said he was.

Still, even if he was a little... mean, he'd gone out of his way to try to feed her. Instead of 'follow prisoner, or else,' he'd allowed her to have a few minutes to quickly bathe so she felt cleaner, healthier, better.

It was obvious he was spiteful. Not towards her, but at something else entirely, and she wanted to know what that was. Why did he hold hate so dearly that he was brash and callous with his words and behaviour?

She was realising the Merc she'd come to know was completely falsified, and that Merikh was someone else entirely.

From what she'd touched on the outside, he was a monster. Raewyn wanted to know if he was a monster through-and-through. Was he something unholy and evil all the way to his core, or was there perhaps a goodness beyond his self-centred goals?

She would only learn these things if she was open about her people, about her world, about herself. She needed to be the one with few secrets if she had any hope of understanding him in the short time she would be with him.

Right now, she could sense she just needed to remain quiet after the whole fishing incident.

He seems to be in more of a hurry to leave this realm than I am. It was hard to imagine with how homesick she was, to the point her heart and stomach felt as though they wanted to switch places.

No, it was he who didn't want to deviate from their path unless necessary. Yet, he was heading to this farming town for her sake.

He was a conundrum.

Raewyn and her people had long ago discovered that someone's exterior meant very little, and it was their actions that should be judged. A Demon was only a monster if it caused devastation within their city.

The Delysian were proof of that – people who were once

monsters but no longer were.

Sure, her people could judge them for their past transgressions, but then there would be no chance for healing and peace.

Could Merikh and his kind be the same? Could they not be monsters at all, but people who could peacefully live among them if they tried?

She was so uncertain, especially since he was hot and cold in every action he took, a complex creature she had little time to pull apart.

She needed to learn, not just for her own curiosity, but also to know if he was a danger to her people or not. It was obvious he was going to force his way into her realm alongside her, so she better have a plan if things went flip-side.

For the first time in what had to be hours, Merikh finally spoke. "We're almost there. The town is in view."

Even though she was completely averse to the idea, Raewyn sighed and asked, "Does that mean I must put those horrible shoes on?"

He was still carrying them for her.

"Yes, I think that would be wise."

Merikh halted, so she did as well when her guide rope went slack. He gently pressed her shoes against her stomach. Raewyn went to undo the ties lacing them together, but he'd already done so in consideration of her.

She shoved them on without any socks, hoping she didn't have to wear them for long. He explained the town was small and they wouldn't be remaining there for long. Get her food and get out was the plan.

Once her shoes were tied on and she'd secured a small cloth over her eyes, he led them down their path. She also propped her hood over her hair and ears to hide them.

"That's odd." He hummed, slowing when they must have gotten close. "The gates are closed. The humans usually keep them open in the day for travellers."

"Are you sure your glamour is working?"

She imagined they'd shut the gates if they saw anything like a Demon or Duskwalker's bony skull approaching.

"Yes. It has never failed."

Her ears shot back at the heavy banging when he bashed the bottom of his big fist against the wooden gate.

Clanking and chiming, like someone wearing metal armour, echoed from above. "Hail, travellers," a soldier yelled.

"Why is the gate closed?" Merikh yelled back, but it was grungy, almost like a roar.

"We're not allowing travellers to enter our grounds currently. Turn back."

The quietest rumble vibrated from Merikh. "What do you mean, you're not allowing travellers entry? We seek refuge within the town temporarily to resupply our rations so that we can continue our travels. No town has ever turned away weary people."

"Well, we are. Leave, or I have been ordered to shoot."

Her ears twitched under her hood at the sound of a knock and then creak, and she stepped behind Merikh. The soldier was aiming at them with a bow and arrow.

"You will let us in the town!" Merikh yelled as he bashed his fist against the gate. "This woman is tired. She needs rest, she needs water and food. Are you so heartless as to turn her away?"

He grabbed her from behind and pulled her forward, so she was in front of him. Then, he cupped underneath her jaw to push her face upwards towards the guard. The ends of her blindfold swayed against her cheek.

Her lips thinned with annoyance at being used in this manipulative way, but she would accept it if it meant she could resupply.

A small length of quietness impregnated the air. The guard was reconsidering, and her shoulders eased their tension.

"I'm sorry," the guard shouted. "But I can't disregard orders, no matter the reason. Our people have received word of a murderer currently making their way through the southland villages."

"Are you implying we are murderers?" Merikh asked with a quirk of humour. "Look at us; do we look capable of such things?"

"How do I know that this woman is truly blind? This could be nothing more than a ruse to ensure your admittance."

"How do you know it is not a Demon?"

"Because a Demon wouldn't leave a corpse. This person – or there could be more than one – has been leaving headless and heartless corpses around, and a warning has been delivered to all nearby towns."

Raewyn gasped and jumped back when a thunk sounded on the other side of Merikh. The guard had released a warning shot! *They truly shot at us!*

"Leave, or I'll shoot you next," the guard said as he nocked another arrow.

"Fine," Merikh bit before stepping back.

He took them away from the town, and Raewyn couldn't stop the crestfallen slump of her shoulders, nor her expression. *But I'm hungry. How can the humans so easily turn away those in need?*

"We will have to wait here," he said as he stopped and swiftly turned to her. "You might as well sit and rest while you can."

Raewyn tilted her head. "Why?"

"You think I'm going to let that stop me? The sun will go down soon. I'll scale the wall once night falls."

"You can do that?"

She'd heard most villages had walls that were at least five, if not six, metres tall. That sounded impossible to climb.

"Nothing the humans do can or will stop Duskwalkers," Merikh stated, his voice coming from below, as though he'd sat upon the ground. "They are just lucky we *generally* don't want anything to do with them."

Raewyn reached her hand forward to find a tree to lean upon

as she once more removed her shoes.

I guess we're waiting, then. I hope no Demons find us.

Merikh spooked the Elf when he landed right next to her grassy barrier. Her scent of fear trickled into the night air, but it calmed when she must have realised who it was.

He'd preferred to not have frightened her, but he could only scale up the town's wall, not down it. He'd jumped from the top and landed next to her after ransacking their crops.

"Any Demons?" he asked as he looked around and listened carefully. His sense of smell was far too diluted to be useful with long distance enemies.

He usually didn't wear his scent-masking cloth, but he was required to because of her. If she smelled of fear or blood, there was a chance he could turn on her.

Her grassy barrier faded as she unfurled herself from her protective huddle. "No."

He dug through the bag of food he'd collected to make sure it was still all there before giving it to her. Their hands touched with the exchange. Her flesh was warm, her skin as soft as silk against the abrasiveness of his calloused palms.

"Lucky," he stated. "Towns are a lure. I was unsure of leaving you out here by yourself, but I hoped you'd be able to protect yourself."

"You weren't gone long," she answered as she took a turn digging through the bag herself. "Oh wow, there's so much here. Thank you for this. You left so quickly that you didn't give me time to give you money to pay for them."

"Pay for them?" Merikh bit in disbelief. "All the shops are closed, Raewyn."

She blinked her spellbinding eyes before they widened, and her bottom lip fell. "You stole it all? You can't do that!"

"Then they should have let us in when I asked. I had half a

mind to go find that guard and bash his skull in while he was asleep."

He almost wanted to chuckle – warmly, rather than his usual dark and cruel laugh – when her face twisted with guilty concern. The corners of her eyes were crinkled as she bowed them in aversion, her white brows shaped into little wiggles of upset.

"It's not nice to steal."

Merikh rolled his head on his shoulders before he sighed. "I picked everything I know is edible without cooking it first. This should suffice until we make it to the temple."

Her lips pursed, as though she wished to keep berating him for his theft. Then, she turned her face up and glared in his direction.

"I heard you threaten people in Clawhaven. Do you often bash people's skulls in?"

"Once or twice, but they usually deserve it."

"Is that even true?" she whined, her head falling back like she was praying to some god above.

"Sure." It absolutely wasn't.

He was sure he'd bashed a handful of people's heads in simply because they'd irritated him. *He* thought they deserved it, but many moments later, he'd reflect on it and then change his mind. He held not an ounce of regret, though, for he couldn't take back what he'd done, and he often liked to whimsically look back on his actions.

Sometimes, he drew great enjoyment from doing so.

He'd definitely enjoy reflecting back on his short visit to this town. He'd destroyed half their crops in retaliation for not allowing them entry when he so *politely* asked for it.

He would have left the fire burning, but he had an Elf he needed to protect. The light and smoke of the flames would only draw nearby Demons her way.

Since she'd had a small nap as they'd waited for night to fall, and now had food, he expected they wouldn't have to stop again for quite some time.

    One step closer to freedom, he thought as he handed her the guide rope.

ELEVEN

Raewyn winced when yet another sharp rock jabbed into the sole of one of her aching feet. For nearly three days straight, they'd walked. That was three days of random bouts of drizzle with lots of sun. Three days of never stopping, never slowing, even in the night.

She was tired of it. She was over it.

I've never walked this much in my entire life.

The bottoms of her feet were tender from stepping on jagged rocks, sharp sticks, and hard dirt. She imagined they were undoubtedly disgusting from all the mud she'd trodden in.

She'd only get a reprieve when the environment became soft, plush grass, and it only made the random sticks more surprising and somehow more painful.

Somewhere along their journey, Merikh had picked up a bit of spirit. Perhaps because he was heading towards the temple, he was inclined to not be unpleasant in any way.

Still, there was an unbreakable wall around him.

She'd managed to learn of five adult brothers he had, all of whom had different skull, horn, and body features. She'd learned that they became partially what they ate, except Demons gave them no new characteristics. Baby Mavka were essentially nothing; they looked like blobby infants with a jagged mouth and nose holes, having no other distinct features in their dark grey, nearly void flesh.

She'd learned that his mother was a human who had become a Phantom after giving Weldir her soul. She had been gifted the use of power by Weldir and acted as his physical self in this realm.

There was no doubt in her mind the Gilded Maiden would be rather upset about that fact – given that she'd only allowed him the power to control his own realm. He wasn't supposed to interfere with Earth. He was meant to be nothing but a collector of souls for those who had been damned by the Demons who ate them.

In acquiring a mate, he'd technically violated the deal he'd made with the Gilded Maiden, the one he'd made to escape his imprisonment realm.

He was not supposed to experience joy, life, or even love. Without a true body to possess, they'd all thought he'd be incapable.

Oh, how wrong they were.

Merikh had also told her much about the humans and the way they lived. He'd explained the differences between the north, south, east, and western lands of the Veil.

The southland's border made this area of the continent safer from smaller Demons, which meant more humans lived here. However, the Demons had discovered this, and it was often the bigger, nastier ones that hunted this area.

Yet, in all her findings, she'd learnt very little about him.

This Duskwalker shared no details about what he was seeking. He'd been travelling the world the moment he'd gained the ability to leave his home permanently. He apparently went back to it every ten years to lay down a protective ward, refusing to allow any creature to take the one thing that belonged to him, but he always left again once he did.

I guess every creature feels comforted knowing they have a place to return to, she mused.

Whenever she asked Merikh what he'd truly been up to over

the years, why he had a glamour to enter the human towns, or what compelled him to keep moving, his answer was always vague.

He often just grunted, informing her he'd heard her, but wouldn't answer. That, or he'd just tell her she would be better off not knowing.

She couldn't tell if he was good or evil unless he revealed something about himself, something that wasn't in self-interest, like caring for her only because it got him what he wanted.

Currently, she was leaning towards... evil.

He'd destroyed crops when he didn't need to, just to be spiteful. He'd threatened multiple people's poor skulls with a thorough bashing. He'd... eaten humans, had already admitted to it, and yet, it didn't sound as though he held even a shred of remorse.

She'd learned he gained intelligence and humanity by eating humans. Just. Like. Demons.

Should I tell him the truth about why that is? She was considering it, thinking a person should know themselves when it was important, but she'd gotten the impression that he didn't like talking about his family.

Not his brothers, not his mother, and there had always been a growl in his tone whenever he explained something pertaining to his father.

Now that she was no longer wearing her blindfold around him, she'd even seen sparks of red right where she thought his face was, like a glow of anger before it disappeared. It was magic that allowed the orbs to change colours, and she was able to see the sparks of the change – and sometimes a trail of colour if it seemed like an emotion gripped him tightly.

They were often red, even when she hadn't spoken for a long while. Even his thoughts were hateful.

I don't trust him. How could she?

She wanted to, desperately wanted to, but she couldn't.

Raewyn had always been told she was too trusting, especially when she employed Cykran as her assistant, but she'd never been an idiot. She didn't foolishly trust those she was uncertain about.

She always weighed the pros and cons.

Merikh was a liar.

So what if his orange and cinnamon scent was delightfully delicious? So what if his deep and grumbly voice was pleasant and made her ears ring happily? So what if his big hand was so warm and rough that it made her skin tingle just from the meagre contact?

So why did she want to get closer to him so she could smell him better, or hear him better, or hope he would hand her something again so she could be blessed with the warmth and touch of his hand?

How can I like anything about him? It didn't make sense.

She'd been bewildered the very few times he'd touched her or grabbed her. His touch had only ever been gentle when he'd saved her from those Demons many nights ago.

His pace was also something she could keep up with. Although she was tired – three days of non-stop walking was exhausting for any creature, except him, apparently – it wasn't because of the pace. The path was usually quite flat, with little to nothing for Raewyn to trip over.

A cruel captor would usually drag their captive through any treacherous path, at the speed *they* chose.

In some ways, this was just a pleasant stroll through an unknown world. It wasn't a march.

If he's so strong, I wish he'd carry me. She wouldn't have minded. She'd considered slowing down to whine constantly, just to see if she could get him to do it.

Raewyn thoughtfully hummed. *If he did carry me, though, would he carry me nicely by cradling me, or would he throw me over his shoulder like a food sack again?*

There were so many questions, and not an answer on the horizon.

"Are we there yet?" Raewyn whined, pulling on the rope so she could lean back as she walked, her face pointing towards the sky so she could rest her neck. "My feet huuurt."

"We'll be there soon," he answered plainly.

He'd been saying that for hours.

Raewyn let out a sigh, no longer sure if he was actually taking her to the temple or was just planning to walk her to death.

With her neck craned back, she tried to feel the sunlight peeking through whatever foliage was above them.

"Merikh..." she slowly stated to get his attention.

Her ears twitched when he let out a weird, raspy, "What?"

"What colour is the sky here?"

The silence that radiated between them only highlighted the noise of their footsteps through the forest – the way sticks snapped under their weight, or when he brushed back a branch to make sure it didn't snap back to whack her.

It was such a small detail, him holding that branch, but it was one of the many tiny things that had her wondering if he was a good person deep down inside. She also doubted it.

"The sky is a pale blue on a sunny day, whereas at night it's such a dark navy, it appears black. There are sometimes white clouds, but they are a dark grey when it rains. The sky is the prettiest when it is either dawn or dusk, and it is rarely ever the same. The sky starts to turn purple, and the horizon starts to turn orange because of our yellow sun. Sometimes, though, it is such a deep colour of red, it appears as though the very edge of the world is on fire."

The corners of her eyelids crinkled with a small amount of joy. She hadn't expected him to be so detailed, and it caused her heart to swell in tenderness as she tried to picture this world's sky.

"What about the trees?" she asked, worried he'd grow bored of answering her questions.

"Depends on the time of year. Currently above you, the

leaves are a deep green, and the trunks are brown. Yet, many of these trees in the autumn will turn red or yellow, and their leaves will fall to the ground."

Her smile grew, and she thought it may have been the first real one she'd shared in his presence since learning he was a monster.

"What about the grass?"

"It's green. So are the shrubs we've passed. Most of Earth is brown with green leaves. It's the flowers that bring colour, and they vary in size, colour, and type. I imagine snow is white for your realm, since it's nothing but frozen water."

Raewyn shrugged. "We can create ice with a spell, but I've never seen snow fall before. It's too hot in Nyl'theria, but we do know of a few ice realms."

Bringing her head forward, she let her imagination run wild as she pictured the world. She imagined the trees were shorter here, so with the colours he gave her, she made up her own version of Earth.

She could almost see it, like a murky painting.

"Thank you," she softly whispered.

She received no answer from him.

Then, after what could only be an hour, he said something that almost had her weeping in relief.

"The town is just ahead of us, so you'll need to put your boots on."

"Oh, thank the holy maiden," she sighed before she tugged on the rope. "Could we stop here a moment, then? I'll need to wrap my hair and cover my face as well."

In her dark vision, a flicker of yellow appeared. "Why do you need to cover your hair? Just keep your hood on."

Raewyn shook her head. "What if it gets knocked back?"

Merikh gave a grunt, which she figured was his way of saying okay. She donned everything she needed, but her awareness of him prickled.

"What does it mean if your orbs or whatever turn yellow?"

Once more, twin sparks of yellow glowed in her vision before one disappeared, as though he'd covered it with his hand. Then they were both gone, and she wondered if they remained that colour or if they returned to his usual red.

"You can see them? How?"

"Kind of," she answered with a shrug. "It's only for a moment, but I can see magic when it's being used."

He never answered what the colour signified, but she thought it may have been curiosity or confusion.

Entry into the city was difficult, as the gates were also closed, but the guard was far more lenient about letting them inside. They were issued a warning: if any deaths happened while they were within the city's walls, they wouldn't be permitted to exit and would be imprisoned as the culprits.

"You can read and write?" Raewyn asked in surprise when he was made to fill out their details in a ledger. She hoped it didn't come across as rude.

"You'd be surprised what I can do," he stated in a dark tone.

Once Merikh had written their names, the guard wrote down a full physical description of them. He didn't force her to remove anything – since she pushed her hood back to show her face – apparently more interested in the big 'human' next to her.

Raewyn wished she had a glamour as well. She'd love to be able to walk around with her hair and ears out without a care in the world.

She felt *shady* entering the town with her hood propped so far over her head that it was likely shielding most of her face. She didn't know if it made her less conspicuous or more so.

It's busier here than Clawhaven and that farm town, Raewyn thought as she stuck close to Merikh. She no longer held the length of rope, opting to curl her hand around the rope circling his waist instead.

She gauged his confident strut through the humans to make sure she didn't step on the back of his heel, walking slightly behind and to the side of him. She didn't know if he minded, but he didn't stop her.

Keeping her head down, she tried to remain as small as possible. She wasn't shy or bashful, just nervous about humans in general.

As soon as they'd entered the town, all she could hear were the voices of hundreds of people clustered together. They were chatting merrily, which was a different atmosphere than Clawhaven.

"What's that smell?" Raewyn asked, lifting her nose slightly.

There was the generic smell of food cooking, as well as sweet pastries. Of course, there was the general scent of so many bodies that came with their own odours – some pleasant, some not. There were flowers and herbs littering the air.

There was also something else, something strange and unusual, a fabricated musk.

"It's incense," he answered as he navigated through the dense crowd.

From what she could tell, whenever she accidentally bumped into Merikh, his back was straight, his walk determined. Not a single person bumped into them, as though the crowd was parting for him.

"The temple acolytes have created the incense to hide the scent of humans," he continued. "It lowers the risk of Demons coming here. They have also placed charms all along the brick walls spanning around the entirety of this village. It's effective against the Demons, but not so much against Duskwalkers."

She almost shushed him for speaking about his kind but concluded that he absolutely did not care. Otherwise, he wouldn't have spoken so openly about it.

Music emanated from all around her, though none of it was in sync. Someone was torturing a poor guitar, while a woman sang her heart out in some sort of establishment.

Many tried to offer them food or wares with cheer in their voices.

The town was alive, filled with hope and joy. She never

expected such a place to exist on Earth.

A pang twisted in her gut. *It sounds like home.*

The beachside city she came from was filled with laughter, as though the Demons beyond their magical barrier didn't exist. People danced and sang in the street without a care in the world, happy to be alive and sheltered.

This town smelt and sounded so similar, a beacon of hope for the humans, just like her own city.

Once her homesickness dissipated, relief washed over her like a gentle wave. She even smiled for these people, overwhelmed by their happiness despite everything they obviously faced.

If they could be like this, live like this, then there was a chance the Elysians could repair their wrongdoings and make things right again. They could help the humans heal once they ridded them of the dangers that lurked in the darkness just beyond the walls.

Everything began to quiet the further they walked down the path they never deviated from. The noise echoed over the distance as Merikh took them away from the main areas.

"We're about to go through the first temple gate, so watch your step," he warned her.

He slowed to allow Raewyn to toe the edge of a stair, so she didn't trip. Then they climbed the stone staircase, and the rock tapped under her boots.

They climbed and climbed, then climbed some more, as though the ascent was never-ending.

"Holy maiden," she gasped. "Just how many stairs are there?"

"There's always a large staircase leading to each of the main temples. This being the only temple in the southlands, it's the tallest one. The building is situated on the very top of a hill overlooking the rest of Ashpine City."

Raewyn nodded, smiling in thanks at him for explaining this to her. The ground evened once again, and after a few steps, they halted.

"There are two gates. The first is always open unless there is an invasion. The second is always closed. The Anzúli you speak of don't allow outsiders to enter their temples."

He finally pronounced their name correctly, probably because she'd said it several times over the past few days.

The boom of his fist on the gate was so loud, she was certain everyone within a mile radius would have heard it. There was a tiny *shink*, as if someone unlatched a lock, before a quiet squeak.

It was clear the gate hadn't been opened, but rather a small peephole instead.

"Yes, hello," a man coldly greeted, his voice raspy, as though he'd been half asleep. "How may we assist..."

Trailing off, he cleared his throat, as if it suddenly had become dry.

"Allow us inside," Merikh demanded, his tone forceful and refusing denial.

Raewyn didn't like the silence that followed. The man shuffled his feet on the other side of the gate, as if he was unsure of how to respond. He cleared his throat again.

"I'm sorry, *sir*, but we don't allow outsiders within our temples. If you require assistance, we are more than happy–"

Merikh shoved Raewyn's hand away from the rope coil around his waist, and a resonating *boom* exploded, like he'd slammed his entire forearms against the gate. His claws scraped against the timber.

"I know you can *see* what I am," Merikh growled. "I have a female here who needs to speak to your people, and you will allow us inside."

Raewyn's ears flattened against the sides of her head. *The glamour doesn't work on them.* It only tricked the humans.

She tried to push Merikh out of the way, who didn't budge an inch for her, so she wedged herself between him and the gate peephole.

She didn't care if she angered or annoyed him, or if she got hurt in the process of shoving him. He was messing this up!

At this rate, they'd never get permission to enter.

Merikh growled as the Elf shoved herself in front of him.

He had this sorted, so he saw no reason for her to intervene.

"Please," Raewyn begged, as she patted for the hole with her fingertips. When she found it, she pulled her hood back and lowered her blindfold, revealing her eyes, her brows, and her pointed ears. "I'm an Elysian, and I seek your help to get home."

He expected the man, who had a white clay mask covering his face with a red stripe going down the very centre, to immediately reject her. Instead, he gasped and stumbled back, as if he couldn't believe what he was seeing.

Then he bounced forward and reached his arm through the small square hole to cup the side of her face. That was dangerous, as Merikh could easily snap his arm in half with the window's frame.

He considered it.

"By the gods... how did you get here?" he asked in awe.

Merikh didn't know why, but the way Raewyn leaned into his touch trustingly grated on his nerves. She bent forward as she curled her fingers around the bottom of the peephole to be closer to the man.

"I accidentally opened a chaos portal to Earth. I've been stranded here for over a month and a half, and I *desperately* want to go home. Please allow us inside."

The man's clay mask turned to look up Merikh's bony snout through the eye holes' mesh, seeing him for what he was, before directing the mask back to Raewyn.

"You will always be welcome inside our temples," the man stated warmly. Then his voice turned frigid as he said, "But *he* must remain outside."

The laugh Merikh released was filled with malice.

"She is not leaving my side. Either we both may enter, or neither of us will."

Raewyn turned to him with her mouth open, as though to refute him, but then she wisely shut it. He'd already made it clear he wouldn't accept her fleeing from him, leaving him behind, or betraying him.

She bit at her bottom lip, her brows knitting deeply. Then her head bowed downward in defeat before she turned to the man.

"Please. He's my guide in this world," she pleaded. "He helped me get here."

Merikh bet under that clay white mask and the white mesh-covered eye holes, the man was glaring at him. He wished he could bare his fangs to appear more sinister, but they were always visible due to the lack of flesh on his face.

"You know what he is, right? A monster."

With anger swirling in his chest, Merikh snarled. He fucking *despised* being called that.

"I prefer the term Duskwalker, you stupid piece of Demon bait."

Not even the lightest touch of Raewyn's palm resting over his sternum managed to quell his anger. He did tilt his head at her for it, though.

"Yes, I know what he is," she stated, her calm, sweet voice managing to ease the tension. "I swear on the Gilded Maiden that he won't hurt anyone. I promise you this."

She shouldn't be making promises she cannot keep, he thought as he leaned back and folded his arms across his bulky chest.

"There, see," he snapped. "I'll be as harmless as a newborn kitten."

The man looked back at the stone temple before sighing. "Okay, I will allow you inside."

He closed the small door, locked it, and then worked on opening the gate.

"You didn't have to be so rude to him," Raewyn bit, the

bridge of her nose adorably scrunched up.

"I wasn't rude," Merikh snapped back, clearly offended. He crossed one of his arms over his chest and pointed at the opening gate with the other. "He started it."

If he remembered the start of their interaction correctly, he'd asked to be let inside and the Priest rejected him. The man had judged his bony face immediately upon seeing it and decided Merikh wasn't righteous enough to enter their *lame* temple.

A temple he could have scaled with ease and decimated everyone inside of. Yet, he'd never chosen to do so – although he'd considered it many times.

See? He was perfectly virtuous.

Guiltless, no, but they didn't know the depths of his crimes against humankind.

"Why didn't you tell me they could see through your glamour?"

With her hands balled into fists at her side, he thought Raewyn looked one move away from childishly stomping her foot.

He shrugged a shoulder, his voice nonchalant. "Must have slipped my mind."

It hadn't. He just knew there was always going to be a battle over him gaining entry. He hadn't expected to obtain permission, even with her help.

The Priest recognised what she was right away. Their people must have a good relationship with each other.

She rolled her starburst eyes with an annoyed groan in Merikh's direction. Humour filled his chest; he was becoming smitten with purposefully annoying the little Elf. She always responded with an adorable pout or a cute brow furrow.

Merikh had never had anyone act this way towards him. He'd always received hatred, or fear, or tears for his actions, and her annoyed tantrums were so devoid of those things that he found it hard not to like them.

She'd never cursed at him or spoken coldly to him. She'd

never tried to hurt him or run away from him again.

Actually, he noticed earlier that she'd almost huddled into him protectively. No one had ever sought his protection in a crowd full of people – usually, people were seeking protection from him.

He'd been curious to know if she would immediately out him for what he was to the humans in order to escape from him. The Anzúli were close by, so he thought she might try to go to them by herself if he was overrun by soldiers and guards.

She hadn't used that tactic, nor had she tried an alternative. Instead, she wisely made sure he could enter the temple with her. It seemed she had accepted the cold, foreboding shadow of his presence looming at her back.

"We need to work on your people skills," Raewyn grumbled as she huddled into him so she could grab the guide rope around his waist.

Merikh grunted, disagreeing with her completely. His people skills were just fine. A little brash, but he always got what he wanted, and that's all he cared about.

The gate door finished opening, and the Priest ushered them through the black iron gate.

There was a small, flat, grey cobblestone pathway that led to ten steps. Two inhuman-looking statues appeared, like part rabbit and part water deer at the bottom.

There were a handful of trees that spanned all the way around the temple, the grassy field lush, as though it was maintained with the most fertile soil and nutrients.

At the top of the steps was a monumental temple made of grey brick and black iron. Above the black iron double doors, a stained-glass window of a world totally and utterly different to Earth had been cut and shaped. In the sunlight, it glittered, and he was sure it smeared its colours against the floors inside.

The temple's roof was pointed in the middle, but there were two towers on each side sporting white flags with purple runic symbols painted on them.

The flags matched the heavy white robe the Priest wore. There were purple runes painted along every seam, as though the very cloak itself was a cloth of protection.

When they reached the door, the Priest turned to them and paused for far longer than Merikh found comfortable. It was obvious he was looking between him and Raewyn, but his clay mask gave no insight.

"If you would like," he stated, turning his clay mask to Raewyn, "he can remain with us, but I would be happy to guide you through the temple."

As long as Merikh was able to remain by her side so they couldn't plot against him, he wouldn't stop her from making her decision. He waited for her to step away from him to take the guidance of another – a stranger, someone more human-like and less... him-like.

Merikh wasn't foolish enough to not accept the reality that Raewyn was only being familiar with him out of necessity. He'd been her only option for the past week, so when given what *most* would consider a better choice, why wouldn't she take the offer?

He expected her to shy and shirk away from him like he and his feelings didn't matter. In their minds, why should a 'monster' care?

She was hesitant, her response slow to come, but she gripped the rope she was holding tighter.

"No, I'm fine as I am."

Merikh twisted his head at that, his orbs shifting to bright yellow in surprise. She'd chosen him, and a strange kind of pride puffed his chest.

It may have meant little to her, but she'd given him just a small sliver of something he'd never been given before: acceptance that wasn't through his own deceit.

"Are you sure?" the Priest pressed. "I'm sure you'd be more comfortable w–"

"She said she's fine with me," Merikh cut in with a growl, snuffing the urge to curl his arm around Raewyn's shoulders and possessively keep the pretty Elf glued to his side. "Hurry up and open the door."

The Priest swiftly turned and shoved open the black iron doors.

Musky incense burned in the back of his throat, but it was pleasant despite its oversaturation as it billowed past him.

Although the outside of the temple was made of bleak stone, the inside appeared warmer and more inviting, due to the wooden carvings etched into timber sheets. On every surface of the back wall were candles of varying colours, as well as a large ring of them in the very centre of the sanctum.

Black cloth tapestries hung from the ceiling, a language he didn't understand painted on them in purple.

He'd thought everything would be light, with more white and purple, but the inside of the temple appeared darker. Black seemed to be their preference, as though they honoured and revelled in the darkness of it.

It was the polar opposite to how they dressed.

Upon their entry, a small choir in the back right corner abruptly stuttered to a halt, as did the walk of a person who glanced up from the text they were reading to look their way.

None of them wore the masks connected to their sashes by a loop, and Merikh noted the same people he'd seen many times.

Their skin colours were similar to that of humans, their hair similar as well, but their three glowing eyes revealed they were of a completely different species. Two of their eyes sat where a human's would, but they had an additional one in the middle, right above their brow bone.

All three eyes moved in unison, and they often glowed pink, blue, or gold, with a downward slitted pupil.

Merikh knew from experience that if you removed everything but their masks, they looked human. If you opened one up, their blood was red, their heart and lungs the same.

It was their faces that were different, as were their scents.

Everyone gasped upon seeing Merikh's towering form. One

even ran through a side door to escape the sanctuary. If it weren't for the incense and his nose covering, he was sure they'd all reek of delectable fear.

In his peripheral, he watched Raewyn reach up with her free hand to unwrap her hair coverings, allowing her two thick white braids freedom.

Chattering echoed. If he could hear their curiosity about the Duskwalker and the Elf, he didn't doubt she could as well.

The Priest led them into the centre of the candles on the floor, where Merikh examined the runic circle, not only painted, but carved into the ground. An aversion to entering it filled him, as such magic symbology could be used to harm or trap him, but he entered it anyway.

The man's earlier behaviour gave him the impression they wouldn't harm Raewyn, considering his awe and desire to assist her. If they were to attack Merikh, they would know she could be put in potential danger.

He hoped they remained wise.

Just in case, though, he warned, "Try anything funny, and you'll make the Elf regret coming here."

The man's back stiffened, as did Raewyn's.

A Priestess with dark, fawny skin and straight black hair came running into the sanctuary, her robe, black rather than white, fluttering behind her. She skidded to a halt, her eyes a bright pink before they settled into their normal dim glow.

The person who had run out earlier was behind her, and they bumped into her so hard, they both almost fell forward. Their feet squeaked as they stumbled and righted themselves, both chests heaving with panted breaths.

The Priestess dressed in black had a different kind of mask tied to her belt sash. It was painted completely red, with a golden triangle where he thought her third eye would be if she were to wear it.

There was something about her, though, as she quickly calmed her breathing while looking them over. She straightened her robe, lifted her chin, and gracefully walked forward.

She's different, Merikh concluded after examining her. Her shoulders were pushed back, as though to convey a sense of superiority. *She must be some sort of leader.*

The Priest who led them inside turned to the approaching Priestess. Since he'd removed his mask upon entering, he closed all three of his eyes, crossed his right arm over his stomach, and placed the side of his index and middle fingers of his left hand over his third eye.

"Holy overseer," he greeted, his tone light and filled with the utmost respect. "I can understand why you must have been alarmed, but I'm sure you can recognise why I permitted them entry."

Her lips were pursed in Merikh's direction, and he folded his arms in response. He nodded his snout in Raewyn's direction.

Her glare didn't fade, her eyes remaining on his bony skull even as she moved her face towards the Elf. Then she smiled brightly towards Raewyn, likely knowing by her starburst pupils that she wouldn't be able to see it, but did so regardless.

"Hello, my name is Maia Sheltier. I am the holy overseer of Ashpine City's temple." Her voice was deep, lacking in femininity, yet it radiated kindness and respect. "May I ask you both your names?"

"I am Raewyn Daefaren, and this is Merikh," Raewyn answered, presenting her own smile.

"It's a pleasure to meet you," Maia said, never taking her eyes off Raewyn. "Never in my life did I think I would be bestowed the honour of meeting an Elysian Elf. Us Anzúli have not greeted your kind in centuries. What are you doing on Earth? Has the great change finally come?"

There was hope in the woman's voice. It even brightened the faces of those pretending they weren't eavesdropping on their echoing conversation.

Raewyn's smile snuffed out within the span of a breath, and her head lowered, as though with shame.

"No. I'm sorry, but I'm not an emissary for my people," Raewyn responded in a small voice. "I'm actually one of the eighteen from the *synedrus* council, specifically one of the three heads of the scientific divisions."

Merikh reared his head back in surprise, unaware Raewyn was a person of power, or a scientist. Her personality already appeared far too playful and light for this kind of profession.

Then again, what would he know? His assumptions were based on stereotypes, considering he'd never met a scientist of any kind before – other than maybe himself. He guessed what he did was theory work and studies, since he'd always known he'd need a freaking portal to get off this world.

Any human leader he'd met was usually someone cold and unfeeling, bearing the burdens of their people.

"While I was working in my laboratory," Raewyn continued, "I accidentally constructed a chaos portal and was transported here, to Earth."

Maia and the Priest's hopeful expressions fell, but Maia was the one who looked truly concerned. She'd even gone a little pale, which only highlighted the brightness of her glowing pink eyes.

"I'm truly sorry, but if you have come here seeking a way home, there is nothing we can do for you."

Merikh could hear the way Raewyn's heart stuttered before pumping wildly. She stepped forward, her brow crinkling in confusion, and he thought even fear. The overpowering incense in the temple made it near impossible for him to smell anything clearly, no doubt even if he removed his snout cloth.

"What do you mean, there's nothing you can do?" Raewyn asked, a tremble in her voice. "If-if you take me to your portal, you should be able to redirect it to Nyl'theria. I'm sure I can help you."

Maia nodded her head to the Priest while waving her left hand, and the man bowed before leaving. He'd been dismissed, and once he was gone, she dropped any superiority she'd held.

Her shoulders slumped, and her chin fell just enough that it was no longer jutting. "Much has happened in the three hundred and forty-three years since your people were here last. Our portal is gone, and we Anzúli that are left were stranded here a hundred and ninety-three years ago."

"How?" Raewyn asked.

Merikh, who was choosing not to insert himself into a conversation that had little to do with him, tilted his head at the crack he noticed in her voice.

"Our head temple was attacked in what we believe was a targeted raid by the Demons and Jabez, the Demon King." Maia turned her head away, looking off into nothing as her eyes bowed with obvious sadness.

Raewyn's shoulders turned inwards, like someone who had been caught red-handed in a crime or lie, which was odd, since she was usually so forward and open with her expressions.

"When the Demons began entering the portal, those in Anzúla chose to permanently close it to protect our world from being infested. Since then, we have had no contact with our people, no help or assistance, and every generation, we grow weaker. We have begun reproducing with the humans to avoid mixing the same genetics. In another generation or so, we will completely lose our ability to perform magic. Some are already being born without our third eye or glow, and currently, we can do little more than create advanced medicines and basic protection for the humans. Our mission here is failing, and soon, the humans will be left with no one to protect them."

"B-but you can still produce magic, right?" Raewyn beseeched as she lifted her face, her eyes bowed with a plea. "Maybe I can help you open a new portal, and we can both contact our worlds. We can bring more Anzúli here to help."

Maia sighed as she shook her head, her black hair dancing as it swayed.

"Only a rare few of us can even create the elements. Those who can become holy overseers, but our powers are limited. It would require every holy overseer on this continent to band together, and then we would need to hope you were able to draw the correct navigational runes to take us to our realms. Do you know the specific Anzúla or Nyl'theria geographical pinpoints that would be the safest?"

Raewyn fisted the skirt of her grey dress with both her hands, the material crumpling with how tightly she held it. "Well, no. Portal magic is forbidden to the Elysians. All our texts regarding it have been sealed away."

"Anzúla is lively with both ice and lava. If you were to open a portal into one of our many volcanoes, you'd be submitting us to death. As for Nyl'theria... would you be able to accurately open a portal to somewhere safe?"

"I'm sure we could figure out a way," Raewyn argued, but Merikh could already read the writing on the wall.

All the anticipation, the excitement, the fucking *hope* that had grown within him as he travelled steadfastly to this temple was twisting into a knot of despair.

"Perhaps I can help," Merikh offered. "I am able to produce magic and can assist the Elf. I'm sure there is a way we can all work together."

He'd give and do anything to achieve their collective goal. Hell, he'd give every drop of blood if needed – nothing was too great of an ask.

Maia, for the first time since greeting them, looked upon Merikh. Her glare was sharp and hateful, her eyes glistening with the tiniest hint of tears.

"And just how did you obtain your *magic,* Duskwalker?" she nearly growled through clenched teeth.

His orbs flared a deeper red, and the snarl that echoed from him was malicious and unholy as it echoed off the walls of their temple.

Maia's glare disappeared the moment her eyes fell back on Raewyn, choosing to ignore his very existence. She never gave him time to voice his callous response.

"It wouldn't matter. We have already tried everything, and we know there is nothing we can do. I want to help you, but unless you want us to heal you or give you charms, there's not much more we can do."

Merikh lifted his skull to the ceiling, trying his damn hardest to stem the vengeful roar building in the back of his throat. Had it not been for Raewyn, he may have already destroyed this temple for its utter uselessness. They didn't deserve to be a beacon of hope for the humans.

When something upset him, Merikh had a deep desire to eradicate it from this world, to destroy and maim whatever had birthed his ire so he could sit in its destruction with pride.

He didn't, because for some stupid reason, he didn't want to upset the Elf.

He also had no desire to claw or bite at her like he did with every Anzúli who currently stood in this sanctuary, even though she had allowed him to believe there was a chance he would be free. She was the centre point of why he felt so desolate. She was the reason invisible hands of rage were massaging his brain, and yet he didn't have a single shred of anger towards her.

They were *both* going to be fucking stuck here on Earth. Raewyn wasn't the key he'd been looking for; she was just as lost as he was.

"O-okay. I'll figure out another way then," Raewyn conceded. "Thank you."

"You're fucking thanking her?" Merikh barked as he lowered his head to look at her in disbelief. "She did absolutely nothing to help you, so why the hell are you thanking her?"

Raewyn turned to him and shined the fakest smile he'd ever seen. Her lips wobbled like they wanted to uncurl.

"Because that's what you do when someone has politely informed you of the situation." She turned back to Maia and bowed her head. "I think it's best we leave."

"Leave?" Merikh bit. "Just like that? Neither one of you are going to think about a possible alternative? We've been here all of ten minutes – there must be another way."

"I have already informed you we have already tried," Maia answered coldly. "There is no alternative."

Raewyn reached forward and patted his side until she found the rope. She tugged on it.

"Please, Merikh," she whispered with a shaken voice as she gave her back to Maia. "I wish to leave."

"Raewyn," Maia beseeched as she reached for her shoulder. "You are welcome to stay here. I know you'll outlive all of us, but we can try to make your life comfortable here on Earth."

"S-sorry, but I must find out if there is another way."

The woman's hand tightened. "Please. I ask that you stay. We could really use your help in protecting the humans. The other factions of Anzúli would appreciate your guidance just as much as us. We are failing, and we are dying here."

Her white braids fell forward over her shoulders as her shoulders turned inward. "Please, let go of me."

When the woman didn't, Merikh grabbed her wrist and squeezed as he snarled. She winced, then glared up at his orbs darkening their red hue.

"Your companion is a monster, and part of the reason the Anzúli's numbers are dwindling rapidly. I fear if you go with him, you'll discover just how *evil* his kind can be."

Priests and Priestesses alike ushered forward before dropping back when he raised his skull in their direction and parted his fangs.

"Come closer, and–"

"Merikh, stop," Raewyn demanded quietly, and yet it was stern and unwavering. He snapped his head in her direction. "Please. Just take me from here."

With a grunt, he shoved Maia's hand, and she almost fell back.

The only reasons he led them towards the exit was because he could see she was trembling and her dark complexion appeared ashen, like she was tired or sick.

Fine. Screw it. We'll leave. Merikh bashed the heavy black iron door open. *What am I supposed to do now?*

He'd been searching for hundreds of years for a way to leave Earth, and he'd never found a single answer. If he couldn't find one, how was she going to?

And what was he supposed to do with the Elf he now had?

The one he weirdly felt compelled to... keep. She could still help him find a way. It would be better than foolishly walking across the continent he'd already circled multiple times.

He was sure that was why he wouldn't let her escape him, or why he wouldn't kill her just yet.

TWELVE

When the metal door to the temple shut behind them with a definitive slam, Raewyn tugged on the rope again so she could stop Merikh. He'd been walking a little faster than normal, likely due to agitation, but that wasn't why she stopped them.

There was someone following quietly behind them. She wondered if it was to make sure they actually left – or rather, that Merikh did.

"A-are we going to a place where I can rest?" she asked in a small voice, trying to control herself while her eyes and nose tingled. "If not, I'll need to put my hair wrappings on."

"I'll take us to an inn," he answered back in a dry, curt tone. "I'll think of something else while I'm there."

With a nod, she propped her hood over her hair and dug her blindfold out of her bag, since her face might be seen.

Still, she only gripped it, held it in her hand as each footfall down the temple's steps boomed within her. *Boom. Boom. Boom.* Each one resonated straight to her heart, clutching at it so tightly, she worried the tendons holding it in place would snap under the pressure.

However, it was when the doors of the temple's outer gate closed behind them that Raewyn choked back a sob, and tears she was unable to hold back a second longer filled her eyes. Every step they took down the stairs seemed to go on forever.

Every step they took away from what was supposed to be her only way home made her feel hollow.

Raewyn let go of Merikh when heavy tears began to spill. She stopped walking, unable to bear taking another step, and covered her eyes.

She'd managed to fight her sadness, loss, and disappointment while facing strange Anzúli. Now that she was alone with Merikh, she couldn't hold it all back anymore.

She didn't care if it made her appear weak or pathetic. Raewyn's hurt was far too gut wrenching to ignore.

"How am I supposed to get back to Nyl'theria now?" she cried, knowing she sounded like a homesick child crying for their parent. "They were my only hope. They were the only ones who could have helped me."

When her legs buckled, she crouched down so she could cuddle her knees while pressing her face into them. Raewyn made herself as small as possible, wishing she could push down her pain and be her usual cheerful self.

She couldn't, not with the way her heart ached like it was moments from bursting.

She didn't know how Merikh was reacting to her breakdown. Would he be irritated? Would he even understand just how much she was hurting? Did he hold any sympathy towards her at all, or were his own thoughts for himself and the failure this brought?

Would he stop helping her now that she couldn't be of assistance to him, leaving her alone in this frightful, unknown world? Was he just staring down at her, empty of any kind of emotion?

"We came all this way for nothing." Her shoulders heaved as she wept, shaking her head in denial, desperately wanting to reject the truth – despite knowing it was hopeless. "I don't want to be stuck on Earth!"

Raewyn began screaming out her sobs. Her tears stained her face and the skirt of her dress that she'd crumpled in her fists.

Her eyes stung and her nose was clogged. It was messy and gross.

Even after many minutes, he said nothing. *Did* nothing.

Most people would have tried to pull the one suffering in for a hug, maybe even patted their back, said something, anything, but silence was all that greeted her, like he wasn't even there.

She grew worried he'd just abandoned her without even saying a word. Had he just left a weeping woman on the stairs to cry by herself, in disgust of her unruly behaviour?

"M-Merikh?" she asked through hiccupping breaths.

He grunted in response, and she hated how much relief it brought. Then, he pulled her shoulder back, and her backside fell to the stair behind her. He'd sat on the step next to her and forced her to sit as well.

Raewyn wiped at her face with the sleeve of her dress, uselessly trying to remove tears that wouldn't cease. She lifted her head properly as she hugged her midsection.

"I'm sor-ry," she sobbed, her lips quaking, mirroring the trembles that wracked her entire body. "I promise I'm trying not to cry, but the tears just won't stop. W-we can leave in a moment."

A small gust of wind cut through her dress, chilly, like the sun was going down. It reminded her of how warm home was and how it was utterly different to here. Even the air didn't feel quite as fresh or inviting.

"Whereas most villages have wooden stakes that make up their protective walls," Merikh started, his voice quiet and stoic, "Ashpine City's are made of stone and smoothed out with clay so it can't be climbed easily."

"P-pardon?" Raewyn asked, wiping at her cheek.

"You can see that the clay is a light grey, but over the years, the rain and dirt have made the top of the walls look dirty with grime drips. They've expanded the city twice, but you can still see where the old walls used to be by the ring of gaps between the houses."

Raewyn had no idea what was going on. He was talking about this town's stupid walls like one would the weather.

"The steps we're sitting on," he continued, "are mostly made of grey cobblestone, but at the very bottom, the path becomes dirt. The path is straight, and if you follow it, you'll greet the main entrance into the city, where they have the black iron portcullis we passed when we arrived. It's the only entry into the city, and the temple sits on the other side, as far away from it as possible. There's a river that runs like a cross-section through the main path, but nothing can swim through it to invade the city because of the water gates. There are multiple bridges that allow people to cross the river."

Raewyn's tears didn't slow. Actually, they increased in severity when she felt he was ignoring her pain. Perhaps it was childish, but Raewyn just wanted someone to bring her in for a hug and make her feel like she wasn't alone or had any reason to be scared.

"Why are you telling me this?" she choked out, her face twisting.

"I don't know," he grumbled. "You asked me earlier what the sky and trees looked like." When her brows drew together tightly, he added, "I have never been comforted, nor have I ever comforted another. I'll stop."

Oh, she thought as a remorseful pang lanced her gut. Her tears bubbled more, but for an entirely different reason. *I'm such a terrible person.*

She covered her face in shame while turning her knees inward to make herself smaller, realising she'd been thinking the worst of him. That, because he was a monster and a little mean, he couldn't hold an ounce of compassion for her. She'd thought that way inside the temple's sanctuary as well.

Yet, here he was, sitting beside her and trying to be supportive in his own way – obviously uncomfortable and unsure of *what* to do.

He wasn't abandoning her, mocking her, demanding that she

stop crying and get up so they could move on. He wasn't trying to drag her around. He was letting Raewyn release the dam of her emotions, and he'd even tried to calm her.

Is this why he hates people? Because they treat him like nothing but a heartless monster? She couldn't believe she'd been doing that as well.

His abrasive personality didn't aid his case, but she wondered if that came from hundreds of years of judgement. She was sure she would have started resenting the world if it treated her badly.

Shaking her head in her hands, Raewyn shuddered a breath. "P-please, don't stop."

He was silent for a long while, like he'd been assessing her reaction. Raewyn bowed her head at the thought that she'd trampled on his kindness, acting so aghast and rude by asking him what he was doing.

She truly feared she'd ruined the moment, but his deep, rumbling voice cascading over her had her chest filling with warmth. It eased some of the ache she felt.

"The horizon looks like it's on fire while purple stains the clouds. The sunset is making everything look as though it's orange or yellow, but most of the houses have auburn, brown, or yellow timber slates. Some are straw, though."

Merikh continued, explaining that the houses were all made up of different materials. Some were built from grey stone, others red brick, and many were made of wood. People had painted their houses varying shades of blue, red, and yellow.

Despite all the neutral colours, he told her there were long banners hanging over the walls, and she could almost picture them fluttering with the soft wind that danced across her clothing. There were also banners hanging from flagpoles that lined the main street.

The way he explained everything gave her the impression the town was more colourful than other places on Earth.

A few people were beginning to light their chimneys, and

some were only just heading inside to hide from the oncoming night. However, these townspeople were apparently more confident about being out later than others, due to the charms and protections given to them by the Anzúli.

The longer Merikh spoke, his voice surprisingly gentle, the more her pain ebbed... until her tears eventually dried. She still hurt. Nothing could remove it, but at least it had calmed to a state where she could tuck it away.

As he was explaining the circular shape of the city, the forest beyond it, and the expansive landscape further away, Raewyn's eyes began to droop, exhaustion threatening to pull her under.

She braved leaning to the side and resting against his thick, strong arm. She was tense, ready to pounce away if he gave any indication he didn't approve of it.

Then, for a moment, she swore she *saw* the city.

She saw the blinding orange, red, and purple glow of the sunset. She saw the blob of the city, brown and grey, but it was clearing with every second.

However, when she flinched and lifted away slightly, she was shoved back into darkness.

What was that? She blinked rapidly and then cautiously leant into his side once more to see if it would happen again. It didn't.

Perhaps her mind had truly painted what he was explaining.

When he didn't nudge her away, Raewyn relaxed and let his heat melt into her. His close scent calmed her further, and she soaked in the physical contact as much as she could. She even rested her head against his shoulder before she let out a shuddering breath – the last one she released from her crying stupor.

Merikh went quiet, and she wondered if he sensed she needed a moment of peace to collect her thoughts. He didn't touch her. Rather, it was like he'd turned to utter stone.

It ended too soon.

"We should get going," he stated. "We will need to find an inn before all the establishments close and lock their doors."

With a defeated sigh, Raewyn sat up straight, checking her clothing and hood to make sure nothing was showing. She patted the stairs until she found her blindfold to hide her eyes and brows and tied it around her face.

Just as she tensed to get up, Merikh said, "I have my hand out. It's your choice whether or not you take it."

Raewyn paused, her lips parting in surprise. She gingerly reached up, and instead of making her look for his hand, he grabbed hers to assist and gently pulled her to her feet.

His palm was massive, swallowing her thinly boned hand nearly completely, but the roughness and warmth of it was comforting. His claws lightly stabbed into her forearm, but she didn't mind them.

Her knees wobbled a little, unsteady from sitting for so long, and from feeling weak in general. Three days of non-stop walking and then bursting into tears could do that to a person.

Merikh continued to hold her hand until she was steady, then he released her so she could find the guide rope around his waist.

Once they were at the bottom of the stairs, Raewyn huddled into the back of Merikh's side when she could hear there were still plenty of humans around. She gripped the edge of her hood to make sure it didn't fall back somehow.

Even though she wanted to thank him for what he'd just done, Raewyn's jaw stayed glued shut. She didn't want to bring attention to it, in case it made him feel awkward or if he took it the wrong way – as though she was mocking him because it 'seemed' out of character for him.

She was more thankful than he could ever know or realise. Her opinion of him had significantly shifted.

A heartless person wouldn't have tried to comfort another.

Maybe he cares more than he shows. A sad smile curled her lips; she was still incapable of showing any true cheer. *I wonder what else about him I haven't been paying attention to.* Or ignoring, rather.

How often had Merikh shown her kindness and consideration

that wasn't just from his own self-gain, and she'd mistaken it?

Could he be hiding it because it makes him feel vulnerable?

When she thought about that question, she shook her head. No, he didn't seem like that kind of person.

Maybe–

Raewyn's musings were cut short when someone shoved into her so hard, she would have fallen if it weren't for her slamming into Merikh's side. An exclamation gasped out of her.

"Watch it," a man slurred, his voice giving away just how inebriated he was before the oversaturation of alcohol washed over her senses. "Y-you silly" – he hiccupped before he backhanded her arm and caused her to wince – *"bitch."*

The slap may have been an accident from him turning suddenly, but Raewyn wasn't prepared for it. She was also just so worn out that tears easily sprung in her eyes at his rudeness, when usually she would have ignored the man or given him a snide remark in return.

A quiet, rumbling growl was the only warning either of them got.

The drunken man gurgled out severe choking noises. Raewyn heard him struggling as he slapped at Merikh's hand that was obviously around his throat, his feet kicking at the dirt like he'd been lifted to the tips of his toes.

"Apologise," Merikh snarled, his tone so different, so inhuman, a cold shiver ran down her spine.

"Holy shit," the man wheezed out, struggling for gasps of air. "I-I'm sorry."

"Not to me, to her!"

He jingled like he'd been shaken. His voice was in her direction this time as he said, "I'm really s-sorry... miss."

"You know what? Maybe I don't think that's good enough," Merikh bit. "And I am in a *killing* mood."

"Please stop! Let him go." Raewyn shot forward and gripped Merikh's biceps to tug on his arm, just in case those dangerous quills he warned her of were extended. Of course, it didn't budge an inch. "I'm fine. I just want to go to an inn and rest."

People were probably staring at them!

Whispers flew around them, and although no one intervened, it would be terrible if a soldier or guard got involved. She didn't want to spend the night in a cell or be thrown out of the city, when she dearly wanted a good night's sleep that wasn't out in the forest.

She hadn't slept in a bed for a week, and her pampered butt would get on her knees and beg for one right now.

With one last tug from her, the man thumped against the ground as he was dropped.

"You're lucky she asked so nicely."

Raewyn's cheeks burned in embarrassment, realising he'd retaliated so harshly because she'd been about to cry, after he'd just helped soothe her earlier tears. She squeaked when Merikh's large palm slipped over her slender shoulder, and he shoved her into the nook of his side.

Her cheeks burned hotter when he palmed down to her biceps, never actually letting her go. It was almost like how a man put their arm around a lover's shoulders, but Merikh was just ensuring no one else bumped into her.

She couldn't stop her pulse from racing.

She'd never had someone choke another on her behalf. Having his arm around her, she felt vulnerable. It was sending her heart into a weird, panicked flutter.

She didn't stop him, not when some part of her, a little secret piece deep down inside, a place within Raewyn that wasn't all good virtue, revelled in it.

The embrace was protective, dominant, and it almost felt... possessive. She'd never experienced that in the arms of another.

Nibbling at her bottom lip, she whispered, "You didn't have to do that."

"I'm not in a good mood," he thundered, his voice dripping with hostility. It was so dark it wrapped around her, sending a tingle through her body. "I don't like humans, and the drunk

ones tend to be even more infuriating."

Even though he was feeling hateful and violent, he hadn't turned those emotions on her, even when she could very much be the source of them. Currently, she was within the bubble that was safe from his ire.

What a titillating thought, one that made Raewyn curious.

"If you don't like the humans, then why do you have a glamour and travel among them?"

"It's not because I want to, if that's what you're thinking."

"Then why?" she pressed.

Merikh turned them, and the ground shifted in texture to stone and brick, like they were on a pathway. "I can't learn anything if I sit in the dark twiddling my thumbs like an idiot."

The handle of a doorknob rattled as it turned before the creak of a door followed. A mixture of scents spilled out from the building they were walking into, all of which were pleasant: wood, fire, food, and cleaning supplies.

"I want to hire a room for the night," Merikh demanded as the jingle of a coin pouch hit the table.

"Oh wow, you're a big fucker." The woman behind the counter awkwardly laughed. "I can give you a room, but none of our beds will fit you, let alone both of you."

"That's fine. If you have a room with two double beds, I'll just push them together. If not, I'll sleep on the floor. Don't care how I sleep as long as we're not outside for the night."

"You make an excellent point." The attendant laughed again, this time a little friendlier. "If you're willing to wait a few moments, I'll have one of my staff sort the room out for you, so you don't have to. Although you don't look like you'd have any trouble doing it yourself."

A little nervous about being alone in a room with him, especially since she'd probably pass out the moment she laid her head down, Raewyn squirmed. She expected she would sleep deeply, which meant she would be vulnerable. Yet... after today, her trust for Merikh had grown, and she didn't think he would do anything to her.

He grunted in response. Then he shook slightly, as though he nodded his head, and the woman slipped a piece of paper in front of them.

"Fill this out while I make the arrangements."

Her footsteps tapped against the timber floor as the attendant left while Merikh filled in their details.

Within minutes, payment was made, and they were taken down a short hallway. Merikh was too big for them to fit down it side by side. With his hand on her back to push her forward, his breath washed over her shoulder like he was bent forward to clear his height.

She reached up to feel how tall the ceiling was, and her fingertips easily grazed it. A frown marred her features until she remembered that, although his voice came from not even a few inches above her own, Merikh had bull horns atop his bony head.

Since they were in a human town, it was easy to forget he was a Duskwalker.

When the attendant opened the door and wished them a good night, the big comforting hand around her waist fell away. Raewyn entered the room with her hands out so she could walk into the unfamiliar space.

"It's pretty small," he commented as he closed the door. "You won't have to worry about me sleeping next to you, as I'm sure you don't want that. The rooms with the double beds tend to have more space to move around in, and I wanted them to make room for me to sleep on the floor."

Raewyn just nodded.

The idea of him sleeping on the floor didn't sound comfortable, and she was sure he was just as exhausted as she was. However, she didn't know how she would feel if he were to sleep beside her, to the point she didn't even offer – despite partially wanting to out of kindness.

Were they past formalities? *What if I accidentally turned and tried cuddling him in my sleep?* How embarrassing!

"There's a bath I can fill with my magic," he stated from the door.

"I can fill it myself," she rebuffed as she searched for the bed. He said the room was small, but even after a few cautious steps, Raewyn hadn't touched a single piece of furniture. "It's not hard to do water and heat magic."

"Do you have food or should I... A little to the left, Raewyn."

At the mention of her name in his gruff, handsome voice, Raewyn's brain twisted, and she stepped right. Her foot bashed something thigh high, and the next thing she knew, she was falling forward.

She tried to right herself, but whatever she'd tripped over was hollow. Her small scream was accompanied by her heart tightening, then a meaty arm wrapped around her waist, catching her before she could faceplant.

"I said go left," he huffed.

Raewyn searched with her hands and found the rim of the bathtub. She bit her bottom lip, unsure as to why she had such a strange reaction to him saying her name.

"Thanks," she offered as he let her go and backed up. "I would really like to have a bath before I go to sleep. I feel filthy." Raewyn fidgeted slightly. "Would that be okay? I might be awhile, since I want to take my braids out and wash my hair properly."

He didn't say anything for a long while. She'd noticed Merikh sometimes took his time answering her, like he was weighing his thoughts.

"Do what you want. I've decided to buy some things before all the stalls close. I'll also see if this inn offers warm food."

Raewyn shined an appreciative smile at him. "I would adore a bath, a warm meal, and a good sleep. Thank you, Merikh."

With a grunt, he stepped out.

Raewyn's chest felt lighter as she turned back to the tub, pushing her hood back. She unclipped her dust-covered cloak from her neck.

Her exhaustion could wait until after she was clean to pull her under.

THIRTEEN

Forced to bend forward to clear his massive height and imposing horns, Merikh stood next to the two double beds pushed together and stared down at the pretty Elf while she slept.

She hadn't finished bathing when he'd returned. He'd opened the door while she was in the tub and running the bristles of a comb through a long sweep of white hair. It was crinkly but straight due to the heaviness of the water saturating it.

Her back was facing him, and she gasped as she covered her chest.

Merikh immediately closed the door at her startled reaction. He didn't expect her to still be bathing, considering he was gone until past sundown.

He informed her he would place the food he ordered on the ground just past the door, and that he would return later. He chose to sit in the hallway and listen for when she was finished.

When there were no more sounds for a long time, he entered the room again to find she'd climbed her way under the covers and was already asleep.

The bathtub was still full of water. Even though he wore his snout covering, he could scent the air was sweeter than before from her cleaning products.

For the first time since meeting her, Merikh had shifted into his more monstrous, four-legged form so he could sleep. Against the ground, he'd curled into a ball on the opposing side of the bed, so she wouldn't step on him by accident. Laying like that tended to make his quills stick out from his body.

Turned out, he never needed to worry, since he towered over her still-sleeping form much later.

It's been nineteen hours, he thought, for some reason compelled to rub the side of his forefinger and claw against her round cheek.

Her slightly parted lips didn't twitch at his touch, nor did her closed eyes or white brows. He allowed the softness of her long, thick eyelashes to tickle his knuckle before he moved higher.

With her laying partially on her side and back, her body twisted, he was able to press the back of his hand against her forehead. Her temperature wasn't raised, nor was she sweating.

She doesn't appear to be feverish or sick.

She'd been sleeping a hell of a long time, and it didn't appear as though she'd be waking soon.

Merikh tapped a claw at the navy bonnet around her hair, noting the silky material, curious as to why she was wearing such an apparatus on her head. Did Elysians often wear these for sleeping?

He must admit, he'd never been interested in watching anyone sleep, yet... he didn't back away from Raewyn.

Her pointed ears caught his attention, as they often did.

He ran the back of his knuckle over the rim of one. A strange emotion bubbling in his chest almost caused him to chuckle when her long ear flicked wildly under the light touch.

Is she sensitive here? He did it again, and it flicked.

Raewyn let out a soft groan, before burying her face against the pillow, as though that was enough to escape him. She was only lucky he didn't wish to disturb her.

The blanket she was wrapped in was lowered, revealing the roundness of her shoulder. Her sleep garment had slipped.

He drew the tip of his claw down the arch of her neck, over the length of her shoulder. Raewyn shivered.

Merikh growled at her, at her reaction to a simple claw, at his own nagging desire to keep touching her so she would let out another raspy moan.

She's too fucking pretty. He grabbed the blanket and brought it up to her cheek, covering her more from his sight.

He'd checked that she wasn't sick, which was why he'd approached her in the first damn place. So why was he admiring her face and shoulder? Even now, he considered touching her face more.

Merikh was a Duskwalker, a faceless *freak.* Why did he think he had the right to touch a female with a face carved by an angel?

Her round features, dark freckles, pouty full lips, and flawless brown skin... He didn't think a single human could compare.

And her eyes... He envisioned their mesmerising colour of rich brown with an incandescent white starburst in the middle. How could any*thing* not be stupefied looking into them?

He backed away from the side of the bed, his orbs a brighter hue of red than usual as he sat down against the wall.

Since he acquired a few things yesterday he'd never purchased before, he was trying to figure out how to make the tool he wanted.

He hadn't liked how that drunken fool had run into her, nor did he like that she was so hesitant in unfamiliar environments. The fact she almost went arse up inside the bathtub caused him alarm.

Although the tool he was crafting would mean she'd require less of his assistance – something he was weirdly content with – he was sure it would make life easier for her. He just hoped she didn't take him giving it to her the wrong way.

If she wished to cling to him, then he would be more than accepting, maybe even a little... prideful. Still, he wanted to give her the option, especially since he'd rarely ever been given a choice in his life.

There were many things he would have chosen not to do but

was always forced to, one way or another.

Merikh examined the item he'd already pulled apart in order to understand how it was constructed so he could recreate it. He'd tried to do this as quietly as possible while she slept. He picked up a broken rod of timber and turned it this way and that.

Maybe it was a part of his nature to destroy things to understand them.

Now that he somewhat understood how it was made, he began fashioning his own version – one that would be better suited to its possible user.

After about two hours, Raewyn finally stirred.

Since he'd restarted his task multiple times, he wasn't finished when she rose to sit up in the bed. Her white sleep dress dropped down her shoulder. Merikh quickly looked down and away when he couldn't stop himself from staring at her starburst eyes – almost like he'd missed them in the hours they were closed.

Foolish, his mind spat, yet his sight kept drifting away from his task to her against his will.

She never righted her dress over her shoulder, even after she rubbed at her eyes and lazily blinked them. She looked like a lazy bunny peeking out from the grass, docile and guileless.

Sitting up but leaning on the arm with the shoulder exposed, she was unaware that a predator was tempted to lick at his snout in her direction.

Resting, then watching her sleep, had twisted something in his mind.

So had the previous day.

Watching her cry and then being able to calm her himself... had been a new experience for him. He'd never been someone's comfort, nor had he ever had someone choose to lean against him so openly like she had. And she'd clung to *his* side.

It mattered naught, though, which was why he wished to reject it and turn whatever affections he had stupidly allowed to grow towards the Elf into self-loathing and emptiness.

She would eventually reveal that whatever kindness she showed him was from a place of fear or wariness. Of isolation and desperation, rather than of comfort.

"Merikh?" she asked, her voice so raspy and sleep-laden that his fur and quills began to stand on their ends from its pleasantness.

"Here," he answered, although it came out more like a grunt.

Her drowsy smile was small, but it was faced in his direction. It made Merikh completely uncomfortable, since he didn't think he'd ever received a smile from someone who knew what he was.

"I feel a lot better," she sighed contently.

Raewyn reached up and slipped off the bonnet that he realised had been keeping her hair tamed so as to not mess it in her sleep, and out spilled her white hair, loose and no longer braided. There was a glossiness that must have come from the product he could scent in her hair. She'd obviously applied a fair amount before going to bed.

Although he knew it to be longer, since her braids came halfway down her back, the newly unbound corkscrew curls made her hair appear shorter. They bounced around her shoulders, brushing the backs and sides before they settled their fall.

He reared his head back in surprise, not sure what he'd been expecting. He'd thought her hair was nice before – the braids had suited her – but he liked this more, where her curls were free and loose. Her hair looked soft and shiny, innocent and playful at the same time.

"You were asleep for almost an entire day," Merikh commented casually, not hinting at anything he may be feeling.

He looked down, *needing* to look down – not only so he could watch what he was doing with his task, but... to make his gaze move away from her.

"Oh," she answered sheepishly. "Did I forget to mention I sleep longer than a human? I was also really tired, as I haven't slept properly since we started travelling together."

"It's fine."

"Are you sure?"

He peeked up to see her shoulders had lifted, as though she was nervous.

"I said it's fine," he bit out before soothing his tone. "I slept as well, and I have been busy."

She *finally* fixed her damn sleep dress. Then she reached down beside the bed and pulled her bag onto her lap so she could dig through it. She retrieved an apple from her bag and ate it as she placed two hair ties on the blanket between her legs.

For someone who had just woken up, she was more bright-eyed than he'd expected. Merikh was often quick to get to his feet, but that was because he had a goal, a mission on his mind. Every second wasted was a second longer he'd have to wait for what he wanted.

Once she'd finished her apple, she began braiding her hair like she had before, in preparation for travel.

"So..." she started slowly. "What are we going to do now?"

"No fucking clue," he abruptly answered, trying his hardest to not over-screw a bolt he was tightening in anger. He'd been wondering what the hell they were going to do now for the whole day, and he'd come up with absolutely nothing. "I have been searching for a way off Earth for years. Don't ask me for answers because I don't have them."

Her shoulders slumped as her lips turned inwards in disappointment.

"I have searched every corner of this continent, have been researching for years, and there's nothing," he continued. "There's no text I can find that teaches me how to make portals myself. There are no hidden pockets that will take me elsewhere. There are no other creatures besides the Anzúli, Duskwalkers, or Demons on this planet that can make them, or even use magic."

"There *must* be something," she beseeched, and all the docile drowsiness from before was destroyed by the reality he shared. "There's always a solution."

He'd be upset with himself for ruining her contentment within minutes of waking, but she'd started this conversation. With the way she cried on the temple steps the day before, she must know he didn't have any answers; otherwise, he would have given them.

"There's only one damn option, but unless you can somehow make us intangible, or teleport us to a place you've never been to, it's pointless to even consider it."

Her lips tightened again. "You're talking about Jabez's portal."

"Precisely. That bastard's portal has been like a taunt for years. There's a way out, but it's so deep inside his castle, getting to it is impossible." Merikh then let out a bitter laugh. "And trust me, I know it's impossible. I've tried."

Raewyn's ears twitched alongside her face as she thought deeply, her sightless gaze moving side to side.

"What... what if it could be made possible?" Raewyn asked softly, her face pointed to the side.

"I would be willing to try anything at this point."

Once she finished the first braid, she paused. She lifted a hand and brushed her lips, obviously weighing her options.

Then she reached up and covered an eye.

"You've never asked me how I lost my sight," she commented quietly. "Why? Most people do."

"My morbid curiosity does not validate me asking such a personal question when it does little to be helpful or useful. It makes no difference to me whether or not you can see, or why you cannot," he answered plainly. "If you wanted me to know, you would have told me."

He wasn't sure, but he *swore* her lips twitched like they wanted to curl into a tiny smile. It didn't last, her expression turning solemn.

"I don't really mind talking about it," she said as she began her second braid. "But yeah, I don't really like it when people ask me about it because it usually comes from a place of curiosity rather than care."

Merikh grunted with a nod, having already figured as much. Humans tended to have a problem sticking their rude little noses where they didn't belong.

"I, um... as you learned yesterday, I'm actually one of the head scientists for the eighteen synedrus councillors. My work varies from genetic cloning via magic growth to the study of magical creatures and how their DNA interacts with each other, especially with our Elysian genome. Sometimes, I also assist our pharmacologists. In short, I'm a biologist, geneticist, and because of how our magic works and the kind of DNA I focus on, I'm also a herbologist. All our scientists are required to learn herbology before they can enter their desired field. I'm currently working on a thesis that will allow me to grow a difficult vegetable with a wide variety of vitamins. It would be an invaluable resource to be able to grow through magic, rather than waiting the seven months it takes to fruit. If I can do that, I can work backwards with other edible plants that have been difficult to clone. It requires a molecular-level understanding of the plant."

Merikh tilted his head. "What does that have to do with anything? What do you want to do? Grow a potato in the middle of Jabez's castle?"

Her lips vibrated together as she let out a 'pfft' and then a giggle.

"No! Not at all. I guess I feel it's just important I explain that to you first." Then, her laughter was gone, and she rubbed her biceps self-consciously. "I have been a synedrus councillor for around seven Nyl'therian years. Six years ago, which is around ninety Earth years, we were discussing a way we could destroy the Demons in large quantities, or at least provide protection that would allow us to take back our home and drive them back to their own."

Even though he was, hopefully, nearing completion with his task, Merikh paused and lowered it to his lap to stare at her.

"It's hard to call it a weapon when it could have been nothing more than a protective charm, but when our astronomer made an off-handed comment about wishing we could harness the power of our three suns, since the Demons burn when exposed to them, everyone had laughed, except he and I. We'd shared a look, realising we might actually be able to replicate the suns with our magic."

He tilted his head sharply. "Would that even be possible? It's not like you can just float into the sky and scoop a drop of it."

"No, but if we combine the right elements, we could clone its impact. I was placed as the leading scientist, since it would require most of my skills, knowledge, and experience." Her laughter was empty. "I almost did it, too. I almost made something like it, but it was too much. The magic was unknown, its effects unknown, the mathematics unknown. It was unstable, and instead of being a controlled power source within a mana stone, it shattered. I lost my sight and suffered severe radiation poisoning that almost killed me. I was only lucky we still had a few healing stones remaining. That was the sole reason I was saved."

"You use stones for magic?" Merikh asked as he scratched at the back of his neck, not really understanding.

"Our land is very fertile in both ore and magic, and there is a stone that has managed to absorb that magic. We call them mana stones, and if we tweak them, we can direct their use for various things, such as power conduits, healing, and growth. They are the only reason we were able to survive the Demon attack; otherwise, we all would have been eaten. To cast the kind of barrier we have in place to protect our people requires constant power. We use conduit stones to help maintain its longevity and strength, and people willingly donate their own magic to keep it going."

"You Elven people sound complex," he said as he shook his

head and worked on wrapping the end of the hollow metal rod in his hand to make a comfortable grip. "Even your lives and city sound complicated."

"It can be. Our people work together to ensure we not only survive, but thrive," she admitted.

"What happened to this 'sun stone' you were trying to make?"

"The entire project was cancelled, as it was too great of a risk. I wasn't the only one who succumbed to radiation poisoning, although I am the only one who lost their sight, since I was in the direct vicinity of its blast." Raewyn then lowered her head. "I almost killed our central tree. Without it, our city will die; we need it to survive. It took nearly a year to repair the damage I'd caused, although no blame was put on me, as I was just doing my job."

Merikh placed his completed task on the ground, folded his arms, and leaned back against the wall. It didn't take a genius to understand what she was getting at.

"You think you can recreate it."

She shrugged her shoulders. "I don't know. Maybe?"

"Here, Raewyn?" Merikh scoffed. "You're on Earth. We don't have mana stones or items like that."

Raewyn lifted her chin with a stubborn pout, her ears pulling back. "But you do. I'm staring at one right now."

He looked around, wondering what the fuck she was talking about. It was only them and this room, and nothing seemed out of place or unusual.

Her twisted smile was almost teasing, mocking even. She tapped at her forehead, and Merikh reached up to touch his own. A cool gem flicked under his claw.

"My glamour?"

"I didn't see it at first because of my blindfold, and it appears as though it's only active when humans are nearby, but yes. I told you earlier I can see magic when it's being used, and I would know that glow anywhere."

Fiddling with it as he eyed her, Merikh thought deeply. "What would happen if I gave it to you and it didn't work?"

"I would be changing it, so it'll either no longer be useful for its current purpose, or I would destroy it. It's difficult to wipe a mana stone, but it's something I've already done. However, the last sun stone I made shattered, as it's a highly volatile component."

Merikh continued to finger it as a coldness washed over his chest. This diadem was precious to him. It was the only thing he owned that he would give his life to protect. It was the only thing that made his existence worth living.

Without it, he'd have to go back to hiding in the shadows.

Would he give it up if it meant he could leave Earth?

Some sacrifices were often worth it, but if this resulted in failure... he wouldn't be reverting to step one, but to a life he refused to return to.

"What's the likelihood you'll be successful?"

"I can't give you those calculations. The charging time and radiation was the problem, and even exposing the stone to our three suns for a single second made it too powerful, but I can *feel* the sun is weaker here. With the right ingredients, which I can test before I do any changes to the mana stone, I'll know if there's a chance."

"Why should I give you my diadem when you can't be certain?" he asked, uneasy about taking that kind of risk.

Raewyn let out a heavy sigh. "I am offering my life here. If this fails, not only will you lose your glamour, but the radiation could kill me."

"I will be able to take any illness or injury that affects you. This will come at no cost to you, only me."

Her little brows furrowed. "But then you'll be the one to die from the poisoning."

"I can't die, remember?" Merikh said while rolling his head, knowing she'd hear his exasperated tone. "Once twenty-four hours are over, I'll heal, as long as my skull is intact."

Raewyn dropped her hands and gripped the blanket laying over her legs. Her eyes bowed as the outer corners crinkled, her forehead forming deep lines.

"*Please,* Merikh," she pleaded in the same beseeching tone he'd only heard from humans about to die by his claw. It was filled with the knowing end, of the pain and definitive nothingness to come. "I know I'm asking for a lot. I know you have no reason to help when I can't be sure, but I don't think I can survive it if I don't at least try. I know I'm being selfish because I want to go home, but please, I'm begging you."

His silence weighed on her. Her hands clutched the bedding tighter and tighter until the backs of her knuckles went taut.

It was her next 'please,' with tears filling her transfixing eyes, that finally caused him to make his decision. It shouldn't have mattered. Her pain shouldn't have mattered to him, nor her tears or the way her lips quaked, but in that moment, he couldn't deny her.

Some gouging emotion dug its way into his chest, and he finally uttered, "fine." The way her face brightly shined afterward made him turn his head to the side dismissively. "But you will conduct your experiments where I see fit. If this works, you *will* use whatever power you have over your people to allow me through that portal. Do you understand? I will not be left behind on Earth with no way off it, and with no glamour."

Merikh stood, scratching at his neck in agitation. He was annoyed. He needed to go for a walk before he turned that anger towards her.

"Yes, yes! Okay!"

Raewyn dug her way out of the bed and ran towards him. She skilfully sidestepped the tub, and he stepped back in surprise when she flung herself against him.

To be fair, he had to catch her, but it was as if she knew he would. When she fell against him, his anger fled out of him.

"Thank you," she exclaimed. "Thank you so much."

He was much wider than her, so her arms barely reached

behind him. She buried her face against his chest, and he was so astonished that he just raised his arms in the air, unsure of what he was supposed to do.

It didn't help that if he lowered his arms, his quills would come back down and slice her.

"I was so scared that there wasn't another way, but if I can create a sun stone, no Demons would be able to come near us when we try to enter Jabez's castle. If you know where it is, we could just walk right in and through the portal."

A thought crossed his mind. "Won't it affect me?"

Raewyn shrugged, leaning back while still holding onto his sides so she could speak properly. He was finally able to lower his arms.

"I am already aware that using such magic is destructive to its user. We both might be a little sick afterwards, but my people can heal us. You can walk in the sun, so hopefully you won't be affected by its power the same way as the Demons."

Her exquisite face, filled with joy shining in his direction, because of him, had his throat clogging. She was so close, he could feel her heat and breasts pressing up against him, and his barrier cloth did little to hide her drool-inducing scent.

His orbs threatened to turn white when his cock stirred, and his seam twitched. Merikh quickly stepped back to break contact, and she easily let him go.

His mind fumbled for a way out of receiving her gratitude, to remove the look she had. His sight found what he'd made, lying on the ground.

Merikh picked it up and thrust it at her, almost punching her in his panic, but thankfully managing to soften the impact. Raewyn fumbled and held the pole with two hands.

"This is for you," he stated, wishing his voice wasn't strained.

Like she often did at him, she frowned.

"What is it?" she asked as she began feeling the length of it.

"I've seen humans with visual impairments use these. A

guide cane, I believe it's called." He scratched at his neck, before looking at his claws, which he realised he'd done a lot more than usual lately. "I tried to find one that would suit your height, but everything I found would be too short."

Her lips parted as her eyes widened. She fondled the very end of the cane that had a stone ring he'd managed to lock to the end using bolts. It spun freely when she turned it.

"Did... you make this for me?"

"Yes," he said as he looked at the wall – anywhere that wasn't her. He wasn't sure why his pulse was still racing, whether it was desire, or just because he felt as though he was out of his depth. "I think it will make it easier for the humans to avoid bumping into you, and you won't fall into a bathtub again."

She was quiet for so long, her high-pitched, tearless sob was deafening. Startled by the sound, confused by it, he turned back to find she was clutching the grip section of the cane with both hands and pressing it against her forehead.

"Merikh," she softly whispered. "Thank you. I used to have one back home, but I couldn't grab it to bring it with me. Not having one has been difficult." Her grip on the cane tightened. "You have no idea what this means to me."

Fuck, I made it worse!

This was too overwhelming for a creature who had never done a nice thing in his entire life, who wasn't used to receiving such sincere gratitude. He wanted out of this situation, uncomfortable with it in its entirety.

"Hurry up and get ready. I want to leave this city as soon as possible."

Her smile was odd when she directed her expression at him, seemingly torn between hollowing sadness and happiness.

Merikh headed to the only exit available. "I'll obtain everything we need while I wait for you."

"Wh-where are we going?"

"The Veil."

Her stunning eyes widened in shock and fear. "What? Why?"
"Because I have everything you'll need at my cave."
For the first time in years, Merikh was going *home*.

FOURTEEN

Raewyn loosely held onto the guide rope around Merikh's waist as he took them to the busy town's exit. Although the cane he'd given her was a little too long, she'd rather that than it be too short.

The loose ring stone he'd connected to the end spun as she swiped it side to side, and it allowed her to see, in her own way, what was in front of her. She was no longer huddled into his side so she wouldn't bump into anyone, feeling more at ease in the crowd.

Her cane acted as a visual aid for others, as well as for herself. If someone didn't see her, it was their fault for not paying attention and being complacent in a crowd.

She only held onto Merikh to be guided in the direction they needed to go.

Holding the leather-bound grip, Raewyn's heart felt lighter.

She'd always been good at adjusting to her circumstances and making the most of what she had. Still, it was a relief to have this tool.

He even thought to add a securing loop. Currently, her wrist was threaded through it, so if she dropped it, she didn't lose it on the ground.

Was it as nice to hold or as fancy as the one she'd had back home? No. It didn't even collapse into a smaller piece so she could tuck it away if she wanted to. Still, it was perfect for its intended use, and the fact he'd been considerate enough to make this for her warmed her heart.

Merikh was currently carrying many bags for her. When he'd left earlier, he obtained a large amount of food, some new clothing, and even some cleaning products.

With the tip of her cane, she felt the ground change. The noise of the city grew more distant until they were buried in the forest.

It was warmer today, still cool to her, but she knew the sun must be bright. A light breeze fluttered her cloak as they walked.

Without warning, Merikh stopped abruptly.

"We're far away enough now. Pass me your cane," he demanded.

"Why?" she asked, her brows furrowing deeply as her grip tightened. He'd only just given it to her, and now he wanted it back?

"You're not going to need it."

She gave it to him, even though her chest hollowed at doing so. However, that feeling passed within seconds, and she almost squealed when he picked her up.

He secured Raewyn to his side, his big hand spanning her entire thigh. She was seated, her arse pressed firmly across his forearm with his bicep supporting her back, her legs spread around his side.

"What are you doing?" she asked as she pressed against his chest and shoulder to back up from him.

"It is going to be a nearly two-week walk at my usual pace. With you, you'll make that longer. I'll be carrying you most of the way."

Her hood fluttered back, and she didn't have time to catch it as he began their journey. The wind cutting through her clothing gave her the impression they were going really fast, even though she could tell he was only simply walking.

Her braids tapped against her back with every step, and after a few minutes of uncertainty, Raewyn relaxed. Who was she to pass up a free ride?

She reached down while straightening her leg and untied her boot. Before she could toss it, he said, "We'll need to keep those. We will be stopping off at the last town so we can sleep before I take you past the border wall. I will need to rest, and so will you."

"Ughhh," she groaned, taking her boot off and tucking it under her armpit as she undid the other. She tied the laces together, and he stole her boots from her before she could do anything more.

"Finally, I can remove this," he stated.

She was just about to ask him what, but his breaths became clearer. She reached forward and touched his snout, feeling no cloth covering his nose hole. Her forefinger curled inside, and she was surprised and a little grossed out to find it was wet.

Then she realised what she'd done and yanked her hand back. After the first night she'd discovered he wasn't human, she'd never touched his bony face again. She was beginning to get a little too comfortable with him.

She closed her eyes when his orange and cinnamon scented sniffs puffed over her jaw and neck. He was sniffing her!

Raewyn tightened her thighs when her stomach clenched in reaction to it. His breaths were ticklish, and his own draflium flower scent warmed her senses. She often had that reaction to it, a hint of desire, but it seemed to have worsened since their short stay in the city.

He drew away from her to watch where he was going, but she'd noticed his grip on her thigh was stronger, as though he was tense. Even his claws were stabbing through the material of her dress.

I guess he's never smelt me properly before. Raewyn nibbled her bottom lip. *Did he like it?* Her cheeks heated when she registered what she'd just thought. *Oh, holy maiden, where did that thought come from?!*

Why did it matter if he liked the way she smelled? Or if he liked holding her thigh and having her pressed against him?

Raewyn was by no means a saint, but she barely knew him! Well... she kind of did, and after his actions in Ashpine City, her opinion of him had changed substantially.

But this much? Where she was kind of hoping he'd sniff her again to deliciously tickle her? Raewyn tightened her thighs when she clenched a little lower and *naughtier* than her stomach.

"So," Raewyn started, in an attempt to run away from her own thoughts. The word came out a little more heated than she wanted it to, and she hurriedly cleared her throat. "I've been meaning to ask, what did the Anzúli overseer mean when she questioned you about how you obtained your magic?"

Merikh grunted. "I was hoping you didn't catch that."

A coy smile spread across her lips, her eyes crinkling with something she was sure appeared puckish. "Have something to hide, do you?"

"I have no shame nor guilt for any of my actions, but yes, I will hide things from you for your own safety." His casual, nondescript tone neither denied nor confirmed his statement. "However, you should consider the questions you ask. You may not like the answers you receive, should I be willing to give them."

Raewyn's eyes narrowed into a glare that held little animosity, but perhaps a little judgement. "Did... did you eat the Anzúli?"

His chuckle was *dark*, answering her before he said anything. "Like I said, I have been searching for a way off Earth. I needed to obtain more magic, and they were the only way to do so."

"Would you have eaten me if I were not an Elf?" Raewyn joked.

"No. I knew you could be useful, since I could sense your magic was strong."

She was just about to tease him, a playful remark on the tip of her tongue, but she slowly pressed her lips shut. Instead, she faced forward, her eyes wide as realisation struck.

Is... is he lying? Had he been intending to eat me when we first started travelling together? She tried to remember to back then, to nearly two weeks ago.

His very own words echoed through her consciousness. *"I'm not your friend. By the end of this trip, you will see that."*

He did, didn't he? He wouldn't have said that if he didn't have any bad intentions.

Her ears flattened as she felt his body moving against hers while he walked.

But he didn't. He didn't do that. He hasn't hurt me, nor has he been cruel. He was rarely mean to her. Yes, she'd witnessed him being callous towards the humans, but he rarely, if ever, turned that hostility towards Raewyn.

Even if that had been his intention originally, even if it was still possible, she decided she would just... trust him. It was better than the alternative – being fearful.

"You've got a look on your face. I don't trust it."

"Have you eaten a lot of people?" She bit her tongue when she realised she'd just made the conversation darker. She should have asked something else, but it just slipped out.

"Do you really want the answer to that question?" His tone was aghast, but also hesitant.

"Sure," she answered in a small voice.

"Fine." His grip was tight again, but for an entirely different reason. "I have eaten around a hundred and ten humans, perhaps a little more."

Raewyn gasped. "That's so many! Why?"

This time, when he cruelly laughed, it was echoed, as if he'd parted his jaws to let the full malevolence of it resonate.

"Because I needed humanity, and that was the only way I could obtain it. Plus, I'm not particularly fond of the humans, or anyone, for that matter. Their loss was my gain. We would not be having this conversation coherently otherwise."

Raewyn turned her head away, unsure of how she felt about

learning this. At least with Demons, they were mindless when they ate people until they fully formed and grew skin. Only then could they suppress their uncontrollable desire to feast on flesh.

That usually happened after only a little more than a dozen, perhaps more with the humans, since they were smaller.

What he was talking about was killing just because he *could*, because he wanted to.

"Remember that farming town?" he asked. "How they wouldn't permit us entry due to the recent murderer in the southlands?"

Raewyn didn't like where this was going. "Yes?"

"He's currently holding you."

Her face drained of warmth. "But why? They-they said he... you... were going around removing people's heads and hearts! How could you do such a thing? You're basically a serial killer!"

If he wasn't eating the whole person, it wasn't out of hunger or insatiable desire to consume them. He was thinking rationally. It was immoral. Wrong. That was... pure *evil*.

When he didn't answer, clearly not intending to, Raewyn pushed at him. "Tell me why or put me down."

A reddish-pink glow sparked in her vision. Then, in a quiet, almost shy voice, he grumbled, "I got fat."

Raewyn paused, not believing what she'd just heard. "What?"

The glow got brighter before it faded.

"When I was first fully formed, I was hollow. I had no muscle, no fat, and all my bones sat outside of my skin, as if I was so thin there was barely any room for them. As I gained mass from consuming flesh, I got bigger, fuller, until all my bones sunk beneath my flesh. Once I achieved a certain size, my muscle continued to grow, but so did my fat content."

Her jaw fell. She couldn't believe what she was hearing! It was as though he was *insecure* about it.

He was much wider than her, bigger, stronger. Even now, she could tell her knee was digging into a muscled, yet thick gut.

Her legs were parted wide just to accommodate his side.

"So, I wondered if there was a way to achieve humanity without having to gain more muscle or fat. I learnt eating their heads and hearts, although slower, was just as effective."

Okay, so what he'd done was still wrong, but why did such a simple insecurity soften her opinion of it? It made him seem... normal.

She'd had her fair share of feeling too thin and incapable of gaining weight. She imagined it was the same for him, just on the opposing end of the spectrum.

She'd always been self-critical about her own height, weight, and even foot size, but she'd never turned that same judgement on another. Who cared about a person's body size or weight? She'd never minded, since all that mattered was their heart.

However, since she'd lost her sight, a person's textures, sounds, and scents were how she decided if their external was attractive to her.

She kind of liked them soft, although not many Elysian Elves were plump due to their genetics and food consumption.

Her nose had strengthened, so they needed to smell pleasant to her. Merikh's orange and cinnamon draflium flower scent was intoxicating in a way she'd long ago realised she found uncomfortable – only because it sometimes made her eyelids flicker with bliss and her pussy flutter.

Her hearing had sharpened, and his gruff voice was darker, rumblier, more brutal than any other she'd ever heard. Sometimes, it caused the little hairs over her body to stand on end as she was struck with waves of goosebumps.

Another reaction that often had her cheeks burning.

His hands were warm and relaxing, especially since he'd never been violent with them towards her – not since the night she discovered what he was. They were large, even compared to her, like big, meaty paws that gripped her thigh nearly completely while he held her against his side.

Pressed against him now, he wasn't soft, instead dense with

muscle, and yet he felt... doughy. If she wasn't careful, she could mistake that frightening strength as protective.

Still, even if she liked all these outside qualities, even if sometimes they made confusing heat rush between her legs, he, himself, was alarming.

Cruel, but kind. Evil, but good? What kind of serial murderer went around guiding a lost woman like her?

"I feel like that's a waste of life," Raewyn finally said, trying to push her thoughts to the side.

"Don't sympathise with the humans," he practically growled. "They don't deserve your righteous pity."

He'd said it so sternly, as though he truly, *truly* believed that.

Sure, Raewyn's interactions with them hadn't always been pleasant, but there had been many in Clawhaven who had supported her when she needed it. It was her own fear of being discovered that hadn't allowed her to let anyone closer.

She turned her head away from him while nibbling at the inner flesh of her cheek. It wasn't a pout, but her heart was aching.

"If you hate the humans so much," she started, "then why continue to be around them? Why not go to the Demons?"

The scoff he released was so razor sharp, her shoulders turned inward self-consciously.

"You think the Demons are any better? They are the same. If you aren't a Demon, you are food, and if you can't be food, you're the enemy."

Raewyn lowered her head, wishing she hadn't asked. It made her seem naïve, but she truly thought they would have welcomed something like him.

"There is a war in this world, and I tire of being in the middle of it."

"You say that," she bit lightly, narrowing her eyes into a glare, "yet you go around killing humans just because you *can*. You have a glamour that allows you to live among them, yet your actions are callous when they don't have to be."

"Oh, look. The Elf has decided to take it upon herself to speak of something she knows little about," he snapped back. He paused his walking, and she sensed he was staring at her, his orbs sparking a brighter red. "You think just because I can parade around as a human that it's like living? My identity is split in two, one where I am accepted not because of what I am, but because of what they think I am. Then, there is the side of me they fear the moment they look upon me."

"Have you ever tried to remove your glamour and speak with them to change their minds?"

That's what the Delysians had done.

"Of course, I fucking have!" he roared, making her ears flatten. "Do you have any idea what it's like trying to strike an understanding with people, only for them to turn on you within seconds? That, when they think they have killed you, solely because it was either you or them and you chose it to be you, they *laugh* and *cheer* your death? Only to survive because you can't die, and remember their laughter?"

His growl was so close that his breaths brushed over her jaw. She couldn't help lifting her chin to escape the intensity of this moment, of him.

"I tried. One hundred years ago, I tried, and that was the reality I faced. My apparent 'death' was something to be celebrated, not grieved over. When I spoke, no one cared to listen. I walked around without my glamour, minding my own business, and I was attacked by Demonslayers. I threw myself into the river just to quieten my own rage before I slaughtered them all, and have worn my glamour ever since, because there is *no* other alternative for me."

He faked his own death, and they cheered it? Raewyn's chest tightened in pain and understanding.

"Merikh, I'm sorry."

"Save it," he snapped as he walked again. "I have every right to hate every creature that breathes in this world, especially when they all wish to see my own breaths cease."

Tears prickled her eyes, and she hid them by turning her face downward. *How... lonely.*

She couldn't imagine how it would feel to walk among those she was surrounded by and know that if they discovered what she was, they'd be hateful.

His acceptance was built on a lie. He understood that, which made it all the sadder.

"This world wanted to see a monster, so I gave it a monster," he added, his voice a croak and heart-achingly sorrowful. "If I'm lucky, maybe I'll be better in the next one."

He must have added that last part for her, like he was only doing all this because of the way Earth treated him, and if he was faced with a different world that was more accepting, he wouldn't do these things.

Is that what he meant by freedom? Freedom to be himself, without being judged by his appearance, by what he was? *He said he's lived for over three hundred years.* That kind of rejection for so long would have weighed on anyone's heart and mind.

"Is there no one who cares for you?" she asked, her tone hopeful but filled with sadness because she feared the answer.

"No one."

"What about your mother, or Weldir?"

They had to care for him, accept him... right?

"If I were to die, no one would sit at my grave," he answered, his voice devoid of emotion. "Not that I would have one."

Her heart broke a little for him.

This was the first time she truly learnt something deep about Merikh, and she wished she hadn't. Some things were just too dark and painful to discover.

His killing... she couldn't fully forgive it, but she could now understand it. She saw it as desperation; everyone, no matter their species, did insane things when afraid and desolate.

"Can you at least promise me not to do it while I'm with you?" she pleaded.

"Fine," he immediately stated. "I have no reason to, since I was only doing it as a way to gain intelligence, to figure out a way off this realm. If I have you helping me, then I see no reason to."

Her smile was the result of panic flipping into relief. "Really?" It was that easy for him to make that kind of promise? "Could you also stop swearing? It kind of makes me uncomfortable."

She squirmed almost every time.

"Fuck no."

Ughhh! She groaned and tossed her head back. She'd known she was asking for too much with that one.

"You should try it. Are all Elves this stiff? Like they have a stick up their arses?"

Raewyn's face flushed so deeply, even the tips of her ears were hot. "You can't just say that! The conversation of my posterior is *not* one we should be having, especially not of something being up it."

"They are just words," he sighed, like she was being ridiculous. "They only have meaning if you give them meaning."

Raewyn lifted her chin. "I give them meaning."

"Prude."

Her cheeks heated again. "Well, you're mean, and rude! I am not a prude, thank you very much. I've had sex plenty of times. I just don't think you need to be vulgar."

"Once doesn't count, and I was *made* to be vulgar."

"It was more than once!"

If only he knew the truth. Then, he'd be eating his words with his sharp fangs and choking on them. She, by no means, was shy or bashful, nor had she been with a lot of sexual partners. The only reason she'd been strange around him regarding her nudity had been more out of surprise than nervousness.

She'd had a handful of lovers. Sure, she could literally count them on one hand, but they'd been long-term companions. She'd gained plenty of experience with them.

"You know what?" he said with a quirk of humour. "I'm going to get you to swear at least once by the end of our journey. I think you could do with a good bout of corruption."

"I think you could do with some cleansing," she grumbled.

"Are you offering?" he asked, most likely just to get a rise out of her.

Raewyn squirmed in his hold, unsure of why her body decided to pulsate at the idea of 'cleansing' him herself, with soapy water and her hands. From what she'd briefly felt, his fur would be soft, and his muscles squishy – two wonderful textures.

"I don't want to talk to you anymore," she grumbled while turning her face away.

"Oh no, whatever shall I do? She no longer wishes to speak with me. I'm so torn up inside."

She could almost imagine him rolling his eyes if he had any. She did feel his shoulders move, like he'd rolled his head.

Raewyn bit her lips to stop them from curling in humour. She had a soft spot for sarcasm – which is why she'd enjoyed Cykran's company so much.

"I could talk your ear off instead," she warned.

"That would require me to have fleshy ears, which I do not." Okay, he had a good point. "However, I am curious about your world. So, if you wish to talk about it, my ear holes are open. Perhaps that would be a better travelling discussion for you?"

"*Now* you wish to be chatty with me?" she asked, just wanting to poke his ire.

"Things have changed. There was no point in our knowing each other when we had been planning to separate after the temple. There is much I wish to know, and there are things you *must* know about me. Just as I said earlier, choose your questions wisely, for you may not like what you discover." Then, with a tone that held a deep and foreboding warning, he added, "And I am not forgiving, Raewyn. Your reactions and words are not something you can take back."

She took his warning to heart, having already uncovered that truth today.

Merikh stared down at the sleeping Elf, cradled in his arms. Her face was smooshed against his chest, her body limp as it bounced, her legs swaying. Merikh ignored the fact that one of her hands clutched his shirt.

He'd never had a soft spot for... well, anything before. Raewyn, however, was funny in a cute sort of way.

She's bubbly. He hadn't expected that of her.

He'd also never had anyone be that way with him. It often stumped him because he was unsure of how to react.

Her world sounds beautiful.

She had explained what it looked like from when she'd still had her sight, and he could almost picture it in his mind's eye.

Apparently, their foliage was a mix between dark blue, bright purple, and medium pink. Some tree trunks were black, their centres a sticky brown, but there were many that were white, as though sun bleached.

Those blue, purple, and pink leaves, as well as many of their flowers, would glow in the night, due to absorbing the radiation from the suns. They used it, rather than polluting the air with toxins.

The grass was blue, and their sky changed from green to purple, depending on which sun was closest.

The world seemed alive, just by its environment.

Even if he had to spend the rest of his life alone in that world, at least it would be pretty – rather than the darkness Merikh was accustomed to here.

She'd also told him, in detail, about the city in which she lived. Most of the roofs were painted white to keep cool from the three suns that beat down upon them. Yet, many also had glass domes, or they painted their outer walls in various colours.

Gold, silver, and bronze were common throughout the city. They were resources not used for trade, but rather for housing, since their world had an oversaturation of it.

Their central tree was their main shade, and they'd used magic to grow it so they could live within it before they built the city surrounding it. Outside the city's protective, oily barrier was a valley with mountains on three sides and a river running through it, whereas the other side was a beach.

Finally, she informed him they had begun allowing Demons to live among them, once they had fully evolved past their base instincts. Those who had fully formed skin, were of thought, and wanted nothing more than the destruction to stop, lived with them as equals.

When she'd told him this, Merikh, in his opinion, had foolishly allowed hope to swell within him. He'd once promised himself he wouldn't feel true hope, to be excited for it, but it was hard not to let it birth inside him after what she'd told him.

Could they accept me?

His heart would stutter when he remembered they had accepted Demons who had formed a face. It would be easy to blend in that way, but Merikh would always stand out among a crowd.

He was tall, his face of bone, and even he knew his appearance was frightful to most.

Hope twirled like a tornado, mixing with his longing and low expectations.

Even if he were an outcast within their city for a long time, it would have to be better than never being able to show his own true face. Someone would eventually befriend him... right?

He'd need to change his personality for that to happen, and he didn't see that coming any time soon.

Then again... Merikh glanced down at Raewyn once more. *She doesn't seem bothered by me.*

He *swore* she'd giggled a few times at him, and she'd

definitely smiled more than he was used to... Or was she just feigning friendliness towards him?

Fuck, I don't know, he thought with a growl.

All he knew was that he was growing annoyingly infatuated with her beauty. Pretty things like her shouldn't exist, much less sleep so trustingly, peacefully, and sweetly against his chest.

It was difficult to be sour towards someone who shined a certain kind of innocence, despite being quite bratty when she wanted to be. She pouted a lot, blowing her cheeks out in annoyance, her eyes narrowing, which only highlighted her long eyelashes.

She also liked to lift her chin, but he noticed her ears often flicked with unease.

It was hard to imagine she was a scientist of anything when she often sounded naïve, but he thought that might be because she was thrust into a world she didn't quite understand, with a person she didn't understand.

Still, he liked her, not that he would tell her that.

She had been kind towards him, open with him.

Except for his murderous tendencies, she seemed more forgiving than he could ever be. He didn't think anything he'd done should be forgiven. Not that he regretted a single action – he held no remorse for the lives he'd taken, and he would gladly take more, as long as it got him what he wanted.

Merikh lowered his head so he could sniff her cheek, and he immediately shuddered.

The fact she smelt like lily of the valley, a flower so wonderful yet also so toxic, was chaos to him. He never should have removed his scent-diluting cloth, but he needed to be able to sense their environment better to protect her.

Despite her height, she was small, delicate, and he would protect her with every piece of him – quills and all.

Yes, she was his way out of this realm. However, a growing part of him just wanted to keep her safe, to protect her, to be her shield. Odd, considering he'd only ever been that for himself.

She was a bright spark in a dim world; he wouldn't mind being the reason it kept shining.

Merikh lifted his head when she gave a little mewl, and he realised he'd just been greedily taking in her intoxicating scent. He'd tickled her ear and neck with his breaths.

Embarrassed by his unusual behaviour, his orbs turned a reddish pink. It'd been a long time since he'd seen this colour, and it was only because of her. He turned his focus back to the sunny forest around them.

Raewyn had been asleep in his arms for about eleven hours. He didn't mind holding her, content in doing so, when a week ago, it would have annoyed the absolute shit out of him.

We should reach the last town before the southland border in around two days. They'd now been travelling for four days, and they had many, many more to go.

The last town would be the final place she could rest comfortably, obtain more food, and gain whatever she needed before a long journey.

We're making terrible time.

He would have preferred to walk on his hands and feet, since it was faster. He could have run the distance in a day if he truly wanted to. His quills made that impossible, since she couldn't sit on his back. He *absolutely* refused to wear a saddle like a damn horse.

Giddy up? More like giddy go-fuck-yourself.

He pictured her giggling at his speed, though, and suddenly, the idea didn't seem so abhorrent to him.

FIFTEEN

When a second drop of liquid splattered upon her cheek, Raewyn's closed eyes scrunched up. Not quite ready to wake, she curled into Merikh's chest.

She'd barely been asleep for an hour, and they'd already travelled for three days since the last town. Being tired was an understatement, but she'd tried to stay awake for as long as she could stand.

The aches and pains knotting her muscles were from holding onto his body and barely being allowed to move. He did, occasionally, let her walk alongside him, but he would eventually scoop her back up to his side.

She was aware they were in more of a dangerous territory, where there would be all manner of Demons rather than those who could fly or climb over the southland's border wall. They'd already fought against a few. Well, him really, while she just shielded herself.

All this travelling was annoying and tedious. Despite being wary he was taking her to the Veil, Raewyn was over it. They'd now been travelling for nine days! At some point, a person would break.

With a dissatisfied groan, Raewyn cringed as she rubbed her face against Merikh's chest when a third droplet splattered against her neck.

"Five more hours," she pleaded.

"I can't turn off the rain, Raewyn."

She opened her eyes and glared in his direction. "Sure you can."

The *shah* of a deluge of water droplets suddenly hitting the canopy of leaves above was the only warning she got before it rained properly. At first, she fought it, wriggling one way and then the other, as if that would stop her from getting wet.

Pointless, really, with the way he supported her back and her knees from behind.

Within moments, as if they broke through the forest's tree line and into a field, Raewyn was pelted by fast and heavy drops. Her clothing became drenched all the way through. Each drop was icy to her, and she immediately shivered.

"Merikh, can you put me down? I'm getting wet."

"We must keep going." That's what he always said!

"Please?" She tried to give him her best pity pout, and he let out a sigh.

He dipped his arms and carefully placed her feet on the ground. Raewyn shoved her cloak hood on, gripped the guide rope around his waist, and he led the way.

Every minute made Raewyn colder and wetter. Her cloak was doing nothing to keep her dry, and before long, her teeth chattered. Her bare feet felt as though she'd dipped them in icy water.

A crack of thunder boomed, before giving way to angry rumbles. The wind picked up, roaring as it cut its powerful strength through her.

This was the first time it'd stormed properly since they'd started travelling together. It often drizzled, mainly throughout the day, but it was warmer then. From the temperature swirling around her, she sensed it was currently the middle of the night.

"Ugh!" Raewyn whined. "It's so cold already, and m-my cloak isn't keeping me dry."

Her cloak dragged across her shoulders when he fisted the

edge and lifted to inspect it.

"What the fuck kind of travel cloak is this?" he sneered. "Why didn't you tell me it was made of cotton? I would have acquired you a better one. No wonder you're getting soaked. You should have picked something water resistant."

"H-how was I supposed to know that? I just bought whatever was available from Clawhaven."

She wished her eyes weren't so heavy from being sleepy. When her hands began to ache, and her feet became unstable from the numbness of being cold, she hugged her midsection.

"Is there anywhere for us to stop? Nyl'theria is hotter than this, even in the winter."

"Are you really that cold?" Raewyn nodded. Before she could open her mouth to apologise, the rain ceased suddenly. "Come here, I'll shield you."

Raewyn cuddled into his side, since he'd lifted his arm to bring her under his own cloak. It was just as cold, but it didn't feel damp on the inside.

It was his warmth when he wrapped his arm around her to keep her close that chased away the worst of her chills. His palm was gripping her hip, his entire arm resting over her back, and Raewyn clutched his shirt to soak in the heat coming off his torso.

"We've entered a mountain path," he stated with a dark tone. "This is Demon territory. I was hoping to pass it quickly, but I know of a shallow cave nearby. Hopefully it's empty, since it's night."

"Are you sure they won't find us?"

"It's difficult for Demons to smell through the rain. I would have protected us without it, but the rain actually makes it safer for us."

Raewyn bit her lip and nodded.

When a nearby howl echoed in the distance, one that didn't sound remotely like any kind of animal, she had the desire to cut open Merikh and hide within him. The tiny hairs on her body stood on end as fear crept up her spine. She had to use every ounce of willpower to remain unafraid.

Merikh was here, and he would keep her safe. Surprisingly, that was enough for her.

He was big, scary, and he'd already killed multiple Demons while protecting her. Now that she was mentally prepared for such a situation, it didn't feel as daunting.

Just as the wind picked up in velocity, the rain constantly pitter-pattering against his cloak, Merikh turned them. The chilly wind rolled in behind them and fluttered their cloaks forward as he brought them into a dry space.

The ground was smooth rock beneath the soles of her feet. Even though it was cold, it was dry.

She could just make out her breaths echoing against the cave walls, informing her it was small but had plenty of room to move around.

"Make a barrier at the entry," Merikh demanded.

Raewyn came out of his cloak and patted the entryway with her hands. She shook her head.

"It's all rock. Unless there's a living component, I can't make anything grow."

There was a small pause, one that only highlighted how deeply he thought.

"Then I will need your arm."

There was something about his tone that had Raewyn cupping her forearm and huddling both arms to her chest. "Why?"

"I can make a shield, but something must be sacrificed."

"You want to cut off my whole arm?!"

"What?" he said with a concerned inflection in his voice, like what she'd asked was preposterous. "No. Bloody hell... Raewyn, why would that be your first thought? I just need a little bit of your blood, as my own doesn't work. I must make the shield for someone else."

"Oh," she rasped, her ears flattening as she fidgeted in

embarrassment. "Sorry. I'm just a little frazzled."

She was cold, tired, and in a dark cave that probably housed many Demons that could return at any time. He'd never stated if there was a nest, but she had a funny feeling there might be.

Stepping towards him, Raewyn presented her arm. "Won't the smell of blood bother you?"

He gripped her wrist and turned her arm face up. "I'll hold my breath and then take your wounds to stop the bleeding. As long as you wash it away, it will be fine."

With no warning, probably to save her from fretting over the oncoming pain, a claw stabbed into her forearm and drew down. Raewyn stifled her wince when her arm burned from the pain.

He turned her arm back over to let it bleed into his palm. Once he'd collected enough, he healed her skin, and it was as though she hadn't just been cut open. There wasn't even a scar marring her.

Raewyn noticed a bright-red light form before it became a transparent red dome she could see. It never faded, the magic semi-permanent for now, and was bigger than she'd thought it would be.

There was a star crossing over the entire dome, with two lines that went all the way around it with more stars. It did nothing to keep the rain out, but when Raewyn touched it, she couldn't pass.

It wasn't a ward, but a shield that kept anyone from entering or exiting it. It likely wasn't strong, probably temporary. Depending on how long they were here, she bet she would need to give more of her blood to reform it.

Raewyn washed her arm with the water coming through the shield and into the cave. He came up beside her to wash his hands of her blood scent.

Then, Raewyn turned to escape the howling wind and rain, shivering as she rubbed her arms for warmth. Although she wasn't getting wet anymore, this wasn't much better.

"Can you make a fire?" he asked, and she once more shook

her head.

"I'm too cold to cast any kind of flame or heat magic. It comes from within."

He let out a long, exasperated sigh. "You'd be utterly useless in a blizzard."

Raewyn lifted her chin at him. "Well, can you? Or will you require something else from me, like my hair or heart this time?"

"No, I can't 'cast' fire, but I can use tools to make it. You're lucky there's a nest here. The wood is dry and old, perfect for burning."

Oh, thank goodness! She was freezing her boobs off!

When he got a fire going, Raewyn sat in front of it.

It wasn't as warm as she wanted it to be, the chilly air blowing in from outside. She couldn't get too close to the flames, or she'd start to feel like she was burning, but if she sat a safe distance away, the heat was barely enough.

It was a miserable feeling, but she didn't want to complain when it was obvious he was trying to be accommodating.

Raewyn nibbled her bottom lip. *I can't get warm because of my clothes.* She folded one foot on top of the other as she hugged her knees.

She needed to strip – she *knew* she needed to. Yet, for some reason, she was nervous about doing so.

On the other side of the fire, Raewyn heard a heavy *plop,* as though he'd laid out a wet bit of material. Her ears twitched at a second *flawp*, and she wondered if he'd come to the same conclusion about stripping. Perhaps he just wanted to dry the clothing he'd worn.

When a rather brutal wave of goosebumps assaulted her spine, Raewyn gathered the courage and stood.

"Do you have my spare clothes?" she asked.

"No. I'm laying them out along with mine to dry by the fire."

Raewyn clenched her jaw and swallowed a lump in her throat. "Why? Shouldn't they be dry?"

"They were, until I had to pull my cloak over you instead.

All our clothing is wet."

Her mouth went dry, and she wished her body would follow suit. Instead, she was forced to untie her cloak and let it fall to the ground.

Her hands were clumsy as she undid the ties at the back of her dress, her ears and cheeks burning. When she slipped it over her shoulders, she had the undeniable urge to turn and give Merikh her back, so she did.

Why am I being so shy? she thought, her lips pulling to one side.

Elysians were usually rather open with nudity and their sexuality. Both men and women had a tendency to prance around without a top on. It was only because of children and their rude little eyes or hands poking at people's privates that they covered them.

Underwear was virtually non-existent, as they liked to let the body breathe naturally. She wasn't wearing any now for that reason alone, especially since she'd never had any intention of letting anyone know she wasn't wearing any.

Raewyn had never been shy in her life, unless she was stripping for a partner she was interested in. Her sudden bashfulness didn't make sense to her.

It was when her dress was around her hips that she let out a silent gasp.

Wait... Am I attracted to Merikh?

What other explanation was there? She liked the way he smelt, his rumbly, gruff voice, his thick and muscled body. What his face was had little meaning to her.

His hands were rough but pleasant, his personality considerate when he wanted to be but mean when given the choice.

Raewyn kind of liked that he could be a jerk. Sometimes, things were a little scary, like his murderous tendencies, but she tried to ignore them. Whenever he was rude, she had the desire to needle him further until he growled or did this strange, low, snorting huff.

People had treated her like she was precious from the moment she became a councilmember. Merikh, on the other hand, treated her like he couldn't give a damn what he did or said to offend her, or anyone, for that matter.

He was also... sweet in his own way. She never needed to ask for help, like when he'd offered to shield her from the rain. He just did it without thought or expectation.

Raewyn let her dress fall as she chewed her bottom lip until it swelled.

Is it weird I feel this way about him? Sure, they hadn't known each other long, and there were obvious issues to work out, but she couldn't deny it.

There had been fleeting moments of desire in his presence that she'd unwittingly suppressed – especially whenever she got a close whiff of his delectable scent.

She wished she could ignore it now that she realised what she was feeling. She covered her chest when she grabbed her dress from the ground, rather than just presenting herself like normal.

But Raewyn wasn't the kind of person to ignore something just because it was uncomfortable to discover.

It didn't mean she'd voice it or do anything about it, as she had no idea what Merikh felt. He was hateful towards everyone indiscriminately. What were the chances he'd feel any kind of desire towards her?

There were truths she was hiding, things she knew that he wouldn't.

After laying her dress out near the fire, Raewyn sat on the ground, trying to ignore the wind cutting against her bare flesh while she thought.

I've never denied my own desires for another before, though. She was carefree in this regard.

She was by no means easy or not selective. Actually, she was insanely picky, which made her desire towards Merikh a bit of a head scratcher, but that was why she'd never not pursued her attraction to someone.

He's a monster, Raewyn, she tried to tell herself. Eh, not that big of a deal, truthfully. *A big monster who said he had a cock.*

What did it look like? What did it feel like? Her saliva thickened when she thought it might be big like he was.

Stop it! At this rate, she'd start turning herself on, and she just *knew* the big guy would sense it and pick on her about it. At least, she hoped he would pick on her about it, just so she could purr at him until he caved.

That's it!

"I'm going back to sleep," she mumbled. Her tiredness was allowing perverted thoughts.

"Do whatever you want," he bit, obviously cranky about being stuck here.

It was funny, though, and she couldn't put her finger on why, but she knew where he was even before he'd spoken. Usually, she struggled to sense him when he was far from her.

Giving him her back as she curled into her body, she began a silent mantra. *Feel the cold.* That should kill the confusing wet heat between her thighs.

She focused on the cold air brushing over her, and a wild shiver had her whimpering. *No! Don't feel the cold. Think warm thoughts.* Her realm's heat, the sun burning her skin, Merikh's warm hand wrapping around her side.

Welp. That wasn't helping.

Just as she was beginning to calm from her strange, desirous thoughts, although not enough to go to sleep, Merikh let out an annoyed sigh.

"Come here," he demanded.

"P-pardon?" she whispered with chattering teeth, twisting so her face was in his direction.

"You won't sleep like that."

She shook her head. "N-no, I'm fine like this."

Her heart nearly stuttered in her chest. *Did he really offer for me to come lie down with him?* With how warped her thoughts had been, she didn't know if she could handle that right now.

She was calm now; she'd gotten over it. It was okay if she liked his thick, dense exterior, his voice and scent. It was okay if she felt desire towards these qualities, but she didn't want to act on them.

At least, she didn't think so.

Merikh was a Duskwalker, and she was an Elf. They came from two different worlds, and their hearts would never align. She didn't know if she wanted to touch someone when their interior was mostly cruel and hateful.

Right now, lying next to him might cause her to do something she shouldn't, something naughty and foolish.

"I won't offer again," he stated, far too sternly. "Either allow my body to warm you, or freeze."

Raewyn drew her lips into her mouth and bit down hard. She shook her head again. Although she wanted heat more than anything, she just couldn't do it.

Her eyelids eventually drooped, but the shivers that wracked her never allowed her to pass out. His soft growl echoed before the whack of his feet patted against the ground.

She gasped when he scooped her up. "W-wait! W-what are you d-doing?!"

"You're being a pain, you know that?"

She covered her body as he walked her to the other side of the cave and laid her down. She stiffened when he got in behind her to block out the wind.

"When the rain stops, I want to leave. It'll be better if you're not tired, and watching you shake for the entire storm will be depressing."

The heat that pressed against her from behind had her melting. It was touching her spine, and she hadn't realised how much the bones of her vertebrae had been aching from her chills until this very moment.

The stiffness in her nipples stayed taut for a completely

different reason as goosebumps cascaded over her flesh, like a wave that came from the centre of her back. Her eyelids fluttered, and she found herself leaning into him more and more. She even wiggled against him when he lifted his knees behind hers until her backside was pressed into his groin.

She didn't even move away when something... twitched against her backside. She was too busy trying to shove her icy toes between his warm calves. The shy and apprehensive Raewyn had turned into a heat seeking parasite.

He didn't wrap his arm around her, but her chest still felt frozen. She patted his leg and found his hand, then yanked it over her.

"Watch my quills," he bit, trying to pull his hand back.

She refused to let go.

"You're *so warm*," she moaned, wriggling against him. "I wish I could wear you like a blanket."

His short fur was so soft against her back, legs, and side. It even tickled her cheek, since he'd pushed his meaty bicep underneath it to pillow her head from the hard ground.

The tension in his own body dissipated at the same time hers did. He hissed as she tried to get closer, continuing to wriggle, as though she wanted to bury beneath him – which she did. Gosh, if it wasn't insane, she would have cut him open and crawled inside just to be completely cocooned.

"Stop that," he coarsely bit out. "Stay still."

"Sorry, I'm just trying to get comfortable," she whined, but she did stop moving, especially when something moved against the cleft of her backside.

She pressed her thighs together when her inner walls clenched in reaction to it this time. His scent surrounded her, penetrated her mind, and she panted to take in more oxygen, only to further drown herself in it. It only made her nipples tighten even more, and, along with their throbbing, her clit pounded.

Squeezing her eyes shut, she pleaded with herself to not grow horny and excited. He was just doing this to warm her; she shouldn't be the one having a weird bodily reaction to it.

Yet his heart was beating against her shoulder blade, and it sounded so big, so strong, as it drummed into her. She couldn't help focusing on it, on the way she'd fit into the nook of him, how his massive and wide body had surrounded her like a cocoon of comfort.

She couldn't even feel the wind anymore.

Please don't smell me. She shoved her hand between her thighs and clenched them tighter around it, hoping to stop any scents from escaping.

She grew distressed when his rough palm wrapped around the shoulder she was laying on. His claws scraped her, and for the first time, they'd tickled her. She almost shivered in reaction.

Since she hadn't allowed him to pull his arm away, he was giving in to holding her. The thick limb was nestled between her breasts, and she tried to ignore that fact, or that something long and thin had wrapped around one of her calves. His tail, maybe?

It should have freaked her out, but the feathery end had brushed over her skin delicately.

Not once did he try to touch her, caress her, or do anything perverted. Why did that make her both relieved and disappointed at the same time?

With saliva clogging in her throat, she whispered, "Thank you for this."

"Just go to sleep."

Such a cold answer, and she wished it had cooled her, but it didn't. Raewyn was nearly vibrating with desire. It'd been ages since she'd felt any kind of release, as she preferred to do so with a partner than by herself. The lack of it was warping her mind.

"I'll stay awake, so don't worry about my quills."

Oh, right. His quills... His deadly, deadly quills that she suddenly wished she could touch and explore. She also wanted to explore him and how different he truly was from her.

His chest expanding and contracting pushed and pulled her with his breaths, like waves to lull her. Sometimes, his fur tickled her back when it slipped against her.

Tired and aroused, Raewyn permanently closed her eyes. *Sleep. Just go to sleep.*

SIXTEEN

The moment she'd wiggled her pert arse against his seam to get comfortable, Merikh regretted his decision to warm her.

He just hadn't been able to stand the miserable sight of her violently shivering as she lay upon the cold, hard ground.

He should have known better than to help.

Especially since the sound that Merikh had produced when she dropped her dress and revealed her naked body was not quite a purr, but a chest-bubbling soft growl. It wasn't filled with anger, but with heat he wasn't accustomed to.

He tried to look away, throwing his head to the side, but his skull would drag forward, as though he was compelled to look. He knew her arse was soft yet firm from the occasional times he'd 'accidentally' held it while carrying her, but he didn't know it would be so round or plump.

Her dress and thin frame were deceiving.

Licking at his snout in interest, he used every ounce of willpower to stop his orbs from shifting to purple. He didn't like that she could see the magic in her vision, and she had a thing about questioning what the colours meant.

He'd rather chew his own foot off than tell her it was a reaction to his desire.

He almost lost the battle with his orbs when she'd turned, her arm doing very little to hide her breasts. The undersides were showing, and they were just as soft and round looking as her backside. She'd covered her pubic mound with her hand, but he could still see the curls covering it matched the colour of her hair.

Her body was tall, petite, willowy, and yet her feminine qualities were much more appealing than he thought they'd be. Her magical black body markings, woven into lines, knotted shapes, and mainly hexagons, were exotic and alluring.

It is like an angel carved her, from every single strand of hair on her head, all the way down to her cute feet. Then again, he doubted an angel would have given her such sinful, sensual curves.

He also thought a devil would have more fun torturing him with something he couldn't have. He currently felt tortured with her in his arms.

For just a split second, he swore her faint scent – diluted from the rain cleaning it away – ripened with something that *immediately* made his cock jerk and his seam twitch. Sweet but spicy, and absolutely delicious.

He didn't like that her scent was ripening in desire, but he assumed it had nothing to do with him. She was warming, and sometimes, the body did strange things without meaning to, like getting excited.

He had to admit, she'd felt like ice when she first pressed up against him.

It would've been easier to ignore his own pulsating thoughts with a frigid and frightened prey. Instead, she'd boldly wrapped herself in him.

How could his throat feel so dry and yet his mouth be on the verge of drooling?

When she'd finally settled and started snoring, he hadn't intended to fall asleep as well. His quills had been too close for comfort, and if he hurt her by accident, she'd be dead before she even opened her eyes.

Perhaps it was that once she'd warmed up, she'd gone all

pliant and relaxed in his arms, which made her comfortable to hold. It could have even been her pretty scent slowly dazing his mind as he drank it in on each inhale. Was it both her breaths and her heartbeat that had lulled him under with their rhythm?

He couldn't remember the last time he'd slept so deeply.

All musings aside, he was awake once more. It was dark within the cave. The fire was gone, leaving no light or heat. However, he hadn't slept very long, and his awakening wasn't peaceful.

He was panting, on the verge of choking. Her scent was sweet, spicy, and so saturated in arousal that it was almost overpowering.

It even made his sight hazy, as though he was affected by some kind of poison eating at his mind from the inside out. His waking thoughts were muddled, like he was trying to swim through thick mud, or quicksand, that was doing everything in its power to suffocate him.

It took him far longer than it should have to realise there was movement. It was subtle, but it was her little mewl that brought his attention to it. Something wet and malleable rubbed over the side of his thumb.

His body was heavy as he assessed his position. It was similar to how he'd fallen asleep, except for one detail – his arms had moved. At some point during his sleep, his hand had moved between her thighs to grip one from the inside. The other laying underneath her was now clamping the arm she wasn't resting upon.

She was *rocking* against the side of his hand, both of her own grasping his wrist.

Her breaths were panted, but they still sounded deep, like she may be asleep. She subtly rocked on his hand again, and he felt his thumb pressing between her folds, her clit rubbing against it.

Had he moved his hand there, or had she? Her thighs were trapping it, and when he attempted to gently remove it, they clamped down tight.

The threads of her scent stole his attention, and he lost his focus to sniff her neck right below her ear, pressing his snout against her. *Shit. She smells amazing like this.* His fur and quills ruffled, standing on their ends as he shuddered.

Toxic. Addictive. Enough to drown all thoughts that didn't involve her. He could lie there and smell her forever.

When his quaking breath brushed over her, Raewyn trembled and ground against his hand again. A sharp moan came from her parted lips, lips that looked malleable and tasty.

His quills were already agitated, and they only stuck up more at her little sensual noises. With how he was holding her, one wrong move from either of them, and they would gouge at her buttery skin.

Temptation lay before him, and Merikh was considering letting it win, to touch her until she gave him a delightful song of cries, until her slick had completely coated his hand, until she squirmed against him.

His cock was throbbing behind his seam, encased completely in his tentacles that were struggling to hold him back. If it wasn't for her arse pressing directly against his engorged erection, his seam would have split apart already. If she were awake, she would no doubt feel its hardness shoving through his skin and into her.

However, as much as he was tempted to, Merikh wouldn't touch someone who was unaware. He preferred those he was playing with to know that it was him, a Duskwalker, teasing them.

Once more, he gently tried to bring his hand out from between her thighs, making sure his arm was twisted in a way that wouldn't cause his quills to harm her. Her thighs tightened, and her hand on his wrist shoved downwards to keep it there.

The motion caused him to rub against her, and she bucked into his hand in return.

His claws lightly stabbed into her flesh.

"Raewyn," he rasped, his lungs moments from collapsing.

Fuck, he needed away from her before it was too late. The storm was still thunderous and intense, booming and flashing light inside the cave. He was sure throwing himself into it would cool his insanity.

"Mmm," she responded. It was almost like a moan rather than a response of alertness.

He leaned over her slightly. "I need you to let go of my hand."

Her eyelids fluttered, showing they were somewhat open. They closed again, just as she deeply bit into her bottom lip. She shook her head slightly, clenched her thighs, and then ground into his hand again.

"Just a little longer," she whispered with a pleasure-laden rasp, her chest quaking as she quivered out a pant. "Please. Your hand feels really good."

Her cute, pointed ears not only flattened but pressed back slightly. He noted how hot her body was in his arms, how flustered she had gotten.

He realised she had been awake for a little while, and that his hand placement had not been unwanted.

The growl that rumbled from his throat was not of anger but of profound lust, and he moved the hand holding her arm to cup her throat. He lifted her chin, arching her neck into a submissive, open position.

"You naughty little nymph," he snarled, twisting his head as he licked from the centre of her throat to below her ear. "Just how long have you been fucking my hand?"

Her strangled moan started out quiet. He deliberately rubbed against her swollen, wet, needy clit himself, and it turned into a little cry.

If she wanted his touch, then Merikh was willing to take advantage of that. With how mind fogging her scent was, how sweet her sounds came out, and just how beguiling she looked all pent up and needy, nothing could have twisted him more into immediately giving in.

He'd woken up hard, his cock aching, heavy pumps of blood rushing to it. The profound throb in it took away all sanity as to why this might not be a good idea.

Right then, he didn't care.

Damn his quills; he would be careful. There was an exquisite creature in his arms who wanted pleasure.

His pleased growl didn't cease. It grew when he realised that his forearm was sitting between her exposed breasts, both moulding around his arm to pillow it. Her dark-brown nipples looked unbearably hard, tight, and begging for attention.

He sheathed his claws and then twisted the hand between her thighs by force until he was cupping the slit of her cunt. The other lowered until he was able to grasp one of her breasts, and she arched into his hand like she'd been waiting for them to be petted.

Merikh ground his palm against her clit, and he gave no warning as he shoved his middle finger knuckle deep through the puddle of her hole. Her pussy clamped down on it as her lips parted on a sharp gasp. She let out a long moan as she ground against his hand, stirring him inside her.

He moved it back and forth, drenching his finger in her arousal. She was so wet it slipped in and out with ease, her entrance leaking so much that everything felt slick.

Considering she wasn't snug around his thick finger, when he ground against her clit again, he quickly added a second finger. Now she was tight, and he was satisfied she'd feel that stretch by how she arched into him, her eyes flinging open.

"Merikh," she moaned, gripping the back of his hand to try and get him to press even deeper.

His quills lifted at his name being called so seductively from her pretty lips. He groaned in return as he shoved his groin against her arse, hard enough that he accidentally opened his seam by force. The tentacle-covered head extruded. Once it broke free, Merikh didn't have a chance in hell of holding it back.

He tried to clench it back down, but she moved her arse against it purposefully. Each rub had his control on it slipping, until it was pressing into her back. He shuddered at the tension of his tentacles struggling to hold him back the last few inches.

"It's wet?" she asked, but there was no hesitation from her as she teased the base of it between her firm, plump cheeks.

No, instead, her scent deepened to the point that his tongue swiping over her sensitive ear was moist with drool. He was panting against it, and it flicked each time.

Merikh didn't answer her, not when her question was immediately forgotten as he speared her channel repeatedly with his fingers. He moved them in a wave, making sure he rubbed the tips against the hot and swollen ridge at the front of her pussy.

He couldn't move his arms too much, otherwise he could hurt her, but that didn't stop him from clamping her hard nipple between his index and middle fingers. He rolled it side to side as he squeezed her mound, weighing her breast and letting the memory of it burn into his palm. He purposefully tickled the underside with his fingertips.

The arm she was lying upon shot up to grip the back of his hand playing with her breast, her other one safely clamped to her side. Both dug their nails into the backs of his hands.

Her chin lifted, exposing her neck as her features furrowed, her body bowing. Her thighs twitched before rubbing side to side, demanding more friction he couldn't risk giving her. Raewyn squirmed as she let out a cry, her pussy sporadically clamping around his fingers.

The moment he felt her inner walls swell, as though she was about to come, Merikh quickly slipped his fingers from her. He used the backs of them to guide his way through the lips of her folds so he could pet her clit.

"No. Don't stop." She bucked into his hand while trying to push it deeper between her thighs, desperate to get him to penetrate her again. "I was so close."

His quiet chuckle likely sounded diabolical, but he just wanted to see what she would do when she was robbed of her orgasm.

He hadn't expected her to try and shove his fingers back inside her, for her to grind so openly and wantonly on his hand. She lowered her face to nuzzle against his arm crossed over her chest, but immediately threw her head back when the tip of an extended quill stabbed into her chin. He was quick to heal her to minimise her blood scent.

"You can be a needy thing, can't you?" he nearly purred, despite not being able to make the actual sound.

He clamped her swollen clit between his fingers, and when he squeezed, she let out a gasp. He rolled it side to side, just like he'd done with her nipple, which he was now plucking.

Her pants were so shallow, sharp, and quick that she appeared as choked as he did. Her brown and starburst eyes rolled slightly before she gave a little shiver.

Then, weakly, she whispered, "*Please*, Merikh. Please don't tease me."

The way her Elvish accent played with his name always sent a thrill through his body. He ground his cock against her as he pulsated, spreading a drop of precum within his tentacles. They hurt, struggling to keep him down, and felt stretched, but he didn't relent the control he had on them.

Merikh uncurled his fingers and speared through the dense pool of arousal overflowing her entrance. Raewyn spread her thighs so she could try to keep him there. Trying to reach her orgasm faster, she bucked wildly as he moved back and forth.

He hoped she was worried he'd deny her again, realising her pleasure was currently at his mercy. She wouldn't know her sweet plea had touched his merciful side.

She's so hot inside, so snug, so soft. He shoved his fingers in deep and then wiggled. *She would feel amazing around my cock.* Since she liked that motion, he did it repeatedly. *Gods, I want my cock in her. Want to spread her thighs and watch her bounce as I fuck her hard.*

Her cunt clamped his fingers as her back arched into a tight bow. He had to hold her straight so she didn't curl into his quills, just as she let out the loudest, most erotic cry he'd ever had the pleasure of hearing.

Merikh let go of her breast, laid his arm straight, and then ripped it out from underneath her. He came out from behind her, causing her to roll onto her back, then he shoved one of her thighs to the side.

He moved his fingers in and out of her more forcefully, faster, dragging out her orgasm until her cry turned into a scream. Raewyn's legs kicked, but her strength was nothing compared to his own as he held her in place.

Braided hair swirling like a halo around her head, her lips parted and swollen from biting on them, her body spasming and twitching... it was a beautiful sight to behold. He looked down, riveted to the sight of his own thick dark-grey fingers slamming inside her.

She truly appeared lost to her pleasure.

Her brown and starburst pupil eyes rolled before they closed, and he couldn't help but be disappointed by their disappearance.

When she calmed, her orgasm fading, Merikh let out a sigh of relief as he relaxed his tentacles and his cock shot forward the last few inches it could. Everything was oversaturated in lubricant from his constant swells and pulsations.

A few drops of his lubricant mixed with precum dripped onto the stone ground. He removed his fingers from her and groaned at the alluring white tuft of hair over her pubic mound.

Her entrance was pink, her clit many shades darker, and everything was puffy from his playing with her. His sight couldn't stop bouncing between it, her round and perky breasts, the flat plane of her stomach. Not even her delicate hands or the smooth curves of her shoulders escaped his attention.

On his knees, Merikh grabbed the backs of hers and yanked her closer, forcing her thighs to spread around his wide hips. Her hair became a river instead of a pool against the ground as he lifted her.

Vibrating with excitement and anticipation, Merikh thrust the head of his cock through the lips of her pussy. Just that contact had him shuddering, his pants so heated they were fogging, despite the warmth in the air.

Raewyn choked out a huff and shoved her hand against her pussy to shield herself. There was worry, uncertainty, and mistrust in her expression.

"No, I-I don't want to have sex."

The anger that bubbled in his chest had nothing to do with the denial. Her rejection stung, but the heavy ache in his cock and embedded seed sacs was far too prevalent. Between her orgasm, arousal, her juices, and his own lubricant, Merikh was suffocating on these scents, on his own need.

He was far too gone to care right then about the negative emotions she'd brought forth.

"I wasn't going to fuck you," he lied. He was absolutely about to ram his cock into her tight little cunt until he'd stretched her, knowing she'd feel him there for *days*. "But I made you come, so now you can lend me your thighs."

Merikh grabbed her calves, straightened her legs, and shoved them together until they created a tight squeeze around his cock. His tentacles wrapping around her thighs from behind made her flinch and bounce forward to escape, which only made his shaft slip backwards.

She gave a mewl when her action rubbed her clit deep inside the groove on the underside of his cock. She bit her bottom lip as she stopped trying to run away and instead explored him with her thighs and pussy.

Now that she knew he wasn't going to fuck her, there was almost no hesitation. When he shoved her back down, she even brought her hands forward so she could feel the few inches of his thick shaft jutting between her thighs. Then she touched behind her arse to explore his tentacles.

Her brows furrowed in thought, and he could almost read her expression.

She's a curious thing, he mentally groaned, after she finished exploring his tentacles and moved to rub the head of his cock again.

Her touches were like teasing little flutters. He swelled as a bubble of precum spilled from his cockeye and into one of her palms.

Raewyn pulled back. Then she let out a sharp gasp and lifted her hips up to greet him when he must have lashed her clit just right. His cock spread her lips apart, and the twisted knot near the base firmly rubbed over the entrance to her pussy.

In his purple sight, watching her, he wished he could show her what she looked like right then.

Although they were sightless, her eyes were filled with heat, interest, desire. The way her breasts bounced as he began to mindlessly thrust was cute, so precious as they swirled. The vision of his dark-purple cock appearing and disappearing between her now lubricant-covered thighs while his tentacles gripped her...

His head tilted back for a moment as he basked in the heaven of this.

Her moans were soft, the slapping sounds of his hips hitting against her lewd. Even his own breaths and groans echoing off the walls brought him pleasure.

The four thick, wide ridges on either side of his cock right below the head, appearing like a braid that wrapped around it, were teased by her pliable skin. But what had him panting to the ceiling before he looked down was that the sensitive knotted ring near the base of his cock was being massaged.

He doubted he would have been able to fit all the way inside her pussy for her to take that twisted ring, which made his deep slams between her thighs feel all the better.

His quills quivered as they rose and fell, his fur standing on end as his long bull tail tapped against the ground, curled in tension. He rested one hand on the ground to lean over her while his arm hugged her straight legs against his torso. Her feet kept tickling behind the corner of his jaw.

I wonder what it's like inside her.

From his fingers delving earlier, he knew she was plush, malleable, hot, wet. Would she perfectly cuddle his cock, or would he be too big and overstretch her, making her feel too tight?

Just the idea of her squeezing him all the way to his core of his cock had another drop of precum welling. *I want to fuck so bad right now.*

Hard, fast, rough, without a shred of gentleness, have her bouncing around and too lost by his thrusting to do anything more than moan. Merikh shuddered, his lustful thoughts causing his flesh to tighten over his muscles. It even clutched at his bones.

Staring down at her, towering over her like a looming shadow, Merikh started thrusting faster, his own orgasm not far from overcoming him.

Raewyn covered her mouth to hide the noises coming from her lips. She couldn't believe how perverted they sounded! Or that she was enjoying this so much.

She had half a mind to call whatever his cock was an *it*, since it had split into five parts, from what she could tell: four tentacles and this giant thing in the middle that was currently setting her poor, pounding clit on fire.

Everything was slick and slimy, and somehow it made every sensation even more *amazing*. Nothing was abrasive or dry, which was what usually caused rigorous movements to feel like sandpaper against her sensitive flesh. Instead, the friction was deliciously damp.

The glides were easy, his cock hot between her thighs,

pressing against her. It was shoving hard, gouging against her clit, but the deep groove underneath his cock made it feel as though she was being petted from all sides.

Then there were these ridges, and every time he sent her clit through the valley of them, Raewyn thought she was about to combust. She couldn't stop herself from grinding back into him, her inner walls spasming and clenching wildly each time.

Holy maiden, I've never felt anything like this. It was better than a tongue, fingers, or even a normal cock.

Raewyn squeezed her thighs around the engorged, hard rod between them, refusing to let it escape.

She'd barely registered that she'd smeared questionable liquid across her lips, chin, and cheeks. She was too busy panting, trying not to suffocate on her own aroused breaths.

Her nipples were tighter than they'd ever been. The only reason she wasn't playing with them was because she didn't want him to know just how much she was enjoying this, not after she'd just rejected him and now wished she could eat her own words in regret.

It wasn't her fault!

To be fair, what had been subtly rocking against her back had been frighteningly huge. What had been slipping over her entire lower back had felt like the thickness of her thigh. She doubted it was going to fit inside her, no matter how much they tried.

She hadn't known the swirl around it would break apart into four tentacles with soft insides that now gripped her legs. She hadn't known it was only shielding his cock, and that it was far easier to manage.

It was still big, but not as scary as before.

She was also nervous about being *that* intimate with Merikh. This... petting was okay. Well, she *made* it okay in her mind, but full-blown sex with someone she barely knew, half-trusted, and who had some questionable tendencies was worrisome.

She was considering it.

His cock felt so good just rubbing the lips of her folds, and she wondered if she'd just melt into a blissful puddle of goo if he started shoving that texture inside her.

Her thoughts were split. She was too busy trying to grind into his cock until their combined movements sent her hurdling into another orgasm to truly think about anything else.

It didn't help that his groans were gruff and so masculine it made her ears tingle.

Every nerve ending was sparking.

His scent was just as mind-numbing. When she licked at her lips, she brought a small taste of his slick and a hint of something else into her mouth, and her entire body throbbed all at once. Her breath hitched, and her pussy clenched tight.

Just as she was about to come, something strange happened that stole her complete attention: an image began to form.

Raewyn covered her eyes. *I-I can see?*

Dizziness swam through her head, her mind not adjusted to having any kind of physical sight in years.

His thrusts and her pleasure were the reason it took her hazy mind longer to register what she was actually seeing. She covered her eyes as she closed them, and yet the image didn't fade.

There was a fiery purple ring dancing around the edges of her vision. It gave the outside of the image a purple glow, whereas the middle was hyper focused, too clear to be normal.

Raewyn was looking down at herself. She couldn't change where she was gazing, no matter how hard she tried.

"What's happening?" she whispered through pants.

"The fuck kind of question is that?" he growled. It didn't truly sound negative, but rather raspy and broken.

His hips moved faster, slammed harder against her backside, and his lubricant dripped down her thighs until it was pooling on her pubic mound and dripping down her cheeks.

Why could she see herself bouncing up and down from his movements, her breasts swirling from them? Why could she see her braids trying to tangle with each other, or that his dark-grey hand was right next to them?

She hardly believed it was real until she moved her hands from her face and saw the action herself.

Then it changed, and Raewyn's breaths hitched when she was now staring down at her legs. She truly saw what was shoving between her thighs.

His cock was purple, as were the tentacles she could just see the tips of. The ridges near the head almost looked like duplicates of the rim of his cock, but they were darker, nearly black.

Raewyn couldn't help herself. She lifted her hands to the tip of his snout, seeing the white of the bone in his vision.

He-he's sharing his sight with me, she thought, when she saw her fingers grazing his bony snout.

Everything became tighter, like he pulled her closer because of the open touch to his face. His fangs parted against her palms, and his warm breath pleasantly wrapped around her skin. His cock became thicker as he let out the tiniest growl, before it went back down to normal, and he let out a deep huff.

His movements slowed but became more forceful.

Raewyn's eyelids flickered at the new depth. Her body arched, her hands falling away to curl into fists against her chest, and her lips parted.

Any embarrassment she suffered at watching herself come, hearing her haunting scream echo against the walls, was devoured by the pleasure that struck her. Her pussy swelled with liquid and clamped down on nothing.

Each empty spasm had her craving to be filled.

Oh my... gosh! Her back twisted when it was too intense, and Raewyn's hips lifted to escape, only to be shoved back down by his arm as he thrust.

She couldn't flee, not from him, not from her own orgasm that went on and on.

"Are you coming from me fucking your thighs?" Any humour that might have been in his teasing question was drowned out by the intense shudder in his voice. "*Fuck...* you are."

Watching her breasts jiggle from above, her stomach then caved in when she stopped breathing properly, and her thighs twitched as they tried to open. Seeing her head stretch one way and then the other as her body bowed uncontrollably was too much.

I feel like I'm going to explode!

She covered her eyes with her fisted hands, wishing the perverted image would cease. It didn't.

When her orgasm did soften, she was oversensitive. Small, broken cries fell from her as she twitched each time he thrust, her body heavy and relaxed while he used her thighs to masturbate. Her hands fell beside her head, and she could do nothing else but lie there.

Aftershocks assaulted her, each one causing all her muscles to jerk.

"You have no idea how tempted I am to come all over you right now," he rasped.

Would it be warm? How much could he produce? Raewyn wriggled, curious to find out. The air was a little chilly; she wouldn't mind it blanketing her right now.

Maybe that was just her depraved satisfaction giving her silly thoughts.

The disappointment that washed over her when he shoved her thighs apart and pulled away was fleeting, only because she was still forced to watch. Merikh held one of her thighs down to keep them apart as he gripped his cock.

The back of his hand was dark grey, his extending claws glistening black as he grabbed his purple cock and stroked it. Raewyn bit her lip at him masturbating over her, because of her.

His woofing growl palpitated with rapture right before the first splatter of voluminous white liquid hit the ground right below her.

Still able to see through his sight, she could tell it was

flicking between staring at her pussy that he had exposed for his own viewing and his orgasm spending against the grey cave floor. Then, he slipped his thumb into her pussy, like he was imagining he was spending inside her. She was drenched in both their fluids, and the sight was hard to bear, but she didn't cover herself.

She didn't want to rob him of the power of his orgasm.

His growl eventually morphed into a groan, and the sound of it was wonderful.

He stopped stroking his cock once he'd created a white puddle against the ground, more than she could have even imagined. It was almost threatening to touch her backside.

He sat back to frantically huff, his head turning towards the ceiling so he could catch his breaths, and he slipped his thumb from her pussy, pulling away. The moment he stopped touching her, darkness swallowed up her vision, and she saw nothing once more.

She didn't know what to start freaking out about first: the fact that she'd been able to see through his eyes, the fact that they'd just done this together, or the fact that she'd started it all.

At some point, whether it was her or him, one of them had slipped his hand between her thighs. She'd woken up rocking on it, and she'd been so damn turned on that she hadn't stopped even when she'd woken up, long before he seemed to have awakened.

Raewyn's cheeks grew so hot, she thought her hair might catch fire.

Not her most honourable moment, grinding against his hand when he'd been asleep, but she'd been unbearably aroused when she'd woken. Like... 'she might die if she didn't come right then' kind of turned on.

She blamed him for every bit of it – not that he could have helped it.

He literally smells like a Nyl'therian aphrodisiac flower, she thought, wishing to combust to hide from embarrassment. *It's all his fault.*

Not really, and she knew that. It would take more than a placebo effect to do this to her, which meant she liked him a little bit. Okay, maybe a lot, but it was difficult to pull her feelings apart. There was a lot to consider, many things she didn't understand about him.

But... Raewyn nibbled her bottom lip, assessing how utterly satisfied she was. Gosh, her body was vibrating from it. *I don't regret this at all.*

She guessed she wouldn't mind if it happened again. It's not like it had to mean anything... right? Just two people getting off – it didn't matter who or what they were.

She'd never had that kind of relationship before, though.

Sex was a funny subject for her. She usually liked to have some kind of intimate relationship with someone before she allowed them to touch her.

It was nice to know she wasn't the only one who felt desire though. At least, she was hoping she wasn't the only one, that he hadn't used her just because he *could.*

Raewyn bit at her bottom lip, her brows knitting tightly, when something painful pinched at the inside of her chest. She didn't want this to be so hollow.

"We shouldn't have done that," he softly barked, like the haze of his own thoughts had suddenly lifted now that he'd spent.

She heard him scuffle away.

Raewyn's heart shrivelled as she skilfully rolled to the side to avoid laying her legs in his impressive amount of cum. She leant on her elbow and hip as she sat up.

She opened her mouth to say something, anything, but too many reactions shoving past her lips rendered her silent. She wanted to be angry he would coldly say that after using her thighs, she wanted to voice her hurt, she wanted to convince him otherwise. She wanted to playfully tease him for it, be sensual and naughty. She wanted to demand that he come back over here and cuddle her.

Raewyn shut her lips at the scraping of sticks against the ground. Not long after, he re-lit the fire that had gone out.

It was him coming back over, lifting her about a foot to the side to make sure she avoided their mess, and wrapping his dry and slightly fire-heated cloak over her that swelled her heart again.

"Go back to sleep," he demanded. She noted the richness of his pleasure-laden voice. "You woke up too early, from what I can tell. We'll be leaving as soon as the rain lets up."

"Merikh," she started, wanting to understand.

Was it because of the face I made earlier? She didn't want him to get the wrong idea. She was just a little lost and confused.

He went from hot to absolutely weird in the span of a heartbeat.

"Don't," he bit. "It is what it is, and you can't take it back."

Then he moved away. She couldn't place why she could tell he'd gone to the entry of the cave, where she could still see the glitter of his red shield protecting them.

Does he think I'm the one who regrets it?

Whatever it was, there was something deeper going on in his head than she could fathom. She didn't know him well enough, but now, she was determined to.

She opened her mouth, but he cut her off before she even began. *"I said no."* His tone was off, animalistic and reverberating.

Her cheeks puffed in annoyance and anger, and Raewyn laid down and curled into his cloak to hide from him. *Fine.*

However, once she relaxed, she slyly brought it to her nose to bask in his smell. It kind of felt like a thin cuddle from him, and the cloak was big enough and thick enough to keep her warm, with the fire helping to chase the worst of the chill away.

It's time to ask the hard questions, Raewyn thought with determination, clutching his cloak.

She couldn't help the mischievous smile that tugged at her

lips, knowing he was going to hate them. It was time to poke and prod her subject until she'd cracked the code.

SEVENTEEN

Raewyn felt like a dead body rolled up in carpet as Merikh cradled her in his arms, his cloak bundled around her.

The rainstorm had taken hours to settle, and it only gentled.

When too much time had passed, he'd told her to wrap herself in his cloak and then just carted her through the constant drizzle. To be fair, the multiple wrappings kept her dry and warm, especially with him holding her. She was also dressed in layers.

He said he didn't mind getting wet, so long as she was comfortable and they could keep moving. Any time the large hood slipped back from her head, he nipped the edge with his fangs and pulled it back over her face to keep it shielded.

They'd barely spoken in the few hours since they'd set off. He'd only informed her they were at least three days away from the Veil.

One minute, he'd be holding her loosely, and the next, he'd accidentally squeeze the life out of her. When she squeaked, he'd grunt and loosen his hold.

Was he thinking about their sexual interlude in the cave the previous night? She hoped so. She hoped it was driving him crazy because he wouldn't be the only one suffering in their awkward silence.

Now that she'd slept properly, due to multiple satisfying

orgasms, her mind was abuzz.

Does he regret it? Did he like it? Does he want to do it again? He seemed to know what to do... Does that mean he's done something like this with someone else?

Gosh! She had so many questions, and her cheeks heated at the next one that blasted her thoughts. *Does he think I'm pretty?*

Her heart stuttered in nervous hope.

Raewyn wasn't the most stunning Elysian. She actually thought she had a childishly round baby face with too strong of a chin and cheek bones. Her nose was like a button her mother enjoyed booping in affection.

Although her frame was thin, her breasts and backside were on the larger side, so they felt disproportionate to the rest of her. She often hid her butt underneath long, flowing dresses that showed off her shapely thighs.

Her feet were too big, her ears not long enough, since they just reached the top of her head. She was too big and too small everywhere!

She also didn't like her freckles. She wanted to appear majestic and classy, and she thought they made her appear too 'cute' for what she wanted. People tended to think they made her appear ditzy, which probably wasn't aided by her forward, bubbly attitude.

Everyone called Raewyn 'cute' when she'd much rather be alluring or sexy, the kind of woman who elicited fierce erections rather than a head pat.

The weird thing for Raewyn was that when other women had these same features of hers, she loved them. Soft bums, sexy freckles, perky breasts that only slightly jiggled when they walked. In the past, when she still had her vision, any time she saw another woman's curls bounce with their steps, her heart had soared, because her own would do the same.

She appreciated the smaller, daintier ears just as much as the larger ones.

Her self-consciousness had grown tenfold, since she couldn't actually *check* her appearance here.

Back home, she was able to apply her make-up slowly and carefully by memory. She knew her different articles of clothing by their textures, so she could match them.

All of that was stripped away on Earth. Raewyn was forced to wear what she had, she had no make-up to suit her tastes, and the last time she'd washed herself was from the rainfall that had her freezing her toes off.

She didn't imagine she was in her most seductive state.

I must have done something right, since he'd gotten hard. Her lips then pursed. *He didn't kiss me, though. Wait... could he even kiss? I can't kiss a bony snout. Awww, I like kissing.*

She guessed she could just kiss it and he could experience it.

Has he ever been kissed? She was back to her original thoughts on if he'd done anything like what they'd done with another.

Honestly, she wanted to know so badly, it was burning a hole in her head. She was bound to give herself a headache soon if she didn't let some of her thoughts free.

"Have you ever had sex before?" Raewyn blurted out, immediately wishing she could eat her words, then mentally shrugged off the regret in the next moment. It'd been asked, and she might as well go confidently into the conversation now.

There was a reason they called Raewyn blunt.

"Who the fuck starts a conversation like that?" Merikh practically shouted in outrage, almost tripping over his own feet.

Slowly, almost coyly, she sang, "Is that a no?"

Okay, so why did the fact that he might be a virgin make her want to fan herself? *I don't think I've taken a man's virginity before. It sounds like fun.* Should be easy to rock a man's world when he had no one to compare it to.

"Of course, I have," he growled, his voice having an embarrassed hike to it. She even saw red-pink sparks glitter. "How else would I have known what to do?"

Well, poop. There goes that idea. Was she even considering it to begin with?

Then, a dark thought struck her, one that could have her hating him with no chance of mending it.

"With a human?" she squeaked.

"No. I would rather not fuck something that has no idea what's fucking it," he stated with a huff. "It'd be impossible for me to hide that my anatomy is different, as you've already discovered."

That settled the worst of her concerns, but she still had others.

"A Demon, then?"

"Why are we having this uncomfortable conversation? I said I didn't want to talk about it."

Raewyn struggled to fold her arms underneath the cloak, since it was a tight fit.

"I've already told you I've had sex, and not just once, as you so rudely implied. I'm just curious, after what happened."

With his fangs, Merikh clamped the end of her hood and tossed it back enough to reveal her face. She couldn't reach up to fix it even if she tried.

"Fine. If you are so nosy to know about it... yes, with a Demon." When she didn't say anything, thinking on what she wanted to ask next, he said, "You don't seem bothered by that."

Raewyn's brows furrowed. "No, I'm not. Like I already told you, there are Delysians – Demons – that live among us. As long as it was consensual, then it's whatever."

His snarl was far more menacing than Raewyn appreciated. "Are you implying it wasn't?"

"Oh no!" she quickly interjected, trying to wave her hands and failing. "That's not what I meant at all. I didn't mean that you would do something so horrible. It's just... Demons aren't always pleasant, and there have been some cases where they... you know. Anyway! I thought you said you had no one who cares for you, but what about this Demon, then?"

"She's dead," he quickly and coldly answered.

"Oh." She couldn't tell if he was bothered by that fact or not.

"I'm sorry. Was she close to your heart, then?"

Merikh shrugged as he stepped onto something – maybe a fallen tree. He jumped down, a lot further than they'd risen, like he'd walked off an edge. He made no sound as he landed, and he just kept moving.

"Not particularly. She was curious about Duskwalkers, perhaps a little too curious. She liked collecting skeletons. Half the time, I thought she would try to kill me to collect mine, but she never did."

"Okay," Raewyn said with a weak smile, horrified by the idea of being intimate with someone like that. "H-how did she die, if I may ask? Demons are hard to kill if they are that intelligent."

She didn't like the eery silence that fell over them.

"Merikh?"

A flicker of orange sparked in her vision before the usual red took over.

"The other Demons killed her upon learning what we were doing," he answered in a dull voice.

"Oh." Raewyn couldn't keep the hint of sorrow from her voice, her ears drooping.

"It's why I'm not fond of them. Even to them, I am something to be disgusted by, despite their own despicableness." She bounced in his arms when he tossed her. "Why the hell do you look sad for? This was over a hundred and eighty years ago. It's over, and there is no point in feeling anything over it. I got her revenge."

He hates humans. He hates Demons. He doesn't even seem fond of his own kind.

"Do you hate Elysians for leaving the Demons here?"

"Can't hate what I've never met," he easily answered. "Then again, maybe I should, considering a particularly annoying Elf."

Raewyn pursed her lips when they tried to curl in humour, but her darkening thoughts won. *I need to know. I have to know.*

"Was Jabez one of the reasons she died?" What had her kind

truly set upon this world?

"I thought he was, but no. I discovered he had no part in her death."

She turned her face down to hide it. "How do you feel about him?"

"Jabez?" Yellow sparked at the edge of her sight before it faded. "My relationship with Jabez is complicated."

She hadn't expected that response. Honestly, she thought it would be a boast of hatred, that he'd start spilling the terribleness of Jabez's crimes.

"How so?" she dug, trying to come across nonchalant. She even lifted her chin, weirdly defensive despite the curiosity that ran rampant.

"It's nothing."

What a terrible answer!

Raewyn whined as she threw her head back, then made sure to roll her eyes so he would see it. "You can't say it's complicated and not tell me."

When she punctuated her statement with a glare, he snorted a huff.

"He was once my friend..."

"What?" she shouted. "You were friends with him?"

Merikh stopped walking and sighed deeply. "You are very frustrating, you know that? Why all these questions now? A little dick rub, and suddenly, you're chattier than ever."

Raewyn's jaw dropped. *He did not just say that!*

"You-you can't just say you were friends with Jabez and leave me hanging!" she said to deflect the whole dick rubbing thing, since he'd used it to deflect her own question!

"Sure, I can. What are you going to threaten me with?"

Raewyn managed to dig her hand out of the cloak so she could present her palm. "I'll... I'll smack you on the nose!"

"That'll hurt you more than it will hurt me."

"Oh, come on, Merikh!"

He let out another sigh, this one more annoyed than before.

He began walking again as he said, "It was a long time ago. It no longer matters."

He must have looked down and noted her deepening glare.

"You won't let this go until I tell you, will you?"

She shook her head, and the 'ugh' that left him was one of deep frustration.

"Fine. It was around two hundred and fifty years ago. I'd been alive for a while and had already gained a little bit of humanity, but not truly a lot. Most of the Demons back then weren't smart and had only just begun forming their stupid village. He was curious about me, about what I was, where I suddenly came from. I know he watched me. He figured out that the more humans I ate, the more intelligent I became, so he kept finding me forced sacrifices to eat."

"And you just... ate them?" She tried to hide the astonishment in her voice, she really did.

"Well, yes. They smelled of fear, and if that didn't get my mind clicking over into an uncontrollable hunger, he'd bleed them. After a while, he began talking to me, and when I started responding properly, he became fascinated. There were only two Duskwalkers alive at that point, and I don't think he'd stumbled across the other yet. Orpheus was fresh, incapable of understanding anything beyond what an animal would."

Orpheus? Is that the name of one of his brothers? She assumed they were all related if they shared the common parentage of Weldir.

"His interest was superficial at first, but the more intelligent I became, the more he kept me by his side. I had found a companion, and I didn't care what he was. I think he enjoyed that I wasn't like the Demons. He felt comfortable talking to me about his frustrations, his past, his plans, because I wasn't mindless and bloodthirsty like the Demons at the time."

They spoke to each other, became friends?

Merikh's voice then deepened into something dark when he added, "I had planned to help him in his war with you Elves."

Raewyn gulped. The Demons were scary enough, but in their travels, especially right before coming to the mountains, he'd killed six Demons in total. Each battle had been short. She'd asked if he was injured, and most of the time, he'd answered no.

Merikh was strong, fast, *dangerous.*

If he had joined Jabez's army and helped invade her world, he would have annihilated a lot of her kind before they took him down, if they were even able to.

"What happened?"

"A woman," he answered. "Many years after we met, he became obsessed with a woman another of my kind was keeping. Orpheus, the Mavka I just mentioned, had found a human to live with him. The longer he kept her, the more intrigued Jabez became with her. He wanted her, rather than the Demons he was surrounded by, and she wasn't afraid of anything. So, when the opportunity presented itself, he offered to take her, and she willingly went with him."

"She willingly went?" Raewyn asked in disbelief.

"Katerina hated Orpheus. Therefore, she hated Mavka. She just wanted an escape, one that might not hurt her."

"Oh."

I still don't understand, though. Who would go with Jabez?

"She quickly drove a wedge between us," Merikh continued. "I think, in his own way, he loved her. He pampered her as much as he could because she was a gigantic fucking bitch. She knew she could use her 'unhappiness' against him. If I wasn't in my cave or hunting humans on the surface, I was in his castle, watching them interact. She fought with me a lot, called me a beast, an animal, a monstrosity. She often lied to Jabez that I was trying to eat her, steal her from him, rape her, despite me not wanting a thing to do with her."

"What? Really? Who would make such lies?" She couldn't imagine anything more horrible.

"Katerina, for some reason," Merikh answered with a sigh. "After a while, he became paranoid and distant, but he wasn't sure who to believe, since he'd only known her for a short period of time, and he'd known me for years. I told you I become what I eat, that I gain humanity. My desires had not awakened then, and Jabez knew that."

The strangest chuckle fell from Merikh. It was so warm and light, and so different to his usual self. She barely believed she'd heard it.

"He explained what a dick was to me, and I had no idea what he was talking about, since I didn't think I had one. It's rather funny when you look back on it. He tried to show me what sex was through a demonstration, and I thought he was just brutalising the female Demon at the time, even though she'd been enjoying it."

Raewyn's lips curled in weird humour. She couldn't imagine being taught what sex was by someone literally showing her.

Despite this sad conversation, he was reflecting on his time with Jabez rather fondly. She'd never heard Merikh make a warm sound before this.

The only time he'd chuckled at all had been in the beginning, when she'd just discovered he wasn't human. The sound that had come from him had been pure evil – like a madman cackling before going on a killing spree.

"It was only when he discovered my relation to Weldir that he turned on me. He thought I was a spy who was alerting my father to his actions, keeping him trapped on Earth. My mother approached me one day to tell me what I was doing was wrong, that Jabez was not my friend and was evil. She'd explained how Weldir was the reason Demons could not go back through the portal, since neither one of us knew that."

Merikh's arms tightened around her, and Raewyn winced.

"When I told Jabez what I'd learned, he'd raged at me, and we almost fought to the death. Katerina had twisted his thoughts, so he thought I was using him. Since then, I have avoided him, as he has me – until the death of my Demon companion. I stormed his castle, thinking he'd ordered the Demons to kill her to get back at me. He'd had no idea and only laughed at me, Katerina sitting on his damn lap while he sat on his throne."

"And you believed him?"

A small gust of wind blew past them, highlighting the quiet as he thought. "I know Jabez. He would have gloated about it if he had done so."

"Even if she sounds pretty nasty, at least Jabez has someone?"

His body shaking informed her he shook his head. "No. Katerina died about a year and a half ago, as did the woman who killed her. Although they have left me alone, due to lingering feelings from our past, Jabez and Katerina stole one of Orpheus' newest companions so they could kill him. Instead, the woman killed Katerina, and Jabez threw a dagger into the woman's back in revenge."

"So, they both died?"

"As far as I know. Then again, I haven't been back to the Veil for two years and only learned of this recently through a rather chatty Demon. I doubt a human can survive a dagger in the back, and Orpheus doesn't know healing magic like I do."

"That's really sad. Did Orpheus really deserve that?"

"Katerina believed so, but she was a chronic liar and often twisted the truth to be manipulative. It's hard to take her side when she often spoke untruths about me to get Jabez to turn on me. Orpheus probably messed up a bunch, his level of humanity very low at the time, but no, I don't think his actions would have been done with malicious intent."

Raewyn's heart broke in so many different ways for *all* of them. Merikh losing someone he kind of cared for. Orpheus losing someone. Jabez losing Katerina. There was so much death and sadness.

"The problem is," Merikh continued, "since Katerina's death, Jabez has become unhinged. I had considered returning to his side to see if I could rekindle our friendship, but he has truly burned that link with me."

Raewyn's chest tightened, not liking his tone, his words, and that they had a terrible implication. "How so?"

"He has ordered his minions to attack all Mavka, including me. It's why I have stayed away. He is now out to eradicate my entire kind in hatred and revenge, and me along with it. I hate him for what he is doing to my brothers, how he has treated me, and that nothing I do will stop him. Every time a Demon attacks me purposefully, the more my resentment grows. You Elves are to blame for his mental state. You know that, right? You kept him in a cage for years."

"It wasn't a cage," Raewyn muttered defensively. "It was a prison cell, one we had to quickly make. It was his own fault for going crazy in our city. He tried to eat everyone."

"That's not what he said," Merikh rebuffed. "Apparently, you experimented on him while he was a boy because he was half-Elf and half-Demon."

"We did no such thing!" Raewyn shouted, her face heating with indignation. "Yes, we examined him, but we didn't experiment on him. That wouldn't be morally right."

"How old are you? Were you even born when this was all happening? People often twist the truth of history to appear like their wrongdoings weren't so terrible."

Her heart rate spiked in apprehension, her own secret bubbling to the surface, moments from being blurted out. She wanted to tell him the truth. She'd started this conversation to gauge how he would react.

She wasn't sure.

Merikh wouldn't kill her or harm her, since he needed her to get out of this world, but she also didn't want him to hate her. She was growing fond of him. It was hard to sever that before it had truly finished blooming.

"I-I may be younger than him, but only by six years. I was five when he turned on everyone."

Raewyn shut her eyes, wishing the memories of the day Jabez was locked in his prison cell would fade. She had been

there, had witnessed his carnage in person, seen the blood that
not only covered the walls but also his hands, feet, and *mouth*.
She hated that she could remember his sickening chuckle as he
walked the halls, searching for his next victim.

The moment his red eyes connected with her own in the long
white-and-golden hallway still haunted her dreams.

"You were five years old?" Merikh scoffed, ready to take
Jabez's side when he didn't know anything. "You would've had
no idea what was happening to him from when he was born to
when he was what... eleven? You really think the scientists at
the time wouldn't have poked and prodded what he was, since
he was a half-breed? He told me how advanced your people
were."

Raewyn shook her head, feeling her hood slipping further
back until it fell away completely. There were so few drops that
the rain had practically stopped.

"I know they didn't. My parents were the ones who examined
him, and they were just trying to make sure he was okay, since
he'd bitten a few people in the past and everyone was worried.
They were the head scientists at the time, which is why I
followed in their footsteps. They wouldn't have done anything
to harm him."

"Your parents? That changes nothing. Parents lie to their
children all the time, and I'm sure they covered up what they
were doing, since you don't seem to know about it. The humans
here want to open up every freak they can find. I doubt you Elves
would be much different."

May the holy Gilded Maiden save her, he was truly shoving
his heels in. She was surprised by just how deeply he was taking
Jabez's side after everything he'd said about him, how he'd
turned on him.

"Merikh, whatever Jabez told you... it wasn't the truth."

"How can you know that with absolute certainty? What–"

"Because he's my brother!" she yelled, before immediately
covering her mouth, her eyes wide.

Merikh halted, and she only knew he twisted his head at her when the spark of yellow in her vision tilted to the side.

With her hands trembling over her mouth, she eventually lowered them as her head turned this way and that. It'd slipped out, but it was a secret only her parents and the synedrus councillors were aware of.

She could almost feel his gaze stabbing through her.

"He... Jabez is my brother. Well, half-brother really," she softly uttered. "I was there for most of his treatments, that's how I know. I would play with his hair, brush it while our mother drew blood to check on his wellbeing. He-he was really sick as a child, and both our mother and my father couldn't figure out why."

"He told me his birthing was not consensual, that it was due to terrible circumstances. Your mother was attacked?"

Rubbing her arm, Raewyn lowered her head.

"No. The truth is... his creation was an experiment. They discovered that Demons are half-formed creatures. They have all their organs, but their skin is made up of energy – it's why they look like the night sky. They technically don't have flesh, which is why it glistens like a void, a black hole, like nothingness. However, they are *technically* Elves, just a different sub-species – one that must eat other humanoid creatures to finish forming. My mother wanted to see if naturally combining their DNA together could be a way to help the Demons, to aid them in their growth. The councilmembers at the time rejected the project, so she worked behind their back. She inseminated herself with Demon sperm to see what would happen, since she didn't want to risk anyone else but herself just to prove her theory."

"Your mother did something like that? She sounds insane."

Raewyn laughed, but it bubbled with awkwardness.

"People often call her mad. You wouldn't be the first." She bit at both her lips until her teeth almost cut through them. "My mother said Jabez was born a healthy child, with all his flesh but

with Demon qualities like horns, claws, fangs, and red eyes. A-
and before you say anything, the Demon father was already dead
from trying to attack our people."

Merikh's silence was unbearable, heavily weighing on her.
Her ears flattened as she tried to make herself smaller in his arms
by drawing her knees up.

"My father bonded with my mother years later, and I was
born relatively quickly. We were loved equally. If I got a new
toy, so would Jabez. If I wanted a treat from the market, Jabez
would get one too. They would hold our hands when we walked
the streets, proud of us both. They didn't care he was half-
Demon, only that he was my mother's child and that he seemed
perfectly normal. To me, he was just my older brother, and he
protected me, did everything a good older brother is supposed
to do."

"Then what changed? Something must have happened to
make him believe what he does."

She sighed. "I was four when he got in trouble for biting
another child. He started getting sick, and he was often hooked
up to different medical lines to make him healthy again, but it
only lasted so long."

Raewyn cuddled herself, wishing this story didn't exist. But
it did, and now that she'd started talking about it, she couldn't
stop rambling. Every word made the cold ball in her stomach
grow.

"When he'd get sick again, he'd bite people, and no one
understood why. He didn't seem to understand why either; he
just couldn't help himself. I remember him crying a lot. He kept
saying he couldn't remember why he'd done it. He'd just say his
fangs ached and his stomach hurt, and then suddenly, he was
hurting people. Other children grew afraid of him, and they
would tease him, bully him, and he got into a lot of fights that
would end in the child getting bitten."

"He was a Demon, whether your parents ignored it or not,"
Merikh stated.

"We know that now. It was only after the second time we introduced the Delysians into our city that my parents understood what they'd done wrong. He was eating our diet when he needed meat like they do."

Merikh's scoff cut Raewyn sharply. "Let me guess, he went on a hunger-filled rampage?"

She pursed her lips and shook her head.

"Yes, but also no. After people discovered he was a biter, they became afraid, started resenting his existence. No matter how much my parents tried to shield him from it, they couldn't hide it. More and more, their glares weighed on him, and I watched him turn from the happy big brother I knew into someone hateful. He stopped wanting to play with me and kept himself locked up in our study. One day at school, he just... snapped. He purposely attacked the other students, and he killed all those who bullied him. When the teachers tried to stop him, he attacked them too, until he killed one. He'd eaten many of them, and they just thought he was acting like a Demon because he wanted to become what they were accusing him of."

Raewyn would always remember that day.

The terrified screams of other children who ran away while she was almost trampled in their fright. How five-year-old Raewyn sprinted to the source when she heard it was Jabez. How she paused when she saw him covered in blood at the end of the hallway, and her little heart had dropped to her stomach.

How she sprinted to him, wrapped her arms around his neck, and pleaded for him to stop hurting everyone.

Jabez put his arms around her midsection to hug her, smearing blood all over her clothing as he petted her hair with his cheek. He begged Raewyn to forgive him, said he was sorry for frightening her, that he couldn't bear how others treated him.

That his stomach hurt, and he couldn't handle it anymore.

Raewyn calmed him down, until a teacher snatched her from his arms protectively. He became enraged. Jabez leapt onto the teacher, slit his throat with his claws, then dragged Raewyn out of their school by her hand.

He hid them both away in the dark.

Despite his violence, not once did he ever lay a claw on her. Instead, that day, he petted her hair, cooed at her, and even sang. She cried in confusion at his actions, and worried about how much trouble he would be in because of them.

He protected her from himself, and Raewyn, at the time, had no idea how to protect him from getting in trouble.

"After that, despite fighting for him, our parents were forced to hand him over to the councillors. They put him away, afraid he would continue to be violent, but they didn't want to cast him out into the world to be attacked by Demons."

Raewyn didn't realise she'd started crying until she needed to sniffle because her nose was blocked.

"We were allowed to visit him, and my parents tried everything to find a way to help him, but... after being locked in that cell for too long, he rejected them. He wouldn't allow them to draw blood, wouldn't allow them to try anything. He'd growl and swipe through the bars at anyone who got too close to his cell... even me. He called me pampered, spoilt, and lucky. Said he hated my existence because we were different, and there was no point in pretending anymore. He said I was just feigning care because I was interested in the 'freak.' Truthfully, I just wanted to see my brother because I missed him. My parents and I continued to visit him, but it was never pleasant because he didn't want us there. He said he'd rather be alone."

"He said he escaped with the help of other Demons," Merikh stated. "That they were all caged."

"A few Demons had asked for sanctuary, having eaten enough of my kind who hadn't managed to get to the city and were stranded in other parts of the realm. They acted like us, spoke like us, were truly afraid to be in the wild, since other Demons would attack them because it aided their own growth. So, we allowed them to integrate with our people. Everyone was wary, but we truly hoped one day we could all live in peace together. Yet, just like Jabez, one of them turned on my people after months of eating like us, and they were all put away. We thought it was best if they weren't out in the world, being dangerous. It was only when we figured out they needed to eat meat, which was an absolute abhorrent idea to us, that we understood *why* they weren't able to assimilate with our people beforehand. We don't know how Jabez and those Demons escaped, but they wreaked havoc within the city before we just threw them outside the barrier. He managed to steal a mana stone and opened a stable portal just outside our city. Since then... well, he's been here, and we've been afraid of what we know he can do."

"Our current plan is to make a sun stone with the use of my glamour spell. What are you going to do when he realises it's you trying to fight your way to his portal?"

Raewyn turned her face away.

"I have no interest in seeing him hurt – I know why he turned out this way. It's our fault we didn't do enough for him." Her drying tears bubbled to the surface again. "I-I know he's good, deep down inside. When one of the Demons he let out tried to hurt me, he saved me before snarling at me and killing someone right before my eyes. But I want to go home, that's all I can care about. There's nothing I can do to help him anymore."

"As long as you understand that."

She was shaking now. "If... if we do face him, please don't hurt him."

"I won't make promises I can't keep. It will be us against him, and if he has chosen not to protect you, then you must face the reality that it's your death or his."

"But he was your friend! C-couldn't you speak with him, make him see reason to let us through?"

Merikh let out a deep growl. "He *was* my friend. He no longer is, and if he has truly become a madman out for blood, there is nothing I can do. You must accept this, because I don't want us failing because you have uselessly tried to reach out to him. My friend is dead to me, just as your half-brother is dead to you. Accept it or get yourself killed."

Raewyn covered her face as she sobbed. "My gosh, how can you say something so heartless?"

She'd always held out hope that Jabez could be saved. She didn't want to accept he was lost, not when she could remember him holding her after his massacre when they'd been children, how he'd wrapped her in his arms and soothed her until she stopped crying.

Jabez had always been strange around blood because it made his stomach 'hurt,' but he'd be the first to wrap her scrapes and bruises. Then he would cart her in his arms to their parents, frantically rushing like he worried her leg or hand might suddenly fall off.

He'd played hide and seek with her. He would wear his best outfits and her silly crowns when she wanted to have a tea party. He would hold her hand when she was frightened at night because she'd had nightmares about the Demons outside the walls, knowing she didn't mean him.

Jabez pampered Raewyn even more than their parents. Even when she kicked him in the shin or pulled on his long hair, he'd never once hurt her. He'd never shoved her or ever said a mean word towards her until he was locked away for nearly six years.

Her brother was in there, somewhere.

"Am I being heartless, or am I being *honest*, Raewyn?"

She hated how much that stung because he was likely right. She didn't want to believe Jabez might be lost forever, but the last time she'd seen him still gave her nightmares. The way he'd roared at her, and his hateful glare of red eyes even after he'd saved her; it was burned into her memory.

It had been a little over twenty-two Nyl'therian years since Jabez created his portal, which was three hundred and forty Earth years. She couldn't imagine how much the time dilation difference could possibly be weighing on him. Did time feel like it was moving too fast here? Was he suffering as he watched every day pass by?

She didn't want Jabez to die just because she desperately wanted to go home.

EIGHTEEN

She's Jabez's sister, huh? Merikh thought, his sight yellow as he twisted his head to her for the umpteenth time. *He never mentioned he had a sister.*

Actually, he hadn't mentioned he had a family, one that, supposedly, cared for him.

Merikh figured it was either because Jabez was ashamed, or his time in his 'cage' or 'prison' had twisted his memories. Maybe he hated them so much because he felt as though they'd turned their backs on him, and he refused to accept them as his family.

Whatever the case may be, what were the chances it was *his* sister who found her way to Earth?

What Merikh *did* know was that Jabez was known for going back to the Elven realm. Merikh had no idea what he truly did there, whether it be to stare at the city in resentment or figure out a way inside it, but he did hunt for Elves to eat to increase his magical power.

Full-blooded Demons couldn't cross through. Merikh never ventured through it because Jabez refused to allow him to. Perhaps he'd worried that his 'friend' would leave him permanently.

Maybe he worried Merikh would gain too much magic by eating an Elf and become stronger than him. Jabez didn't like anyone to be more powerful than him.

He was trapped for so long, now he wants to feel like he's the one in control. Hell, neither one of them were really in control of their lives, both somewhat stuck here, never moving forward.

Raewyn's tears eventually eased. The rain had stopped, but she hadn't asked to be moved yet from the cradle he held her in.

Her face was swollen, her nose shinier than normal. It was a testament to how much she truly cared for Jabez, even after everything she'd explained. In its own way, it made him envious; he wished he had someone who would spill tears on his behalf.

The issue was, Merikh could relate to Jabez's hate.

Had Merikh been in Jabez's position, he would have done the same thing. He would have raged upon the city once he was freed from his imprisonment and destroyed everyone he could. He probably would have also saved his siblings while simultaneously turning his back, and heart, on them.

He would have tried to forget their existence, his parents' existence.

He'd technically already done it.

Merikh wanted absolutely nothing to do with his parents nor his brothers. If the situation ever came to it, if it was them or him, Merikh would always choose himself.

He'd been alive the longest.

He'd suffered the longest.

Much of his own suffering had become their knowledge. *He* had been the experimental child. He had been the one his parents stumbled through learning how to be a mother and father with – while failing horribly for so many reasons.

So much of his pain could be blamed on them.

No number of apologies could erase what he'd been through. Nothing Lindiwe, the Witch Owl, or Weldir, the spirit of the void, did could ever make Merikh forgive them.

He was sure it was the same for Jabez.

So, even if she and their parents had done everything with the best intentions, whether or not her version of the story was closer to the truth than what Jabez had told him, Merikh could only side with Jabez – while at the same time wanting to snap his neck and rip his head from his shoulders.

Maybe that would change if Jabez stopped trying to kill him. That was doubtful.

What was bothering him right now, though, was Jabez's actions had made this woman cry. He also didn't like that he'd had a part to play in her tears, and Merikh grumbled to himself.

He didn't often tell himself off, but he was currently doing so as he looked away from her tear-stained face.

Actually, the adorable state of her inflamed cheeks was causing his heart to do this weird squeezing flip in his chest. One minute, his sight was flickering yellow in joy because she looked really cute, and the next, it was a reddish pink due to shame.

He couldn't remember the last time he'd been ashamed.

"Why don't you tell me more about your realm?" he offered, hoping to distract her.

Raewyn shoved the cloak up from underneath to rub her cheek, and then snapped her head away from him.

"No. I don't want to talk to you right now."

Merikh bounced her lightly in his cradle, trying to stir her into being playful like she often was. "Come on. Why don't you explain to me how Jabez was able to steal a portal crystal? I'm curious to know about that."

Her arms folded underneath the cloak, and she lifted her chin even higher. "I don't want to talk to a big jerk."

His fangs parted in disbelief, before he shut them with a clipping noise. "What are you, five? Stop acting like a bratty child."

"Make me," she answered cheekily.

Those two words paired together, with her disobedient attitude, had the strangest heat shooting to his gut. Even his cock tingled, and his tentacles squirmed in reaction.

Merikh's head shot back in surprise at himself, but heat continued to slowly spread throughout his body. He leaned forward with a small growl, unsure if it was in anger for her disobedience, or desire.

"I could, you know," he rumbled.

She had the audacity to roll her starburst eyes. "Oh, yeah. How?"

His fangs parted, before he shut them with another clip and a grunt this time. He didn't know the answer to that question.

He could threaten her, but Raewyn would have to know it was empty, since she was a valuable asset to him right now. He could hurt her, but that would only make her trust him less, and they were already on strange terms.

What do the humans do to their younglings when they're in trouble? Oh yeah, that's right.

"Well, if you continue to act like this, I could spank you for being troublesome."

He didn't understand why she suddenly bit her lips shut, twitching like they wanted to curl in humour.

She finally loosened them and said, "Did you really just threaten me with a good time, Merikh?"

He jerked his head back in outrage. "How the fuck would that be a good time, Raewyn?"

From his knowledge, children hated being spanked! They would cry and scream, promise to never be naughty again, only to be a little shit ten minutes later.

The way she burst out with laughter at his expense wasn't appreciated.

"Holy maiden, you really don't understand the meaning behind what you said, do you?" Raewyn wheezed, trying to get her breaths under control before she bellowed out more laughter. She even kicked her legs and held her stomach like it ached. "Spank me, Merikh. I dare you!"

Is there some kind of joke I'm missing here?

The fact his orbs turned a reddish pink in embarrassment was just as humiliating as her laughter.

He practically dropped her to her feet, making her gasp in surprise, before he ripped his cloak from her.

"You will stop laughing, or else I will make you walk through the rain when it returns."

The night sky was still grey with clouds, and the storm could either fade or return.

"Oh no, whatever shall I do?" she falsely cried as she threw the back of her wrist to her forehead and turned away dramatically. "If you do that, I will have to make us stop moving again because I won't be able to walk from the cold. Whatever shall you do then? Spank me?"

She's mocking me!

Merikh's snarl was feral, a warning for her to stop immediately. He bared his fangs and claws, just as his quills raised to stand to their full height in aggression, tearing at his clothing. His orbs glowed a dangerous colour of red, haloing her in his potential violence.

Instead of being frightened, she turned to him with her hands curled into fists at her sides and leaned forward slightly. With her nose bunched, her teeth gritted in her own anger, she said, "*Grr.*"

Merikh paused, his head tilting to the point it almost went upside down as his orbs flashed to bright yellow. His anger deflated out of him like a swift gust of air, and his quills flopped.

"Did you just..." He twisted his head the other way. "Did you just *growl* at me?"

He stood up straight and covered the end of his snout when a weird noise escaped him.

A smile twitched her lips. "Maybe?"

That weird noise finally finished building, and Merikh let out a warm chuckle, one of adoration for what she'd just tried to do.

"Did you just laugh? Like... an *actual* laugh?" she asked, her sweet voice turning higher pitched in surprise, as though she couldn't believe he was capable of such a positive and pure emotion.

Even her white eyelashes fluttered in disbelief.

Merikh stepped closer. He towered over Raewyn, his snout inches from her nose, as he allowed a loud, deliberate, and menacing growl to bubble from his throat and chest.

Her nose bunched as she gritted her teeth. This time, she shook her head up at him as she said, "Grrrrr."

She sounds like a fucking puppy!

It was hilariously endearing. He didn't know whether to laugh at her or nuzzle her damn beautiful, scrunched-up face.

Merikh snarled again. She did her growl in return, and his hands came up to cup her entire head. He lifted her face, unsure of why he was compelled to bring her closer, but something tender was playing with the strings of his heart.

He snarled again.

When she growled in return, one of his conflicting desires won, and it wasn't his laughter. Merikh rubbed the side of his snout and cheekbone against her cheek and jaw to pet her.

His snarl softened into rumbles before all went silent, except for a few crickets that had decided to come out of hiding.

He hadn't realised his sight had gone black from a delicate emotion closing it until he opened his vision and his usual red flashed. When he registered what he was doing, Merikh grunted and yanked himself away from her.

"Sorry," he rasped, scratching at the side of his neck. "I'm not sure why I did that."

Her eyelids flung open wide. She looked confused and awkward, and he wasn't quite sure if that was a bad thing or not.

"I-it's fine," she said, offering him a reassuring, broken smile.

This day had been filled with so many highs and lows, and Merikh wasn't quite sure how to deal with them.

Their sexual interlude the previous night had not truly left his thoughts, and he was still unsure how he should feel about it. He was well aware he'd allowed himself to get caught up in the moment, her scent, her touch, and the fact she'd been using *his* hand to pleasure herself.

He'd enjoyed every damn second of it, especially because her noises had been cute, her body sensual, and her face beautiful, filled with an erotic, heated gaze. It was hard to believe she'd been the one to instigate it.

He refused to talk to her about it.

He didn't want to know how she felt, not when it could make him reflect negatively on that memory. If she regretted it, she'd ruin it for him, so he'd rather not speak of it.

Then, speaking about his past, learning of her connection to Jabez, and now this embarrassing outburst from him?

Merikh scratched at his neck, kind of wishing he could disappear in that moment as his orbs continued to deepen their reddish-pink hue.

What is wrong with me? I've never acted this way with another.

He didn't allow anyone to get under his skin, instead remaining rather distant with everyone he met. Whether it be a human or Demon, Merikh didn't allow anyone to twist his gut like this.

So why her, of all people?

By the holy Gilded Maiden... I can't believe he just did that to me, Raewyn thought, as he basically shoved her guide cane at her.

"I think you should walk by yourself for a while," Merikh stated in a strained voice before he gave her other hand the end of the guide rope.

Raewyn clutched both items in her hands, her cheeks heating. As soon as she positioned both so she could walk, the rope tugged, and he led the way, while she was a few steps behind.

Tapping the round end of her cane against the ground to make sure she didn't trip over any roots or forest floor debris, she couldn't help lowering her head.

Not in shame or embarrassment, but in hopes of hiding the strange expression twitching her face. *Does he not want to carry me because he feels awkward? Maybe he's feeling too comfortable with me because we keep touching?*

Of course, her thoughts ran rampant. He'd practically nuzzled the skin off her face!

It was Merikh. He didn't seem like the kind of guy to rub against another affectionately, and yet he'd done so to her. All because she playfully growled back at him?

Her heart had nearly tumbled out of her chest, confused but utterly delighted. His bony face was hard, and he'd pressed it rather deeply as he rubbed it against her cheek, but it reminded her of one of the pets they had in Nyl'theria begging for snuggles.

If she hadn't been so startled by it, she may have rubbed back.

He got all shy and awkward.

She'd almost 'awwed' at him when reddish-pink sparks flared in her vision. She found it sweet, but she hadn't wanted to make him feel uncomfortable. She was kind of hoping he'd do it again in the future, but intentionally.

Merikh's insides were just as hard and jagged as his outsides.

To have witnessed even just a shred of tenderness seemed impossible. She wasn't surprised he'd instantly deflected and made them start walking, as if to ignore what had just happened.

Which, of course, had her mentally pouting.

Why is he the one to throw up a wall? He was the Duskwalker, not her, so why was he quick to shove a barrier between them?

Shouldn't she be the one who hated such actions from him?

Instead, she couldn't stop her pulse from racing every time

she felt a tingle on her cheek, like the ghost of his cool touch was freezing it. It only made her remember what had been sliding between her thighs less than a day ago.

Suddenly, her entire pussy went warm in memory.

He'd thrown up a wall after that too, perhaps more than one.

Raewyn clenched her eyes shut. *I feel kind of pathetic,* she thought to herself with a humourless laugh. *He shows me a few moments of kindness, and suddenly, I'm like a creature in heat?*

She knew that wasn't true, since she wasn't trying to climb him now.

Merikh was usually so rough, short, and mean, that when he wasn't, it always took her by surprise. She'd snatched this strange thread in her head that maybe he was only like this with her, but she doubted that was true.

There had to be someone, somewhere, he was affectionate with freely.

She wished the idea didn't make her stomach knot with mild jealousy. Raewyn, despite being a head scientist, had never been special to anyone other than her parents. Even then, her parents had been obsessive with helping Jabez, so much so that, sometimes, Raewyn had been pushed to the side until he came to Earth.

She didn't tell Merikh that because she hadn't wanted him to think she was envious of her half-brother. It was just a fact that, as a young child, she wasn't the interesting one, or the one who needed help, or extra love and care.

She hadn't minded at the time, since she'd been able to garner all the affection she'd wanted from Jabez. She annoyed him, and he let her freely. She'd violate his space, and he'd accommodate her as best as he could. Even though he hated it when she braided his hair and put flowers in it and around his horns, he'd wear them proudly until they all fell out.

She'd had many friends, but they went off to do fun things while she was studying. She adored school, and when Jabez was locked away, she'd thrown herself neck deep into it as a way to cope.

Loneliness wasn't an issue on her radar.

Someone had to care that they were alone to be bothered by such a thing. Still, it didn't mean, in some moments of her life, the space next to her didn't feel a little empty.

That was, until she lost her sight. Then people became overwhelming.

That's why she'd adored Cykran. He wasn't like the other Elysians. He didn't get under her skin, didn't pester her, and if it wasn't for his breathing, she'd barely notice his existence.

I guess I kind of feel that way about Merikh.

Travelling with someone for so long would have bothered her by now, but she wasn't bothered by him at all. She had no filter with him, was as flamboyant as she wanted to be, and he'd just grunt. He never stopped her, didn't seem to care to, and it just made her... worse – which made her want to laugh at herself.

Laugh, until she realised she'd never, not once, been aroused by Cykran.

I really do hope he tries to spank me. The big goof had absolutely no idea what he'd just offered.

Raewyn had only ever been spanked once in her life by a sexual partner, and they went about it so awkwardly it had sapped all the fun from the moment. A light tap, then he checked to make sure she was okay, worried he'd hurt her when that was the point.

She'd almost yawned and fallen asleep.

Raewyn didn't want to be treated like she was made of glass, and yet most of her partners had done so. Everyone seemed to think she was some kind of innocent saint.

She hadn't necessarily done a lot of kinky stuff, although she had done some. She wanted to try new things and see if they were things she was into, experiment with her sexuality. It was hard to do that with a partner who she worried would feel pressured to try for her benefit. What was a little spanking and biting between friends?

Rolling her eyes, she sighed. *Apparently, that's asking for too much.*

She didn't mind a little pain; although she didn't want to mar her near-perfect skin, but there was plenty to do in between that.

A little thankful the wind was brushing towards them rather than from behind, which was likely stopping her scent from wafting towards him, Raewyn sidled a smidge closer.

I wonder what it would be like if he stopped putting up walls and just let things happen. Would Raewyn grow bored because it was no longer exciting, or would his overbearing personality have her wanting more?

Did she want that?

One minute, there was a cut of dread across her chest at the thought of being intimate with him again, and the next, anticipation. Another, hurt when he could be so 'honest', then thankful he didn't want to coddle her feelings. He was mean in one moment, and more considerate than most people the next.

Did she want him to be kinder, more affectionate, perhaps even more sensual? Or stay being a big brute?

He was different from her, from humans, from Demons, from anything she'd ever known. Even just the large space he took up felt different. Overbearing, and somehow warm.

Maybe I shouldn't think about things I may not want.

At a rustle of leaves, she knew he'd moved a low-hanging branch. Her ears twitched, and she ducked to stop it from whacking her in the face when he let it go. It whooshed above her head, a few leaves falling in her hair.

His dark chuckle warmed her, as though he'd known all along that she'd dodge it. Was he testing her reflexes or just trying to distract her?

She answered him with a conniving smile.

Do it again and watch what happens. Her head and heart were all over the place, and she was happy to fight dirty against a bully.

If he was throwing up walls, she'd make it her goal to climb over them until he was truly on the back foot.

Currently, she wasn't even trying. *He better watch out.*

NINETEEN

It hadn't taken long for Raewyn to be carted through the forest once again by Merikh locking her to his side or cradling her. The closer they got to the Veil, the quicker he rushed them.

Considering the forest's occupants, getting closer and then into the safety of his supposed ward didn't sound like a terrible idea. She was a sitting duck out here.

They had been attacked once upon their approach, but Merikh disposed of the Demon swiftly and they moved on. She experienced guilt over its death, since it was likely her scent it'd been chasing.

Knowing they could truly become a person, that they could change and be good, meant it felt almost... wrong.

Explaining that to Merikh had proven pointless, and before long, they were at the very edge of the Veil.

When they arrived, he put her down close to the canyon and reshuffled his bags in preparation to climb down. After placing their bags on the ground to double check everything was secured, he removed his cloak, already informing her it would just get in the way.

Raewyn, on the other hand, covered her nose with her sleeve.

"Holy maiden, that smells awful," she commented with a nasally hint to her voice. "It doesn't smell like this back in Nyl'theria."

"It's Weldir's magic," Merikh stated, as items clanked and clinked together. "There are two types of mists that move through the Veil: a recurrent white one, and a black one."

"And the black one is Weldir?" Raewyn grimaced. "Please tell me it doesn't smell like this down there. I don't think I could bear it for longer than an hour."

It smelt like animal rot, and decay, both sickly sweet and sour. It almost had a fruity scent to it, which only ever emitted from a corpse because of bacteria.

"It doesn't. It's Weldir purifying the souls he's captured, the ones Demons are ferrying into the Veil every time they eat a human. They don't know they're carrying it, but they warp and infect the soul, which he then needs to purify before he can take them to Tenebris for safe keeping. The black mist is both his reach and the physical manifestation of those toxins. The smell is part of that process, and it lifts upwards and fades. It's actually a good thing."

Raewyn tilted her head in his direction. "How do you know all that? Not even I do."

"There's a lot I know that most don't," he answered plainly. "When you've immersed yourself with every side of people, you become privy to shit you wish you didn't learn."

"I couldn't disagree more. Even if it isn't good or feels burdensome to discover, the more knowledge you have, the better."

His growl was quiet, but no less menacing. "That's because you've never learned something you wish you could forget."

Raewyn opened her mouth to disagree and then shut it. *I guess that's true.* She'd never been faced with something so terrible, it weighed heavily on her conscience.

Sure, there was her brother, but she wouldn't forget Jabez no matter what the world threw at her. Even if he had been absent, he was always in her thoughts. A lot of what her scientific experiments were about was bringing him home – preferably not to be buried.

She'd even taken over some of her mother's work on how to splice genomes of her people with Demons, hoping an injection could give them a proper physical form. All tests had come back inconclusive so far.

Letting the conversation go, she turned back to the canyon just beyond her feet. She noticed a red glowing ball in her vision, like there was a spell being used or cast nearby in the direction of rushing water.

There must be a waterfall nearby.

"We know of the Veil," she mumbled as a soft breeze blew around her, threatening to make her gag. "But I don't actually know what it looks like."

"It's nothing but a canyon with thousands of trees. It's not special."

A sigh flittered past her lips. "I wish I could see it."

The silence that bled between them was heavy. Saying things like this often weighed on the person next to her, but she didn't want to hide how she was feeling to protect them.

She wanted to know what the Veil was like. She wanted to know where her brother was living, if it was bright or dreary.

Then, in true Merikh fashion, his big warm hand patted the top of her head. "If I could lend you my sight, I would."

His pat and then slow stroke wasn't condescending. Rather, it was like the awkward attempt of someone who had no idea how to comfort another, but who was at least trying to, like someone saying 'there, there' while internally freaking out.

He would have no idea just how soothing she found his attempt, how much she appreciated it, and that it softened her towards him.

She considered telling him he could share from his perspective, like he'd done in the cave, but decided against it.

I saw something when we'd been sitting on the steps of Ashpine City. For just a second, when she'd first leaned against him, she'd seen the city in a blur of colour.

A small smile curled her lips. *I guess he wanted to share his sight with me then, too.* It was like having a secret peek into his thoughts.

Raewyn turned her head to give a half-hearted thanks, only to jump sideways with a gasp when red flickered in her vision.

It was the strangest sensation, like something cold pierced her eyes. A red light sparked, as though it was right in the centre, before it burst in a circular wave until flames danced on the outside of her vision.

The red flames were constantly in her peripheral, and it took her a moment to realise there was an image in the middle. It was hyper clear in a way that was completely unnatural.

Blinking rapidly, she covered her face, and the image of rocks, greenery, and a blue sky faded. When she moved her hands away, it returned.

This wasn't like before, when Merikh had shared his sight.

It was her own viewpoint. She could change it and move where she focused it, but it was disorientating. It'd been years since she'd truly seen anything physical, and it was an overload to her senses.

The red ring never faded, but it also never impacted her vision. It did make the outer rim of her sight glow, but the middle was utterly clear – clearer than she'd ever been able to see before.

What she saw took her breath away.

When she'd imagined the sky, she hadn't pictured such a light shade of blue. The fluffy white clouds were like those back home, but the singular sun beyond was yellow. The three suns at home were green, blue, and red, which often shaded the world in different hues, depending on which was closer in its yearly rotation.

The lush greens were also varying shades. The grass was lighter than she expected, but some of the trees were darker. Their bark was truly brown, when she'd thought it would have a redness to it, like the sap in her realm.

And finally... the canyon was far larger than she could have

ever expected it to be. It was like a planet-sized giant had
stabbed the ground with a knife and cut through it.

Raewyn let out a sharp gasp and backed away from the edge
Merikh had let her be dangerously close to. The fall looked long
and fatal.

Her gaze shot to a waterfall spewing into the canyon not too
far away. She'd been able to hear it, but she hadn't appreciated
how close it truly was.

Movement caught the corner of her eye as an arm reached
up, covered in a red flannel shirt.

"What the fuck?" Merikh spat, covering his own face with
sharp black claws. "Why can't I see?"

Her lips parted as she, for the first time, truly saw her
travelling companion.

His feet were bare, the flesh of them a dark grey with little
black claws on his toes. His pants were black, loose, fitted to
him by a brown belt. His shirt had been altered on the sides to
fit his massive frame, two triangles of cream cloth making it
bigger, like he'd sewed them on himself.

Short glossy-black fur poked out from his pants and shirt
cuffs.

What had the warmth draining from her expression was
when he removed his dark-grey clawed hands from his head,
and she saw his face.

It was a pure-white bear skull covered in what she could only
imagine was his version of scarring. The dark-brown curling
horns on top of his head almost appeared devilish, like he'd
come from the pits of damnation. His eye sockets were empty
though, when he'd told her he had glowing orbs there.

She covered her eyes once more.

Uttering under her breath, she whispered, "You gave me
your sight?"

She couldn't believe this. She could literally see!

It had been over six Nyl'therian years since she'd been able
to see the sky, the ground, her own hands! She'd almost

forgotten what her hands looked like! She stared down at the backs of them, her eyes widening.

Holy mother... She brought her fingertips closer to inspect them. *I really need to clean my nails.*

It was the weirdest thing to focus on, but it immediately made her smile.

"What do you mean, I gave you my sight?" Merikh growled, before blindly reaching in her direction. "Give it back."

Raewyn's feet moved of their own accord as she stepped back to escape his reach. She hadn't meant to, she really hadn't, but she didn't want him to take it back... yet?

When he stepped forward a second time, her heart swelled with guilt as she purposefully stepped back again. She panted as anxiety gripped her sternum.

The way Merikh's bony head twisted was unnatural. It tilted until it was nearly upside down.

His following snarl sent a spike of fright through her, but she quickly squashed it down. He knew, whether because he missed her twice or because he could hear rock shifting under her feet, that she was retreating.

"Give it back, Raewyn," he demanded, stepping further away from the bags he'd been checking.

His head snapped back into an upright position, as did his spine, as he towered over her. He practically blocked out the beautiful sun, casting an ominous shadow over her.

He was so... massive. He was wider than she'd pictured, and his imposing skull had the ability to loom over her with the height difference.

There were moments in time when someone recognised they were making the wrong decision, were doing the wrong thing. It didn't stop them from making it; they were just aware of it.

This was one of those times for Raewyn.

Despite how deeply her guilt and shame twisted her stomach, she still shook her head. Raewyn dropped her cane.

"No," she whispered.

Raewyn didn't want to give it back.

When he parted his deadly fangs, his snarl lowering in depth as it echoed, she darted into the forest.

As if she was going to give him back his sight! She could freaking see! She'd searched for a cure this entire time, and it had been floating right in her face for the past month and a half.

His roar made her shoulders turn inward. She risked looking over her shoulder as she sidestepped tree after tree to see him knocking into multiple as he gave chase. She was used to navigating environments sightless; Merikh wasn't.

That didn't make him any slower, since he just rebounded and kept moving. He even trampled a bush that would have tripped her.

Raewyn squeaked when she thought he was gaining on her.

If I can see, I don't need him anymore. I can find all the ingredients I need by myself. If he has a mana stone, then there must be more. She pumped her arms as she sprinted, and her soul took flight. *I can walk through the human towns easily now!*

She no longer needed Merikh's guidance or help.

She was no longer trapped, confined to her situation, because it had drastically changed.

If she played her cards right, she could wear him out today and pluck the blue jewel she'd seen on the crown of his forehead. *I can be home within the month, I'm sure of it!*

She could make the sun stone, run through the Veil with it as protection, and then storm Jabez's castle – once she found it. She may even be able to talk to her brother, perhaps even change his mind, bring him home.

She could stop the war he was obviously trying to incite.

The possibilities were endless.

Though she could hear Merikh's snarls, not once did they frighten her. Instead, she swiftly moved through the forest, as if she'd always lived in it. She breathed it, sensed it through her feet, her fingertips, how it swirled with wind and blew through the core of her being.

She reached up to grab a low-hanging branch and used it to swing herself across a fallen tree trunk. The impact to her bare feet when she landed had her catching herself on her knees, but she grinned at the slight lance that radiated up her ankles.

I can't remember the last time I moved like this.

The wind cut through her clothing, her speed so fast, it lifted the ends of her braided hair as they tapped against the back of her shoulders. It was chilly, but exhilarating, and her movements warmed her through it.

There were little yellow and white flowers littered on the ground here and there. She'd remembered smelling them as they came through near here.

She looked up, watching as the canopy of leaves glittered with the sunlight poking through the gaps. The bark was rough, and momentarily touching it to catch herself or push off a tree reminded her of how much she'd enjoyed playing.

The faster she went – not having to be cautious – had her laughing, as she could examine each hazard as she approached it.

Probably not the wisest thing to do with the Duskwalker still steadily chasing her, but she couldn't deny how much *fun* she was having.

Not once had it occurred to Raewyn that she should be running from him because her first glance at him had been scary, or that she should be fleeing because he was a monster.

She should be running away from what he was, not because she wanted to selfishly keep what he'd accidentally given her.

For the first time in years, Raewyn was able to push her body to its limits. The longer she ran, unused to it, the more her lungs tightened painfully, her thighs stinging with the strain. She revelled in the ache.

She jumped to grab a different low-hanging branch, then climbed on top of it. She crouched down onto it, waiting for Merikh to pass underneath her. She needed a few seconds to catch her breath, to ease the rapid heave of her lungs and the beat of her heart going into overdrive.

Her eyes nearly bulged out of her skull when he skidded to a halt between the trees, haloed by a glow of dancing red. She'd expected him to run off into the forest, allowing her to backtrack and then eventually lose him.

He'd been following her scent, and when it had cut off, he, too, had stopped. He may have even heard her quick huffs.

Him stopping wasn't what had her eyes widening.

It was the fact that all his clothing was gone, and he had been running on all fours. Jutting through the black fur on his back were hundreds of grey quills with sharp, dark points. They appeared deadly, sticking up in obvious aggression, and were just as nasty looking as the ones protruding from the backs of his forearms and calves.

His grey tail curled before flicking to the side, as though the black tuft of fur at the end was weighty.

The noises that came from him were animalistic; a rabid and enraged predator sniffing and woofing like a bear.

"I know you're there," he growled.

Raewyn shivered, never having heard his voice drop so low and split between tones – like he was so close but also far away. There was almost an echo to it, which just made it that much more unnerving.

No wonder the humans were afraid of his kind if they were able to run like this, sound like this, *hunt* like this.

So why wasn't she afraid?

No, she was the opposite of afraid.

Excited, exhilarated, focused. She was the prey hunting the beast.

His bony white skull turned one way as he huffed out snorts, sniffing the area. It turned the other way, then creepily lifted in her very direction.

"Found you."

Raewyn squealed and leapt to another tree when he shot for the branch she'd been resting on. *He reached it in one leap!* His claws had been millimetres from slicing her, had she not jumped. He didn't even grab the branch; he merely sliced it in half with a distinct *crack*. It'd been thick and strong enough to support her weight!

She continued to leap from tree to tree as Merikh followed on the ground.

"Even without my sight, I'm faster than you," he snarled, just as he climbed the side of a tree she was clambering up to escape.

She was lighter, and she'd been hoping to evade him by going up. His weight bent it, and she dropped herself to the low branch of another tree when she had to hang from the bowing trunk.

Raewyn didn't respond. What could she say in this situation?

The crunch of bark being pulverised under his claws twitched her ears, and she began having a strange reaction to it. They sounded sharp, like they had the ability to rip anything into shreds. Yet, the closer he got, the more her nipples hardened at each crack, each slice.

Either her fight-or-flight reaction was acting up, or she was turned on by being chased. The more excited she got, especially when she was *forced* to jump to the ground because the closest tree was too far away even for an Elysian, the more heat pooled in her stomach.

Her breaths were growing into pants, and a flush spreading across her entire body warmed her against the chill of her speed, cutting through the wind.

Raewyn ducked just as Merikh was at her back, and his claws stabbed into a tree trunk above her. She somersaulted to the side, got to her feet, and didn't look back as she ran around the tree to go back the way they just came.

I shouldn't have waited for him to run off. She realised that now.

At this rate, she'd tire out before he did.

She was also losing her enthusiasm for being chased.

Suddenly, she wanted to be caught, her mind snagging on the random thought of him grabbing her by the ankle and dragging her beneath him.

Trapping her in, pinning her down, his orange and cinnamon scent washing over her as he let out those thrilling snarls and growls.

Raewyn licked at her lips before wiping them with the back of her wrist. Her lips were parched, but her mouth was damp.

Would he eat her? Would he rip her clothes off and take her against the ground hard and fast in a fury? The unknown was freakish, both frightening and frighteningly arousing.

Merikh let out a roar not far behind her, and her pussy clenched so hard, she stumbled. Her gasp was so sharp that she almost missed what she thought might have been a groan coming from him.

Can he smell that I'm getting turned on? Because Gilded Maiden help her, it was leaking from her, coating her inner thighs. It somehow made running faster, now that her thighs were lubricated.

Something is wrong with me. How could she go from running away so she could steal his sight, to wanting him to catch her? *How can I want him after finding out what he looks like?*

She'd had an inkling from what she'd detected on the rare occasion by touching or bumping into him, but it couldn't compare to the otherworldly oddity of what was actually *there*.

Why did her breasts have to suddenly ache and feel heavy because of *him?* Why did her stomach clench, causing her core to spasm, because of Merikh in beast mode?

Any *sane* person would be freaking out right now, and she was having the opposite reaction.

It all came back to that night in the cave. Whether she wanted to be or not, she was attracted to Merikh's brutish personality and hard body. She wouldn't have ground against his hand while sleeping in his embrace if she wasn't.

"Stop," he demanded, but it was shaky, like he'd said it with

a deep shudder wracking his entire body. Even his huffs were louder and breathier than before.

Okay, he could definitely smell how turned on she was.

Does that mean I can stop without being mauled to death?

No matter how much she ran, she wasn't going to get away. He was surprisingly agile, even without his sight, and he was obviously used to running through a forest. Even if he bumped into something, he just charged on. He was a rolling boulder, annihilating everything in its path.

Even though the idea of being grabbed by the ankle nearly had her biting her lip, she didn't want him to accidentally hurt her. He'd already told her the scent of blood might make him go crazy.

If he grabbed her or even tackled her, she could accidentally be cut.

So, Raewyn did the safest thing she could think of.

After running for a little longer, right when he was only a few dozen feet behind her, she picked a thick trunk. Raewyn turned, slammed her back against it, and waited for him.

"Merikh," she called, huffing wildly. "I stopped running."

She clenched her thighs at the image of him running on all fours in her very direction. He was almost a black blur with a floating white skull. Within *seconds,* he was directly in front of her, his claws stabbing into the tree, causing bark to flake off underneath the points of them.

The heat radiating off him was intense, waving across her body every time his chest expanded and decompressed. It was even hotter coming from his parted fangs, and the sweetness of the scent in his breaths brushed over her.

The end of his bony snout was inches from her nose as she looked up at him. He was visibly quaking. In rage, or perhaps his desire, she couldn't tell. She did duck her eyes down to his groin, but other than a noticeable bump coming from within him, his cock wasn't exposed.

If she hadn't felt it rub against her, touched it, had it slipping between her thighs, she wouldn't have thought he had one.

A constant growl emitted from the back of his throat, and her ears tingled.

Her stolen sight flicked back up to his bony face.

Now that he was right in front of her, she expected her senses to come back and for her to be scared, wary, or at least put off. Instead, she was falling deeper into whatever spell he had cast over her.

If it weren't for his claws cutting deeper and deeper, or his quills remaining sharp and raised over his body, she would have thought he was calming.

Merikh seemed on the very edge of his tether, trying to rein in his emotions but failing.

Everything hung on whatever she chose to do next.

Raewyn tentatively reached out to place her hands on the bridge of his snout. There was a cut there that looked like a sword wound, and he had four claw marks cutting down over his right eye socket.

It was the face of someone who had been hurt by two different kinds of people.

"So this is what you look like," she whispered around soft but quick breaths.

What she examined was magnificent.

Whether it was her touch or her words, one of them snapped him into action. Within the span of a heartbeat, Merikh wrapped his massive, clawed hand around her throat and lifted her to the tips of her toes.

"Don't ever fucking run from me again," he snarled, a purple tongue coming out to slide across his sharp fangs. Then, he actually squeezed her throat, and her entire body pulsated while her tongue fell forward to pant erotically. *"Because next time, I might just kill you. Now give me back my sight."*

Raewyn's sight flickered. As it dimmed, two red orbs began to form where his empty eye sockets were. Just before her sight completely faded, she watched the fiery vortex of his orbs turn to bright purple.

Once again, Raewyn was faced with the same darkness as usual.

She didn't have time to digest that loss as her hands fell to rest against his firm chest. Not when Merikh leant forward and slipped his tongue from right under her chin, all along her jaw, to her ear. A sharp moan caught in her throat.

"Why the hell do you have to smell so good?" he groaned, which conflicted with the growl that continued to rumble from him. Even his monstrous voice softened but didn't fully disappear. *"You smell very wet here."*

The gasp that came out of Raewyn was drowned out by the moan that followed it as he shoved his fingers between the tight press of her thighs. Her hands came down to grip his, which only stretched her neck further in his chokehold as she ground into him.

"What's with this expression?" he asked with a shudder. *"Who the fuck gets turned on by a Duskwalker chasing them?"*

Raewyn shivered. *Me, apparently,* she thought, wishing it wasn't true. It was impossible to deny it.

She could feel it in the way her wet pussy spasmed from his tongue, her ears twitched from his deep voice right next to her head, and the way her nipples and clit both pounded at the same time.

She could even sense it in the way the tiny veins in her wrists fluttered faster and harder than normal.

His forefinger lifted from the hold on her throat, and he slipped his fingertip and claw between her parted lips. Her tongue brushed against the hard point as the tip of his snout ran up the side of her face, caressing it, before he drew back slightly.

Then his voice softened a few decibels as he said, *"We should not be doing this."* Merikh retracted his hand, even as she clung to his wrist and tried to pull it back. *"Shut your mouth, Raewyn."*

"Make me," she rasped. Then she bit down on his finger to

stop it from escaping, licking the tip and the claw.

His snarl was the only warning she got.

Raewyn's eyelids, lazy from desire, shot open when he curled his finger inside her mouth, shoved her teeth apart, and something filled the gap. It was soft, long, flexible, and it tasted so sweet her mind instantly dissolved.

Merikh's fangs scraped both her cheeks as his tongue swirled within the cavern of her mouth. Her mewl was stifled as she tried to playfully twirl hers in return.

He removed his hand from her throat, and before Raewyn knew it, he'd lifted her skirt and her legs along with it. With her thighs spread, he shoved his big frame between them, and *slammed* her against the tree. The wind knocked out of her as a gasp, and he pushed more of his tongue deeper.

His hands slid up until he was grabbing the very apex of her thighs, where they met the softness of her backside. His claws dug into her flesh, and he growled, grinding his groin directly against the spread lips of her pussy.

Her legs twitched as he ground again, and something wet and hard came from him.

Raewyn felt the swirl of his tentacles release, and his cock shot forward, fast and hard, against her unwitting clit, grazing his entire length against it. She tried to throw her head back to whimper, but Merikh's mouth followed.

"Stay." She couldn't believe he'd spoken with his tongue in her mouth! *"Your saliva tastes delicious."*

He kept thrusting against her, making her eyelids shudder closed and her legs twitch. Her pussy tingled, aching and needy. His tentacles wrapped around her thighs, but they stretched whenever he pulled back.

The groove underneath his cock caressed her clit from all sides, and the three ridges made her want to scream out already.

"Why do you keep doing this to me?" he practically whined before his right hand moved up to knead her backside. His palm was so warm and calloused that she wiggled in delight.

He was making it sound as though it was her fault! She could say the same thing. He was the one who kept turning her on when she really shouldn't be.

Rather than fight this, she went to wrap her arms around his neck but was forced to retract them when his quills made it difficult. There were a few short ones just beneath his skull.

Instead, she wrapped them around the back of his head. His hard chest massaged her breasts, finally giving them some attention, while his thick stomach caved hers in.

She didn't mean to bring his fangs closer, but they pressed more firmly against her, threatening to cut into skin.

Merikh must have taken that as an invitation because one minute, he was swirling his tongue within every crevice of her mouth, and the next, she was swallowing it.

So deep. His tongue is so deep. She arched, her knees lifting up in surprise, just as he let out the most wonderous groan.

I'm going to come... Her pussy clenched and stayed tight as he thrust faster. *Holy maiden. Oh, I'm coming!*

Whatever noise came out of her was so damn obscene even Raewyn was surprised by it. She didn't know what she did after that, whether she clawed him, bit his tongue, kicked her legs. All she could perceive was her own orgasm leaking from her in a hot, wet squelch, while both his cock and tongue moved back and forth without relenting.

Only when she went lax, did Merikh draw back his tongue. She panted heavily when he slipped it from her and drew it over the corner of her mouth, across her jaw, and then down her neck.

"This is not enough," he rasped as he ground his cock harder against her. *"I need more."*

"Yes," Raewyn whispered, not quite sure what she was agreeing to.

Just as she was spreading her thighs even further and bucking against him, hoping he might try to sink that big, girthy cock inside her, Merikh dropped her legs. She stumbled, barely able to stand after her orgasm.

Her discontent was short-lived as he turned her around. He lifted her dress with his right hand and pulled it to the side, pinning it with his palm against the tree trunk. His other arm dived underneath her skirt, shoved up, and grasped her breast with a rough knead.

He used his arm squishing her against his torso to lift her to her toes. She assisted by arching her back to tilt her hips and give him better access, resting her arms against the rough bark of the tree.

All her inhibitions had disintegrated. Not once did she think about the fact that they were outside, doing this in the forest, not far from the Veil's cliff edge. She wondered what she would have done if a Demon came along, but right now, she didn't think anything could stop them.

Merikh's cock slid between her cheeks, lubricant smearing all over them, and the air brushing over it had a wonderful shiver tickling her spine.

Then it shoved between her thighs. The head caught along the slit of her pussy, and she bit her lips in disappointment. *I thought he was going to put it inside me!*

"Keep your legs together," he demanded. *"Nice and tight for me."*

She gave a little nod and clenched her thighs just as his tentacles wrapped around her hips from behind.

However, the moment he started moving, Raewyn noticed the difference in him gliding the top of his shaft against her rather than from underneath. Her knees buckled, Merikh forced to hold her up as his ridges petted her clit over and over again.

They were spongey so they didn't hurt, but they flicked the sensitive nub instead. She squirmed; she couldn't help it. Raewyn lowered her left hand so she could gouge her nails into her stomach, wanting to shield her pussy when it was too intense.

Her lips parted as she let out cry after cry. Her ears tipped back, and her nose tingled as a wild haze settled over her. She even started grinding in the opposite direction to him, making it faster.

She completely leaned against the tree as she sagged.

"I said keep your legs tight!" he growled, deepening in treble, right before his thin tail coiled around her legs so he could force them together himself.

His hips picked up speed, snapping against hers harder in what felt like anger at her disobedience. His hand wrapped around her breast, too big and struggling to play with her, kneading in rough grabs.

His cock feels so good. A cock isn't supposed to feel this good just rubbing against my clit. She kept trying to rock on it while bowing her back further and further. *What would it feel like inside me?*

The more she tilted her hips, the more the head gouged against her entrance whenever he pulled back, only to push forward.

In, she thought. She wished her voice would work, but she could do little else but pant. *Please go inside.* If she could just line them up, maybe she could get the head to prod deeper against her entrance, where she could shoot her hips back and mount it. *I need it inside me.*

She didn't care if it hurt, if it over-stretched her, ruined her. Her core felt empty; it needed something, anything.

"Your cunt is so wet that my lubricant feels slicker than normal."

He grabbed her hair with the hand holding the end of her dress up and shoved it to the side. The strands pulled on her scalp in delicious pain.

Then he glided his fangs over the nape of her neck as he parted his jaws and sinfully rasped, *"Let me give it something to suck on."*

The top two prehensile tentacles currently wrapped around her backside slithered between her cheeks. Their little tips tickled her entrance before they both shoved inside her at the same time.

"You were fine with my fingers, so how about these?"

Raewyn choked, her entire body seizing. Her knees buckled inwards, her hand raking at her stomach shot up and back as she attempted to grab the short fur on his chest, clawing at him.

The limbs were tapered, the tips thin, the bases thick enough to stretch her. They wriggled inside her, repeatedly pressing against the front of her channel like they were desperately searching for something to grip. What they did keep gripping, keep assaulting, keep twisting and swirling against was her G-spot.

Within seconds of having them inside her, Raewyn let out a haunting scream. She milked them, her channel quivering as she came. From her clit to her inner walls, she was in utter bliss.

By his gruff voice echoing through her orgasm, she registered he'd said something. Raewyn shuddered, even though she couldn't make it out, too busy experiencing every nerve ending in her body sparking to life all at once.

Something about her smelling good, maybe even wanting to taste it?

Don't stop. Raewyn squirmed, twisted, and turned. At one point, she knew her feet had left the ground, as her knees momentarily lifted. He just held her up, her slick running down her legs, tickling her all the way to the sides of her ankles.

Something on his cock was spreading her thighs apart, a ring-like ball that thickened, but his tail kept them together. It seemed too big to pass through properly, but she barely registered it.

Then, just when she thought she'd disintegrate, her ongoing orgasm starting to dry out like she had nothing left to give, Merikh shoved forward and paused.

His tentacles pushed down as the ones around her legs clamped onto her. Then, his entire cock swelled, beginning to pulsate and throb. Merikh's tail and hands tightened on her as he shook her with his intense shudders.

Her ears picked up the heavy splatter that hit the tree in front of them, as well as the woofing roar he released up towards the canopy over them. Raewyn felt each time he released a heavy spurt of seed, heard the liquid splatter that followed.

He gave little absented-minded thrusts, soft and shallow.

He's coming. There was a cock between her thighs coming, and the idea of it twisted her mind and made her nipples ache.

His scent, his roar, his heat, all of it made her breath hitch, and his ending groan had her eyes closing in contentment.

I don't care if it's wrong. It was amazing.

TWENTY

As the last quake rippled across Merikh's flesh, causing his quills to quiver, his thoughts and body split apart into two fragments of warring internal conflict.

He was satisfied, since he'd emptied himself against the tree supporting them. He'd practically watered it in his seed, his release heavy and mind scrambling.

Yet, his cock was still unbearably hard, and his tentacles were still gripping. He wanted to turn this woman, lift her, then shove her body down on top of his aching shaft. He wanted to screw her until neither one of them could move.

The scent of her arousal, her orgasms, her skin and hair – it was all heady and intoxicating.

The moment he'd gotten a whiff of it while chasing her, his mind had split between hunting his prey to devour it, and hunting his prey to mount it.

While he was in his enraged state, *nothing* had ever brought him back to reality. Usually, he was a mindless, hungry, uncontrollable beast – Merikh always let those squeezing invisible hands massaging his brain win. Willingly, he gave himself over to the worst of what he was.

Her scent was the only thing that truly saved her today, and currently, it was poisoning him.

She reeked of it, of her own sex. It was dizzying.

He didn't understand it. *Do all Elves produce this kind of intense scent?* He'd been fine around the hundreds of humans he could smell fornicating through the walls of their houses. Although pleasant in their own way, it never bothered him before.

He'd never been frenzied for it, desperate to smell it, taste it, feel it, have it cover his fur until it masked his own damn scent.

What the fuck was she getting all hot and turned on for? Being chased? Sleeping in a cave? He wondered if it had something to do with him, or if Elves were usually such perverted, horny creatures.

Whatever the case may be, it was fraying his nerves.

He liked being in control of his desires, or just himself, until he decided to let his aggressive instincts take control. This? This he wasn't accustomed to, this he didn't know how to navigate, and he didn't know if he particularly liked it.

Merikh had no interest in obtaining a bride. He'd rather not wish for things he couldn't have, because if he were being honest with himself, what idiot would agree to bond with him? Putting aside the fact he was hateful and spiteful, he was a Duskwalker, for pity's sake.

He was a monster – deemed ugly, disgusting, and despicable by every sentient creature, humans and Demons alike.

He wouldn't start feeding those fantasies when only a fool would think it was possible, especially with such a *bewitching* female. He was sure the moment they were in her realm, she'd stop becoming aroused in his presence when she had her own kind to fornicate with.

After meeting two of them – her and Jabez – he was under the impression they were all pretty fuckers. Why would she choose him when there were better options?

He didn't want to be a masturbatory tool for a selfish Elf who had no idea how her actions might be hurtful to those who had given up hope. He'd given up on the idea of friendship, lust, love, or anything pleasant at all.

Huffing deeply, Merikh pulled back his cock to release it from the lovely press of her thighs, hoping it would go soft now that it was no longer trapped. His tentacles pulled out of her, and she gave a mewl that made him growl in frustration when his cock jerked in excitement.

I need to calm down.

He removed his hand from under her dress and placed it against the tree. The other let go of her gathered skirt so he couldn't see her supple, round arse anymore.

Raewyn didn't turn around, instead choosing to rest her entire upper body against the tree trunk. Her contentment only infuriated him more.

At least he hadn't killed or harmed her. He needed her to escape this vile world, so something truly positive had come from this.

He still couldn't believe they'd done this with Demons possibly close by.

However, salvation was on the horizon. Maybe if he stopped touching her, stopped having to be anywhere near her, her pestering arousal and his own would cease. They were too familiar, constantly in each other's presence.

Once they were in his home, he could finally have some space, some semblance of normalcy.

She ran away from me.

That was something that made his cock soften and caused his orbs to shift to blue – a colour he was used to seeing.

It was to be expected, really, but it just made him unable to truly trust her. They'd made a deal; he would help her get home, and he'd been planning to adhere to that promise. Merikh didn't often make bargains with others because he had a weird compulsion to submit to them.

Perhaps, in their own way, even verbal contracts were something Duskwalkers were stuck obeying. Their magic was completely built on sacrifices and bargains.

Yet, when given the choice, Raewyn had opted to fuck off

into the forest. Not only that, she'd chosen to do so with his sight! She'd attempted to steal from him.

Even if he understood why, it didn't negate the fact it would have made him vulnerable in a world where he had no one to turn to. He couldn't turn to anyone for help, for guidance – whereas she could at least turn to a human.

He had no one, even with his glamour.

Merikh likely would have found himself dead within a week's time, with the way Demons would hunt him. They'd faced eight on their travels since the moment they'd set off together.

Even if Raewyn came across guileless, with her angel-like appearance and soft personality, she'd shown him today she could be just like every other despicable creature in this world: cruel, selfish, and untrustworthy.

Still in his monstrous form, he wrapped his hand around her throat and turned her enough so he could see her expression.

"How long have you known I can give you my sight?"

She'd only begun travelling with him in the beginning because she'd thought he was human, but what about when he'd revealed what he was? Did she always know and had been waiting for the perfect time to steal it from him? Had this been her intention all along, the reason she was being so obedient with him?

"Only today," she answered in a small, raspy voice, broken from crying out so much.

It shouldn't make his skin tighten with a thrill that he'd brought her to this sloppy state.

His orbs flared crimson. ***"Don't lie."***

She gave a mewl and a shiver, and he tilted his head in confusion at her reaction.

"I'm not," she whispered. "B-but I knew you could share your sight with me from the cave."

"What do you mean?"

She licked at her lips nervously. "You... uh, when we were

intimate in the cave, I was able to see everything from your perspective. Y-you didn't give me your sight like today, just shared your own."

Merikh's gaze slipped to the side as he thought.

I had wanted to lend her my sight today. When he'd said it to her earlier, he'd truly meant it. *What had I wanted last time?*

It hit him.

Fuck. She'd looked so erotic beneath me that I wanted her to see how perverse she looked with my cock sliding over her.

So, he could do both? That was at least interesting to know. He generally discovered the capabilities of his magic through accidents, by deeply wanting something.

"Merikh..."

"What?" he bit, his settling quills lifting suddenly. He hadn't liked the way she said his name, all soft and gentle.

"I'm really sorry," she apologised in a small voice. "I don't know what came over me."

And just like that, the deliciously wicked scents in the air he'd been secretly huffing in became unpleasant, as did the wetness of her orgasms clumping the fur around his groin.

He let go of her, resisting the urge to toss her against the tree supporting her. He averted his gaze when the reddish pink of shame lifted into his orbs. He hadn't had this many orb colour changes in years!

At least his tentacles had swirled protectively and pulled his cock back within his seam.

"It's fine. I didn't stop either."

Raewyn finally turned, and in his peripheral, her brows drew together tightly in either deep thought or confusion – maybe even both. Then, her lips parted, and she fidgeted slightly, as though she was feeling bashful.

"Oh," she said before wringing her hands together. "No, not that. This was fine. I wanted it. I mean I'm sorry about running away."

Merikh grunted, unsure of how to respond.

The petting was okay? What was he meant to make of that? She was just adding a deeper layer of confusion to the whole situation.

Raewyn's head lowered. "Doing something like that... It's not something I would usually do. It's just..." She scratched at the side of her neck before toeing the ground. "I've spent the last six years trying to reverse the magic that took away my sight, and when I could see... something just came over me and I wanted to keep it. I'm really sorry. It must have been very upsetting for you."

Must have been? It *was* upsetting, and he was still rightfully angry about it. He didn't know if he could trust the words that just came from her pretty lips – the ones he'd just had his tongue delving between.

He was conflicted about them, and he scratched at his own neck. She was the second person who had ever apologised to him, but she may be the first he could forgive. He didn't want to, though, as he wasn't a very merciful creature.

"Whatever. It's fine."

"Please, I really mean it," she said as she bounced forward to grab his arm.

"Don't touch me!" he roared as he leapt away from her, causing her to stumble on her feet.

Her starburst eyes filled with tears, and he didn't like the way it made his damn chest feel. Right now, his emotions were all over the place. He took in a deep, calming breath.

"Currently my quills are extended. Don't try to grab at me when I'm in an agitated state." Then, just for good measure so she understood, he added, *"That also includes sexually."*

Raewyn had almost grabbed his arm, and with the way she'd been coming at him, she would have impaled both her hands. Although he could heal that kind of injury, he didn't particularly want to walk around with bleeding hands – that's if he didn't eat her because of her blood scent.

When her face lifted in his direction, he averted his gaze once more when she appeared relieved.

"Give me a moment and I'll revert to my normal form. Then I'll be able to carry you into the Veil before a Demon comes."

The sun was still bright, but they were just asking for trouble remaining in one spot much longer. He'd need to find where he left their bags.

"So, you forgive me?" she asked, a beseeching and pleading smile lifting her face – one that made it hard to deny.

He wasn't sure if he'd forgiven her or not, but at least he discovered this kind of magic was something he could do. He wouldn't make the same mistake twice, and she would have to know that.

"Sure," he grumbled with uncertainty, just as his clothing seeped through his fur and covered his body once more. The change also soothed his quills and made his mind feel more composed. His voice had returned to normal when he said, "Why not?"

Raewyn tried not to scream as Merikh jumped from cliffside boulder to cliffside boulder – she really did. It was just every time her stomach dropped, she thought her heart was going to give out.

He was cradling her in his strong arms, and although she was secure within them, it didn't stop her mind from thinking of the worst. One wrong move, one underestimated drop, and they'd go plummeting. He could even slip and toss her by accident.

"Control your fear," he demanded when he landed on another boulder. "Even a small amount will attract Demons."

"I'm trying!" she whined. "Are you sure there is no other way?"

Merikh leapt and spoke at the same time. "Not one that would be this fast. The next walking point is a three-hour walk from my home, so you would be travelling on the outskirts of the Veil's forest for that long."

Getting eaten by Demons or splattering against the ground – those were her options? *At least I'll probably die if I hit the ground.* The idea of being eaten alive was horrifying.

"C-can you go slower?" He was barely giving her a moment to adjust to the next landing before he would run off the edge!

"We're almost there. Stop your fussing."

Then, just like that, they were at the bottom.

Merikh never entered the forest. He took them around the border towards the red glow she'd been able to see from above. The closer they got, the more she could make out what it was, hear the crashing of water.

Before them was a half-kilometre-tall magical dome with a multi-pointed star. There were two rings, one a border ring and the other one slightly further in, with star-like symbols encompassing it. There were other, smaller circles within the border rings.

It all glittered red.

The dome didn't appear fully formed, since it was pressing against the cliffside, but she bet it went all the way through the rock to stop Demons from clawing their way in.

"Your magic is the same colour as your orbs?" Raewyn asked, already concluding his base orb colour was red.

"Yes. It's the same for all Duskwalkers," he answered plainly before he walked straight through the dome's edge. "The fact that you can see it means you won't accidentally wander out of it."

Raewyn expected to feel a brush of coolness, or at least something to signify that she passed through his ward, but nothing happened.

Like she was a hot coal he'd been holding for far too long, Merikh placed her on her feet. He backed up enough that the heat constantly radiating off him dissipated.

The handle of her cane gently tapped against the side of her wrist, and she grabbed it.

The air here was cool and fresh, like it was filled with condensation. Even the grass beneath her feet was soft and moist, and she dug her toes into it to explore the plush carpet of life.

"Be careful where you walk. I'm sure you can hear the waterfall, but there's a large lake at the bottom of it that makes up two-thirds of the area."

The waterfall's soft melody wasn't harsh or overbearing. It was just enough to create a pleasant background noise, like moderately heavy rainfall. Raewyn's lids lowered as she listened, pleased.

"To your left are two trees with some boulders underneath them for you to sit on, if you choose to. To the right is the entrance of my cave."

Her heart swelled. *His home sounds pretty.*

"Can you show me?" she softly asked, wanting to know if what she was picturing was right.

"No," he flatly rejected.

Raewyn's cheeks puffed outwards as she pouted. "Oh, come on. Please show me?"

His chuckle was dark, and it, along with his words, stung. "No. I don't trust you."

Maybe what she was asking for was too much after she'd tried to run away with it, but she really wanted to see! He was the only person, not just in this world but in so many others, who could actually give her a brief moment of sight. The least he could do was share it with her for just a second.

"I said I was sorry." She turned to him with her hands on her hips, a little awkwardly with the one holding her cane.

"I forgave you, but it doesn't mean I trust you. Those are two different things."

With an internal groan, she grabbed at his shirt and pulled on what she thought was the front of it. She shook him.

"Just do it, you big cranky pants! You don't even have to give it to me. You can show me through your perspective while keeping it to yourself."

She was accustomed to him giving her light growls, so she 'grrred' him back this time. He let out a warm chuckle, and she stopped shaking him when her ears went hot. He really seemed to like it when she did that.

"Fine, here."

He placed his massive hand on the top of her head, and Raewyn smiled as she waited. She kept her face pointing towards him, and after a few moments of him thinking – likely trying to figure out the spell – the first thing she saw was her own expression.

Raewyn looked like a mess. There were sticks and leaves in her hair, as well as a dirt smudge across her cheek. *Holy maiden. I need a bath, immediately. I can't believe he touched me like this!*

Then, his sight drew away from her and spanned over the entire area.

The Veil looked spooky, despite the treetops glowing with the sun shining over them. It was far denser than the forest above, and the white mist made it appear haunted and dreary.

She could do nothing to change the focal point as he drew his gaze over the three boulders he'd spoken about earlier. They were between two trees relatively close together and weren't far from the lake's edge.

The water was a crystal-clear blue, clean and not muddy at all, from what she could tell. Already, she wanted to go for a dip and scrub her body from head to toe. The water raining into it was frothy near the bottom, and it sprayed a mist over the water's surface, seeming to blow into the Veil to make it more prominent through the trees.

Then, finally, the decently sized entrance of his home came into view. A cream burlap curtain was latched to it by loops and hooks to keep leaf debris from blowing inside. Although she couldn't make out what it was, there was a charm hanging from the very centre of the rocky, round archway. It was purple, blue, and red, fluttering in the wind like ribbons.

The cliff wall here wasn't straight; it had its own concave pattern before bulging out to the right, close to the entrance of his cave. She couldn't see where the ward ended because of the wall that became convex there, especially with the small group of four or five trees.

They'd walked past those trees as they'd entered.

There, Merikh's sight spun at a dizzying speed, making her stumble, as he twisted his head back to her. She hadn't even realised he'd been looking over his back with ease, like a bird would, until he'd done that.

He removed his hand and the image of her woozy, greening face disappeared.

"There. Now, let's go inside."

Using her cane to tap against the ground, Raewyn followed him with no physical contact. She didn't know why, but for the past week, whenever they weren't touching, she could always tell where he was.

At least, not by any normal means; she still couldn't hear his footsteps or breaths. It itched at her brain – being able to sense him like this was nagging at her.

Don't get me wrong, I appreciate the change. She just wanted to figure out why.

Before she could even ask, he placed his hand on top of her head again.

His home rushed into her vision, and Raewyn blinked rapidly in surprise. The entire process was disorientating, and the more he did it, the less she liked it.

"There isn't much," he commented as his gaze roamed.

She couldn't help thinking he was just being modest. There was far more here than she'd been expecting.

Carved like an oval, the cave was long and deep, both ends having a curve to them rather than giving the room corners.

On the left was a chair covered in animal fur that looked surprisingly plush, far too big for her thin frame. At the very back was a bed that would have been completely circular if he hadn't cut off the very top pressing against the wall. It looked kind of soft, with leather laid over it to hide what it was made of.

What really caught her attention, though, was everything to the right: two long shelves filled with leather-bound books and odd knick-knacks. She wouldn't say the knick-knacks were cute, considering two of them were skulls, but some were large crystals.

There was a thinner shelf that held an assortment of ingredients. From what she gathered, most of it was dried herbs, ground-up crystals, and other various earthy materials.

The last pieces of furniture were a long, rectangular stone island bench and a decently sized cooking hearth. There wasn't much on top of the bench currently, perhaps a knife, a mortar and pestle, and a cutting board made of the same stone.

There was an animal skin rug underneath the bed, and it took up most of the floor space. Nothing hung from the roof, no chandelier for light. She also couldn't see many candles lying around.

She figured he could see perfectly in the dark.

The sight faded, and Raewyn was left wondering why he'd choose to abandon this place when he'd obviously styled it. There were a few pieces of décor, and the bookshelves gave her the impression he collected books that interested him. Why do all that to just leave it behind?

She sighed, wanting to ask, but she knew she'd get some dark or sad answer. It was something that had bothered her over the many weeks she'd been travelling with him.

Not once, except for when he'd spoken of Jabez, had Merikh said anything positive about his past. He had no friends, and his family was a touchy subject for him. It didn't seem as though he enjoyed anything.

I guess that's why he wants to leave so badly.

Raewyn couldn't imagine doing that. She'd miss the many

people she'd leave behind. Her family, her friends, some of the other councilmembers and people who worked within the central tree; she could name twenty people without even thinking about it.

Was there really not a single person in this whole world he would miss or would miss him? *There must be someone.* She didn't want to accept that he truly had no one.

It was too lonely of a thought, and it made her heart ache for him.

Suddenly tired and weighed down, she rubbed at her cheek, before doing the same to her eye.

"As much as I'd love to bathe, I'm really tired."

They'd been travelling for a few days since she'd slept in the cave. Adding her sprint through the forest and then coming a bunch of times, and she was out of energy.

"Eat," Merikh said, the bags he'd tightened to his torso rustling as he placed them against the stone benchtop. "You can have my bed for the duration of your stay."

Her heart decided to shyly flutter. "You want me to sleep in your bed?"

"Don't worry. I plan to sleep on the floor in my monstrous form."

Her chest swirled with a cold rush. She didn't know if she was disappointed because he didn't want to lay next to her in his own home, or because she was kind of hoping to steal his warmth. One thing she did know was that guilt radiated within her.

"But it's your home. The floor will be hard and uncomfortable."

"Not while I'm in that form. I actually find enjoyment being like that, and I sometimes choose to sleep on the floor for my own contentment. That's why I have a rug laid out."

With her lips tightening, unsure if he was lying or if she was just annoyed, she used her guide cane to walk over to his bed.

Now that she knew where all the hazards were, she would be

able to map the area out with her feet over the course of the next few days, not just inside, but also outside. She'd use the magical red glow of his ward dome to learn her placement within it.

Once she was at the foot of the bed, she unthreaded her wrist from the loop of her cane. She and it both freely fell to the bed.

She remembered spotting a big pillow, like two sewn together in size, and she crawled her way up to it. Raewyn face planted into it as she mumbled, "Good night."

"You *know* it's the middle of the day." She shrugged in response, Earth's sun cycle useless to her Elysian sleep cycle. "And I told you to eat first."

It was too late for that. As soon as she was horizontal, her eyes grew heavy, and her eyelids began to shut. She hadn't even cared about all the dust everywhere.

"Fine. If I'm not here when you wake, it's because I've gone to the closest town to obtain you food."

Raewyn didn't respond, and she heard herself snoring before she'd truly fallen asleep.

TWENTY-ONE

Covered in multiple bags filled with plants, fertiliser, and food, Merikh hadn't expected the sight that would await him when he returned.

He didn't know what he was expecting when he walked through his cave entrance – perhaps her sitting on the bed or going through her bags.

It surely wasn't for Raewyn to be on her hands and knees, patting around the base of the bed. Her round arse was pointing to the sky and facing his direction, and he may have gazed at it a little longer than he should have.

He'd held that arse in his hand, touched it, kneaded it, and it was a lot softer than he thought it'd be.

The ground at his feet was wet. From the mixed scents of cleaning products, he could tell she'd chosen to bathe in the lake, or at least next to it.

The stone bench was covered in an array of items. It was neat, like she'd taken care in her placement once she pulled them from the bags. *She must have taken her bathing supplies from them.*

The urge to laugh tickled his chest when her arse wiggled at him while she patted the ground, just because he thought she might be mortified if she discovered she'd done so towards him. He immediately sobered from his humour when she turned her face and he saw her expression.

Tears were pooling in her eyes, her nose red and glossy.

"What are you searching for?" Merikh asked, since she was on the hunt for something.

Raewyn screamed, and her entire body jumped.

Merikh flinched in return.

He shouldn't have been so shocked by her reaction, considering he'd given plenty of people a fright because he was usually silent upon approach. It was more that it was done in his own home, where it would make sense for him to be there.

"You nearly scared me half to death!" She wiped at her cheek with the back of her wrist, looking utterly defeated. "I can't find my cane. I tried earlier but got frustrated, and I knew I didn't need it while I was washing. I thought if I came back to look, I'd find it."

Not wanting to bring everything inside, Merikh dropped the multiple bags he had across his body. Dirt sprinkled from the bottom of the burlap sacks as he placed them down next to the entryway.

The entrance was permanently open, with one side of the closing sheet hooked to the opposing side.

His orbs turned a flaring orange from guilt. *I shouldn't have touched it.*

It'd been laying on the bed with her. He thought she might kick it off, break it, or roll on top of it, which would be uncomfortable.

"It's here," he said, walking inside and taking it from its upright position against the wall next to the bed. He handed it to her while she knelt on the ground. "Next time you're not using it, I would like to alter it to better suit you."

He'd made it without measuring her height, and it was longer than it needed to be. Now that he had the time and the tools to make another version, he'd like to improve it.

Merikh then held his palm forward. "I have my hand out. It's your choice whether you take it."

She reached up, and he directed his hand to clasp her own before he helped her to her feet.

"Did you move my cane?" she asked as she clutched it.

"Yes, but I won't do so again without informing you."

With the way she was holding it, he now understood it was a very precious item to her. He wouldn't mess with it again, even with good intentions.

The fact she didn't have one when I first met her must have been upsetting for her. Yet, even so, she had found a way to navigate her way around Clawhaven without one.

The smile of relief she shone at him was hurtful, simply because he didn't like doing the wrong thing for the right reason. He wasn't used to helping others, and he often felt like he was making a mess of it with her.

"Thank you," she said, pushing her hand through the loop.

"While I was gone, I obtained some vegetables and fruits that would survive the trip. If you are going to remove my glamour enchantment, I won't be able to buy you more food, as I won't be able to walk into a human town again."

Just the thought sent a numbness through him. Even his orbs tried to flicker to white, but he pushed down his unease as best he could.

He didn't want to give it to her. He didn't want to give up the one item that gave him a sense of normalcy.

"I thought it was best if I bought plants rather than buying the vegetables themselves. I can go back and sneak in throughout the night and steal whatever else you like to eat."

Some plants had been too delicate and wouldn't have survived being uprooted and then travelling such a large distance on his back.

"You have a lot of forethought," Raewyn complimented.

Merikh scratched at the back of his neck.

"It's best if you let me know what else you'll need for your experiments before you destroy my enchantment." When she opened her mouth to probably start rattling off some kind of list, he said, "Tell me outside. The longer the plants are exposed, the less likely they'll take to the soil."

She followed him to the entryway, where he checked on the plants before unstrapping everything else he was carrying. He took what he needed to a section close to the Veil's cliff walls, where they would get adequate sun throughout the day, close enough to the lake and waterfall that he doubted he'd need to water them.

Then she gave him a list while he dug into the ground with his claws. He had no idea what some of what she needed was, some ingredients unknown to this realm.

Most of it, though, he did know, like a scale, heat padding, a flask, and various other items. He even already had a lot of it, since he'd been experimenting with various charms and had stolen a few books from the Anzúli – some illegible because they were in a different language.

"You'll have to use what we have here. I don't know what a *solisflores* is," he answered plainly.

"I'm sure any kind of flower will work, to be honest. I just need to teach the mana stone to absorb sunlight and photosynthesise it into radiation, heat, and light. Doing this with a solisflores is easier because they are one of the flowers that glow the brightest. I guess it would translate to sunflower?"

"We already have a sunflower, and it doesn't glow, Raewyn," Merikh answered with an exasperated tone. "None of our plants glow, and only some animals do."

"I glow," Raewyn stated, catching him off-guard. "Biofluorescence happens in Elysians during certain spells, depending on how powerful they are. That's why our hair is white and no longer dark like our ancestors. We've lost all our colouring, and it's technically transparent now."

He lifted his head up to her. "What are you going on about?"

"When we use certain spells, only the symbols that relate to them will glow. When I do earth magic with my feet, my feet markings will glow, but if I do them with my hands, my hand markings will glow. However, if I do spirit magic, like fire and other things that come from within and don't require a source, my hair will glow along with my markings. I can use a few strands of my hair to teach any kind of flower to harness magic, and then I use the flower to teach the stone. It just needs to be a flower large enough to encompass it completely."

"Bloody hell, that sounds complicated," he grated, shaking his head. "Are you sure this will even work?"

Her lips tightened and pulled to the side. "I guess it is, but what else can I do? I have to teach the stone, and if I don't have all the ingredients, then I will have to try other things. I've only had to use my hair once, because I can usually use another plant to obtain my goal. It worked, though. My hair is not just dead cells; its lack of colouring comes from years of exposing ourselves to magic – sapping the pigment through evolution. It's technically a negative by-product of magic use, and instead of it toxifying us, we've adapted to using it."

Merikh waved his hand in annoyance, not liking the way his gut twisted in uncertainty. "If your point was to reassure me, you haven't."

Just the opposite, in fact. *Shit. If she fails, then we're both screwed. Me, more so.* He didn't want to go back to living the way he had before, not after he'd obtained the humanity he currently had.

He'd go mad, he just knew it.

He dug at the ground more forcefully before almost snapping a poor tomato plant he yanked from a burlap sack. He put it in the hole he'd dug.

"Why a flower? Wouldn't any plant do?"

She shook her head, her drying hair bouncing around her head. "The plant must be alive. Would you be able to source one with its roots intact and then plant it in a pot? I need to be able to move it around in the sun."

He had to add a pot to his list of items to get.

Merikh turned his skull towards the sky, noting the hour. The sun was going down, but he thought he'd be able to make it to the closest town if he ran on all fours before they closed their gates.

Her stomach chose that moment to gurgle loudly. She covered it with both arms, her shoulders lifting bashfully.

"Sorry," she laughed. "I ate when I woke up, but I didn't actually have a lot of food left."

"I grabbed you plenty to eat, and these plants still have vegetables and fruits on them. They aren't fully ripe yet, so that'll give them time to grow." Merikh sighed as he looked down at the plant in front of him. "Do you know how to garden? I've never done it before."

"Not really, but I'm sure we can figure it out together." Raewyn offered him a warm smile, and he averted his gaze completely. "Speaking of figuring it out together... could you help me cook?"

"Me? Why would I know how to cook? I've never cooked a thing in my life. If it wasn't obvious to you, everything I've eaten is usually so fresh, it's still screaming."

Raewyn rolled her eyes at him, but he noticed how she shuddered as well. Perhaps he was a little graphic, but he just couldn't fathom how she wouldn't understand that by now.

"Can you at least cut a potato, or is that too hard for your Duskwalker butt?"

Merikh grunted. "Of course."

"I don't actually need you to cook. I can do that myself. I have tastebuds," she said, more curt than usual. "It will just be easier if you give me the food rather than me figuring out where or what everything is right now. Your home is new to me, and I'll end up spending hours trying to find what I need when you know where it is."

She had a good point, and the bags of food he'd brought were all mixed together.

"Fine," he answered. "Just let me plant these and then I'll come inside."

He expected Raewyn to leave his side and give him some peace, but she didn't.

She began explaining a whole bunch of math. He didn't know if it was complicated or not. He may be decent at reading and writing, but his mathematical skills were subpar.

There was something about calculating the absorption rate of the mana stone, explaining that each stone was of different quality. Then, she would have to feed it more spirit magic, which, apparently, would give him a demonstration of her hair colour change. She needed to give the right amount, or the thing would shatter.

Then, there was calculating how much radiation, heat, and light it absorbed from the sun, and each one needed to be balanced or it would fail. Her face had turned crestfallen when she explained this to him, and he figured it was one of the reasons why her sight was the way it was.

Despite only understanding half of her mathematics and procedures, Merikh's faith in the whole process was waning. They hadn't even started yet, and he was worried.

What would he do if it failed?

Would she ask to be taken to a human town and learn to live among them? The idea of letting her go had both its pros and cons.

He wouldn't want to let her go, in case she figured out another way to get home. They could figure out something together, a new plan – he was used to being met with failure. He'd sulk for a while, but if he kept her, the potential was more probable than if he were alone.

She also had a lot of magic he could consume, but he'd completely lost the enthusiasm to eat her.

She'd gotten under his skin with her smiles, kindness, and just general mirth. The idea of snuffing out her brightness for his own greed would probably weigh on his conscious.

He didn't regret much in his life, but he thought he'd regret harming her.

However, he would like to dump her in a town so he wouldn't become attached to her, especially if they both ended up stuck here. They'd already been together for almost a month, and his tail was twisting into knots.

He didn't like the idea of being a horny woman's masturbatory scratching pole. He didn't want to be used to fulfil some weird, fucked up desire towards a monster, only to be discarded when she grew bored or had someone attractive like herself to play with. That's if that was her intention.

He still didn't understand why everything had happened between them while travelling to his home.

Just because he desired her, and she had been aroused in his presence, didn't mean she actually wanted to be his partner – in any sense of the word.

I'm her only option to get home at the moment. In the same way, she was the only potential key to his freedom. *If that no longer becomes the case, she'll want to leave my side.*

Turning his gaze up to the sky, he waited for his orbs to shift to blue in sadness at that thought. It never happened.

Merikh was just so used to being alone and rejected that he'd stopped caring. He was so used to it he never even allowed a flicker of hope to spark, so it couldn't then be violently snuffed out like it always was.

Raewyn pursed her lips as she hacked at the carrot she was preparing for her dinner in annoyance.

He's avoiding me, Raewyn thought as she chucked the food into the fry pan, cautiously reaching for the handle to know where to place it.

It'd been three days since she'd woken up here, and after he'd helped her make food that first day, her interactions with Merikh had become almost non-existent.

He showed her where all the food was after he placed them

into their own bags. He'd given her all the tools he had, along with the ones he'd gone to obtain the following day, so she could get familiar with them for when she started working on the sun spell. He'd given her a notebook and a strange pen she wasn't familiar with – it had a quill tip she needed to dunk in ink – and she was thankful she was able to use her elbraille spell on it.

Once she could function on her own, he ceased being near her.

I know he's there.

He'd informed her he would be sleeping in the cave and for her to watch out for him – he didn't want her accidentally kicking his quills. Other times, she'd call out to him, and he would approach from goodness knows where to help her.

He was there, just not in any way permanently close to her.

Now that they'd arrived at his home, the constant separation was getting to her. She wanted someone to talk to, and she realised today that she kind of... missed conversing with him.

Sure, he wasn't the most social of people, but he was a good listener and occasionally asked questions. It wasn't one-sided, but she did most of the talking. For a person who was overtly chatty, this was a wonderful quality.

Raewyn also missed his closeness. His lingering scent was mild, since it was obvious he hadn't spent much time living here over the years. She liked his orange and cinnamon scent and wished it was stronger, like when he was by her side.

She liked the warmth of him, and his big hand holding her up as he carried her around. Then there was his gruff, ear-tingling voice and his lulling deep breaths she could only hear whenever she was pressed against him.

They'd essentially been glued to each other's side for a month. Now, it was like there was a void next to her.

A big, spiky, irritable void she'd enjoyed skirting around.

Pushing his buttons, asking uncomfortable questions, confusing him – Raewyn enjoyed all of it. She found his reactions, or that grunt he did, funny and cute.

She was a bunny poking a big bear who didn't know what to do with the soft little thing annoying him.

And she knew he didn't want to harm her, at least not anymore.

He was too considerate of her. He'd fixed her cane and now it was even more comfortable than the one she had at home – although she bet this one was ugly in comparison. It was the thought that counted, especially from someone who could just be cruel to her.

Merikh had the opportunity to treat her as nothing but a captive, some kind of prisoner, but he didn't.

Considering he had a dick and could experience desire like any other male, there was truly nothing stopping him from attempting to use her in a perverted manner. If he wanted to, he could force her to please him just because she was there, alone and vulnerable, with no one to save her.

Raewyn threw basil and garlic into the frying pan and then stirred everything with her cheeks heating.

She wasn't against that, so long as her consent could be given and adhered to.

Then she paused. *Maybe he doesn't see me that way?* If she looked back on both times they'd touched, Raewyn had instigated it in some way.

He said he likes the way I smell. The prickle of shame caused the hairs on her nape to lift. Did his kind react fiercely to pheromones, and he'd gotten caught up for that reason?

Unsure of the truth, Raewyn dug her nails into her loose curls and scratched the side of her head. *I could always ask him.*

Gosh, that conversation was too embarrassing!

"Hey, Merikh. Are you interested in me sexually, or have I been taking advantage of you by accident?" Yeah... that was *not* a conversation she wanted to have.

She would be more conscious in the future. He was intelligent, which made the whole thing confusing.

She was used to being around people who didn't succumb to

the more animalistic urges like heats and ruts, but there were some species of Elves that did.

The Taihee clan were, for instance, a species of Elf affected by periods of uncontrollable desire. It was almost like their bodies were a perfect blend of humanoid and animal, and each subclan was different.

A few chief representatives had briefly come to Nyl'theria before the Demons arrived. There had been an adult male who had a feline face with a humanoid body, yet his legs were digitigrade, since he'd walked on paws. There had also been a female with a giant flock of feathers and a beak.

Her parents had been the ones to study their DNA to find they were half-Elf, just like the Bansu clans who were basically half plant.

I hope Merikh didn't just get caught up in my pheromones. Self-consciously, her shoulders turned inwards. She liked Merikh for a bunch of different reasons, and not all of them were physical.

He was her friend, and she hoped he felt the same way. She found his companionship easy, since she didn't need to hide any part of who she was.

It was hypocritical of her, but she was pretty intolerant of others, and she hated anyone who talked over her. She didn't like competing for the spotlight. It probably came from Raewyn's intelligence as a scientist, and the self-assuredness in her position on the council.

It was why she'd chosen to separate herself from normal society and focus on her career. She couldn't offend or upset anyone if she was too busy working on the next breakthrough. The other councilmembers had their own issues they had to battle as well – none of them were perfect.

Whatever. If he won't come to me, then I'll go to him.

Once Raewyn was finished cooking a delightful vegetarian meal, if she did say so herself, she scooped herself a plate. With her hand supporting the underside of it, her cutlery in her other hand with her cane, she left the cave.

Once the cane tip encountered the roughness of grass in comparison to the smoothness of stone, she knew she'd made it to the entrance. With the lack of warmth, it must have been late into the night.

Now, where is he?

Wandering the area was a terrible idea, especially if she didn't want to throw her food to the ground by accident.

"Merikh?" she said loudly.

"Over here," he called back.

"Stay there." Raewyn headed to where she thought the three boulders and two trees were next to the lake.

When she got halfway, her ears twitched at whatever noise it was that indicated his location. She followed it, and it got softer before the tip of her cane hit the boulder he was sitting upon. She hit one foot but not the second, so she figured he had one folded up.

"Do you need something?" he asked with a gentleness, making Raewyn's lips pull into a small smile.

Had it been a month ago, he probably would have snapped, "What do you want?" It was hard not to think deeply on small differences like that.

"Nope," she stated as she lifted her chin and simultaneously sat while folding her legs into a crossed position. She rested the back of her hand holding the plate against her calves and stabbed into her food. "What are you doing?"

"Sitting here, looking up at the sky." There was a shrug in his voice.

"Mind if I ask why?"

"Because I can? I currently have this pest in my home, taking up all the space. Where else am I to sit and have some peace?"

Her lips pulled into a bigger smile; she didn't believe he thought she was a pest.

"I actually happen to think I'm great company, thank you very much, Mr GrumpyBear."

"You know what? From now on, that shall be my name. However, I think we should make it more formal. Sir GrumpyBear, just so you understand the hierarchy of our relationship."

"Then I shall be Queen RaeOfSunshine. Just so *you* understand the hierarchy of our relationship."

"I kneel for no man, your *highness.*"

Ooh, he was being rather condescending.

"Luckily, I'm not a man," she answered, poking her fork in his direction.

"Not what I meant. Man as in all of humanity."

"Luckily, I'm not human, either." When he grunted in answer, her smile grew so bright it hurt. She took another bite, pushed her food to her cheek, and asked, "So, Sir GrumpyBear, why are you avoiding me?"

"I'm not. Just giving you space in case you wanted it. You're the one who hasn't searched for me."

Raewyn's jaw fell ajar. Well, damn, he wasn't wrong about that. Still, she couldn't help thinking that might be a lie. There was much he'd said that might be a lie, but she was choosing not to think on those things.

"You know you have to give it to me eventually," she stated, her smile falling.

A light gust of wind chose that moment to wrap around them, foreboding and full of the heavy silence he sat in.

Quiet and solemn, he whispered, "I know."

The fact that Merikh hadn't given her his diadem with the mana stone in it yet showed he was concerned she'd fail. To be fair, she was nervous about it, too.

It was the first time Merikh had truly shown any vulnerability, and it was the sign of someone who might be a little scared. Picturing him frightened wasn't an easy task, but she understood the weight of what he'd be giving up.

Her heart swelled in tenderness.

He wasn't as infallible as he seemed, and it deepened the

many facets of him. He wasn't a two-dimensional jerk riding his spite as a cop-out. He had fears, worries, and dreams – some he'd shared, and many she imagined he hadn't.

"Why is it you can't create another portal like the one that brought you here?"

He was looking for an alternative, a way out of giving up the one item she didn't think he could live without.

"Because that was a chaos portal. They are usually created without a mana stone and by accident, and they can take you anywhere. Mine happened to bring me here."

"You couldn't accidentally create another one?"

She swore she saw a flicker of white, but it quickly flashed back to red before fading.

"No. After speaking with the leaders in other realms we were in contact with, they asked us to close all our portals and not to open them again until we'd dealt with the Demons. Out of respect for them, and for the safety of others, we've chosen to agree so we could gain their help in the beginning. For instance, the Anzúli sacrificed a few of their people by sending them here, to Earth, while another realm helped us build the first part of our stronghold city. Another gave us resources to help feed the large influx of people, while others helped to save as many as they could and bring them to the city before retreating."

"You were in contact with other places?" Merikh asked, and a spark of yellow flashed in her dark sight.

"Well... yeah," Raewyn said while tilting her head. Had she not told him yet? "About thirty-one years ago for us, which is around four hundred and sixty-five years here, we figured out how to open permanent portals rather than chaos ones. We were able to teach mana stones to open them with astronomical points to make gates. There are a whole bunch of calculations I don't understand, since it's not my area of expertise. I just know the portal will always find land, so we don't just pop up in space. Still, it doesn't always mean the other side is safe or breathable. Most worlds aren't."

"This is how you found Earth? The humans have known about your kind in some way for thousands of years."

"No. Earth was found many years before that through a chaos portal. We were able to recreate it, but it was always temporary, and it brought us to a different part of the world every time. Earth is really big, which is why it was so easy, whereas many other realms are small. You can literally travel around our realm in the span of a Nyl'therian week with nothing but your own legs."

"What about the Demons? Was that an accident too?"

Glad she was most of the way through her food, Raewyn placed her plate on the ground when her stomach twisted.

"No. We created a portal to their world on purpose, not knowing what we'd be facing. When a team of explorers went inside, they never came back, and instead, a horde of Demons exploded from within."

"Couldn't you just close it?" There was an accusation in his tone, one that cast justifiable blame.

Raewyn shook her head with her shoulders falling. "We must be able to access the portal, and the Demons' numbers are dense around it. There's too many of them, and they've built nests around it. That part of the forest is impenetrable now."

"And these other realms wouldn't help your people?"

Once more, she shook her head. "What you don't understand is that we are one of the most technologically advanced races of people. What humans have here is nothing in comparison to what we have discovered, or what we can do. Out of the five realms we've had stable contact with, the only ones who can compare to us are the Anzúli, but they are essentially humans with magical capabilities. They aren't fast, nor strong, and their magic can't compete with the horde – Demons are resistant to magic, although not impervious."

Raewyn leaned back on her hands and turned her face up towards the sky to rest her head. She wished she had more positive answers for him, or that the history of the Elysian people didn't turn out the way it did, but nothing could change it.

It was what it was.

"The Bansu were the first we were able to reach, and they were primitive. They were basically one with their realm's flora, so they didn't need any advancements. Everything they could need or want was provided by their planet. The Taihee were a little more advanced. The difference between them and the Bansu was that they were overjoyed when we shared our knowledge with them, whereas the Bansu, although happy to share a connection with us, didn't want to change their lifestyle. There was a race of Elves named Nanteth, and they had an opposing sun cycle to us – more night than day, and it was basically winter all year round. They were pale because their melanin was different to ours, so they could absorb more of their weak sun, whereas our three suns are too strong and we live in a permanent summer. We couldn't handle their world, and they couldn't handle ours – even though we did try."

"Why bother doing all this?" he asked, like what they had been doing was absurd. "Why bother trying at all?"

Raewyn snorted a small laugh.

"Because we wanted to be friends! We wanted to connect with people, no matter who they were, where they came from, or how they lived. We respected everyone's culture, never pushed anyone to make changes, but we wanted to expand. We wanted to learn what was out there, *who* was out there, and our hope was that we could build a bigger world, where we were all connected through peace."

Quick to respond, Merikh curtly said, "That's foolish. Peace only lasts for so long before differences create war."

"Not for us. For nearly a decade, so a hundred and fifty years here, not once did we have any issues. Everyone understood we were all different, and that stepping into someone else's realm meant we adhered to their culture, unless they approved otherwise. There was balance and unity. It's possible when your heart isn't filled with judgement and hate."

"No wonder you didn't keep in contact with the humans here, then. They are the complete opposite of that ideology."

Raewyn bit at the inside of her cheek, and then picked at grass stalks as a way to distract herself.

"I wish you weren't right, but you are. When our people visited here, we were hunted for being different. They saw a tall, pointed-ear creature who could cast magic, and the humans wanted to hurt us, experiment on us, turn us into prisoners so we could fulfil their greedy desires. We tried, many times, to establish peace, but it just wasn't possible. We were going to try again in the future, hoping they'd change."

"Humans know of centaurs, mermaids, golems, and other weird creatures. Did you meet them as well?"

Her expression brightened with the curiosity in his tone, which made it less gruff and more boyish.

"Golems I've never heard of, but are you talking about centaurs as in half-horse people?"

"Yes."

She nodded. "We did meet a race like that, but they weren't as friendly. Actually, they were rather rude and had a superiority complex. We kept the gate open, but no one ventured to either side. Mermaids were a little more friendly, but we can't breathe underwater, and they couldn't walk on land, so we only traded with each other. They did teach many of my people how to swim, and a large group of them moved to Nyl'theria since they wanted to give their ecosystem a break from overpopulation. See?" Raewyn gave him a coy smile. "Unity that benefitted both parties. They came to our sea, and we were able to venture to their small land."

"Ugh," Merikh grunted, and she imagined he would have rolled his eyes... if he had any. "You expect me to believe your kind is so forgiving and understanding, but I'm sure that can't be completely true. There must be a point at which you Elves couldn't accept another."

"Were you not listening at all?" Raewyn's brows drew together tightly as her lips pulled to one side. "As long as the people were understanding of cultural differences and accepted the bond of an open gate, we were happy to have that connection. If they were set on changing us, we would close it with the intention of trying again in the years to come. The idea was placed in their heads, and we hoped the next contact would go more smoothly. We never forced the issue. If they were violent people and wished to control or harm us, we would have closed it immediately without discussion."

"All the people you have spoken about are similar to you."

Raewyn tilted her head to the side. "I don't understand."

His singular laugh was dark, lacking in humour. "What do you think your people would do if I came banging on your gate?"

"Talk to you?" she asked in confusion.

"Raewyn, that's delusional. They would see a creature who has a dead thing on their shoulders and would likely perceive me as evil, or some omen of death."

"I don't think so," she stated in a quiet tone. "We always gave everyone a chance."

"Children don't like looking at dead things; they find them frightening. Adults are no better when it comes to things they don't understand. You are speaking from an experience of dealing with people who don't appear like Duskwalkers do."

Perhaps she was biased, because she truly thought her people were accepting, but her entire chest swirled with anger. She turned her face towards him, so he knew she was glaring.

"You're wrong. We've allowed Demons who have asked for sanctuary to live among us."

"And you imprisoned them once they succumbed to their hunger because you forced them to eat your way. I would be faced with the same issue if I smelt blood or fear, and I doubt I'd be forgiven, even though I cannot help it. It's easy to forgive a face when its similar to your own."

"Because we didn't know that before," she bit, slitting her eyes in his direction. "We now have a section of the city that holds livestock for them, because they can't change what they require to eat any better than we can."

"Do they look like you? Smell like you? Talk like you? How are they treated? Are they subjugated, living in their own section as outcasts?"

"They chose that out of comfortability. They wish to live closer together because they are wary of themselves and don't wish to endanger anyone else. They are welcome anywhere in the city. Not everyone chooses to live there."

"Did they choose that, or were they pushed to make that decision based on how they were treated or looked upon?"

I don't understand, she thought, shaking her head in disbelief. He was defending people he didn't know, had never met. *It's like he wants to see evil in us.*

"No," she answered with complete resolve. "Just because their housing is together doesn't mean they don't work with us, eat with us, play or converse with us. They shop in the same markets, put their children in the same schools. There is no divide in that sense. There is no difference between us, to the point where my assistant is a Demon and I hand chose him. We even call them Delysians, because even though they are different, they are just like us, and as long as they aren't hungry, they've never harmed another."

"How can you be so certain?"

What more could she say? She'd eaten at Cykran's table with his neighbours. She'd played with their children and spent time in that part of the city as Cykran's friend – while he boasted about working in the councillor palace.

Just as she opened her mouth, Raewyn shut it when a striking realisation hit her like a thunderbolt.

This has nothing to do with the Demons. She rubbed at her cheek before doing the same to the back of her neck. *It's about him.*

Merikh, in his own weird way, was trying to find out if he would be accepted among her people, despite his appearance.

"Merikh... as long as you truly tried not to harm anyone, I don't see why you wouldn't be accepted," she said as she softened her features. "We're not like the humans. You've been able to walk among them, speak with them without accidentally hurting them. As long as you were able to make that same effort with us, you wouldn't be forced to hide your face behind a glamour."

"You cannot say that with absolute certainty." When her brows twitched, he added, "You were frightened of me the moment you met me."

"That's different!" she shouted in outrage. "You were cackling like a psycho and acting aggressively. You'd lied to me, made me think you were someone else entirely."

"If I had revealed what I was to you in Clawhaven, you wouldn't have walked out that gate with me. Admit it."

"Well, no," she pouted. "But that's because I didn't know you, or what you were. I do now, and I can speak on your behalf." Then she bent her arm, as though she was flexing her biceps muscle. "I'll be your strong arm and you'll be welcomed in no time. I am synedrus councillor Raewyn Daefaren, lead representative for the Duskwalker people."

It started off quiet, like someone trying their hardest to suppress it, but it grew louder and louder until a yellow flame burst. Merikh's chuckle grew in depth, like he couldn't help himself.

"A representative for a Duskwalker? Never in my life did I think I would hear something as absurd as that."

"It's not absurd," she grumbled, trying not to grin in triumph.

He's laughing. I made him laugh. It was sincere and genial, making her heart flutter in its wake.

"Fine, Raewyn. I'll let you try, but don't be too disappointed if you fail."

"I won't fail," she stated with absolute certainty. She

wouldn't let herself fail. "So, you'll give me your diadem now?"

"Not yet. I must get a few things from town before you play with it."

Raewyn rolled her eyes. "I don't need to change the enchantment yet. I can check its absorption rate without doing so, and I don't need to do anything else until you have the flowers and I make them bind with my hair."

"I'll give it to you tomorrow, since I know you'll likely sleep soon."

She rubbed at her eyes, like him mentioning it made tiredness wash over her. She sat there with him for a little while until she once more wanted to fill the silence.

Honestly, she was just hoping she could get him to talk for once.

"Why are you looking up at the sky?"

"I don't know," he answered. "It's actually pretty fucking boring if you ask me."

Raewyn was sent into a fit of giggles. "Then why are you doing it?"

"Because I'm bored, isn't that obvious?"

"You could always come and hang out with me."

"Why? So I can stare at you? Most people would find that... weird."

Her shoulders jerked as she shrugged. "Better than staring at the sky. At least you could have someone to talk to. I think I'm pretty interesting."

"So modest," he stated with a playful sneer. When she raised a brow, he gave her a deep huff. "Fine, I will come inside for as long as I can stand you."

Raewyn used the boulder to get to her feet and retrieved her plate. With her cane in one hand and her mostly eaten food in the other, she headed back the way she came.

The sound he produced stayed with her, so she knew he'd not only followed but was walking beside her. She snuck a little closer, hoping to feel his heat, and her elbow snuck a feel of fur.

Then it struck her, and she dropped her plate as she halted.

Merikh paused and turned back. "What's wrong?"

"That's it," she uttered under her breath. "That's what I can hear."

She raced forward and ploughed straight into him, causing him to stumble back in surprise. Placing her ear right against the centre of his chest, the sound became louder.

"You're vibrating! You're producing a sound that isn't obvious, so it's not overbearing and easy to tune out, but the frequency is one I can hear if I search for it."

Now that her ear was pressed against him, it was like a purr as it rumbled deep within him. If she took it away, it would dull exponentially.

"You mentioned you couldn't hear me, and I wasn't keen on changing my walk to accommodate you. I'm used to being light on my feet to hunt."

"I could tell something was different. I just couldn't figure out why."

She didn't smile out of joy, but she did close her eyes as she listened, finding solace in it. His heart pounded loudly, and it'd been quicker when she'd first touched him. Now, it fell into a deep, easy rhythm. It sounded so big, and he was so warm, she would have loved to crawl inside him and fall asleep straight inside his chest cavity like a cocoon of security and comfort.

"Thank you for doing this for me."

She was basically hugging him. Since he wasn't pulling away, she didn't stop – although he didn't return it.

Raewyn finally smiled when he gave an awkward grunt in response.

TWENTY-TWO

Sitting on the large boulder situated underneath two trees right next to the lake's funnel point, Raewyn combed her fingers through her curls.

She was reflecting on the previous day's conversation.

After speaking with him about the history of her people and their plains for connectivity between worlds, then telling him she would stand with Merikh to help him live within the city, he was *still* funny about giving her the diadem.

He did give it to her though, after she slept, and she thought he may have rested as well.

She didn't need to remove the mana stone from the piece of jewellery, which he was relieved about.

The central piece was simple in design. The stone was locked into place by a metal coil that ran around its edges and back. The coil had a loop at the top where the chain, knotted and twisted in design by tiny rings, ran through it.

From what she'd briefly seen of the diadem, he locked it in place by wrapping it around the bases of his upward protruding horns. The stone was a deep blue, like the ocean.

He complained in a low murmur about not having removed it in over a hundred and eighty years as he handed it to her.

She'd placed it on the stone bench and then began working her feeler magic into it.

Merikh commented on how the roots of her hair turned grey, which was the base of her magical properties. That was her spirit magic, although it was different for everyone.

Then, her hair, as well as the markings over her sternum, began to glow multicoloured as she examined all the stone's components, from all elemental magic to spirit magic.

The only reason she knew the diadem floated between her spread hands was because of the magic essence that glowed within her sight.

It allowed her to see the mana stone's properties up close, check its absorption rate, and if it had any flaws – of which it had none. It was in perfect condition, although not very strong or large. She'd need to feed it her own magic for a few days once she'd neutralised the current enchantment.

A glamour enchantment wasn't easy to achieve. She'd wondered at first who had given it to him, but only one name came to mind – Weldir.

That demi-god was doing things he wasn't supposed to. He was messing with the circle of life by creating his own children, creating enchantments, and apparently, he'd figured out a way to steal a mana stone from Nyl'theria without being able to step foot on it, probably using his mate.

Weldir's history was a part of her own, and most Elysians learnt of it growing up.

She was uncomfortable talking to Merikh about him. He may not appreciate learning what he did about his semi-divine father, or the truth of their origins.

The more she came to understand Merikh, the more she wanted to tell him, especially since it was obvious he didn't know the truth.

She didn't want to blindside him when they went to the city and he was questioned, and she didn't want to upset him with *who* might question him.

Once she was done checking the mana stone, she'd given it back to Merikh. The big Duskwalker had run off with it like his tail was on fire.

A soft laugh bubbled past her lips.

His tail had given her a fright at first when it swatted the back of her thighs. Now that he was home, he was freeing it from the inside of his pants, and it seemed to have a mind of its own.

It'd brushed the side of her legs a few times, tickling and swaying against her, before darting away. She wondered if that was just because it was swaying as he turned, or if he had a thought. Hard to know, since she didn't have a tail of her own to compare it to.

She turned her face up towards the heat of the sun. It was late in the afternoon, tilting in her direction under the cover of the tree.

I wonder if Merikh will be back soon.

He'd left to go to town with the intention of obtaining a flower with the kind of bulb she required. It needed to encase the entire stone.

Then, she could begin her experiments.

Just as Raewyn tilted her head down and off to the side where she thought he may eventually come from, she bounced on her perch, having been startled. For a moment, she swore she saw a transparent woman in her sight, clear and white like a Ghost.

The moment she was spooked, though, the ghostly woman disappeared. A scent took its place, one unfamiliar and close.

"Hello?" she called, her ears flattening. "Is someone there?"

It was strange asking when she hadn't heard anyone approach, nor had she smelt another person nearing. She wasn't sure if there could be someone there, not even a few feet from her.

"Hello?"

Her pulse settled when the wave of paranoia softened.

From what she knew, no one could enter Merikh's ward, so she wasn't sure why she thought she saw someone through some magical essence. Maybe she was imagining the scent, or hadn't noticed it before because she'd been distracted?

It smelt kind of floral, although she couldn't remember if she'd seen flowers when Merikh had used his sight to show her the area.

As she turned her face away, shaking off the idea that someone was there, the white essence returned in the corner of her sight.

Raewyn didn't get the chance to turn and look. On the opposite side of the stream through the Veil's forest, the crunching of earth debris and snapping of sticks drew her immediate attention.

Something, or rather, multiple somethings were heading this way.

Raewyn stood and turned towards them as she slowly crept towards the cave entrance. She wasn't afraid; she had no reason to be. Merikh's ward was keeping her protected in one of the most dangerous places on Earth.

She just wanted to be able to leave quickly, in case it was more Demons. They liked to loiter around the ward and hiss at her, saying cruel and unpleasant things from a distance. She'd rather avoid them if she could, especially since they always made her skin crawl.

Keeping her eyes on the red ward's boundary, she knew the moment the strange creatures broke through the tree line.

Then two shadows hit the ward as they passed through it. There was a shuffle, one snapping its fangs while the second snickered, followed by a loud thud.

Raewyn sucked in a sharp breath and froze. *They're inside...* Whatever they were, they sounded massive and hostile. *How did they get inside the ward?*

"Do you see her?" one asked.

"I don't see her, but she went this way," the other answered.

They had similar voices, a warm baritone that swelled with a totally inhuman roughness.

Both had a different, strange timbre when they spoke, growly but at the same time mixed with a human's voice. She'd only ever heard Merikh speak like that.

"She did not stop to play with us."

"Maybe she did not notice us."

Then, at the same time, they said, *"Strange."*

Unsure of what to do, considering they hadn't noticed her or perhaps didn't care, Raewyn snuck an inch closer to the cave.

One of them had been speaking but quieted as soon as she moved, and she cringed. Did they see her? Perhaps she shouldn't have done anything and pretended to be a tree.

Two pairs of yellow sparks flashed in her vision, leaving a glowing trail as though they'd tilted their heads in opposite directions. Unfortunately, they'd obviously been facing her.

It did, however, highlight what they were.

Only Merikh's orbs create such magic. They were Duskwalkers, two of them, from what she could tell.

"What's this?" one of them said while slowly moving in her direction.

The other followed, practically in time with the other's footsteps. It was like they were one moving unit.

"There's a human here."

"What's a human doing here?" He sniffed with deep, snorting huffs. *"It doesn't smell human, though."*

Raewyn slowly retreated backwards but was forced to halt when two pairs of flame sparks flared red before fading. She couldn't flee, not even slowly, or she'd ignite their hunger like Merikh had warned her.

She stood her ground, hoping if she didn't agitate them, or smell of fear or blood, that they may be 'friendly' like Merikh.

"H-hello," she said, offering them a weak smile.

Yellow sparked in her vision.

"It spoke!" one exclaimed. *"It spoke to us!"*

"It is she," the other snickered.

The closer they got, passing over the stream and onto her side of the lake, the harder it became to hold her resolve. She took in a deep, calming breath and kept her smile in place. 'Fake it until you make it' was going to be her motto right now.

One thing she did notice as they neared was that they actually didn't sound the same. One's voice was raspy and coarse, while the other's was slightly higher in pitch, although still deep.

Their colour flashes changed, one going purple and the other going... pink? She'd never seen Merikh's sparks go that colour, but the purple one made her wary. Hopefully, that was just his natural orb colouring, since she had a theory that purple meant desire.

At least, that's if their orb changes were the same emotions for all of them.

"Yeah, but the humans never speak to us," the one on the left said, his orbs sparking purple and his voice the coarser one.

"Only scream and cry," the one on the right said, his orbs pink and his voice higher.

Their steps were quiet, but nothing like Merikh's. They were too close for comfort, but she remained where she was.

"She is on Merikh's lands," Pink said.

Purple sniffed at the air. *"He has been here recently."*

"Why is he keeping food alive?"

"Maybe she's not food?"

They both burst out laughing.

"No!"

"Never!"

"Humans cannot be friends with Mavka."

"S-sure we can," Raewyn interjected. "I'm Merikh's friend."

They paused, and the silence only made her more nervous. That was until they both burst out laughing again, this time even louder than before.

"Impossible," Purple stated, his voice stern, like he may have shaken his head. The sound of rattling bones came from him.

"Merikh does not have friends."

"He likes no one, not even his own kind."

"He'll be really angry if he returns and finds I'm not here," she told them, turning her head to the side when Pink crept behind her.

"He is always angry. This is nothing new," Purple stated.

"Are you sure she is human?" Raewyn flinched when her hair was grabbed and yanked upwards, like Pink wanted a better look. *"Her hair is white."*

"Humans don't usually have white hair unless they are old."

"Yes, and she smells different." She tried not to let out a cry when Pink tore at her hair to sniff it.

"Her ears are strange. Pointy and wrong." Purple grabbed her ankle and lifted her foot off the ground. She bounced, having to balance herself in an odd position. *"Her feet are the same, as are her hands."*

"I-I'm an Elf!" she yelped when she almost tripped. The only thing saving her was Pink holding her hair, and it made her wince further. "You're hurting me. Please let go."

Neither did, not seeming to listen as they had a conversation between themselves.

"Could she be like the Demon King?"

"But the Demon King has horns and red eyes. Hers are strange, like she has stars in her eyes."

"Why does she have stars in her eyes?"

"Not sure. Do you know why?"

"No, but I like her hair. It smells nice, and it's a pretty colour."

"Smells nice? She smells awful! Her scent is too sweet."

"Please let me go," she pleaded, trying to pull her foot away when Purple started wiggling her big toe. She also reached up and gripped her hair to take the worst of the pain away.

At the same time, they both dropped what they were holding, and she fell to the ground from the lack of support. Raewyn's face twisted into a wince when she landed on her side and elbow, but she didn't have time to recover.

They circled her, poking and grabbing different limbs as they inspected her. She was like a fish, and they were two predators circling the water, checking their prey before they attacked.

They seemed just as big as Merikh, since they'd spoken from above her, but she was questioning their intelligence. She was used to Merikh and the way he clearly articulated himself. It was hard to imagine they were all the same species.

"His smell is on her," Pink stated from near her feet.

"But it does not seem like he has claimed her," Purple said as he moved down her left side.

"What does this mean? Is she his bride or not?"

"Bride?" Raewyn asked, hoping to the Gilded Maiden that Merikh would turn up and save her.

"Do you have to like someone to make them your bride?"

"But Merikh hates everyone. He only lets us rest here."

"We must be careful. We do not want him to rip your arm off again and smack you with it." Purple chuckled.

"Hey! That is not funny. That really hurt."

"He smacked me with it too."

Weirdly enough, they both chuckled.

"What's a bride?" Raewyn shouted, wishing they'd stop ignoring her.

They stopped again, and yellow flashed in her vision, darker with curiosity.

"We do not know. You tell us."

"We can have a bride, this we know."

"But we do not know what that means. Mother explained it, but we do not understand."

"A friend? Someone we will cherish who is not Mavka? Someone who will make us whole?"

"But we are already whole," Pink stated, his orbs flashing a much brighter pink than before.

"We have each other." Purple's orbs must have flashed pink as well, since there were two pairs of matching sparks. *"How much more could we want?"*

Wow. That answered absolutely nothing and just made her even more confused. Although... she did find what they said about each other rather sweet, and some of her unease faded.

They cared about each other deeply. It was hard not to find that tender.

She let the bride subject go, since it was obvious it was pointless.

"Okay. Well, I'm Raewyn. I'm not a human, but an Elf from a different world."

"What's an Elf?"

"And what's a Raewyn?"

She couldn't help the small giggle that left her. Yep, these two definitely didn't have as much humanity as Merikh. She kind of found it cute, now that it seemed like they weren't going to harm her... at least, for now.

"Raewyn is my name."

A small silence fell upon them, yellow sparking in her vision. They'd done it at each other, from what she could tell.

A glowing trail informed her they'd both turned to her, and at the same time asked, *"What's a name?"*

She explained it to them as best as she could, even though they were slow to digest it. She had to say the same thing multiple times and in different ways. They didn't even realise Merikh was a name and thought it was just something he'd preferred to be called other than Duskwalker, or Mavka.

They'd thought it was some kind of strange descriptor.

The longer she spoke to them, the more she liked them. They were a little goofy, and they liked to answer each other's questions and finish their sentences. They were so in sync with each other but obviously disconnected from the world.

"Could you name us then?" Pink asked, coming a little too close to her face.

Raewyn tilted her head before grabbing her feet while crossing her legs. "Sure, I guess." She gave a shrug. "Can I touch your faces, though? It might make it easier for me to figure out what to name you if I know what you look like."

"What do you mean?" Purple asked.

"You are already looking at us."

Her eyelids flickered, but she gave them a weak smile. "I can't see," she told them. "That's why I have stars in my eyes."

A whoosh of air in front of her face informed her one had waved their hand millimetres from her nose.

"She did not see it."

"No, she did not."

"Did you know creatures could lose their sight?"

"No," Pink answered, before throwing her a question. *"You do not heal in twenty-four hours like us? This is permanent?"*

Raewyn nodded. "Yes. Humans and Elves can't heal wounds like this with magic."

"We see... Well, if you must touch my face to name me, then you can do so," Purple offered.

Raewyn raised her hands up and waited for him to place whatever kind of skull he had in her palms.

"No! I want to be named first," Pink exclaimed right before Purple was shoved to the ground with a thud and a thwap.

Just as Pink placed his skull in her hands, it was gone as he was tackled. *"I offered first!"*

Dread crept up her spine, since she'd obviously started a fight between them. It worsened when one grabbed her ankle and yanked her towards them, while the other growled and clasped her wrist.

Oh no. What have I done?

She hoped they didn't plan to play tug-o-war with her body!

Raewyn let out a high-pitched squeal when her worries were proven right, and they yanked in opposite directions.

"Me first!" one of them snarled, just as a deafening roar bellowed from the side.

Their orb flashes turned white, the glowing trail moving towards the sound. Heavy footsteps pounded against the ground, frighteningly fast and bolting in their direction.

"It's Merikh."

"He has returned."

Then, at the same time they said, *"And he is angry with us."*

Hanging from one shoulder was a bag filled with more food for Raewyn he hadn't been able to carry before. The other had a satchel of clothing for her, since he'd noticed she only had two dresses and one was filthy from their travels.

Humans liked to regularly change their outfits and had different kinds. He imagined it would be the same for her, especially since she bathed more regularly in comparison to them. She didn't have anything to sleep in, something she'd whined about.

When he hadn't managed to find the last tools and the kind of flowers she needed, he'd gone to a different village that wasn't too far from the first. Thankfully, he found them.

In his right hand, he held a decent-sized pot with multiple yellow tulips dancing in it.

Although he'd sprinted on all fours to both villages, he'd walked back to minimise damage to the flowers. Other than Raewyn, he didn't think he'd ever held something so delicate before.

His ward was in place, so he thought all would be well. No Demons could get inside, and the chance of another Duskwalker entering his territory was low – especially since most of them lived on the north-west side of the Veil, whereas he was south-east.

He'd been wrong, so very wrong.

Merikh hadn't taken into consideration the twins, who had no home and ventured everywhere within it, leaving destruction in their path. They weren't inherently violent, but their version of playful was aggressive, and their curiosity often got the better of them.

As soon as he saw them in the yard, within the protective dome of his ward, panic struck him. He couldn't smell blood, so

Raewyn hadn't been eaten, but they'd been blocking his view of her.

The moment she screamed, and he saw her lying on the ground between them, his panic turned into rage.

Merikh was in motion, dropping his bags and the pot to the ground as he darted forward and roared. The *chink* of ceramic breaking barely registered as he swiftly crossed the distance.

Of all fucking days, these two had to show up?!

Merikh and Raewyn had been here for days, and he'd only left briefly for two of them to get supplies. Today, he'd been gone the longest, and they had decided to come now?

The twins often came to his lands when he wasn't here. Since he rarely occupied his home but had a ward in place, they found it a safe haven to truly rest. They had nowhere else to go, so they came here occasionally.

When Merikh had first discovered them on his lands, he'd been angered by their annoying, playful presence. Over time, they'd worn him down, refusing to leave him alone despite how much he fought with them.

They were persistent.

He'd eventually given up and told them they could come here, so long as they left him alone, and as long as they didn't touch his things or enter his cave.

This moment was the first time he'd considered Raewyn to be 'his', although not in a truly deep sense. She was more someone he was supposed to be protecting, someone they couldn't touch, because they could destroy her within seconds.

"Run!" the twins shouted in unison.

It was too late. They were too slow to turn around and bolt in opposite directions.

He grabbed the bat-skulled one, who usually had pink orbs, by the base of one of his useless feathered wings. Merikh could tell he'd never used them, since the muscles around the base hadn't finished forming.

Then, he grabbed the lizard tail of the raven-skulled Mavka

who usually had purple orbs. He didn't have wings like his fraternal brother.

At the same time, he yanked to grab some part of their heads. The short-nosed, fruit-bat-skulled Mavka had goat horns that curled up and back over his head. It was easy to grab one. The other had smaller horns that pointed upwards, too little to be grabbed, so he just curled his hand around his beak.

Raewyn was between his feet as he put himself into a protective stance above her. She crawled from underneath him as his orbs flared a crimson red, causing the other two to go white in fear.

He lifted them to their feet, and neither were able to hold the position comfortably in their monstrous forms. They were always like that, and Merikh had once wondered if they knew they could turn more humanoid.

Perhaps they didn't even want to.

"What were you doing to her?" His rage deepened his voice to what it was like when he was in his monstrous form.

"Nothing!" the bat-skulled Mavka yelped, just as the raven-skulled one claimed, *"We did nothing!"*

"Then why the fuck did she scream?" he roared, shaking both their heads violently when they tried to push at him.

"We don't know!" they shouted in unison.

Merikh was so agitated, he'd torn his clothing, his quills quivering at their highest points. He'd freed his tail upon his walk home, and it curled and flicked to the side.

Their answers weren't good enough. He squeezed his hand around the raven skull's beak, clamping his jaw together until he was sure it hurt. It was a warning, a threat, one he'd given before. He yelped, causing the bat-skulled one's orbs to whiten even further in understanding.

"We did not mean to make her cry," the bat-skulled one said. *"Isn't that right?"*

"Yes. We did not mean to hurt her. We were not thinking about eating her once we were done."

"No, never. We would not eat Merikh's things."

It was like they shared the same brain, and it wasn't very smart. They'd basically just told him an obvious lie, which revealed the truth of what could have happened.

They'd been considering it, and if he had come any later, he may have found her eaten. The rage he would have unleashed would have been so acute, he doubted he would have held back.

He tightened his fists in realisation that he could have lost his own path to escaping this world because of these two half-brained Mavka.

I should never have trusted them! He should never have allowed them to come here and rest.

He didn't like them any more than the rest of his wretched kind: all fucking dumb, filled with foolish hopes and dreams that couldn't be obtained.

The only one he held any kind of sentiment towards was Orpheus. He was the only one who saw this world with the same foreboding, melancholic lens. Orpheus was the only one who understood the dark truth of the humans, the Demons, of every living, breathing thing uselessly desperate to live.

He understood just as Merikh that they were nothing but beasts to them all, that they were hated, that there was no kindness for them.

Yet, he still fucking hated him, because he held out hope that he could find a bride.

Duskwalkers weren't meant to find happiness, find love, or someone to hold them tenderly in the dark of the night. There was no one who wanted to be sheltered in their claws.

Even if offered, no one wanted to use them as their shield. They were never seen as someone who could be trusted, and they were treated as nothing more than horrible, despicable creatures.

Orpheus and he had the same perspective on the world, but where Orpheus allowed his loneliness to fester into foolish hope, Merikh had twisted it into spite.

Towards him, to other Duskwalkers, to the Demons and humans. To everyone, including his own damn reflection.

The twins being here, meddling in his affairs and almost ruining the one potential he'd found to escape? *That* was a startling reminder of why he'd never wanted them here in the first place.

They were too afraid of him to turn it into anger. Their minds were scarred from the memories they had of fighting him in the beginning, where he'd won, temporarily killing them over, and over, and over again until he gave up bothering.

His sight sunk deeper into crimson as his growl became more pronounced.

Then it began to soften as he took in their orbs, their skulls, their horns, and the submissive way they were letting him hold them.

Even if he didn't like them, there was a reason he'd never killed them. There was a reason why he'd never crushed their skulls when he'd had ample opportunity to do so.

They were his brothers.

It wasn't easy to rein back his anger. As he started to calm, he registered that Raewyn had been shouting at him. He'd been too focused on them.

Once he opened his senses again, the thread of a familiar scent caught in his nose hole – one that instantly ignited the flames of his rage.

Not at the twins, but at someone else entirely. Someone who had come here, was likely the reason the twins had come here, even though he'd asked her to never be within his presence, his home, his territory ever again.

The Witch Owl, he mentally snarled.

He turned his head to search for her, and a whisp of white ducked within the Veil.

"Merikh, I said stop!" Raewyn shouted from behind him. "Leave them alone! They weren't doing anything wrong. They just got a little excited."

She was too quick to defend them, especially when curiosity from a Duskwalker could result in death.

"Please don't hurt us. We won't do it again."

He didn't know which one spoke, but it still sliced at him in a way he found deeply uncomfortable.

The twins took his new bout of aggression as being directed at them, even though his grip was loosening. So had Raewyn, who bounced forward with the intention of trying to stop him.

Unfortunately, he'd tossed the twins back, letting them go, and Raewyn grabbed at his arm he'd just dropped. She'd likely been going for his side to pull him back.

She sucked in a sharp, pained breath.

The scent of blood lifted into the air.

All three of their orbs turned red in hunger.

Shit, was all he could muster.

Holding his breath the moment he got a whiff of it, Merikh only had *seconds* to spin in a circle. He caught her in his arm, making her gasp as he impacted her stomach, and tossed her into the lake before the twins attacked.

TWENTY-THREE

Her scream was swallowed up by deep water as Merikh continued to spin.

He wrapped his arms around the shoulders of the raven-skulled Mavka who had dived after Raewyn. The other was scratching at the grass where drops of her blood had fallen, licking at it and diminishing the scent.

It allowed Merikh to breathe through his mouth.

He threw the raven-skulled one to the ground, and he rolled across it for a few metres, his limbs and thick lizard tail flailing.

Raewyn broke the surface of the lake and sputtered water as she searched for the edge in panic.

"Stay in the water!" Merikh shouted, worried that if her hand was still bleeding, she'd become a target.

Unfortunately, the quills on his left arm were coated in her blood scent.

The bat-skulled Mavka lunged for his arm and bit down around it with Merikh's hand deep in its mouth. Some of the quills broke inside its mouth, the top part having very little flesh to destroy. The Mavka yelped when the broken shards must have lanced his tongue.

Merikh faced no damage from his quills being broken. They were painless to break, since they were like hollow hair follicles.

He did, however, roar at the deep cut of fangs slicing through his flesh.

Merikh dug his claws between the Mavka's fangs to dislodge the jaw from his arm, the pressure becoming unbearable as it tightened. The bat-skulled Mavka begun shaking his head while tugging backwards, which only made the pain more severe. At this rate, Merikh was going to lose his hand down the Mavka's throat – he could almost feel it.

Merikh did the only thing he could think of.

With his fingers flat and together, Merikh sliced his claws into the side of its neck like a blade.

The bat-skulled Mavka's yelping cry caused the other's orbs to flare a brighter red in rage for his twin. He sprinted for Merikh, who was still being held immobile, and barrel-rolled into him.

With his caught arm still being tugged and his body being shoved to the ground the opposite way, his shoulder dislocated, and the popping pain sent him over the edge.

The small thread of control he had on his instinctual rage snapped, and his sight darkened to its red hue.

What happened next was faded, hazy images and senses, as invisible, invasive hands squeezed at the squishy meat of his brain. It was like he was being manipulated, controlled to lose his sense of reasoning, to just battle until he'd ravaged everything within his path.

Bloodthirsty and angry, *everything* was a foe.

His body shifted into his monstrous form to better fight. It heightened his senses, his speed, his strength. It extended his quills and made him even larger than he already was.

While he was on his side, Merikh let out an agonised yelp when the bone in his arm was snapped. Claws went to slash at his back, but the raven-skulled Mavka jumped back when he was impaled by Merikh's quills. Instead, he slashed at Merikh's side until Merikh booted him in the head.

He spun and sat on his arse, grabbed the bat-skulled Mavka's horn, and tried to twist his head to get him to let go. He just wanted it to let go, his arm in so much agony that it radiated all the way to his spine. It felt like he was trying to pull Merikh's body inside out through his left shoulder as the Mavka yanked and bit, slowly climbing higher up his arm with chomping bites until he was near Merikh's elbow.

Twisting the Mavka's neck and head did nothing, since their heads could rotate nearly three-sixty degrees. It was the only thing that saved him when the raven-skulled Mavka yanked on Merikh's own horn with his fangs and tugged him the other way.

Merikh clawed at the underside of his neck to free himself, but to no avail. He was being torn in two from his shoulder joint, and he let out a bellowing roar.

He did the only thing he could.

Flattening his hand once more, he shoved his claws into his own shoulder and pulled. His yell only highlighted how much effort it took to rip his own arm from his body in desperation, freeing himself in a spray of blood and snapping tendons.

The bat-skulled Mavka tripped back, not expecting the sudden release. Once he regained his footing and shook his head from side to side, the upper part of Merikh's arm wiggled in the air from his maw.

Now freed from the nuisance of his arm, Merikh rose to his knees to keep himself stable and then shoved his claws into the raven-skulled Mavka's throat, piercing his trachea and windpipe.

His strangled choke only grew worse as Merikh swiped and tore the front of his neck completely open.

That didn't put him down; it only made him weak. Blood poured from his wound faster than it leaked from Merikh's shoulder, but the raven-skulled Mavka was still quick on his four limbs as he leapt for Merikh.

Merikh turned, dodging him completely. He spun, grabbed his beak and twisted it as he stood on top of the Mavka's spine. He pulled back until the little bones in his neck caved in and snapped before exploding through the front of his wounded throat.

The roar that exploded from the bat-skulled Mavka was too late, as was his sprint to save his twin. Merikh tore the raven's head from his body and then proceeded to carry it backwards as he was chased.

In the midst of his bloodlust, despite how little he could truly formulate a thought, he'd always done one thing when fighting these two.

If he temporarily killed one, he'd carry their skull and toss it away from the fight so the other couldn't accidentally destroy it.

Perhaps, on a subconscious level not even he could hear, a voice was telling him to protect his siblings – even when he wanted nothing more than to destroy them.

He ditched raven skull's head when he couldn't support himself on his bowed, bear-shaped back legs for too much longer. He dropped back down to all three limbs and then sprinted towards bat skull, who was already heading in his direction.

It only took a few moments for Merikh to wrap his thick, meaty legs around the Mavka's flailing arms and trap them to his sides. He wrapped his only arm around bat skull's face to keep him in place as he squirmed and snapped his jaw with sharp clicks.

Then Merikh tore into the Mavka's injured neck with his fangs, spitting away muscle and bone until he'd decapitated him as well.

Although his quills were useful in any fight, a Mavka would just keep fighting. Even if their heart was pierced, even if they were down to no limbs, they would keep fighting, would keep moving, growing more and more lethargic until the fighting had stopped.

The only way to stop one was to remove their head, and hundreds of years of knowledge had imbedded that into his subconscious. Even when his mind was muddled, he went for the weak spot of every creature.

For a Demon, it was their spine and throat. A human's was their heart and throat. Animals were generally weakest at their soft exposed underbellies.

Once the fighting stopped, Merikh was in far too much pain to return to his normal state, both physically and mentally. He sniffed at the ground, at the blood that wasn't enticing at all, searching for a safe place to lie down.

Darkness was taking hold, the cliff wall making it seem like night was falling long before it actually did.

Two fully intact Mavka skulls lay metres away from each other without their orbs. Their bodies eventually disintegrated into black sand.

Merikh limped over to the entrance of his cave and lay down next to it against the wall.

He whimpered, licking at his shoulder in hopes of getting it to stop bleeding. When it did, he rested his head against the ground, too agitated from fighting to sleep, too panicked to let himself be vulnerable.

Any sound caused him to growl in warning, even if it was only a fluttering leaf.

If anything approached him... it would die.

Raewyn remained in the water after Merikh had thrown her into it to hide her scents of both fear and blood. The sounds they produced as they fought were awful, and the smell of their blood was like sweetness and iron. She wanted to gag.

There were things she was never supposed to hear, like yelping cries, whimpers, skin and body parts tearing.

She'd shuddered every time and just buried her face against the dirt, waiting for them to finish.

Once the fighting stopped, only one remained. She didn't know who it was, but she thought it might be Merikh. His echoes of whimpers and growls made her heart burn.

None of this was her fault. It didn't take away from the fact that she was the cause of it, even though she hadn't meant to injure herself.

His whines drifted over the area, and she had no idea where he'd gone, since she was thrown off her placement within the ward. She thought it might be near the entrance of his cave due to the dome's edge disappearing through the cliff's rock, but she wasn't quite sure.

The heat from the sun faded, but the water was warm from being bathed in its light all day. That didn't stop her from shivering from the cold that came from blood loss, or the pain that radiated up her hand.

She could barely move it. Not just because it stung – she'd also damaged something vital in it. The only fingers that could move were her thumb and pinkie, and trying to move only made it ache more.

The water stung, but she kept it submerged to minimise her blood scent.

The water was so deep there that her toes barely skimmed the muddy ground. She floated and held on to a rock jutting from the edge.

He's in pain, Raewyn thought with sympathy as his high-pitched, quiet whines continued. *He must be really hurt.*

She waited until they faded before she lifted her head over the side. *I hope the other two Duskwalkers are okay.*

The tears that pooled in her eyes during the fighting had long ago abated, and they started up again at the thought that Merikh might have killed them. They were siblings. She couldn't imagine killing her own family.

She didn't want her being the cause to weigh on her conscience.

"M-Merikh?" she cried, wondering why he hadn't come to fetch her from the water yet.

She wanted to get out, to see if he was okay.

His answering growl had her shrinking momentarily, until

she lifted her head over the edge again. She growled back like she sometimes did, hoping that would help calm him.

His deep, echoing snarl was so frightening that she submerged herself completely, head and all. When a few seconds passed and he didn't approach to attack her, she came up for air.

She didn't know how long she stayed there. Minutes? Hours? She eventually grew tired and held onto the ledge as she rested her head on the crook of her elbow and closed her eyes.

Everything went quiet, and she thought Merikh may have fallen asleep, like she was beginning to.

"I'm sorry. I didn't mean for this to happen," a feminine voice whispered. She sounded so far away, and yet Raewyn could tell she was right there, beyond her hand.

She opened her heavy eyelids, and a ghostly, human-shaped white wisp darted away. They had loose, curly hair, and sharp but kind eyes.

Just as she was beginning to drift off again, a groan carried over the short distance. She peeked her eyelids open but didn't move.

"Shit," Merikh wheezed before letting out a curt whine. *"Everything hurts."* His voice was groggy, like he was tired or dizzy. *"Shit! Raewyn!"*

He sprinted over to where she was within a few seconds of shouting her name. It was odd to hear him approaching, since he was usually so light on his feet.

"Are you alright?" he asked, his voice back to its normal bass as one of his hands wrapped around her thin wrist.

The dull ache in her hand instantly faded, and she became stronger, like the blood she'd lost was returned. He'd healed her before he'd taken her out of the water, probably wary of her scent right now.

"You didn't have to do that," she admonished quietly, as he slid his hand down her biceps to pick her up at a stronger point in her arm. She grabbed the torn shirt around his shoulders to help support her weight. "You're injured. You didn't have to add to your pain. I stopped bleeding."

"Don't worry about it. I didn't feel it, since I don't have that hand right now."

Sitting on her hip against the ground between Merikh's crouching knees, a cold chill crept down her spine. Dread took hold, and her eyes widened as she patted his chest.

"What do you mean, you don't have that hand right now?"

Just as she touched his left shoulder joint, her hands retracted when he hissed out a breath.

"Holy maiden, Merikh, your arm is gone!"

His answering chuckle was surprisingly filled with humour before he let out a groan. "Yeah. Noticed that myself."

This was what he found funny? Raewyn burst into tears, wishing to wipe this day from her memory completely.

"I'm so sorry," she apologised as she covered her face, too worn out to care if he found her tears awkward. "I should have been more careful."

"The fuck you apologising for? Do you know how close you were to dying?"

She had a feeling she was close to death with the three Duskwalkers around. "Yeah, but–"

"I brought you to my home with the intention of protecting you, and I almost failed on that promise today. I didn't realise the twins would come here. If I need to leave the area, I'll take you with me, so you aren't attacked again."

"N-no, it's fine. I kind of liked them."

"You *liked* them?" His tone was aghast.

"Sure. They asked me to name them and then got into a fight about who would be named first. It was silly, but was also kind of funny, like two kids fighting over a toy." Then she rubbed her arm as she said, "I just didn't like being the toy."

His silence was uncomfortable. She could almost feel him peering at her in a certain way.

"Merikh... Did you... Are they..." Gosh, she couldn't even

bring herself to ask the question.

Would she judge him for it? She wished that wasn't one of the reasons she was so hesitant about asking.

"No, I didn't kill them. Even if that is my intention, I can never bring myself to do it – whether I'm in that enraged state or not." Her shoulders sagged in relief. "They'll grow their bodies back in a day, like I will with my arm."

"Their bodies?" she asked as she wiped at her face to remove the stain of her tears.

"I beheaded them," he answered without a shred of remorse.

The idea only made her dizzy. "Can we go inside? I really want to go inside."

"You can. I, on the other hand, am covered in blood and will make a mess."

She nibbled at her bottom lip, wishing there was something she could do for him. Unfortunately, she didn't have any healing magic.

Then, her chest ached as she said, "I lost my cane. I think it's in the lake."

It must be lost forever, but she really wanted it back.

"I'll find it for you. If not, I'll make you a new one."

She wished she could offer him a thankful smile, but she couldn't muster one right then. "Thank you."

He helped her to her feet and guided her back towards his home. Her ears twitched the entire time, hating that he was suppressing his whines like he was ashamed of them. She could tell he was limping, and she thought he might be more wounded than he let on.

"I think I broke the flowerpot when I dropped it," he grumbled quietly when they made it to the entrance.

"That's fine. If it's mostly intact, we can strap it back together."

TWENTY-FOUR

Standing near the entrance of his cave, Merikh watched the Elf and the two Mavkas spending time together. Raewyn was sitting on the ground with the raven-skulled Mavka acting as her back support, while the other had his bat skull resting in her crossed legs.

When Merikh had tried to chase them away from his home after they'd grown their bodies back – and his arm returned – Raewyn had intervened with a loud shout. When they slowly scampered away, their tails down in submission, she'd managed to coax them back.

Their surprise had been unmistakeable, but their dark yellow orbs of curiosity had turned bright in joy.

She'd offered them sweet smiles and head pats, and they'd grown smitten with her. They'd spouted a hundred apologies and tried to give her head pats in return, which caused her to explode in a spout of soft giggles.

Since then, they'd been talking. When she sat, they'd each found a way to nuzzle into her.

There had been a small fight about who would get to lay their head in her lap, which she'd managed to control before another incident occurred. From a distance, Merikh listened to them asking her questions about what she was, where she came from, why she was on Earth.

It was obvious they didn't understand all of it, but they didn't mind. They'd found a friendly creature to talk to who wasn't like them, and they were curious about her.

At first glance, had he not known better, it would have appeared like they'd known each other all their lives. Raewyn was exceptionally patient with them.

Any time Merikh tried to approach, the twins would shirk away, lowering themselves after their defeat yesterday.

He was forced to remain away from them, from her.

He felt like a fucking outcast.

He couldn't remember if his orbs had ever turned green in jealousy, but the emotion clawed at his chest like a rabid beast. It wounded him deeper than the arm he'd torn from his own body.

Forced to stand on the other side of the yard, he watched to make sure she didn't come to harm. Arms folded and back leaning against the wall, he dug his claws into his arms in annoyance.

Any time she laughed, his sight would become green with envy that they had managed to make her so content while he struggled to do so. Then his orbs would turn red in anger that he was experiencing these negative waves of emotions because of her... in his own territory, his own damn home!

The sun was bright today. Although it was dropping down the horizon, it bathed them in light like a pretty, warm scene. Merikh was in the shadows, like usual.

It was just a reminder that he'd always been in the dark, alone, while others experienced joy as he watched.

Covering the side of her mouth with one hand, Raewyn whispered something, causing the raven-skulled Duskwalker to look up at Merikh.

"Yes, he still stares," he said.

The other added, *"He always stares."*

Merikh rolled his head and tightened his arms across his chest. He was being watchful, which could be the difference between her life and death.

"He does not like us being here," the bat-skulled, pink-orbed Mavka stated.

"We have rested. We must leave soon before his patience wears thin."

It was already thin! The only reason he hadn't chased them away by now was because of her.

"Come with us. He is mean."

"You do not have to stay here."

He noted that Raewyn's ears flattened, and the joy she had been wearing disappeared. "That's not a very nice thing to say."

"But it is true," the purple-orbed, raven-skulled Mavka said.

"Come with us." The bat-skulled Mavka had gotten up and began tugging on her arm. *"We will protect you within the Veil."*

That was enough. That was the line Merikh had to draw for these foolish Duskwalkers. He made his way over to them.

"No," Raewyn said with a stern voice, pulling her arm back. "I will stay here with Merikh. If it weren't for him, you two would have hurt me yesterday."

Both their orbs turned a deep blue as their skulls lowered. At least they understood the truth of that.

"He comes," the raven-skulled Mavka whined, jumping to all fours so suddenly that Raewyn fell to her back as her support disappeared.

"We were not doing anything," the bat-skulled Mavka said when he was almost to them.

"No, nothing. Just talking. Right, Rae?"

Once more, Merikh's sight flared a deep green.

Wasn't 'Rae' the special name her friends called her? Not even Merikh had crossed that line with her, unsure if they were even friends. Why did they take it upon themselves to call her that?

Was it *that* easy to become her friend? Even after they'd tried to eat her the day before?

"It's time you leave," he said to them before turning his snout in her direction. "I'm ready to give you my diadem, so you should start your experiments now."

He'd only just made that decision upon seeing them all together. It was an excuse to break them up, so he didn't have to watch this weirdly painful scene anymore.

"But she has not named us yet!" the bat-skulled Mavka shouted in protest.

"She promised us she would."

"It's difficult to name people I don't know." Raewyn laughed as she sat back up, turning her face in Merikh's vicinity. He was producing his vibration for her. Then she grumbled, "And they didn't like the first names I gave them. They said they were too hard to pronounce because they were Elvish."

This was the hold up from them pissing off?

"Fine," Merikh bit. "I will name you, then."

"No," the bat-skulled Mavka whined as he backed up to stand next to his brother. *"We do not want you to name us."*

"They will be bad names. Mean names."

Merikh rolled his head. This time, he turned his snout to the sky to hide his orb change that had flared red. When he'd snuffed out his anger and they returned to normal, he lowered his head.

Ignoring their complaints, he said, "How about... Ingram for you." He pointed his snout at the raven-skulled Mavka, before moving it to the bat-skulled one. "And Aleron for you."

They tilted their heads in opposite directions to each other, their pinkie fingers overlapping.

"What do they mean?" the bat-skulled one asked as he turned his head to his twin.

"Probably something terrible," the raven one answered. *"Like annoyance or destruction."*

"Ingram means raven of peace," Merikh told the raven skull. Then he turned to the other Mavka while eyeing his feathered back. "Aleron means the winged one. To fly."

"Then should I not be named Aleron?" the raven-skulled one

said. *"And he be named Ingram?"*

"Yes. That makes far more sense," his twin answered. *"Since I have a raven skull."*

Raewyn giggled off to the side, obviously coming to the same conclusion Merikh did.

Idiots! They're both idiots!

"You have the raven skull," Raewyn said to the purple-orbed Mavka.

"What you see is not what you have," Merikh sighed, realising they thought they had each other's heads because that's what they were always looking at.

They had no trouble deducing that with other Mavkas, but apparently, between them, it never registered.

"Then what do I have?"

"You have a bat skull, and bird wings."

"Wings?" He turned his head over his shoulder and then subtly wiggled them up and down. *"That is what these things are called?"*

"I see..."

"Yes, so do I."

"Ha! I cannot believe you did not figure that out."

"You did not either!"

They shoved at each other as they chuckled.

"So, are you happy with them?" Raewyn asked as she clapped her hands together once to gain their attention. "In-grem and Ale-ron?"

The way she sounded them out was funny to Merikh, but he found her Elvish accent made them even nicer.

They both nodded.

"Yes, we are," Ingram stated.

"We are pleased," Aleron confirmed.

"Good," Merikh lightly snapped. "Now that the matter is settled, go away. We have work to do."

"Merikh!" Raewyn cried, which only made him chuckle when her face was scrunched in displeasure. It was cute, the way her brows furrowed and her lips pursed.

After some back and forth between him and the twins, they did eventually leave. They shoved each other playfully, speaking their new names, and an unidentifiable emotion swirled in his chest.

One that made it puff out with warmth.

"That was nice of you," Raewyn commented as she held her hand out, as if she was expecting him to offer. She was right, he would have, and he took it so he could help her to her feet. "I like the names you gave them. They were really thoughtful."

His sight moved back to where they'd disappeared into the forest.

"I didn't give them new ones," he answered. "Those are their names."

She pushed her hand through the loop of her cane – he'd found it for her yesterday, near the boulder. Once steady on her feet, she frowned up at him.

"What do you mean?"

"Those were the names given to them by our mother. They just don't remember, as most of us don't." When she nibbled at her full bottom lip with a strange kind of concern on her features, he couldn't help tilting his head. "What's with your expression?"

"I just don't understand. Why would she name them so sweetly but give you a name that means... something so hateful?"

"Ah," he gave a singular, dark chuckle. "That is because I renamed myself. Most of us will find our own names, ones we like or are given when we are ready. The twins may even forget the ones we've just given them."

"Do you know what yours was originally, then?"

Silence stretched between them, his answer slow to come, his heart burning with each beat. He was hesitant about answering.

"It was Orson, meaning bear cub. She named us each after our features, like Aleron's wings and Ingram's skull." He turned his skull away, wrapping his hand around his snout as he rubbed it. "I ask that you never call me that, as that name is dead to me."

He expected her to ask him why, but was thankful she didn't. In doing so, by her showing him more respect than anyone else had in his entire life, a different emotion swirled in his chest. It was utterly tender, and he was utterly terrified of it.

He grunted and cleared his throat.

"So, are you ready to begin your experiment? I will give you my diadem, and hopefully, what we've done to put the flowerpot back together will last until you are ready."

Her lips twisted to the side in thought, but a mischievous smile played at the edge of them. He liked it when she looked conniving; it didn't match her guileless features.

"Can I borrow your sight while I do it?"

"No."

"Oh, come on!" she exclaimed, while stamping one of her feet. "It's not like you need it more than I do."

"It's mine," he tried to roar back, but instead, it came out as a chuckle when she gave him a glare.

Raewyn placed her hands on her hips. "Sharing is caring. It's the nice thing to do."

Merikh leaned over her until the tip of his snout was just a hair's distance from her nose. Her eyelids twitched when his breath told her how close he was.

With his voice filled with a malevolent kind of humour, he said, "When have I ever said I was nice?"

"Jerk," she lightly bit, before using the heel of her foot to kick him in the shin.

Then, with her nose turned upwards, she walked off.

"A little to the left," he stated, and she readjusted her path to align better with the entrance to his cave.

"Thank you," she said, all snooty-like. "But I still think you're churlish."

His chest rumbled with a laugh he didn't let out. He couldn't remember the last time he'd found someone so funny, or someone who could make him want to laugh so freely.

"You should consider my rejection as faith in your capabilities, little 'scientist.'"

When she lifted her nose even further and she was practically facing the sky, his fangs parted, and the chuckle finally left him.

She's cute when she does that. The fact that she was unafraid to be so cheeky in a high-handed, superior way always caught him off-guard.

No one was playful in the way she was.

His humour was cut short when he noticed a ghostly figure at the edge of his peripheral. When he turned his head that way, it disappeared within an instant.

We're being watched. He snarled in that direction. He even took a step forward to tell them to get lost – but changed his mind.

The Witch Owl would eventually understand he had no interest in speaking with her and would, hopefully, fly away. Merikh would rather not speak to her, or even see her, if he could help it.

Raewyn dropped her smile when Merikh entered, refusing to let him know that she'd only been teasing him.

She didn't think he would allow her the use of his sight. Although it would be welcomed, since it would make things faster and easier, she didn't *actually* need it. She was completely capable on her own, and the fact he'd felt the same way was actually... nice.

Raewyn didn't like anyone looking down on her. She was strong – physically, emotionally, and mentally – and she'd always hated when people doubted her. Whether that be because of her scientific capabilities, her sight, her athletic abilities... she'd always had this flaw where she needed to prove herself.

Merikh didn't make her feel that way. He just silently

supported her without needing to receive gratitude.

That's all Raewyn could ask of a person.

However, because it was Merikh, and it was obvious he was uncomfortable every time she either apologised or thanked him, she always did it.

At his soft vibration, she turned her head the other way while forcing a pout to her lips.

"I would like for you to do me a favour for a few days," he said as he entered his cave.

Raewyn scoffed as she yanked the flowerpot closer from across the stone bench.

"Why should I do anything for you when you won't do something for me?" She put her hand out. "Diadem, please."

"I'm being serious, Raewyn." By the sternness of his tone, she dropped the act, as well as her hand.

"Is something wrong?"

"I would like for you not to go outside when I sleep."

He slept a few hours every day, while Raewyn only needed to do so once every two or three days. It was an odd request, and one she didn't understand.

"If it's about Ingram and Aleron, I'll be fine if they return. It's one of the reasons I got to know them today."

Raewyn had an inkling he hadn't liked her spending time with them. She, on the other hand, didn't care if he thought they were dangerous. They were funny, and oddly sweet.

It was unfortunate the relationship between the three Duskwalkers was obviously poor. She'd been hoping she could help mend it a little, but it seemed impossible to bridge that gap.

Every time he tried to get close, the twins would shirk away. Merikh also wasn't friendly towards them. He was imposing, even to his own kind.

"Just do as I ask," he snapped, more short-tempered than usual. The clink of metal hit the bench, followed by the scrape of claws. "There, have the diadem."

He'd slapped it down, and then stood there. Her shoulders

turned inwards. *He's really angry for some reason.*

Had she poked the metaphorical bear too much?

Keeping her head down, she pushed it back at him. "I-I don't actually need it yet. I still need to get the tulips you brought me to absorb magic and change their photosynthetic structure so they will do what I need them to."

"Take it," he bit. "The quicker I give it to you, the quicker you'll figure everything out so we can leave."

Why does he suddenly want to rush? He'd been dragging his feet about this for days.

"What can I do to help?" he added, completely surprising her.

"Pardon?" She was under the impression he'd thought she'd be able to do this on her own.

"You said you had an assistant, yes?" His tone was colder than usual, but at least his question eased her. That was, until he said, "Or is my assistance not good enough?"

Something is wrong with him. Merikh could be rather curt with her – well, with everyone apparently. Usually, it wasn't too brutish, but that last question had been a sincere jab at her.

Raewyn slapped on a forced smile and tried to be blasé. "Sure, your assistance would be much appreciated. You can do the honours of pulling your diadem apart while I begin the flower process. It'll be much faster with both of us working."

"That's what I thought," he said, and the chime of him picking the diadem back up rang in her ears.

Raewyn began plucking a few of her hairs out. She checked each one by pushing magic into it while she held each end. Then she wound them around each flower stem, only needing one strand of hair per plant. Once she was done, she checked to make sure each one was securely in place for the next step to work.

Merikh was silent beside her; it was taking quite a while for him to warm back up to her. She was wary of being near him, in case his quills were extended.

Let's just say, the whole impaling her hand and then having

to be tossed into the lake had taught her a hard lesson about being close to him. His physical aspects were far more dangerous than she'd given them credit for, especially after being safely carried by him for weeks. But now she knew otherwise, even though it wasn't a lesson she'd wanted to learn.

"Okay, hopefully, this will be enough," she said. "Now for the hard part."

"Hard part?"

"I was actually going to ask you for your help either way." Raewyn rubbed at the side of her neck. "I don't know how long this will take – it really depends on the flowers themselves, but I'm going to need to pump them full of my own spiritual essence."

"What do you need me to do?"

Her cheeks heated. "I need you to take care of me. Don't worry, I'll make myself some food and rest first, but I won't be able to stop the concentration of magic; otherwise, I may have to restart."

"So, you'll need me to what? Watch you and make sure you're fed?"

"Yes, that." Among other – possibly embarrassing – things. She turned away and touched a few of the tulip bulbs. "But you'll also need to cut away anything that doesn't survive the process, so they don't kill or infect the others. You can't let me fall asleep, and... and even if I get sick, I need you to keep me going and lucid."

"What do you mean, if you get sick?" His forearm thudded as he slapped it against the table. "You never said anything about you getting sick."

"What I'm doing is changing this plant's natural state into one that can handle magic. To do that, I have to insert some of my own essence and delve into it. I must connect with it, and that has its dangers; one of them being that whatever may be wrong with this plant could infect me. Another is that it could require so much of my magic for the shift that it drains mine completely. Don't worry, though! Mine will come back over time, and it shouldn't be too bad, but that depletion can be quite scary for those who have never seen its effects."

When he didn't say anything, she couldn't help stepping towards him. "Merikh?"

"Is there any way for you to teach me how to do this, then?"

Her eyelids flickered, surprised he was offering to take her place in this role. She couldn't help the way tenderness lifted into her expression. *He cares enough about me that he doesn't want me to come to harm.*

To know he was willing to make that sacrifice meant a lot to her. He didn't need to offer, he didn't need to care, and yet here he was, doing so.

She shook her head, even as the tender pang in her chest refused to dissipate.

"I'm sorry, but this is something that requires someone with years of experience in magical herbology, cell restructure, and just magic in general."

"Don't know why you're the one apologising," he grumbled. "But fine. Whatever you need from me, I'll do what I can."

Her smile brightened. "Thank you, and thank you for offering. That was really sweet of you."

"What the hell?" he exclaimed, his tone flabbergasted as reddish-pink sparks flashed. With the way she heard his claws running through fur, she imagined he was awkwardly scratching at himself. "Sweet? I just didn't want to take care of a sick person, let alone one who bitches and whines all the time."

She stamped her foot at him. "I don't whine!"

"She shouts as she whines."

Raewyn rolled her eyes, wishing her cheeks didn't ache in humour. "Oh, just grab me some food to cut up, *Sir GrumpyBear.*"

"I'm really starting to dislike you calling me that," he said as he moved away. Raewyn stuck her tongue out at his back. "I saw that."

She instantly sucked it back into her mouth. She'd thought he looked away.

TWENTY-FIVE

Merikh held Raewyn's form as he sat on his bed with his back against the stone wall. For someone so weak, her uncontrollable shivering was powerful.

From head to toe, she was covered in slick sweat. Though it was blistering hot outside, her little body was like ice in his arms.

Over the course of two days, she'd held the tulip flowerpot within her arms and never let it go as she fed it her own magical essence. Her usual lily of the valley scent had been saturated and overpowered by her magical, clary sage one.

During that time, she'd been almost incapable of doing anything herself. Sure, there were things on that list he'd rather not have done, like helping the woman go to the toilet in the designated spot she'd picked within his yard. Since he didn't produce waste and absorbed his food completely, he had no other amenities for her.

He'd hand fed her, given her water, and even when she began to grow tired, he'd carried her wherever she wanted to go.

In reality, Merikh really didn't mind doing all this for her. She needed his assistance, and what she was doing benefitted them both.

What he did mind... was this aftermath.

The tulips had required more essence than she thought, to the point she'd had to squeeze the last of it out of her body just to finish the task.

She couldn't feed it too fast or she'd kill them, as proven by two of the five tulips he was forced to cut away. If she did it too slow, it had been ineffectual. Raewyn had found the safe balance, but they took more than she'd accounted for.

When the tulips began to faintly glow after two days, the transformation complete, Raewyn finally let herself collapse. Whatever she'd done, it'd been so toxic to her body that it was rejecting her current state. She'd vomited foam as she convulsed, before going non-responsive.

Since then, for the past night and day, she'd been feverish.

Her clammy skin had an ashen tinge to it. Her pulse was so slow and soft, he worried that at any moment, her heart would cease beating. He constantly had to put his fingers over her mouth to make sure she was still breathing, since it was so light.

He'd seen humans die from sicknesses not as terrible as the state she was in. Part of him fretted, Merikh having no clue on what to do.

He'd never cared for another through an illness, and he was utterly useless. When he tried to help, more foam had frothed from her blueish lips, and his orbs had turned orange in guilt.

The only thing he could do was hold her, since her chills lessened with his heat enveloping her.

Staring down at her, he gently moved a clump of curls stuck to her face behind her ear with one of his claws. Her pointed ear didn't twitch.

You fucking lied to me, Elf. She'd said it wouldn't be too bad, that he hadn't needed to worry, but he'd been panicked since this started.

His gaze dropped to her hand, and the orange in his sight deepened.

He hadn't known what else to do, but he'd made it worse by trying to help. Since she'd told him the sickness might come on due to a depletion of magic, Merikh had gripped her hand and tried to figure out a way to give her his own.

Red glowing lines formed through her veins, and with the dark complexion of her skin, her hand looked as though it had lava streaks. It went up just past her wrist, and it was a terrible reminder that whenever he helped someone, it always came back to bite him in the arse.

Her entire body had contorted at the time, and her scream made him stop. Her heart ceased beating, but it eventually started back up on its own.

Raewyn's fever had intensified.

Occasionally, his orbs would flare a brighter red, like they did now. *You should not have pushed yourself.*

Merikh was beyond furious.

He was angry that she'd done something so foolish; it looked as though it could have killed her. He was pissed she hadn't further explained the effects of this, especially since his interference had only hindered her.

He wanted to believe it was because he didn't want to lose his only escape off this world. He wanted his anger to be because of self-serving concern – pure selfishness, and nothing more.

Unfortunately, it was hard to deny his own feelings of guilt, especially when his orange orb colour refused to permanently recede over the last few hours, always coming back. It was even harder to deny it when his chest ached in sympathy for the pretty female, wishing he could bear this for her.

Merikh had tried, but he wasn't able to transfer the illness to himself. Instead, he was forced to bear witness.

He understood none of his reactions, or maybe he just didn't want to understand them. In the few months he'd known Raewyn, she'd flipped his damn life upside down.

He'd experienced more unpleasant emotions in that time than he had in the last few decades. He'd also laughed more than he could truly remember.

There must be something I can do to help, he thought, lifting his sight to the dark entrance of his cave.

There was something he could do, but he didn't want to. More than anything else in the world, he didn't want to. He'd rather cut off his hand, his arm, his own head, than do it. Had it not been for her wellbeing, he wouldn't even be considering it.

It was only when she'd stopped shivering, going completely limp like she was losing even more strength, did he finally gain the courage to lay her down on the bed by herself.

Worried that her sweat-soaked hair would suffocate her, he moved it away from her nose and mouth. He turned away.

Then, Merikh's orbs flared red, not in normality, but in hatred. He took himself outside and into the night.

At first glance, it appeared as though no one was there. Sniffing at the air, it was empty of unusual scents.

He knew better.

"Come out of the shadows," he demanded, his gaze roaming over the tree line.

The woman he sought immediately poked her head out from behind a tree trunk, knowing better than to annoy him by playing any hide-and-seek games. Her ethereal form was transparent, white only due to her current ghostly nature.

When he saw her, his quills shuddered in revulsion as his fur stood on end. Thankfully, he wasn't wearing anything more than a pair of shorts; otherwise, he would have torn his clothing.

The silence that hung between them was so heavy, it was like a blanket attempting to snuff him. He hadn't looked at this woman in nearly a hundred years, and he'd told her he didn't wish to look upon her ever again.

Yet, there she was, right when he needed her the most.

Her gaze upon him was not unfeeling, to those who could identify her tells.

A soft growl rumbled from his chest without thought – an instant, uncontrollable reaction. She turned her eyes up to the ward she floated on the other side of, before bringing them back to him. Her brow raised in question, and he gave a curt nod.

The moment she passed into the safety of it, she changed her form to one that appeared human, although smelt entirely different. Brown skin formed when her bare toes touched the grass, and it grew up her limbs. Her white dress appeared, as did her white feathered cloak.

Merikh folded his arms when she was almost to him, and he tapped a claw against his biceps.

"I told you to never come here again," he sneered as he lowered himself down to her stout human height. "Yet, you not only disobeyed me, but you brought the twins here with your stupidity. You entered my ward the other day when you realised my guest could not see you."

"You called for me. I imagine it was to do more than confront me when you could have done so sooner." Her rich-brown curls, looser than Raewyn's, fluttered in the wind. "What is it you seek from me?"

"There is currently a female within my home who needs aid I cannot provide. You will help her, then you will fuck off back to the void where you belong."

The only indication of hurt she gave was the flickering of her long eyelashes. Her eyes moved around him as she leaned to the side.

"She's an Elf." Her eyes darted to the corner of her lids to look up at him. "You could only imagine my alarm when I saw you bring her here."

Merikh released another growl, hating that she watched him through one of her spells. It appeared like a floating mirror with a black dust border.

His arms tightened defensively across his chest. "You *will* help her. You owe me that much."

Once more, her eyelids flickered, the corners of her lips drooping with them. She nodded as she stepped around him. "I will do what I can, but you know my power is limited."

He carefully watched the woman go past him before he turned and followed close behind. He kept his distance from her so not even a single strand of fur brushed her.

His apprehension grew as she approached Raewyn, who still rested in the same position as when he'd left her. He was unsure if her lack of shivering meant she was getting better or worse, but his concern was palpable as it thickened in his throat.

As the woman placed a single knee on the bed next to Raewyn, she looked small compared to the Elf. Yet Raewyn was the one who appeared fragile, delicate, and frail in comparison.

From the foot of the bed, Merikh was vigilant as he watched the Witch Owl place the back of her hand against Raewyn's shiny forehead. Then she turned so she could place her ear centimetres away from her nose and mouth.

"She said she could become sick from depleting her magic. That is the current cause," Merikh stated, hoping to give her as much information as he was willing to offer to get her out of his home.

No doubt, she'd watched them all day performing the task.

"This is not something I have ever dealt with," she said as she placed her other knee to steady herself.

Then, she hovered her hands over Raewyn's chest and muttered incoherent words. Black mist glittered from her fingertips. It also filled her eyes, as if working in tandem with her sight, and they went completely black.

A few unbearable seconds passed, and his worry grew that she might trick him and harm her further.

She let out a deep expire before ceasing whatever magic she was doing. The scent of it was unpleasant. It was too sweet, like sugar that had been added to honey.

"Her magic has already begun replenishing itself."

"Then why isn't she getting better?" he bit as he stomped forward.

She flashed him a calculating gaze out of the corner of her eye before returning her focus to Raewyn. "You care about her."

Merikh's growl was so feral that even *he* thought it sounded barbaric. His orbs turned crimson when his torso tightened at the possible truth of her words, at how much he was against her knowing anything about him.

"She is nothing but a means to an end, one I will not see perish before it is complete."

The Witch Owl grabbed Raewyn's wrist and wiggled her limp hand at him. The streaks of lava-like veins flared at the movement.

"This is the action of someone who cares. You attempted to inject your own magic into her body to quicken the process, and in doing so, you've blocked her natural circulation." Then, she narrowed her gaze into a fierce glare. "You can hate me all you want, but you cannot lie to me, *Merikh*."

Fuck, of course he couldn't hide his feelings for the Elf from her. He'd rather she think he was just using Raewyn.

His snarl almost overshadowed her words. "Then. Remove. It. Surely, you can at least do that."

She turned her head away dismissively and took Raewyn's hand in both of hers. Slowly, the glowing streaks retracted, and instead grew up her own arms. She hissed in what he thought might be agony, and he gleefully admitted that pleased him.

As soon as his own magic was gone, Raewyn's colour improved significantly. She let out a sigh, and her breathing returned to a semi-normal state. Even with the small distance between them, he noted her heartbeat had strengthened.

Then, she curled into a ball as her eyes peaked open for just a second before closing.

Within seconds, she already appeared a hundred times better. Merikh looked at her arm, and orange flared when he realised he'd been the reason she hadn't been getting better.

I shouldn't have interfered.

The Witch Owl looked down at her hands and opened and closed them, wincing as she did. Lava streaks had grown over them.

"Weldir will heal you if you go scampering back to him," Merikh coldly stated.

Then, he stepped back and threw his arm in the direction of

his cave entrance, showing her he wanted her to leave.

He wouldn't offer any thanks. She had a mountain of emotional debt she owed him. A person wouldn't thank another for returned money, and he considered this the same.

She stood and faced him. "I must speak with you first."

"There is nothing I want to say to you, and I'm not interested in anything you have to say." He stepped back so she could better see he'd pointed to outside. "Now, get out."

Her left jaw ticked. She stood her ground, lowered her head slightly, and glared up at him.

"What are you doing with this female? How did you find an Elf on Earth, and why did you bring her here?"

"What I do and who I keep within my home is none of your business." When he reached to take her arm, she turned incorporeal and evaded him.

Her voice sounded distant, despite standing so close to him in her ghostly form. "You cannot have an Elf as your bride, Merikh."

His footsteps stumbled when he slipped through her, and he twisted his head in her direction.

"You have no right to tell me what I can and cannot do. Now get your wretched Phantom arse out of my fucking home!"

He didn't chase her; he wasn't an idiot. He couldn't touch her, so there was simply no point.

"You shouldn't speak to your mother that way," she bit back, floating around his home like a fly he couldn't squash.

Merikh's laugh was dark. "You and I both know I stopped thinking of you as a mother, Lindiwe."

"She is from the Elven world. You cannot keep her, Merikh. She needs to go back there."

"That's exactly what I'm trying to do!" he yelled, wincing when Raewyn curled up tighter and rubbed her face against the bedding.

"And you must stay here."

His rage was like an inferno, swirling tighter and tighter until it was strong enough to swallow up everything and spit out destruction.

He left his own home, knowing she would follow. Whatever damned conversation they were about to have, that she was *forcing* on him, he wouldn't allow it to disturb the unwell woman on his bed.

Once he was outside, he turned left to go around the bend of the Veil's cliff. The ward ended right next to three trees, and he thought this was an appropriate place to speak with her. It wasn't out in the open, and hopefully, they were far enough away on the other side as to not bother Raewyn.

He stood with the swell of the cliff just behind him and to the left. The trees were at his back, and he waited for the Witch Owl to flutter herself in front of him.

"If you wish to speak, you will do so human. I will not speak to a Ghost." Once she became corportal, he folded his arms. "What I do and where I go is none of your concern. The fact you haven't learned this yet just makes me question your intelligence."

"You cannot go there, Merikh. You must stay on Earth or find somewhere else to go. It cannot be there."

"Why?" he chuckled, allowing yellow to fill his orbs in true humour. "Because Weldir will be punished if it's discovered he created his own children?"

Her eyelids flickered, giving him the truth.

"The problem is, *Mother,* I don't give a fuck what happens to that demi-god." Then he raised a hand so he could tap a claw to the side of his snout. "Actually, the idea of him being tortured by his own creators brings me immense joy. Now that you've put it in my head, I hope there is some form of trial where I can tell them all about what he has been doing here on Earth."

She curled her hands into tight fists. "It is far more likely that they will destroy you. I am telling you this to protect you."

"No," he said as he refolded his arms. "You are doing this to protect him, and yourself, and all that power you gained from him. This has nothing to do with my life."

"And what if you go there and find out I'm right?"

Merikh tilted his head to one side. "I think I would gladly accept my death if it resulted in both your destructions."

"Neither one of us deserves this much hatred from you," she bit out.

"You and I both know that's not true," he said with humour, happy to see her all riled up.

"What happened was not my fault!" she yelled, throwing her hands forward before brushing one of them over her hair. She turned her head away from him in *shame* and in hurt. "I was thrown into this just as much as you were. I had no idea what I was doing back then, how to take care of you. I had been alive for what? Fifty years? I still considered myself a human. How was I supposed to know everything? I have never been all-knowing."

"It doesn't matter. I was still the one that suffered. I wasn't the one who asked to be born into this world, and not by a mother who did not want me."

"I have never said that." Her eyes twinkled with tears, but she quickly stemmed them.

"No? Your actions were enough."

"I tried everything I could to take care of you to the best of my abilities. I thought you were indestructible. If you were hurt by a Demon, I tried to give you aid or heal you. I watched over your skull until you grew back. I fed you when I realised that helped you to grow. What more could I have done? You didn't want to be in my home, preferring to wander the forest by yourself."

"Quit defending yourself," Merikh snapped. "You only birthed us for your own selfish gain. *He* wanted children, and you accepted to keep your magic. That was not want, that was you obediently following your master. Well, guess what? I won't bark and bite for him like you, not after everything."

"You know that was only in the beginning. It didn't take me

long to grow to care for you."

"It was still too long." Then Merikh's orbs shifted to blue, and he wished he could stop the way his heart turned to ash in sorrow. "And it was too late." Her lips tightened, reflecting his own pain. "Then you turned your back on me."

"I didn't mean to," she muttered as she turned her head to the side. "I was just upset and grew afraid of you. I know it was unfair on you, but I've tried everything I can since then to help you, show you I'm sorry. I've watched over you, tried to share as much information as I can with you, even when you wouldn't speak to me. I even begged Weldir to find a way to give you a glamour so you could travel with the humans when I could see you wanted to fit in somehow."

"That doesn't bring him back. You blamed me for it, and yet all that blame rests on your shoulders."

Merikh's heart pumped unsteadily, fluctuating between hurt and anger, slow and painful, fast and anxious. Not once had they ever broached this subject, both of them avoiding it over hundreds of years.

He'd always wanted to. He'd wanted to cruelly shove it in her face and see her regret, to hurt her. Yet, even in the few times they'd spoken, especially since she fed him information and he listened before turning away from her, not once had he brought it up.

He didn't want to speak of the past, not when he'd rather forget.

Her eyes narrowed in rage. "You can't cast that on me, just as I shouldn't have done to you. How was I supposed to know that would happen?"

His orbs flashed orange before they burst into crimson red.

"Because you could have asked him!" Merikh was so close to reaching out and swiping at her – even knowing she was quick with her Phantom abilities. "You could have asked Weldir about us, who and what we were. Instead, you avoided him as much as possible!"

"Because his magic was weak! He could only call for me when he had enough souls to risk bringing me to Tenebris."

It was an excuse, one he thought could be true. However, she still would have had ample time to ask Weldir.

Merikh absentmindedly clawed at his own chest.

"Why did it have to be me?" he roared, stomping a foot forward so he could tower over her. "Why did I have to be the experiment? If you had taken the time to ask how one of us dies, I wouldn't have been the one to find out!"

His skin crawled as he covered his skull, considering obliterating it into dust with his own hands. *I killed my own fucking brother!*

Not a day had passed that he'd not regretted it, wished he could forget it, wanting nothing more than to take it back.

It hadn't even been on purpose.

And then she, his damn mother, had grown frightened of him. At his confused rampage, at his agony-filled roars, at his panic. She'd blamed him for it, hated him for it, and it was too late to forgive her when she finally accepted that it had been an accident. He had no way of knowing he was about to kill his own brother, because how could he?

He'd been young, not long an adult Duskwalker, and none of them knew that crushing their skull would result in their everlasting death. They always grew back and thought they always would – no matter the cause.

It was Merikh's actions that had shown them all.

It was his pain that became their knowledge.

"It's not your fault, Merikh," Lindiwe said, her voice growing soft and motherly. "I've told you this."

"Shut up," he said as he drew his hands from his face. "I know what I did, even if I didn't mean to, and it's just as much your fault and his for not informing us. You could have prevented it."

She turned her head away. "He didn't know either, but you're right. I didn't ask because I thought you were incapable of being killed, just like him. I *am* sorry, for everything."

"I don't care if you're sorry. I don't care how many times you try to apologise. It doesn't change it, nor does it fix what happened afterwards. It doesn't change why I was created in the first place, nor does it negate what I have suffered since I took my first breath. Your sorry is just as worthless as mine."

It should have been me. If Merikh could go back and choose, he would rather be the one who died. His life had been nothing but miserable. At least his brother could have lived a different life to the path he'd walked.

"I know life hasn't been the easiest for you," she said as she rubbed at her arm. "But you *do* have a chance to find happiness."

Merikh gave a saddened laugh. "What a ridiculous statement. Mavka are not destined to find anything good in this world."

"That's not true," she said, stepping forward as she shook her head. She went to reach out to him comfortingly, but retracted her hand when she knew it was dangerous to touch him – especially since he'd lifted his quills on purpose. "Merikh, you will find someone. Orpheus found a bride, and he holds her soul."

His orbs shifted to a deep blue. He took a step back, as though he'd been punched in the gut – and it actually hurt.

"What?" The blue deepened. "Orpheus has a bride?"

She raised her sharp brows at him. "You don't know?" Oddly speechless, he shook his head. "It's almost been two years since Orpheus found Reia. Even Magnar and Faunus have found females."

"Who the fuck are they?"

Her dark brows knitted together tightly. "I thought you would know all this by now," she said, baffled. "Magnar is the antler Mavka, and Faunus is Kitty."

He knew of Kitty, but the antler Mavka had always been nameless to him.

Merikh wrapped his palm over the side of his snout in thought, the well of blue in his sight deepening. He'd been gone from the Veil for two years, but nothing like this had ever happened in the hundreds of years he'd been alive.

A Mavka gaining a bride? Impossible – that's what he'd thought.

The female who killed Katerina... She must have survived.

Even if this was good news for his kind, the reality was too clear.

"Good for them," he said slowly, before holding her gaze. "But no human will want to tie themselves to me." When she opened her mouth to argue, he let out a warning growl while throwing his arms out. "Look at me! Not only am I frightening on the outside, I'm just as terrifying on the inside! You and I both know I hold too much hatred. I destroy everything that gets close to me."

"You can try," she offered. "There is someone out there, but it cannot be that Elf."

Merikh tilted his head. "Why are you bringing her up again?"

"Because of me, you're part human, even if you don't look it. That's why, when you make a human your bride, you're compatible." She rubbed at her cheek awkwardly. "I don't know if she would be able to give you a child. It's not impossible, but I thought I should at least let you know of my doubts."

Merikh burst out into a fit of laughter. "It's just too bad I don't want one, then." At her shocked expression, his laughter deepened. "You think I want to bring another Mavka into this world? I'm not interested in watching my own spawn suffer."

Her opening and closing mouth reminded him of a gaping fish.

He hated how hollowing his next words felt.

"And you think that female would want to be mine? You saw her. Why would someone that beautiful consider becoming my bride? I am hideous, inside and out. She is too kind, too smart, too... perfect, and she can have someone who is just like her." Then a gust of wind from behind her pushed its way through both of them as Merikh quietly said, "I know that once I go to her realm, she will want nothing to do with me. All I can hope for is that her people allow me to live among them in peace."

He didn't understand why her gaze turned sympathetic.

Did she really think I would be so silly as to have that kind of hope with Raewyn? Not once had it crossed his mind.

Even if his face wasn't the problem, Merikh knew his heart was ugly. He was too twisted up and broken inside to think something as wonderful as love was achievable. He might be capable of loving, but it was doubtful anyone would love him in return.

He was thankful she didn't argue with his statement; he didn't want her pushing false hopes onto him. In its own way, her silence on the matter was comforting.

Still, dashing his own hopes before he'd even considered them was more painful than he thought they'd be. Saying it aloud only made him realise just how lonely his future would be, even if he went to Raewyn's world.

His rage faded, snuffed out by his own truths, and the fire he'd had for the conversation died. He was losing enthusiasm to argue when he was now just... tired.

He was tired of her, tired of living like this, tired of all the suffering he'd dealt with. Merikh was exhausted.

"Think of your brothers, then. If you go there, you could bring death to all of them."

Merikh raised his skull superiorly. "The Elves would have to come here to do that, and I highly doubt they will. I will leave with her, no matter what you say."

"How?" she asked.

"You think I would tell you, so you can let Weldir know and then try and stop me?"

"I'm trying to help you. What if you're wrong? What if you bring about your own death, your brothers' deaths? Do you really not care for them at all?"

He didn't respond, not when he truly didn't know the answer. It wasn't fair for her to push that onto him. He was seeking his own happiness, to not feel desolate or like an outcast. Yes, he cared that they continued breathing, but other than that, he didn't want to know them, speak with them, nothing.

He pretended they didn't exist until they rudely shoved themselves into his life.

He waved his hand dismissively. "I'm done talking to you."

When she didn't leave, he swiped his claws, and she turned incorporeal just before he could make contact with her. The fact his hand went straight through her intangible body showed he hadn't been feigning an attack.

She backed up, her face twisted in too many emotions for him to distinguish.

She returned to her physical form and drew her feathered cloak onto her head. Within moments, she'd morphed herself into a human-sized owl and he watched her fly off above the trees towards the centre of the Veil.

Whether she was truly gone or not, Merikh wasn't going to stand there staring after her.

He was annoyed, all the inhuman parts of him ruffled and irritated. His heart and mind burned, wishing he'd never given his mother the chance to twist his insides into knots.

Funnily enough, he found himself wanting to seek out Raewyn. He wanted to check on her, maybe even soothe her while she slept.

He thought being near her might make him feel better. She was the only creature in this damn world he just couldn't seem to hate.

Merikh turned around to make his way past the trees and the convex shape of the cliff next to him. It was like the wind behind him was pushing him forward to go to her so she could comfort him, even if she was unaware she was doing so.

As he rounded the bend, his heart nearly stopped in his chest as his orbs turned a stark white.

There stood Raewyn, leaning weakly against the wall. She was covered in a sheen of sweat, and she was trembling on wobbly knees. She still looked awfully unwell.

Fuck. The wind had been pushing in the other direction, so he hadn't picked up on her scent. He may have also been too focused on his argument to be aware of anything.

The moment she shrunk into herself, her ears pressing down, she knew she'd been caught. She *knew* he'd be furious that she was there. His deep, rumbling growl only made her step back in wariness.

"The next time you eavesdrop, make sure you're not stupidly caught," he bit out.

Then he spun away. Where he was going, he wasn't sure. Just anywhere away from her and the embarrassment of what she'd likely heard.

It didn't matter how long she'd been standing there; every part of that conversation had been incriminating. The last thing he'd spoken of... was her.

If he didn't want to leave Earth so badly, he may never have returned.

TWENTY-SIX

He thinks I'm beautiful... For the umpteenth time, Raewyn patted her cheeks, as though she was trying to wake herself from a dream.

It was hard to concentrate whenever she sensed he was nearby, even if it was only fleeting moments. Her mind was too preoccupied with what she'd learned.

Merikh had left her leaning against the cliff and had disappeared for a long time.

She only went out there because he was yelling at someone to leave, and it jolted her awake. When she cracked open her weary eyes, a ghostly figure was dancing around in her vision before it left with him.

Even though she was weak, she managed to drag herself off the bed to follow them.

They weren't quiet, so she didn't need to get too close, but she overheard everything.

When the conversation ended, Raewyn wanted to flee before he found her. She had ample time to, but she was barely able to stand. The warmth she regained was fading, and every second she remained there, she got weaker, until she was incapable of movement.

She'd even collapsed after Merikh left and had fallen asleep against the wall – only to wake up on the bed, almost fully recovered.

Since then, she couldn't stop thinking about it.

He thinks I'm beautiful, and smart, and kind? He'd even uttered the word *perfect,* and she had no idea what that meant, but dear holy Gilded Maiden, she wanted to fan herself. What a way to make a woman feel special.

It didn't matter that he had barely uttered a word to her since, or that he'd been exceptionally standoffish. He made no mention of it, as if he was hoping she'd been too unwell to remember it.

Tough, because she did.

The question was... what did she do now that she knew he felt that way?

So, he likes me, I'm guessing? She didn't know how deeply, but she thought that might be enough. *He's never tried to bring it up, though.*

It had always been because of Raewyn that they'd had any form of intimacy.

'I am hideous, inside and out.' Her heart sank a little to find out he thought that way about himself. Sure, he was pretty prickly, both literally and metaphorically, but he wasn't hideous. He could be kind in his own way, thoughtful and considerate.

When she'd barely been conscious, she could remember the feeling of someone stroking her hair from her face, rubbing her back soothingly. He'd tried to force sips of water down her throat.

When it wasn't his psycho, madman, or morbid, dark chuckle, his *real* laughter was scarce, but it just made it far more sincere when she heard it. It was rare, and she had a funny feeling he hadn't done it much in his life. She also thought she might be the source of it.

'I know that once I go to her realm, she will want nothing to do with me.'

I never said that. She'd been running headfirst into being his friend because of how he'd treated her, even more so when she'd seen he could be cruel to the humans but had never turned that towards her.

Groaning, she planted her face against the stone bench and covered the back of her head. *I'm kind of horny.* She squeezed her thighs together. *How can knowing how he thinks of me make me even more attracted to him?*

And he didn't call her cute! It was the word *beautiful*, and that's all Raewyn ever wanted to be. She would have skipped everywhere if he'd said sexy, or hot.

The moment vibrations came closer, she shot up before he could enter the cave. Pretending she hadn't been having a sexual existential crisis, she patted the bulbs of the tulips.

He took something from the shelf and then left again, and Raewyn went back to trying to work. She fretted instead.

What do I do now? They could continue like this until she finished making the sun stone, then they could go to Jabez's portal. She was fine keeping things how they were.

There was no real reason to change it.

I kind of want to know what would happen, though.

She one hundred percent could have sex with him and then wave goodbye like it never happened. It didn't *have* to mean something, although usually she preferred there to be some kind of relationship first.

What she wanted to know was how he would act *afterwards.* Would he continue to be the prickly Merikh, or would he blossom into someone who would be tender? Was this as deep as his kindness could go, or was she just scratching the surface?

He's thrown up walls around himself. More like shoved them six feet into the ground so they couldn't be destroyed.

Raewyn was game.

Walls didn't need to be broken, not when she could use her wiles and sweetness to get him to lower them himself. That, or she could just crash-tackle him by climbing to the top and forcing him to catch her when she took the metaphorical plunge.

That's it! I've decided! She slapped her hands against the stone bench, wincing when she hurt her palms. *I will come to regret it if I don't discover what it's like to have sex with a Duskwalker. For scientific reasons, I have to know.*

She really couldn't call herself a scientist if she didn't experiment... right?

It was really every excuse she could give herself to gain the courage of what she knew she must do. If Merikh wasn't going to strap on his big-boy panties and try to touch her, it meant she had to lower her non-existent ones for him.

It was mainly that his cock felt so good rubbing against her clit that she just *had* to know if it was even better inside her. She'd wanted it in the forest; she'd even gotten turned on by him.

Raewyn cupped her chin as she began to scheme. *Okay... so how do I start this with him?* Obviously, she was going to do this today, before she let her nerves change her mind.

She went to her designated shelf. Merikh had emptied it for her so she had a place for her clothes – he hadn't even asked her, he'd just kindly done it.

Going through each article of clothing, she tried to find something enticing. They were all boring and long. *Ugh, none of these feel like they would be nice or sexy.*

She grabbed her sleep dress, since it was silkier than the others, and just hoped it was a nice colour. She took a pair of scissors to it so she could shorten it, as well as make an actual neckline that wasn't almost to her throat.

It feels like it was made for an old grandma.

Now that she was done brutalising her clothing, she needed to have a bath to help with her nervousness. Also, his nose was so freaking good that she was self-conscious if she didn't smell nice.

Raewyn tied her hair up to stop it from getting wet before she slid into the lake. It was warmer than the air, and she soaked it in as she turned to place her cleaning products on land. There was only one section of the lake where she felt comfortable bathing, since it was shallow enough to come to her waist.

She didn't know where Merikh was, nor did she any other time she'd bathed. Since the first time she'd done so at his home, she'd secretly hoped he'd been watching.

I bet he's not though. Coward.

Once she was clean, she hopped out of the water and donned her, hopefully, enticing sleep dress.

She'd meant to cut it so it would sit mid-thigh rather than down to her ankles. Unfortunately, she'd never been a good seamstress, and she'd made it so short it barely covered her backside.

She should have gone longer and cut incrementally rather than just taking a pair of razor scissors to it.

It was her first mistake of the... evening? She didn't know what time of day it was, since Earth's sun cycle threw her off completely and she still hadn't adjusted.

No matter her mistake, she wouldn't let that hiccup stop her.

She did begin to rethink her choice at the second hiccup of the evening. She'd been planning to present herself on the bed in some kind of pose, but Merikh was already inside the cave. He must have heard her coming, since he was doing his vibration for her.

It was in that moment she knew she was the most awkward person she'd ever met. Okay, so she'd also never gone this far to have sex with someone, but she was willing to try.

She placed her cleaning products on the ground and her cane as well.

Unsure of what else to do, she played with her hair to make sure it was framing her face. Then she felt for the rocky entrance. When she found it, she put her arm above her head and leaned her elbow and side against it while crossing her ankles.

"H-hello there," she attempted to rasp, except it got clogged in her throat. Her greeting wasn't as sensual as she'd hoped.

He grunted in return. A few unsteady heartbeats later, since she'd fumbled this completely already and was internally panicking, two yellow sparks flashed.

"What the hell are you wearing?" he asked in disbelief. "I just bought that for you, and I cannot go back to a village to get you a new one."

Embarrassed, she accidentally stumbled forward when her elbow slipped.

She hadn't considered he'd be upset that she cut up the clothing he'd given her. No, it was hers, and if he didn't like what she did with it, then that was his problem.

With how things were going so far, she thought about abandoning her entire plan. Then she dug deep, remembering he was only being curt and grumpy because of what she'd learned.

A good orgasm should calm him right down... hopefully.

Taking the biggest, deepest calming breath she could, she swaggered forward. Brushing her hand over the corner of the stone bench helped to orient her, and she made a slow beeline for him.

Merikh backed up when she got too close, until he had nowhere else to go but up against the wall parallel to the bed.

"You've been avoiding me."

"No, I haven't," he *blatantly* lied.

Raewyn *tsked* and reached up to fiddle with the button seam of his shirt. "You haven't even let me thank you for taking care of me when I was sick."

"You shouldn't thank me," he bit. "I happened to make things worse for you."

Her brows twitched, unsure of what he was talking about. Regardless, it was pointless. She could ask her questions later, of which she had many. Like why his mother was here, and everything they'd spoken about.

"Can you step aside so I can pass?" he asked, gently pushing her shoulder sideways.

Raewyn held strong. Instead, she pushed her arms up so her forearms were resting on his shoulders and slid her chest against his.

"So, you like me, do you?"

Raewyn had prepared herself for the answering snarl and red sparks she received. He even leaned forward, as though he wanted to be taller, more dominating.

"What you heard the other day, forget it."

She pouted her lips into a sultry smile, and even brushed her fingertips into the fur just above his collar. "Would it help if I told you I like you too?"

She didn't like that she could feel his fur raising beneath her fingers, or the fact she could hear clothing tear like his quills were rising. He was growing very agitated, and she was a lot more wary about his exterior after being hurt by it.

"What the hell are you doing?"

Okay, so playing subtle definitely wasn't working.

"I'm trying to seduce you." She laughed, hoping to hide her uncertainty, her awkwardness, and to defuse the situation. "I thought that would be obvious."

It probably wasn't with how terrible the lead up to this was.

Raewyn choked out a gasp when his hand wrapped around her throat, and he practically lifted her to her toes. It wasn't painful at all, but it was a show of dominance. His growl was menacing, and he was so close to her face that one of his front fangs brushed the tip of her nose.

"I'm not interested in what the humans call a 'pity fuck,' Raewyn. I don't need or want your sympathy."

Her ears flattened as her brows furrowed. "That's not why I want to be intimate with you," she whispered, hoping to hide the hurt in her voice by speaking softly.

Did he really think she would open her legs just to make someone else feel better about themselves? Raewyn had never been that kind of person.

She wasn't so shallow.

"Then what else would it be?" he growled. "Because you currently don't smell like a female who is aroused, begging for a cock."

He brought his face closer and drew the end of his snout over her cheek, just in front of her ear, and then down her neck. He sniffed her, and his warm breath over the sensitive places such as her ear and neck had goosebumps tickling down her back.

He also squeezed her neck a little tighter, and just him doing so had her panting. She wanted him to squeeze a little harder.

Her nervousness had been too strong before, but funnily enough, his warm hand and breaths were helping. Especially since his scent was right on the tip of her nose, so close that she wanted to lean forward and taste it.

What would he do if I just... licked him right now?

"I'm not doing this because I pity you, Merikh," she whispered, her voice finally becoming raspy like she wanted. "I'm doing this because I want you."

He gave her another growl, and her nipples hardened against her thin dress. Just as she brought her hands down to palm his chest, he pushed her head back while rearing back his own.

"Look at me, Raewyn," he darkly rumbled, and her eyelids flickered when the world began to open before her eyes. Within seconds, the fog cleared, and she was looking up at his bony face and horns. "Just because you don't stare at it every day doesn't change the fact that this is what I look like. You can pretend as much as you want that I'm not a Duskwalker, but I will not allow you to drag me into your delusions. So, say it again, while actually staring at my face."

Like a snake striking before its victim could notice, Raewyn bounced forward and pressed her lips against his sharp fangs. She also placed her hands on the cheeks of his bear skull.

"I know what you look like," she said softly as she pulled back from her kiss. The vision of him faded like a swallowing pit of darkness, as though he was so shocked that he took back his sight. "And it doesn't bother me."

His hand loosened, and it gave her the opportunity to start giving the tip of his snout and his front fangs little kisses.

"It doesn't bother me that you have a skull for a face, Merikh. Or that you have horns, fur, or claws." Then, she laughed against his fangs as she said, "Actually, I kind of like it."

For Raewyn, it had never been about overcoming his exterior. She didn't like him *despite* it. She didn't consider him ugly, or monstrous. He was just... Merikh, who may look a little different to her, but was pretty in his own way.

"I... don't understand," was all he could say, but he'd stopped growling, stopped holding her throat so aggressively.

"You don't have to understand it," she answered as she continued to rain slow but deliberate kisses to his bony face. He'd backed his head up as if to escape, but the wall behind him didn't let him flee far. "I wanted you in the cave, and then again in the forest. I was just... nervous, and uncertain, like I was a few minutes ago."

"I'm not interested in being an experiment for you, little Elf," he bit out, throwing another pathetic wall between them.

He even tightened his hand, and she pulled on it so it was more forceful.

"Do I smell turned on enough for you now?"

She sincerely felt it, even more so when she clenched her thighs, and it pressed the lips of her dampening pussy together. As if mentioning it made him finally take it in, his breaths grew slightly shallower.

"I won't let you use me as a masturbation tool again." Then he leaned forward, breaking away from her kisses to utter right next to her ear. "If you start this, it will end with my cock inside your ripe little cunt."

If it was meant to be a warning, it was a terrible one. Instead of inciting fear, it only heated her further. Desire coiled in her belly and pooled at the entrance to her core, and she nibbled at her bottom lip.

"That was kind of the point," she said in a raspy voice.

Merikh backed up with a grunt, and she wasn't sure if it was because of her words or her deepening arousal.

"Fine. Prove to me that you want me." His hand slowly dropped, and the points of his claws slipping against the bare skin of her exposed sternum had her shivering in delight. It fell away completely. "Seduce me then."

Her brows twitched. "P-pardon?"

She thought she was already doing that!

"I want you to initiate. *Lead*, rather than make me take over so you can ride out any uncertainty in my control. Make me want you, despite my doubts."

Raewyn froze when understanding dawned. She'd been hoping he'd take over to make this easier for her. Usually, men helped to strip so they could get to sex and feel good.

He was telling her he wouldn't be doing any of that, and instead, she would have to do it all.

Honestly, if it were anyone else, this might have been the moment she'd bow out and say they were being too difficult. She'd question if they wanted her at all.

But this was Merikh.

After what she'd learned, she knew why he was doing this. It was because he didn't believe she could desire him. He was unsure, didn't know if he could trust her, and maybe it was even his own way of showing he was... scared?

Lucky for him, Raewyn was determined. She'd made her mind up today, and she wanted to finally find out if his weird cock felt just as good inside her as it did rubbing against her clit.

If seducing the big Duskwalker was what it would take for her to show him she desired him, then she would gladly do so.

TWENTY-SEVEN

Merikh stared down at the scantily dressed female before him and waited to see what she'd do.

The moment he'd seen her in a cut-up nightgown that had revealed far too much of her long, shapely legs, his sight had wanted to shift to purple. She'd cut the neckline too, so it sat lower, threatening to spill the cleavage she was incidentally highlighting as her breasts squeezed against his torso.

Most of the dresses he'd selected were red, because he wanted to see her in his favourite colour, the colour of his orbs. Even unaltered, since the first night she'd worn it, he'd realised his mistake.

This was the first time in years he'd been truly stumped in a situation. He barely believed Raewyn was not only standing before him in this skimpy outfit but was pressing her chest to his in the hopes of enticing him.

She didn't need to even *try*. Half the time, looking at her face had his blood pumping and his shaft twitching – which is why he tried to avoid her as much as possible.

Her beauty made him uncomfortable.

This whole situation made him uncomfortable.

Yes, he could scent she'd grown aroused. However, right now, that meant very little to him.

She likes me? What is that supposed to mean? His face, his body, his personality – none of these were 'likeable' qualities. Hell, if he met himself, he knew he'd try to kill him.

How was he supposed to believe this pretty *fairy* from some magical world wanted him?

He was standing here, hoping she would convince him.

Because, even if his words or actions said the opposite, he wanted her touch more than he wanted his next breath. He wanted to have her hands upon him, her sweet and unfamiliar kisses, her warmth, her taste. He craved her pussy wrapping around his cock so he could finally give in and rut her like he'd wanted to from the very first moment he'd looked upon her face.

But he wouldn't give into a female who didn't truly want him. She'd rejected his cock once, so if she truly wanted it now, she could take it from him.

He'd been purposefully holding his breath to save himself from her scent, and he gently let it out when she ran her hands up his torso.

She's not pulling away? Deep down inside, he'd been expecting her to.

She grabbed the underside of his chin and pulled his snout down. "Come here then," she said, before she brushed her soft lips against his fangs.

He stifled the shudder that wracked him. No one had ever *kissed* his skull before, and he was tempted to part his fangs and lick her in return. He didn't, only because his control on his need was thin, wet paper thin, moments from disintegrating.

When she dragged her hands back down, they followed the button seam of his shirt, and he worried his frantically beating heart would give away his excitement. She had to be able to hear it with how close she was, especially when she began undoing the buttons of his shirt.

His head turned and tilted so he could watch her undo each one, and she continued to press her lips against any part of his skull she could reach: the side of a longer fang, his jaw, his cheek bone. Even though his short fur made it harder to feel it, he still reacted fiercely when she kissed at his neck.

Then she skated her palms up and began pushing his shirt off his body. With his hands curled into fists at his sides, he watched her flinch at the tearing of his clothing.

"Stop," he quietly rasped, reaching up to halt her hands.

Before she could say anything, Merikh tore his shirt from his body. His quills helped to ensure he ripped it to shreds. They'd raised before in his irritation and had gotten caught within the fibres of his clothing.

Understanding why he'd take over this part, she gave him a small, somewhat broken smile. Then she placed her hands on his uncovered chest, and his muscles leapt to her touch, his bull tail curling to one side.

She slid them higher and higher, before enveloping them over his skull. She touched his snout, going up to stroke his horns, the back of his skull, before sliding over his shoulders.

He didn't understand this exploration.

Shouldn't she be trying to get to his cock? Although her hands were wonderful, soft and soothing, she was highlighting everything different about him. It heated him as much as it left him cold.

Then, she tried to go down his arms, and he had to halt her again. "My quills face up my arms. Don't go in their opposite direction."

He didn't like that he had to warn her of something when she was in the middle of touching him. It ruined it. How many more times would he have to tell her to stop, or watch out, before she gave up trying?

She just nodded and then moved her hands to his sides. Just when he thought she was about to put her arms around him, and he would have to stop her once again, she ran them downwards.

Merikh jumped in her arms, his sight flashing a reddish pink.

"Did you just grab my arse?"

He turned his head to the side to look down to check that he really could feel her hands kneading his damn backside through his pants.

Her giggle had him snapping his gaze forward.

"Yes?" She gave his cheeks a big squeeze. "Women can like butts too, you know. Yours is really nice, all soft and squishy, and yet somehow still firm."

Should he be offended or pleased by what she just said?

Then she did something that made understanding unfold. She grabbed near the base of his tail and pulled it forward so she could feel the entire length of it.

Is she showing me she accepts all this? His heart caved in a little, and some of the tension he'd been holding within his body eased out of him, tension he may have been holding for centuries.

He gave in and stopped holding back the orb change that had been nagging at him. They shifted into a purple, already deep in desire, and his cock jerked along with it. He could feel his tentacles moving to swirl tighter around his shaft, and it pressed against the back of his seam he was clenching shut.

There would definitely be a noticeable bulge there.

When her hand came to the tuft at the end of his tail and let go, she finally reached for the front of his pants. She unbuttoned them, opened them, and then slowly drew them down his thick thighs so they could fall to the ground. He used his tail to unpick the fabric from his quills around the backs of his calves, so she didn't know they were caught.

Merikh swallowed his groan when she placed her hand against his groin in search of his cock. Her teeth nipped at her lips when she didn't find it exposed like on most creatures, but she fingered the fur seam there, and her features softened.

Her fingertips traced up it and tickled his tentacles covering his cock where they were bulging from within. He couldn't contain his groan when his seam twitched, threatening to open as she traced back down.

"It's in here?"

Gnashing his fangs, drool collected in the cavity of his

mouth. She was touching him so lightly, teasing him, and he felt the hold on his inaction, on his very control, slipping.

Bumping the end of his snout against her cheek, he quietly said, "If you're expecting me to be gentle, Raewyn, then you should reconsider. I am not gentle, and this will only end in me taking you hard and fast."

This was her last chance to turn back.

Raewyn rubbed her cheek against his snout, seeming to take anything he did as a sign of affection, and dug her fingers around the bulge within him.

"How do I get it out?" she whispered up to him, her breaths fanning over the side of his fangs.

He'd warned her, and she wasn't shying away.

In that moment, he knew he was weak to this pretty little Elf. His seam parted, and his cock *quickly* shot forward into her welcoming, open palm. He let out a raspy exhale of relief, since the pressure had been unbearable.

Then, he released his tentacles for her, and the last inch of him pushed forward so his erection was jutting to its full length. The tentacles were almost as long as his cock, reaching to just below the head, and they wriggled back so they could cling to the base.

She was gentle with him as she brushed both palms over the sensitive head, and Merikh had to lean back against the wall as he pulsated at the contact. His claws dug into rock, and he had to use every ounce of his will not to lunge at her.

If he gave in, he'd tackle her to the bed behind her. He would be shoving himself inside her within seconds.

Her fingers overlapped to form a ring as she pushed her hands down, vibrating sensation to the core of him as she went over the ridges behind his head. She smeared his natural lubricant, thick as it collected in front of her hands and eventually dripped from him.

Then she went over the knotted ring that was just over three-quarters of the way down, and Merikh let out a pleased rumble.

She went even lower and found the two oval protrusions at the very base, pushing his tentacles back to do so, and petted his embedded semen sacs.

His lungs almost seized as they sunk inwards at her touch, before dropping back to their bulging states.

"You're really big," she rasped, rubbing her hands back up. "Kind of makes me nervous."

Red flared in his sight at the chance of her backing out, only to be swallowed up by purple when her scent deepened, and she nibbled at her bottom lip. She wasn't going to.

Then she let go so she could reach for his right hand. In curiosity, he gave it to her, and she dragged it towards the apex of her thighs.

"C-could you sheath your claws for me?" she asked, her voice small and shaking. He didn't know if that was from her arousal or nervousness at what she'd been planning to do.

Merikh's cock thickened momentarily, and a drop of precum welled. His entire groin tightened as a deeper clutch of desire lanced it.

"That's enough," he bit with an undertone of a heated growl.

What she'd done was more than enough to prove she desired him. He didn't think his sanity could survive watching her masturbate with his hand and stretch herself to take his own cock.

Sheathing the claws of his right hand, Merikh shoved it forward and slipped the tip of his middle finger against the swollen nub of her clit. Leaning forward, he wrapped his arm around the back of her curls, moving his hand to the other side, then pressed the still-extended claws of his left hand to the underside of her jaw so he could lift her head.

"You've done enough," he said as he licked from one cheek to the other with his flat tongue, catching her soft, malleable lips with it. "I'll take it from here."

With her gown crinkled around his wrist, Raewyn let out a broken gasp as he stroked her clit. She bucked into his finger, the slit of her pussy so wet, her arousal so strong, that she soaked the tip.

She grabbed around his wrist as he gently played with her, her thighs twitching and clenching around his hand. Just by her reaction, he could tell she'd been aching for a while. So, he shoved his hand deeper and speared her with his finger to help ease her.

Raewyn moaned and tried to lean into him for support, but he didn't let her as he continued to lick across her lips, 'kissing' in return for all the ones she had gifted him before.

She was so relaxed, she was loose enough for him to be able to spear her with a second digit without too much resistance, and he panted against her for it.

She's so hot inside. He moved his thick fingers back and forth, her pussy tight and slick, like she was sucking on them. Her core was quick to quiver, and Merikh dragged her closer, his tongue becoming more incessant, even when he sunk it into her mouth. *She's so hot, and wet, and tight.*

She was like a snug little pool of inferno; one he was about to be inside of. He hoped she scalded him.

His pants deepened at the idea, choking in his lungs as he forced her to take a third finger.

Her shaken moan tingled his ears, and her scent clogged his brain. His fur and quills lifted as a swirl of need began to cyclone within his chest.

She tried to rub his cock for him, but each touch was sloppy as he thrust his fingers. She was too busy shivering against him, too busy turning inward, rocking on her feet so she could buck into his fingers for more. He spread them, stretching her further in preparation to take his cock, and she pulled her head back.

He didn't let her escape, his tongue twisting inside her mouth, stealing every drop of saliva to quench his yearning to taste her sweet cunt.

Her moans grew sharper, and she dug her nails into the back of his wrist. He didn't even mind when her other hand did it to his cock. Her movements became more jarring, her core spasming like crazy as her back arched.

"Don't you fucking dare," he growled, yanking his fingers and tongue from her. She cried at the loss, but Merikh ignored it as he fisted her dress and slipped it up over her head. "The next time you come, it'll be around me."

He darted his hands down and grabbed the backs of her thighs, lifting her until her legs were spread around his hips. She wrapped them around his arse, and, despite his warning, ground her clit against the groove underneath his cock.

Merikh climbed his way onto the bed and turned so he could lie down. She knelt over him, nestled over his shaft, and nibbled her bottom lip as she selfishly moved. He grabbed her arse and halted her.

"I thought you would be on top," she whispered as she leaned back.

Merikh's gaze fell on her chest. Her breasts were round and firm looking, with stiff nipples that were shades darker than her smooth, rich flesh. He wanted to nibble at them with his fangs.

"I will only be able to hold back for so long," he rasped, licking at his snout.

If she wanted *time* to adjust without being violently rutted, then she needed to be the one on top. The moment he started thrusting, he wouldn't stop until he was spent.

Her nails dug into his abdomen as she tried to shift forward so she could keep grinding. He didn't let her, and her eyes crinkled into agonised bows.

"Please, Merikh. I want to come."

Fuck, she wasn't making it easy for him not to snap.

I want her to see how obscene she looks right now. With her digging her nails in to sit on his cock currently jutting up and resting against her stomach. His tentacles were trying to circle her, to drag her closer in the hopes she would sink him into bliss.

He wanted her to see how needy she looked for his monstrous purple dick – each ridge, the thick head, the knotted ring at the bottom. How her lips were parted on panted breaths, wet and swollen from him playing with them. How her expression appeared dazed as she sat on top of a Duskwalker's fur-covered body.

He wanted her to see what she was tormenting him with, how beautiful and sinful she appeared.

"Nooo, stop," she whined, raising both her hands to her face to cover it.

He didn't mean to share his sight with her, but he shuddered all the same at knowing she could see herself.

"Tell me you want to fuck me," he quietly demanded, as he lowered her hands.

He wanted to look at her cute face covered in freckles, to see her starburst eyes, and her nose, her lips, the roundness of her cheeks, and softness of her jaw.

He wanted to see all the geometric markings that looked as though they were painted over her body, mostly concentrated around her hands and forearms, feet and calves, her sternum, and the sides of her neck.

Even the gold chain around her waist, tickling just above her navel, caught his eye.

"I want you to say those words to me."

Her curls bounced around her face when she shook her head.

"Tell me you want to fuck me, Raewyn," Merikh growled as he palmed his dick to push it more firmly against her. "Tell me you want my cock inside your tight little cunt, and I'll give you what you want."

What *he* desperately wanted more than anything right now.

Since he'd released her, she slipped forward and subtly grinded. There was some internalised panic, her ears slowly pushing back.

With her hips, she pushed his cock down to lie against his stomach and played with him. Going higher so she was rubbing against the four ridges and the rim of his cockhead, her breaths turned shallow. Whether it was courage or her care lessening, she moaned and licked her lips before she spoke.

"I want to f-fuck you," she uttered softly. She placed her hands on his muscled gut and turned her head down to concentrate – or to hide from her own face staring at her. "I-I want your cock inside my... pussy. Please, I can't take it anymore. I've wanted it since the forest."

Even though she hadn't said exactly what he wanted, he still let out a pleased growl. Merikh grabbed her waist to steady her. Raewyn had to shuffle her knees on top of his hips and thick stomach as he lifted her, but she was quick to steer his shaft and nestle it at her entrance.

He grunted at the tightness that greeted him.

The moment he felt the kiss of her, he shoved her down through the pressure. He tried to be slow, tried not to hurt her, but he couldn't stop his claws from flexing.

He could fit, he knew he would fit, but it didn't make it any easier. At least her pooling arousal and his dripping lubricant were helping. His back bowed, and a yelp tore from his throat when the head popped inside.

Oh fuck. Raewyn winced, her core crushingly snug when she tightened. Yet, she pushed her hips forward and back to help ease herself, to loosen even as he popped the first ridge into her.

I need more, he mentally pleaded. *I need deeper.*

He needed it now, to soothe him before he lost it.

The moment the first ridge went inside, it stretched her enough to take the others that followed, and she quickly went down until he bottomed out inside her.

Merikh hadn't even realised he'd closed his sight until he was forcing his orbs open again to stare and pant at where they were joined.

Shit. I'm inside. I'm actually inside her! She'd taken him most of the way, at least three-quarters. The twisty knot sat just outside, and her lips were resting upon it.

She was trying to climb up and away, so he held her down. "Stay."

"You're too big," she whimpered.

Trying to reassure her he wasn't 'too big,' since she'd taken him, he wished he didn't swell as he said, "I'm inside you."

She winced, but he couldn't contain how thrilled he was that he was buried in this sinless-looking female. He had an angel around his cock, one who appeared more ethereal than he could have ever dreamed up.

Despite his growing desperation, Merikh didn't like that she looked uncomfortable seated on him.

"Come here." He wrapped an arm around her slight waist and dragged her up his cock until the bottom ridge was just at her entrance.

He hoped the lack of deep pressure helped, and he curved her back so he could lick across one of her stiff nipples. She pressed her hands against his shoulders to keep herself upright, which gave him the freedom to bring his other hand between them so he could tease her clit with his index and middle fingers.

Merikh fought every urge to thrust, to move her, so he could ease her pussy into loosening. She was on his cock, and he wasn't going to let her get away from it, but he wasn't going to hurt her when he could just be *slightly* more patient.

If he was, he would get what he wanted. When she was ready, he could finally give in.

It was why she was on top of him in the first place.

Plus, he was kind of fond of his tongue doing swirling patterns around her left nipple before he lashed it over the right. She seemed to like it, especially with him teasing her clit, and she eventually softened.

It was lucky she was tall enough for him to be able to do this – and that was saying something, coming from a nearly seven-foot Duskwalker.

When she began moaning and stirring the first quarter of him inside her, Merikh pulled back. Then, just so he could watch her reaction, he pushed her hips down so she had fully mounted him again.

They both shuddered.

He lifted her halfway before he pushed her back down and groaned, his fangs parting. Swelling from just that minor movement, he stopped and held her.

"Move on me," he demanded.

She slid forward up his cock, then waved her hips back down. He didn't know when he'd begun digging his claws into her arse, but he gripped her cheeks hard.

One of her knees slipped off him, and she had to drag it back up so she could keep moving. She gave little moans, her head falling back as she supported herself on his stomach.

Each sound from her was high-pitched, decadent, and just potent enough to eat away at him. She smelt wonderful now that her arousal had returned in force, and the longer he breathed her in, the drunker he got on it.

He didn't think he'd ever experienced something this profoundly pleasurable. She hugged him all the way to his core, so hot she was almost searing, and her moulding plushness tickled every ridge and thick vein of him.

It wasn't enough. Not for Merikh, who was trying his hardest to stop himself from thrusting. Raewyn was using his cock right now, rubbing down his resolve, but he wanted to see her bring herself to orgasm.

He desperately wanted deeper.

"Faster." He needed faster if she couldn't take him deeper.

He *could* change her body to mount every inch of him, but he didn't want to do that. She'd swallowed most of him; he'd take what he could without permanently altering her.

Raewyn tried to be swifter. Her leg slipped again, so she placed the other down so she was pushing off the bed with her toes. When that didn't work, she tucked them back underneath herself on top of him and tried to use his arms to help her. She hissed in a breath and threw her hands away when she stabbed herself with his quills, and he healed her.

"I can't," she cried. "You're too big."

His body was too large in comparison to hers.

She may be tall, but he was two if not three times wider than her. His hips were wide, so she struggled to move while straddling him properly. His stomach was round, and although it was a good place for her to rest her hands, it made resting her knees on him difficult.

It didn't help that she couldn't sit back completely on his cock, since she hadn't swallowed all of it.

Merikh assisted her, but each time his hands moved, his hips wanted to go with them. He gnashed his fangs, trying to keep himself still beneath her.

Fuck, she smells so good. Feels so good. Sounds so good. A small growl rumbled from his chest. *I need more.*

Her breasts bounced as she moved, catching his attention, before it was stolen when he looked down and watched her riding him. The purple hue at the edges of his sight danced and darkened.

"Faster, Raewyn," he demanded, just as he thrust up and felt a deep pounding against his cock.

His orbs flashed red momentarily just as she let out a moan.

He did it again, and she shivered as her pussy spasmed. His angle was different, hitting somewhere wonderful for her. Then, her movements became shallow, short, and *impossibly* slower. He was only halfway inside her when she just rubbed his cockhead and ridges over a swelling spot.

Raewyn's spine arched as she threw her head back, and a sweet, euphoric cry fell from her wet lips. She squeezed him as her cunt clenched and quivered, drenching his cock in her slick.

The way she looked while visibly trembling... her scent, her cry, the squeeze he felt, all while she was stuck, barely moving on his cock... Merikh's patience snapped.

His quills and fur stood on their ends, as a bout of aggression shot through him and clutched at his groin like a set of malicious claws.

He shot forward so he could wrap his arms around her, one

hand supporting her shoulders while the other remained on her arse. Merikh snarled as he pinned her down against his torso and rammed his cock through her orgasm.

Her cry was cut short, the breath knocked out of her, as Merikh pistoned. His thrusts were fast, hard, and unrelenting, but even when she stopped squeezing him and went lax in his arms, he didn't stop.

Remaining inside the heaven of her, he rolled them, shoved her back to the bed, grabbed her thighs from underneath, and spread them wide as he wildly thrust.

A groan mixed in with his permanent snarl.

Finally, he was getting speed. Finally, he was getting depth and hard slams. Finally, he was obeying the nagging need of his hips to pound into the naughty little Elf who had been driving him crazy.

I'm going to fuck her senseless. I'm going to fuck her until she can't think of anything else but my cock. Until she can do nothing but cry and beg for me to stop. Until the only thing she can scream is my name.

He gazed down at the female, who had an angelic white halo of hair around her head, and yet her spread pussy being railed by a monster said she was a nymph. Her face looked guileless, cute and innocent, yet her lips were parted and moaning like a bitch in heat around his purple cock.

She was perfectly misaligned.

A contradiction.

Scalding him as much as she was soothing him, his salvation as much as his demise. The image of her burned deep within his mind, winding him into a frantic, twisted ache.

His cock swelled within her as he pulsated, leaking a heavy drop of precum. *I want to mark her in my scent.*

When Merikh had entered her, he'd taken back his shared

sight. Raewyn was thankful for that.

She didn't think she would be able to handle watching herself through his eyes, not with the way she was under him.

Not with the way he'd lifted her backside completely off the bed and spread her legs apart so he could freely thrust into her. Her upper back and head were the only things still laying down, and she could feel her breasts bouncing wildly.

She knew what her face looked like right then, feverish with desire, flushed, sweat-slicked, incapable of having a coherent thought beyond her pleasure, both amazed and stupefied by how fast he was going and how good it felt.

Her brows were furrowed in bliss, her lips parted to moan. Her eyes were crinkled as she tried to survive this sudden onslaught.

Her curls were caught underneath her head and shoulders, but they helped make her quick, back-and-forth slides easier. He was mostly holding her in place, but she constantly rebounded. She was naked, completely exposed to him.

Honestly, she feared she looked like a drooling mess.

Raewyn revelled in it. He hadn't stopped thundering out a growl, and the very sound of it washed over her and tickled the most sensitive places on her body. Her pussy, her clit, her nipples, her ears.

His cinnamon and orange scent was drowning her, and she greedily took it in. His body was so warm, it relaxed her all the way to her very core for his pounding, from the *inside.*

She adored the way his tentacles constantly wanted to wrap over her hips and around her waist. They were lengthy, and it felt like a cuddle, even though he was so far away.

He was so thick and long that she was filled to capacity. There wasn't a place inside he wasn't touching, wasn't petting, and her poor G-spot was being wonderfully annihilated.

Yet his lubricant didn't make her feel like she was being chafed. Everything was slippery, and the only thing they had to fight through was her tightness against his impossible size.

It wasn't long before she knew he was about to screw her into another mind-shattering orgasm.

She couldn't hold back her cries as they became more erratic. Her toes curled, her feet arched, and Raewyn searched for something to hold onto.

Pain lanced her hands when she tried to grip the only part of him she could grasp: his forearms.

Any pain in her palms disappeared in a cool rush of red magic that glittered in her sight.

Raewyn gasped, her eyes widening in distress when he yanked his shaft from her. A sob broke from her at the loss. She didn't mean to hurt her hands! She didn't want him to stop because of it.

There was no chance for her to make a complaint, for her to plead for him.

Within seconds, she was turned over onto her stomach, dragged back so her arse was in the air, and she was devouring his cock again. She pushed up onto straightened arms and, with the underside of her perky breasts jostling from his thrusts, she turned her head to the side.

"Like this?" she asked in surprise, as each breath was shunted out of her by a slamming thrust.

Doggy-style wasn't the most 'romantic' position, and she couldn't believe someone had put her in it for their first time.

The sharp, pained cry that came from her next was one of complete and utter delight. His claws scraped her scalp as he shoved his fingers into her coily curls, fisted them, and yanked her head back until she was barely able to touch the bed with her fingertips.

"Someone doesn't know how to keep her fucking hands to herself," he snarled directly into her ear.

Raewyn clenched around him, the delicious pain and his rough snarl twisting her mind into fraying rope. She poked her tongue forward, like that would help her to breathe through her pathetic pants.

He was so spikey and dangerous right now, and she bet he looked like a menacing creature behind her, all puffed out and scary.

She wasn't afraid, not when she was too busy wringing her next orgasm. He was being so rough, going so hard and fast. Liquid gushed, and the squelching between them intensified.

"Merikh," she moaned, never having been taken this forcibly before.

Raewyn didn't have many inhibitions, but any she did have had long been thrown out the window... cave entrance? She thought they'd been thrown so far that not even the Veil could find it.

"Don't stop. Please don't stop."

Licking across her ear and causing goosebumps to shiver throughout her entire body, he rumbled in a gruff, raw voice, "You seem to like my cock."

Like it? Raewyn was *adoring* it.

She *knew* those ridges would feel just as divine inside her as they had teasing her from the outside. With him pulling back so far, they stimulated her all the way along, with textured waves against her most sensitive places. They rubbed her tender aches and had her squirming beneath him.

The base of one tentacle had slipped between the sopping wet mess of her lips, drenched in both their fluids, and it grazed along her clit.

Her mind struggled to accept she was taking something like this. He was so hard that her body was forced to give way, and yet he was so soft on the outside that it didn't feel like she was being assaulted by stone.

He was the perfect texture, heat, wetness to turn Raewyn into a needy ache who just wanted more, more, until she was so raw that she couldn't stand it.

The only thing missing was that she wanted him deeper. She wanted to feel how thoroughly he was taking her by how hard his hips slapped against her thighs. She wanted to be swallowed up by his tentacles and learn how far they could reach.

She wanted to know what that ring kissing at the lips around her entrance would do, what it would feel like, if it, too, was inside her.

There was no relief, no chance for her to calm down and think, just Merikh and his desire to ease whatever pent-up frustration was inside him. Was he always this domineering?

"Harder," she demanded.

She didn't care if it meant he split her in two, if he broke her. Raewyn needed more.

He pulled on her hair until she was forced up to her knees, and the pitiful mewl that came from her only gave away how much she relished it. She'd always liked biting and scratching, but she'd never had someone almost threaten to pull her hair out to know she *needed* something like this.

He pulled until her ear was next to the side of his bony snout, and she could feel his entire thick body against her back and jiggling bottom.

"Harder?" he asked. She sucked her bottom lip into her mouth and bit on it, second guessing her demand. Maybe she shouldn't poke the bear while he was already pounding her. "Like this?"

Then he gave her exactly what she wanted, and any tension she had left in her body melted. She gave herself over for him to hold, to support, to do what he wanted as she just took it. If he let go of her hair, she'd fall on her face.

The sounds that came out were incoherent moans, gasps, and cries, and she didn't care to try to make them out. Raewyn was gone, and she was absolutely fine with that.

With deep, feral grunts that matched every time he hit the end of her, Merikh moved his free hand from her hip. Then, he cupped the side of her head with her lips resting in his palm.

"From the first moment I saw your beautiful face, I wanted you," he rasped, before his claws dug into her flesh like he wanted to cut her apart. Then he drew them down her neck, her chest, catching a nipple along the way with a sharp sting. He dug them into the thatch of hair on her pubic mound. "I didn't know you had such a greedy hole. Otherwise, I may have tried to fuck it sooner."

His groan was haunting when she started coming, her body agreeing with him in tight spasms.

"It feels so good when you do that," he said, his hips jerking and losing their rhythm when he thickened within her. "Your cunt is so wet and hungry, it keeps trying to milk my cock. Should I give it what it wants?"

Raewyn whimpered in answer, and she fell forward against the bed as he released her.

Treating her like she was a doll to be thrown around, Merikh turned her by her thigh. He caught both her hands in one meaty hand and shoved them above her head so she couldn't hurt herself again. Then, her body arched into a deep bow when he also lifted her hips to meet him. His entry was so smooth now since she'd adjusted to him that he slipped right in.

She pressed her foot against the side of his thigh to steady her leg from bouncing, doing nothing to fight him.

His hips weren't so fast, although still deliberate and rough.

It just gave her freedom to focus on all of *him*.

Everything about him was different. His clawed, calloused hands felt different pinning both her wrists down. His fur against her inner thigh was wrong when she was supposed to feel bare skin.

His tongue was rough, flat, and long as it swept over her neck sporadically. It left delightful streaks of saliva in its wake and made her shiver when his breath rolled over them.

Nothing about this was normal, not in taste, not in scent, not in sound or feeling. Raewyn had never been more turned on because of it, had never been this fretful for her next heart-stuttering orgasm.

"Merikh," she coarsely whispered, unsure of what she was trying to say.

She wanted him to keep going. He still felt so good inside her, but her last orgasm had worn her out. She hadn't come this much before, never had someone wring her almost dry, and changing positions so that she was on her back had her eyes growing lazy.

Like he understood, his hand stopped gripping her wrists. Instead, he dived his fingers through all of hers and tenderly held them to pin her down. Her heart melted at the gesture, especially when he let out a woofing exhale as he shuddered, and then gripped tighter.

Raewyn let out little mewls every time his cock swelled in thickness before going down. It was like a wave, one that had her toes curling.

Then, it happened one last time as he thrust in deep and held still. A sharp cry came from her, just as he let out a deeper woofing exhale. Liquid heat began to spread within her, hot and heavy.

I can feel him coming. She adored it, spreading her thighs in welcome.

"Fuck, Raewyn," he groaned deeply.

His thrusts softened as he pumped, his hips shuddering violently. She quivered around him every time heat burst right against her cervix before he drew back. He was making sure he came deep, but was also helping to push his seed out.

Merikh shuddered above her, his hands tight as they clasped her fingers and thighs. He sounded euphoric, and even his breaths were choppy and elated.

There's so much of it.

Right when she thought she was about to overflow, he violently yanked back so he could unlatch his clinging tentacles.

She winced, finding it burned her skin, and then instantly forgot about it when a heavy spurt of heat splattered against her clit. His cock followed, the groove lining up against her and sending her into a twitching mess as another splatter of liquid shot over her sternum.

He placed both hands against the bed and rocked, coming over her body as he ground his cock. One rope of seed streaked across her right nipple at the same time it leaked from her pussy. She lifted her chest, wanting to feel a little bit more of both, as more spurted over her.

With one last deep groan that made her tingle, he was done. Her thighs were resting on top of his as he panted down at her.

She didn't have the energy to smile, but her entire body was singing with satisfaction. Her eyes were drowsy with it.

"I couldn't resist filling you," he said with deep huffs. "But I have been wanting to cover you in my seed since the night in the cave."

Raewyn wiggled when the multiple, thick pools of warm liquid rolled down the curves of her torso. "Why didn't you then?"

She would have been one hundred percent on board with being covered in warm, thick spunk. She imagined there would be twice as much as what already heavily coated her torso if he hadn't half spent inside her pussy. She wiggled when more leaked, tickling on its way out.

Her eyelids flickered in surprise when his claws gently moved over her arms until he cupped the side of her face. His thumb stroked over her cheek.

"Because you had just gotten dry after freezing from the rain. I did not want to make it harder on you."

Her heart fluttered in response like it had been replaced by an eclipse of fuzzy moths. He'd been sweet and considerate of her in a time she hadn't even realised. It just made her wonder how often she didn't notice something trivial like that.

Despite how lethargic she was, Raewyn tentatively lifted her hands and pressed her fingertips to the sides of his jaw. She'd touched it earlier, but desire could make people more comfortable with something.

Now that he was spent, she wondered if his diffidence would return.

He didn't flee from her touch, but he didn't lean into it either, like she'd hoped. Still, she cupped the sides of his hard cheeks in her palms, the bone warmer and somehow feeling alive.

"Well?" she laughed, since he was still looming over her. "Are you going to lie down with me or are you just going to kneel there and sleep?"

She was tired, and she imagined he was as well, since he slept more than she did. He often laid down on the ground when she went to bed, and she really wanted to be held by him right now. She wanted to bask in his warmth, his scent, and even his fur now that she was thoroughly sated.

Her forehead knotted when he took his skull from her happy hands.

"I won't lie down with you," he stated as he backed up to sit on his haunches.

"P-pardon?" Did Raewyn need to clean her ears out, or did she actually hear him correctly?

"I won't lie down with you," he repeated.

Her lips opened and closed in disbelief. He rejected her, like seriously rejected her. It wasn't a 'can't', it was a 'won't' – like he didn't want to.

It kind of stung.

He'd just had sex with her – the least he could do was cuddle her so she didn't feel... used. Sure, that was a weird thought coming from someone who'd started it, but not holding your sex partner even for a moment afterwards was pretty hurtful.

She'd never been a fan of men who would be intimate and then once they came, they shoved their pants on, saluted, and left while she was still naked.

She turned her head to the side, but then let the issue go. She imagined he had a reason, not that it changed how she felt; she was just choosing not to be angry over it.

It did change how she felt about being saturated in his release, though. Before it had been titillating, but if she was going to be laying down by herself, she didn't want to be covered in it.

It would have been fine if they were both laying in his mess.

"Could you get me some water from the lake, then?" she asked quietly as she covered her chest and pubic mound. "I'd like to wash up before I sleep."

It'd be a lot faster if he did it, and Raewyn wasn't sure if she could walk right now. At least, not without wobbles and aches.

"You... want to wash my seed from you?" She didn't understand his grim but surprised tone.

"Well, yeah." She tried to laugh it off, since that was a fairly normal request. "I'm all sticky and gross right now. I can help you wash up as well since you're covered in my come too."

She would be embarrassed about saturating his groin, but she was just so elated by their coupling that she couldn't wrangle up the emotion.

Since her head was turned to the side, she didn't know if she saw the sparks of blue in the corner of her peripheral correctly. However, when she turned her face forward, she knew for certain she saw red, *deep* red.

Why is he angry?

"No," he bit out as he shuffled backwards.

With her brows shooting up her forehead, Raewyn sat up. "*Excuse* me?"

"Get your own damn lake water," he growled.

Then he stormed out of the cave – his footsteps for once making deep, pounding thuds.

Her jaw dropped so quickly it threatened to unhinge and fall off.

Oh... my... gosh! He did not just leave me here to wash all this off by myself! If he wasn't going to do a shred of aftercare, the least he could have done was get her water so she could do it herself.

Raewyn went to cover her eyes when tears formed and instantly smeared his seed over her face. She removed her hands with a cringe, her tears fading as she came to her senses.

I thought he'd be sweeter after sex.

Instead, he was so rude and thoughtless that she regretted doing it with him at all.

TWENTY-EIGHT

With an annoyed huff, Raewyn got to her feet. She found her cane near the cave entrance, picked up her toiletries, and walked towards the lake.

The idea of dousing herself in lukewarm water wasn't what she wanted to do, especially since she would have rather stayed laying down, all relaxed. Her thighs *ached* with every footfall, and each one thumped inside her tender core. She was aware she was limping on certain steps.

That should elate her! She should be grinning at the pain, and instead, her internal hurt just made each twinge annoy her.

Not long after getting into the water, a soft growl growing closer informed her of his approach.

"What do you want?" she quietly bit out, hoping to unnerve him. It wasn't as powerful as she'd have liked it to be, since her throat was hoarse from crying out earlier.

She didn't bother covering her chest like she was tempted to. Although she didn't want to show her body to someone who didn't deserve to see it right now, she just washed her arm while giving him her back, pretending she didn't care.

"Enjoying your *bath*?" He had the audacity to sneer the words at her.

"Very much so," she answered with an air of nonchalance. "All squeaky clean and no longer covered in your cum."

His growl stuttered for a moment before returning. "I'm leaving."

That made her pause. "Pardon?" she said as she turned around slightly. "Where are you going?"

"Stay away from the ward." His sounds began to fade as though he was walking away.

"Hey!" she yelled, reaching over the ledge. "When are you coming back?"

She received no answer, and once more, tears stung her eyes.

Merikh had never just up and left like that before, except for when she'd eavesdropped on him. Usually, he let her know how long she could expect him to be gone for, and where he was going.

What's he mad at me for? she thought, looking off in the direction his body made a shadow when he went through the ward. *I'm the one who should be mad.*

Now, Raewyn wasn't just royally pissed – she was livid!

He had the audacity to screw her brains out, then turn into a jerk within the span of minutes. And after leaving her by herself to clean up, she was forced to have this bath in the lake when she would rather be asleep. He was such a... a dick! He was being a dick, and he must know it – if he didn't, then he was an idiot.

Which meant he was doing it on purpose.

He'd never truly turned this kind of hostility on her before. Gosh, she knew he'd probably kick a small puppy if it suited him, but currently, she felt like the puppy.

He'd never made her feel that way in the past.

There was a lot she could forgive, but this treatment wasn't it. She wouldn't reward it, but she also wouldn't accept it with a smile.

So, whenever he decided to turn back up, she hoped he didn't plan for her to be a ray of sunshine. It was time for her to show him her ire.

With that thought in mind, she exited the lake and went to

bed after changing the sheets. Her sleep was fitful, as she expected. She woke up in a fouler mood than when she'd laid down, her eyelids heavy and achy.

Her desire to return home strengthened in her want to get away from him as soon as possible, and Raewyn finally put her mind to the mana stone.

It was weak. She didn't know how long he'd been using the stone for his glamour, but it was nearly depleted of magic. It had also been a poor quality stone to begin with.

Whoever had mined it obviously hadn't known that. They also likely didn't have a lot of experience with these kinds of stones and how to read them.

It took her most of the day just trying to unravel the glamour. Despite the stone's lack of quality and magic depletion, whoever had created the glamour itself was vastly powerful, able to weave a tight, perfect spell.

Weldir, she mentally sneered.

This kind of magic was nearly divine in construct, and for a lowly Elf like herself, it had taken her hours just to learn its woven craft. Then, she had to loosen the threads in the opposite way he'd wound them. If she didn't do it correctly, the tension could destroy the stone.

A sad thought crossed her mind. *I wouldn't be able to do this so well if I still had my sight.*

She could see the magic, could see the glamour's seal threads, and the darkness surrounding it made it easy to identify each tiny fibre. There were hundreds of them.

Many people who had lost their sight didn't always lose it completely. Many saw blobs or had such a blurriness they couldn't make out a single thing. She considered herself as somewhat sightless on the spectrum, since she could see this.

It heightened her magical abilities, and it made it both harder and easier to do her work.

Once she was done, Raewyn placed the stone on the bench with a sigh of relief. The spell was gone, but now she was mentally, physically, emotionally, and magically exhausted. Even her eyes hurt from staring at grey glowing threads for what could only have been a full night and day.

What greeted her was silence.

She kind of wanted someone to complain to about what she'd done. Usually, she would have rushed off to go annoy the Duskwalker into giving her attention, but he wasn't there.

She leaned her elbow on the bench, placed her chin in her palm, and fingered the stone so it rolled back and forth.

He would have listened to me, though.

He would have let her ramble on and on until she thought his ears might have bled. He would have asked for clarification on things he didn't understand, or given his own short opinions, but he usually just let her do and say whatever she wanted.

Her lips drew into a hard line. *Hey, no!* she yelled at herself. *I'm angry with him. I'm not going to sit here and miss him because I'm bored.*

She walked off so she could finally make herself some food: a vegetable stew with plenty of spices and herbs to make it tasty.

It was while she curled up in his too big of a chair and was halfway through eating that she heard movement.

She snuffed out the urge to get up and greet him. Instead, she turned her back to the entryway, leaning her back against the arm rest with her feet pressed into the other.

Something thudded against the ground just outside, and he left what he dropped to enter his home. The warmth and freshness of his orange and cinnamon scent billowed into the cave.

"I've returned," he said, his vibration surprisingly giving her comfort. Her ears twitched.

She relied on it, even if she didn't mean to.

"Okay," she answered before turning her chin up. "Where did you go?"

"Hunting." The chime of tools, like metal and wood, clinked and clanked as he rummaged through his shelves. "The fainthearted Elf would be wise to stay away from me until I've skinned my deer."

Raewyn shrunk into herself. She didn't like that there was a dead creature just outside, the whole idea abhorrent to her. She also didn't like his deep, displeased tone.

"I-I thought you didn't eat, since nothing sustains you. What was the point of hunting?"

"Creatures are used for more than just their meat. I'll feed it to the Demons loitering around the ward, and then once they're done with it, I'll get rid of them."

What needless bloodshed and slaughtering. No wonder he'd named himself something so malevolent as *Merikh.*

Just as he was leaving, she said, "I've removed the glamour."

His tone was so icy it was lethal as he stated, "Then you better make sure your experiment works. For both our sakes."

Then he was gone, leaving Raewyn feeling worse than she did before. He didn't even seem to care that she hadn't been her usual self towards him.

Did I possibly do something wrong?

She thought he'd left to take out whatever thing he'd shoved up his own butt, but it seemed to be still firmly in place, which meant he wasn't just angry over nothing.

It was either that, or this was his personality when he got what he wanted. Now that they'd been intimate, was he no longer being kind to her because he'd finally gotten his dick wet? Could a Duskwalker be that... crude?

I don't think I did anything wrong.

Either way, whether it was something she'd done, or this was just him, both left her feeling like someone had burned a hole in her chest. She didn't think she deserved this cold-shoulder treatment.

It wasn't often someone could wound Merikh. He'd suffered

a lot in his life, from the moment he was born to the next breath he was about to take in.

He'd suffered multiple temporary deaths, had been in situations where he'd needed to remove his own limbs, had killed people. He'd had the light shone on how much the world hated him, what it thought of him, and how it would always treat him.

He'd long ago built deflective barriers to it, and just accepted whatever life would throw at him next.

So, for Raewyn to wound him in a single statement meant it had been a deep cut. It wasn't something he'd prepared himself for, especially after experiencing something he also hadn't thought possible.

Having her seduce him, to be inside her, to have her ask for more so he truly hadn't needed to hold back... It had been like a heavenly dream. Even when he'd been rough and had to heal her multiple times, Raewyn hadn't asked him to stop, slow down, be gentle. She'd taken him at full force and then came the entire time.

When he'd been kneeling over her, his chest was so full of euphoria for the first time in his life that he hadn't known what to do with the emotions slamming inside.

Then, in just one statement, she'd tainted it.

He'd gone from an ecstasy-filled high to a soul-crushing low.

With a grunt at the cold lance of pain that radiated behind his sternum, Merikh yanked the last of the skin from the deer corpse in front of him. He was kneeling on the ground, his nose blocked by a satchel filled with garlic, basil, and lemon that he'd shoved into his nose hole.

He sat back and looked down at what he'd completed.

Why am I even doing this? he thought with his sight shifting to blue.

He was doing it for her, but he wondered if there was even a point to it. He guessed it was just because he liked to prepare for anything and everything. Even if she'd wounded him, some small part of him hoped it would be something he'd require in the future.

With the earlier interaction, he doubted it.

She hadn't wanted to speak with him, and that was his own fault.

He knew he was being callous towards her, even childish, but he didn't know how to deal with how he was feeling. He was angry with her, but he also recognised that he shouldn't be, as it wasn't his place.

I am nothing to her.

It made sense, but she was the one who had decided to start their intimacy, only to dash any hope he could have for more before it'd even started forming.

He grabbed the leg of the deer and dragged it out of his ward to throw it at the Demons, then stepped back into safety to watch the two of them eat it together. They were fairly small and stupid, but he'd rather not have them running back to Jabez and enlightening the half-Demon that he had an Elf here.

His *sister*, no less.

Once the Demons were done, he made short work of killing them. He threw them into the river so they could wash down to the swamp Demons, who would feast on them. Leaving behind corpses would only bring more Demons, which is what he was currently trying to avoid.

Then he turned back and picked up the deer's hide. *I guess this would be useful to have even if I don't utilise it for her.*

Merikh started up the vibration in his chest as he entered his home, finding Raewyn resting on the chair still.

Since he'd cleaned his hands of blood, once he lit the cooking hearth and placed the deer hide in boiling water, he removed the horrible satchel from his snout. The only reason he'd obtained a cooking hearth in the first place was so he could boil whatever he wanted. Whether it be spell ingredients or turning hide into leather like he was currently doing, it was an invaluable tool.

Since he'd never actually made leather before, he obtained

the book that detailed how from one of his shelves. When he turned back around, he found Raewyn at the stone bench, fiddling with the crystal from his diadem.

His earlier behaviour wasn't aided by the fact that she'd finally taken away the one item he cared more about than his own life.

Once more, he was a creature forced into the shadows.

The silence between them was so heavy, it was nearly crushing. He was so used to Raewyn being bubbly and chatty that the lack of both weighed on him.

He wanted to fix it, but the moment he considered pushing his thoughts forward into sound, the cold pain behind his sternum intensified.

Merikh placed the book onto the table's furthest side and searched for what he wanted.

Once he found the instruction page, he read he was supposed to add salt to the water and quickly did so. It should be fine, since it hadn't been on for longer than a few minutes.

Over the many years he'd been walking this continent, he'd obtained all kinds of books. Most of them were about how to craft things, but he also had a handful of spell books made by humans. Most of those spells were useless, but there was a tiny handful that surprisingly worked – like his dill and bell charms.

He'd taught the Witch Owl how to make the barrier charms, so she could show Orpheus how to make them when his human offerings kept dying on him. Merikh had taken pity on him.

Thinking of that Mavka had his sight turning blue. *I cannot believe he managed to find a bride.* The only reason it saddened him was because he doubted he would find one for himself.

In reality, he was happy for Orpheus, Faunus, and that barely intelligent Mavka named Magnar. Three of his brothers had found brides, and Merikh was just seeking a way to flee.

Funnily enough, he wasn't surprised about Faunus.

Merikh didn't like him, simply because he was so optimistic and cheerful that it annoyed the absolute shit out of him. Faunus had always been that way, curious and hopeful – which was the exact opposite of Merikh. His personality was warm, so it was no surprise he'd managed to find some deranged bride to fawn over him.

I hope she drives him up the wall.

"I'm just letting you know I'm going to be working on the mana stone some more now that I've rested a little."

It was only when Raewyn finally spoke that he realised he'd been just standing there, watching water boil, lost in his own thoughts. *What was I planning to do? Fucking watch it boil for the next twenty-four hours?*

Much was bothering him, and he was feeling listless.

"Do what you want," he answered quietly, wanting to walk away from the pot but also having no idea what else he wanted to do.

"The stone is almost depleted." When he didn't say anything, she added, "I have to inject my own magic into it."

That made him rear his head up. He turned his bony face towards her.

"Don't be foolish again," he demanded, making sure his tone was stern enough to show he wasn't messing around.

Taking care of her while she'd been ill had been distressing. He didn't like feeling helpless, and her constant feverish shivering had deeply worried him. He didn't want either one of them to go through that again.

She rolled her starburst pupil eyes. "I won't need to. Last time, I had to feed it until the magic had taken, but since the stone already has its own source, I'll just be making it stronger."

Now that he was looking upon her, his sight threatened to shift to purple. The memories of the other night, although tainted, were now permanently burned into his memory.

Her sultry cries as she bounced, her wicked scent that made him feel drunk, her flesh breaking out in goosebumps that spread down her sides. The image of his cock pumping in and out of her overstuffed pussy. All of it instantly had his shaft jerking behind his seam.

Knowing that sweet face covered in cute freckles hid how devilish she could truly be, his attraction to her had grown tenfold.

When she parted her soft, full lips to say something, it reminded him that he'd tasted her mouth, had explored it, knew every one of her tastebuds personally.

Desire fiercely clawed at his gut, while also hollowing out his chest cavity. He realised he didn't want to be anywhere near her right now while he was having this reaction.

Even her pretty, curling hair was enticing him to claw his way into it so he could be tangled like in a spider's webbing.

"Hey–"

Before she could finish speaking, he moved to the other side of the bench and walked towards the entryway. Some strange emotion was clogging his throat, as though he was being plugged from the inside.

It was like he was being buried alive and was breathing in dirt.

"Where are you going now? I was trying to talk to you."

"Outside." Anywhere that wasn't near her and her beauty, her poisonous lily scent, her melodic voice. Just... away.

"Merikh, stop," she shouted in a bout of frustration.

His feet halted, but he didn't turn.

"Why? What do you want?" His tone was curt and swift, only so he could quicken this and leave.

If she required his assistance with something, he wasn't going to just leave her by herself. He would put up with his own dark thoughts if it meant he could help her achieve their collective goal.

"I don't know if I gave you the impression I'm a doormat, but I'm sorry to inform you that you're wrong," she said dryly. "I don't like the way you're treating me."

He turned his head to the side to look at her, and found she'd folded her arms across her chest. She was tapping a foot on the ground, her eyes narrowed into a glare.

He couldn't deny he'd been treating her coarsely.

"Noted," he stated, confirming he heard her.

It only soured her further, and her expression deepened.

"I don't like that you're avoiding me, either."

He also couldn't deny that. Unlike his usual stance, he wouldn't.

Her tone and aggressive posture only made his hackles rise, and his fur and quills lifted to mirror it. He'd foregone clothing the last few days to avoid the probability he'd just tear them.

"I may do what I like around my home," he stated truthfully. "If that is to be alone, then so be it."

With that, he stepped forward.

"Merikh!" she yelled, leaping forward.

He only had enough time to turn and raise his arm to stop her from foolishly grabbing at him.

"How many more times must you be hurt before you learn not to touch me?" he roared.

Her features flinched in fright at his sudden loudness. She backed up when he stepped forward, and her back hit the bench.

"When will you learn that the outside of me is *dangerous?* Every time you bleed, you are only courting your own death."

Once her initial shock faded, her own ire rebounded.

She took a step forward and accidentally knocked her chest to his own. Her stance reminded him of one of those yappy little dogs that always barked at him in the human towns, a silly little thing riling up a monstrous bear.

"Whatever your problem is, you need to get over it," she snapped up at him. She could be quite feisty when she wanted to be, and he found that oddly cute – especially with the way her ears had darted back in aggression. "I don't deserve to be treated this way."

It took a while for those words to sink in, to register. His hands opened and closed into fists, but he could feel his anger rising on the back of his neck.

The rumble that came from him was low, deep, and sinister as he lowered his head to be more level with her.

"Don't you?" he growled, his claws digging into his palms until they had pierced the plump flesh, blood squeezing through the creases. "Because I have another opinion on the matter."

"Excuse me?" she said in disbelief. "I'm not the one being an a-asshole! I asked you to lie down with me, and you acted like a jerk!"

"No." He raised a hand and risked loosening a single finger to tap her cheek with a claw in a *very* threatening manner. Merikh usually killed and destroyed what angered or hurt him; the female was lucky this was *all* he was doing. "I denied your request, and then you became spiteful."

Her brows twitched. "No, I didn't."

"I said I won't lie down with you, and apparently, that was enough for you to reject me."

That rejection had stung ever since.

"I have no idea what you're talking about. You're the one who couldn't even give me a shred of care afterwards. I asked for something as simple as a cuddle, and you stormed off because apparently, that was too much for you." Then she muttered, "Even though you'd already done so in the cave. It just meant you didn't want to."

Is that what she thought? He almost wanted to laugh.

"And you were *millimetres* from death," Merikh darkly added.

"What do you mean?"

"If you had moved in a certain direction even slightly that night, you'd be dead." He placed his hands on the stone bench behind her, trapping her in so she couldn't run away. "We were insanely lucky that night. If you had cut yourself on my quills while I was asleep, I wouldn't have been conscious enough to cut off my own breathing to save you. My reflexes are fast, and you probably wouldn't have even woken up to realise you were about to be eaten."

Her lips parted and then closed, her brows twitching like her thoughts were scattered. One moment, she looked angry, the next hurt, the next confused.

"I am a Duskwalker, Raewyn. That is why I could not lay with you – I thought that danger would have been obvious. I just thought you were being your usual reckless self, and I wanted to protect you, but then you turned spiteful towards me."

"Oh," she blurted out, making it known the reasoning for his denial had never crossed her mind.

That did little to change how much she'd bruised him.

Of course, he'd wanted to hold her afterwards! He'd wanted that more than anything else, and he'd been quite self-hateful because he *literally* couldn't. He'd wanted to painfully rip his quills from his own body just so he could.

His selfishness to just... hold something in his embrace, to keep it warm and safe, wasn't enough for him. He didn't wish to harm her or be the cause of her death.

"And, since I am so *offensive* to you," he sneered, his orbs shifting to blue before he forced them back to their usual red. "I thought it would be best to leave you alone, especially since you so callously rubbed it in my skulled face afterwards."

Now that he'd cleared that up, maybe she could reflect on how her words were harmful. He backed up.

"Wait, I don't understand," she said as she reached forward. Then, realising what she was doing, she pulled her hand back and cupped both to her chest. "Why would you think I find you offensive?"

Merikh's head twitched as it tilted, taking in the more submissive way she was presenting herself. All her anger had deflated out of her and left her usual softness behind. There was also deep confusion reflected in every forehead crinkle.

"Do you really not know?"

She shook her head with wide eyes.

He turned his head away as he thought, tapping a claw on the side of his snout.

Was she not trying to be spiteful?

What she'd said had been eating him up inside, but if she truly had not known... then she really didn't deserve his anger. It was still upsetting, and he would still sulk about it, but his behaviour would be unjustified.

He peeked at her expression again, finding it had deepened, and Merikh released the tension that had been rolling off him.

"I am sorry, then," he offered, feeling saddened. Shame prickled down his spine, and his sight turned a reddish pink. "I will do better." He'd learned something, and he wanted to come to terms with how that was his own fault. "I'll be outside. If you need me, call for me."

Since he'd apologised and would fix his behaviour, he thought she'd leave him alone. Instead, she chased after him as he moved towards the cave entrance.

"How many times do I need to tell you to stop and wait today?" she huffed. "I want to know how I upset you."

He let out a sigh. "Don't worry about it. If you don't know, then it is not something you need to worry about."

"Stop being so difficult and just tell me."

He paused and then quickly dodged to the side so she didn't run into the quills on his back. She turned to him with her hands on her hips. She was a feisty little Elf when she wanted to be.

"I can see this is an issue that has to do with me, and as an Elf, you do not have the same desire. Even a human wouldn't understand."

He felt like a coward, since the only reason he didn't want to explain it to her was because he was embarrassed.

She tapped her foot against the ground again. "Don't make me follow you around this whole area. Don't test me, Merikh. I'll even follow you into the Veil if I must."

Why did he have a funny feeling she wouldn't let it go? He grumbled to himself as he rubbed at his sternum, trying to remove the cold ache behind it.

"Duskwalkers are instinctually territorial," he admitted

quietly. "We are possessive of everything: our territories, our homes, our things." Her lips pursed, and she shook her head to show she didn't understand. "I marked you."

Her eyes lit up in a weird way, and she lifted her arms to rub at each one. She even rubbed her neck. It was like she was searching for something. "Did you?"

"You immediately wished to remove it, stating it was gross and offensive."

She paused, her starburst eyes flicking side to side in thought. It registered with her, and her ears slowly pushed back as her features fell.

"You rejected my sexual scent. It's something Duskwalkers internally crave to do to deter others. It is our way of staking our claim."

He'd discovered this about himself from the past, and he'd had this sense of completion from doing so – one that touched his senses. Demons had a similar inclination, which had made him all the more feral to do it.

It stated *mine,* without having to make it official.

"For instance, if the twins had returned here, they would not have tried to pull you into the Veil like last time."

For many reasons, he hadn't liked that they'd tried to steal Raewyn from him. He was putting all his faith in her, but he also just... didn't want them to have her. He didn't want any of his kind to have her if he couldn't.

"Merikh," she whispered, stepping forward.

"It is also our way of showing the person is under our protection. That they are *ours,* at least in body. You also asked that I remove yours, meaning you did not want to have your own scent upon me."

He'd washed it away because she'd obviously wanted him to, and he'd also wanted it gone after her rejection. It had shown a clear line between them. That, despite their desire, there was nothing more between them, and there would never be.

It'd been the same way between him and his female Demon

companion, but for some reason, this stung.

He'd known from the start that his companion had only sought him out in curiosity and liked his skull head – since she liked collecting them. He, on the other hand, hadn't minded her and was just curious about desire altogether. He'd also liked her company, even if they hadn't spoken much.

It often made him chuckle, thinking how quickly both of them could have turned on each other, but neither had tried to.

With Raewyn, she had initiated each time they'd touched and had never put forth a boundary. It had allowed him to foolishly have strange thoughts and feelings.

He wouldn't have them again.

"I'm so sorry." She shook her head, her expression beseeching. "I didn't know. I didn't mean to make you feel that way."

"I can see that it is nothing more than a misunderstanding," he said quietly, stepping back. "We are different."

He should have realised sooner that it was a clash of two different creatures. She was an Elf; why would she understand anything about Mavka and their behaviours?

Merikh prided himself on being smarter than the rest of his kind, but he'd been undoubtably idiotic the last few days. He'd been harsh to a female who hadn't deserved it, all because he'd been feeling vulnerable and sensitive.

"I had originally been hoping to do it again with you," she muttered, turning her head down to hide behind her hair.

His sight morphed to blue, unsure how he felt about that right now. He could no longer deny how much he wanted her, but the aftermath had been messy between them. What was the point if it would just end painfully each time?

None of their other intimate moments had ended well, and he was becoming acutely aware that he was the one to blame for it. He was the problem. He was always the problem. He destroyed anything and everything that tried to get close to him, one way or another.

"If you still plan to work on the mana stone, do so wisely," he said as he turned his head away, wishing to escape the conversation. "I haven't slept in a few days. I will be outside near the entrance should you need me."

He headed back towards the outside of his home, shifting into his monstrous form along the way so he could be comfortable. She must have known that he no longer wished to speak on the subject, because she followed him without saying a word. She found the wall, patted for the entrance, and opened her mouth...

But she shut it again and slowly retreated inside.

TWENTY-NINE

Distracted, Raewyn grabbed a curl and brushed it back and forth over her lips to tickle them. It'd been an hour, maybe two, since she'd spoken with Merikh, and she'd been thinking heavily on it ever since.

She couldn't believe that their whole issue had been a damn misunderstanding – from both sides. It annoyed her greatly because she was usually perceptive, picking up on miscommunications and squashing them. People who fought over them tended to make her eyes roll, and she gave herself one for being so unaware.

But she'd learned a lot from it.

Lesson number one: If a Duskwalker wanted to cover her in his sticky cum, she needed to adjust quickly to the idea if she wanted to keep him content.

Lesson number two: If Merikh was being unusually callous towards her, there was likely a reason, and she needed to figure it out before letting her own anger get the best of her.

Lesson number three: His quills were a big issue for him. He didn't like being touched because of them.

Lesson number four: *Merikh hates himself,* she sadly thought.

She didn't think he was insecure, but rather, he held hundreds of years of self-loathing.

Raewyn had been tossing the assumption around in her head for weeks, but what she'd learned from eavesdropping, and the fact he wanted her to seduce him, plus this terrible fight... She could no longer deny it.

It was hard not to feel sympathy, although she'd never tell or show him that. She did *not* want to discover how he'd react.

Still, it was sad. Inside and out, he didn't like who he was.

She kind of liked that he was a bit mean to the world, so long as he didn't turn that on her. It was like having a big bodyguard, and she did like the idea of being protected. She wanted to feel safe, no matter where she went.

Sure, she would like for him to see the world more positively, but that was just because she wanted him to be happy. The more he showed of himself, his deep feelings, his hurt and past, the more she was rooting for him.

When she'd first discovered what he was, she'd thought he was evil and deserved the world being cruel to him.

Now, she understood that he'd only been evil because the world had made him so. Inherently, he was really sweet when someone didn't treat him like the very ground he walked on became tainted.

So how could she show him that she didn't think he was bad?

Could I make him my assistant? She wondered how Cykran would feel about that.

Cykran was her friend before he was her employee, but she'd chosen him because of that. She'd known him even before she'd lost her sight. He'd taken on the role as soon as she'd asked him; there had been no begging from her side.

Then again, I was never attracted to Cykran.

Merikh, on the other hand... She couldn't deny the way her body reacted to him, how it liked his warmth, how her lungs greedily took in his scent, how her ears tingled whenever he spoke.

I can't work with someone I want to play with.

She'd never get any work done.

She stopped tickling her lips with her hair to assess the fact that she wasn't getting anything done, since she'd been just standing here, doing nothing. However, she kept doing it when she decided her current thoughts were more important.

Funny, considering she desperately wanted to go home.

I don't think I'll be able to seduce him again. She also didn't want to.

It wasn't because she didn't desire him. Since they'd cleared up their issues, she once again wanted nothing more than to grab that Duskwalker by his horns and grind on him in the hopes of being gifted more mind-scrambling orgasms.

His dick was a ten out of ten, a chef's kiss, in her opinion. *Mwah.* It hit every good spot all at the same time. It even hit sensitive spots she hadn't known existed. Her G-spot was like the holy grail that most men couldn't find, yet sitting on his cock had made it feel as though her whole body was an erogenous zone.

She also thought his tentacles were *cute.*

They were like four cuddling limbs that wanted to squeeze her in affection. Since they were so long, they held her nice and tight, and their little tips even swayed back and forth, like they wanted to pet her.

By all means, Raewyn didn't indulge in a lot of kink. She hadn't experienced being tied up or orgasm denial, and she didn't want to be subjected to severe pain, but she did like scratching, biting, and now apparently... hair pulling? Maybe even a little amount of spanking, if it came from him?

She still wanted him to discover why she thought being spanked was so funny.

Now she understood why he'd made her be on top. Once he took over, Raewyn didn't think anything would have stopped him.

Merikh had been rough, but it hadn't been painful between her legs. He'd obviously been holding back enough to give himself whatever speed and depth he'd needed, but she knew, with how strong he was, he hadn't used his full force.

Most importantly, he'd obviously cared about her pleasure.

Raewyn stifled a moan and cupped herself between her legs through her long dress. She was turning herself on with her thoughts.

What is wrong with me? she whined as she placed her face against the stone bench. *I'm not usually like this.*

People would start to think she was a pervert if she kept this up. By people, she meant him.

Holding onto the edge of the bench, she crouched down to hide. She was having an internal crisis. Someone needed to come and save her from herself.

There was an issue, though. Raewyn no longer wanted to chase him; she wanted to be the one chased. She wanted him to come to her.

She wanted him to stop being a coward.

She'd made her feelings obvious. What more could she do beyond that? She was over the constant hesitation on his part.

An idea crossed her mind.

If scents are such an important thing to him... what if I drive him crazy with mine? In the forest, he said he liked the way I smelled. Would that work? She wasn't against playing dirty, so long as it had him finally coming to her.

Hell, she was likely already producing a light arousal scent. What if she fed it?

For the time being, she'd begun to see this cave as her home; why shouldn't she treat it like hers? It was private, besides him. No one else would hear or see her.

Raewyn bit her lip, humour crinkling her eyes. *If he won't take care of me, I'll just take care of myself.* It was a win-win, for her at least.

The giggles echoing within his cave were loopy and unhinged, but she couldn't help them.

She was lucky that injecting her magic into the stone would require very little concentration – because she was about to be *very* distracted.

Merikh reached over his shoulder and clawed at his back, breaking a handful of quills in the process. His shudder started out light, then it struck him from skull to toes.

I cannot enter my own home.

Raewyn had taken over it so totally that he could barely stand to be inside of it.

It had started out subtle. At first, only the little Elf herself smelt like the tastiest morsel known to Merikh, something that didn't stir hunger in his gut, but in his groin, and in his throat that became dry even when he was salivating.

It had been easy to ignore then. Just light enough to tell him she was excited, a soft hint but not demanding.

However, as two days passed, it grew and grew, until his entire cave *reeked* of her delicious scent. Entering his own home was like barrelling through a wall, and that dryness in his throat would become a sweet strangulation.

It was begging him, trying to lead him to her like a collar and chain. Like an animal in the heat, Merikh would instantly pant with his fangs parted and his tongue falling forward.

It was constant, like she was *always* aroused, but he didn't think that would be enough to do this. It should only be localised to her, not his entire cave.

Since she bathed in the lake every day, he'd attempted to duck inside while she was preoccupied so she couldn't torment him. The lingering scent of her arousal had hit him like a boulder; he thought his lungs were going to cave in.

Not even the presence of her magic-induced clary sage scent diluted it.

He'd taken the deer hide he wanted and fled as fast as he could.

Avoiding going inside at all had been impossible. Raewyn

would call for help to do even the simplest of tasks, like aiding her cooking, or helping her find something. She even asked him to take the tulips outside when he'd once seen her pick up the flowerpot with ease.

Merikh slept outside. He spent his time outside.

He was out in the fresh air. It shouldn't be bothering him anymore, but it was. It clung to his fur, to the inside of his nose hole, like it was a parasite that had latched onto him.

His sight regularly switched between its normal red hue and deep purple.

It worsened whenever she searched him out to speak with him, but she behaved as though she had no idea she was producing it. She didn't try to touch him, didn't action anything, but was just her usual, chatty self.

She was a female who would laugh and talk about some strange, Elven nonsense while her nipples were so taut, he could see them through her clothing. Her lips were always wet, and her pupils blown.

He'd told himself he would put distance between them, and instead, he would sit there and drool. He'd grow so enraptured with her as she spoke that he would be as still as stone, hoping she might reach out to him.

She didn't.

She torments me. It's not fair.

Even now, she was doing so.

She was having her daily bath, but instead of wading in waist-deep water, she was sitting on the lake's edge. Flaunting her body, as though he might not be nearby and able to watch her, she rested back on straightened arms and turned her face up to the sun's heat.

She was naked, her back arched, pushing up her chest so her breasts almost pointed up to the sky while the ends of her wet hair brushed the grass behind her. With the light bathing her, she appeared lovelier than ever.

It was hard to look away. He thought he may have been

content to gaze upon the scene until time ended and he withered away into dust. He didn't even need to involve himself to be entranced by her, deriving pleasure in just being able to look.

He didn't mean to stare, and at first, he'd tried not to, but the more her scent clogged his brain, the less of a hold he had on himself.

While she was there, he tried to continue his task, to pull his sight to it. Then she made just the slightest movement and caught his full attention.

Merikh yelped when he speared his thumb with a sewing needle so deeply, he thought he might have scratched bone. He accidentally flung away the ball of string connected to it. Since he was resting against one of the trees next to the lake, he watched it roll.

The fact it'd happened was so damn stupid of him, proving just how terrible his luck was, that he just stared at the spot it'd plopped into the water.

Shit. He still had the needle side, but there was no point in him chasing after a wet ball that was likely unravelling. It would damage the leather he'd finally finished curing after days.

He'd split the skin, dried it, rubbed it with oils, and even hung it out to stretch. Wetting it when it wasn't quite ready would be foolish. He'd ruin it.

He clawed the string to cut it and placed his skull in his hands with a sigh. *I'd only just started sewing this.*

It was a test piece. He'd cut it to a specific size, but he did worry he'd made it too small. He also didn't know if it would be thick enough, even though he'd double layered it.

Maybe I can hold my breath as I go inside this time? It would be better to do it while she was bathing. She wouldn't find a reason to keep him in there until he was forced to suck in oxygen.

His orbs turned white when he lowered his hands and found where she was sitting was empty. He let out a distressed whine, realising she'd gone inside.

I should have grabbed my herb satchel while I had the chance. He could have blocked her out if he shoved it into his nose hole.

Instead, all the blood in his body had drained from his brain straight into his dick. He'd just taken the belts and sewing instruments he needed and ran off with his tail so kinked, he thought it was going to snap off.

I could go in silently. If he didn't produce his vibration, she wouldn't notice him there.

A trickle of shame ran down his nape. He didn't want to do that; it felt wrong to trick her and sneak around her.

Food wafted into the air, the Elf beginning to cook her lunch. See? She was more than capable of doing it by herself. He didn't know why she regularly asked him for assistance.

Staring down at the leather between his spread legs, Merikh eventually growled at himself. He was acting rather pathetic, and he was growing annoyed with himself.

What was one woman against a Duskwalker? He'd fought harder battles than this; actually, he usually revelled in the fight. So why was he currently being so... feeble?

With his resolve renewed, he rose to his feet to obtain new sewing instruments.

Her scent was so thick, it reached him before he'd even come to the entrance of his cave. He cut off his breathing, hoping to keep his sanity for as long as possible.

Just as he started his vibration and was about to enter, Merikh's feet halted of their own accord at the sight that greeted him. All sound from him dissipated.

The stone bench was just in front of him, the sunlight pouring in, and Raewyn was between it and the cooking hearth.

Leaning her entire torso over the bench, her arm beneath her face so she could bite into her forearm to hide most of her noises, her other hand was beneath her skirt. Even with the layers of material hiding it, he could see her fingers were pumping in and out of her pussy. Her legs were twitching, her slim torso heaving.

His orbs flashed to purple, just as his already-hardening cock burst from his seam so fast, not even his tentacles were prepared. The sensitive head was instantly abraded by the inside of his shorts, and his breath slammed out of him.

Frozen, unable to do anything but pant and watch, he knew the moment she came.

Her eyelids wildly flickered, her snuffling moan was distinct, and her knees turned inward.

No wonder his cave had turned into a cesspool of her scent. She'd been masturbating inside it! She'd been leaving little droplets of liquid behind – like she did now, as some dripped to the ground between her feet and darkened the stone with its wetness.

He hungrily eyed those droplets as he licked across his snout. His fur and quills raised, a profound blaze of lust lighting beneath his skin. If this continued, he was sure to combust into flames, or at least begin to steam from his maw.

Screw this, he thought with a growl, stomping forward.

THIRTY

Raewyn unlatched her teeth from her arm with a whimper as she withdrew her fingers from her core. She was slow to rise, having to palm the edge of the bench to steady her wobbly legs.

That's better. She gave a hum of contentment.

Now that she'd gotten off, she could go back to cooking.

Or so she thought.

In her satisfied state, it took her longer than it should have to hear Merikh coming. His growl was deep, brassy, and so unnervingly quiet that it speared her right to her still-throbbing clit.

She'd been caught red-handed, or rather... *wet*-handed.

An 'oops' would have been uttered if it hadn't been the whole point. Really, she should have been found out sooner, considering she'd done this quite a few times in the last two days.

She didn't even show a shred of decorum by pretending to be bashful, not when her thighs were still shaky and her nipples were hard. There was no fight as he turned her, lifted her arse to the bench, and pushed her skirt up.

"I cannot take it anymore," he groaned in an agonised voice, his movements jarring, forceful, rushed. There was no patience as he pushed her thighs apart by cupping underneath them to expose her pussy for himself. "You win, Raewyn."

She just panted, waiting for him to sink his cock inside her with a lopsided smile of triumph.

I knew it would wor– Raewyn squeaked out an 'eek' as her toes curled and her knees shot up.

That's not a dick!

Pushing at what was between her thighs, she touched bone, then arched when she gripped his horns. Merikh had spread his fangs around her and sunk his tongue inside.

It was soft, and so deep she swore it'd folded.

Adjusting to the sudden intrusion, her spine relaxed. Then her brows knotted as she turned her expression to him.

He wasn't moving it.

Actually, he wasn't moving at all. He didn't even seem to be *breathing*.

The only thing happening was that she could see purple sparks constantly flickering in her vision, like he kept closing and opening his sight. Was he having a mental breakdown?

"M-Merikh?" she whispered, wondering why he'd turned to stone.

"Nnhn," he finally groaned, a full-body shudder going through him.

It shook her legs and reverberated directly inside her, causing her to tingle and tighten around the soft and flexible limb. He clawed at her to get her deeper within his fanged maw.

He drew his tongue back agonizingly slowly. It twisted and swirled, grazing everywhere inside her all at once, like a cyclone. Her eyes widened at each movement, before it darted forward in the same fashion, but so much faster. Then, he pulled back slowly again, and her hips bucked to get it to go faster, only for it to penetrate her swiftly and bottom out.

Her breaths turned higher pitched with each one.

It was the strangest sensation to have something moving within her like this. It was foreign, inhuman, and Raewyn found herself liquefying because of it.

She gripped his horns tighter, thankful to have something to hold onto so she could move her body in a wave to greet it. Placing her feet against his shoulders, she tried to split her thighs further apart.

Her backside was almost hanging off the edge, and the only thing keeping her from falling off was the grip of his rough hands.

She could barely believe he was doing this to her. He'd once told her he'd kneel for no man, and yet here he was, on his knees for *her,* just to taste and tease her like this.

"Faster," she pleaded.

He was savouring her, but she was so close already that she needed more.

Her head fell back, little cries cracking past parted lips, when he gave her exactly what she wanted. The cyclone of his swirling tongue picked up speed. The swishing and squelching of it was so terribly vulgar that it became erotic, a sound only made by this, by him and his wicked tongue.

Her legs clamped around his skull like she wanted to crush it as liquid ecstasy burst from her. She came hard, her back arched as she hung from his horns, and she grew so hot, she feared she'd pass out. Merikh gave her an appreciative snarl that tickled her insides as he shook his head like he wanted to spur her on to give him more.

"That's it, Raewyn," he rasped against her, making her toes curl until her calves cramped. "Drown me in your taste. Give it to me."

He didn't stop thrusting, even after she stopped.

She tried to push his head away, her body twitching in aftershocks, but there was no relief. He withdrew his tongue so she could feel the entire length of it slip over one side of her folds, tickling it as he swiped over her swollen clit before going to the other side.

He did it repeatedly, like he was seeking more.

"How can something taste this good? It's like liquid heaven."

"Merikh, please," she begged, her legs jolting each time he

stroked and rubbed her clit. "I'm too sensitive now."

He didn't stop licking, but he at least moved away to steal what he could from the creases of her thighs before he followed a path down her legs. He was tracing where the orgasm she'd given herself earlier had trickled down.

He was completely cleaning her, pressing deeply to make sure he took every speck that she constantly felt his fangs and snout brushing over her. She was surprised by how much she enjoyed the scrape of bone caressing her skin.

Then, when he was done, he came at her pussy from the side as he swiped it one last time. His rough tongue abraded her with his tastebuds, but it only left pleasure in its wake.

Merikh stood and gingerly let her feet touch the ground before he placed his hands on the stone bench on either side of her. His breaths fanned over her like a wave of orange, cinnamon, and her essence, each one heavy and shaking with need.

His demand was quiet, soft, like a husky plea. "Get on your knees."

Raewyn's stomach flipped.

If she were to reach forward right now, would his cock be jutting between them and greeting her palms? Raewyn nibbled her lip nervously, knowing that his dick was impressive, and she was unsure if she'd be able to manage its size.

When she took too long to move, claws scraped into the stone behind her, and the tiniest whine echoed from his chest.

"*Please,* don't leave me like this."

He sounded like he was in so much pain, like his cock was unbearably hard and aching. Her stomach flipped again. Her satisfaction was ebbing, rubbed away by rekindling desire.

Having no qualms about complying, she slowly pushed off so she could kneel for him. She didn't particularly appreciate it when a stray tentacle lightly slapped her on the cheek.

She expected him to chuckle like any man would, but he grunted and shifted slightly. Caring more about her comfort, he said, "Sorry, I'll hold them down."

Once she was on her knees for him, there was a sweetness to the air, one that had her mouth watering.

Dripping wetness greeted her as she encompassed the head with both hands. The moment she made contact, he let out a woofing, low exhale as he thrust nearly the entire length into her hands.

With one twisting stroke of both hands, she explored him.

She felt the round, bulbous head, the rim that seemed to multiply four more times with his ridges. There was little in the centre, just thick veins that throbbed heavily against her sensitive skin. About three-quarters of the way down, she brushed her hands over the twisted ring, and his entire cock swelled in thickness. Finally, she stroked near the base where his tentacles were connected and stroked over two embedded ovals that were hot and firm, and something dripped onto her knee as he let out a deep expire. A heavy drop of precum, perhaps?

Coming back up, she stroked everything again, but also pressed her thumbs into the deep groove on the underside as she went.

His cock was saturated in liquid, but it was so hard, she *knew* he must be in agony. Even her just touching him was making his knees shake.

Feeling sorry for him, she held him halfway and darted her head forward so she could strike the very tip with her tongue.

Two different tastes hit her tastebuds, one liquid thin, the other thick. She'd taken in both his lubricant and heavy drop of overflowing precum. Both were sweet, both tasted like his scent, and both had her moaning wildly against the tip of his dick.

Merikh widened his stance as he uttered a low, *"Fuck."*

Maybe it was just the feeling of everything, the hardness, the heat, the liquid, and even the shape, but her hands and mouth were already adoring this. However, it was his aphrodisiac draflium flower scent and taste that had her mind going blank, like her brain was being wrapped up in a dizzy haze.

Raewyn started licking at him while kissing at the same time, going over the head before moving over the sides. She tried to sweep her tongue everywhere, to collect it all, but more of his lubricant kept seeping through his skin, an infinite source.

Merikh made constant groans, and his hips twitched like he wanted to thrust.

He was being such a good boy, controlling himself.

As a reward, she placed her lips on the tip and spread them over it, like she was trying to sink him into her mouth. His breath hitched before it came out low when she was able to take the entire head inside. She was even able to take him past the ridges and almost halfway down.

It was tight, with very little room, and she could barely move her tongue, but she was surprised it actually fit when it hit the back of her throat.

"You took me into your mouth," he muttered in surprise. Then he let out a sharp groan when she sucked on it, his entire body shuddering. Purple sparks fluttered like before, like he was opening and closing his sight as he looked down at her. *"Fuck, Raewyn. That feels so good."*

She darted her hands down and pressed them over his fingers holding his tentacles. He removed them, and she let the waving appendages wind around her digits so he could have more freedom to do whatever he needed.

Like he wanted to hold it, he pawed at the back of her head. Then he thought better of it and placed his hands against the bench.

Now that she was in place and knew she could suck him properly, thankful she wasn't some small, feeble human, she smirked.

Raewyn leisurely pulled back while sucking, letting him think that she would be slow. Then she began to move back and forth fast.

His hand darted to the back of her hair again, his breaths

fanning over her fading like he'd thrown his head back. His groan was so close to being a quiet roar that it resonated in her ears, and she grew giddy.

"Not so fast," he warned as he grabbed her hair to stop her. "Go slower."

She almost popped him from her mouth, grinding the tip against the textures on the roof of her mouth, then swirling her tongue around it. Right when the tension eased out of him and he stopped fisting her hair, Raewyn sunk him all the way in until he hit the back of her throat.

Then she increased her speed again, pumping her head even harder.

Merikh growled as his hips started moving, drawing back and darting forward as she did. Claws stabbed into the sides of her scalp.

His breath billowed over the top of her head like he'd turned his skull back down to watch her. His shaft swelled, and the taste of his precum was lost in the motion between them.

Then he leaned over more and thrust harder.

When she stopped moving to let him take her, he must have thought it was a sign that it was too much for her. He halted, but his shudders and shakes were just the physical symptoms of how much she could tell he was holding back.

"Be good," he rumbled, lowering his hand to wrap around her nape until he'd completely enveloped it, his fingertips and claws ending under her jaw and chin. "Be gentle. Because if your mouth can take me..." His hand tightened on her neck from behind, before loosening. "No. Just go slow. I've never been sucked like this before. I don't know what I'll do."

Raewyn's eyes widened. *He's never been sucked?*

That only made her want to be ruthless with him, take him to a height he'd never reached before. *That makes me want to scramble his brain.*

She pulled back to lick and tease him so she could speak. "I can be slow and gentle," she said coyly between kisses. "If that's really what you want."

"Yes," he answered, moving his hand from the bench so he could push some of her curls behind her ear to see better. It tickled the tip and made her shiver. "You look pretty with my cock in your mouth. I don't want you to take it away."

His words – tender, sweet, and honest – were the reason she wouldn't stop until he came, no matter what.

What was the worst that could happen?

Raewyn sunk her lips around him and cupped the base of his cock with her tentacle-covered hands. Massaging the ovals where she thought his seed might come from, she renewed her earlier depth and speed.

She thought he might have growled her name in warning, but it was so distorted, she could barely make it out. His hand tightened on the back of her neck, his claws stabbing into the soft skin under her jaw while the other slammed against the bench.

Red sparks flashed before purple returned. "Raewyn," he snarled.

When she didn't soften her motions, instead trying to get her tongue to help by moving in waves, she didn't need to add anything else when he began thrusting. He came in far harder, more forcefully.

She was thankful when the cool sensation of his healing magic swirled around her. Instead of feeling pain in the back of her throat, there was only pressure. It allowed her to just take it rather than reconsider her actions.

Merikh stepped back, the movement arching her body forward. She had to lean her hands on his groin when his retreat stretched her out and straightened her neck. She practically squished his tentacles against him.

She should have taken his snarl as the forewarning it was, but his thrusts picking up speed had her just trying to steady herself through it.

Merikh pushed her head down at the same time as he thrust

forward.

Raewyn's squeak of surprise was cut off by his cock popping past the back of her throat. Her hands fell away from his groin so she could dig her nails into his thighs.

He halted the moment his four tentacles wrapped around her entire head, cuddling her in their limbs, when she'd swallowed every inch of his cock. With it lodged deep into her throat, her lips pressed against his oval seed sacs, the twisted ring sat against her tongue.

Tears bubbled in her eyes from the pressure of his girth, but there was no pain. The only discomfort was that she couldn't breathe.

Raewyn did not care.

Not when Merikh was absolutely losing his mind.

His yelp had been loud, but his strangled pants were even louder. His legs were shaking, like he'd almost gone to the tips of his toes as he arched, yet his hips twitched, like they didn't know what to do with the pleasure that assaulted him.

She could hold her breath. She could handle this because of his healing magic. She just wanted more of that, more of him doing whatever he wanted for once to feel good.

Raewyn cupped between her legs with both hands, wanting to ease the profound throbbing by pushing her palms down on her clit. Her entire body had clenched at the intrusion, and even her pussy had clamped down hard. In its wake, it left her more turned on than she'd ever been.

She felt undeniably empty.

So fucking tight, Merikh internally groaned, as he was suspended in a moment of complete and utter stillness from the constriction around his cock. It felt like his heart was about to stop.

Merikh shouldn't have let the intrusive thoughts win, but

he'd known that if he could fit in her mouth, then he could fit in her throat. He was deeper than he could reach within her pussy unless he altered her body, but he didn't need to with this. Considering the pain that was softly throbbing in his own oesophagus from the transfer, it was likely uncomfortable for her.

Under his fingertips, her throat had expanded.

She'd tensed below him, but she couldn't back away with his tentacles keeping her down in a tight huddle.

He should back out. He should pull away. He should apologise, but the bliss of the tightness, the hard texture, the warmth of her tongue upon his knot... He started softly thrusting as his brain dissolved and grew fuzzy.

He barely needed to move, since just lightly rocking back and forth was sprinting him headfirst towards release.

Her nails dug through the short fur on his thighs and tried to cut into his flesh. His head darted to look down, but he could barely see her face. His entire cock had disappeared inside it, and she likely couldn't breathe.

Uttering a curse at himself, at what he was doing to her, he began to withdraw. He went slowly, knowing if he yanked it out, it would drive him to shove back in.

Any thread of control he'd gained back was unravelled when she started bobbing her head around the end of his cock.

Her breaths were short and fast as she tried to catch them. Instead of being upset, she began to 'make out' with his shaft, kissing, licking, and sucking everywhere she could. She even wrangled a tentacle into her mouth and bit the side of it.

She's driving me crazy. How could he resist such a seductive female? Merikh's sight was such a dark purple, he could barely see.

Moving his hand to the back of her head and making sure he kept contact with her so his magic would work, he thrust into her mouth. With his other hand on the bench, he supported himself as he just let his hips take over.

Thoughts were muddled as he produced incoherent groans, growls, and rumbles.

With his fangs parted so he could pant down at her, drool leaking to drip down her cheek, he watched his cock moving and the scene before him. He felt every single movement: her teeth, the roof of her mouth, her soft tongue trying to play.

Merikh mostly only gave her what would fit in her mouth, but he couldn't help himself from taking her throat again, not when it had felt so damn amazing. He was slow as he thrust, not needing to be fast when the pleasure was more intense than anything he'd ever felt.

Closing her eyes, the moan she produced vibrated straight into the centre of his cock, like she enjoyed it. He even felt the motion of her trying to swallow.

He pulled back to find one of her hands was pressing against her clit through her dress, while the other hand reached up to cup a breast.

She didn't mind that his tentacles had latched onto the hair framing her face, very content to curl inwards while holding it.

Fuck. I'm so close. He'd been on the verge of coming since the first time he'd gone deep, but he'd gnashed his fangs to stop himself. He didn't want to come, didn't want to stop, didn't want this to end.

His cock constantly swelled as his seed sacs ached. Everything was hot as they throbbed along with his erratically beating heart.

He didn't mean to whine at his own thoughts. He was torn. *I want to come in her mouth so badly.* But if she was just going to reject it afterwards, spit it out and wash it away, it would just upset him. He'd rather come against the ground.

He wanted her to taste him, to dirty that pretty face of hers. He wanted his scent in her, on her, to stain her in a predatory marking of *'mine.'*

His thoughts were all over the place, his mind turning to goo, while it felt like he was going to melt in her mouth.

The bubbling rumble in his chest and the tingle at the base of his spine told him he was about to come, whether he wanted to or not.

His knot began to inflate down his shaft, and he was unable to go deep because of it. He couldn't knot her face, not if he wanted her to *survive* past this.

His seed began to rise, his cock in absolute blissful agony. His mind blanked, and he was unable to pull away from the heat of her mouth.

Merikh shoved her down on him, breeching her throat and forcing her lips to his knot as he let loose a loud, bellowing roar. Seed exploded from him in thick, spurting ropes as he came down her throat and into her stomach so she could hold it for him.

The pleasure of doing so... Merikh left permanent and deep gouge marks in his stone bench. His quills lifted, his tail slapping against the side of the kitchen hearth behind him. Even his sight closed, unable to keep it open under the onslaught of this profound pleasure.

When his orgasm slowed, he pulled back so he could at least coat her tongue with the last two ropes of liquid.

Merikh withdrew to stare at her, his still mostly hard cock dropping downwards. He cupped the side of her face and parted her panting mouth wider. With a seed-covered tongue, she licked at her lips and made him shudder when she swallowed it all down.

Would she have swallowed my seed if I had come in her mouth? If there was a next time, he'd like to find out.

He hadn't known his lubricant had dripped down her chin and throat to wet the top of her dress. It was even glistening between her breasts.

The issue Merikh found himself with was that her scent was buzzing with deep arousal. She was dazed with it.

"Merikh..."

The moment she whispered his name, undeniable need, lust,

and craving struck him. He missed the taste of her essence already.

Within *seconds*, he'd rent her dress into two pieces, tearing it from her to expose her beautiful, naked body. Then, she was on her back, laying on the ground parallel to the stone bench as he lowered himself and spread her legs.

He shoved his tongue deep into the well of her flooded cunt and drank from it. He lifted her slightly by her thighs, groaning as he tried to take every drop. He shuddered when she grabbed his horns, finally finding a safe place to hold on to him, and just let herself go, her feet securely on his shoulders.

Sucking him had turned her on, and the deep satisfaction of that had him wanting to ease her in return.

Her taste was divine, and from the first moment he'd finally had a sample of it, he knew he was obsessed with it. Her sweet little cries were his reward as he pleasured every inch of her with his tongue.

He swirled deep, then lashed her pretty clit so her legs would twitch for him. He explored her tasty merlot-coloured folds, her lips, just to make sure he touched anywhere and everywhere that could feel good for her.

By the time she came for him, his cock had hardened back up and rendered his mind fucking *useless* unless he spent again. He rested himself on one elbow and his knees so he could reach down and grip his shaft. He stroked it, content to do it this way if he could keep delving his tongue.

If heaven existed and he was allowed into it, and it wasn't him in this exact position with Raewyn's spasming cunt around his tongue, he'd burn the place to the fucking ground.

Whether it was his feverish groan or the fact that one of her legs bounced from him pawing at his cock, she eventually realised what he was doing.

She tugged on his horns to stop him, to pull his skull from between her thighs.

The snarl he produced was so feral, it even turned his orbs

red for a moment. Right now, her pussy was his, and he was tasting it. It was his to feast on, to drown in.

"C-come here. You don't have to do that," she pleaded, unafraid of his threatening sounds, like she knew he wouldn't hurt her.

She shivered, her eyelids flickering as he petted the swollen, textured ridge inside her. She moaned, then bit her lip as she turned her face down to him, as though she was trying to think through muddled thoughts.

She looked just as heated as he felt, just as desperate and undone.

She opened her mouth and then chewed at her lip again. She looked conflicted.

"Fuck me," she panted.

Merikh paused, surprised she'd offered that as her word choice.

"This is fine, Raewyn," he reassured as he gave her adorable little clit a gentle side swipe. She'd already done more than enough when she sucked him.

With her cheeks puffed and her eyes narrowed, she yanked as hard as she could on his horns.

"Oh, just fuck me, you big, silly Duskwalker." Then she self-consciously closed her eyes as she half-yelled, "I want you to shove your cock in my pussy and pound into me until my eyes cross and I can't think of anything else! I don't care how hard or how fast. Please. I need it. I need *you*."

Merikh nearly mangled his cock in his fist, especially when it swelled in enthusiasm. *Fuck,* that was hot; he couldn't believe someone had said that to him.

Screw it. She was trying her hardest to get him to bend to her will, and he couldn't deny her anymore.

Still on a straightened arm, he roughly pawed one of her thighs to grab it. He slid her across the ground while tilting his hips, and with an enthusiastic snarl, he mounted her fully by the time she was completely under him.

Raewyn arched with a surprised moan, her lips parting wide.

Before she could do anything foolish, he grabbed both her hands within his own and pinned them down.

Spreading remnants of her come across her lips and cheek with his tongue until he reached her ear, he grunted, "Fine."

Then, with her arousal coating his fangs and the tip of his snout, he started thrusting, moving in and out of her hard and fast.

If she wanted him that badly, he'd give her whatever she wanted. She'd been so good to him earlier, so forgiving and naughty while she sucked him – even now, while he slammed into her, just the memory made him shudder.

If she'd rather come around his thrusting cock than his tongue, he'd submit and let her. He'd let this pretty little fairy have whatever she craved right now, so long as he could keep touching her.

Merikh was tired of holding back.

Although he'd been hiding it from her, he desired Raewyn like a sickening ache. He'd wanted to taste, to touch, to feel from the first moment he'd properly seen her face, but it was her shiny personality, so completely opposite to him, that had him stuck under her spell.

For weeks, she'd been nagging at him, wearing him down until he felt raw. The last two days had been unbearable. She'd been driving him insane, warping him until he thought his mind and heart would switch places. He was still pent up and frustrated, and for once, he just wanted to stop caring.

He wanted to pretend he didn't have any troubling thoughts and have one good, pleasurable memory in his life.

Being inside her was wonderful, like rapture and beautiful torture at the same time. She was so soft, so warm, and she smelt so nice, it was soothing any aggression within him.

His hips were still fast, his thrusts still hard, but instead of growling and snarling, he just groaned her name like he was calling for salvation. *"Raewyn."*

Each time she came, trying to milk his cock in hungry little clenches, his head sagged more and more until he rested the side of it against one of their connected hands. He buried his entire face into her curls.

He was at her mercy and was thankful his tormentor was kind enough to let him slake his lust on her.

At some point, she'd managed to free one of her hands. Since she'd wrapped it around the back of his skull, a place where it couldn't be hurt, he let it stay free. It gave him the freedom to hold her arse in his hand and keep her still when his tentacles began to forcibly latch on.

It gave him the freedom to detach them from her right as he was about to come so he could pull his cock from her. He did it in a way that pushed him downwards, and he groaned as the top of his shaft rubbed through her soaking folds.

He groaned and quaked as the first rope of seed left him and splattered against the ground. He'd already used his fist to bring himself close to release.

"Wait, no," she whispered.

She darted her free hand between them and gripped his cock, causing him to blank out when she squeezed his sensitive and engorged knot. Merikh didn't have a chance of fighting. She redirected his cock head, and instead of him coming against the ground, she made him do it over her.

He thrust into her hand, his head turning up as she stroked him at the same time. He was overcome by each of his senses simultaneously obliterating him.

His lungs caved in as his heart tried to give out, and he shook as his tail flicked and slapped the ground.

The aftershocks that assaulted him were violent and intense. He hadn't even realised he'd arched his back until he was falling forward and trying not to crush her.

Supporting himself on all fours and rising, he looked down to see she was covered from navel to neck in his seed. Not even her face had managed to avoid being hit by a stray streak. It was everywhere because she'd been bouncing him as she stroked.

With deep pants, he asked, "Why did you...?"

He wondered if she'd realised the cold pang from the aftermath of last time had still been nagging at him.

Her smile was so pleased and triumphant. "Because I wanted to." Then she leaned up and pressed a kiss to the side of his snout. "I guess this is what I'm wearing for the rest of the day."

Merikh grunted as his cock jerked at the idea of an outfit made solely of his release.

He looked down at her body, her thighs still spread around his waist. If she didn't watch out, she was in danger of him sinking his tongue back into her.

He'd only come twice, and his stamina was superhuman.

She should watch how she teased him.

THIRTY-ONE

Gazing down at the comely female curled up on her side across his lap, Merikh radiated contentment.

She'd originally asked if he would mind taking her to the bed so she could rest for a while, worn out from their intimacy. As she was prattling on about how she didn't think she could walk there herself, Merikh's insides had twisted.

Like last time, he could tell she wanted to be held.

She had gone out of her way to reassure him about the things that had bothered him, and he had wanted to do the same for her. What she yearned for was something a normal person could give her. Her request wasn't absurd – if it had been given to anyone other than *him*.

So, Merikh had done the only thing he could think of.

He'd carefully picked her up into a safe cradle within his strong arms, lifted her while he stood, and crossed his cave. He sat down in the only chair available and placed her across his lap.

He'd waited to see if she would oppose it. Only when she curled into him, laying her head on the inside of his arm and the chair's rest, did he finally relax. Then he drew his arm from under her legs and crossed it over her so he could hold her hip.

The front of her was still covered in his seed, and he didn't mind that it was spreading over his torso. As long as it was still staining her in his scent, he was pleased.

Raewyn cupped her hands near her chest to nestle them between their bodies. She didn't close her eyes. He thought she may not actually be tired, just physically exhausted.

He didn't know what he was supposed to do now. All he wanted was to stare at her, but he was unsure if that would make her uncomfortable.

"Thank you," she softly whispered as she gently rubbed her nose and cheek against his round but firm stomach.

A tingling emotion spread through his entire body, something he was totally unfamiliar with. He was still full of tension until she spoke those words.

His hand curled so he could hold the back of her exposed nape, and he was surprised by her light shiver. "You're so warm."

It was summer. Perhaps it was because he was a Duskwalker, but no element bothered him. Most humans couldn't stand the current heat that billowed on the wind. Her skin, however, always seemed to have an iciness to it, so he pressed his forearm more firmly over her to give her warmth.

The longer they sat there, though, the more his limbs nagged at him. Even though he was greedily drinking her in with his sight, the stillness was bothering him.

"May I touch you?" he asked hesitantly.

Raewyn groaned while burying her face into the side of his stomach and shook her head. She brought her knees higher to prevent him from having any chance of touching her between her thighs.

"I don't think I can take anymore right now."

Bloody hell, she was painting him as a deviant who had no other thoughts than sex.

"Not like that," he huffed with a slight bite to his tone. "Like this."

He demonstrated what he wanted by slipping his claws down the arch of her nape. As a little mewl fell from her lips, her neck arched, and her head tilted in a way that gave him more surface to play with.

She nodded, and with her lips closed, said, "Mhm."

Delighted, he drew his claws down her nape again, then down her shoulders and back in an arc. She let out a contented sigh and brought herself closer to him. As he kept doing it, she eventually rested her hands against him and subtly did the same back and forth over the fur on his stomach.

Her coily curls were draped over him like a cotton blanket, and they looked so soft and fluffy, like a cloud – although a complete mess from earlier. He couldn't help but reach up above her so he could bury his clawed fingers into them.

His plan had been to brush them into being neat, but she winced just as he was forced to halt an inch down the length or he'd rip her hair out.

She let out a soft giggle and touched the underside of his wrist to draw him away. "You can't do that with curls," she chided playfully. "You'll just get caught in my hair and put it in disarray."

His sight shifted to a reddish pink in embarrassment. He wished he'd known that sooner.

He still wanted to touch her soft, springy curls, so he just brushed his hand over the top of them. He even picked up a few strands so he could rub their silkiness together.

Growing bolder, as he drew his claws up her back so he could glide them across her neck, he took his hand from her hair so he could caress her rounded cheek with his thumb. Her skin was smooth, soft, delicate. He explored her mesmerising features with his fingers, going up the straight of her nose until he brushed over one of her eyebrows.

It was strange that he was doing this. He'd never just... touched another, but her smile was worth it. She was enjoying it, and that was all that truly mattered.

Once Merikh was done petting her face, he brushed his palm down her arm, her leg, touching her everywhere he could. His claws at her back never stopped, and he was quite content to keep petting her there.

Sometimes, he glided his fingertips over the length of her pointed ear, and it would flick under his light touch.

They were very expressive, which fascinated him. He liked watching her eat because of them. Her left ear would always twitch whenever she was truly happy with what she was consuming.

"Merikh," she started, her voice croaked and groggy. "Can you tell me a story?"

"Like a fairytale?" he asked, his throat thick from his earlier sounds of pleasure and the current emotions roiling around inside him. "Sure. I don't see why not, but I would have to put you down and search if I have any."

Her brows furrowed, like that wasn't what she'd been seeking. "You would sit here and read me a book?"

He tilted his head, unsure of why she appeared puzzled. "If that is what you want, yes."

She smiled so sweetly but shook her head. "That would be nice, but that's not what I meant. I wanted you to tell me a story about you. Something good."

He lowered his head so he could bump his snout against her cheek. "I don't have anything like that to share."

"Not even one?"

"I have funny moments," he admitted. "I once told a human I was friends with a Duskwalker, and that if he met me outside of the gate, I would introduce them."

"You did not lure someone like that." Her lips pressed into a disappointed line before she turned that expression up at him. "Tell me you didn't."

Humour swirled in his chest, unwilling to deny it. "Here, let me find a story. I think I even figured out a way where I don't have to put you down."

He wound his arm around her back and gripped her thigh tightly. His quills were awfully close to her, but since they were laying down, he thought it might be okay. Then, crushing her to his chest, he got to his feet and went to his shelves.

He had a few story books here. When he found one, it was so covered in dust and brittle from disuse that he had to be careful with it. Some man named William had written the story, and he cared very little about the author in general.

When he sat back down, he held it up with the hand behind her so he could hold her hip with the other.

It was one of the books that had been given to him by Jabez when he'd been teaching him to read. The ghost of the recently deceased king tells his son to avenge his murder by killing the new king – the hero's uncle. It was a bloody tale about death, murder, and deception, but he had little else to offer her.

As he was reading it, he wondered if Jabez had learned to speak English from his parents, like Raewyn had. He'd also tried to teach him math, but numbers often made him scratch at his head – they still did.

Raewyn didn't seem to mind the tale's gruesome tone, but she did do something that stole a piece of his heart.

While he was reading, Raewyn held the back of his hand before slyly stroking up his quills. Like with her kisses up his skull, he'd never had anyone *willingly* touch his quills, let alone stroke them.

He paused to watch her, unsure how he felt about it. She was petting them from their base up to the sharp points, going with their grain. Since she wasn't causing herself harm, he let her be and continued to read.

It wasn't hard to tell she'd fallen asleep by her soft snores, and he eventually placed the book down.

He resumed his earlier touching, although much softer, and just admired the pretty female in his arms. Eventually, he lightly grabbed around her jaw so he could steer her face until it was pointing upright at his own.

He currently had a well-pleasured female on his lap, covered in his seed, who was peacefully asleep as though she wasn't being held by a monster.

A burning sensation, both pleasant and painful, tried to sear him from the inside. *Why are you doing this to me?*

He thumbed her lips, remembering how they'd sweetly moulded against his skull, and hoped to feel them again.

The burning sensation was unwelcome, as it only lived to show him he was being foolish. The likelihood of Raewyn ever becoming his was low – lower than any lustful acts they shared together. It was doubtful their hearts would ever align, and this would probably end up with him feeling lonelier than he ever had before.

Yet, he couldn't deny he didn't particularly want this to stop, too weak to the charm of this ethereal fairy to not submit.

Not just the sensual touching, but also this. Holding her felt oddly wonderful, and her curled up to him in trust did strange things to him. It soothed his mind, quietening all his terribly despondent and painful thoughts.

He didn't even want to wake her to move, not when it would disturb this contentment. This might be the happiest moment of his life, and not even the realisation that it might be his *only* happy memory diminished it.

Raewyn rubbed her face against the sheets in hopes of removing any sleep or possible drool – only to discover that fur tickled her cheek. She patted her hands forward and touched something warm, moving from breaths.

She realised it was Merikh's stomach.

"Sorry, I didn't mean to fall asleep," she grumbled, rubbing the tip of her nose against him. "How long was I out?"

"Two hours, maybe more," he answered, his gruff voice lazy, as though he was utterly relaxed.

Two hours? She couldn't believe she'd napped for that long!

His voice, warmth, and scent had lulled her into a trance. She hadn't even known she was passing out until she woke up.

"Why didn't you lay me on the bed?" She felt bad he'd been stuck where he was.

"You looked peaceful," he said as he brushed the back of his hand across her cheek. "I didn't want to move you in case I woke you."

Raewyn nibbled at the inside of her cheek. She felt like a pet asleep on its master's lap, keeping them there forever until the pet decided to move. Would he have sat there for eternity so as to not wake her? Why did just the thought make her heart dance?

Sex was a useful tool to show someone you liked them both inside and out. She had been wondering if using it to break down his walls could make Merikh sweeter, could soften him.

He was proving she was right.

She made no comment, knowing if she did, he'd want to get up to flee. Instead, she selfishly rested there a little longer and just petted the fur on his side.

"Should I have laid you on the bed?" he asked, second guessing his decision.

"No. This is nice," she reassured.

Since he seemed fine to let her stay there, she let her mind wander for a while. Raewyn had questions, so many of them. She'd wanted to broach them for days, and she'd tried to earlier when she asked him to share a pleasant memory. The fact that he didn't have any was sad.

Should I ask him now? This seemed like a vulnerable moment. It was far more likely his heart was open to her now, and that would make it easier.

Raewyn, not one to hesitate, spoke. "Merikh, can I ask you about the woman you spoke to while I was unwell?"

His answer was sharp. "No."

She felt guilty about pushing it, but she wanted to know. What she'd learned was only the surface of who he was, why he was the way he was, but it still left so many empty spaces. Learning about him was difficult; he only shared things that didn't go too deep.

Like his skulled face, he bore scars, terrible ones, within the depths of himself. Raewyn wanted to help him heal some of them.

"She was your mother, wasn't she?"

She knew she was, since Raewyn had overheard him call her that with a *sneer*. It was like he'd only said it to insult her.

"Yes," he answered coldly. "She is likely the reason why the twins ended up coming here." He was trying to change the subject.

"Why do you hate her?" Raewyn pressed.

"Why are you asking me all this?" he asked, appalled.

"I guess I just want to know you better." She offered him a small smile. "Am I not allowed to be curious?"

He raised his hand from her backside, since he'd been holding it, and she thought he may have scratched at the side of his neck.

"It's complicated, Raewyn. I've never shared my feelings about this before."

"I'm happy to listen." She carefully reached up so she could hold the end of his bony snout, showing her acceptance of him. "Please?"

Once more, he grabbed her arse and shuffled her closer. "Will you stay like this if I do?"

She nodded while burying her face against him, and he let out one of his usual sighs.

Ha! She'd won.

"It's not that I truly hate her," he admitted while grumbling. "She did take care of me most of the time. It's just... the main reason I don't like her is because of Weldir."

When he went quiet, she poked him by saying, "Weldir?"

He let out another sigh. "It is hard to think of him as a father, but more of a creator. I have only met him a few times, and he is distant. I don't know if he cares for us, but why he wanted us born is what bothers me."

He began skating his claws back and forth over her nape. She wondered if he was doing it as a way to distract himself.

"After how I reacted to learning of it, I think she has kept this from my brothers."

"What did you learn?"

"That we are nothing but a tool for him." Blue sparked in her vision, and her heart tightened in worry. "Cleansing the souls he harvests from Demons is draining for him, as is maintaining the shield around Jabez's portal and his realm. He sought out a mate, one he could breed, so that he could make children. We don't taint the souls we accidentally carry once we've consumed the flesh. So, when we return to the Veil, he's able to harvest them, and they strengthen him exponentially."

Raewyn's ears shot back in surprise. *This is why Weldir wanted them made? For power?* His reasoning could be either malicious or righteous, depending on what it was.

Since he was as stuck on Earth as everyone else here, if his magic dwindled too low, he wouldn't be able to maintain the barrier on Jabez's portal. He could be doing it to protect the Elysians, which would upset no one.

There could be other reasons, but she chose not to think on them when Merikh continued speaking.

"To learn that I am nothing but a slave for a master, that I am nothing but a messenger of souls for him, was painful. I thought we were created in want, in love, and instead, this horrible truth left me feeling empty." His hands tightened on her. "I know she was used as we were. She is like his hands and feet in this world, but still, she went along with it. Like I said, she did try to care for us, for me, but so many other terrible things have happened between us that I cannot find it in myself to forgive her, no matter what she has done to try and rectify it."

"Like what?" she asked, despite having an inkling already.

"Can this not be enough?" he asked instead. "There are some things I just do not wish to share with you, Raewyn."

"Why not? It will not change anything."

"You cannot make promises when you don't know the truth about them."

"Sure, I can," she said with a coy smile.

When he didn't say anything for a long while, it eventually fell. She brought her hand forward and drew swirling patterns on his stomach to distract them both.

"Is it... is it about the person who died?"

His next breath sounded more like a distressed wheeze with a quiet whine. It struck her all the way to the very core of her essence.

"You said it was an accident. I could never be upset with you for accidentally hurting someone."

"Raewyn–"

"Please, Merikh? I want to know. I've shared things with you I haven't told others. Only the other councillors know Jabez is my half-brother, and about how I lost my sight. I've shared my secrets with you, even if they were painful."

She would have threatened him she would get up if he didn't tell her, but she didn't think that would work in her favour. Her patience in his silence was rewarded anyway.

"I am not the first Mavka," he mournfully admitted, more blue sparking. "We were not born far apart from each other, and we acted similarly to how the twins do – although not so closely."

"They do seem like two halves of one person," she giggled, hoping to ease him, even though she didn't really feel any light-heartedness right now.

He wasn't the first Duskwalker, and already, she knew what that meant.

"When I was small, if I was not clinging to Lindiwe, she told me I was clinging to him. She said it was hard to get close to him, but having me around seemed to ease him – like he could just sense I was young and in need of protecting. So, one day, he took me away by accident, and I returned fully grown. From then on, all I knew was him. Wherever he went, I went. If he gained more humanity, so did I. When we played, we played rough. If I won, I would protect his skull until he grew back, or vice versa, and then we would play again."

Her eyes widened in shock. "You played a game where you killed each other?"

Merikh's chuckle was empty. "Death means nothing to creatures who don't die. The game was about strength, in which I was regularly the winner."

"I thought you said breaking your skull kills you?"

"That's because we didn't know that yet. In twenty-four hours, we always came back to be teased about losing. Except one day, he didn't. The play was often accompanied by our bloodlust, and when it had been a particularly ruthless fight, I had crushed his skull in my hand. Then I sat there, waiting for him to come back, and he never did. I probably would have sat there for forever if Weldir had not come to collect his skull and inform me he'd died. Lindiwe had been with him, and I think I remember her crying and screaming at me, but I was so overcome by my own emotions, denying his death, that I ended up frightening the shit out of her. I even hurt her."

His hands tightened on her, and it allowed her to feel the strength of his regret.

"I tried to attack them because I had thought them telling me meant they were the source of my pain. For years, anytime she came near me, I would instantly attack. I gave her no room to get close to me. I hated her for telling me, and she hated me for killing one of her children. There never was, and never has been, a chance for us to bond. The pain we share is too great, and I hate the way she looks at me, full of sympathy for the pain his death caused me. I hate how she sees that in me."

Raewyn didn't know what to say. She could try to soothe him, but she didn't want him to know that she, too, felt sympathy. It was hard not to.

She couldn't imagine what it was like to accidentally kill your own beloved sibling, but she did know what it was like to lose one.

"It is the only time I have regretted taking a life," he added. "And now, being near my kind brings back memories I do not want. I am envious that they get to learn about our weakness when I was not gifted with that knowledge, which likely would have saved him. So now, I am the oldest Mavka, but not the first, and everything I have suffered is shared to protect them, whereas I was not shielded from that suffering."

"That's not fair on you," she whispered.

"No, it's not, but that's what happened. Our mother didn't know anything. I don't think Weldir knew either, but I don't care. We are nothing but soul harvesters for him, and I wonder if he cares at all that one of us died, or if he only mourns the loss of a servant."

"Do you really think he could be that heartless?" she grumbled.

"He doesn't have a fucking heart," Merikh snapped. "He's made of mist and cloud. I doubt he even has a cock with which to make us."

Raewyn's cheeks heated in embarrassment at his words. Then she patted his chest. "Thank you for telling me. It explains a lot. Can I hug you?"

"No," he bit, instantly crumbling her heart. "My quills make that impossible."

"No, they don't." She wrapped her arms around him, bending her elbows so her arms went up his sides. She squeezed him. When he didn't do so in return, she pouted. "You're meant to hug me back, you know."

Merikh grunted before sliding his arms around her to hug her. He was tense at first, but he eventually eased into it. He even brushed the side of his snout against her.

"I think this is the first time I've hugged someone," he admitted with an awkward mumble.

"I figured as much. Feel better?"

"Not at all. It changes nothing." Most people would have

lied, but she guessed Merikh didn't have enough social etiquette to know that. "Have any more painful questions you want to ask me, or can we go back to before?"

Raewyn bit her lips shut when they tried to curl in humour, especially since she felt guilty. "Actually, I do."

"I told you to forget what I said," he rumbled, so close to a growl. "What I said matters little, and I don't like that you overheard it."

He was speaking of what he said about her.

She shook her head. "Don't worry, it's not about that." She didn't need to bring it up. What he said had painted a *very* clear picture. "It's just... you said something about a bride, and so did Aleron and Ingram. I don't know what that is, and I was hoping you could explain it to me?"

While still hugging her, his hands tightened on her to the point his claws dug in – dangerously close to cutting her.

"You don't need to know about it. It has nothing to do with you."

Why did that not feel like the truth?

Raewyn rolled her eyes. "Is it like the Taihee people I told you of? They often bite their chosen partner as a claiming mark, and it's held sacred to them. Violating it, without good reason, can lead to banishment."

It wasn't solidifying, but it was far more complex to undo a claiming than it was to enact one. Most tended to be overly cautious about their partner of choice.

"We could never do that. The moment we taste blood, our insatiable hunger would take over. It is solely a Mavka problem, one you don't need to worry about." When she opened her mouth, he must have felt it against his pec because he snarled and pulled away from their hug. "I won't tell you more about it, so don't try. If you do, I will put you on this chair by yourself and leave."

See? Her earlier idea of threatening him with the exact same words wouldn't have worked in her favour.

"Fine," she pouted, realising he was more sensitive about this than anything else.

When his snarl only turned into a soft growl, probably worried she'd try anyway, Raewyn growled right back.

He quietened completely, like the wind had been knocked out of him.

After a few moments of heavy, uncomfortable silence, he tickled his claws down her nape, forcing a mewl from her. Then he said warmly, "I really like it when you do that."

A small, but disappointed smile curled her lips. *I know,* she thought, which is why she enjoyed doing it.

THIRTY-TWO

Raewyn hummed contently as she cleaned up after her meal, happy she'd finally finished injecting her mana into the stone.

It'd taken longer than it should have because Merikh's insatiable hunger wasn't just apparent in his stomach, but in his groin as well. Although she could tell he was wary about being overbearing, it seemed he was no longer interested in denying his desire.

Raewyn was thankful for that, as she was finding she was even cheerier than usual because of it. Merikh was proving to be charming now that he felt comfortable with her.

He no longer avoided her.

He'd taken up a section of the stone bench to work on whatever secret task he was trying to complete so he could be near her. He still wasn't as forthcoming and talkative, but she had the feeling that was just who he was, preferring to quietly fill up the space with his prodigious presence rather than with idle chatter. It gave Raewyn the freedom to talk until her tongue turned dry.

He would assist her with any task, sometimes doing small things before she needed to even ask. He'd taken it upon himself to figure out how to cook, so she always had food ready. He cleaned the cave almost daily – he didn't like that their mingling scents, mainly those of a sexual nature, were making him foggy-headed.

What she liked the most was that he was more affectionate: not with his words, but with his actions.

Like now, he stood behind her, his hands on the bench on either side of her, and plonked the underside of his jaw on top of her head. Then, he shared his sight with her so she could see what she needed to clean without having to feel for it.

They both knew she didn't need him to do this, and it was actually disorientating. His sight didn't match up with her face, so she often had to overreach for everything. When she shook her head, he moved his jaw away to rid her of it, then plonked it back.

He said nothing, offered no explanation. He was just silently seeking attention, since she'd been ignoring him for most of the day while she was busy.

Next was the final stage, the one that scared her the most.

"Your heart has been beating faster for a while," he said in a soft but gruff voice. "It is not like how it usually is when I'm close, and neither is your scent. Is something wrong?"

"No. Everything is fine," she answered as she grabbed her plate to place it in a wooden bucket she'd later use to clean everything with.

Merikh moved his head so he was looking at the side of her face and used his claws to pull her curls behind her ear.

"There are other tells, like your ears and brows," he rebuked, since her ears were pushed back and her eyebrows were furrowed. "If you do not tell me, I will begin to think I have upset you, and I would like to know if I have."

He was rather particular about that.

If she didn't like or want to do something, he was quick to adjust his behaviour. If he said something that upset her, he would figure out a way to rectify it.

His anger had essentially become non-existent, and his aggression was only present in his lustful actions, rather than in general animosity.

Merikh hadn't changed. He was still hateful and spiteful, but it was only towards things of his past or anything beyond his ward.

After everything that would not require her to move from between Merikh's arms was put away, she sighed and turned her cheek towards his snout. She tapped it with the side of her face to steal a bony, lipless kiss.

"I'm nervous," she admitted. "I'm worried about failing. I don't want to upset you if I destroy the stone and we can't figure out a new way for me to go home."

"I have been thinking on that, and if it comes to it... I may be able to obtain another."

Raewyn gasped as she turned around. "There's another stone?"

"I am not the only one Lindiwe gave a stone to. Orpheus has one, although it has a Demon protection charm in it."

Hope blossomed in her chest. "Do you think he would be kind enough to give it to us?"

"I don't know, but I also don't care. I will steal it if he won't, and I will harm him, and anyone he is close to, if I must."

"Merikh!" she whined. She would say she was surprised at his hostility, but she absolutely wasn't.

While she was facing him, he plonked his head on top of hers again to silence her. "I didn't say I'd kill him, not permanently at least. Is there anything else about your task that is bothering you?"

The way he pried, she had a funny feeling he already knew the other reason. He was just being considerate of her feelings and giving her the option to share and speak about it.

She leaned forward and pressed her forehead against his chest. "This spell is the reason I lost my sight. I can't lose it a second time, but if it becomes too volatile, you or I could be hurt."

"Don't worry about me. I will be fine. I will heal within a day, and if you come to harm, I will take your wounds so you don't have to bear them."

She wished something so sweet didn't have to be clouded with such darkness. Still, he'd managed to ease her when she didn't think that was possible.

"I don't feel like working anymore today," she admitted.

She was tired and would likely sleep soon. The next step could wait.

Licking across her lips, over her cheek, and then dragging his tongue over her ear, Raewyn shivered when he rumbled, "I can give you something else to think about."

Despite the sharp stab of desire that clutched at her abdomen, she reached up to his face to stop him. She wasn't quite in the mood, since her emotions were all over the place.

"Could you read me more of that story?"

"If that is what you'd prefer." She liked how he didn't get all pissy when she denied him.

Instead, he leaned back and pulled her into his lap once he was seated against the wall next to the cooking hearth. Then he reached up to the table and grabbed the book, as though he'd placed it nearby. She often asked him to read to her, since she couldn't, and he always complied.

Like she always did when she wasn't sleepy and he read to her, she asked him a million questions about the book. She wasn't particularly fond of angsty mystery stories.

She also just adored annoying him.

When she knew she had asked him one too many ridiculous questions, like why the curtains were red or the carpet blue, he shoved the book at her.

"Here," he said with a small, half-hearted growl. "You read it to me then."

Her eyelids fluttered when the world opened up in her vision. She looked around, finding she could control the sight, which meant he'd given it to her rather than sharing his own.

It was rare that Merikh did this. He'd only ever done it twice; the first time when she'd run off with it, and the first night they'd had sex and he wanted her to look at him, thinking it would make her want to stop.

She blinked up at him in shock.

She was always taken aback by his otherworldly appearance. When she pictured his face, she always saw his bear skull and upward curling, near devil-like bull horns. She even pictured the claw and sword scarring on it – she'd touched it enough to know every nook and cranny of it.

"You gave me your sight? I know you don't like doing this."

"I didn't like it because I thought you'd run away with it again." He blindly reached up and petted her hair. "I will *always* take it back, Raewyn. Always. However, I don't mind lending it to you if you truly need to borrow it."

A small smile crept up her lips, and she gave him a surprise kiss – one he couldn't see coming.

Then she settled in, wiggling her back against his crossed legs until she was laying down more as she read the book to him.

It was after only two pages that he *rudely* stated, "Fucking hell, you're so slow. You'll put me to sleep at this rate."

"Hey!" she shouted. "I learned how to read and speak Earth languages when I was a child, thank you very much. I was slow at speaking when I first arrived here. I don't even know what language we're speaking. Español, I think?"

"It's English, Raewyn. English."

She rolled her eyes and threw her hands up. "How was I supposed to know that? Feel lucky my father was a linguist and learnt every language he could to teach me; otherwise, we wouldn't be able to speak to each other. I only know a handful of the languages from here, and I wasn't particularly good at learning them as a child."

"You talk so much it may have benefitted me. I could have tuned you out better."

Raewyn smacked him in the chest with the book. "You're such a bully," she whined, knowing he was only being playful.

"Only to you," he said as he cupped the back of her head and nuzzled her cheek. "You're the one creature I do not wish to be harsh towards, but I don't mind teasing you."

Her stomach swirled with tenderness. "Do you want me to keep reading or not?" she pouted.

"You could slowly read to me until the world ended, little fairy. Your voice is soothing, and I'm enjoying this."

"Then why'd you poke fun at me for?"

His chuckle was so warm and light her ears tingled from its pleasantness. He'd begun laughing with her more freely lately, like he found her humorous. It was odd, considering he'd rarely done it before.

"Because I thought it would be funny."

"Ha ha," she said with a sneer. "When did you get so jolly?"

"When a strange female came along and decided to annoy me with questions about a book I didn't even write."

Her lips parted in disbelief. He'd gotten revenge! To her dismay, it had her melting for him.

"You better watch out, Duskwalker, or I'll make you regret meeting me."

He chuckled again, this time while licking at the side of her neck. "I already know I will."

She was about to giggle back and keep reading, but suddenly paused. Was he poking more fun at her, or was there a grim undertone of honesty to his words?

Before she could ask him about it, a loud, booming, and near-heart stopping crack of thunder had her jumping in his arms. A waving *shaa* then spread just beyond the entrance, highlighting the sudden outburst of rain as the cloud passed over the area.

Her shoulders drooped as she turned her face to listen and watch with Merikh's borrowed sight. The world now looked less colourful, instead a dreary grey in appearance.

The wind was pushing away from the cliffside they resided in, but a wet, icy temperature softly billowed.

The book forgotten, it fell to her lap as she stared at the miserable outside world.

She grumbled, "I hate the rain."

Since it was obvious she'd lost interest in the book, Merikh glided his claws just behind her ear as he took back his sight. He turned his head towards the rain to stare at it.

A sense of peace washed over him.

When she shivered, he stood and placed her on her feet. He almost chuckled at her crestfallen face; it was apparent she'd been soaking in his warmth and was upset she'd lost it.

However, she didn't need to wait long for him to rectify upsetting her. He stripped the bed of its blanket, steered her to where he wanted her, and sat back down right near the entrance while facing it. They were a safe distance away from the pooling rain as he drew her back into his lap like before, this time with the blanket covering her.

She didn't smile, which is what he'd been seeking, but she did look far more comfortable than before. She also didn't shiver again.

He could have asked her why she didn't like this weather, but it would just be some kind of drivel complaint. She liked to complain, and it was hard to tell if she was serious or just purposefully and playfully trying to annoy him.

"I like the rain." Since he had his back resting against the side of the bench, he was able to freely view outside. "Sure, it's annoying to be wet, especially with my fur, but I find it soothing. It removes the quiet and replaces it with its own music."

He said this, but it wasn't the whole truth. Merikh didn't want to tell her the real reason he liked the rain, why he often threw himself into any storm to greet it.

It's like being held by the world. It was a cold, wet hug. He turned his sight down to her momentarily. *Although this hug is much more favourable.*

He held her a little tighter.

In all his life, even with his first memories, he couldn't remember ever being held or holding another like this. He'd never held anyone soft or warm, nor had he been held in return. He'd never had someone's lulling breaths puff against his bare chest or had their heartbeat fluttering against him.

He'd never held someone alive without it ending in bloodshed.

This was all new to him, and already, it had become an addiction he knew he wasn't going to enjoy weaning himself off of. Would he suffer through cold shivers with the loss of her warmth? Would he seek out someone to replace her scent, her body, her kindness, just because he was now enamoured with being touched?

He'd lived his touch-starved life repelling all this – not that it had been difficult, since no one had truly been interested in becoming his companion.

He turned his face back to the rain.

I don't want to become like Orpheus.

He didn't want to become obsessed with how lonely he was, only for it to end in failure every time he tried to fix it. Except it apparently didn't end in failure this time, although Merikh knew that likely wouldn't be his own future.

Merikh shook his head of his darkening thoughts, wishing his mind didn't always twist that way. *No. I will be fine.*

A few pleasant weeks with Raewyn wasn't going to change the fundamentals of who he was. He'd been fine before her, and he'd be fine without her once she was gone.

He'd been so distracted by his own thoughts that her sniffle echoing in his cave startled him.

She'd been feeling a little off today, but when he looked down to see tears rolling down her cheeks, he had no idea what to do.

Shit, shit, shit. She's crying. He tilted his head one way and then the other. *Did I make her cry?*

He didn't think he'd said anything hurtful towards her. Then again, he wasn't always aware of how his words could be taken – which was often negatively.

Was I insensitive to how she was feeling? He'd just been trying to make conversation in the hopes of veering towards a more positive one. *Should I apologise?* He was doing that a lot lately.

Unsure of what else to do, he cupped the side of her face and brushed a flowing tear with the pad of his thumb. "If I upset you..."

"What?" she choked. "N-no. I'm sorry. I'm not crying because of you." Then, with a false, broken smile, she added, "Weirdly enough."

That was a lie, considering he didn't make her cry often. It was why seeing her do so now was puzzling.

She wiped at her face to remove them, but they didn't cease, no matter how she tried. She even sobbed into the sleeve covering her wrist.

"I just miss home, and I feel like the rain coming now is a bad omen. I'm scared I'm going to mess this spell up like I did before, that I'm going to be stuck in this stupid realm where it's cold when it rains, even in the summer. I miss how warm it is no matter where I am, and that it's only winter when I feel a chill in the air. I miss my house, and my friends and family. I miss Cykran's stupid sarcasm and how he always makes me laugh when I should be concentrating."

The more she listed off how much she hated this world, which had been his home all his life, the more his chest sunk. She was usually so happy and cheerful that hearing her so unhappy was baffling.

His sight shifted to green when he thought, *I don't like hearing of this Demon, Cykran.* He refused to admit it was partly jealousy that she was able to easily get close to others who were so different from her, when Merikh had found it hard to be close with even his own kind.

It may also be because he thought he would have enjoyed

taking the Demon's place. Watching her work was enjoyable, calming even.

"I-I miss my jewellery and what they represented to me and my culture, how each band was given to me for my achievements inside and outside of my work. Not wearing them feels like a piece of me is missing, but I had to sell them so I had money here, since humans don't support those in need."

"I could find a way to get you new jewellery?" he offered, wishing to be of help. He'd just steal it.

She sobbed harder, making him wince when he realised he'd said the wrong thing.

"They can't just be anything. Each band on each limb has a meaning and an engraving. They're special. I don't mean to sound ungrateful; I just miss everything about my home. I miss eating good food and wearing clothes that aren't itchy, going out into the sun and feeling warmth."

"I didn't know you found it so unpleasant here."

It was all he could say, since it wasn't his fault Earth was the way it was. Should he apologise for something he couldn't control? Was that how sympathy worked?

"I'm sorry," she exclaimed. "I d-don't mean your home. I know you've tried to be as accommodating as you can be. You've been so helpful, and I don't know what I would have done without you. Please, just give me a few moments to collect myself. I don't know what's come over me."

She went to get up to be on her own, but Merikh let out a soft growl as he yanked her back to his lap.

"I have no issue with your tears, Raewyn. If you wish to cry and explain why Earth is terrible, then you are free to do so."

"I don't want you to think I'm blaming you, or that I'm unhappy because of you," she said as she turned up a beseeching expression towards him.

"Even if that were the case, I'm sure you would tell me," he said, unsure if that was true. He began patting her head, hoping it felt soothing. "I don't know how to comfort another, so if I say something that could be misinterpreted as something thoughtless, understand I don't mean it that way, unless it is obvious."

"I'm sure it's uncomfortable to have someone crying on your lap when you're trying to enjoy something," she replied softly, rubbing her wet cheek on the back of her wrist.

Does she think I care that much about the rain? He wasn't so shallow.

"Not as much as you might think. Whether you are crying, angry, or happy, I enjoy your company." His orbs threatened to turn a reddish pink in embarrassment at his own words, but he managed to snuff out the urge. "I am not used to it, and unsure of what to do most of the time, but if you wish to feel homesick and cry in my arms, I will hold you, if it makes you feel better. If you wish to go off and cry by yourself privately, I will go into the rain. Like I already stated, I find it pleasant, so doing so would not upset me."

"No, please stay," she sniffled as she hugged his midsection without putting her arms around him. "I promise I'll stop crying soon."

Despite the terribleness of her mood and how it made his gut twist, his chest was light from her desire to stay exactly how she was – upon his lap.

She continued to cry while he petted her head.

"Does it rain a lot in your realm?" he asked, hoping to distract her after some time passed.

She nodded. "Yeah, but it's really refreshing. It's not miserable like it is here. Although, I do like the way it sounds hitting the lake."

"I like it, too. It's like the waterfall has grown."

When her tears began to settle, he knew she was listening, since her face was pointed towards outside. He shared his sight with her once more and pointed.

"I like the way the grass smells after it rains. Everything smells fresh and more alive, and the lake is much deeper afterwards, so it has a different colour."

Her lips twisted. "I wish I could swim in it."

He tilted his head as his orbs turned yellow. "I guess I didn't notice that you didn't swim, only bathed. I could try warming it for you, but it might take me a few hours."

If he could make warm bath water with his own blood, he was sure there was a way he could warm the lake for her.

She shook her head, making her curls bounce around her head.

"It's actually warmer in the lake than outside it." She wrung her hands against her abdomen. "It's just... water is really disorientating for me. I haven't swum properly since I lost my sight. In Lezekos City, we have a beach we can swim in, but the barrier only stops things from outside coming in. Since I can't see which way the city is, I've always been worried I'll accidentally swim outside the barrier, even though we have things to prevent that. But what if it's somehow broken one day? I also don't want to get tired and drown, nor do I want to have to ask for help and need rescuing. I don't mind when it's a controlled environment like a small pool, but from what I remember when you shared your sight with me, it's really big."

"Wouldn't you know where to go because of the waterfall? You also said you can see the ward."

"Yeah, but what if I don't come out where I think I have? The stress just doesn't seem worth it to me."

I see. He didn't know she had such reservations about his home. What else was she hiding?

"I cannot swim," he admitted, and her face shot to him in surprise. He rolled his head. "I know how to by what I've seen, but I don't think any Duskwalker can float. I'm too dense. I just sink, like a rock tossed into water." He cupped the side of her face before tucking her hair behind her ear. "But I know the deepest parts of the lake, so I can be there with you if you wish to swim in it."

"Really? You would do that for me?"

Merikh shrugged, not understanding why that would make a slim smile appear on her face.

"Sure. When it's sunny again, we can swim if you'd like." Wanting a distraction because he was uncomfortable with the way she was looking at him, he reached behind him to obtain what he'd been working on from the stone bench. "I wanted to show you something."

He handed her two large pieces of thick leather with thinner strips attached to them. She ran her fingers over them reflexively, looking puzzled as to what they were.

"They are arm guards," he stated as he took one from her so he could strap it on. "The back one is being difficult to create, since I don't have enough belts to make the straps and I will need to obtain more, but I have tried and tested these. You shouldn't harm yourself on my arms again if I wear them."

He rested his arm over her, hugging her, as he used the other arm to move her hand on top of his forearm. The leather guard protected her from his quills, and she curiously brushed her hand over it.

It wasn't perfect. If he were truly enraged, he'd rip them to shreds, but he doubted that would happen.

"You were making these to wear for me?"

She turned her face to him with an emotion he couldn't decipher, since she was a little swollen from crying, but it was one that definitely bruised his heart.

"Once I make the back piece, I should be able to lie down with you. Since I doubt I will need to defend us within my ward, I can wear these for now."

She was silent for a long while as she touched his arm, feeling the guard and how it was made. It wasn't tan, since he didn't care for the usual leather colouring made by humans. He only desired functionality. It was two layers, thick and sturdy, and attached to belts he'd threaded between the two pieces so he could strap it to his arm in three places and stop it from shifting.

When her face turned mischievous, he should have prepared

himself for her next words.

"Does that mean you can wear them during sex?"

Merikh nearly choked on his own saliva. He grunted in answer.

That had not been his intention when he'd begun making them, but yes, they would be very useful for her to have more freedom during that.

I don't think I want her to have more freedom.

He was already smitten with touching her. If she were able to be more forward without fear of being harmed by his quills, how was he meant to survive this toxic lily? Especially when she was already poisoning him.

His bull tail curled in apprehension.

It wasn't even her fault anymore. She'd ceased trying to seduce him, since there was utterly no point. All she had to do was flash him a certain sweet smile or brush her hand over his knuckles, and Merikh was lost.

She'd opened a gate, showed him it was okay to crave her like an ache, and he finally felt comfortable enough to just be himself. Unfortunately for her, it meant she was experiencing all sides of him, especially those of his long-denied desires.

Every time he touched her, tasted her, fucked her, Merikh knew he was infecting himself with her. Every time she allowed him to hold her as he was now, which he tried to do often, the more he was succumbing to her gentle poison.

And Merikh didn't give a single damn if it killed him.

THIRTY-THREE

Merikh licked at his snout while his hand reached outwards, allowing Raewyn freedom to swim with an anchor: him.

The silly little dress she'd cut far too short did very little to hide her shapely thighs and backside. If she turned to her back, it gave him fleeting little peeks of the tuft of hair on her pubic mound, her hip bones, her navel.

With the golden sun shining over her beautiful, rich-taupe skin, the water made her glitter with sparkles of light and warmth.

If he hadn't licked almost every inch of her legs, hips, backside, and torso, he may have preferred she'd worn one of the longer, heavier dresses. Now, instead, he just marvelled at the pretty mermaid swimming in his own private lake.

She wasn't very elegant, otherwise he might have thought she were a swan. Then again, his little fairy could become whatever she wished to be.

Her hair was tied up into a ball near the top of her head, keeping it safe and dry.

He had no desire to playfully splash her or dunk her. They were deep enough that the water was almost to his shoulders, and he'd rather just peacefully watch her.

They'd already learned his vibration was impossible for her to hear like this, so if she disorientated herself, he just tapped at the surface of the water. He barely moved, just allowing her the comfort of his presence while she swam around.

He didn't have to join her. He could have stayed near the shoreline, but he'd promised to do this with her. Merikh was thankful for that, as he was surprisingly enjoying himself.

Raewyn hadn't wanted to do this yesterday. The water had been chillier than usual, and he informed her the loose sediment from the surface world above the Veil would need at least a day to settle.

She'd worked on one of the final steps of her spell preparation while he'd snuck to the closest town to steal some belts to finish his back quill guard.

He turned his sight up to the flowerpot currently sitting on a ledge of the cliff wall. Most of the tulips had died from her attempts at working the stone and the flowers together. Two remained, and even now, one was glowing, despite the sun shining on it.

She said by the time the sun begins to truly fall away, it'll be done.

Apparently, the issue she'd had in the Elven realm was that when she put the stone in the sunlight for even a second, it had been too strong. She'd been impatient, despite it being late summer there, and she'd thought she would be quick enough.

It had ended in an accident that almost killed her and her colleagues.

However, Earth didn't have three suns. Even in the summer, the solar radiation, heat, and light were nowhere near the same. She even said the winters in Nyl'theria were warmer than this.

Fucking hell, I hope my fur keeps me cool. He'd heard shaving certain creatures could make it harder for them to regulate their temperatures, so perhaps he shouldn't try that.

Plus, he'd look weird if he shaved himself.

Either way, she was taking her time measuring the amount of sun that the stone, currently wrapped in a tulip's petals, needed. It hadn't been enough yesterday, but she thought it might be by the end of today.

He'd offered for her to swim in the meantime. When she grabbed his tail to yank herself closer, which felt awfully playful, he was glad he'd done so.

She didn't grab his arm, since he wasn't wearing his new guards, and instead waited for him to hold his hand out to her again. He followed hers until they clasped.

She dragged herself closer until her breasts bumped against his hard chest.

"I'm sorry you're not having any fun," she said, although her expression lacked any truth in her apology.

Her small smile revealed that she was enjoying this too much, and his tail flicked under the water.

"Who says I'm not having fun?" he rebuffed, holding her elbows, since she didn't seem to want to part right then. "I've been considering drowning you this entire time."

His tone was filled with humour, and the urge to chuckle tickled his chest when she glared his way.

"You better not. I don't want to get my hair wet; otherwise, I'll have to wash it." Then she fiddled with some of the fur on his chest. "It's just... you're standing there while I swim."

"I told you I sink." He tilted his head slightly. "I can pretend, if that will make you feel better."

Her lips curled. "No, that's fine. I think it's odd you can't float. Even Demons can swim."

"Well, I'm not a Demon," he answered plainly.

Her warm smile died, and she turned away from him.

"About that. I wanted to talk to you about something," she uttered quietly, her expression grim. "Actually, I've been meaning to bring it up with you for a while, but I wasn't sure how you'd react."

His hackles rose, and he had to forcefully make his fur and quills relax. He didn't want her to accidentally reach out and hurt herself.

"Should I be scared?" He chuckled warmly to hide his

apprehension.

"How much do you know about Weldir?"

His head cocked, while a swirl of anger spun in his chest, as it usually did when hearing his 'creator's' name.

"I know enough."

"What about how he was... born?" She swam casually around him, her anchor, and her face grew solemn.

"No, I know very little about that."

Great. What more terrible things must I learn? Why did he have to become the keeper of knowledge for his kind?

"Do you know anything about the Elysian deities?"

"No. Not a single thing."

She paused and turned to him. Her little lip nibbles caught his attention for multiple reasons. Every time she did it because of a desirous thought, he craved leaning forward to lick at them, to soothe them.

In this context, it was nervousness. It only made his apprehension grow until his tail curled.

"Do I want to learn this, Raewyn? As I told you, sometimes there are things I wish I had not discovered."

"I don't know?" she answered honestly. "I just would want to know if I were in your shoes... well, paws, I guess?"

Was she seriously making fun of his clawed toes right now? She'd nearly tickled the spirit right out of him when she'd gone exploring.

His silence, unsure of how to answer, was her opening.

"You're not a Demon, Merikh, but there is a reason why you and they seem to share so many similarities." She turned away from him, tilting her face to the sun. "When the Demons first came to Nyl'theria, the Gilded Maiden tried to help them grow fully formed. In doing so, she accidentally absorbed their void and only ended up hurting them. She began to lose her power, like an infection eating away at her holy essence, and she ceased trying to help when she nearly lost her divine status. The infection was like a contagion, and many other deities died."

"What does this have to do with anything?"

Her features tightened. "She was pregnant. She gave birth prematurely, and what came from her was Weldir – a half-formed god. She hadn't meant to harm him, never expected him to save her life by absorbing the worst of the Demons' void. Like them, he had no physical outside. His early birthing meant he didn't have anything internal, either. He was born as an essence."

The coldness that rushed through his pulsing veins was like a razor.

"Great. So not only am I a servant, I'm also a fucking mutant."

"No!" she exclaimed as she swam closer. She patted him until she pressed against his torso once more. "We never considered Weldir that. He was her son, but it's complicated. He is a demi-god only because of his lack of power, and the Gilded Maiden gave him a duty which would help strengthen him. But..."

"It was also one that meant he couldn't be near the other precious 'gods.'" Merikh scoffed as he turned his head away. "Say what you will, but the intention was to get rid of him."

"I wanted to tell you this so you knew why you were so similar, and that I worry what your existence will mean for him when the other gods learn of it. I'm sure he is aware of that as well." Her ears drooped as she lowered her head. "I don't like that you hate him. He was an outcast, just like you, and I want you to know that you probably mean more to him than you think. If he gains enough strength and does what he is supposed to here, he will be granted a position with the rest of our surviving deities. The Gilded Maiden has been weak for a long time, but her strength is returning, and she'll be able to help him once it does."

Merikh gently cupped her throat so he could lift her chin with his entire hand. He liked holding her there, and that she trusted him with a place so fragile and delicate.

"Whatever his reasons are, nothing you say can erase how I feel. I have met my father three times, and it has been nothing but information and pain. Thank you for telling me *why* I am the way I am, but it does nothing but weigh on my conscience, as does everything else I am forced to bear."

"I'm sorry. I shouldn't have said anything."

He didn't like the way his chest burned at learning all this, nor how her expression had turned so solemn. She'd been mystical to him before. He'd like to go back to how they were just a few minutes ago.

He removed his hand from under her chin so he could brush the backs of his claws up over her cheek. He moved them behind the point of her ear while flicking it, making her shiver, then brought the points of his claws down her throat.

He made a path down the flat of her sternum.

"You could always make it up to me," he rumbled, hoping to ameliorate the situation – in a way that would make him very delighted.

Her eyes squinted in suspicion, her lips thinning. "What do you want?"

"Take this off while you swim." He tugged at the poorly cut neckline. "I'll even hold it for you."

Her features brightened. "Oh. Is that all?" She was quick to wiggle it down her body and hand it to him. "Although I don't mind if you lose it. I kind of ruined it."

"No, I like it," he answered as he stared down at her floating perky breasts. Her brown nipples were stiff, and he flicked one with the side of his foreclaw, causing her to cover her chest as she swam backwards. "The next time you wear it, I'll tear it from you."

He liked how teasing it was, since everything else she wore was long and mostly hid her.

"If you like that," she teased with a smile. "Then you should see what kind of outfits women can wear in my home realm."

"If it's more revealing than this, I think you should consider how dangerous it is for you."

"Maybe you'll find out."

Doubtful, he sadly thought as she swam circles around him – like she had already been doing metaphorically for weeks.

She poked her tongue out at him, but her smile had returned and that's all he cared about. He could ignore everything else now that he had his mermaid back.

Swim, swim, little fairy, he thought as he eyed her naked body through the ripples of the water. *Swim as fast as you can from me.*

Raewyn cheerfully hummed as she double checked her workstation. Everything was completely out of the way, but she just wanted to triple check.

It'd be terrible if something happened and other ingredients were nearby as she activated the mana stone for its new function. Wouldn't want to oops another chaos portal into temporary existence.

What are the chances of that happening again?

With her apparent luck, who knew? The odds definitely weren't in her favour.

Okay, so she was really checking everything for the umpteenth time because she was anxious.

She was happy, since their long swim in the lake had turned into something much naughtier. Being taken against the lake wall hadn't been on the top of her list, but at least he couldn't complain that she was clean of his seed!

She was also now dry, dressed, and ready to work.

It was likely she was feeling much more relaxed than she would have because of their heated moment of intimacy. Plus, he'd been kind enough to just... be there with her while she swam, and she appreciated that more than he'd ever know.

She'd also gotten off her chest something that had been

bothering her. Raewyn had assumed Merikh would take learning more about Weldir terribly, but it had been bothering her that she knew something about him he didn't. It'd felt wrong to keep that in, and she'd been considering telling him since they'd journeyed here.

Merikh was an enigma, and even when learning about such things, he seemed to bear the weight of everything with ease. She was sure it was just a façade, but it showed his inner strength.

Said stoic Duskwalker entering the cave broke her out of her thoughts.

"Alright. Here's the pot."

The clink of the ceramic hitting the stone bench made her ears twitch, only because he seemed to manhandle everything. It was broken, barely held together via rope. He should be more careful.

Still, she thanked him as she brought it closer.

In the dark of her vision, she could see the tulip holding the stone was glowing with activating magic. She gingerly loosened the ribbon keeping the flower closed and let the stone plop into her hand.

She couldn't see the stone, but she could feel its warmth, the way it tingled her senses with power.

I must be quick now that I've removed it from its absorption tool. The flower had taken some figuring out and reconstruction on her part, which is why she'd fallen so ill after days of trying to change it.

They had a mechanical tool made back in her realm, but it had been designed off something similar.

"Will you need any help?"

"No," she answered after she took a calming breath. "You don't have to stay and watch. It might take me a while."

"It's fine. I'm interested in what you're doing."

Raewyn held the stone flat between both her palms and poured magic into it. It began to float, as did her hair around her face, as she used a hovering spell that would allow her to rotate and work it on all sides.

Once it was floating, and she could finally see the stone glowing black – a neutral colour similar to her own grey base magic – her heart raced.

No. It's okay. I can do this. She strived to take in another calming breath. *I promised Merikh we'd go to my realm, and I really, really want to go home. Just take it slow. Don't be impatient like last time.*

Raewyn had been too young, cocky, and impatient when she'd done this last. She wouldn't make that mistake again – she refused to.

Around the stone, a clear ball of essence formed. With her mind, she drew circle runes and symbols all throughout it. Multicoloured lines formed, white, black, blue, green, red, and every colour and tone possible.

The markings all over her body began to glow, and she was able to see them, too.

Then came the difficult part, one which would take hours.

She needed to thread the tiny fibres of the spell – she'd successfully done so before, which had ended in near catastrophe for her.

There were thousands of micro-threads that needed to be woven together into patterns. The central piece was a sun, but it looked unusual – like a geometric, twenty-four-pointed star.

With sweat dripping down her back and forehead, she didn't know how long she stood there with Merikh watching her. He moved around, since his vibrations became louder and softer at different intervals, but he didn't disturb her.

It wouldn't have mattered either way. She was hyper focused, concentrating so deeply on her task that if he had tried to push her, touch her, anything at all, she would have been rigid and unbending.

"Raewyn," he called, but she gave no answer. She couldn't, not when she was slipping a thread underneath another before coming out above, only to slip back under a different one. "Whatever you do, stay inside. Don't leave the cave."

She wanted to ask why, but her lips wouldn't move. If she deviated her thoughts from her task too far, she could ruin the spell. She could destroy the stone.

Despite this, she would heed to his warning. If it was his mother again, Raewyn didn't want to get involved. She was done eavesdropping, and she didn't want to violate his trust again.

It's working, she thought as she continued to fabricate the sun spell. *It's working!*

The stone's black glow began to turn red in the middle.

Okay, okay. Red is still too weak. Even the heat that was emitting from it wasn't strong. It was the equivalent of a three-thousand-Kelvin sun, although only a tiny droplet of it.

However, it was better than what she'd done the last time. It'd started off white, and since their warmest sun was blue, she'd aimed for that. Not again, not after last time.

Starting this low did bring about its own problems. Either the stone's low quality, even though she'd injected a large amount of mana into it, was hindering it, or she hadn't left it in the sun for long enough.

Regardless, she pumped it with a small amount of her own magic, and it turned orange – mimicking a four-thousand-Kelvin sun. It still wasn't enough, not to protect them both. It may just protect the wearer if it were to be turned into a necklace.

She worked on injecting it with small amounts of her own essence to strengthen the stone while also creating the spell. Both had to be in balance with each other. Otherwise, it would either be a dud and only so strong, or the lack of stone strength would cause it to shatter if its energy was overly strong.

It didn't occur to her that Merikh had been gone a long while, not as she worked on perfecting that balance.

Then, when the stone glowed a subtle white, reflecting a droplet of a ten-thousand-Kelvin sun, even Raewyn could feel the heat in her fingertips.

She stopped injecting her own essence into it and wove the final threads, pleased that both had ended near each other.

Once she was done, the stone stopped glowing as it dropped into her hands. Rather than just racing, her heart was so swollen with fear and uncertainty that all she could do for a long while was just hold it.

Now, to test it.

Either it would work, or it wouldn't. She feared the outcome.

Do it. All you have to do is activate it.

She willed herself, but she just bit at her lip.

Her ears twitched, checking to see if Merikh was there. She heard nothing, and she didn't know if she was thankful for that or not. She didn't want to hurt him, but she was also afraid of doing this alone.

She closed her eyes, her brows furrowing as she gripped the stone tight. Then she opened her eyes and activated it.

An explosion of heat and light threw her into complete brightness.

THIRTY-FOUR

Merikh couldn't contain his growl once he left his cave.

Not only was he being disturbed, but he was being disturbed from watching Raewyn. He'd been utterly fascinated with what she'd been doing, considering he'd been able to see everything.

He hadn't expected that, and thought she'd just be standing there with little indication as to what was happening.

However, he'd seen the magic circles form on a ball of essence. He'd seen her weaving threads. He'd seen the tasty bead of sweat dripping down her temple, her jaw, before it finally dipped into her low-cut dress. What a tantalising drop.

Instead of remaining to observe her in awe, he was being dragged away – by someone he'd rather punch himself in the face than talk to.

Danger was lurking, and it was best to give it what it wanted before it was too late. Hopefully, if he shooed it away, it wouldn't return.

There was no need to be cautious as he approached the long-eared, white-haired, Demon-fanged man. Merikh was completely protected within his ward, and there was absolutely nothing even *he* could do.

Except be meddlesome, which is *why* he figured the red-eyed, horned fucker was standing there.

His grin, which highlighted a mouth of fangs eerily similar

to a shark, flashed. He knew Merikh would come.

It was because he understood Merikh better than most.

At the opposite side of his ward to his cave entrance, Merikh folded his arms and raised the tip of his snout while twisting his head so he could still see him.

He was thankful they were in a place that made it difficult to peer inside his home. He didn't want the half-Demon to see Raewyn.

"You have some nerve coming here," Merikh warned with a snarl.

"Is that any way to greet an old friend?" Jabez chuckled as he waved his hand to the side.

"We stopped being companions when you turned on me for Katerina, and any goodwill between us was lost the moment you set your Demons on me."

Jabez's cheek twitched, likely due to the mention of Katerina.

"Yes, well," Jabez nonchalantly said while overlapping his clawed fingers. "We all have our reasons."

"You look like shit," Merikh answered, and his jaw knot clenched in reaction.

Despite his dark-taupe complexion, which had a similar Elvish grey undertone to Raewyn's, the soft creases under his eyes looked deeper and bruised. It was obvious he wasn't sleeping, and he just generally looked... unhinged.

His long white hair was neatly brushed. His maroon pants were clean, as was his body. Perhaps to any other, he would look put together, handsome even, but Merikh knew better. It didn't matter that two hundred years had passed since they'd truly been face to skull.

He knew the man. He also knew when he was up to something.

"So, Katerina got herself killed," Merikh stated with far too much humour. Jabez bared his fangs in a warning growl, which he, of course, ignored. "By Orpheus' new bride, no less? You can bet I got a kick out of that."

"Cease speaking of her," he bit. "I came here for a reason; don't make me change my mind."

"Come to try and steal another female from one of us?"

Perhaps taunting the man while he had his half-sister hidden away wasn't wise, but there was no other reason why Jabez would approach him. Why now, if not because of that? If a Demon had wandered past, they may have seen her.

Hopefully, they were just too stupid to know *what* she was.

"Are you keeping a female here?" Jabez exclaimed while cocking his head, just as a grin curled his lips. "I was not expecting that, Orson."

Fuck. He shouldn't have said anything.

Merikh's orbs flashed red. "That is no longer my name, and you know it."

Jabez raised a claw to tap at his lips in thought, his naturally red eyes lifting to the dusky sky. "Ah, yes. It's been so long that I'd forgotten. Merikh, is it?"

"You're the one who gave it to me!"

"Temper, temper," he chuckled, turning his sight back to him. "I'm only playing with you. Trying to break the tension, if you will."

"What do you want?"

"Sit with me." Jabez waved his hand towards the ground. "There is much we should speak about."

Then, like he expected Merikh to do as he was told, Jabez plonked himself onto the ground in a cross-legged position. With his hands on his knees, his bare feet poking out from under them, he stared up at Merikh expectantly.

"Sit, Merikh. I will stay here until you do, whether that is a day, weeks, or months."

"Why should I listen to you?" Merikh scoffed.

His eyes darkened, his lids lowering as Jabez let out a rumble in warning.

"You know defying me will get you nowhere. You know I

will stay here until I get what I want." He looked around Merikh's legs before his malicious gaze cut up to him. "Then, perhaps, I can see this apparent female you have here."

Other than a battle of wits, which Merikh didn't know he had the intelligence to win, there was no harm in speaking with him. It was also true he would remain, and Merikh didn't want him seeing Raewyn.

It was *that* threat that had him obeying.

He sat as well and folded his hands between his legs. He said nothing, knowing Jabez would start prattling when he was ready.

Seemed it was a trait shared between siblings, and it was something he apparently appreciated in both.

However, Jabez lifted a claw, pointed it at him, and covered his mouth with the other hand as he laughed.

"When the fuck did you get so fat?"

Struck by the suddenness of it, Merikh's orbs turned a reddish pink in embarrassment. "When did you get so skinny? Look at you! You look as though I could snap you in two by blowing at you."

"Skinny?" Jabez chuckled, flexing an arm. "I've grown much since the last time we met. You just got so big that everything looks small to you now."

His tail flicked as red once more filled his sight. "Get to the point, Jabez."

"Know what your cock is yet?" the man laughed. "Smells like you do. That female's scent lingers on you, but I'm surprised it's so familiar. Have I perhaps met her? Is she another Demon?"

Merikh tilted his head. He would have been embarrassed if something didn't become apparent. It'd been so long since he'd been near his sister that he couldn't remember her scent properly.

Although he'd technically bathed in the lake, her scent lingered everywhere within his home. He'd picked up remnants of it before he came outside, but not enough to specify what species she was.

Instead of answering, Merikh just waited for Jabez to get over himself and finally tell him why he was here. He tapped a claw on his knee, catching Jabez's attention.

His humour eventually died, seeing Merikh wasn't the same foolish Duskwalker he once had been. He'd changed vastly in the last two hundred years.

Jabez sighed as he tossed his head side to side to push his long hair back. He used to have it tied up, but it seemed he no longer desired to keep it contained.

"As you mentioned, Katerina was killed by Orpheus' new bride." Mimicking him, although it was originally his own trait Merikh had picked up, Jabez tapped a claw on his knee as well. "In retaliation, I have ordered for your kind to be eradicated."

"That much was made obvious by the Demons who have come after me, even above the surface."

Jabez narrowed his eyes, hating being interrupted – which is exactly why Merikh would make it his mission during this conversation.

"Honestly, I was angry and wanted revenge for her."

"Revenge? You and I both know it was her own fault. There was no reason for her to be so hateful of my kind, and yet you let her, fuelled her. Her death is on your hands more than it is on Orpheus'."

His cheek twitched, along with his jaw, and the way his pointed ears shot back revealed he was growing agitated. Merikh wouldn't have known if it weren't for him observing Raewyn's own ears in fascination.

"You know I cared for her, which is the only reason you wish to blame me."

"You have been out here hunting my kind. What were you expecting? I have been waiting for you to wake up. I had been waiting for you to realise she was venomous and discard her, to bring me back to your side. Instead, you severed all possibility of that the first moment a Demon shot out from the forest with your *regal* demand in place, hissing about how they would get the glory for killing me and bringing back *part* of my skull to you."

"Perhaps I let my emotions get the better of me when I told them to target you after her death, but that doesn't negate the fact that removing your kind would weaken Weldir. Every time one of you brings back a soul by accident, the stronger he gets, and the harder it'll become for me to send my army through my portal. You once told me you wanted him gone, but I refused to listen." Jabez roamed his eyes down Merikh's body before darting them back to his skull. "I want to know if you still feel the same way."

He grunted in answer, not wishing to give him a real one.

Jabez, mocking him, grunted in return before grinning. It was a creepy smile, one that showed just how deeply he could see into Merikh. It almost felt like he was peering beneath his very flesh and at his twisted soul.

"I can see that has not changed."

"I have no desire to get in his way anymore. I do what I can to avoid strengthening him. Eating the heart and head of a human benefits me, but it also stops me from consuming their soul. There is nothing else I can do to hinder him."

"Perhaps not." He raised an arm to shrug. "But what I'm offering will damage him from the other side. His task is to prevent Demons from crossing from this world into the Elven realm, but it doesn't stop me from controlling those present on the other side."

Yellow filled his sight, and Merikh tilted his head. "What are you proposing?"

"I *tire* of being here, Merikh. I tire of this realm, the humans, the Demons here. I already tire of hunting your kind. I kill one, and it comes back to life, and suddenly, there are two more for me to have to take into consideration. I killed the cat-skulled Duskwalker, and somehow, he lives, and now he has his own child – another for me to contend with."

"You started this," Merikh answered as he folded his arms, hiding the fact that he hadn't known he had more... family.

Faunus has a youngling?

"Yes, but I still seek to finish this. What the Elves did to me" – Jabez started as he held his hands up to open and close his fists – "I can't ignore it. I can't forgive it. When I was locked away, I began to forget who I was. All I saw was darkness. I was mostly alone until they put Demons inside with me, and their voices were just as distraught as the ones within my mind. You can't fathom what that was like. They made me, and then they discarded me when they couldn't control me."

This story sounded familiar. "Are you sure that's what happened?"

Jabez cocked his head. "You dare try to insinuate I don't know my own memories? Weldir and the Elves wish to keep me away as though I am some kind of villain, without taking into consideration what they did to me, to my fellow Demons. Why must I be painted as the 'bad guy'? In many stories, I would be a liberator for those who have been made outcasts. Of course, real evil wishes to stamp out those who would disobey them, but I refuse to allow it."

Merikh rolled his head. Yep, that wasn't going to work. If he revealed what he'd learned, Jabez might grow suspicious of the little fairy he had in his keeping.

However, the Elves were at fault for his unsettled mind. From what Raewyn told him, they'd turned a man into a monster.

Merikh also knew Jabez was normal. He still sought happiness, humour, love, and kindness – unfortunately, it was now only limited to his own.

It had once included Merikh as well.

"I'm well aware of how it feels to be in the dark, Jabez. You were the first to pull me out of it, and the one who shoved me back into it."

"Then why not join me again?" Jabez asked as he offered his hand out. "You can save your kind by doing so."

Merikh's arms loosened. "What do you mean?"

"I can't take any of the Demons here, but you can cross that portal with me." Jabez's mischievous grin was full of malice, but it was obvious it wasn't towards Merikh. It was towards his goal. "I need someone on my side if I face the Demons who remain in the Elven realm. Once they see how strong and fast you are, they will not attempt to harm me, not with the magic I wield along with your strength. You are far more intelligent than your dim-witted brothers, which makes you *dangerous.* If we work together, we can take control of an army already present in the Elven realm and finally destroy them. Their pathetic city will become mine to live in, a place where all of us, Demon and Mavka, can be at peace. Your brothers can have a place there where they won't be scorned by the humans in the way the Demons have been scorned by everyone. A place where none of us need to hide."

Merikh was rendered silent.

Jabez was offering everything he'd once wanted: a place away from here, where he would be accepted, perhaps even respected. A place out of Weldir and Lindiwe's control and touch.

Jabez had once been his friend, and he'd enjoyed being by his jovial, although pampered, side. The man was funny in his own morbid way.

He lowered his skull so his sight could dart over the ground. *What do I want?*

"Think about it, Merikh. Forgive what has happened in the past, and we can return to the way we were before. In doing so, your kind will be freed from my hatred, and we can leave here and make our own world."

"Do not place that burden on me," Merikh bit as he turned up his white sight. "Don't give me no other alternative, or I will see my brothers harmed if I choose to reject your offer."

"I wouldn't, but unfortunately, they are the only two options available to me. Either I'm forced to stay here and figure out a way to disable Weldir's ward, or I leave with the only person who can leave with me. I've already offered your *brothers* to join me, but they have chosen not to. You can save them from their stupidity or die along with them – but know I do not issue that with animosity towards you. This is war, and even those who choose no side can fall from their inaction."

Merikh would have thought this was some kind of ploy or trick to trap him, but his stern expression said it wasn't. Jabez was being truthful, and Merikh was the only one who could, or even would, cross that portal with him.

I grow tired of fighting. I grow tired of blood, death, and hatred.

The path Jabez was offering was a bloody one, but it was one he'd already been walking. Just a few months ago, he would have leapt at this chance. He'd been pleading for something like this to come along.

Perhaps protecting his siblings and their spawn would have been part of his reasoning for accepting, but he would have done it just to escape. He would have done it for himself.

But now?

He no longer wanted to feel blood cooling in his hands when he could feel warm strands of coily white hair. He no longer wanted to dig his claws in to shred flesh when he'd rather tickle them along the indents of Raewyn's spine, or thigh, or the nape of her neck. He'd rather his tongue be coated in her, every part of her, rather than the tangy, coppery taste of blood and entrails, or stomach acid.

He hadn't realised he was giving up on his hatred – until a pretty Elf tried to smother it in her kindness.

I don't want to disappoint her. I don't want to... hurt her.

If Jabez wished to destroy her people, that meant her as well – unless he chose to spare her.

Raewyn would never stand for that. She wouldn't stand idle

while those around her were harmed. She would try something, anything, to get the fighting to stop. If he joined Jabez, he would become part of her suffering.

Fuck, why does my chest hurt so much?

He clawed at the pectoral muscle over his heart until he'd drawn purple blood, wishing to rid himself of this pain. It deepened at the picture of her covered in her own blood, with blue lips and a lifeless stare he'd seen far, far too often in his life.

A stare he'd been the reason for.

"I can see you need some time to think about it," Jabez said quietly, which startled Merikh out of his thoughts. He stood and brushed off his maroon pants before rubbing one of his backward-curling horns. "For now, I'll call for the Demons to back off. You have a week. If you don't come to my castle by then, I'll know you've made your decision."

"My home is the furthest point from your castle," Merikh snapped with a growl.

Jabez shot him a knowing smile.

"We both know it will take you a little over a day if you run really, really fast. Unless your new gut slows you down, of course." His chuckle was warm as he began to disappear, teleporting away like he often would. "I know you'll come, so don't leave me waiting too long."

Merikh, unsure if his legs could take the weight of the burden that had just been cast upon him, stayed where he sat.

What the hell do I do? How was he supposed to pick a side? *Why can I never just pick my own side?*

Why must he be put in the middle of everything? Why must he be the one to know everything, deal with everything, be tormented by everything? Why could he not have just one moment of peace in his life before everything went to shit?

If I choose Jabez, Raewyn will come to harm. I promised to get her home, and I don't wish to change that simply because of this. But what would be the point in getting her home if he planned to help Jabez destroy it anyway? *She's his sister. Would he let me protect her if I convince her to join us?*

He could already see what would happen. Raewyn would hate him if he even tried to bring it up to her. His only option would be to get her home without letting Jabez know of her existence here, and without telling her if he changed sides.

Yet... he wanted to go to her realm with... *her.*

The life she was offering, even if it meant he could never see her again, was far more pleasant than the blood-filled path Jabez wanted him to walk.

But if I do that, my brothers will continue to be attacked.

He may dislike them, want nothing to do with them, but the last thing he wanted was to be part of their destruction. He, in his own way, wanted to protect them.

What if I convince the Elvish people to let them come?

It would also weaken Weldir, since he needed his 'servants' to bring him clean souls. Then again, it may not matter in the end.

If I travel with Raewyn to Jabez's castle and use his portal, I now have a week to do so safely. He may even be given permission to freely walk inside, and with a good plan, they could shoot for the portal before Jabez even noticed.

Merikh reached up while crossing his arms and grabbed his horns to yank on them. A sharp whine hollowed his chest. The last time he'd been this distressed was when he'd discovered he'd killed his own brother, and that he wasn't going to return no matter how long he sat by his broken skull.

It was pure and utter agony.

His orbs broke as droplets began to float around his skull, and he snarled and snapped his fangs at each one. He hated the evidence of his ethereal tears, that they physically represented the twisted emotions eating him up inside.

Should he return to his old friend, or trust the female who could only give him promises – without actually knowing if she could fulfil them?

Both seemed selfish and yet selfless at the same time.

Merikh didn't know how long he internally struggled for, but sitting there in the disappearing sun would do nothing. For some reason, all he wanted was to watch Raewyn in the hope it would comfort him.

In the hope it would help him make his decision. What was good or what was right?

Thankful his orbs turned solid again, he finally stood. Every step closer to his home only deepened the hollow pit that had formed in his chest.

I don't know what to do anymore...

Just as he stepped into the entryway, the smell of clary sage wafted towards him, and a bright light flashed. An immense amount of heat caused him to step back, his fur threatening to singe.

It was too hot, too bright. The pressure was so immense that when he lifted his arm, he saw it shaking as he tried to protect not his orbs, but his face, as his senses were annihilated all at once. There was even a *sound* coming from it, like someone had bashed a metal pole against a hard surface, and the vibrating *ting* of it radiated.

Something red and black shook in his sight, and he realised it was his own arm. Except something strange was happening to it, to him. His arm began to separate, his physical self and his red-spectre self pulling apart, like his body and soul were vibrating in two different directions on separate wavelengths.

Everything else had gone white, his red spectre leaving him, and he feared the worst. She'd killed them both, and he was about to enter the afterworld.

It only took a few seconds for the light to dim, for the vibration to gentle, and for the heat and pressure to soften.

His body stopped trying to split apart. The world came back to show him the brown and grey of his cave walls, and the stone bench that matched them.

He didn't get the chance to assess what strange thing had just happened to him, how he'd seen the red ghost of his arm, because there Raewyn stood.

Above her palms, a drop of sunlight floated. It lit up everything, threatening to absorb all colour.

The heat was so intense, he was unable to step much closer, or he'd begin to wither away. The radiation that came off it itched his flesh.

He was within its dangerous radius, but just on the fringes of it, where he could survive.

She, however, had a grand smile upon her face, seemingly unaffected by its power. The starburst pupils of her eyes were glowing, multicoloured, as were her floating hair and body markings.

She was utterly, heartbreakingly beautiful.

With just one spell, she'd chased away the constant darkness that had been present in his cave – as well as within the corners of his heart.

He realised what he'd been seeking for years was something to chase away everything that hurt, everything bleak and dark. He'd been seeking his polar opposite so he could finally feel wanted and accepted.

He'd been seeking his own little light, a star to shine in the shroud of darkness and endless void of his life.

I want her.

Whether it was here in the safety of his ward or in her realm filled with all the magnificent things she'd told him of, whether it was by Jabez's side or by her people's side, Merikh wanted the one thing that had ever allowed him to feel... hateless.

His orbs turned a bright flamingo pink as he stared at his own personal piece of light – and it wasn't the one she was holding.

I don't want to let her go. I want her to be mine.

He thought he could handle being anywhere, in any world, so long as she was there to brighten it for him.

THIRTY-FIVE

The moment Merikh looked upon Raewyn, he'd made his decision.

Unfortunately for everyone else, it was the most selfish decision he could possibly make.

Whenever she wasn't looking at him, his orbs couldn't decide whether they wanted to be bright pink or a deep orange.

I will keep her... here... where it is safe. Where no one could touch her, not Jabez, not the humans, Demons, Mavka, or other Elves.

Because he had chosen her. He would convince her to become his bride. Then, they could do what they wanted, go where they wanted, and she would be a Phantom who couldn't come to harm. Jabez couldn't harm her, and once she gave him her soul, no one could permanently take her away from him.

They would be forever entwined.

Just like her body, her soul would be his to guide.

Through the darkness and the light, the pain and the pleasure, the happiness and the anger, she would be his. He was hoping she could guide him in return, so he didn't fall back into the bleakness from before she came and upturned his life and heart.

How do I convince her?

He wrapped his hand around the side of his snout while he sat on the shore and watched her swim.

Splashing water around as she kicked, she looked content. She'd been much happier since she'd figured out the sun stone spell.

In her excitement, thinking she'd been alone at the time, she'd run on the spot, squealing in joy while holding it.

He'd never been so overwhelmed with happiness that he'd done anything remotely like that, but it only gobbled him up even more. He wanted that, with her. He wanted her to share that with him, for him to be the reason she did something so silly.

The problem was, he didn't think he could convince Raewyn to become his. He still had his doubts, but if he kept her in his home for long enough, he wondered if she would warm to the idea.

Did he plant the seed first, or wait until she revealed her own feelings? *Will it even be possible for her to love me?*

Merikh grimaced. *Fuck, I wouldn't love me.*

Was it still possible though? He sincerely hoped so.

Without knowing it, she had become a captive in his home.

Two days had passed since he realised that all the tender, aching sensations in his chest he'd been feeling towards her were much more violent than he'd allowed.

Every time she tried to talk to him about the plan to go through the Elven portal, he'd found a way to redirect the conversation. Now that she had successfully created the sun stone, she was ready to face the Demons, go home, and share her 'scientific' breakthrough with her people.

His orbs would always threaten to turn orange, but he worried the moment they were in her city she'd come to her senses, and she would leave him.

He palmed his bony face. *I'm the worst. I think this is the most selfish thing I've ever done.* It wasn't going to stop him, though, not if it meant he could hold her soul – all by her willingness to give it to him.

He considered just taking it. It's not like she could stop him, but he'd rather not take that choice away from her. He didn't want her resentment when he was hoping he could be charming.

I don't know how to be charming. He just knew how to destroy things.

Should I get her a flower? Don't human women like gifts? He already got her tulips, though.

She will start questioning me.

His avoidance about them leaving. Why he was being different. Even touching her had become a strained task, since it felt like his heart and stomach were trying to switch places... and maybe his brain, too.

His cock jerked in excitement behind his seam, much needier than usual. It didn't help that he hadn't released in a while. She was also swimming in that red dress she'd ruined, the one he promised he'd tear from her next time.

For some reason, it was like his cock and heart were linked. His desire to bond them was making him more sensitive, and he'd held off touching her when he thought he might do something stupid in the middle of pumping into her.

He didn't know what it was, but it was either take her soul or reveal his feelings – both were disastrous. He'd rather explain it to her while he was clear-headed.

To distract himself from his thoughts, he finished working on attaching the last strap to the quill guard for his back. As if he couldn't help it, once it was attached, and he only needed to finish closing the two large leather pieces together, his sight drifted to her.

He tapped his tail against the water's surface to let her know she was swimming the wrong way, and she redirected herself with a smile upon her face.

It was currently nighttime, but the sun hadn't long disappeared.

He continued sewing the guard together, then sighed once it was done. He threw it over his back and worked on strapping it across his torso to check that it was suitable. Even though it was good enough for now, he sighed heavily.

He thought it would have brought the joy he'd been seeking.

Instead, all he could ask himself was, *How am I meant to ask for her soul?*

He wanted to come right out and ask so he could get it over with. It would be easier than living with the guilt that was already festering, and he didn't understand why his tender feelings for her had to hurt so fucking much. It was like his heart had a barbed-wire ball inside it that kept stabbing the soft muscle on each pump.

Like anything that had to do with her, he found himself hesitant when he'd never really been that way before.

I don't have time to hesitate.

Either her patience would wear out, or the clock for Jabez's amnesty would – which would make things harder. He had a window of freedom for both of them.

She's smart. Much smarter than him, that was obvious. *How long do I have before she realises what I'm doing, that I plan to keep her here?*

An hour? Another day? He could almost *hear* the clock ticking.

For the first time in his life, he truly felt like a bad guy, a jerk, a... selfish monster.

He looked down to his claws. *What will I do if she says no?* Or even worse, a definitive *never.*

Fuck, he finally found something that made him feel good, would make him happy, and it just so happened to be something as unpredictable as another person. He'd been striving this entire time to find it on his own.

His hands clenched into fists, realising it was doubtful he would have found it on his own. He was cursed to experience little else but anger.

I needed someone else to show me how to feel something other than hate.

"What are you thinking about?" Raewyn asked him in a singsong, yet nonchalant, voice.

She was swimming his way, and he tapped his tail so she knew exactly where he was.

"Nothing, just watching," he lied before thinking better of it. "I finished making my back guard."

Her lids lowered. "Then why have your orbs turned blue?"

He raised a hand to cover one eye socket, only registering now that his sight had turned a colour reflecting his melancholy thoughts. He wondered what she saw when his sight shifted.

"Actually, I wanted to ask you something."

She came directly between his folded knees and jumped up on straightened arms to hover outside of the water.

"Do you now?" she asked with a sly smirk, barely an inch from his snout. If he wanted to, he could have stolen a kiss from her sweet lips.

His sight darted down to look at how her wet red dress moulded perfectly to her body: the vee dip of her pubic mound, the arches of her hip bones, her navel and sides. Her cleavage was attempting to spill from the slit of the neckline. Her dress only hid her flesh. It did nothing to hide the undercurves of her breasts, or her hard nipples jutting from her mounds. He could even see the little bumps of her areolas.

His sight instantly turned purple, and his cock jerked from just staring at her tits – like he was some ill-minded human who couldn't keep their thoughts straight. Then it dipped lower to look at her navel and the flat of her stomach.

Her scent tingled his nose, clean and fresh from her swim, but just as brain fogging. Already, he wanted to mess her up until she smelt utterly of him.

"I want to knot you so badly," he absentmindedly said, subtly licking at his snout.

He'd been wanting that for a long while.

"Pardon?" Her arms buckled, and she slipped back into the water.

His sight instantly turned reddish pink.

"No. Wait." Did he really just say that? That's not what he

meant to ask at all! "I mean..."

He turned his skull to the side in the hopes of hiding the shift, but his sight flickered back to purple when he peeked at her.

Then again... If she rejected having all of him inside her, it might show if he were to make a mistake asking for her to bond with him. If she accepted it, wanted it – something that was permanent – would it reveal if she had deeper feelings for him?

He didn't want to damage whatever was happening between them by asking for her soul too soon. But this? He could play with it, test her, see if it was safe for him to lay his craving desire before her.

There's only one way to find out.

THIRTY-SIX

Why did Raewyn get the impression that wasn't what he'd been intending to ask? It hadn't really been a question, either.

Still, she was a little confused by his statement.

Knot me? Like the Taihee? It was a sexual function that only certain species could perform.

The heat drained from her face, not in trepidation, but in realisation. *So that's what the twisted ring at the base of his cock is!*

It was the biggest face-palm moment she could've had.

She'd held it, licked it, felt it swell, and she'd never put two and two together. Then again, how was she supposed to know? She'd never experienced one before.

Purple sparks flashed in her sight. Whatever awkwardness Merikh had just uttered fell away, and he reached forward to cup under her chin.

He slightly lifted her until she was halfway out of the water and slipped his front fangs against her cheek. His breath washed over her, dancing into her hair around her ear.

"Yes, my little starshine, I want to knot that pretty body of yours," he rumbled in his gruff voice, causing her to shiver.

A quiet squeal left her when he slipped his arm around her waist and lifted her completely from the water. He folded her onto his crossed legs so that her knees were resting on his thighs while the backs of her feet were over his shins.

My little starshine? He's never called me that before.

He'd called her a little fairy, but nothing with 'my' in front of it. Who was this possessive Duskwalker and what did they do with Merikh? She didn't think he'd ever give her a playful pet name.

"My little starshine?" she rasped when he slipped his tongue from her collarbone up to her jawline. "Can't you call me Rae?"

"I don't want to call you something everyone else does," he uttered as he licked across her ear. "I want to name you after something bright and mesmerising, just like you."

Such sentimental words had her turning to putty in his big hands.

Her nipples, which had softened due to the warmth of his body pressing against hers, tightened again. Tenderness pooled in her belly, and it only grew as he began licking drops of water from her sternum and shoulders, as though every part of her was tasty.

"So how about it?" One hand gripped her backside to knead a cheek, while the other palmed her thigh before cupping her entire pussy. "Will you take me deeper here?"

"That's not possible," she whispered, dabbing her tongue at the seam of her lips as she ground against his rough hand in welcome.

He took in a deeper breath than usual, and she wasn't sure if it was to take in her scent, or a breath of courage. Who knew with Merikh; he could be both hot and cold at the same time – difficult to read.

"But it is," he said, gently rubbing her clit between two fingers as he drew away. His sharp claws tickled her abdomen when he palmed it. "I can change you so that my cock can fit, my little starshine, and I would... *adore* it if you would hold all of me."

Merikh had changed much over the past two weeks since they'd truly started touching. He could be endearing when he wanted to be, could be direct, but not like now. Something was different.

Raewyn had a funny feeling he was asking for more than just deeper pleasure.

She leaned back, and it gave him more freedom to slip his hand further under her dress until he was cupping a breast. Raewyn flinched the first time his thumb flicked over her nipple before she settled into its teasing rhythm.

"Why didn't you tell me about this sooner?" she panted, wishing her voice wasn't so coarse already.

"Because it may be permanent," he answered, licking up her throat. She lifted her head as goosebumps broke out in his tongue's wake. "I don't know if I can undo it."

Was that why he was being so coquettish? It was like he was trying to bring her into a heated state where she'd be more inclined to do whatever he wanted, so long as it felt good. His touches, his words, his persistent but teasing licks, they were distracting.

This is the first time he's asked me for something I haven't instigated. She could understand why he hadn't asked her before; there was a high likelihood she may have denied him.

To alter her body in a way that may not be reversible... sure, that was a little frightening. It was like taking a leap with him, a big one, considering his massive size.

Raewyn could have chosen to be playful or teasing with him, but she didn't want to crush his confidence, not even a little. He pushed the hand gripping her backside between her thighs to pet her entrance and clit at the same time, and a small moan broke from her.

Then he sheathed his claws and buried two fingers within her core. She tensed around them.

"Already so wet for me," he groaned as he pumped them. "I want to feel you take all of me."

It wasn't an easy to decision to make.

Had it been anyone else asking her, she would have closed

her thighs and run for the hills. But it was Merikh, and the thing was...she liked him much more than she'd probably showed him.

When they got to her home realm, she'd been intending to kick Cykran to the side as her assistant – although gently, since she wanted to maintain their friendship – so Merikh could take his place. She was sure her home could fit the big Duskwalker, and since she lived alone and they'd already had a trial run here, they could easily live together.

The other councilmembers would want someone to 'keep an eye' on him, and Raewyn was intending to be his watcher. They wouldn't know it was because he was... special to her.

She'd never desired someone as much as she did him. She liked all parts of him, the good, the bad, the mean, the sweet. He was endearing, only because many of the negative sides of him were from what she considered a terrible past. What if she nurtured him, healed him?

Just look at him now.

The growly, silent, scary Duskwalker she'd met was now a rumbling, teasing one as he carefully touched her – being so light with all the delicate places of her body when he could rend anything to pieces.

Was she certain of him? No, but they had *time,* and plenty of it. Nothing had to be decided now, and they could discover more about each other in her home realm, where she was comfortable.

This step was obviously important to him, though, and she didn't wish to snuff out his flame of hope. He'd even taken the courage to ask her; how could she deny him?

"Will it hurt?" she whispered, grinding onto his fingers, feeling how wet she'd gotten by how she coated them.

"Maybe a little," he answered honestly. "But that will be because of my claws cutting into you. I will heal you, but I think you might enjoy the feeling of swallowing more of my cock."

He's done this before. She nibbled at her bottom lip, a little relieved that he at least knew what he was doing.

"Okay," she conceded, darting her hands forward to unbutton his pants – she needed to be quick before she changed her mind.

She hadn't expected to feel his cock bulging against it, already extruded but thick, like it was sheltered by his tentacles.

The moment her palm gripped underneath it, his tentacles released, giving her his slick-covered shaft to hold.

He swiftly withdrew his hand from between her thighs, fisted the back of her dress, and tore it from her. The fabric ripping across her skin burned a little, but it was more pleasant than it was painful.

Within seconds, Merikh gripped her arse to push her pussy against the underside of his shaft while licking across her nipple. Her legs wrapped over his thighs until the sides of her feet touched the grass, reminding her that they were outside.

"S-shouldn't we go inside first?"

"I can't wait that long," he groaned. "I don't care if anyone sees me fucking you."

She stroked her clit with the groove on the underside of him, teasing herself, and it made her wetter. Her breaths became breathier, especially when he drew his tongue over the column of her throat.

Before long, she was the one to whisper, "Inside. I need you inside me."

He ground her hard against him before slipping her higher. He gave her an appreciative growl when she helped to direct the head of his cock against her entrance. Then, she was falling onto it. The head popped through, and each ridge caused her breaths to turn higher pitched.

His tentacles softly wrapped around her hips.

Like usual, once he was seated as deep as she could take him, heated shivers swept over her. She trembled as she began stirring him inside, needing movement, unable to help rocking on the hard girth within her.

Her eyelids flickered as his cock grazed against her most tender places, and she leaned into him. With messy kisses, she let out little cries against his skull.

"Wait," he bit as he gripped her arse to stop her when she tried to pick up speed, rubbing him deep back and forth. "I need to explain that once you take all of me, I won't be able to stop once my knot is swelling."

"That's fine," she whispered as she fought against his hold so she could move.

I already feel so full. How would it feel to have more?

Feeling close to him, she buried her face against the side of his neck, stealing his warmth. His orange and cinnamon scent tangled within her mind, and all her fears and worries slipped away. A desperate need began building, and her inner walls spasmed around him.

"Raewyn," he growled in warning. "I will be different. I need you to understand this. I won't *want* to stop."

His growl and warning were ignored. "Okay, whatever you want."

Her hands danced over his chest. She detected the straps there, and she pushed them higher until they were slipping over his shoulders.

He finished the guard.

She tentatively put her arms around his neck, and her heart shyly fluttered at the fact it was safe to do so. She put her weight into her rolling hip movements, her arms around him like an anchor. A sharp moan escaped her, and she clung tighter, liking the way his fur tickled her chest.

She'd never held him before, and it felt so different.

She stopped caring about anything but the way he felt inside her, against her, trapped in her arms. Her bucking was only slight; there was barely any motion, but she knew two things: Merikh was inside her, and his cockhead and ridges were hitting her absolute favourite places.

At this rate... "Mmm," she moaned.

His pants were heavy, laboured, drowsy, like he could feel her pulsing around him. He grated, "You haven't taken all of me yet. Don't you dare come."

Raewyn's eyes rolled back as he palmed her stomach. *Too late,* she thought, just as she pressed her face against him and let out a loud cry.

Her legs twitched as she came around him, and she moved faster as liquid heat spilled from her while she tried to milk him of his own.

She clung tighter, moved faster, and her hips jerked.

That was until she felt a sharp stab of claws in her abdomen and then the sudden jolt of him shoving her all the way to the bottom of his cock – the twisted ring was difficult to push past, the rest easy. Raewyn clutched the edges of his back guard as she let out a pleasure-filled scream like she'd been sucker punched in the G-spot.

She stopped moving with her lips agape and just trembled and twitched against him. Her feet lifted off the ground, arching as she dug her heels into his back. Her pussy walls clenched him hard, squeezing him.

Moments ago, she'd been wet from the lake, but she was now covered in a layer of sweat.

His choking snarl was all that remained once her orgasm, which had exploded in intensity, finally faded. He was gripping her arse with both hands and pushing her down hard. Quaking just as much as her, his guard had lifted, like his quills were agitated and trying to rise.

It held, thankfully.

"Merikh?" Raewyn whispered, her pulse pounding around his shaft. She was throbbing everywhere, but he never stopped being tense.

With his head resting on her shoulder, his breaths were even heavier than before, like he was barely able to breathe. Quiet whines burst from him; she'd never heard him make those noises before during sex. He felt impossibly hard within her.

"You don't know how long I've wanted to do this," he rasped, his voice husky. "You don't know how *amazing* it feels.

So warm, and wet, coming around me while your tight pussy sucks every inch of me." His claws dug into her flesh a little too deep for comfort, and she bounced forward to escape. "Fuck. I feel like my heart is about to stop beating."

Good, because he was currently cock deep in her heart; not physically, but metaphorically.

She reached between them to touch how deep he was now.

The only thing not within her were the two oval sacs at the very base of him she was pressing against. She slipped her hand up her body, wondering where he ended within her – perhaps just past her navel?

The closeness between them now allowed her to feel his rounded stomach pressing against hers when he breathed in, and somehow, it was more intimate than before. His tentacles also wrapped around her more, hugging her, and she wiggled into them.

He hissed in a breath, but his exhale was shaking. He pulled back and licked at her lips, since they were almost the same height with her on top of him like this. When she parted them to allow his tongue within her mouth, he held the back of her head, his claws stabbing through her hair to scrape against her scalp.

With his other hand still supporting her arse, she started falling to the side. Merikh placed her back upon the ground. As she wrapped her legs freely around his waist, the heels of her feet against his guard, he laid over her by straightening his legs.

Supporting himself on his elbows, his tongue swirling within her mouth, he ground in deep, and Raewyn moaned against his fangs.

It was a different kind of fullness, one that had her tightening in bliss beneath him. Keeping her arm around his neck, the other wrapped around his back, she dug her nails into the leather.

This is the first time I've held him like this. He was massive in her arms, but Raewyn forced him to give her more of his weight.

When he finally began to move, she winced each time he

tried to pass the twisted ring through her. He let out sharp groans, his body tensing each time, while he thrust surprisingly slow and measured.

She wished it didn't feel so uncomfortable, like that part of him was just too thick to keep moving through her entrance, especially when he threaded his arm under her knees to spread her legs further apart, trying to ease his way in for her. He must have noticed how tight it was, that not even his spell had saved her.

Turning her head to the side to remove his tongue from her mouth, she gulped for breath. "I-I'm sorry, but it hurts. Can you not move your knot through me so much?"

Merikh's thrusts didn't change in speed, but he did draw back. She was surprised he didn't bury himself deeper.

He lifted her hips up, one of her legs bent over his right elbow, and placed both his hands against the ground to steady himself, forcing her back to curl.

"Better?" When she nodded, relaxing beneath him once more, he licked across her exposed neck. "Good, because it'll be yours soon enough."

Why did that sound ominous?

Raewyn didn't care, not when she was forced to hold his forearms for dear life when he began to thrust fast. With the way her hips were tilted towards him, the head and the inches of ridges behind it bombarded a spot that had her moaning.

She appreciated that he cared for her wellbeing, even when he'd been enjoying it. To show him her gratefulness, she reached up, found a horn, and yanked him closer.

Raewyn kissed whatever part of his skull made contact with her lips, and then just gave little cries against the cool bone. Sweat dripped down her back and chest, his heat and her own arousal smothering her.

Why did he have to smell so good, sound so good? Why did every part of her body sing for him? His thick stomach rubbing against her own kept spreading warmth throughout her. His fur always made her skin tingle whenever it touched her. His tentacles were clasping at her skin, but she liked how soft they were, how they didn't bruise her. Even his breaths huffing over her had her breaking beneath him.

Why did he have such a strange cock that felt this wonderful?

There wasn't a part of him, from tail, to horn, to claw, that she didn't thaw for.

His subtle groans made her want to tangle her own lewd noises with them so they were one harmonious song.

It wasn't fair. It shouldn't be this easy to disarm her, and yet, here she was, about to lose her mind to another mind-scrambling orgasm.

"Merikh," she whimpered, her voice hoarse and airy. *"Merikh."*

"I like it when you call my name like that." His cock swelled momentarily and sent her into the depths of bliss.

His growlish groan from her spasming and clenching around his cock was drowned out by her loud, unhidden cry. Her head tilted as she arched, which only made his shaft gouge deeper.

Her eyelids flickered as her eyes rolled before she closed them altogether to clench them. Her nails cut into his forearm guard, while her other hand tore down his chest and dug into his flexing muscles.

Merikh let go of her leg and curled his arms across her back, holding her tightly as he laid down on top of her. Locked into place, just as her body was softening and she was turning limp, he began shoving all of his cock inside her.

It was even tighter to squeeze the twisted ring at the base of his cock through her entrance. Before she could ask him to wait, he tilted his hips one way, then the other, and popped it through.

Raewyn gasped, just as a choke tore from him.

Once more, he was seated deep, but any uncomfortable pang was annihilated by his jerks. There was a wonderful pressure, one that was unusual but had her legs twitching like crazy.

It was growing as he stroked her insides. Her eyes flung open in surprise and tension, and she wrapped her arms around his torso to hold him, hug him, just... anything to help steady herself through this.

Oh, holy maiden. I can feel it. She could feel his knot thickening, ballooning inside her, and it was pushing into spots that were too much.

She just came, and yet each stroke was sending her into a lather. It was so wonderful, it almost bordered on pain; no person should feel something this pleasurable. Her mind, her body, neither could handle it. It was too intense.

And he was getting *bigger.*

Tears dotted her eyelashes as she started orgasming again, but this time, it didn't stop.

Merikh shuddered wildly the moment he buried the entire length of his cock within her. Pushing past her pubic mound had been a challenge.

He'd been intending to push his knot into her before it began swelling, but her coming suddenly started the process of his own oncoming release.

This would usually be the point when he'd begin slamming into her, hard, fast, trying to ease the ache in his cock and exposed knot. Usually, when the twisted ring thickened, the growing heat in it against the cool air would plead with him to bury it within her. It would be agony, a craving he couldn't satisfy.

Now, though... Merikh's feverish shudders became violent as he slowed his thrusts. He rammed in hard, grinding his way in as he laid over her, their tightly clasped bodies slipping over each other.

His groan was one of utter bliss, shaken, low, and dazed.

His knot was one of the most sensitive parts of him, just like the head of his cock that kept lightly bumping against her cervix.

Having both snuggled within her, two intense erogenous zones, broke him.

So warm. She's so warm. His pants were strangled, and his mouth filled with drool that dripped through his fangs and onto the grass. *So wet and tight.* She was getting wetter each time he moved, milking him in heavy, quivering spasms that didn't cease.

He couldn't think of anything other than the way his groin radiated in pleasure, except for the tingles that kept racing up and down his spine.

If he wanted to speak, he was incapable. Breathing was becoming optional, and he was certain his heart was about to give out.

Any control he had on himself was obliterated. Gone. Non-existent.

His sight was such a deep colour of purple, it was like seeing through a dark fog, and all he could see was white hair. All he could scent was her, not the grass, the air, the dirt, or the lake. It drowned him, suffocated him, *ate* at him.

When he scented blood, he stopped gripping her and turned his arms so he could claw at the dirt. Her legs were wrapped around his sides, kicking and squirming, and he felt each of her contortions around his excitedly jerking shaft.

It feels so good. Nothing had felt better. His tongue fell forward so he could taste the air and breathe better.

"Merikh," she cried, which only made his knot jump in size and force a gasp from her. "Wait. Please. I-It's too much."

Her words were inaudible to him, like his mind couldn't process anything more than what was happening inside her. Her voice frolicked around him, lulling him even further.

His thrusts became shallower. His knot was descending downwards and giving him fewer inches to pull back with, and no more time to play.

Nothing right then would have been able to separate them.

Even if he wanted to stop, he was too swollen to pull out of her. They were locked together.

Yet the pleasure was so enormous and consuming that he wouldn't, *couldn't*, pull away. He wouldn't stop moving until he spent inside her, even if she begged, pleaded. Not even a Demon, human, or another Mavka would stop him – he would have just extended his quills and protected her from harm as he mindlessly rutted her.

Merikh was thoughtless, incapable of control, exactly like when his rage and hunger took over. Nothing was going to pull him out of this – which is why he'd warned her in the first place.

Since he wasn't listening, she reached behind him and grabbed one of his horns. She yanked his head back, tilting it and bending his neck unnaturally, and he only quaked in bliss from it. He hoped she would pull harder, so he tried to fuck deeper.

Although the word never truly formed in his mind, his body, his soul, his heart, each one of them radiated the essence of *mine.*

There was no violence in his thrusts. He didn't even have the strength to growl. There was not an aggressive bone left in his body. Instead, he had been replaced by a creature completely numbed by pleasure.

He was just a pulsating ache, a pathetically needy male.

Her orgasms continued to gush from her, and they dripped down the length of his tentacles. Everything was saturated in her, and the squelch of their bodies was loud as it rung in his ears. She kept milking him for his impending liquid bliss.

Merikh was about to flood her with it.

A pleasure-stricken sob broke from her, right as he perceived something moving against his stomach with the way he was crushing her beneath him. His knot had swelled to the point it was bulging from within.

Poor little female. What else did she think was going to happen? She'd explored it, touched it, knew what it was – she should have realised what it would do inside her, how it would feel pressing against her inner walls.

Oh god. So close. Can't stop. Can't stop. He lost track of his sight completely.

She gave up tugging him and just held him with all her limbs. She even bit into the side of his neck, muffling her moans and cries.

The desire to bite back struck him, but it was overshadowed by what her little flat teeth caused. His hand shot down to grab her arse to keep her still, while the other ripped apart the dirt right next to her head.

His quills tried to lift. They pulled on all the straps covering him and threatened to snap under the strength of his body.

Just as he pulled back to plug her, his tentacles did something they'd never done before. They pushed her away, giving into the same desire rather than trying to pull her down him like usual.

He sucked in a breath, right as his lungs collapsed. His heart paused, just as his cock took over the pumping. His sight blacked out and she let out a gasp at the first heavy burst of seed that exploded from him.

Merikh accidentally clawed the bottom of her arse as he let out a strangled roar. He trapped her beneath his body, curling around her like he wanted to crawl into her. His hips jerked with quakes while he filled her with his liquid ecstasy.

He didn't think his cock had ever been this hard before, his knot this swollen, or if he ever came as hard or as much as he did right then. Nothing could compare to filling Raewyn's soft, giving pussy like this.

His head collapsed next to hers, resting like it was too heavy for him to hold up while he pumped into her. His elbows shook, threatening to buckle and truly crush her under his heavy weight.

She was so wonderful, so perfect for giving him this, for letting him experience this kind of rapture with her. She was a paradise for his heart, as much as his body. For someone who had only experienced the pain of damnation, he knew, all the way to the very core of his being, he'd destroy anyone who tried to take her away from him.

When his cock ceased twitching within her, Merikh couldn't move a muscle. Raewyn went languid, and her arms fell to the sides.

Both panted, but his were laced with whines as aftershocks caused tiny extra drops to come from him – like his body was confused. Fuck, it still felt like he was spending each time. At this rate, he was going to hurt his own cock.

It gave a painful throb.

After a few moments, Raewyn gained a little strength. With it, she started punching at his sides with the bottom of her fists.

"I-I told you to stop," she weakly howled.

Did she? He hadn't heard that.

Merikh wrapped his arms around her so he could hug her. He spread questionable liquid from her arse to her lower back, some of it thick and sticky, some of it watery. What he did know was that he could smell blood.

Thankfully, her arousal was overpowering it, but he healed her of any wounds and gained a decent cut over his own arse.

"I'm sorry," he whispered, hugging her tighter. "I can't help it when I'm this deep. It's one of the reasons I didn't do this sooner. I can't think at the end." Literally.

"I came so much, it hurt," she moaned. "I thought my pussy was going to fall off or explode."

Despite the pounding in his head, like blood was rushing back to his brain, Merikh choked on a laugh. He finally lifted his head so he could lick at her tear-stained cheek.

"Does that mean you won't let me do this again?"

Her lips tightened as her eyes squinted into a glare. "I didn't say that."

"Good, because I want to do it again. Now, even."

Gods, he'd want to do this every minute of the day with her.

At that thought, Merikh pulled back so he could look down. He rocked back and forth once to check the state of everything inside her. His head darted up when she slapped at his chest.

"Not yet! I need time. Everything is tingling and sensitive

right now." Then she lowered her hand to her abdomen. "And I feel... really weird inside."

Staring down at where they were joined, Merikh licked at his snout. He didn't doubt she felt 'weird.'

His knot was no longer creating a bulge, since it was going down, but she did look... swollen with his seed. Not a *drop* had spilled from her cunt, his knot keeping it inside. When he moved even a little, his cock barely grazed her walls, since she was overflooded and stretched with his cum.

"I would like to show you something," he said in a teasing tone filled with so much *heat*.

The shudder that came from him was out of fierce lust and joy for what was about to be revealed.

"Oh no," she cried as she covered her eyes – like that would save her when he began sharing his sight with her. "What is it? What have you done to me?"

Merikh thumbed her clit and then smeared a wet line all the way to her navel. Everything was softer than usual, and her stomach didn't appear so flat. He was rather thankful she had the contraceptive chain around her waist, since he wondered if her holding this much of his seed could potentially defy all odds and accidentally impregnate her.

"M-Merikh?" she nervously asked when he bounced his thumb against the flesh of her stomach, pushing his seed around.

He worked his softening knot, and yellow filled his vision when he finally yanked it from her. A waterfall of white semen gushed behind it, pouring onto his cock and the ground as a flood.

Purple instantly replaced his sight, and he was tempted to bury his thick cock back within her. It looked a little veinier than usual, still unbearably hard – but only because it seemed to be stuck in an erect state.

That probably *wasn't* a good thing.

"Oh my gosh! That... that was... You did not just show me that!" She closed her legs and turned to the side. "That was so perverse. Why *me*?"

"Whine all you like," he warmly chuckled, dragging her closer. He stopped sharing his sight with her, but he was rather happy with himself that he'd shown her something so perverted. "But you came around me the entire time. I didn't come this much on my own."

She'd drained more from him by her pussy constantly quivering and spasming around his shaft.

She played dead, acting all limp and lifeless, as he picked her up while he was on his knees. It wasn't the first time she'd done this.

He was forced to wrap her legs around his waist himself, then worked on getting her arms over his shoulders. Merikh hugged her, thankful he could do so properly now because of the guards he'd made. He rubbed the side of his skull against her ear, cheek, and soft curls to nuzzle her.

He couldn't purr, but he did give her light, appreciative rumbles and growls.

She accepted all of me. Does that mean she would become my bride if I asked her?

He pressed her sternum, which was where her soul was hidden away, right over his heart. *I've never wanted anything as much as I want her to be mine.*

His own piece of starlight.

THIRTY-SEVEN

Basking in everything that was the big Duskwalker, Raewyn brought herself a little closer. Currently, they were lying in bed on their sides, chest to chest. His arms were around her, and his cuddle was so intimate that even his tail had curled around her thigh.

Her left arm was wrapped around him while the other was locked between them. She'd tried to throw her leg over him, but the guy was just too big for her to do that. So, he'd placed his top knee back so she could rest it on his lower thigh.

I've never properly lain with him before. It was no wonder he was already softly snoring, and she liked to think it was because he was utterly content. *I've never been able to touch him while he sleeps.*

Although she was lying with him since she *finally* could, her mind was racing after everything that had happened tonight. The second time had been just as intense as the first. Physically, she was limp as could be.

Having to be taken away from the bed so she could be popped like a freaking bottle was embarrassing, but it was still better than making a mess on the bed. She also kind of liked the feeling of his knot breaking free and then releasing what she'd been holding.

His slower thrusts during sex made it feel more intimate.

She'd gotten to hold him the entire time, claw and bite at him however she wanted. And his sounds... how enamoured he was during it. Well, she would have suffered a third time as long as she got to experience that – even though he'd wrung so much from her, she didn't think she had a drop left to give.

Thank goodness he could lubricate them both. She was raw, but not chafed, a thoroughly taken woman.

In reality, physically, she radiated a level of satisfaction she didn't think was possible. She'd never achieved it before.

Unfortunately, it was her thoughts, her *heart*, sprinting. She'd tried to calm them, tried to ease them so she could just lie there with him, but she was unable to.

She drew her arm back so she could cover her face with her hands and bury both against him. Her ears darted back in anxiety as she bit her lips shut to stop any noise of distress.

I think... I think I'm falling in love with you, Merikh, she thought, unsure if it was a cold or a warm shiver running down her spine. Her heart skipped in her chest, as both shyness and uncertainty tugged at it.

She wasn't averse to loving Merikh. Even if he didn't know it, he was lovely both inside and out. Maybe it was only towards her, but he was kind and considerate, and after today, she knew he could be tender.

He'd stroked her back until he'd fallen asleep, had tried to soothe her, had removed any pain she could have had. He'd checked on her, made sure she was comfortable, asked her if there was anything she needed before he'd started quietly snoring.

The issue was... how could she know if she cared for him for real without going home first?

She could make him fit in her life. She'd even started making plans. But she just didn't know if she could be certain she felt so strongly towards him without having some space. Currently, he was her lifeline; she was utterly dependent on him to help her get home.

Was it some kind of appeasement? She definitely wasn't a captive, but what if her feelings had grown from comfort?

It didn't matter that he was different, but their current situation wasn't normal. Was she attaching herself to him because she was homesick and just needed some way to pacify herself? Her heart said he was her new home, and she didn't like that at all.

Is he even capable of love?

He had to be. He had all these other emotions, but he also wasn't human or an Elf. She worried that love was just too strong of a compassionate emotion for him, especially since it was so vastly opposite to the obvious hatred he held within.

She'd overheard the term 'bride,' but what did it mean? Was it a mate or some kind of bond partner? When she'd asked him about it, he'd shut down the conversation so hard, she wondered if he would even seek something like that. Maybe it wasn't something he wanted, and he was just interested in pleasure rather than anything deeper.

Why did the idea of that hurt?

Trusting him, loving him – she couldn't fully do it here. She needed to see how he treated her people. She needed to see how he treated her when they weren't stuck in the confines of his cave. She needed to know if he wanted more, or if she was just being foolish.

Currently, she was his only option. What if he went to Lezekos City and found another partner he'd prefer? Raewyn was pretty, but there were both men and women who were even more stunning, who had better social skills than her, who weren't work obsessed.

He may resent her when he discovered she'd prefer to be in her laboratory with an experiment in her hands. She was also a synedrus councillor. There would be times she would be busy with long meetings and tasks that required her to drop everything.

Love had never been on her radar – it had just been too

bothersome. She'd been a career-driven woman who hadn't cared if she was alone or not.

What if it bothered him she couldn't give him as much attention as she was able to now? What if she... wasn't good enough?

Raewyn had failing qualities, but they would be better proven when she was back in Nyl'theria. Only then could she trust anything Merikh said – if he felt anything warm and tender towards her that wasn't based purely on getting his dick wet.

Gosh, to think of him like that was tearing her insides apart, but she'd met plenty of men like that. Just because he was a Duskwalker didn't mean he couldn't be the same. His humanity came from *humans*, and they were cruel and selfish in their own way.

What if he incidentally shared in those ideals?

She wanted to ask him, but she also wanted to wait and see.

Raewyn flinched when claws scraped over her scalp as he petted her hair.

"What's the matter?" he asked, his voice husky and groggy. It was so nice, her chest tried to cave in on itself.

"Huh? Nothing. Sorry, did I wake you?"

She tried to settle her heart rate, her breaths, her mind spinning around in her skull.

"Hard not to when your heart is beating so loudly." He wrapped his arms around her tighter, smooshing her against him. "You also smell mildly of fear. You're lucky the other scents on you are so distracting." Then he rubbed the underside of his bony jaw over the top of her head, his maw splitting apart as he yawned. "Don't worry, my little starshine. I promise I won't hurt you."

He softened around her and immediately started snoring again.

Did he think she was scared his wards wouldn't protect her? Raewyn wished his words didn't make her want to toss all her apprehension to the side and just let her feelings take control.

She refused to, and for once, she was the one throwing up a wall between them.

Raewyn didn't know how long they stayed like that. The hours that passed only twisted her stomach further, but not a single part of her wanted to move away from him. If she could have, she would have adored remaining there with him forever. If only the world could fall away and disappear, so she could keep him to herself.

Unfortunately, reality didn't work like that, and eventually, Merikh stirred. She'd barely slept a wink, too many questions plaguing her.

Raewyn had hurt her own feelings so many times, she could feel it festering inside. It nipped away at her centre, her essence, her very *soul* with venom.

"Good morning," he grumbled, before his head shifted slightly. "Well, afternoon."

He started playing with her curls, lifting them up and placing them on his face like he wanted to blanket himself in them.

"So soft." He placed more on top of his skull. "I don't think I've had such a sweet waking. It makes me not want to get up."

It was too sweet, too much. She'd always wanted to experience this side of him, but she couldn't handle it right then.

Raewyn dug her hands into his chest as she placed her forehead against him, her ears drooping. "When are we leaving, Merikh?"

He rubbed his fingertips up and down the side of her neck. "Soon."

That wasn't a good enough answer.

Escaping his arms, she sat up on her hip. "How soon?"

Orange sparked in her vision, and her brows furrowed, since she'd never seen that colour come from him. Then again, he often tried to hide his colour shifts from her.

When he didn't say anything, she could almost feel his stare all the way to the essence of her being, and her frown deepened.

"I made the sun stone. We should be able to travel through

the Veil safely now. So, how come we haven't left yet?"

"I still need to get supplies for you," he said while sitting up himself. "It'll take a few days of travel."

"I've seen you run on all fours before. You're really fast like that," she offered. "You've made your guards, so I should be able to ride on your back."

"What if I don't want you to ride me like I'm a horse, Raewyn? The idea is utterly degrading."

Shame rested on her shoulders. She hadn't considered he might find that offensive. She was the kind of person to find a solution, often willing to do just about anything to solve a problem efficiently.

"You say you need to get supplies, but don't we have everything here? There's plenty of food, and you have all the tools we should need here."

"Have you considered what you will do if we must face off against your brother?" Merikh deflected. "What if the sun stone doesn't work against him?"

Raewyn lowered her head. "I don't know if it will be fully effective against him, but..." Tears welled in her eyes as she said, "But I can throw it against the ground, and it will act as a bomb. It'll shatter, and the heat and pressure will knock everyone away – just like when it shattered last time."

"What of me, then? I couldn't be near you when you first activated it. It was too hot. I thought I was going to disintegrate if I took even a single step closer." Then, he cupped her face as he said, "And what if you get hurt in the process?"

Biting at her lips, she thought that was a fair concern.

"I'll protect us," she offered. "If we take any plant, I can form a shield, but if we throw the stone far enough, we can just use it as a diversion and shoot for the portal. I don't want to harm Jabez, but I really want to go home, Merikh."

I want to know if my feelings for you are real. She wanted to know that more than anything.

"We'll leave soon, Raewyn," he said softly as he stroked

over her cheekbone.

She smacked his hand away, and white sparked.

"It's been three days." She rubbed at her biceps, feeling nervous and anxious. "I'm starting to feel like you're keeping me here on purpose."

She was surprised he didn't growl at what she was insinuating. "You forget I want to leave here just as much as you do," he answered in a dark tone.

She guessed that was true.

Yet, the fact that he *didn't* get angry weighed on her. Anger was his usual go to emotion, and orange sparked in her vision again.

Why do I get the feeling something is wrong?

Merikh sat on his rump with his legs straight, tilting his head, trying to decipher whatever emotion was currently resting upon her pretty face.

This was not what he expected upon waking up.

To be fair, he hadn't expected to still be holding her if she were awake, but he'd been delighted by it. Having a warm, soft, lax female in his arms had never been a part of his fantasies, and he realised he should have wanted that sooner.

So why were they having this argument when he'd rather go back to a few seconds ago when he'd been experiencing joy?

He knew this conversation would come sooner or later, but he'd also been hoping for just never.

He didn't like that his orbs, which had been pink upon waking, were now orange from the heaviness of his guilt.

I don't want to lie to her.

He'd actually been intending for today to be the day he explained what a bride was, to see if she would be his. He'd wanted to pamper her when they both woke, feed her and watch her do her little happy food dance that always tickled him with humour.

Once she was rested, fed, washed, and content, he'd planned to ask for her soul. Then, this conversation wouldn't have been necessary – because for once, he just wanted to have hope. Hope that she would say yes. Hope that she would choose him.

Now didn't seem like a good time at all, especially when her face turned suspicious, and she directed that towards him.

"What are you hiding from me?" she bit, the little Elf perceptive.

How could he answer that? Because, as it stood, he was hiding much from her.

Why they weren't leaving. His explanation as to why he was only giving her a vague answer. That fact that he wanted her soul.

That wasn't even the worst of it.

Even though he'd made his decision on what he wanted, which was her, there was still the decision on what side to pick: go with Jabez and keep her with him, or go to her realm with her and abandon the safety he could provide his brothers.

The choice was too hard for him to make on his own.

Decimate her people and protect his fellow Mavka, or join her people and never know if he was the reason another died. One had already died from his actions; he was afraid to have more of his brothers' deaths on his hands – even if he wasn't the one to cause the killing strike.

What he needed was for her to take that choice away from him, to take the responsibility of that burden. What she wanted would be what he would do, but only after she was his.

If she denied him...

He'd already made his decision on that. Merikh would take her home, leave her there, and return here.

Not to be by Jabez's side; he didn't think he'd want to look at another Elf again after she tore his bruised and bleeding heart from his chest. Instead, he would forcibly round up all the Duskwalkers, then guard them until something came along and killed him – likely the Demon King himself.

If Raewyn didn't want to be with him, he wouldn't be happy no matter where the fuck he went.

He'd been seeking a light in his dark, dim world. Now that he had it, he knew nothing would brighten it again if she disappeared.

But if she died... If he tried to take her home and he wasn't able to protect her, he didn't think he'd forgive himself. He didn't know what he'd become. Would he abandon all his humanity and wander the world as a self-loathing ball of spikes?

He'd probably try to annihilate everything in his path.

Lost to his thoughts, unsure of how to answer her, he watched as she stood. She tried to take the blanket to cover her nudity, but he was currently sitting on it. Instead, she went to her section of the shelf and grabbed a towel he'd acquired from the human town close by.

"Answer me," she snapped as she covered herself and searched for her cane.

Merikh stood as he curled his tail around the length of it resting against the wall. He gently handed it to her, and she took it to put space between them.

"I don't know what you want me to say," he lied, wishing he didn't feel so rotten. "I don't know why you're upset. You were fine when we laid down."

They were more than fine, to be precise: satisfied, seed-covered, warm.

"Because I want you to tell me the truth! Something doesn't feel right, and I want to know what it is."

I can't do that, he thought as he grabbed a horn to rub it in annoyance at himself. Maybe it was cowardly of him, but he didn't want to tell her anything out of frustration just because she was yanking it from him. Had she just waited, been slightly more patient, everything would have been revealed.

He'd say the wrong thing if he just blurted it out. He was always putting his pawed foot in his mouth around her.

"Maybe we should speak when you've calmed down," he stated, turning his head away.

I can't wait any longer. She'll only get more upset and realise what I'm doing. Merikh needed to tell her everything today; otherwise, things weren't going to bode well for him.

He needed her calm. He needed time to think on how he should word the most important question he would ever ask in his entire life.

One he wanted to be hopeful about but couldn't help being utterly terrified of.

"Did... did you just tell me to calm down?"

He didn't like her tone, how it was high pitched and full of disbelief. He shot his head to her to find her mouth was agape and got the impression he'd just absolutely said the wrong thing.

"You know what? Fine." She felt around on the shelf and grabbed a dress. "I'll go calm down for you, *your highness*."

"Raewyn," he started as he reached forward with a wince. "That's not what I meant. I just need to think."

She stepped backwards as he approached her, and he only halted because her expression was a mixture of hurt and anger. He'd never seen that from her before, at least not turned towards him.

"For once, Merikh, *I'm* going to be the one to storm away." She turned and literally stomped her feet as she navigated her way outside. "I'm going to go have a *bath,* and if you don't give me some sort of explanation when I return, I... I..." She gave a huff. "Well, I don't know, but you'll regret it. I'll try to rip your tail off or something."

The moment she was gone, he covered his bony face with his palm as he crossed his other arm over his chest.

I'm an idiot. How? What? Why? How am I meant to fix this and ask her now?

He should have told her everything last night, but he'd been a... cowardly chicken. Did he eat one in the past or something? Should he start bawking and flap his arms?

THIRTY-EIGHT

Clean, dry, clothed, and sitting near the lake, Raewyn covered her face in shame and embarrassment. *I can't believe I exploded at him like that.*

She had no proof whether or not he was lying or hiding something, but she had worked herself up. If her past actions didn't already prove it, she usually wasn't one to do that. She liked to come at issues with at least some kind of backing, but she'd been bursting with a mix of emotions and they'd just... *boom.*

Yeah, okay, not her proudest moment, but she also thought she wasn't completely unjustified.

I just shouted at a Duskwalker. He'd sounded confused at her behaviour. Considering how they'd gone to sleep, what they'd done right before it, he definitely hadn't expected her to behave like that.

To be honest, neither had she.

He obviously wants to tell me something. He'd asked her to calm down, and then they'd speak. *At least, I hope he wants to tell me something.*

Right now, she'd take any explanation.

Having a bath had calmed her. She thought it was really the space that made her feel better. She was clearer headed and in better control.

She toed the water with a pout. *I ruined what could have been a good day.* She regretted that now.

She wasn't used to having all these kinds of emotions swamping her. She should be drowning in bookwork, not in her conflicting feelings over a big Duskwalker who was as confusing as he was sturdy. She wanted to lean on him, and she wanted to run away.

Most of all... she didn't want to be alone in this. She didn't want her growing affections to be unrequited, especially since she'd never allowed herself to feel them for another.

How could an Elysian male fail to win her heart, but a Duskwalker could? It made no sense, and yet that was the reality she was facing.

One that could only just be enjoying her until they made it to her home world. It wouldn't even be his fault, since she technically started it all. He'd been hesitant about it in the beginning.

I should go inside. She'd been sitting here for a while now, and she couldn't avoid him forever. Not talking to him wasn't going to solve anything. *I'm not going to apologise, though, since he has some explaining to do.*

Just as Raewyn was about to stand, quiet crackling from the left filled her ears. Then, an aqua light began to form, cutting through the air not far from her.

With a gasp, she stood and backed up, careful not to fall into the lake.

That light, which had turned into a seam of lightning, then opened into an oval. A shadow passed over it, and many more followed after it.

Fear caught in her throat, unsure of what it was or what was happening. Along with the crackling, a familiar sucking sound penetrated the air, and it softly pulled her hair and skirt in its direction.

Two voices called to her.

One was far away, Merikh's gruff voice, while the other was

gentler.

"Raewyn?" The tone was deep, yet soothing. She would know him anywhere.

She stepped forward with her brows furrowing. "Cy-Cykran?"

"Rae!" he yelled back in joy, his footsteps quickly approaching her as though he was running.

She squealed and bolted for him, knowing the tall but strong Demon would catch her. They collided, and he instantly spun her in a circle while she hugged him tightly. She took in his familiarity, the smell of home that lingered on his clothes, his very skin.

"Do you know how long we've been searching for you?" he said in the Elvish tongue.

"How did you find me?" she answered back.

Just as he was about to answer, a snarl caused them to separate. It was also moving towards them with heavy, quick footsteps, and when she turned her head to the sound, white sparks flashed.

Merikh. She made it a step, intending to ward him back, but Cykran threw her behind him.

"A monster!" someone shouted. "Guards, form a shield. Protect her."

Metal and leather ground against each other as a group of people shuffled to act as a barrier, while more moved behind her, towards the portal. She knew they would be holding polearms with blades on them that could be activated to cover the blades with deadly energy.

Each of them would be a Delysian, besides maybe two or three. They had taken it upon themselves to become soldiers, since they had no problem with bloodshed and killing, unlike the Elysian people, who were far gentler.

Dread sunk into her like a viper with venom, and it filled her veins with ice.

"Wait!" Raewyn shouted in Elvish. "Wait, stop. He's not a

monster."

No one listened to her. Why would they when Merikh let out a blood-curdling roar that had even her shrinking away from its hostility?

She hoped he didn't think she was planning to abandon him now that her people were here to save her. She would never do that. She'd made a promise, and she had every intention of bringing this big, secretly soft-hearted Duskwalker back with her.

Cykran dragged her away in the opposite direction, towards the intense crackling. "We need to leave. The portal will only last so long."

"Let go of me, Cykran," she bit.

She struggled in his arms, but she was too disorientated to realise she'd spoken English and he wouldn't understand her. The Delysian was also too strong for her to get free from, and no matter how much she slapped at his forearms or pried his fingers from her waist, he just wouldn't let go.

"Merikh!" she squealed, hoping he could make it to her so she could drag him through the rift as well.

Raewyn realised two things after she shouted his name and he roared in answer: she shouldn't have called for him while panicked, and things were about to go *horribly* wrong if she didn't intervene.

Red sparks flashed. Merikh let out a yelp as the smell of copper tangled into the air. He'd been hurt, and her fighting redoubled.

I have to go to him. I have to calm him before it's too late!

If he turned into his mindless state, they would get themselves all killed – her along with them.

"Let go of me, you stupid jerk!" She bashed on Cykran's arms harder. She even tried to stamp on his clawed toes. "I want to take that Duskwalker with me, and I will throw you off the top of the highest point of the central tree if we don't! That's an order!"

Her being a councilmember had to have *some* sway.

Cykran halted and must have looked at her, since she could almost feel his gaze boring into her. He gripped her shoulders tightly in what could only be disbelief, nearly crushing her.

Through clenched fangs, he hissed, "You want to take the monster with us?"

They're taking her away from me.

Merikh fretted as he tried to get around the soldiers – *without* hurting them.

He was also concerned for how they might hurt him as well. Their weapons were long, with blades running down one side. Coloured ribbons were attached to the satin-looking white metal.

Eight spears were being pointed directly at his face, with three more towards the back protecting two other Elves, the sharpness of them shining in the moonlight. A few of the weapon wielders had smacked the handle bottoms against the ground, and energy flared to life around the blades.

The soldiers stood in an arc around a sparking aqua portal, protecting Raewyn and her captor as they fought. He was dragging her while she squirmed, fighting to get away, fighting to get to *him*.

Merikh paced at the end of the blades, assessing each of the white-haired, dark-skinned Demons holding him back. They looked fairly similar to Raewyn, but their red eyes, horns, claws, and fangs only reminded him of Jabez.

They had satin-white metal armour shielding their chests and shoulders, yet it was minimal. The rest of their bodies had green, blue, or red leather garments underneath.

I can't hurt them. It was the only reason he wasn't trying to get through them. *They're her people.* She wouldn't forgive him if he were to harm them, and the smell of their fear was already doing funny things to his mind.

He needed to stay calm.

"Let me through," he demanded with a snarl.

He backed up when a wide-eyed one stabbed at him and he narrowly missed it. It was obvious they'd never come across something like him, something as large as his body or as ominous as his skull. They appeared to be inexperienced soldiers, trembling in their pants and about to wet themselves.

Merikh had seen more courage and resolve in battle-hardened humans, like the Demonslayers.

They spoke to each other, but he couldn't understand a word they said. All he knew was that they were discussing him, refusing to take their eyes away and growing more uncertain and frightened with each second.

They backed up when one looked over their shoulder to check in with Raewyn, the male holding her, and two other people who appeared to be Elves. One was frozen with his eyes wide, while the other was tugging on his shoulder and signing with his hands.

"Merikh!"

Raewyn called to him, and red filled his vision. If he didn't do something, they'd take her away from him forever. He'd never gotten the chance to ask her if she'd be his female, had never told her how he felt.

He didn't want to be stuck here, wishing to go to her, without knowing her answer – or trying to change it if it wasn't what he wanted.

He couldn't handle not knowing, knew it would eat him alive for the rest of his life.

With a spike of fear clapping through him like a thunderbolt, Merikh sprung for her.

He managed to smack one of the Demon soldiers to the side, but another cut their sword right over his side. He or she gouged deeper than any human weapon ever had, and he didn't think an Earth Demon had ever cut so deep.

Pain caused his orbs to whiten before they flared red.

Invisible hands tried to reach through the bone of his skull, massaging his brain to lull him into a rage. His whine was the physical show of just how hard he fought to keep them at bay.

His form shifted into his monstrous one, giving him strength and agility, but it did little to save him as another soldier stabbed their polearm blade straight through his thigh.

The weapons with glowing energy did far more damage and cut through his usually tough skin like butter.

When another stabbed him straight through the stomach, a roar broke from him.

He spun around and pinned the soldier to the ground, accidentally shoving the entire weapon through his midsection until he'd impaled himself all the way to the pole section her hands were clamping.

Some kind of rope or vines threaded around his horns and head, and they all worked together to pull him off the woman as she screamed in terror. It was palpable; he could taste her fear like it was the richest treat he'd ever eaten.

Merikh wound his arms around the green ropes, twisted them around the vines, and tugged. He disarmed all of them as they fell to their stomachs, unprepared for his overbearing strength.

His thought was to kill what was currently in his way, pests keeping him from Raewyn, but he shook his head.

No. Can't hurt them.

She shouted in a foreign language, and he turned his focus back to his pretty little fairy, his own personal piece of starlight.

She was arguing with another Demon while he was pointing in Merikh's direction. He was explaining what Merikh was doing, likely how he'd just attacked everyone.

Had they not pulled him off the female soldier, he would have bitten her head off. He'd been about to.

Was he painting Merikh as an uncontrollable beast? That wasn't fair, not when he was trying his hardest to *not* be. He didn't want to be a monster, something to be frightened of, to hate and spurn.

Blue flickered in his vision. *Raewyn.*

He took a step towards them, to her, but the green ropes still attached to his head were yanked. Merikh turned, his orbs flaring crimson as he roared.

He wanted them gone! He wanted them out of his way and to leave him in peace. He'd done nothing wrong. Why did they have to cast judgement on him when he'd never harmed them? Or when they'd never seen him before?

Suddenly, he was flipped upside down, landing on his fucking face! They'd wound the rope around his legs and tripped him. His neck kinked, and he was thankful it was so flexible. Otherwise, he'd likely have broken it with his own weight collapsing on top of it.

The Demon yelled at Raewyn and then everyone else. He tugged on her arm and pointed towards the portal guarded by three other soldiers.

His blood ran cold. It was closing, shutting, shrinking.

They were going to leave him here.

Their argument hadn't been settled, and he was trying to drag her through it before it was too late. Even one of the Elves had begun helping him.

Raewyn reached for Merikh, screamed his name again, and the white of fear, of anxiety, of the potential loss he'd feel if she disappeared, filled his vision.

I want her. She's mine. They were stealing her, trying to take her away from him. He didn't care what anyone said – not her, not his mother, not the rest of her people, or anyone on this stupid, wretched planet – Raewyn was his, would be his, and he wasn't going to be apart from her. *She's fucking mine!*

His quills tore apart his leather, unable to be held back by the intensity of rage, fear, and utter adoration for her that overtook him in that moment.

He wasn't going to lose her.

He would find a way to get her to forgive him for what he

was about to do.

His quills destroyed the rope trappings around his legs, and he bolted for Raewyn. He took a spear being thrown at him from behind, and it cut deeper into his injured side. He didn't care; he barely registered it.

The Demon holding her shouted before he put Raewyn behind him. She must have heard Merikh running, because she turned to him.

He knew grabbing her himself would result in her pain, in her coming to harm from his claws in his panic. He'd hold her wrong, she'd grip him wrong, and he'd likely impale her with his quills.

They wouldn't even get to him in time before he turned on her, not with how agitated he already was. That, or someone else would try to separate them, and they'd bleed and shove him into mindless hunger.

His own body was stopping him from taking her, and his own self-loathing redoubled. Why couldn't he just be fucking normal? He doubted any of his brothers had to combat the deadliness of their own bodies the way he did.

Merikh was skating on the edge of his control, and it was too close to snapping for him to do anything else but what he planned.

He wasn't even sorry about it.

"Please, it's not what it looks like," she pleaded. "I promise I'm not going to leave y–"

He bypassed the Demon, her hands, and shoved his claws straight into her chest. She gasped, her lips parting.

"You are mine, my pretty starshine," he growled, his sight turning bright pink. "I won't let *anyone* take you away from me."

At the same time, she was pulled away after only seconds of him being close to her, and he yanked her soul from her with a chuckle. He gave her his sight in the process so she could watch, so she could have him with her, even if it was only in spirit. He *would* take it back; he'd promised her that.

At the same time as he took it, soldiers pushed their way between them.

It was obvious he wasn't going to get the chance to go through the portal with her; he didn't want to barrel through it and potentially have her be killed by all the weapons these fools were holding.

If he couldn't go with her, then he wouldn't let her be gone forever. They could take her for now. Then, within a day, she could come right fucking back here as his bride.

They could work on going to her realm, or whatever they planned, once she was with him again. They could play this day over and over again, forever if need be, but he wasn't going to lose Raewyn.

Not now, not ever.

With his sight black, Merikh lifted his hand above his head, parted his fangs, and dropped her soul into his maw.

THIRTY-NINE

Raewyn didn't know what was happening when she looked down, and with his borrowed sight, saw Merikh's entire hand had disappeared into her chest. Her skin waved like rippling water. It didn't hurt, but it was oddly invasive, like he was gripping her spine.

Then, he pulled something from her, and a blue flame flickered in his enclosed fist.

She didn't know what to do, or even say, as he held his hand above his fangs and dropped it into his mouth.

She let out a heart-wrenching scream when he didn't even get the chance to close his fangs around it. One of the Delysian soldiers had leapt up with an energy blade, swung in a swift arc, and removed his *head* in one swoop!

The blue flame floated in the air as his body disintegrated in a plume of glittering black sand. His skull plopped against the ground like someone had dropped it, and tears instantly welled in her eyes.

"No!" Raewyn screamed.

She fought Cykran to go to Merikh's skull. *Is he dead?*

He couldn't be dead. There was no way. He said he'd come back from something like this.

"There's no more time!" one of the other councilmembers shouted.

"I can't hold it for much longer," the other yelled back.

"It's dead now. Just get her through the portal!"

Cykran shoved her into the arms of her fellow Elysian just as the flame floated back within her. With a hard, unbothered expression, the bearded face of their head of security shoved her through the portal, despite her protest. Earth was swallowed up in a bright light before she was spat out the other side. From the way she'd been pushed, she fell straight onto her backside before rolling onto her back.

She nearly flipped over with how hard she'd been tossed.

The welcoming heat surrounding her did nothing to warm her of the dread that chilled her bones. On her hands and knees, struggling to get to her feet, she darted for the portal.

I have to go back. I have to get him.

"Raewyn!" a woman shouted as people grabbed her arms.

Someone drew her in for a forced hug, and her mother's floral scent cascaded over her. Despite how much she'd longed to be in the shelter of her mother's arms again, there was someone else she wanted more.

"Please wait," she rasped, pushing her off with her eyes glued to the rift.

Raewyn was disorientated from coming through the portal, her stomach queasy like last time. She also wasn't used to the utter brightness that was Nyl'theria. The suns pouring through the glass ceiling, triangular in shape due to the branches above, were too blazing.

It didn't matter that it was obviously late afternoon and the three multicoloured suns were descending. It hurt her eyes, and having Merikh's sight always made it difficult to orientate herself. It'd been easier on Earth, where everything was dim.

Her mother, who she hadn't seen in weeks, and even longer due to her lack of sight, stumbled as Raewyn carelessly tossed her to the side. Panicked, she headed for the portal, but Cykran and everyone else coming through it blocked her path.

With a crackle, it closed behind them.

Her heart shattered into a million fragments.

How could Merikh forgive her for leaving him behind? They were supposed to come here together!

"You jerk!" she screamed as she flung herself at Cykran. She punched his chest with the bottom of her fists. "Why didn't you listen to me? I told you I wanted to bring him with us!"

More people grabbed her, and she kicked to get free and punish the foul Delysian she'd called her friend.

She didn't care that his expression appeared betrayed, or that she was able to see it. She didn't care that there were at least three dozen people in the room watching her.

Her tears stung, her chest burned, and her stomach was so knotted, she thought she was going to vomit right there on the obsidian floor. She wanted to purge the crawling heartsickness burrowing inside her like a parasite.

"How could you do this to me?" she cried. "You didn't even give him a chance and just attacked him."

Now he was stuck on Earth while she was here.

Merikh had the sun stone, but unless he could figure out the key spell, he wouldn't be able to activate it.

I'll never be able to go back to him. She couldn't make another portal, and entering Jabez's from this side was suicide.

"Someone take her from here," Cykran demanded, turning his head away from her. "She needs rest. I think that realm or creature did something to her mind."

"I'll give you rest," she hissed as she lunged for him again, only to be pulled back.

She just kicked her legs and yelled, fighting desperately for an outlet. She'd never been violent before, had never truly tried to hit or attack anyone, but she wanted to beat the ever-living hell out of him right now.

She also wanted to turn to Mericato, the head of their security division, and show him what her small fists were made of. He'd shoved her through the portal and had done nothing to stop his soldiers, no matter how much she'd begged him to.

They could all go to hell right now. She'd happily send them there.

Tears were flinging from her face, and her hair was waving around her like a mess. She probably looked like a shrieking banshee as she fought against the people holding her back.

"Let go of me!" How many times would she have to say this today?

"Raewyn Daefaren, calm down this instant," a booming voice bellowed, echoing off the palace chamber they were in.

Her spine went rigid, and all heat washed out of her from the sternness of her father's voice. She turned to him with her head lowering, simultaneously clenching her fists at her sides.

"I raised you better than this," he said as he stood there with his arms folded, his lips flat in a disapproving line. "Cykran spent days helping the people who were able to save you, and this is how you repay him? Them?"

He loosened an arm so he could wave it to those on the right of her.

Her tears bubbled faster as she looked over to her father. He looked so tired from the last time she'd seen him, and she hated the disappointed scowl he gave her. She always felt a certain way about his neatly cut, bearded face, especially when it looked that way at her.

She'd often strived to never receive it.

He was usually so cheerful, caring, and protective. The kind of man who was easy to make laugh, and who found it even easier to make others laugh. His anger was exceptionally rare, which made it more frightening.

"You don't understand," she said through gritted teeth, her fists tightening. "None of you understand."

"Come, petal. Let's get you looked at," her mother cooed as she placed her arm over her shoulders and steered her. "You look so skinny. You're worrying me."

"I always looked skinny!" Raewyn's outraged yell was loud, but she bit her lips shut when she finally looked up to see all the eyes gawking at her.

The other seventeen councilmembers were watching her act immaturely, and she'd always held herself with such composure before this. She had to, as they could often be judgemental. Embarrassment soared, and it only made her feel more pitiful.

She'd had an outburst in front of them, in front of her parents, and the soldiers who had worked so hard to help. They thought they'd saved her from a monster, when really, they'd just separated her from someone she cared for dearly.

Raewyn just cried into her hands and let her parents guide her. Footsteps followed them, but she didn't turn to check who it was.

She didn't care right then. She just wanted to weep and be heartbroken.

Not even the comfort of being home brought her any joy at the loss she suffered. With red outlining her sight like a glow of flames, she didn't bother to look at the white walls of the tree palace, or the bronze, silver, and gold melted into the gaps. She didn't look up to examine the purple and pink leaves through the windows, or downwards to marvel at the obsidian ground.

"You should be happy," her father sighed. "Do you know how difficult it was for Thorill to find you?"

Thorill was a portal expert. He was old, but that gave him the experience of once working with them. He'd been a portal stone maker and navigator in the past and had opened many portals to find people to connect with.

He was wise, and Raewyn had always respected him and his field – despite the fact that he wasn't allowed to experiment with it any longer.

"It took him and his chosen team weeks to figure out where you'd gone," her father continued, his back straight and proud as he walked beside her wrapped in her mother's arms. "Of all the places you could have gone to, I don't know if you were lucky or unlucky you ended up on Earth. We feared you would be eaten before we found you."

"We were so worried, petal," her mother chimed in.

She was the harder one of her parents, the stricter one, but she was also just as loving. Hearing their concern in the very trembles of their words had Raewyn's shoulders turning inward.

She probably appeared ungrateful towards everyone's care.

"It's still better than going anywhere uninhabitable."

"We knew there was a chance. We held out hope for that."

"H-how did you even find where I was on Earth?" Raewyn asked, her throat hoarse.

She licked at her lips to stop the tickling sensation of her tears and only ended up tasting her sadness.

"Thorill and his team managed to trace you to Earth, but they'd been trying to pinpoint your location when they sensed a large influx of magic. You're smart, Raewyn, you always have been. We knew you were trying to signal us so we could come get you."

Signal them? What were they talking about? She nearly tripped over her own feet when she realised it, her eyes going wide. *The sun stone.*

They'd sensed her when she activated it, since it was such a powerful spell. If they were scrying through magic, they would have noticed it.

Why didn't I think of that sooner? She could have saved herself weeks of work!

Her heart shrivelled. *But I wouldn't have gotten to know Merikh.*

If they had come too soon, she wouldn't have realised how wonderful he was, how much she could... gentle him. Her easing tears redoubled, and she felt like a child with how uncontrollable she was behaving.

I want him back, she thought as her mother steered her into a room and sat her on a healing bed. *What am I going to do?*

"Lay down," her father demanded softly, and Raewyn complied.

Her father was a valued scientist, a medic, and a linguist –

although the last one was more of a hobby, one he had tried to push onto her and Jabez.

He hooked Raewyn up to devices to check on her physical wellbeing, while her mother brushed her forehead soothingly.

"Is there a way we can go back?" Raewyn asked, eyeing the machines.

"In theory, yes," her father answered, staring at a glowing magical ball informing him of her nutritional levels. "But we also can't. The portal stone we used was the last one we had, since all the others have been converted to power the city. It was weak, and it gave out the moment they opened the one to you – which is why it closed so quickly. Thankfully, it was able to take the soldiers to you. Cykran demanded they take him with them, and he wouldn't take no for an answer."

"He loves you, Raewyn," her mother added.

They all knew she meant platonically.

"You should have seen him threaten the other councilmembers," her father chuckled warmly. "Said he would die just to bring you home. How could anyone deny such a proclamation?"

Raewyn stopped listening; all she heard was that she couldn't go back. Her breaths sawed in and out of her like a blade that wanted to sever her in two.

Her mother placed her hand over her forehead, like she was checking for a fever. What was the point when her father was already doing a health check?

Without meeting her eyes, she examined her daughter's face.

It clicked with Raewyn that they didn't realise she could *see*. Weirdly enough, she didn't want to tell them.

It was private, a gift from Merikh, and she feared if she spoke about it, it would disappear. It was all she had of him right now, and it was giving her hope that he was at least alive.

That he would figure out a way to come to her.

I will always take it back, he'd once proclaimed. Did it mean he'd given it to her as a promise?

Why would he do something so foolish? How was he able to come to her if he couldn't see the dangers he faced? He would have to travel the Veil and to Jabez's castle without it.

"What's wrong?" her mother asked, and Raewyn looked up to her.

Her mother had wavy hair, whereas she'd gotten her tight corkscrew curls from her father. She had her mother's nose and lips, but her father's brown eye colour and round jaw and cheeks. Both were tall, both relatively skinny.

"I left someone behind," Raewyn sobbed. "Someone who was supposed to come here with me. I promised him, and he's the only reason I'm here now, yet Cykran just let him be left behind. When I argued with him, he couldn't see past his... his..."

Face. Cykran, the terrible hypocrite, hadn't been able to see past Merikh's bear skull and horns.

Dear holy Gilded Maiden, how was she supposed to tell her parents she'd fallen in love with a monster? A Duskwalker, something completely unknown to them.

"I promised him our people wouldn't turn on him, and yet they cut off his fucking head!"

Both her parents gasped, but she didn't care that she'd sworn – although the word was a little different here, a little *worse*. She did her best to translate the curse closest to it.

"Raewyn," her mother whispered.

"There's nothing wrong with her!" her father shouted as he slapped his hands together to end the spell. "She's perfectly fine. All her vitals are as healthy as ever; she's just acting immature for no reason. She gets it from your side of the family."

"Excuse me," her mother sneered, while narrowing her eyes at him. "You're the one who let her be rebellious when she was a teenager, taking her to the fringes of the city to look beyond the ward."

"You're the one who has always practiced insane experiments," her father rebuffed. "At least I move forward with my work *carefully,* rather than ignoring everyone's concerns."

Just as they were about to *lovingly* bicker, Raewyn sat up between them.

"Just take me home." She'd been wanting to lie in her own bed for many Earth months, and now, she wanted to sob on it. "I want to be alone."

Despite what either of them thought, she was actually controlling the worst of her despair. She wanted to let herself explode, wear herself out, and once she was done processing, figure out a solution.

Because there *had* to be a solution.

FORTY

There was no solution, as Raewyn came to discover.

She didn't even need to waste a lot of time learning that.

After crying for hours, then shovelling food she'd missed into her face as a self-soothing mechanism, she couldn't sleep. Tired, irritated, and just physically incapable of producing another tear, like she was all dried up, she kicked her butt into gear.

It was doubtful her obsessive mind would allow her to sleep, even if she tried. Once she'd set her mind to something, she had terribly unhealthy habits of not caring for herself until she'd completed her task.

Cykran had carried her home one too many times after she'd fainted.

So, with that resolve in mind, she moved.

She'd marched her way through the central tree and bashed on Thorill's office door. When she got no answer, she marched down the central tree's spiralling main hallway and bashed on his front door!

The suns were gone, but she didn't give a damn that it was late into the night.

When a stranger opened the door, the woman looked startled. Raewyn had been bashing on the wrong house and needed to go two homes down. Honestly, it just made her more aggressive.

Maybe Merikh's behaviour had rubbed off on her. She was kind of pleased with it at the moment; she wanted to be big like him, massive and imposing, scaring people into giving her what she wanted.

When Thorill opened the door, one of the faces that had been on Earth to rescue her greeted her. It, however, wasn't the one who pushed her through it. She slitted her eyes at him, rather angry he was part of the reason she hadn't managed to get Merikh.

"Raewyn, dear child," he muttered in a shaken, aged voice. He was almost seventy-five years old, with the wrinkles to match all his wise years. Although he sported no beard, he was fond of curling his long moustache. "It's the middle of the night. What are y–"

"How do we open a portal back to Earth?" She would like to say she asked, but it was really a demand. She also shoved her way past him and into his home.

He furrowed his overly bushy brows. "Another portal? Impossible. The rest of my stones are depleted."

She stood in the middle of his house, turned to face him, and folded her arms over her chest. "Then I'll inject them with my mana."

She barely noticed his home, despite taking in its details.

It held little, as most of their homes did. It was an oval, like a dome with tree roots for walls and a ceiling, with metal ore filling in the gaps. He had one or two pieces of art, and they consisted of historical paintings of him shaking hands with either a Bansu, Anzúli, or Taihee from when the portal gates were open.

Thorill shook his head in disbelief that she'd rudely let herself in, but he didn't ask her to leave.

"It's not that easy, Raewyn," he sighed.

He walked over to a plush lounge to rest his tired bones – likely worn out from coming to 'rescue' her. He massaged one of his knees.

"Once a mana stone has been completely depleted, you and I both know it can't be restored. The one I used to save you was a personal keepsake I'd stolen." Then, he gave her a terrible eye, a stinky one, as he said, "I got into a lot of trouble revealing I had it, and not once have you thanked me. I would say young adults back in my day weren't so disrespectful, but I already know you'll roll those eyes at me."

Raewyn's arms tightened across her chest as she squinted at him in suspicion. "You have another one, don't you?"

"No, I don't. It's been decades," he answered far too curtly. "The others I took no longer work, and I only just managed to keep that one healthy enough in my old age to keep it glowing. Ulair was the one who helped the most in truly restoring it."

"Ulair?" she asked in surprised. She and Ulair never really saw eye to eye, so she scarcely believed he'd had such a large hand in helping her. "Please, Thorill. There must be another way."

He shook his head again, and his balding tuft of hair swayed side to side. "Unless you can figure out how to control a chaos portal to open directly where you want, which not even I've managed to do, there's nothing that can be done."

"Nothing?"

"No, child. Nothing." He waved his hand to the side. "Trying will only see you hurt or send you to another random world, and we won't be able to save you a second time."

Raewyn anxiously bit at her lips. "But–"

"Whatever or whoever it is you left behind, they are gone. Accept this."

She hated the way his words were uttered so definitively, like they were true and there was nothing she could do about it. She hated even more that he was likely right, especially since he was the only person in this city who could strike with such knowledgeable resolve.

He was the only person she could ask, and he was the only one who could have told her if there was another way. He hadn't.

Raewyn's shoulders turned inward in embarrassment that he'd witnessed her outburst in the central palace, but she turned her back on him to hide the pain in her expression.

"Thank you for speaking with me," she whispered, wishing it didn't sound so choked.

"They must have meant a lot to you," he said softly, his voice radiating with care. "I've known you all your life. You haven't been this distraught since..."

Since Jabez was locked away. Since she was a child.

Raewyn tightened her left hand into a fist when pain radiated down it from her heart. "I'm sorry if I've bothered you, and for entering your home without permission."

"You are fine, councilwoman. We all have our days, and I'm sure your adventure has weighed on you. It hasn't even been a day since your return, so I think it's fair of me to say we can all forgive any transgressions, considering the stress you must be under." She turned her head to the side to peek at him, and his expression was one of sympathy. "We all know what it's like to lose someone."

Thorill had been there when the Demons first came. He'd lost many loved ones and had watched the bloodshed himself.

She nodded as she calmly walked to his door. "Thank you. I'll see myself out."

Honestly, she just wanted to escape. She'd been hoping the usually mischievous man would leap at the idea of creating another portal, and his denial meant he couldn't. He had the approval of a councilmember, so the responsibility would have fallen on her shoulders.

Just as she placed her hand on the doorknob, he chuckled as he said, "When are you going to tell everyone you've restored your sight?"

Perceptive old man. Then again, that was Thorill – observant as always.

"It's not mine," she admitted before leaving.

All the strength in her threatened to burn out. Her knees

wobbled in tiredness, in disappointment, as she walked back up the central tree. The main hallway was a long spiral upward, and she looked towards the ground to hide her face under her hair.

It wasn't just to shield everyone from her tears, which apparently *hadn't* all dried up. It was so no one could recognise her. She wanted to be alone.

If Thorill, an expert, told her there was nothing she could do, then that was the truth. Chasing after Merikh by herself would most likely send her to a frozen wasteland or a lava-filled hell, knowing her luck.

That'd help no one.

Once she was safely back home, she let her legs give out and fell to her backside against the door. She wrapped her arms around her legs as she buried her face against her knees. Her ears were so drooped, she didn't know if they would straighten up ever again.

I'm really sorry, Merikh. She hugged herself tightly, wishing she could disappear from the misery drowning her. *I don't know how to get to you.*

Her field of expertise would do nothing to assist her. She'd feel like a toddler trying to push a square block into a round hole. She might eventually get it right, but there were too many dangerous consequences for her to play foolishly.

It's probably been a whole Earth day, she thought, remembering he'd said he'd heal within that time. *Are you angry with me? I don't want you to think I abandoned you on purpose.*

If only she could acquire a new stone. Unfortunately, in order to do that, she would need to go outside the safety of the city barrier. All the mines were deep within Demon territories, which is why none of her people could obtain new ones.

Powering the city, the ward, everything, took all their combined strength. One day, in many years, the stones just wouldn't be able to keep working, and they'd burn out.

Then they would be faced with the burden of protecting the city themselves, with only their individual magic to save them –

and she'd already proven just how weak that was on Earth. Her grass vine barrier would only protect her for so long before a barrage of claws and fangs ripped it apart.

Her people, those much stronger and faster than her, had never returned from trying to get more stones. How would she be able to do that on her own?

I promised to bring you here. I promised to fight for you. She'd promised herself she'd gain the courage to be with him properly once she was home, and yet now she was here alone.

Why did it have to feel so cold and empty? It lacked his warmth, his scent, his imposing presence taking up every corner.

I want to go back to you...

Soft tapping on the door startled her awake, and she flinched. Eventually passing out while crying, she'd fallen to the side to lie on the floor in a ball.

Tree branches had sprouted from the ground and were wrapping around her protectively. She figured she'd subconsciously, in her sleep, sought comfort by being held and had called them to her.

The starfir central tree was naturally imbued with magic, due to the cluster of mana stones that had once been beneath its roots. The Elysians used them to force it to grow. As a result, it was highly receptive to their inner desires.

A few red and purple flowers had sprouted as well, cushioning her from the ground.

When she sat up, the roots and flowers retracted, fading completely as though they'd never been conjured, except for one. A singular red flower remained, and she plucked it from the ground to play with its petals, sadness radiating in her core.

Why did it have to match the fires dancing at the edges of her borrowed sight? Why did it have to remind her of him?

She felt cold, like her very soul had frozen.

Tapping, more incessant and louder, forced her attention to the door. There was a pattern to it, a tap, tap, taptaptap, then tap. She ignored it to look around her brightly lit home with swollen eyes.

My face hurts. With how much she'd cried yesterday, she figured she would have started crying blood. She smeared the dry tracks of salt from her cheeks. *I can't believe I fell asleep on the floor.*

"Oh, come on, Rae," Cykran shouted through the thickness of the door. "I know you're awake. You're usually the first weirdo up before everyone else."

"Go away," she grumbled back.

He opened the door and nearly sent her flying. With a shocked expression causing her jaw to fall, she turned back to look up at him. He'd winced apologetically.

He said nothing about her being on the floor.

"Come on. I brought your favourite: hufflepumpkin and nutberry soup. Can't you smell it?" He waved the shallow bowl around.

Raewyn turned and booted the door with the bottom of her foot. The plate was nearly lost to the ground when his body, which had been half in and half out, was jammed between the door and its frame.

"What in the *Evergreen Servant* happened to you?" he grouched, referencing one of the male deities of her people – the only one left. "First you punch me, then you try to crush me to death with a door. I'm just trying to do my job here."

"You're fired," she half-heartedly stated, turning her head away.

His expression turned to one of hurt. "You don't mean that."

Then, with a sigh, he pushed his way through and entered her home. He placed the food on the ground next to her, then skilfully evaded every streak of sunlight to not be burned as he went to her small kitchen to boil a pot. Everyone in the city ate together in large rooms where they shared the same meals, everyone fed for free by volunteers.

He was making her a flowery tea.

"I didn't see you in the palace eatery," he said as he opened a silver jar and scooped tea leaves into it. "It's unlike you. You're usually the first one there, fighting to get all the best portions."

"You have some nerve, pushing your way into a councilmember's home," she said through clenched teeth, her nose crinkled in his direction while also slyly trying to pick up the plate to eat his offering.

She was hungry, and she did miss this delicious morning soup.

Cykran rubbed at one of his black horns. "You can't possibly be mad at me for something you asked me to do."

"What do you want, Cykran?" she asked, crossing her legs so she could freely eat.

She held the hot underside with one hand and scooped spoonfuls into her mouth with the other.

"I want to talk about what happened. You've... you've never acted that way towards me before." His pointed ears twitched, like they wanted to lower. "I didn't mean to leave that... *monster* behind, but what else could I have done?"

"He's not a monster!" she almost screeched.

Okay, he kind of was, but he was *her* monster, and only she could playfully call him that. Hers was a term of endearment, while Cykran's was obviously an insult.

"What do you mean, it's not a monster?" He placed his hands on the counter and bared his shark-like fangs. "You didn't see it attacking everyone! It was going to kill one of the Delysian soldiers before everyone managed to stop it."

"Because you were trying to take me away," she yelled back. "He was the only reason I was able to survive on Earth, and he was helping me get back home with the promise he could make a home here. He did so much for me, and because you didn't listen to me, your inaction caused him to be left behind."

"He had his hand in your chest! I thought my heart was going to explode," he said as he slammed his palm against the bronze counter. "I don't know what it was he took from you, but you're lucky we stopped him before it was too late. I thought he'd *killed* you, just as we were rescuing you!"

Raewyn lowered her head in thought. *I don't know what he took either.* She'd never seen anything like it.

It had been a blue flame.

She'd felt no different from it being removed, but it eventually floated back to her right before she was shoved through the portal. Whatever it was, he'd tried to *eat* it.

"He was just freaked out," she quietly rebuffed. "Random people with weapons had come to his home. He would not have understood a word of what anyone was saying, and all he saw were people trying to 'steal' me. I made him a promise, and now I've broken that promise because you didn't listen to me, a councilmember, your *friend.*"

Cykran rubbed his horn again in annoyance before pouring boiling water into a cup. He brought it over and crouched to put it on the ground in front of her. Then, he placed his hand on top of her head while squatting before her.

"My job is to assist you. That also means protecting you, but it is our friendship that will make me throw my life away for you. I didn't even care if I survived, so long as I was able to help bring you back."

"I never asked for your protection." She'd never really needed it before.

"No, but you need it. Otherwise, you'll turn yourself purple again."

Raewyn rolled her eyes. "That was one time."

He gave a lopsided grin when she picked up the teacup, happy she'd taken his offering. It fell, his red eyes crinkling in anguish.

"The fact I couldn't stop you from disappearing meant I had failed you to begin with. I was there. I almost had you. Then the portal closed before I could jump through it." He shook his head, the ends of his tied back long hair fluttering behind him. "I wouldn't have been able to stand it a second time. We only had so much time to save you, Rae. My people were freaked out by what they saw."

"*Our* people," Raewyn corrected, her eyes narrowing.

He rolled his own this time.

"They wear armour, but none of us have truly ever needed to fight against anything since we came here. You know just as much as we do that both the Delysian and Elysian soldiers are just for show, to give everyone in the city a false sense of comfort. Those eight Delysians and three Elysian soldiers were the only people brave enough to venture to another world, unprepared for what we were going to face. They expected Demons, unintelligent ones like we used to be, and we came to Lezekos to get away from them. Can't you understand how much we all care for you just by our actions yesterday?"

"I do," she answered confidently. "I don't blame them for what they did, but you are my friend. When I asked you to let me speak with him, you refused to listen. You are the one I'm angry with, not them."

"I'm sorry," he said as he sat on the ground with her. "I thought you'd gone insane on Earth. You wanted to reason with an unthinking beast, one throwing our soldiers around. The rift was closing, and Thorill was barely managing to keep it open."

Raewyn thumbed the sides of the cup. She didn't need him to explain it all to her; she was there, she'd seen it all.

"I made a sun stone," she whispered.

In her peripheral, Cykran's red eyes lit up with joy. "No way! That means you can replicate it and we can start taking back parts of the forest, the realm. People can start going to the mines safely and bringing back stones to power the city."

Raewyn slitted her eyes. "You made me leave it behind."

His cheerful expression fell before it twisted into a cringe. Cykran spouted a bunch of curses in Demonish as he yanked on his white ponytail.

"Why didn't you tell me?" he snapped, glaring in her direction. "I would have allowed you to grab it."

"Because you weren't listening to me! I would have needed to get through the 'monster' to get it, and if he knew everything was fine, he would have grabbed it for me."

"Well, how was I supposed to know?" His bottom lip puckered forward. "You should have stated that's what you wanted."

"Because it wasn't. I only thought about the stone once I got here."

Liquid filled her eyes.

She placed the tea on the ground when she realised she could no longer stomach anything. Even the food she'd eaten earlier felt like lead.

"What are you trying to say?"

"He was more than my friend, Cykran," she sobbed, covering her face to hide the shame of her tears. They were like razors coming from her swollen tear ducts. "I didn't even get to tell him how I feel."

My gosh! The last thing I'd said to him was in anger.

If she hadn't gotten upset with him because she'd been anxious about her own feelings, she wouldn't have been outside by herself. She could have been by Merikh's side, and she could have held his hand as they walked through the portal together.

Everything would have been different if there hadn't been a wall of blades between them.

I ruined everything. It's all my fault.

"Rae?" Cykran said as he pushed back her hair and tried to pull one of her hands from her face. "I don't understand why you're so upset over this. It's probably better that he stays there."

"Because I am in love with him, you stupid, idiotic, silly horn head!"

She bashed on his shoulders with purposefully weak punches. She just wanted to retaliate for all the pain in her chest by hurting him in return. He was too busy trying to fight her off to give any shocked expression.

"That Duskwalker meant more to me than you could even imagine, and I was going to fire your butt so I could make him my assistant!" She grabbed one of his pointed ears and started yanking on it. "And now he's gone, because you couldn't give me a moment of respect."

"Ouch, stop it!"

When she didn't, he gripped her wrists and hissed at her with his fangs bared.

Cykran wasn't often angry, so witnessing it was shocking to Raewyn. She couldn't fight past her hurt to be calm. His anger softened at her expression as she tried to curl into herself, then his eyes widened when he finally took in what she'd said.

"You're joking," he spat as he tossed her hands back and got to his feet. Disgust marred his handsome, sharp features. "You fell in love with that... that thing? It had a skull for a face, Raewyn! A skull!"

"I know that! I know what he looked like." She clenched and unclenched her fists. "I held his face in my hands all the time."

She'd liked how it felt.

How it was smooth except for where he had scars. How it was cool but eventually warmed under her touch. She'd liked exploring his fangs, his jaw, his rough horns. His short fur had tickled her palms, and she'd often drawn patterns in it.

"I'm not so guileless as to not know what I'm befriending, Cykran. You, of all people, should know that."

He put his hand over his chest. "That's not fair. We Delysians are different. We came here because we'd changed, and you could see that in our appearances. If it wasn't for our horns, claws, and eyes, you couldn't tell the difference between us."

"And the Taihee are no different, yet they had fur, tails, and wings," Raewyn argued. "How is he any different? There are even a few Bansu and Taihee hybrids who live here."

"Yes, but–"

"There is no 'but.' It was his heart, Cykran." She held her hands forward like she was holding it. "That's what I fell in love with. It didn't matter that we came from two different puzzles; our pieces fit perfectly."

"His heart?" Cykran eyed her warily. "For you to say that... Was he really that great?" Then his lips turned downward. "Are you even sure he felt the same way? What if he was using you just to get here?"

"I don't know," she answered sadly, fidgeting with her fingers. "I never told him because I just wanted to come home first. I think so, though. At least, I was hoping so."

"Are you sure? I don't mean this offensively, but have you met you? You're an obsessed workaholic who never hides how she feels, which kind of makes you annoying."

She threw her empty plate at him, and he quickly ducked with a chuckle. He'd just been trying to cheer her up, since she was so distressed.

The wooden plate clacked against the ground before it settled.

"None of it matters now," she said as she looked to the ground. "I already asked Thorill, and I can't go back to get him."

"Raewyn... I don't know how to tell you this if you truly feel that way about him," Cykran said in a serious yet solemn tone. He turned to the side as he scratched at his ponytail. "He's gone. One of the soldiers... They, uh, they removed his head. You can't go back to get him."

Raewyn turned her face away to look out of one of the sections of tree branches that acted as a window. She'd always preferred her home bright, which is why anywhere that could allow her to see outside but be private was filled with glass rather than ore.

That was before everything had become dark, of course. She'd barely looked at her home now that she was back and actually able to see it.

Should I tell him there may be a possibility he's not dead? What did it matter? It's not like Raewyn could go to him.

Unless Merikh figured out a way to come here, she'd never

see him again. The less anyone knew of him, what he was or how he came to be, the better it was for him and the other Duskwalkers.

It was better that she didn't reveal he was still alive.

"Cykran, can you please leave? I want to be alone."

His white eyelashes lowered briefly as the corners of his eyes crinkled with regret. "I'm sorry."

"I know," she murmured. "I want to have a bath and just deal with how I'm feeling."

"I wish I could give you that, but I actually came here to tell you the other councilmembers want to have a meeting with you. They want to know about your journey and the state of Earth."

Her lips tightened into a hard line. "Tell them I'm still resting. I'll deal with them when I'm ready to."

"Alright." He went to the plate she'd thrown and picked it up to take it away. "The tea is in front of you. Drink it before it goes cold."

He left, giving Raewyn the sweet, blissful silence she preferred.

She bent her knees so she could hug her legs and attempted to drink the tea. Her heart just wasn't in it. She wondered how she was supposed to go back to work or face anyone when she'd completely lost all will.

She gave up and eventually stood.

It was... weird being home. It felt much emptier than it did before.

The space would have perfectly fit Merikh. It was tall enough that not even his horns would have scraped the lighting. Shaped like an oval, it was twice the size of his cave.

It was an average sized home for her people, and it held everything she could possibly need. There was only one additional room, which held a toilet for privacy, but beyond that, it was open.

Her bed was big enough to fit two of Merikh. She'd opted for more sleeping space, since she often used it for multiple functions, like a chair and table all in one.

She owned two chairs, but their backs rested against her kitchen bench, which had a heating stove in the middle so she could cook snacks and drinks. Her lounge table was round to fit the room, made of obsidian, and it was more a storage space for all the paperwork she always brought home.

Most items were made of either molten ore or obsidian, considering there were veins of both underneath the city.

Many purple and pink leaves had sprouted on the ceiling, which needed to be clipped away. They weren't supposed to be there, but building their homes within a living structure had its disadvantages.

Knick-knacks and ornaments gifted to her by the people of Lezekos City sat on shelves. She'd never had the heart to part with a single piece, each one precious to her.

It was home. It smelt familiar, looked familiar, it even felt familiar, and yet she was out of place within it. Something was missing, and it was his orange and cinnamon scent. It was too quiet, and her ears were listening for tiny vibrations that only she could hear.

Yes, it was warm, but Merikh's warmth had been different. It had seeped into her pores and wrapped itself around her heart.

It hasn't even been a day, and I already miss him.

She turned to the side and made her way to the bath, its edges level with the ground. On the wall was a runic circle, and when she placed her hand over it, it glowed purple before water filled from the bottom.

Steam ghosted over the surface, and she walked down the stairs to greet it once she removed her dress.

After a brief soak, she washed her body using a loofa to scour away all the dirt, sweat, and stress that had clung to her body over the last several hours. She washed her face with products tailored to her skin type, moisturising it.

Then she rubbed a lock of curls between her fingers, grimacing at the coarseness. Her hair needed some serious tough love. Now that she had the proper care products, she was able to give it the attention it deserved.

Raewyn was slow, allowing herself to get lost in thought as she finally had her first real bath in ages.

Months on Earth had only been a few weeks here, but somehow, it was like forever ago that she'd left.

Carefully combing her hair while it was lathered in a detangling shampoo, she started at the ends and worked it through. Then she rinsed it and conditioned it twice, the first time with a deep conditioner to nourish and strengthen her hair, and the second time with a leave-in conditioner to lock in moisture and keep her hair soft and silky. She gave it one last comb through before she just reclined in the metre deep water to her shoulders, allowing herself to be comforted by its warmth.

She closed her eyes so she could truly rest.

Reflecting on her time on Earth was painful, but she had much to think over.

Once she was done, she got out of the bath and wrapped herself in a plush towel. She pressed another rune that would relocate the water to be cleansed through natural soil before it went back into the safe water systems that ran beneath the ground.

Everything was borrowed, and nothing was truly wasted.

Raewyn lightly fingered oils through her wet hair and covered it in a thin satin bonnet that would help to protect her curls. She laid down on the ground, where the only bit of light was still shining, since the last sun was dropping past the horizon.

She'd been home for nearly a full sun cycle.

Just when she thought she was getting better at handling her emotions, her self-care routine helping, something had her eyes welling with tears worse than before.

"No," she rasped, her sight flickering, fading in and out suddenly. "No, no, no!"

She covered her face, almost clawed at it with her nails,

willing it to stop, to keep it. When she pulled her hands away, everything was *gone*.

Somehow, Merikh had taken his sight back, and she felt even more alone than before. She feared the worst.

He'd never been able to take it back without touching her, without physically drawing it back.

No. Please. Rolling onto her side, she hugged her midsection as she wept. *Please don't tell me he died. Please don't let that be the reason it's gone.*

She would never know. She would have to live with the painful, unanswered question for the rest of her life.

It's not fair. I want him back.

Heat stopped warming her when the final sun finished falling away. She curled herself into a ball.

I'm so sorry I couldn't save you.

FORTY-ONE

The issue with regrowing one's body within seconds was that coming to could be quite startling. Coupled with the fact that his environment was completely foreign, Merikh's first glance around was disorientated.

He'd never been able to take his sight back without touching Raewyn before. Was it because he regrew his entire body, or because a day had passed? He'd never willingly given Raewyn his sight for more than a few minutes.

Something shattered beneath his weight, and everything turned upside down as he collapsed to one side. The fading light was too bright, the room completely made of glass on one side.

He clutched at his throat. *I can't breathe.* He clawed at his chest. *The air, it's too thin.*

He took in quick breaths to combat it. Adjusting to it would take time, but it still felt like needles in his lungs in the meantime.

Almost keeling over as he stood in the rubble of the desk he'd crushed, his head darted one way and then the other.

On the opposing side of the glass windows, books upon books were neatly put away on a ceiling-tall shelf. There were at least two dozen random skulls – most of those consisting of Demons and fanged creatures – in crystal domes on benches up against the glass walls.

Where am I? Nothing was familiar.

He hadn't expected to have his head removed, but he also rarely came back *not* in the place he'd remembered being last.

What happened? he thought around choking breaths, stumbling to the side so he could rest his hand against a wooden bookshelf slat. It broke under his strength.

Something was wrong. Something was missing. *Raewyn.* He stabbed between his horns, trying to grasp something he *knew* wasn't there.

I didn't take her soul! A distressed roar bellowed from him as he shot for what looked like an exit. *Fuck. I need to find her.*

He didn't care where he was. He didn't care what world he was running into, not when his thoughts were of his little fairy, his piece of light.

Stumbling, he broke through the door with his shoulder when he found it was locked.

Wood splintered before shattering, and a woman screamed as he burst into a hallway filled with people. He skidded to a halt. Gasps rang from all around as one man on his left grabbed a woman's shoulders to drag her back, since she was the closest. On his right, a man roared out with fear as he fell to his arse.

Through his hazy vision, unable to cope with the light, the lack of air, the *heat* around him, he noticed two distinct features: dark skin and white hair.

Elves? If they were Elves, then he'd been taken to her realm.

Had they picked up his skull to examine it like the others he'd seen in the room he was just in? Thankfully, they hadn't destroyed it in the process, or perhaps they just hadn't had time to yet.

He took a step one way, wanting to get past them. *Where is Raewyn? Is she here?* If she asked them to bring him here, why wasn't she nearby? Why hadn't she waited for him to come back to life?

The moment he stepped towards people, the stench of fear pierced the air like a spear, and Merikh rent out a choke. He backed up when his orbs flashed a deeper crimson and turned the other way to get away from it.

A deeper fear stench struck him, and he covered his snout with a whine. Even though he was oxygen starved, he cut off his breathing.

No. Shit, don't. White flashed in his sight. *I can't let hunger take control. I'll fucking kill everyone.*

More people were collecting in the hallway on both sides, foolishly coming to see what the commotion was. They thickened the air to the point he could *taste* their fear. It'd never been this overwhelmingly tangible before, and his mouth began to drip with drool.

He probably looked like an uncontrollable beast, darting one way and then the other, his claws, fangs, and skull frightening to most. It didn't help that his quills were fully raised in aggression, making him appear like a frightening, spiked animal.

At this rate, his consciousness would fade.

He needed to take a breath, but the next one would clutch at him.

Out. I need out!

He couldn't move through the people, not if he didn't want to murder someone by accident with his quills. The hallway was tall, but it wasn't wide enough to fit his massive body with them in the way.

There was no gap. No way out.

Glass situated between pieces of white branches caught his attention. There.

With a snarl, he bashed his shoulder against it. It didn't break, and the lack of oxygen constricted his lungs. He bashed it again, but it still didn't shatter.

Shit, shit, shit! He needed something hard. He placed his hands on either side of it and used all his strength to bash his bony forehead against it. It cracked, and he did it again.

The moment glass shattered, he shoved his head through and

sucked in fresh air, uncaring that it was thin. More screams exploded, but he ignored them as he broke his way further through the window.

Glass shards cut at his belly and sides as he crawled his way through. He needed to get away from them.

From what he could tell, the entire section of hallway he'd been in was part of a massive tree, bigger than anything he'd ever thought possible. He turned so he could claw his way upwards on a gigantic white branch, already noticing he was miles high.

No wonder the air was so thin. He'd never been this far above sea level before in his life.

Using his toe claws, he kicked and climbed his way higher.

At the top of the branch, he went to stand, but a sharp gust of wind nearly pushed him off it. He had to steady himself with his hands or he'd slide over. Assaulted by wind pushing his body to the side, his quills acting like a sail fin, he crawled to the trunk of the tree.

It gave him something better to hold on to, as well as shielded him from the worst of the wind.

He stood, and with the wind pushing his quills and tail to the left, he finally took in the world.

Holy... spirit of the void, whoa.

He took in the uncanny workmanship of nature, made by an extraterrestrial world.

From as far as the eye could see, the land was covered in trees that reached at least half the magnificent height he was standing at, which meant they were taller than any other on Earth. Some had white bark with pink and purple leaves, which were the prominent colours, but others had splashes of blue and green with black trunks.

In the distance, where the fading sunlight wasn't touching them anymore, their leaves were *glowing*.

There was an open field between the middle of two sets of forest, a large river running down the middle that headed straight below him. The grass was an azure blue, waving like the sea from the wind pushing through its long stalks.

Still, it was what was below that was truly awe-inspiring.

It was a white city, hundreds of miles wide, with cream limestone walls circling it all the way to the ocean behind him. Houses around the base of the tree he was standing upon were mainly made from its white roots, but it looked as though they were *connected*, like the tree itself had made their homes.

Further out were more houses made of cream limestone, many with glass as ceilings. Those made of the tree were circular, but the stone ones came in varying shapes, swirling colours painted into them.

Hills played all throughout the city, with coloured flags and fluttering cloth giving life to it.

A small cliff separated the people from the beach behind him, but there were three stone staircases freely leading to it.

He was so high, he could barely make out thousands of people, all dressed in different colours, moving through the city. The pathways were azure blue grass like he could see around the river – as though they preferred having something living to soften their footsteps.

The sky was difficult to make out through a multicoloured dome barrier that protected the entire city. It was only when he stopped looking through the rainbow of the bubble that he noted the sky was green to match the only sun he could see.

Everything was painted in the dimming light of dusk falling over the water. At least the ocean looked familiar, although a little greener than he was used to.

The sight before him was beautiful – lush, vivid, and overwhelmingly breath-taking. How could a world glow like this?

Another gust of wind tried to push him forward, and it woke him from his maw-gaping stare.

His orbs turned blue. *How am I meant to find her here?*

He was sure she'd find him first, but what he really

wondered... How the hell were they supposed to find each other without him killing someone?

Merikh needed to find her before those soldiers he faced on Earth found him, or before fear forced him into a hunger-filled rage. He had no quill guards, no scent-cloaking cloth.

Hell, he was even naked.

He couldn't stay this high for much longer. He could become accustomed to the thin oxygen, but it would take time. Going back inside the tree to where the people stood in a tight hallway seemed idiotic.

He'd look like a monster barrelling his way through. If he accidentally hurt someone, the already overbearing fear mixing with blood was a sure-fire way to set him off.

I need to go down. From the outside.

Merikh started clawing his way down, occasionally jumping from the hundreds of branches. Some of the leaves were bigger than him – some of the sticks, too. He was like an ant scaling a tree.

He slipped after one leap and began to plummet, only to break his fall when his torso slammed against a thick branch. Spittle sprayed from his mouth, and he already knew his insides were going to be bruised. When he started slipping off the edge, he panicked and dug his claws in, then just stayed there for a moment, huffing.

At least going downwards was helping him breathe, but a fall from this height was sure to shatter his skull in an instant. He didn't think he'd been this close to his own possible death.

It felt like hours before he reached the bottom.

Once he did, he stood on a random home so he could look around and search. Like a looming figure lifting his snout into the air, he hoped he could catch even just a thread of Raewyn's lily of the valley scent.

Nothing, and someone's scream had his sight shifting to white.

Merikh darted to another rooftop, then another, wanting to

get as far from the screamer as possible. He just needed to evade everyone until he found her sweet, toxic lily scent, and hopefully escape being noticed in the meantime.

Despite how quick he was on all fours, whenever he stopped on top of someone's oddly shaped home to sniff for Raewyn, he would catch someone's attention. Whenever they pointed with a shout, he bolted, even if he hadn't scented the air properly.

Where are you, little starshine?

Now that he was in the heart of the city, it looked impossible. It was even bigger than he thought, and it was as confusing as a labyrinth. He didn't know if he'd doubled back or not. He didn't know where he was going or how he was supposed to navigate it.

Lanterns filled with something other than flame lit up without anyone's assistance, even before the sun had finished setting. Everything was getting darker, making it hard even for him to distinguish between people.

He was blindly following his nose now, and only stalked those with long but coily hair – none turning out to be her.

Time passed slowly, but his pulse was quick.

Then it began.

An alarm blared like an ominous chime.

Before long, Merikh was being chased by white metal armoured soldiers wielding those deadly polearms. The occupants of the city had alerted them to his presence.

Different coloured balls of light glowed from their weapons. It looked like ornaments had been tied to the shafts of them by ribbons, and he noted they matched the colour of their leather. They appeared to help them follow each other as they gave chase.

Three became nine, until there were dozens heading towards him from all directions.

Even with the darkness falling on them, his red glowing orbs were like a beacon.

In his monstrous form, Merikh just ran on all fours, sprinting to escape. He was faster, and he tried to pick up Raewyn's scent as he bounced from rooftop to rooftop.

With the alarm chiming, people ran to the safety of their homes. It gave Merikh the freedom to hide within the labyrinth of the city by dropping down to the streets. His quick, thumping paws reverberated off the walls, and the exhaustion caused his huffing breaths to be loud and wet.

The smell of fear grew stronger, then faded as he passed different houses. Each time a particular area was saturated with it, like those within the area were petrified, he ceased breathing until he passed through.

Running down a path, he skidded to a halt at a line of soldiers pointing their blades towards him. From what he could tell, they were a mixture of Elves and Demons, and their blades faintly glowed with misty energy.

He now knew how deadly those weapons were.

He darted to the left but doubled back and went right when more collected that way.

The tree he'd been standing on earlier wasn't the centre of the city, but it was close to it. The leaves were glowing a pinkish purple in the dark, and he headed for it.

He'd go back up until he lost the soldiers.

If Raewyn was here, she would have been alerted to his presence by now. *Will she come find me, or leave me to fend for myself here?*

How the tides had changed.

He was being *hunted.* He hadn't hurt a single person, and they had already pointed their weapons at him.

Not really the warm welcome she'd promised him.

He knew the problem.

He was a strange creature in their home. In their eyes, he was a monster who had trespassed, and they didn't know if he was safe or not.

Worse still, they couldn't communicate. The soldiers back at his home had spoken another language. They hadn't understood him then. He needed Raewyn to translate.

He was moving too fast. How was she supposed to come to him when he couldn't stop for even a moment before being swarmed? Finding her seemed impossible.

There were too many people. Too many houses to check. Too many scents on top of each other for him to even pick up a thread.

He kept his sight on the tree. *What if she's in there?*

He couldn't move through it.

Fuck. What am I supposed to do?

There was an open area between two overarching tree roots, a clear path to safety – or so he thought.

A net burst from the side and wrapped around three of his limbs. His quills were quick to free him, but he still crashed against the ground, his left shoulder and skull first. By the time he was back on all fours, he was surrounded.

Seeing no other alternative, he leapt over the top of them and their long polearms. A vine with two stones on each end wrapped one of his arms against his torso, and he hit the ground with his chest when he landed.

An *oomph* burst from him.

Fighting to free himself, he was surrounded once more, this time by twice the number of soldiers. As he stood on two legs so he could free his arm, they jabbed upwards to keep him from attacking.

He backed up and yelped when someone poked him in the arse with a sharp tip. Merikh roared, his quills standing on their ends, puffing him out and doubling his size.

Shouts rang as they kept him locked in. They gave him just enough space to move back and forth as he searched for an escape, for a space to leap, anything.

There were too many now. He'd be impaled if he moved back down to the ground.

"Stop being afraid!" he roared, wishing the smell of their fear would cease. His voice was distorted in his monstrous form,

a treble to his usual bass.

His sight deepened into crimson, and he was forced to shove two fingers into his nose hole to shield himself from it.

Someone stepped forward and jabbed their blade at him when he got too close.

"Fuck off," he snarled, growing more agitated by the second.

His chest was tight in anger, in fear of what could happen. He spun in a circle, but there was no way out unless he fought them.

I can't. She'll never forgive me.

They wouldn't accept him. He would fall into a killing spree. Shedding the blood of just one person would start something he wouldn't be able to control in such a dense population.

Currently, they were jabbing at a bomb of claws, fangs, and insatiable hunger, and they were moments from setting him off.

If she tries to stop me, I'll kill her. His sight momentarily shifted to white at the thought, panic skittering through him.

It didn't matter how he felt towards her. In that state, he wouldn't see the difference between friend or foe, food or companion. She'd be nothing but meat.

Merikh paced the length of their polearms on three limbs, two fingers still lodged in his nose hole, as he tried to figure a way past, tried to think *rationally.*

He sat back on his haunches and raised a hand to wave down, hoping the sign for calm the fuck down was universal. The person he'd done it towards, although random, had only seen him threaten with claws.

A man came forward and used his hands to speak. A person next to him translated on his behalf.

"I cannot understand you," he answered back, hoping that was enough.

He stepped closer to the one person who was actually trying to communicate with him. Two polearms on either side of them stabbed forward as the one signing retreated. A blade sliced over his biceps.

Merikh roared and backed up. He halted before it was too late. Someone shouted, and a net was thrown over him. They tugged, and his weight shifted to his side as they attempted to trap him. Merikh burst through the vine wrappings when his quills easily ripped them apart.

His sight wobbled as invisible hands clutched at his mind, trying to force his control to slip. His arms and legs quaked, his breaths growing more irritated by the second, sawing in and out of him like a blade.

The invisible hands that massaged his brain felt *so good* that he almost wanted to let them win. His glowing orbs turned a dark crimson with the desire to maim.

Merikh stopped moving, stopped responding to them.

Raewyn. I need to get to Raewyn.

He wanted her to calm him, to save him – from them, from himself.

His sight flickered in and out of consciousness, and he tried to hold it back, to not let his mind shift. His shudders were violent.

She's mine. I want her to be mine. Cannot lose control. Don't destroy.

They were poking a fucking bear, one who usually let anger take hold. If they kept doing so, they were going to reap the consequences of their stupidity.

I need to stay in control for her.

Still curled on the ground, holding her midsection, Raewyn flinched at the sudden frantic banging on her door.

"Raewyn. Raewyn!" Cykran yelled. "For the love of the Evergreen, are you dressed?"

She bounced to her feet and carefully walked towards the sound, knowing the layout of her home by pure memory. She flung open the door, his constant bashing helping to direct her.

"Of course, I'm dressed. It's been hours," she answered as she gave a sniffle. "My bath ended ages–"

He gripped her shoulders so tightly his claws threatened to cut into her skin. "We have a problem, a big problem!"

Just then, an alarm bell began to chime from the heart of the city, informing all of danger.

Her droopy ears stiffened and darted back as her eyes widened. "What's happened?"

Had Demons managed to figure out how to get into the city? Her sadness could wait. She needed to help her people, direct them through an emergency.

"Your creature... he's here." His claws cut deeper, and she would have winced if it weren't for his words. "He's in the city!"

She pushed him away from her. "What do you mean, he's in the city?"

"He's being chased, Rae." She could almost picture him tugging at a horn. "He's not surrendering to Mericato and his soldiers."

As relieved as she was that Merikh was alive, he was alone in an unfamiliar environment with hostiles chasing after him. She understood how badly this could end.

"We have to go." She grabbed whatever she could of Cykran's clothing and shook him. "You have to take me to him. He's not like you Delysians. He'll go berserk and decimate the entire city if we're not careful."

"I thought you said he was good!"

"He is! I promise he is. He wouldn't be able to help it. Just... please, Cykran." Her eyes bowed into a desperate and beseeching expression. "Take me to him, as fast as you can; I don't care how."

He gave a soft, rolling growl. "Fine. Hop on."

He turned and gave her his back as he crouched down. Raewyn touched his shoulders and then wrapped herself around him.

Usually, when she made Cykran carry her like this, she'd make him giddy up in a funny way. This time, she said nothing and waited for him to sprint.

Her home was high up in the central tree. They were fortunate the hallways were empty due to the alarm telling everyone to hide in their homes.

"How did he get here? Do you know?" she asked, clinging to his neck while his arms threaded around her knees.

She could feel how quickly he was sprinting by the air whooshed over them and how vigorously his body moved. She felt as much as she heard how hard his footsteps were thudding against the ground with each foot fall. She constantly bounced on his back.

"Mericato ordered for his skull to be brought here. I heard his translator say he was going to give it to Ulair to study, since we'd never seen anything like him."

Raewyn's lips thinned in annoyance. "Why didn't you tell me?"

"How was I supposed to know he'd come back to life?" Cykran snapped back. "I didn't think it would be a good idea to tell you I saw them bring back your dead lover's head, okay? Your face was all gross from crying, and I was worried you were going to start hitting me again."

"Gosh, you make me so angry." She reached up and yanked on his horn.

He stepped to the side as he stumbled. "Hey! I'm running here."

"Can you go any faster?"

"I'm going as fast as I can!" Just as fresh air rushed against her face, Cykran halted. "I don't know where they are. It's too dark, and I don't see any beacon lights."

Raewyn squinted her eyes, as if that would help her see. Funnily enough, it did. Since no other lights, like those of the city, were able to distract her, she noticed a handful of magical glows to the left.

She pointed. "Go that way."

Cykran spun and headed to the left. As they met the top of a rise, dozens of glows emerged and circled a black spot in the middle – a spot with sparks of red and white.

Merikh.

"I need you to be my voice," Raewyn said as they got closer. "If he hears me, I'm worried he'll try to get through the soldiers like back on Earth. I'll only be able to speak quietly."

"You know Mericato will be leading them."

That will pose a problem. "I know, but you just have to get him to let me through."

Cykran nodded, only a metre away from the mixture of glowing colours.

"Let us through!" he demanded. He shoulder-barged against soldiers' backs, none of which got out of his way. "I bring councilwoman Raewyn Daefaren."

She winced at her name being shouted, but it didn't appear Merikh had heard or understood it.

The first line of soldiers parted, and they were swallowed up by people. The clanking and grinding of metal on leather creaked in her ears, as the smell of armour oils penetrated her nose. With how much sweat was clinging to the air, she worried how much fear they were producing.

"I can't move further in," he said over his shoulders. "There's Rankae blades everywhere."

"All civilians have been warned to retreat into their houses," someone yelled as two sets of footsteps stomped closer. Armour jingled and jangled upon their approach. "Take her back inside the palace."

"She's here to defuse the situation. Let her pass."

There was a silence shared between them as Mericato signed. Raewyn knew sign language, but unfortunately, it became difficult for them to communicate once she could no longer read his hands. When they wanted to communicate privately, he'd write with elbraille ink on a piece of paper, or he'd use his finger to write on her palm, and then she would speak back to him.

However, he often had a translator with him, and Cykran was still learning it upon her request.

"I told you he'd be leading the team," Cykran whispered.

"This is not your jurisdiction," Mericato's translator said, although he lacked the anger in his voice that was surely written on his face. "I am the councilmember in charge of the city's safety. There is no need for you, a civilian, to be here."

She wasn't pleased to hear this. She was also still cranky, since he was the one who'd pushed her through the portal.

"Tell them he can't speak our language. I can calm him down and translate."

"He's from Earth and a friend to her. Let her speak to him."

She just knew Mericato had narrowed his eyes at her, especially when his translator said, "So you're the reason he's here. Of course. You disappear for weeks and bring back a hostile pet."

A deep and booming snarl reverberated off everyone's armour, making it sound hollow and echoey. Her ears darted back, and she gripped Cykran's neck tighter.

"Just let her through!" Cykran shouted at the terrifying noise Merikh made. "Before it's too late. We don't have time to be arguing."

"Her safety is top priority. I'm not letting her through to speak with some beast when we have no idea what it is or what it's capable of."

"Let me down," she quietly bit as she lowered her legs.

When he released her, she headed for Mericato.

"A little to the right," Cykran stated, just like Merikh often did for her.

She diverted slightly.

She patted the man's chest plate, grabbed him by the shoulder straps, and lifted him to his toes – since she was a little taller than him.

Then, morphing her features into the fiercest stare she could muster, she *growled,* "Move."

His laughter was quiet and muffled.

"Fine," Mericato said, his voice raw, strained, and so raspy it was difficult to understand. It was the first time she'd ever heard him speak, and the pain of him doing so was obvious. "You want to die, go for it."

She let him go in surprise, and backed up to give him room to use his hands.

"Three runs in," his translator started when Mericato must have signalled with his hands. "Disarm to let her through."

Cykran patted her on the back to lightly steer her.

"A path's opened up, Rae. Do you want me to come with you?"

She shook her head, telling him to stay as she put her hand out and made her way through the air to make sure it was empty. She knew she'd passed the soldiers when their sounds ceased from all around her and instead shuffled from behind.

"Merikh," she gently called, knowing exactly where he was by the rapidly flickering sparks.

"Raewyn," he said with a growly groan. His relief was so obvious, it was palpable.

She came a little closer, thankful he was coherent enough to speak. It meant it was safe to approach.

She wished she'd been able to see what came next; it might have stopped her from screaming. Green sparks came from him, just as the soldiers behind her gasped.

Merikh grabbed one of her outstretched hands, yanked her forward, and then tackled her to the ground. She didn't know when she'd started screaming, but it was muffled by his chest the moment he laid down on top of her.

Her knees were forced into a bent position when they pressed into his stomach, her arms trapped between them. Merikh curled his entire body around her. His forearms covered her arms with his hands on top of her head, while his legs covered her sides with his feet supporting her backside.

"Raewyn!" Cykran's panicked shout echoed.

"This is why we don't allow civilians to get involved! Everyone stay back. If you attack it, it might turn on her."

"I'm okay!" she exclaimed.

She knew what this looked like, since she'd been in a similar defensive position below him before. She no doubt imagined he looked like a big spikey ball with her hidden inside protectively.

Sounds beyond him were quieter, and it allowed her to hear how frantically his heart was beating, how short and shallow his breaths were. Acute whines burst from his torso, right before his head darted to one side and he let out a feral, bursting roar.

He pulled her in tighter, then tighter still as his head whipped the other way to snarl in warning.

"I need you to calm down, okay?" she gently sang in English, rubbing at his chest in hopes of soothing him. "You're scaring everyone."

"Tell them to back off," he growled. *"Tell them to control their fear."*

Raewyn managed to shove her hands through the gap where the corners of his jaw and his shoulders were. She covered the end of his snout with one hand to block their scents for him while waving the other in the air.

"Please give us some space," she called to her people. "The smell of your fear is agitating him. He won't hurt you, so please ease yourselves." She hoped she wasn't making empty promises. "Better?" she asked him when rattling informed her the small army had backed up.

He grunted in answer.

I feel so bad for him. Has he been running since the moment I lost his sight? That had been two hours ago, if not more.

Silence radiated between them, but it was thick with tension. His snarls and growls hadn't faded, nor had his heart or breaths calmed.

She braved moving her hand from his face and brought them both down to rub at his thick, firm neck soothingly. When she scratched it, he shivered, and the pressure weighing down on her lessened.

Which was good, since he'd been crushing her.

"Did you hurt anyone, Merikh? It'll be much harder to fight on your behalf if you did."

"No, I made sure not to harm any of your people. I knew they wouldn't trust me if I did, and I didn't think you'd forgive me."

Such a smart Duskwalker, on both accounts. She smiled lightly as she placed her forehead against his big chest and took in the comfort of his orange and cinnamon scent. His fur tickled her forehead, and she rubbed into the soft fibres.

Despite her desire to stay with him, her heart blossoming at his return, she turned her head up to the underside of his skull.

"I need you to let me up, Merikh," she gently requested, only to wince when he bared down on her again.

"No." The depth of his unusual, monstrous bass doubled, and it was so definitive, it had goosebumps rising on her arms.

"We can't stay like this forever."

"I won't allow them to take you away again."

She wanted to promise him they wouldn't, but she knew where his next destination was – and it wasn't her home. At least, not yet.

That's if he wanted to stay with her.

"You're here. You made it to Nyl'theria," she said, hoping to reassure him. "If you let me up, we can resolve everything and work on gaining you permission to remain in the city."

"I don't give a fuck where I am, Raewyn."

Her brows drew together so tightly they knotted her forehead. "I don't understand. Isn't this what you wanted? To come here, to get away from Earth?"

"What I want has changed. I don't care where I am so long as I have it."

"What do you want, then?"

His breaths whimpered, anxious and fearful. It was strange. His answer was slow to come, but it was soft, uttered so quietly that it was a whisper. *"You."*

Her heart stammered in her chest, racing for what that could possibly mean. *Does that mean he feels the same way as me?*

"Is... Is that why you tried to take something from me?" she asked, unsure if her voice was shaking from nervousness or excitement.

The silence that followed weighed heavily on her chest. He didn't want to answer.

"Merikh?" she pushed, her voice cracking.

"Yes."

"What was it? I've never seen anything like it."

Under her hands, his heart rate spiked, thumping wildly, like it was moments from giving out. Gosh, it was obvious he was deeply distressed. *"Your soul."*

"My soul?" she grumbled in confusion before her eyes widened. "You're a soul eater, just like Weldir. That's what it means to be your bride."

"Yes," he answered quietly. *"However, unlike him, Mavka can only consume one soul. We become your anchor, and you become ours. We would be tethered to each other for eternity. In this world, and in the afterworld."*

A flare of anger shot through her. "You tried to bond me to you without my permission! How could you?"

She would have smacked his chest if she wasn't aware she had a violently quaking beast above her. She also didn't want to alarm the soldiers, but she did pinch him in the side of the neck.

An acute whimper echoed from him, and he tightened around her to make their shared space smaller. Raewyn had a feeling it had nothing to do with her physical retaliation and everything to do with her outrage.

"I'm sorry. Please forgive me." His breaths sounded as though he was shaking with agony, so much so that he was wheezing. *"I saw them trying to take you, and I knew I wasn't going to be able to get past the soldiers without hurting you or them. If I took your soul, you would have returned to me."*

"Why didn't you tell me you wanted that?" she asked, digging her fingers into his fur. "We could have spoken about it rather than you just... trying to steal it."

What he did was wrong. He shouldn't have tried to do that.

"I wanted to, but I was afraid you'd say no."

Of course, he was. It wasn't like she'd given him a reason to think she would have a different answer.

Raewyn lowered her head so she could press her forehead against his sternum and wrapped her arms over his sides, careful to avoid his razor-sharp quills.

"You big numbskull," she murmured, taking in his warmth, his scent, just... all of him. She let out a contented sigh. "I missed you, you know."

He didn't answer her, but she noticed that his heart slowed – so big and heavy, so powerful and full of life.

"I was so worried when they pushed me through the portal. I thought I'd lost you," she said, her voice breaking on a sob. Tears welled in her eyes, making her want to roll them at herself, but she couldn't help it. Instead, she freely let them flow down her temples. "I thought I'd never see you again or get the chance to tell you I was falling in love with you."

She hadn't known that she already was, and being apart from him only made her realise just how much she wanted him in her life.

All noises from Merikh suddenly cut out: his heart, his breaths, his warning growls and whimpers. The next soft gust of wind was unbearably loud, as was the shifting of the soldiers and a random cough.

He'd gone so rigid and still that she'd almost feared he'd turned to stone. She wished his skull wasn't blocking her sight so she could see if his orbs had changed colour.

"Give me your soul," he impatiently panted when everything washed out of him.

"Can't you ask me nicely?" she half-sobbed and half-laughed.

"Please? I want to hold it, guide it, cherish and protect it, just as I want to do for your body."

Raewyn reached up so she could cup the sides of his bony snout. "There are so many other amazing people here you haven't met, Merikh. What if you change your mind?"

She had her own fears and reservations. Cykran was right; she may be, in her own opinion, cleverly humorous, but Raewyn had flaws. Not everyone enjoyed her humour, and work had been and would always be her priority.

His head reared back so he could stare down at her, giving her more space and freedom.

"I won't. I thought I would be content as long as I left Earth, but I realised what I was searching for was something to bring me peace and happiness by brightening my world. I have sat in the pitch black for most of my life, my bright starshine, and you chased it away with your strange playfulness, your laughter, your tears, your kindness towards a creature everyone else had scorned."

"But someone else can be that for you."

He cupped the side of her face. *"You have scored my heart, Raewyn. I never dreamt of having a bride because I didn't think it was possible, but in your light, in your unconditional acceptance, you made me believe."*

Raewyn leaned into his big palm as he stroked his clawed thumb over her cheek. "Merikh," she choked out, gripping the back of his hand.

"I want you to be my beacon on the days the darkness wishes to take hold of me again."

Raewyn wished such a special moment wasn't being witnessed, but she was thankful none of them could understand what they were saying or the tender words coming from him.

"I have been waiting for over three hundred years for you." Merikh licked across her cheek to erase the stain of her tears. *"If you truly meant what you said, if you have really found it within your heart to love me, I won't allow anyone to take you away*

from me."

A strange hiccup, like a giggle and a sob catching at the same time, broke from her.

Even though this wasn't the time nor place, he wasn't going to let her up until she gave in. Not that it was a particularly hard decision – she'd already made up her mind before coming here. She just hadn't known what it truly was or how permanent it would be.

"How do I do it? How do I give you my soul?"

"I don't know," he answered truthfully. *"Just will it or... Never mind."*

A chomp of fangs clipped right above her before he thickly swallowed.

Wait, that's it? I didn't even see it! Then again, why would she see her soul when it technically wasn't magic? It was essence, something beyond recognition.

"Am I supposed to feel anything different?" she asked, patting at her chest.

"I'm not sure, but my hunger is gone. The scent of fear is no longer bothering me." His muscles tensed, as if he'd winced. *"However, it's so hot, it feels like it's going to burn me from the inside out. Was it meant to be blue?"*

How was she supposed to know? Blue flames tended to be hotter than most others, though.

Raewyn waited, but even as time passed, he didn't free her. "Merikh, can you let me up now?"

He grunted. *"I don't want to. I want to stay here, where I can hold you and protect you."*

She wanted to laugh, realising he could be possessive when he wanted to be. She didn't, though. "We can't do that."

He did eventually pull back to remove his weight from her. *"I know. I can see the worry on their faces. The bearded one waving his hands will not wait much longer."*

Once she was free, Raewyn sat up. She also reached for his hand, subconsciously knowing it would be there waiting for her.

Her cheeks heated when she stood, like she'd been caught doing something she wasn't supposed to, now that her attention was split from Merikh. She turned to him.

"I'll translate for you, okay? You'll need to follow whatever orders the lead guard tells you. I will have very little sway in this discussion."

"I thought you were some important person in this realm."

Raewyn nibbled her bottom lip, feeling a little shy. "I am, but there are seventeen other councilmembers. Mericato is the head of the safety department. He was born without the ability to speak, and multiple surgeries have left his throat permanently scarred. He will have a translator speak on his behalf. Not even the guard commander can overrule him."

He'd changed his form back to the more humanoid version she was used to, and his voice was normal as he stated, "As long as I will not be separated from you, I will do as they ask."

Still holding his hand, she stepped in a random direction. She redirected when she heard movement coming from the left.

"Raewyn," Cykran shouted in relief.

He must have come forward too fast, because Merikh wrapped his arm around her midsection, pulled her back flush against his torso, and bit out a malicious snarl. Raewyn shot her hands into the air just in case his quills had lifted.

"I told you to stand back," Mericato's translator said.

"Everything's fine. He's just a little agitated. I would be too if I had weapons pointing at me." Raewyn sighed, and it only took a small push to free herself once his arm had loosened. "Merikh is seeking sanctuary within Lezekos, Mericato. He will do what is asked of him, and I promise he will not cause anyone harm."

"How can we trust his word after what has happened today? We spent hours chasing him."

Raewyn's features morphed into a scowl. "Did he hurt anyone? He knew attacking would only reflect terribly in his favour, so he fled out of fear."

She doubted it was fear, but she figured that was the safest bet to win Mericato's stoney heart over. He was silent as he thought on his options.

"Please don't judge him on his outward appearance," Raewyn added. "We have made contact with many people who are different from us. Don't allow us to reflect badly on this day in the future. He may look a little scary, but his heart can be gentle if given the chance."

After a small wait while he signed, his translator said, "Fine. Like the Delysians, he will have to be detained, questioned, and assessed. We don't allow risks to infiltrate the safety of our walls."

Raewyn winced. "He has asked that he not be separated from me."

"Until he is an accepted member of society, what he wants matters little. The process is the same for all outsiders of this nature. He nor I have any choice in the matter."

Turning to Merikh, she explained this to him. Red sparks flashed in her vision, and of course, he rejected it.

"Please? It'd just be temporary. The process only takes about a day, since we don't like to keep people detained for too long."

"What if I am not accepted, Raewyn?"

She gave him a broken smile. "You will be. You have me, remember?" She lifted her arm and flexed her biceps as she tapped it. "I'm councilwoman Raewyn Daefaren, the representative for the Duskwalker people."

Plus, she kind of did just give him her soul. Rejecting him would be considered cruel, since they were technically bonded, even if it wasn't by her customs.

This might actually work in my favour. She almost wanted to rub her hands together and evilly cackle.

Blue flashed, and the end of his snout bumped gently against her temple. "Fine. I will go wherever they ask of me. I will warn you that if you are apart from me for too long, you will come to my side. If it's not a safe place, you will not be safe."

With a nod, she translated what she needed to back to Mericato.

After a little more back and forth between all four of them, Raewyn's heart sunk when Merikh turned to give them his back and be cuffed. His left wrist was tied to his right biceps and vice versa – although they struggled a little with his quills, even though they were lying flat.

Disappointment washed over her, wishing it didn't have to be this way.

When they walked towards the central tree, Merikh wrapped his tail around her midsection and pulled her close.

Curling her hand around the tuft of fur at the end, she took comfort in it, especially since her mind rebelled against where Mericato and his soldiers were leading them.

FORTY-TWO

The silence that surrounded Merikh was deafening.

There was nothing there. Not a squeak from an animal, nor a crawl from an insect, not the distant movement of life just beyond the room he was locked within.

Inside was dark. The only lights were glowing orbs placed inside the stone of a central column. Their green light only illuminated the ceiling and ground where they circled.

There were no windows; Merikh wondered if that was to protect its usual occupants from the sun that would burn them, or to drown them in the abyss.

The walls were entirely made of obsidian and appeared to have been carved from the inside, rather than being placed there. Although he was alone, gold, silver, and bronze prison bars were made to box its occupants in from all sides, the green lights reflecting against their mirror-like shine.

From what he could tell, in this round room there were eight cells.

The ground was hard and uncomfortable. He would have shifted to allow himself to lie down properly, but his arms were still locked behind his back.

He'd tried to break free from the binding, just so he could rest in this long and excruciating wait, but he was unable to. Whatever these simple, flexible threads they'd woven around his wrists and biceps were made from, they had to be enchanted.

That was wise, considering he may have been able to break himself from his cell. With enough strength, any metal could bend.

Raewyn had explained to him why he wasn't allowed freedom from his trappings. They didn't know what he was capable of, whether he could wield magic or not. Mericato had demanded that Merikh remain as constrained as possible until his trial or whatever.

Sitting on the ground with his legs straight, he rested his back against the wall behind him. It was the best he could do to be comfortable.

Although the air was stale, it was at least cool. It also wasn't thin, since he was metres below the ground.

The wait was excruciating.

He was alone, had been alone for hours, possibly days. He'd slept three times out of boredom, and to mentally escape his containment.

Where is she? The small whine that broke from him echoed back.

Raewyn hadn't visited him, which left a yawning hole behind his sternum. She also hadn't returned to him through the bond, which meant she must be close enough to not incite it.

With his sight bleeding blue, he looked around his current home again. It was spotless. There wasn't a speck of dust to be seen, nothing to distract him as he waited.

It was tall enough that when he'd entered it, the very tips of his horns had clanked against the protruding metal bars. His cell width gave him just enough room to mindlessly pace if he wanted to, had he been free.

It was spacious. Yet every minute he spent in it, alone, trapped with his arms behind his back, the more claustrophobic he became. The cool air was turning thick, strangling him in an anxiety-induced chokehold. It felt like granite had filled his chest and was weighing him down.

He was used to freedom, to wandering a vast and open world. His sight darted everywhere. *Is this where Jabez was kept?*

Had his arms been bound like Merikh's while he sat in this fucking hellhole? Already, it was driving him insane, and he'd only been here a short while.

How long did Raewyn say Jabez had been inside it? Six Elven years, the equivalent of ninety Earth years? *No wonder he went fucking mad.*

Each moment he was forced to wait, rage grew like a tornado within the very centre of his being. It was growing so wild, it was beginning to spiral into something physical within his chest. It knocked against the coldness Raewyn's absence had left in him.

Couldn't she visit him, even once? Give him something other than the dark walls, ceiling, and nothingness to stare at? Hear something other than his own breaths and anxious heartbeat? Smell something other than metal, stone, and questionable fluids?

He could even smell his own body, the dirt he'd tracked in from outside – that's how lacking the world around him was.

Only once had he been visited by a person, and they'd attempted to bring him water and food, both of which he rejected since he didn't need them.

That had been in the beginning.

It was probably a good thing no one returned, since the next person who came in would have been snarled at.

Just as his mind was beginning to wind and twist further, invisible hands working with his agitation to render him enraged, white wavered in his peripheral.

A body formed in the cell next to him, hollow, completely lacking of colour – a Ghost. Curled up on her side, he could tell it was Raewyn by the distinct curls pooling around her head.

She turned solid, and her scent washed over him like a soothing wave, even more so when her slow breaths and heartbeat lulled his mind with their fragile gentleness.

How could he be angry at his female when she was resting?

Why did she come to me now, though? He looked around, wishing he had some form of exterior light to inform him what the hell was going on, what time it was.

For a little while, he just watched her.

All his anger, anxiety, his bubbling panic against the claustrophobia, eased out of him.

So pretty...

Like a strike of heat from a match, he sensed she was his bride all the way to the very essence of his being. Her soul sat between his horns, and he couldn't wait for the moment he had the freedom to finally, truly look upon it.

He'd been so impatient before, wanting to consume it in case she took it back, that he'd eaten it without giving it a true glance. A mistake.

I wish she was closer.

If she wasn't in another cell, and his arms had been free, he would have scooped her up into his arms and held her. He would have stroked her cheek, played with her hair while he felt her sprawled across his torso.

"Raewyn," he gently called.

His light sleeper stirred, but it was the coolness and hardness of stone against her sliding cheek that truly woke her.

She quickly sat up and patted the ground, her appearance frazzled and panicked. A wave of fear burst from her scent, and it did nothing to incite his hunger. It only made him swell with sympathy – she had been suddenly teleported to a new environment without warning, no wonder she was upset.

"Vvereh eam ey? Haou diid ey geht ereh?"

Merikh winced. He didn't understand the language, but it wasn't hard to guess what she'd asked.

"You are with me, little starshine."

"Merikh?" she groggily asked, rubbing one of her eyes, like she had sleep sand caught in it. "We're in the cells? H-how did I get here?"

"I told you that you would return to me after too much time had passed." She crawled her way to him, and his muscles tensed. "Wait! Stop. You are in the cell next to me."

She paused right before her forehead could knock into the bars, and she put her hands up to feel them. The silence within the room highlighted how much learning that distressed her, her pulse spiking.

"Merikh." Her eyes crinkled as her bottom lip trembled. "I don't like this. How do I get out?"

"You're a Phantom now." Considering her ghostly appearance before she formed, it didn't matter whether it was a human or an Elf he bonded with. He'd changed her. "You are able to turn yourself incorporeal and float through the bars."

"I can? How?"

He grunted. "I'm not actually sure. This is as new to me as it is to you."

Despite the fact that his mother was also a Phantom, he knew little about them. Perhaps he could have asked her about it, but he'd never expected to have a bride of his own.

She pulled her lips to one side and narrowed her brows in what he thought was a cute expression of determination or concentration. "Maybe I can just will it?"

Just like that, her fingertips turned ghostly, and she dipped forward through the bars. Like it was coming from a faraway place, her scream was quiet and distant.

"No! No!" Her arms cartwheeled as she floated upwards towards the ceiling within his cell. "I don't like it! I can't see or feel anything!"

She suddenly turned physical, and Merikh pushed off the walls with his elbows to catch her with his thighs. She fell on the thick cushion of them with an *oomph*.

A half-hearted sob broke from her quivering lips. "Never again. I don't want to do that ever again. I felt like a floating consciousness."

He'd never considered how a sightless Phantom would

navigate, but he was now realising that it wasn't going to be easy for her. She wouldn't be able to see, feel, smell, or taste – only hear.

Still, his female was resilient, determined, and wonderful; he trusted she'd find a way.

When she pushed off him and knelt between his thighs, Merikh wiggled back. He seated himself upright against the wall once more and folded his legs.

He stared at her in silence, taking in the mesmerising sight of her, the smell of her.

The strap of clothing she wore could barely be considered a dress with how short it was, reminding him of a ruined red one he'd torn from her. It had dark green lace where she'd cut it, while the rest of it looked as though it was made of pale green silk. It hugged her slight curves before flaring around her hips. The cleavage line was cut low, but not enough to let her breasts spill from it.

It was obvious she wasn't wearing anything beneath it.

Her chest flushed under his silence, likely feeling his gaze upon her. Her ears darted back, and she lowered her head as she nibbled at her lips. She looked awfully nervous and shy before him.

"I-I should go back to my home," she murmured quietly. "It's late. I could get in trouble for being here."

Panic clawed at his chest, and a whine slipped from him. "Please stay."

Like that was all she needed to be convinced, she nodded and shifted closer. When she reached up, he placed his skull in her welcoming palms, and once more, all his anxieties faded.

"Are you okay?" She stroked up the underside before a hand rubbed down the top of it. His sight blackened in bliss at her touch, and he freely leaned into it. "I've been worried about you."

"I'm fine," he lied. "I'm used to being in the dark."

She came even closer so she could lift up and rub her cheek

against his front fangs.

"I'm sorry I haven't visited you. You probably feel abandoned, but I've been in a council meeting from the moment I woke up today. They were inquiring about my time on Earth, and they had so many *annoying* questions."

"It's fine," he lied once more. "It's only been a few days. I'm patient."

He'd always been patient. Looking at his bride, he'd never been more thankful for it.

"Few days?" she gasped as she pulled back. "It's only been a *day* here, Merikh."

Only a day? Fuck. It feels like it's been forever. His sight wandered as he thought. *She only came to me now. The cycle has changed to match this realm.*

His twenty-four-hour rotation was now in line with whatever sun cycle was present here. He internally cringed. That meant his time of separation from her would feel longer to him, as well as his healing cycle.

It also meant his allocated time from Jabez had ended, so there was no turning back. He was now on the Elvish people's side.

As he brought his sight back to his bride, he should have known that would happen.

"Raewyn..." he started, licking at his snout in interest. "Would you lay on me? I need to feel you."

A small smile pestered her lips. "I thought you'd already be pulling me to you."

She crawled on her hands and knees into his lap to rest within the space of his folded legs, like she'd already done so many times before. With her knees pressing into one side, her elbows on the other, she was facing his torso as she placed a hand upon his stomach.

"I can't," he said, using the end of his snout so he could push her hair from her face and see her. "My arms are behind me."

"I forgot they kept your bindings on." She tightened her lips before she went to sit up. "Do you want me to take them off?"

He forced her back down with his entire head. "Don't touch my back. I don't want you to hurt yourself with my arm and back quills. I am content with you here."

"You can't mean that," she grumbled, once more placing her hand on his stomach and petting the fur and grey skin she found there.

"I do." He dipped his tongue over the corner of her jaw, utterly thankful he was flexible and his snout was long. "You are all I need, no matter where I am. I would be happy to remain here in this cell with my arms bound behind my back forever, so long as you were resting against me."

Her bottom lip pouted as water filled her eyes, but she was quick to blink her tears away. He continued to lick at her jaw, sometimes going down her neck, and her skin prickled intermittently with goosebumps.

"That tickles," she whispered, squirming a little.

The subtle tangle of heat in her scent told him she was enjoying it.

"I missed you, my *bride*." Fuck, just calling her that instantly had his sight turning to a bright pink. "My pretty, smart, brave, fairy bride."

She gave a small moan as she arched her neck. "I'm not a fairy," she rasped.

"Sure, you are. With your long, pointed ears, glossy white hair, and alluring brown skin, you're the most enchanting thing I've ever seen, especially since you hold stars in your eyes. All you are missing is wings."

"Stooop," she whined as she covered her face to hide her embarrassment. "You don't get to suddenly become charming now that I've given you my soul."

Merikh licked down to her shoulder and used his tongue to push away the dark-green strap of her dress. She tasted clean, like toxic lilies, and his seam clenched, his cock jerking with the desire to dirty her with his own scents.

Spirit of the void help him, he wanted to fuck his new bride – one he never thought he'd have – more than anything. He'd been locked in this damn cell right after she'd given him her soul. He would have preferred spending that time touching her, tasting her, feeling her while their bond was fresh.

Just as he pushed the edge of her dress down enough to reveal a lovely breast tipped with a dark-brown nipple, which he licked across, feeling it grow hard, Raewyn stopped him.

"Not here, Merikh. Please, not here. It's cold, and it smells funny."

Did it? Because currently, he felt hot, and all he could scent was her deepening arousal.

"Okay," he conceded, not wishing to scare her off. "Just... let me lick you."

There was little else he could do, and he was obsessed with the idea right now, almost like he was self-soothing with it.

She didn't cover her exposed breast, but he let it be under her wishes so he could just taste the flesh covering her sternum, neck, ear, and face. He even drew his tongue across her lips, and it was odd when she kissed it in return.

She even... licked it back.

There was one last thing he wanted to say to her, something he was truly nervous about. It didn't matter that she'd already kind of said it to him. The emotions that came with it were so utterly foreign, they were painful in his chest.

He needed to say it, to utter it, before it burned a hole in him.

Her eyes were drooping and falling asleep, like she was content to be with him just as he was with her, so he needed to say it now.

"I love you, Raewyn," he said, the pink of his orbs brightening as he lifted his head back so he could properly see her reaction.

She was his equal, his polar opposite, his strengths where he was weakest, his vulnerability where he was strongest. She was all that mattered, all that would ever matter.

Her eyelids opened slightly. She parted her lips to say something, but considering she closed them again, he had a funny feeling it was to tease him.

She reached up and dug her fingers into the empty space of one of his bony eye sockets. "Is that what this colour means?"

"Yes," he grated.

"I saw it not long before we left Earth."

Merikh's shoulders turned inward under the weight of his emotions. "It's because I loved you then."

A small smile curled her lips, and she used his eye hole to pull him down so she could kiss the side of his sharp fangs.

"I love you, too, and if you don't know this about me yet, I want you to know that once I set my heart to something, it never fades."

"It would be unfortunate for you if it did, because I'm never letting you go, my own personal piece of starlight."

His orbs pink, Merikh petted Raewyn with his snout and tongue until she passed out in his lap. With his arms trapped, and both of them in the cool dark, he'd never been happier.

FORTY-THREE

Raewyn knew this conference room like it had, annoyingly, been seared onto the back of her eyelids. She'd spent hours, days, weeks, *years* in it, to the point that it haunted her with the uttermost boring nightmares.

It was pyramid in shape, the walls reaching a centre point in the ceiling where white tree branches allowed sun to filter glass. However, sheets of gold metal could be moved to the left like fanning blades to hide the sun if they wished. From the middle of the blades' meeting point hung a tapestry flag with the synedrus council's emblem, the Elysian people's universal symbol beneath it, and the city's marking below that.

There were spare spots on the walls where other flags could be placed, had the world not been overrun by Demons and forced them to become one people rather than many.

Like everywhere within the central tree, the walls were white from its bark. In this room, gold mainly filled the spaces, since it was a common material for them. Obsidian was also common, and they preferred laying it on the ground.

Unlike most rooms within the central tree, which was filled with thousands of them, this was at the very top of its trunk. It was also in the heart of it, the only one of this shape.

They were lucky that this kind of tree often grew in unusual patterns with many pockets, twists, and turns – although they did assist this one in particular. It branched halfway up its trunk and covered the entire city with shade when the sun was at its highest.

The city's stone walls, which weren't just for protection from the Demons, protected the Elysian and Delysian people alike from the sun's heat and radiation.

Rich with hyper fertile soil, this world's forestry grew dense and had always shielded them. Unfortunately, that magnificent growth gave the Demons the perfect home to thrive in such a sunny environment.

From the warmth she could feel on her left shoulder, the gold blades must have been opened on one side.

That would be for the Delysian councilmembers and their safety, since they still burned in the sunlight. Since becoming a councilmember was a difficult process and they were still fairly new to the city, there were only four of them. It took great strengths and achievements to gain a position, especially in the speciality they chose.

There were three curved sections of solid gold tables, silver branching through their elegant designs. If pushed together, they would have made a perfect circle, but they were usually spread apart to allow people in and out of the middle freely. Each table could only hold six people.

Seventeen of the eighteen chairs were currently occupied, since Raewyn's was empty.

She stood in the middle with Merikh by her side. He was kneeling to make himself look smaller and less imposing – his idea – while she pleaded his case and translated on his behalf.

The only other person who could speak his language was her father, and despite how much the other councilmembers demanded for him to be his translator, he'd rejected them. Her father had chuckled when she begged him not to accept before they'd even asked him. Of course, he'd sided with his daughter, no matter the reason.

They hadn't wanted Raewyn, who was obviously biased

towards Merikh, translating on his behalf, where she could twist his words to make sure they would benefit him.

She *may* have been doing that. Okay, she absolutely was doing that, but it was because Merikh could be a little brash in his word choice.

It was mostly going well, except for one problem: Ulair and his boorish lack of a heart.

He was always a menace during council meetings. He liked facts, and he completely disregarded a person's feelings and opinions unless they were his own.

Merikh was an unknown, a mystery, an enigma, which meant he didn't trust him. He also had a thing against Raewyn, perhaps because they were polar opposites in personality and *always* butted heads.

To be honest, each member had their flaws and was very protective of their station and speciality. They always fought. It was only when at least seventy-five percent agreed on a topic, a large majority, that they could settle a matter.

There was a reason there were so many people in charge of the city, and it was to make sure every decision was made fairly. They wanted to have the opinions of many, and to make sure they had a diverse council to ensure their choices would be what the people would want. To hear every voice.

If the council could not come to a seventy-five percent agreeance, they would then turn to the people for a vote.

They weren't perfect, nowhere was. If the Demons didn't roam beyond their walls, things would be different, and so much better; they had once been.

However, it was Ulair who was being the biggest thorn in her side right now. It didn't help that he had Mericato's support, who was being translated by one of the other members for Raewyn's sake.

She wished she could walk right over and smack them on their noses.

"You wish for us to allow this... this *Duskwalker* into our city, but we have no idea who he is, what he is, or why he is truly here," Ulair announced loudly, with a steely tone.

Raewyn opened her mouth, but he quickly spoke over her.

"He is one of Weldir's descendants. That he was made at all is an abomination, and we have no idea what that demi-god is up to. How can you expect us to approve of him when he could be a spy?"

"It is known that Weldir was unhappy when he was sent to Earth," Sliveria, a female councilmember, stated in a soft, angelic voice. "We know he still barricades the Demons from returning from Earth, but he may have ulterior motives for creating his children, other than what we have been told."

"If he starts taking Elysian souls via this vessel, there's no telling how strong he'll grow," Cleth, a non-binary councilmember, sighed. "If it's information he seeks, there's nothing stopping him from going through Jabez's portal and spreading it."

There was a short pause.

Just as Raewyn opened her mouth to speak, she was told to wait by Cleth, who most often translated on Mericato's behalf. Cleth was in charge of the city's shield maintenance, as well as the conduit stones that powered the city.

"Mericato has said that he ran and attacked multiple soldiers in both realms. While he did nothing more than snarl and roar, I thought he was a mindless beast. We don't allow beasts to freely roam, as they are likely to attack when provoked," Cleth translated.

Teyen, a female Delysian, said, "I agree with Mericato. If he wanted sanctuary within the city, he should've had faith that we would not hurt him and do the right thing. Instead, he fled, frightening our people and causing alarm in the process. What if he accidentally hurt someone?"

"When given the opportunity to lay all his truths forward, you have denied us that request," Ulair bit, and the sound of him rubbing at the short stubble on his face was loud enough to irritate her ears.

"Because it is invasive," Raewyn rebuffed. "You would not subject anyone else to a mind reading, and yet you want to violate his privacy just because you don't know what he is. Isn't the truth spell enough? That's usually all we do for the Delysians who wish to enter. He's already answered your questions. He's already explained that he intends no harm, and that he is not Weldir's puppet."

"We have too many concerns," Ulair stated. "How are we to know this creature cannot manipulate the spell like the Anzúli are able to? He has already explained he can use magic that he's stolen from the Anzúli on Earth."

Her hand tightened into a fist at her side.

This had never been asked of a Demon before. Merikh was an unknown and had frightened everyone when the portal appeared on Earth. He'd roared and bolted for her, with soldiers between them, and 'attacked' them.

The councilmembers were afraid. For themselves, for the thousands of people they were trying to protect, and for those they hoped came after them.

The rules they had in place gave so much freedom, but they were also designed to protect. The fact that every single councilmember agreed with this mind reading just showed how deeply they were all worried, how scared they were.

They didn't know Merikh like she did, and it hurt her to know that if someone else was in her current position, she would have agreed with them all as well. But she wasn't, and she wished her voice on the matter could convince them.

"Raewyn?" Merikh asked from beside her, since she'd stopped translating.

She turned to him and explained what was happening.

"I am not comfortable with that." Reddish-pink sparks flashed in her vision, and she thought they may be from shame. "There are terrible things I have done, Raewyn. If they learn all of it, they will not trust me."

"The Delysians we approve have hurt people, too, Merikh. They, like you, want a better life, one without bloodshed and pain."

Reddish pink sparked again, this time deeper in colour. "It's not the same, and you know it. I have done things I know were wrong just so I could escape Earth. Lies I have told, ways I have harmed, people I have turned on."

"They will see you don't want to do that anymore. When you enter the city, you are reborn, and your past transgressions are forgiven."

They usually only ever turned away those who were dangerous, who couldn't be trusted. Over two-thirds of their people had been lost when the Demons came, and they feared extinction.

She understood why they were wary of Weldir. She was as well.

Although there was little the Gilded Maiden could do to aid him right now, as she was still recovering, what if he felt abandoned? What if he turned on the Elysians and his mother, the Gilded Maiden, not knowing that she would one day come to aid him?

But I know Merikh would never turn on us for Weldir.

"See?" Ulair cut in. "He does not trust us, so how can we trust him?"

Raewyn hadn't even translated the conversation, and Ulair was just making an assumption because it benefitted him. He was a terrible hypocrite at times.

"If he is not allowed within the city, then I must go with him," Raewyn informed them, hoping her backup plan might work. "For reasons that are our own, we are bonded. I cannot break that bond, even if I wanted to."

"Mericato says it's the flame he holds between his horns. I watched him eat it. I'm not convinced he didn't coerce her into giving it to him, though. She was trapped beneath his body while he had his spikes keeping us away."

Raewyn guessed that would look suspicious to people who didn't understand their relationship.

"Foolish," Zerik, an older councilmember, proclaimed, his voice deep. "She made her choice regardless, knowing there was a chance she would be forced to leave with him."

"The city's safety is priority," Ulair stated on Mericato's behalf, perhaps giving it more bite than he was supposed to. "Your life does not matter against the thousands, even if you are a valued councilmember."

He'd spoken over Cleth so he could put more emotion into it, whereas they were likely to speak neutrally.

"I wasn't coerced," Raewyn snapped back, the heat of rage prickling her neck. "I give you permission to use the spell on me to prove that."

"It's not your truth we're after. It's his," Ulair argued.

Raewyn turned to Merikh. "I don't think you have a choice."

It wasn't the first time a growl had emitted from him, but he ended it on a huff of defeat.

"Fine." Then he coldly chuckled. "I told you on Earth that your people weren't as forgiving as you made them out to be."

"It's only because of your connection to Weldir," she answered back with a wince before she faced the table of councilmembers directly in front of them. "He has agreed."

Since he was the head of security, Mericato switched places with one of the members sitting next to Ulair so that he could go through Merikh's mind with him. Questions were asked in order to incite memories, which Ulair only noted out loud if they were of importance.

Unlike the truth spell, this one required the use of a mana stone because of how complex it was. It glowed red before a ball of energy formed, and she could see the shadows of their hands upon it.

He detailed Merikh's dislike of Weldir, his lack of connection to him, his mother, and his Duskwalker brothers. They detailed some of the horrific acts he'd done to the humans, how he'd lured them from their cities so he could kill and eat them, how he hunted Anzúli to grow his magical capabilities and what spells he knew – none being a deflection for their previous truth spell.

They mentioned how he killed his own brother – although they were relieved to know he had a weakness if they ever needed to utilise it. Her people were non-violent unless it was to defend against the Demons, so she didn't believe the other councilmembers learning of it was any cause for alarm.

"He's a serial killer! Pulling out the hearts and heads of humans just to advance his own intelligence." Then Ulair asked, "Do you know he planned to *eat* you?"

"Yes," Raewyn responded swiftly. "I'd already surmised from what he told me of his past what his original intention had been. I already knew he'd harmed people to increase his humanity. He never hid that from me."

"What about the fact that he had four humans harass you in a human town in order to obtain your trust?"

"W-what?" she rasped, cupping her wrist when both her hands flung to her chest.

"You didn't, did you?" Ulair said with a hike of humour in his tone. "He paid four humans to pretend to rob you."

She knew the ones they were speaking of. She remembered how frightened she'd been when they'd grabbed her, how they'd cornered her in the street. She even remembered how the woman had smelt like burnt food and mouldy hay.

I can't believe he did that to me.

Was this one of the reasons Merikh had been uncomfortable with sharing his thoughts, his mind, his memories?

"He followed you around for a week after realising you were different by your scent. He'd been able to sense your magic, but he knew if he approached you suddenly, you would be wary of him. He tricked you into making sure you'd leave with him, all so he could find out what you were and how to find more of you, with the intention of eating you for your magic to grow his own."

Part of her wanted to shy away from him, while another glued her feet to his side.

She dipped her head and wrung her wrist to soothe herself. "T-that could be true..."

"It is," Ulair said sternly.

"It changes nothing," she answered. "He did what he thought he needed to escape Earth, and not once in the time we travelled together did he hurt me. Whatever he did, whatever his intentions were with me in the beginning, they changed." The more she spoke, the more her confidence bloomed. "He protected me, cared for me, was kind to me. There were so many things he didn't need to do for me, but he did so out of sheer desire and selflessness for me to be comfortable, to make me happy. He showed me more kindness in his actions and words than many of the humans I met there. How could I not forgive him after everything we went through together?"

"What did you say? What's going on?" Merikh asked, but by the orange that sparked, she had a feeling he already knew.

Since Ulair wasn't poking her anymore, allowing her answer to stand as the final stance on the matter, she explained to him what was shared.

"Raewyn, I'm—"

She turned a soft smile at him.

"It's fine, Merikh. I understand, and it doesn't matter anymore." She was surprised by the tiniest whine that squeaked out of his lungs. "We can talk about it later if you want, but it's in the past. We can just look to the future, okay?"

He gave a sharp grunt in response as Ulair and Mericato continued searching.

She hated the idea of them seeing or knowing of their intimate moments that came much later. Mericato did cough a few times, perhaps out of awkwardness, but neither spoke their thoughts aloud.

Most of what they learned, although cruel and bloody, eased

their worries. That was, until they discovered his relationship with Jabez – not of his past, but what had happened most recently.

It was also something Raewyn had been unaware of.

When Merikh bumped the end of his snout against her arm, likely worried about her expression, she couldn't stop herself from ripping it away from him.

With her hands clenched, her voice shook as she translated to Merikh what they were saying. She tried her best to remain composed rather than reveal any confusion or hurt.

Her half-brother had been just beyond the ward while she'd been there, only metres away, and Merikh hadn't told her. A different sense of betrayal cut through her chest.

She'd already had feelings for him then, had already grown to trust and care for him. Why did that sting far worse than anything she'd learned before?

"He'd been considering joining Jabez's side, not even days before coming here," Ulair practically growled, if he could growl. "The only reason he didn't make that choice was because Mericato brought his skull here. He would have sided with the man who had turned on us and helped him destroy our city, helped him command the Demons who still roam Nyl'theria."

"That's not true," Cleth translated for Mericato. "You are leaving out that he was planning on telling Raewyn first if she bonded with him. He was intending to leave that choice up to her."

As the head of security, now that Mericato could see Merikh wasn't a threat, he seemed to be in support of defending him. He'd always been that way; hard when he needed to be, but always ready to side with those who were in need of help.

Orange sparks flashed in her peripheral.

Before she could say anything, ask a single question that hammered its way into her consciousness, Merikh's voice penetrated her thoughts.

"It was either your people or my brothers," Merikh stated. "I have already seen one die, have already been the reason for it. How could I choose between them and the bride I wanted?"

She translated this to the other councilmembers before she answered him. "How could you not tell me he was there, Merikh? I could have spoken to him, seen if I could have changed everything and brought him here."

"Because he is half-mad, Raewyn. I didn't want to endanger you when I learned how much this war means to him. Had I let you speak with him, and things went poorly, getting you through his portal would have been impossible if he became aware of your existence. You hadn't made the sun stone yet, so the only other alternative would have been to enter his castle without it – which could have ended with either one, or both, of us dead."

"Still," she grumbled, finding what he was saying hard to argue with.

"I could not make the choice on my own. I had been intending to ask for your soul the day you were taken, and then I was going to pose what two paths were available had you said yes."

"And if I said no?" she asked warily, worried about how... callous or selfish his answer may be.

"Take you home, then return to Earth where I could help protect my brothers."

Her brows furrowed, and she shook her head. "You wouldn't have stayed here after everything?"

"If I could not have you, then I knew it didn't matter where I was – I wouldn't be happy. I would have preferred to attempt to protect my family from Jabez, to join no one's side but theirs. You showed me what it felt like to not be filled with hate, and I would have preferred to use that gift by being a shield for those who were able to have the love I could not."

Raewyn only translated the first half of what he said, as the second part made her clog up on her own feelings.

"What he says is true," Cleth translated.

"Now you're forgetting to mention that he was technically

keeping her captive until he posed all this to her."

"That doesn't matter. They are here now."

Although it was obvious that Merikh's heart wasn't pure, his reason for being here was: her.

When both Mericato and Ulair agreed he wouldn't be a threat to the city, especially learning that their bond had erased his hunger altogether, the weight of the meeting changed.

It became a discussion about where he would live, which was with her. What he would like to do in the city, which was be with her. How he would prefer to dress so they could tailor him clothing, of which he told them to ask her what she'd like him to wear – so long as they made him guards that would protect everyone from his quills.

It became a little comedic towards the end, when he'd answered each question with 'whatever will make Raewyn happy.'

When she offered for him to make his own choices, he simply stated, "How am I supposed to know what I would like here? I'm still just trying to adjust to how fucking thin the air is up this high. Why do I have to answer all their questions right now?"

Raewyn almost laughed, but she just coughed behind her fist to hide it. She was sure, in time, he would come to learn what he truly desired within the city.

Just as they were ending the meeting, Merikh nudged her. "I want to ask them something."

With a nod, she requested for them to wait from leaving their seats.

"When I first learned the truth of my connection to Weldir, that I was a servant and a soul ferry for him, I felt betrayed by the parents who had created me. I had already lost my brother and been Jabez's companion for many years before I was approached by the Witch Owl and learned of it. At the time, I didn't know telling this to Jabez would be the reason he would turn on me, or that Duskwalkers would later become targeted. I thought he was my friend, and I was venting my frustration because I was angry and didn't know how to process it. It didn't help that I lacked the humanity to understand what was truly happening in the world."

"Are you asking if we will allow them to come here?" Sliveria asked in surprise.

"Yes," Merikh answered.

"No," Cleth answered for Mericato. "At least not those who have not bonded with a human and erased their hunger. In your memories, I saw how you were formed. They will not be able to hold back with the blood and fear scents within the city."

"You act like creatures at first," Ulair cut in. "As already mentioned, we don't allow wild beasts in our city."

"You must also take into consideration that if we bring your kind here, it will weaken Weldir and pose a risk for our people as well," Teyen added. "We would like to help, we really would, just as we have always wanted to help the humans, but we can't."

"We also can't make a portal to get them," Raewyn told him, her eyes bowing in sympathy.

What he was asking for was fair and noble, but she couldn't help agreeing with the other members – at least regarding those who didn't have a bride.

"The solution would be to find a way to help the Demons or make protection charms that would allow us to take back our world and Earth without fear," Zerik offered. "It's what we have been trying to do since their unfortunate arrival."

Merikh grunted, but blue sparks flashed. His silence was haunting and painful, highlighting just how upset he was.

"I'm sorry, Merikh," Raewyn said. "I want to help them, especially since Ingram and Aleron were so cute, but there's little we can do for them, or the humans, right now."

His huff was the only answer she received on the subject. It was all he could give without revealing the depth of his anger and disappointment.

Merikh finally stood. "Can you make them take these bindings off now?"

Raewyn gave a sad smile, wishing this meeting hadn't ended on such a terrible note. "Absolutely. I'm excited to show you your new home."

Particularly her laboratory, where they were going to be spending most of their time. She hoped he was ready to become her assistant, because it was nearly around the clock work, with how much she buried herself in her paperwork and experiments.

Now, with the resolve to save his brothers before it was too late, she knew she would be even more determined.

"My home is standing in front of me," Merikh answered warmly as bright-pink sparks flashed.

Reaching up, she waited for him to place his weighty skull in her palms so she could nuzzle the end of his bear skull snout.

Mine too, she thought.

FORTY-FOUR

With a quiet hum, Raewyn worked on cleaning the main bench in her laboratory. It was currently a mess of paperwork, the result of her catching up on all the different tasks and requests that had piled up during her disappearance. There were also notes from meetings she'd missed and important events that had happened within the city.

Although it was in elbraille, she was able to read the handwriting with Merikh's borrowed sight.

A small smile curled her lips. *He's a good assistant.* Her eyes fell on him, curled up in his monstrous form right next to her legs. *For someone who naps three times a day.* It's not his fault; he was born in a different realm with a different sleep cycle.

That wasn't going to suddenly change in the single week he'd been in Nyl'theria.

She also didn't truly need assistance when she was just reading hours upon hours of paperwork, which, honestly, was half her job.

Although this was the first time he'd done it, he'd given her his sight when she said she wanted to clear her laboratory to make some room. She said it was for new experiments, but it was really so she could figure out a space for him to do his own work.

Merikh was going to learn how to read and speak Elvish.

Besides her father, no one else could translate and teach him, so it was an additional task on her plate – not that she minded.

She'd delegated some of her work to another scientist, palming off almost everything for the time being, except for experiments like growing hufflepumpkin or anything Demon protection related. Hopefully, she didn't accidentally make another portal.

At least if I do go to a new realm by accident, Merikh would call me back here, as long as he doesn't try to save me. They'd already spoken about it, and he made no promises on how he'd react if she were in danger.

Despite hating it, even though she'd only done it once, she explained that she'd just turn into a Phantom and float senselessly through the world until she returned.

At least that calmed his worries, though it elevated many of her own. She'd likely be more reckless now, since she couldn't permanently die. Bonus for her.

It had only been a week, and already, Raewyn was certain she'd made the right choice in falling for Merikh.

He was sweet, caring, naughty, but also considerate.

He understood many were uncertain about him, and he was as patient with strangers as he was with her. He was willing to try anything, and she appreciated him for it.

His big, warm, rough hand had swallowed hers as they walked through the city together. She'd spent two days showing him around, their handholding highlighting the unity between him and her people. No one had to know it was because they were in a relationship, although she had no intention of hiding it.

Many approached them out of curiosity, many didn't.

He seemed awkward and out of place, not used to conversing with those who could see his real face. It always startled him when someone asked if his skull was real, since his jaw didn't move when he spoke.

The first time someone asked if they could touch it, he'd been nervous and put off. It'd been a little rude to ask him in the first place, but he did allow a small handful to curiously touch it – especially children who had been frightened of him at first.

Her ovaries nearly exploded when he got on his hands and feet so a small child could cup his jaw, especially when his orb sparks had gone from a reddish pink in embarrassment to yellow in joy.

Raewyn had showed him the beach, the markets, and all of the central tree palace, since nowhere was off limits.

It'd burned much of their time, so she'd only returned to her laboratory the day before to begin working. Before that, they both just worked on resting in *their* home, bathing and spending time together in peace.

There was lots of touching, since Merikh was interested in 'rediscovering' Raewyn now that she was his bride.

Since she'd already moved everything around and cleared a bench for him in her laboratory, she was confident she could navigate it again without her sight. He'd slept through it, since she'd been relatively quiet for his sake.

I'm glad Cykran didn't mind that I fired him.

Actually, the sarcastic Delysian had been overjoyed by it. He'd enjoyed the work because he was her friend, but when he discovered his replacement would be Merikh, he was happy to step down.

There was also an Elysian he was chasing, and she'd pouted when he refused to tell her anything about who he was interested in. He said he didn't want to tell people, in case his hopes were dashed now that he had time to pursue them.

She was thankful it was easy.

After shuffling the last of her paperwork, she turned to stare down at Merikh, who was completely in the way. He'd curled up in his monstrous form and fallen asleep next to the stool she'd been sitting on earlier.

He's happy here. That brought an even bigger smile to her face.

She crouched down near his head resting upon his bent arm. Wrapping one of her arms around her closed knees, balancing herself on her toes, she stared at her soul flame.

Funnily enough, it was positioned similarly to how she was now, except it had both its arms wrapped around its knees. Its head was also resting in the nook of its knees.

The centre of it was a light blue, with dark blue flames encasing and wisping through it.

"Hello," she whispered, wondering if she could get it to stir from its apparent sleep.

It turned its head up and opened its eyes. They were brown, with white bursts in the middle. It was amazing to think it was exactly like her; her weight, her pointed ears, her coily hair floating upwards, even her eyes.

Raewyn went to touch it, to pat its head, and her hand moved through it. She pouted. Merikh could touch it, so why couldn't she?

Maybe because it no longer belongs to me?

It eventually lowered its head to rest against its knees.

Her gaze then roamed over the flower crown she'd placed around his horns. It was woven together with golden leaves and wire, the main flowers pink and purple with smaller blue ones.

He'd been happy to allow her to make it for him. She thought it would soften the death aspect of his face and make it easier for her people to warm up to him. She hoped it was helping, but she was also fond of the moment she'd made it.

They'd been sitting on the floor, her on his lap and wrapped up in his arms. With his head plonked on top of her own, he'd shared his sight so she could see what she'd been making, since she hadn't wanted to make a mess of it.

She'd never been good at arts and crafts.

It was a memory she cherished already. His willingness to conform to her people and their need for security regarding him just showed what a wonderful person he was. How could someone not fall for that?

She touched a flower petal. *Everyone will love you just like I do, but I know you're willing to be patient until then.*

Her eyes caught the blue sun currently shining the brightest out of all three, haloing him in its light. She stood, placing her hands on her hips as she stared down at Merikh.

It's getting late. It's time you woke up.

There was also one last thing she wanted to move, and he was blocking her path to it. *I did warn you...* She also just wanted to annoy him; it'd become her favourite pastime.

He usually wore either black or red clothing, but he was lucky the guards he was wearing were too thick and dense for his body to absorb during the shift. It meant she could touch him anyway she liked without his quills harming her, no matter his form.

They were made of the same material the soldiers wore. Although it appeared like white metal, it was actually made of one of the strongest and most flexible materials they could get their hands on. The starfir's flowers, the tree they were currently inside of, produced a silk that was precious to them.

This tree provided them with materials, a home, shade, and protection. It's why it was a beacon for her people.

Knowing the big, scary Duskwalker would never hurt her, a humorous grin marred her face. She stood on his head, then his shoulder, then his back, before making her way down to his butt.

Merikh's surprised grunt and jolt informed her she'd woken him. Just as she bounced off him after grabbing what she wanted from the shelf above him, his growl was the only warning she got.

The back of her long white dress was yanked on.

He was fond of this dress, since it both hid and revealed much. It was designed like a continuous, thin white scarf, wrapped over one breast then around her neck to cover the other, before crossing over her back to wrap around her hips and hide her arse and pubic mound. It flowed between her legs to skim the ground.

Her thighs were completely showing, as were her midsection and arms.

It was light, perfect for the current summer weather, and she liked how it showed off her body markings and replacement bangles. She'd been given new silver, bronze, and golden bands to replace the ones she'd needed to sell on Earth, each one with the achievements that came with them inscribed on the inside.

Their chiming and rattling was comforting.

Merikh flung her into his arms, bundling her into his lap while taking back his sight. The metal container holding spare writing apparatuses flew from her hands in a clattering mess.

"Did you really just fucking walk on me?" he groggily asked in disbelief, his voice deeper in his monstrous form.

"You were in the way!" she exclaimed, trying her hardest not to giggle. "I told you yesterday I'd prefer if you didn't lay there."

"You could have gone around me."

"It's not like I hurt you. Did you lie when you said I weigh nothing to you?"

Red sparks glittered in her vision. *"That's not the point. You cannot just walk on top of me like I'm a rug. Wake me next time you want me to move."*

Unable to hold it back any longer, she burst with laughter. She covered her mouth to hide it when he growled.

"You did that out of spite to retaliate, even when I only wanted to contentedly sleep by you."

"I did warn y–"

Raewyn squeaked when he rolled her over and splayed her across his lap. She tried to push up on straightened arms by pressing on his thighs, especially when he tugged the skirt of her dress to the side.

"What are you doing?" she asked as a draft whispered over her exposed backside.

"If my bride wishes to be naughty, then I will have to make sure she's not again."

Her eyes widened, realising what he intended. "Wait, no! I'm sorry. Please, don't."

"I would never actually hurt you, Raewyn," he uttered with hurt in his tone.

He was upset she thought he would actually harm her, since she was wiggling to get free. However, that wasn't the reason she was desperately trying to crawl away.

"I'm more hoping it's the embarrassment that bruises you."

Before she could say anything more, his big palm came down on her backside. It definitely wasn't hard, only enough to tingle and make a slapping sound. He'd put absolutely no strength into it, but she gasped all the same.

Her face heated. *I can't believe he actually spanked me!*

Not prepared for a second one, thinking the first would be enough, she was surprised that it stung a little. She wished a moan hadn't broken from her, and she quickly covered her mouth with both hands.

She'd teased him about this in the past, but she'd never actually been spanked properly before. It wasn't something her people did except as a sex act, and she didn't have the heart to tell him otherwise.

She'd always wondered if it was something she'd like, since she wasn't particularly fond of pain. It wasn't the light sting from the third one that had her squirming, though; it was just the fact that it was being done to her.

"What the...?" he grunted. *"Are you* enjoying *this?"*

As if to punctuate his questions, he ran the fore knuckle of his index finger through her wet folds to collect her pooling arousal.

She moved her hands, and panted, "Maybe? I'm actually not sure."

"I don't understand. You aren't supposed to like it."

The cry that burst from her was paired with her legs shaking when he glided his claws over her now-sensitive backside. The tickle of them went straight to her pussy, like an electric spark.

His hand darted away in what could only be surprise.

Her entire head went hot in embarrassment at the weird, strangled, perverse sound that had come from her. In a panic, she tried to scramble away.

"O-okay," she whispered, unsure why she was feeling bashful. Perhaps because it was new for her, and he was the one doing it? "You made your point."

The chuckle that fell from Merikh was positively evil.

His hand came down on her backside, just a touch harder than before. Her gasp was sharp, but it was his claws immediately after that had her moaning and tightening her thighs.

"I like this," he rumbled, tickling her sting before kneading one of her cheeks and pulling them apart to look at her pussy. *"I like this a lot."*

He did both one last time. A slap had her back bowing before his soothing claw tips had her arching instead. Then she squeaked, her entire body going tight, when he speared her with two thick fingers.

She wished the squelch of them going in wasn't so loud, but her care was lost as she tried to grind back on them.

"You got really wet, really fast."

He removed them instantly, and the loss of them had her fretting. She turned slightly to berate him for stopping, but the sound of him licking what he'd collected from her core had her stomach clenching. His following raspy groan had more liquid pooling between her legs.

"Stand up," he panted, giving her freedom.

"What, why?" She'd been perfectly content on his lap.

"Stand up, Raewyn. Now."

Confused, she got to her feet. Was her punishment not getting pleasure now that she was terribly turned on?

Nope, that wasn't it.

She knew it when he spun her around, pushed her stomach against her laboratory bench, shoved the back of her dress to the side, and spread her thighs. There was no chance to wonder what was going to happen, not when a second later, his tongue slipped from her clit and up the slit of her pussy before bottoming out inside her from behind.

Her gasp was accompanied by her hands fisting between her and the bench. Wrapping his hands around her calves, he spread her a little more and held her still as he worked his tongue in and out of her.

Raewyn turned her knees inwards to help part her legs while she balanced herself on her feet.

"I can never get enough of you," he groaned from beneath her.

She shouldn't have been surprised that this was happening. Almost *all* their intimate moments together involved his tongue inside her. Merikh, in a husky tone, had already stated that it was like his insatiable hunger was only present when he had her arousal on his tongue.

He had a desire to lick and taste every drop from her – even if much of it was mixed with his own lingering seed.

Even though she wasn't completely comfortable with the position, she didn't care enough to stop him. He even made her move, forcing her to stand on his cross legs so she was higher for easier access.

His tongue was firm, warm, and covered in drool, and its flexibility always had her knees buckling. Raewyn went to the tips of her toes as she moaned, letting pleasure take hold.

Why did a single tentacle wrapping around her ankle, revealing that his cock was free and jutting between her legs, have lust stabbing through her? She wanted to touch it, to feel it, hold it and kiss it. She wanted to worship it, and him along with it.

"You know what I want, my little starshine," he demanded in a low tone as he dipped his tongue out to tease the hard nub of her clit before he shoved it deep again. *"And you will give it to me."*

His tongue grew more invasive, swirling and twisting faster.

When she started coming around it, she didn't know whose groan was louder as he swallowed what flowed into his fanged maw.

Her eyelids flickered as her toes curled and stabbed into his furry thighs. He had to hold her up while her insides quivered and spasmed, but he didn't relent until she begged for a reprieve.

"Mine," he growled as he slipped his tongue from her so he could lick her clean.

Her body still tingling with aftershocks, she barely flinched when he nipped the inside of one of her thighs hard enough to draw blood. She bit her lip at the sting.

"Mine." He bit the opposing arse cheek, licking at the blood he'd drawn. *"Every bit of you is mine."*

She was afraid he was going to start biting his way up her stomach when he turned her, but he thankfully didn't. He'd already healed her of his bites by the time he easily yanked the material covering her breasts to the side so he could free them.

Her pants echoed between them as he licked across one breast before circling the nipple of the other. Paper fluttered to the ground when he picked her up by the backs of her knees and laid her on the bench. He didn't stop swirling his tongue over her tight nipple, instead growing more persistent.

"Inside you," he groaned, rubbing the groove on the underside of his cock right over her entrance and clit. *"I need inside you."*

She was surprised he wasn't already burying himself within her.

He was still moving against her while licking at her chest, his breaths hotter than usual. Raewyn grabbed a horn to lift his skull head. She didn't even get the chance to kiss him before he was dragging his tongue across her lips, incessantly tasting them.

"Then be inside me," she whispered, grabbing the head of his cock to help position it. She felt empty, and it was a new kind of torture that only became known since meeting him. "I need you, too."

Without wasting a single second, Merikh pulled back to tuck the head of his big purple cock against her entrance. Letting go of one of her thighs to steady himself in his monstrous form, he held the other tightly so he could *slam* his way in until he was buried to the hilt.

Her back snapped into an arch as her head fell back, her curls dragging against the bench.

Raewyn had taken each ridge and his twisted ring with ease, her body already moulded for him over the past few days. It was still snug, she didn't think that was ever going to change, but it gave her the chance to just enjoy him penetrating her.

His appreciative growl was quiet as he ground deeper, and she gave him a little moan in return.

Then, he pulled back, so she was only taking him three-quarters of the way, before he began thrusting without moving his knot through her. Holding her leg firmly while she held onto his opposing horn, Merikh speared her repeatedly with increasing speed.

Like he couldn't help himself from being rough and aggressive, he took her with unmerciful passion and need. Raewyn spread her thighs further in welcome, letting herself bounce without care.

Since she'd discovered he liked it when she touched herself, she gripped her breast, and his pants deepened. Too much was happening between her thighs for her to feel much else, but she squeezed her nipple, and his hips quickened their pace.

"Lower," he rasped.

She moved her hand down, slipping her fingers over his tentacles wrapped around her waist and hips. She petted her clit, making herself cry out louder than before, and his pistoning cock swelled with excitement.

Deep purple sparked. *"I like watching you touch yourself with my cock inside you. I want to see you come while I still can."*

Even as she pressed down hard on her clit, Raewyn tried

holding back her impending orgasm. She knew what was about to be buried inside her, and she would become nothing but an orgasming mess.

She wanted him wild for it, frantic.

Her orgasm was ripped from her the moment he pushed her thigh forward and changed the angle of their hips. He prodded a single spot over and over again with the head of his cock and his ridges, and Raewyn came in an instant. She removed her hand from her throbbing folds as she spasmed and clenched.

Her breaths turned laboured as she gripped the side of his back plate to hold on through bliss.

"Merikh," she moaned with trembling lips.

She soaked the back of her dress she was sitting on, and the only thing stopping her from falling off the edge of her golden metal bench was him and his cock.

"That's it," he growled, his claws digging deeper into her skin. *"You look so pretty when you come on me."*

Then, just as she was softening, she threw her head back and fell against the bench when he shoved in deep and meshed their hips together. Merikh groaned once his knot was buried, gripping the edge near her head as he laid over her.

Instead of speed and long thrusts, he slowed and gave shallow slams. When he pulled back just a little too far, she could tell his knot was already past the point of no return without breaking her.

So was he.

"Feels so good inside you," he rasped, lost to the pleasure. *"You're so hot and soft around my knot. Fuck, I never want to stop."*

Trapped beneath him as his shoves forced her to bounce, she knew he was gone the moment he laid his head down next to hers. He just mindlessly thrust, rutting into her like a beast, and there was nothing she could do. Raewyn wrapped her arms around his back and held him while trying not to disintegrate beneath him from bliss.

Her moans were loud, sharp, and she buried her head into the side of his neck to take in his soft fur and scent.

"Does it feel good knowing you're fucking your bride, Merikh?" His answering whimper was hauntingly beautiful, and she dozily smiled against him. "It does, doesn't it? I'm all yours."

She liked reminding him. She liked that she was so special to him. She'd grown comfortable swearing during sex because it obviously heightened his pleasure.

So consumed by Merikh and his feral passion, when someone knocked on the door of her laboratory, she couldn't piece her thoughts back together properly.

"Busy!" she shouted.

Mortification slapped her like a tonne of bricks when the double doors creaked open, and two sets of mouths gasped.

At the tension that shot through her, Merikh shoved her thigh further against the bench, splitting her more. He groaned, *"Fuck. So tight."*

His hips jerked and shuddered in euphoria, like he didn't notice two people had entered the room!

"By the holy Gilded Maiden, Merikh, stop!"

He didn't, wouldn't.

She groaned in embarrassment despite the orgasm that was threatening to overcome her.

She lifted her head up so she could shout, "Who's there?"

"You look *very busy*, Raewyn," Cleth chuckled, their clothing ruffling.

"I'm sorry councilwoman," Aurea, a general council assistant, apologised. By her squeaking footsteps, she turned around to stop watching. "Please forgive us."

"You, perhaps," Cleth dismissed, likely waving their hand dismissively. "I, on the other hand, have every reason to interrupt."

She wished a moan hadn't slipped from her. Merikh's knot was beginning to swell and put pressure on a tender spot that usually had her mind going numb.

"Please," Raewyn pleaded, her eyes crinkling from a mingle of distress and pleasure. "Not now."

"I must speak with you. It's an important matter I wish to discuss."

Couldn't they speak to her when she didn't have a giant Duskwalker cock rearranging her insides? He was going so deep and hard that she could almost *taste* it.

"It actually concerns your rutting companion there." Cleth chuckled. "No wonder he is so well behaved within the city. I didn't know this was the level of bond you spoke of."

They came a little closer, which only made Merikh snarl and lay on her more protectively. Thankfully, his guards prevented his quills from lifting as she was holding him.

Cleth halted at his warning. "It doesn't appear he plans to stop anytime soon. How intriguing."

"Get. Out!" Raewyn screamed, only for her eyes to roll and her hitching breath to cut through it as she started to come.

She couldn't hold it back, no matter how hard she tried.

Merikh gave a whine as she squeezed him, and his thrusts became shallower as his knot grew. He let go of her thigh so he could push his arm underneath her and grip her backside, shoving her closer. There was a scrape of claws and grind of metal just above her head from his other hand.

"Please, I'll be quick," Cleth said behind a cough to hide their laughter. "I didn't want to wait for our next meeting, but I wanted to inquire if Merikh would be willing to go to the Codez Mines to acquire more stones. From what Mericato has told me, he is quick and strong. If he could bring back just even one large mana stone, he would ease the fears of many within the city."

Raewyn gave up on trying to shoo the annoying Elysian.

Cleth was lucky that Raewyn considered them a dear friend; it was likely why they were pushing the boundary.

Cleth and Raewyn were like a mirror when it came to their careers. Both obsessed, and often buried so neck deep in work that it was difficult to have free time to speak privately with each other.

It helped that her continuous orgasm was numbing her to everything except the wonder that was Merikh and his cock. His orange and cinnamon scent was also mind fogging, and his warmth, both inside and out, had already eased and massaged out any tension that wasn't pleasure related.

Even her nipples scraping against him was distracting her.

"He doesn't want to fight anymore," Raewyn answered through her airy moans.

"He doesn't need to fight if he's as fast as Mericato said he is."

"What if he says no?"

"You know we would never force someone to do something they're against. That is not our way," Cleth stated. "All I implore is that you ask him for the benefit of our people. No one else can do it. I would beg that you ask him now, but I can see he is in no state to respond."

"Okay, I'll ask later. Now leave!"

They gave a hum filled with mirth. "As you wish. I'll leave you to your rigorous coitus for now."

They did not just say that!

Before she could make a remark, they swiftly left.

She was going to have to catch up to them later and make sure they didn't tell a single person she'd been caught having sex in the middle of her work area. The other councilmembers would tease her about it for years.

"Oh, Merikh," she moaned, gripping him again. "What am I going to do with you?"

"Councilwoman," Aurea cringed.

"Holy maiden, what?" Raewyn couldn't believe she was still there!

"I came to remind you of the appointment you have in half an hour." Could this get any worse? She'd completely forgotten about it. "That's all. I'll take my leave as well."

Just as the doors closed and Aurea left, Merikh's bliss-filled whines ceased. All Raewyn could do was finally give in. His cock ground into her, and even though it was barely moving, it was so thick she didn't need it to. Her body continued to milk him, spasming around his swells and girth.

I feel like I'm going to split apart. It always felt like that when he'd grown this big.

She bit into his shoulder to muffle her loud cry, just as the first gush of hot seed spurted against her cervix. With a woofing roar that never ceased, he shot back and rammed his fangs against the side of her neck.

He bit down hard, returning her bite.

Usually, he pulled back to stop any liquid from coming from her, but this time, he pumped his cock into her as he tightened above her. A small amount of seed dripped and tickled her backside. Whatever ecstasy he experienced in filling her and biting her at the same time was evident in the way his hips twitched.

His shudders were more violent than usual.

The pain of it was nullified by her pussy milking him in heavy, hard spasms, his knot moving within her. The pressure, the heat, his scent and ending groan, everything had her wrapping her arms and legs around him to anchor herself.

I love it, I love it so much. Using all her limbs, she tried to pull him in deeper as he released.

The moment he ceased moving, all tension fled out of her, and Raewyn fell languidly against the bench. Merikh was an unmoving, heavy weight atop her; it was comforting, despite her struggle to breathe.

His furry stomach and chest moved rapidly against her as he huffed, and she heard his racing heartbeat as much as she felt it.

Raewyn eventually covered her face.

"There were people, Merikh," she whined.

He nuzzled the end of his bony snout into her hair. *"I'm sorry."*

It wasn't his fault. Had they interrupted just minutes before, he wouldn't have gone mad with pleasure and kept thrusting. He'd buried his knot, and once he did that, there was no turning back.

She'd explain what Cleth wanted later, but she already knew Merikh's answer. He was tired of fighting, tired of pain and bloodshed. He wouldn't go to the mines unless Raewyn begged him to, and she didn't want to force him to do something just to keep her happy.

No one was allowed to use portal stones. Creating a link between his world and hers would be too dangerous with all the Demons freely roaming around Earth, so she didn't want to give him false hope of saving his brothers. Such a portal would have to be voted on by all within the city, not just the councilmembers, and she could already tell the people would reject it out of fear without a guarantee of safety.

She couldn't give a promise that it might be possible just to gain his assistance.

She didn't want to use the power of their bond in such a dirty way. Her people could last for a few more years without more stones, and perhaps Merikh would be warmer to the idea after he'd spent some time... resting.

It was also exceptionally dangerous. She didn't know if she had the strength to convince him when she wouldn't want him to go. There were thousands of Demons, and she knew he could die if one were to crush his skull.

She didn't know what would become of her if that happened, but she didn't want to discover it.

However, Aurea's matter was entirely different.

"I told you my laboratory is a no sex zone!" she cried. "If I'm in the middle of an experiment, I can't have you contaminating it."

Semen could be a rather potent ingredient. Merikh came so much that there wasn't a chance he wasn't going to get it everywhere when he finally dislodged his knot from her.

"You are the one who started pushing my cock towards your pretty pussy," he rumbled, his voice deep in his monstrous form as he licked at the wound on her neck. *"I was going to ask you if we could leave since I was hard and wanted to bury it in you."*

Was he lying, or was he not? Hard to tell when he was such a tricksy Duskwalker.

She finally moved her hands from her face and gestured to her body.

"I can't believe we have to see my parents while I'm freshly filled with your cum." She almost wanted to tear her face off in mortification. "I hope they can't tell."

Merikh tensed above her, and he darted his head back, white sparks flashing.

"We? I didn't know I was going with you."

With her wounds healing, Raewyn's brows furrowed as she tilted her head.

"Well, the whole point was that you would meet them. I haven't told them you're my life partner, and I wanted to properly introduce you to them before word got out." She pressed her ear to his chest when his calming heart picked up again. "What's wrong?"

"I don't want to meet them," he grated out, his tone so thick with apprehension, he could have choked on it. He used his claws to move a curl stuck to her lips, and he was gentle as he pushed it behind her ear. *"What if they don't approve of me, Raewyn?"*

She snorted a laugh.

"Then that's their problem, and they'll have to get over it." Still, she understood his worry, and she slipped her arms around his big chest. "I don't care what anyone thinks. I love you, I chose you, and I'm happy."

She wasn't going to give Merikh promises that they would adore him like she did. Her parents could have any reaction to discovering she was bonded with a person who had glowing red orbs for eyes, and a bear skull and bull horns for a head.

"Even if they are concerned or don't like you in the beginning, I'm sure they'll warm up to you, just like I did." She reached for his skull so she could cup his cheeks. "They're pretty easy-going, and I'm sure they'll welcome you when they see how much you love me and how much you care for my wellbeing."

"How can you be so sure?"

"Because I know them." She lowered her hands and scratched at the sides of his neck to disarm him – pretty freaking delighted to discover she could do this.

Merikh stretched his neck to give her better access as he shuddered.

"However, there is one question my mother *will* ask." She took her nails away, and he turned to look down at her. "Do you really not want to have any children?"

She'd overheard him say this to his mother, and she wanted to know if his answer was the same.

"No. They will likely be Mavka, and I don't want to bring any more of my kind into the world. They also wouldn't be able to stay within the city, and I will not abandon them in this Demon-infested realm, just like I didn't want to on Earth."

She was a little disappointed by that. She'd always wanted to have her own, and she wouldn't have minded if they were Duskwalkers, a mixture of their love forming something else. Maybe Merikh would change his mind in the future?

"What about adopting then?"

"Adopting?"

"Sure," she said with a shrug. "I still want to have a family with you, and there is an orphanage within the city. Would you be against having an Elysian as a child?"

Merikh lifted up on straightened arms. *"I feel like this is a conversation we should be having when my cock isn't buried inside you."*

Raewyn grinned, gripping the strapping over his chest as she rubbed her calves over the sides of his plump backside.

"It's the perfect time to have the conversation. You can't run away or avoid me right now, and it will be a concern my mother will have when we meet her."

She knew he'd scratched at his neck in thought when his weight shifted to one hand. *"I'm Mavka. I don't know how good of a* father *I'll be to an Elven child."*

"You'll be amazing at it, just like you're amazing with me. You're very patient and thoughtful, Merikh. You were that way with me from the first moment I met you, even when you were pretending to be human, and I've already seen you show that same consideration to my people in the week you've been here." She lifted her hand so she could playfully grab at his eye socket. "However, you do have a temper you need to learn to control."

Merikh huffed at that, and after a pause he said, *"Will it make you happy?"*

Her expression softened. "Yes, it would."

"Does it have to happen now?"

"Maybe soon?" she asked with an uncertain cringe. "I am kind of ready to start having a family. I'm getting older."

"Okay," he sighed. *"So long as I get to keep my bride to myself for a while first."* He laid back down on top of her and crossed his forearms above her head. *"There's much I want to do with her first."*

He moved his softening cock back and forth, which gave space for his seed to start dripping from her. She was thankful she still wore her contraceptive chain around her waist, especially now that she knew Merikh's stance on having his own Duskwalker child.

"No more! We have to go meet my parents, and I'm going to need to get changed first."

He threw his head back and groaned. *"I don't want to!"*

Raewyn burst into a fit of giggles. "I thought you were supposed to be brave. Did I give my soul to the wrong Duskwalker?"

She got what she wanted: a deep growl and red sparks. She

just hadn't been expecting him to yank his cock from her at the same time. She gasped, trying to ignore the mess that flooded from her as she sat up.

With her nose scrunched up, leaning her arms behind her, Raewyn growled right back. Slamming his palms against the bench and towering over her, he added a burst of ferociousness, his growl growing louder and cracklier. She tried to match it.

He quietened immediately.

Then he chuckled, pink sparks flashing as he tenderly cupped the side of her face. *"Fuck, I love it when you do that."*

She adored doing it for him, just as much as she adored her big, spikey, yet secretly soft-hearted Duskwalker.

Also by Opal Reyne

DUSKWALKER BRIDES
A Soul to Keep
A Soul to Heal
A Soul to Touch
A Soul to Guide
A Soul to Revive *(TBA 2023)*
A Soul to Steal *(TBA 2024)*
(More titles coming soon)

WITCH BOUND
The WitchSlayer
The ShadowHunter
(More titles coming soon)

Completed Series

A PIRATE ROMANCE DUOLOGY
Sea of Roses
Storms of Paine

~~THE ADEUS CHRONICLES~~
This series has been **unpublished** as of
20th of June 2022

If you would like to keep up to date with all the novels I will be publishing in the future, please follow me on my social media platforms.

Website:
https://www.opalreyne.com
Facebook Page:
https://www.facebook.com/OpalReyne
Facebook Group:
https://www.facebook.com/groups/opals.nawty.book.realm
Instagram:
https://www.instagram.com/opalreyne
Twitter:
https://www.twitter.com/opalreyne
Patreon:
https://www.patreon.com/OpalReyne
Discord:
https://discord.gg/opalites
TikTok:
@OpalReyneAuthor

Made in the USA
Las Vegas, NV
25 November 2023

81509049R00374